THE
PUSHCART PRIZE, XXI:
BEST OF THE
SMALL PRESSES

THE 1997 PUSHCART PRIZE XXI
BEST OF THE SMALL PRESSES

Edited by
Bill Henderson
with the
Pushcart Prize
editors.

Poetry Editors:
William Matthews
Patricia Strachan

PUSHCART PRESS
WAINSCOTT, NY 11975

Note: nominations for this series are invited from any small, independent, literary book press or magazine in the world. Up to six nominations—tear sheets or copies, selected from work published, or about to be published, in the calendar year—are accepted by our December 1 deadline each year. Write to Pushcart Press, P.O. Box 380, Wainscott, N.Y. 11975 for more information.

Acknowledgments

Selections for The Pushcart Prize are reprinted from 1995 publications with the permission of authors and presses cited. Copyright reverts to authors and presses immediately after publication.

Distributed by W. W. Norton & Co.
500 Fifth Ave., New York, N.Y. 10110

Library of Congress Card Number: 76–58675
ISBN: 0–916366–96–0
      0–888889–00–4 (paperback)
ISSN: 0149–7863

Manufactured in The United States of America
by RAY FREIMAN and COMPANY, Stamford, Connecticut

In Memoriam:

ROBIE MACAULEY (1919–1995)

INTRODUCTION
by BILL HENDERSON

BACK IN 1976, the task of establishing a non-commercial literary project in a world of commercial frenzy seemed impossible. With only a small grubstake and no other support, I needed all the encouragement I could gather.

Robie Macauley, a former *Kenyon Review* editor, was an early mentor. He had been asked by Harvey Shapiro, then head of the *New York Times Book Review,* to have a look at the galleys for this new book from a strangely named, unknown publishing company. Robie's opinion of PP#1 was featured in the *Book Review* on June 27, 1976: "A big, colorful, cheerful, gratifying samplecase of 56 small press works," said Robie, next to a snapshot of me looking rather stunned by the attention.

About this time, I visited Chicago for the annual American Library Association Convention. Lost in the glitz and hoopla of the publishing giants, I sat at Pushcart's table, one of the first such alternative displays allowed at the convention. Robie found me in this peanut gallery and invited me to lunch. I wondered if lunch meant Hefner, the mansion and bunnies—Robie was doing time as fiction editor at *Playboy.* But it was just me and Robie at a small restaurant. I told him how overwhelmed I was by his review and uncertain about undertaking this impossible task. (My track record to date was getting myself fired from two commercial book companies for general noncompliance and utter rejection of my first novel.) Robie, a veteran of the literary seas, and about the same age then as I am now, assured me that *The Pushcart Prize* was "a good thing".

His reassurance, and Ray Carver's short story "A Small Good Thing" (PPVIII), contributed to a motto I carry with me, "a small good thing."

9

This is what I have thought about this project for two decades whenever debts or book returns or busyness seem the only reward. I owe this faith to many people, like Robie. Gentle, dedicated people who keep making it happen.

I heard from Robie infrequently after 1976. He moved on to Houghton Mifflin as an editor, and he published a novel with Knopf in 1979, *The Secret History of Time to Come.* In 1990 he won the John Train humor award from *The Paris Review* for his piece "Silence Exile and Cunning."

When word reached me that he had died on November 20 of 1995, I realized I had never let him know how much that lunch had meant to this new, very uncertain, kid on the block. This edition's for you, Robie.

Pushcart Prize XXI begins our third decade, and it is an extraordinary volume in several ways. Our poetry editors for instance: Pat Strachan was for 18 years an editor with Farrar, Straus and Giroux where she worked with many distinguished authors including Nobel Prize winners Seamus Heaney and Derek Walcott. More recently she was fiction editor at *The New Yorker.* I have pestered Pat for many years to help edit the poetry and I am honored that she is with us.

Her co-editor is Bill Matthews. His poetry has been featured here several times from *Iowa Review, Gettysburg Review, Antaeus,* and *New England Review.* Bill's poetry collections include *Selected Poems & Translations 1969–1991, Blues If You Want* (1989) and most recently *Time & Money* (1995) all published by Houghton Mifflin. In March, 1996 he won the National Book Critics Circle poetry award.

More superlatives about PPXXI: it is among the largest small good things in our history, 69 selections from 44 presses. Twelve of these presses are new to the series, (as are most of the authors herein). *Atlanta Review, The Baffler, DoubleTake, Glimmer Train, Hanging Loose, Literal Latté, Mid-American Review, Old Crow Review, Paris Press, Rhetoric Review, Seven Days* and *Vignette* are represented for the first time.

Finally a note about what is not here: cyberbabble from cyberspace. Last year a reviewer complained about this cyber omission. Those of you who have sampled Pushcart's *Minutes of the Lead Pencil Club* realize that this editor would like to yank the plug on the electronic revolution that is colonizing this culture. Authors who use "word processors" (a damning term to begin with) and then instantly fire off their stuff over the Internet and consider themselves "published" are under a nasty delusion. There's no instant gratification in this vocation. Terrific literature requires a terrifically long apprenticeship. The chore of writing and rewriting and submission and rejection is a painful but important education. Knocking your stuff out on a Mac is too often like playing PacMan or Doom. Words are not to be processed or toyed with. They are the dearest gifts we have. We try to talk to each other and pray to our gods with words. In words we seek an approach to truth. Words are not cheese or salami, and a machine can't process your dreams and visions for you. And it can't see you properly published either, no matter how vivid the temptation to dash off your inspirations around the world on the Net. The result is almost always cybergas.

End of sermon.

Turn the page and meet some real writers. They and their editors flourish in a commercial age that has elevated mindless frivolity to a "lifestyle" and denigrated all of us to mere "consumers."

The Pushcart Prize is not lifestylish, or word processed, or consumer friendly.

But life? It's here, along with ideas, passions, joys, jokes, sorrows: "A big, colorful, cheerful, gratifying samplecase."

Thanks again, Robie.

THE PEOPLE WHO HELPED

FOUNDING EDITORS—*Anaïs Nin (1903–1977) Buckminster Fuller (1895–1983), Charles Newman, Daniel Halpern, Gordon Lish, Harry Smith, Hugh Fox, Ishmael Reed, Joyce Carol Oates, Len Fulton, Leonard Randolph, Leslie Fiedler, Nona Balakian (1918–1991), Paul Bowles, Paul Engle (1908–1991), Ralph Ellison (1914–1994) Reynolds Price, Rhoda Schwartz, Richard Morris, Ted Wilentz, Tom Montag, William Phillips, Poetry editor: H. L. Van Brunt.*

CONTRIBUTING EDITORS FOR THIS EDITION—*Philip Levine, Kenneth Rosen, John Daniel, Kenneth Gangemi, Lisel Mueller, C. S. Giscombe, Lou Matthews, Stuart Dybek, Maura Stanton, Robert McBrearty, H. E. Francis, Jane Hirshfield, Tony Hoagland, Bin Ramke, Eileen Pollack, David Jauss, Sherod Santos, Cleopatra Mathis, Kelly Cherry, Rosellen Brown, Daniel Stern, Maxine Kumin, Molly Bendall, Marie Williams, Rick Bass, Joan Murray, A. R. Ammons, Carl Dennis, Gary Fincke, Dennis Vannatta, Edmund Keeley, David Wojahn, Charles Baxter, Arthur Vogelsang, David Baker, Kathy Callaway, Ron Tanner, Philip Booth, Manette Ansay, Carolyn Kizer, Carol Snow, Norman Lavers, Marvin Bell, Edward Hoagland, Michael Waters, Joe Ashby Porter, Lisa Sandlin, Elizabeth Spires, Jim Simmerman, George Keithley, Kristina McGrath, Mary Peterson, Karen Bender, Ted Wilentz, Wally Lamb, Kathy Mangan, Alice Schell, Susan Onthank Mates, Diann Blakely Shoaf, Arthur Smith, David St. John, D. R. MacDonald, George Williams, Michael Bowden, Alice Fulton, Josip Novakovich, M. D. Elevitch, Carole Maso, Robert Phillips, Stephen Corey, Joyce Carol Oates, Michael Bendzela, David Lehman, Sigrid*

Nunez, Steve Barthelme, Sven Birkerts, Robert Wrigley, James Linville, Susan Wheeler, John Allman, Dan Masterson, Rebecca Mc-Clanahan, Richard Kostelanetz, Philip Dacey, Eugene Stein, Jim Daniels, Steven Huff, Frankie Paino, Lois-Anne Yamanaka, Laura Kasischke, Donald Revell, Timothy Geiger, Stephen Dunn, Paul Zimmer, Rita Dove, Laurie Sheck, DeWitt Henry, Pattiann Rogers, Melissa Pritchard, Henry Carlile, Jay Meek, Thomas Kennedy, Colette Inez, Ed Ochester, Agha Shahid Ali, Ehud Havazelet, Cyrus Cassells, Thomas Lux, Liz Inness-Brown, Lee Upton, Marianne Boruch, Carol Muske, David Madden, David Rivard, Ha Jin, Edward Hirsch, Robin Hemley, Barbara Selfridge, Richard Burgin, Roger Weingarten, Richard Jackson, Walter Pavlich, James Harms, Maureen Seaton, Mark Jarman, Fatima Lim-Wilson, David Romtvedt, Mark Cox, Lloyd Schwartz, H. L. Van Brunt, JoEllen Kwiatek, Reginald Gibbons, Alberto Rios, Dennis Sampson, Marilyn Chin, Michael Dennis Browne, Tony Quagliano, Pat Henley, Stanley Lindberg, Campbell McGrath, Raymond Federman, Brenda Miller, Brenda Hillman, Gary Gildner, Stuart Dischell, Pamela Stewart, Antler, Kent Nelson, Susan Moon, Mark Irwin, Michael Collier, John Drury, Tony Ardizzone, Molly Giles, Lynne McFall, Judith Ortiz Cofer, Marilyn Hacker, Christina Zawadiwsky, Naomi Shihab Nye, Ben Marcus, Christopher Buckley, Gerry Locklin, Linda Bierds, Brigit Kelly, Khaled Mattawa, William Olsen, Sandra Tsing Loh, Sandra McPherson, Ralph Angel, Ellen Wilbur, Andrew Hudgins, Jean Thompson, C. E. Poverman, Gibbons Ruark, Jennifer Atkinson, Maria Flook, Jane Miller, Sharon Olds, Michael Martone, Steven Millhauser, Len Roberts, Gail Mazur, Adrian Louis, Vern Rutsala, Debra Spark, Jack Marshall, Philip Appleman, Sabina Grogan, Clarence Major, Sue Halpern, Joe David Bellamy.

ROVING EDITORS—Lily Frances Henderson, Genie Chipps

EUROPEAN EDITORS—Liz and Kirby Williams

MANAGING EDITOR—Hannah Turner

AT LARGE—Marvin Bell

FICTION EDITORS—Rick Moody, Bill Henderson

POETRY EDITORS—William Matthews, Patricia Strachan

ESSAYS EDITOR—Anthony Brandt

EDITOR AND PUBLISHER—Bill Henderson

13

CONTENTS

THE
PUSHCART PRIZE, XXI:
BEST OF THE
SMALL PRESSES

PROPER GYPSIES

fiction by BOBBIE ANN MASON

from THE SOUTHERN REVIEW

In LONDON, I KEPT WONDERING about everything. I wondered what it meant to be civilized. Over there I was so self-conscious about being an American—a wayward overseas cousin, crude and immature. I wondered if tea built character, and if Waterloo used to be slang for water closet and then got shortened to "loo." Did Princess Di shop on sunny Goodge Street? And why did it take high-heeled sneakers so long to become a fashion—decades after "Good Golly Miss Molly"? I wondered why there was so much music in London. The bands listed in *Time Out* made it seem there was a new wave, an explosion of revolutionary energy blasting from the forbidding dance clubs of Soho. The names were clever and demanding: the New Fast Automatic Daffodils, the Okey Dokey Stompers, Tea for the Wicked, Bedbugs, Gear Junkies, Frank the Cat, Velcro Fly, Paddy Goes to Holyhead. But the dismal, disheveled teens who passed me on Oxford Street made me think there could be no real music, only squall-pop, coming out of the desperation of the bottom classes. Yet I wondered what rough beast now was slouching toward its birth. I had an open mind.

However, I wasn't prepared for what happened in London. I was cut loose—on holiday, as they said in Britain. I had little money and no job to go home to, so this was more of a fling than a vacation. I had abruptly left the guy I was involved with, and now he was on a retreat (on retreat?) at a Trappist monastery. He had immersed himself in Thomas Merton books. Andy was very serious-minded and had high cholesterol. Actually, I believe he found Merton glamorous, but I always remembered the electric fan in India that electrocuted him—an

21

object lesson for transcendental meditators, I thought. I was separated from Jack, my husband. New-Age Andy had been my midlife course correction, but now he was off to count beads and hoe beans, or whatever the monks do there at Gethsemane. When he was a child, my son saw the dark-robed monks out hoeing in a field, and he called the place a monk farm. I didn't know what I'd do about Andy. He was virtuous, but he made me restless. I knew I was always trying to fit in and rebel simultaneously. My husband called that the Marie Antoinette paradox.

I was all alone in London, so in a way I was on a retreat, too. I had a borrowed flat in Bloomsbury for a month. My old college friend Louise worked in London as a government translator, and she was away, translating for a consulate in Italy. Back in the '60s, the summer after our junior year, Louise and I had gone to Europe together—"Europe on $5 a Day." During that miserable trip Louise's mother died and was already buried by the time the news reached us in Rome. We didn't know what to do but grimly continue our travels. We ended up in England, and we took a train to the Lake District, where we met some cute guys from Barrow-on-Furness who had never seen an American before.

Louise's flat was on a brick-paved mews just off Bloomsbury Avenue. It stood at the street level, and all the flats had window boxes of late-fall blooms. There was no backyard garden—just as well, since I didn't want to mother plants. I wasn't sure what I wanted to do. I was supposed to be thinking. Or maybe not thinking. I wondered if I should go back to Jack. I didn't want to rush back automatically, like a boomerang.

Two days after my arrival from Cincinnati, I still had my days and nights mixed up. On Sunday, I slept till well past two. After breakfast I went walking, a long way. I walked up Tottenham Court Road, past all the tacky electronics stores, to Regent's Park. I walked through the park to the zoo. When I got there the zoo was closing. I decided not to head into the dim interior of the park but walked back the way I had come, on the wide avenue. The last of the sun threw the bare trees into silhouette.

As I walked back to the flat, I kept thinking about Louise. I hadn't seen her in five years, and we were never really close. She was always following some new career or set of people. She thrived on people and ideas, as if she hoped that any minute someone might come along with a totally new plan that would radically change her life. Her closet was a dull rainbow of business suits, with accessories like scarves and belts and necklaces looped with them on the hangers and a row of shoes below. Big earrings were stashed in the jacket pockets. There was nothing else in the flat that seemed personal, no knickknacks or collections. She was without hobbies. No stacks of magazines, only some recent issues of *Vogue* and a lone *Time Out*. There was nothing to be recycled or postponed. The cupboards had only a few packages of Bovril and tea, and the refrigerator had been thoroughly cleaned out for my arrival. A maid was due each Thursday. I knew no one back home who hired someone to clean. In my neighborhood, in a small city on the edge of the Appalachian Mountains, if you hired somebody to clean or cook or mow, people would figure you had a lot of money and would hit you for a loan, or they would gossip.

Louise's place was like a lawyer's reception room. The art on the walls was functional—a few posters from the National Gallery and a nondescript seascape. But in the hallway between the living room and the bedroom was a row of eight-by-ten glossy color photographs of raw turkeys. The photos were framed with thin red metal edges. In the first one the turkey was sitting upright and headless, its legs dangling, in a child's red rocking chair. In the second, the turkey was sitting in the child's compartment of a supermarket cart. I could make out the word Loblaw's on the cart, so I knew the photographs were American. In the third one the turkey was lying on a rug by a fireplace, like a pet. In the last, it was buckled into a car seat.

I longed to show Jack these pictures. He was a photographer, and I knew he would hate them. The pictures were hideous, but funny, too, because the turkeys seemed so humanized. I had a son in college, but Louise had no children and had never married. Was this her creepy vision of children?

It was almost dark when I reached the flat. A sprinkle of rain had showered the nodding mums in the window box. Clumsily I unlocked the outer door with an oversized skeleton key and switched on the light in the vestibule. Beyond this was a door with a different, more modern key. I opened the second door; then a chill ran all over me. Something was wrong. I could see my duffel bag on the floor. I was sure I had left it in a hall closet. The room was dark except for the vestibule light. Frightened, I darted out, pulling both doors shut. I jammed the skeleton key into the lock and turned it. At the corner I looked back, trying to remember if I had left the bedroom curtains parted a slight bit. Was someone peeking out?

I walked swiftly to the nearest phone box, a few blocks away, and called the number Louise had left me, a friend of hers in case I needed help. It was an 081 number—too far away to be of immediate help, I thought. A machine answered. At the beep I paused, then hung up.

I might have been mistaken, I thought. I could be brave and investigate. I walked back—three long blocks of closed book shops and sandwich bars. It would be embarrassing to call the police and then remember I had left the bag on the floor. I had experienced deceptions of memory before and had a theory about them. I tried hard to think. Louise had assured me, "England is not like the States, Nancy. It's safe here. We don't have all those guns."

I had some trouble getting the outer door unlocked. I was turning the key the wrong way. I had to turn it several times. When I got inside, I fit the other key to the second door, but it pushed open before I could turn the key. It should have locked automatically when I closed it before, but now it was open. I could see my bag there, but I thought it might have traveled six inches forward. Now I realized that the outer door had been unlocked, too. I fumbled again with the awkward skeleton key. Then I rushed past the bookstores and the sandwich bars to the call box, where I learned the police was 999, not 911.

"I think my flat has been broken into," I said as calmly as I could.

A friendly female voice took down the information. "Please tell me the address."

I gave her the address. "I'm American. I'm visiting. It's a friend's flat."

"Right." The voice paused. The way the English said "Right" was as if they were saying, "Of course. I knew that." You can't surprise them.

"I thought London was supposed to be safe," I said. "I never expected this." In my nervousness, I was babbling. Instantly I realized I had probably insulted the London police for not doing their job.

"Don't worry, madam. I'll send someone straight away." She repeated the address and told me to stand on the corner of Bloomsbury Avenue.

I waited on the corner, my hands in the pockets of my rain parka. People were moving about casually. The street seemed normal enough, and I was aware that I didn't believe anything truly calamitous could happen to me. This felt like an out-of-body experience, except that I needed to pee. Soon four policemen rode up in a ridiculous little red car. I had heard they didn't go by the name "bobbies" anymore. (Not P.C.? I had no idea.) Two of them stayed with the car, and two approached the flat, asking me questions. They took my keys.

"Stay across the street, please, madam, while we check out the situation." The bobby appeared to be about twenty. He was cute, with a dimple. His red hair made me think of Jack when we first met.

They whipped out their billy sticks and braced themselves at the door. It was a charming scene, I thought, as they entered the flat. I didn't want to think about what the cops in America would do. In a few minutes, the older of the two bobbies appeared and motioned me inside.

"Right," he said. "This is a burglary."

Inside, the place was like a jumble sale. All the drawers had been jerked from their havens and spilled out. The kitchen cupboards were closed, but the bedroom was a tornado scene. My clothes were strewn about, and Louise's preaccessorized suits lay heaped on the floor, the earrings and necklaces scattered. I was so stunned that I must have seemed strangely calm. The police might have thought I had staged the whole affair. Louise's place had been so spare that now with things flung around it seemed almost homey.

"Was there a telly?" said the bobby with the red hair.

It dawned on me that the telly trolley was vacant.

"Why, yes," I said, pointing to the trolley. "And there was a radio in the kitchen."

"No more," he said. "Was there a CD player or such?"

I shook my head no. Louise never listened to music. How could she like languages and not music?

"The TV, the radio, and about a hundred dollars cash—American dollars," I told the policeman after I searched a while. The cash had been in a zippered compartment of my airline carry-on bag. I had no idea what hidden valuables of Louise's might have been taken. My traveler's checks were still in the Guatemalan ditty bag I had hidden in a sweater. The burglars must have been in a rush. I had probably interrupted them. The phone-fax was still there. The turkey pictures were hanging askew.

The bobbies wrote up a report. They gave me advice. "Get a locksmith right away and have the lock changed," Bobby the Elder urged.

Bobby the Younger beckoned me into the vestibule. "You see how they got in? The outside door should have been double-locked. See

25

the brass plate of the letter box? They could poke an instrument through the slot and release the handle inside. Then it was a simple matter to force the lock on the second door. It could be done with a credit card."

"It could have been Gypsies," Bobby the Elder said. "There's Gypsies about quite near here."

"Be sure to double-lock the outer door," the younger bobby reminded me when they left a bit later. He seemed worried about me. I tried to smile. I coveted his helmet.

In the telephone book, I chose a locksmith named Smith because the name seemed fitting. His ad said, "Pick Smith for your locks." While I was waiting, I tried to clean up the place. I hid Louise's kitchen knives behind the pots and pans. I looked for clues. Under a book on the floor, I found a framed photograph of Louise's parents. They stared up at me as if I had caught them being naughty.

Smith came promptly, arriving with a tool kit and a huge sandwich—a filled bap, like a hamburger bun stuffed with potted meat. He set it on the dining table.

"You'll be needing a few bolts," he announced, after examining the doors.

"Could I ask you to block up the letter slot somehow?" I asked. I demonstrated how the door could be opened through the slot.

Smith flipped the brass plate a couple of times. He frowned. "How would you get the post?"

"I'm not expecting any letters." Andy might write, but that didn't matter. Jack didn't even know where I was.

"I could screw it down," Smith said begrudgingly. He was a heavy-set man who looked as though he worked out at a gym. He wore clean, creased green twill. Between bites of his bap, he shot an electric screwdriver into the lock plate of the living room door and removed some screws. The sound was insect-shrill.

"Likely this was committed by some Pakis," he said, pausing in his attack. "The Pakis are worse than the Indians."

"I wouldn't know," I murmured. I was trying to remember where Louise's parents belonged. I had tried them out in the bedroom, but they looked too disapproving.

"We have some very aggressive blacks," Smith went on. "Some of them look you right in the eye."

"I wouldn't jump to conclusions," I said. I plumped a sofa cushion.

"But you know how it is with the blacks in your country." A screw dropped to the floor.

I didn't know what to say. I wasn't used to hearing people tossing around such remarks, but as an American I didn't seem to have a right to say much. "Have you ever been to America?" I asked.

"No. But I long to take the kids to Disney World." He scooped up the screw. "Maybe one day," he added wistfully.

After that, I toured London by fury. I walked everywhere, replaying what had happened, hardly seeing the sights. I walked right past Big Ben and didn't notice until I heard it strike behind me. "England swings, like a pendulum do, bobbies on bicycles two by two"—that song kept going through my head. I walked the streets, confusion growing inside me like a ball of calzone. I saw signs on walls of unoccupied stores: FLY STICKERS WILL BE KNACKERED!

It sounded so violent, like "liquidated" or "exterminated."

I found that I was talking to myself on the street. A teapot was a grenade. A briefcase could be a car bomb. There *were* guns. I remembered the time Jack and I went with our little boy to see the crown jewels. It was 1975. We were waiting in a long line—Louise would say queue—to see the royal baubles, and an alarm went off. A group of baby-faced young men in military uniforms materialized, their M-16s trained on the tourists. Any one of us might be an IRA terrorist.

The cacophony on the major streets was earsplitting. On the Pall Mall, the traffic was hurtling pell-mell. The boxy hansom cabs maneuvered like bumper cars, their back wheels holding tight while the front wheels spun in an arc. A blue cab duded up with ads screeched to a halt right in front of me and let me trot the crosswalk. Angrily I marched to Westminster Abbey, aiming for the Poets' Corner. I had a bone to pick with the poets. You couldn't dance to all those old words. And where were they when you needed them? I had to elbow through a crowd of tourists earnestly working on brass-rubbings. A sign warned that pickpockets operated in the area. I never followed directions and refused to ask where the Poets' Corner was. I was sure I'd find them, lurking in their guarded grotto. I walked through a maze of corridors, stepping on the gravestone lids of the dead. A great idea, I thought, walking over the dead. I stomped on their stones, hoping to disturb them. Then I saw an arrow pointing toward the Poets' Corner. But a man in a big red costume steered me away and pointed to a velvet rope.

"Why can't I see the poets?" I demanded.

"Because it's past four o'clock," he said.

I didn't know the poets shut up shop at teatime. Slugabeds and layabouts, I thought vehemently. Pick a poet's pocket—pocketful of rye? Would prisoners have more self-esteem if their bars had a velvet veneer? I wended my way past a woman in a battery-powered chair that resembled a motor scooter. I skirted the suggested-donation box and plowed around a crash of schoolchildren.

I left the poets to their tea and hit the gift shop.

At the Virgin Megastore on Oxford Street I searched for music. Everything was there, rows and racks of CDs and singles of folk and gospel and classical and ragga and reggae and rock and pop and world. The new Rolling Stones blared over the p.a. No moss on Mick! Then a group I couldn't identify caught me up in an old-style rock-and-roll rhythm. I breezed through the store, buoyed by the sound. I had to find out what it was. It was a clue to the new music, all the music I had been reading about but couldn't hear in the soundless turkey decor of Louise's flat.

"What group is playing?" I asked a nose-ringed clerk.

"Bob Geldof and the Boomtown Rats, from their greatest hits CD," he said, smiling so that his nose ring wiggled. "Circa '78."

Where had I been all these years? Why didn't I know this? Did this mean I was old? The song ended. The Virgin Megastore was so huge and so stimulating I felt my blood sugar dropping. There was too much to take in. Whole walls of Elvis.

At the British Museum, I stared at ancient manuscripts. I saw something called a chronological scourge. It was a handwritten manuscript in the form of a "flagellation," an instrument used in ritual self-discipline for religious purposes. The chronicle was a history of the world, written on strips of paper streaming from the end of a stick. There was a large cluster of the shreds, exactly like a pompon. I wondered if Andy was flagellating himself at the monastery. A paper scourge wouldn't hurt. It would only tickle and annoy, like gnats. Birch bark twigs would give pleasure. Rattan would smart and dig. Barbed wire would maim.

For two days I kept telephoning Louise, getting no answer at the villa in Italy where she was supposed to be. Then I got an answering machine, Louise in Italian. I guessed at the message, heard the beep, and blurted out the story. "Don't worry," I said. "There wasn't any damage. Just the telly and the radio and nothing broken. I had to change the locks." I asked her to let me know about the insurance. I didn't tell her about the gagged letter slot and how I found her mail littering the mews because I kept missing the postman. I knew she would say telly and not TV. Louise had gotten so English she would probably have tea during an air raid.

I sat in a cheap Italian trattoria and drank a bottle of sparkle-water. The waitress brought some vegetable antipasto. Then she brought bread. I ate slowly, trying to get my bearings. I knew what Andy would do: purify, simplify, and retreat. He'd listen to his Enya records, those hollow whispers. I felt a deep hole inside, as when a family is shattered by some unspeakable calamity. The family at a table nearby was having a jovial evening, although I could not make out most of their conversation. A young man, perhaps in his thirties, had apparently met his parents for dinner. The father ordered Scrumpy Jack, and the son ordered a bottle of red wine. The mother pulled a package from a bag. It was gift-wrapped in sturdy, plain paper. The young man opened it—underwear!—and discreetly repackaged it. He seemed grateful.

Another young man arrived, carrying a briefcase. The two young men kissed on the lips. Then the new arrival kissed the mother and shook hands with the father. He sat down at the end of the table—diagonally across from the man whose birthday was evidently being celebrated—and removed a package from his briefcase. It traveled across the table. Some kind of book, I thought. No, it was a leather case filled with what looked like apothecary jars. The young man seemed elated. He lit a cigarette just as a young woman swept in, wearing a long purple knit tank dress with a white undershirt and white high-heeled basketball shoes. Her hair was short, as if Sinead O'Connor hadn't shaved in a week or two. She handed the birthday boy a present. I decided she was his sister. But maybe they weren't even a family. Maybe I was just jumping to conclusions, the way the locksmith did.

My main course arrived. Something with aubergines and courgettes. I couldn't remember what courgettes were and couldn't identify them in the dish. I knew aubergines were eggplants. I didn't know why the Italian menu used French words. I wondered if Louise had learned Italian because Italy was where she learned of her mother's death. Maybe she had wanted to translate her memories of those foreign sounds we heard that unforgettable day at the American Express office, near the Spanish steps, when she got the news from America.

29

Finally I spoke to Louise on the telephone. "Don't worry about this little episode, Nancy," she assured me. She had no hidden valuables that might be missing. We discussed the insurance details. I'd get my hundred dollars, she'd get her telly.

"The police said it might be Gypsies that live nearby," I offered.

"Oh, but those are proper Gypsies," she said. "They don't live in the council estates."

Council estates meant something like public housing. "Proper Gypsies?" I said, but she was already into a story about how a cultural attaché's estranged wife showed up in Rome. The Gypsies must live in regular flats like Louise's, I thought. In America, no one would ever use a phrase like "proper Gypsies." Yes, they would, I realized. It was like saying "a good nigger." I had a sick feeling. This was too deep for me.

"Louise," I said firmly. "I'm very disturbed. Listen." I wanted to ask her about the Indians and Pakistanis, but I couldn't phrase it. Instead, I said, "Remember when we went to Europe on five dollars a day?"

"More like six," she said with a quick little ha-ha.

"You know how I didn't know what to say to you when your mother died? I was useless, not a comfort at all."

"Why are you upset about that now?"

"I just wanted to tell you I'm really sorry."

"Look, Nancy," Louise said, in mingled kindness and exasperation. "I know you're unnerved about being burgled. But you got the locks changed, so you'll be OK. This is not like you. I believe you're just not adjusted to your separation from Jack."

"It's not that," I said quickly. "It's the world. And the meaning of justice. Major stuff."

"Oh, *please.*"

"*Ciao,* Louise."

At a little shop, I bought detergent and a packet of flapjacks, just to find out what they were. I went to a laundrette: how did Louise do her wash? The laundrette had a few plastic chairs baking in a sunny window. Two Indian women cleverly bandaged in filmy cotton were washing piles of similar cotton wrappings. They were laughing. One said, "She was doing this thing that thing." She had beautiful hands, which she used like a musical accompaniment to her speech. It dawned on me that Louise's maid did her wash—probably taking it home to her own neighborhood laundrette. I wondered if the proper Gypsies had maids. Technically, wouldn't a proper Gypsy be one that fit all the im-

30

ages? Gold tooth, earrings, the works? I sat on one of the hot plastic chairs. In my pocket I had a fax from Andy—a fax from the monastery! I didn't think I would answer his simple-Simon missive. I couldn't imagine a monk faxing. I waited in the laundrette, eating the flapjacks. They were a kind of Scottish oatcake mortared with treacle. The Scottish called crumpets pancakes. They had tea very late, giving the impression they couldn't afford dinner. But the English had afternoon tea just early enough to make it seem they didn't have to work during the day and late enough to make it appear that they could have a late dinner. The English said "starters" for appetizers, a crude word instead of a French word. It was the direct language of my forebears, a culture that could be proper yet at times strangely without euphemism. They ate things they called toad in the hole, bubble and squeak, Spotted Dick, dead baby. They ate jacked potatoes and drank hand-pulled beers. The English spoke my language, wore my skin.

I threw my jeans and T-shirts and socks into a spin dryer called The Extractor. It was a huge barrel encrusted with ancient grime and thick cables of electricity and with a box on the wall for coins. It looked like a relic from early Soviet technology, a grim reminder of something absolutely terrible.

At Trafalgar Square I was trying to get from Nelson's column to Charing Cross, and I got caught up in a demonstration of some kind. With my plastic bag of laundry, I squeezed among a bunch of punks with electric-blue and orange mohawks. Spiritless teenagers in ragged, sloppy outfits propelled me through a flock of pigeons. I kept one hand on my belly-bag; the pickpockets from Westminster Abbey were probably here. The poets stayed away, mumbling dead words in their niches. I couldn't tell what the protest was, something about an employment bill. I saw turbans and saris and heard hot, rapid Cockney and the lilt of Caribbean speech and the startled accents of tourists. I could hardly move. My plastic bag of laundry followed me like a hump. Although it was scary, there was something thrilling about being carried along by the crowd. My anger started to dissolve and blend with this world of people, and I felt all of us swirling together to a hard, new rhythm. My hair was blowing. I could feel a tickle of English rain. A man next to me said "Four, four, four," and the woman with him beat the air in time with her fists. Her earrings jangled and glinted. The scene blurred and then grew intensely clear by gradations. It was like the Magic Eye, in which a senseless picture magically turns into a

3-D scene when you diverge your eyes in an unfocused stare. As you relax into a deeper vision, the Magic Eye takes you inside the picture and you can move around in it and a hidden image floats forward. Inside the phantasmagoria of the crowd, everything became clear: the stripes and plaids and royal blue and pink, the dreadlocks and Union Jacks. I saw T-shirts with large, red tie-dyed hearts, silver jewelry, gauzy skirts, a large hat with a feather, a yellow T-shirt that said STAFF. I saw a coat with many colors of packaged condoms glued over it. The surprise image that jumped into the foreground was myself, standing apart, transcendent. All my life I had had the sense that any special, intense experience—a sunset, the gorgeousness of flowers, a bird soaring—was incomplete and never enough, because I was always so aware it would end that I would even look at my watch and wait for it to end. This was like that, in reverse. I knew the crash of the crowd had to cease. It was like an illusion of safety, this myth of one's own invincibility.

Finally, I reached a crosswalk where a policeman had halted traffic and was rushing people across the street. I landed in front of the National Gallery. I joined a smaller throng inside and found myself staring at some sixteenth-century Italian crowd scenes and round madonnas. The driving piano of "Lady Madonna" bounced through my head.

I thought about the first time I visited England. It was in the summer of 1966, and I was alone in London for a few days because Louise had gone ahead to deal with her mother's effects. It had been five weeks since her mother died. I was left alone, emptied of Louise and her grief. I was going home soon. The Beatles were going to America, too, to begin what turned out to be their last tour there. Their records were being burned in the States because John Lennon had commented offhandedly that the Beatles were more popular than Jesus. I figured he was right. The morning newspaper gave their flight number and departure time. It was a summons to their fans to wish them well on a dangerous, heroic journey. The Beatles' vibrant rebellion had taken a somber turn. I decided to go to the airport and try to get a glimpse of them because I was young and alone and I loved them fiercely, more than I'd ever loved Jesus. I took the tube to the Heathrow station, then had to catch a shuttle bus. While I was waiting, a motorcade turned a corner right in front of me. It was a couple of police vehicles, with one of those black hansom cabs sandwiched between them. I realized it was the Beatles being escorted to their flight. I could see vague shapes in the back of the cab. I waved frantically. Through the dim glass I couldn't tell which was which. But I knew they saw me, and I knew they were looking to America, cringing with dread at the interrogation they would face. They were looking at me, I was sure, and I was looking at my own reflection in the dark glass.

The rest is history.

Nominated by Joyce Carol Oates

LOVE IN THE MORNING

by ANDRE DUBUS

from DOUBLETAKE

At the weekday mass in my parish church, I see the same people, as in a neighborhood bar. Not everyone comes every day, but I rarely see someone who is not a regular. We greet each other going in, say good-bye leaving. One morning when I parked at the church, an old woman and two old men were standing near the door I can go through in my wheelchair. I opened my car door and pressed the switch to open the box on the roof of my car and lower on two chains my folded wheelchair. The woman and men were talking about their bodies, about tests and medications. My chair descended, and the woman looked at me and smiled and said to the men: "And here comes the one with no troubles at all."

I have been at funeral masses for people I did not know. When many people are expected at a funeral, that mass is usually in mid-morning, after the daily mass. Years ago I walked one morning from my apartment to the early mass and saw a hearse outside. I went into the sacristy where the priest was putting on his vestments, and asked him if I should go home. "Oh no," he said. "It's a very small funeral. Just sit in the back."

"Should I receive Communion?"

"Of course. It's a community. Wait till her family receives, then come."

I kneeled in the back. So did the other regulars, when they came in. That was at Sacred Heart Church in Bradford, Massachusetts. Now I go to weekday masses at St. John the Baptist Church in Haverhill, because it is close to my house, mass is at nine rather than before eight, and it is the easiest church in town for me to push my wheelchair into. It is a brick church with steps at its front; but at both its sides, close to its rear, there are doors without steps or a curb, and the asphalted ground is level. So I roll in, between the altar and the first pew, and park in the middle aisle.

I have taken part in several funeral masses here. I push backward in a side aisle till I am at the rear of the church with the other regulars. I would feel like an intruder, if the priest at Sacred Heart had not instructed me. Now I see a few relatives and friends in the first six or seven pews, flanking the body in the casket; then the empty pews separating them from the rest of us; the priest at the altar; the brown wooden walls and ceiling, and the stained glass windows enclosing all of us; and I think it is good for us strangers to be here as witnesses to death and life, to prayer and grief. During the mass and in the church, we are not strangers. We simply do not know each other. Entering the building has rendered us peaceable; the mass keeps us respectful; we only speak when we pray, and when the priest asks us to offer each other a sign of peace, and we take the hands of those near us and say: Peace be with you.

The mass unites us with the body in the casket, and with its soul traversing whatever it is that souls traverse, perhaps visiting now the people in the pew near the body; perhaps melding with infinity, receiving the brilliant love of God. The mass and the walls and floor and ceiling of the church unite us with the people who knew this person, with their sorrow, like the sorrow most of us have felt and all of us will feel unless we die before anyone we love dies. It unites us with the mortality of our bodies, with the immortality of our souls. The mass ends and everyone but me stands as the family and friends follow the body in the casket out of the church. Then we leave, and tell each other good-bye. We do not say good-bye. We wave, we nod; sometimes we say, "Have a good day." Earthly time is upon us again; we enter it, and go to our cars. Sometimes, in spring and fall, I do not go to my car. I push myself around the church, on the asphalt parking lot, downhill on one side of the church, then uphill on the other; I breathe deeply and look at trees and the sky and passing cars, and I sing.

The thirtieth anniversary of John F. Kennedy's murder was a Monday, a day in Massachusetts with a blue sky, and in the morning I filled a quart plastic bottle with water, put on a Boston Red Sox jacket and cap, and a pair of gloves, and went outside and down the six ramps to

35

my car, and drove to the church. On Sunday afternoon, while I was driving my young daughters to their mother's house in a nearby town, the first line of a story had come to me. I was talking with my daughters and watching cars and the road, and suddenly the sentence was inside me; it had come from whatever place they come from. It is not a place I can enter at will; I simply receive its gifts. I had been gestating this story for a very long time, not thinking about it, but allowing it to possess me, and waiting to see these characters living in me: their faces, their bodies. I do not start writing a story until I see the people and the beginning of the story. In the car with my girls I knew I must start writing the story on Monday, and before writing I wanted to receive Communion and exercise. So Monday I drove to the church, grateful to be out of bed and on the way to mass on a lovely morning, my flesh happily anticipating exercise in the air under the sun. In that space between my heart and diaphragm was the fear I always feel before writing, when my soul is poised to leap alone.

There is only one priest at the church, and he is the pastor and lives in the small brick rectory beside the church. The rectory faces the street and is close to the sidewalk, and it is separated from the church by a driveway of the parking lot, and on some mornings in the basement of the rectory people in Alcoholics Anonymous gather to help each other. I like this priest, but liking him is not important. A priest can be shallow, boring, shy, arrogant, bigoted, or mean; during mass, it is not important. I believe most Catholics go to mass for the same reason I do: to take part in ritual, and to eat the body of Christ. If the priest is an intelligent, humorous, and impassioned speaker, then the mass includes the thrill of being entertained, even spiritually fed. I know that a homily can affect the soul. But a mute priest could perform a beautiful mass, and anyone could read aloud the prayer and the gospel and the words of the consecration of the bread and wine. The homilies of the priest at St. John the Baptist are good; he always says something I can use that day.

I do not remember his homily on that November Monday morning. At mass my mind wanders about like a released small child. It does this wherever I am; it is not mine to hold, and I can either concentrate and so contain it, or wait for it to return. Probably at mass that morning I was concentrating on not writing the story in my mind, for doing that disturbs the gestation, and the life that may come on the page comes too soon. Once, while working on a novella, I came home from teaching and, before writing, I took my golden retriever outside to relieve

36

himself. It was late afternoon and we walked in a grove of trees on the campus. The dog rolled on the ground and chewed on fallen branches, and the work I meant to do at my desk began coming to me: the people and the words I would use and the rhythms of punctuation. I let it come and it filled me and I was not under a blue sky in the shade of a grove with my happy dog, I was a young woman who lived in a notebook on my desk, and the words I saw and hefted in my mind gave her a body and motion and dread and hope, and I was those, too. Then I went inside with the dog and made a cup of tea and went to my desk; but my soul, filled in the grove, was empty. I sat at my desk, but did not write. I had already written, without a pen in my hand, standing under trees and gazing at my golden dog. It is part of my vocation not to worry about what I am working on, and never to think about it when I am not at my desk, and doing this demands as much discipline and focus as sitting at my desk and writing. I also keep a notebook and pen with me, everyplace where I am clothed, for those images or people or scenes that may fall on me like drops of rain.

I hope I prayed for my murdered president at mass; I do not remember. Dead for thirty years, he would not need prayers to help him on that Monday in 1993. But since reading Dorothy Day's belief that prayers for the dead can help them while they were alive on earth, I have believed it. I prayed to Kennedy later in the day, after mass and exercise and a shower and breakfast, when I wheeled to my desk. I had never prayed to him before. Moments before I wrote the sentence that had come to me in the car with my girls, I prayed: Jack, you were an active man, and probably people don't ask you to do much anymore, so will you help me with this story?

When mass ended I put on my jacket and gloves, and hung my leather bag on my right shoulder, the straps angling down my chest and back to the bag on my left thigh, which is now a stump. I left the church and put on the baseball cap and looked up at the blue sky. I went to the passenger side of the car, reached for the bottle of water on the seat, and drank. People got into their cars and drove out of the parking lot. I waited for them to leave; I do not like moving among cars in motion; my body's instincts are to step or jump out of their way, but the chair has no instincts at all. This is something I think about when I am sitting next to the stove, stirring a pot of beans.

When the people in cars were gone I pushed uphill to a tree at the edge of the lot. Behind it the hill with brown grass rose to a brick nursing home. Three young women sat in chairs outside, smoking in the sunlight. I turned right, and pushed behind the church, singing "Glad to be Unhappy." I sing while exercising so that I will breathe deeply into my stomach; I also do it because pushing a wheelchair around a parking lot is not exciting, as running and walking were; but singing, combined with the work of muscles and blood, makes it joyful. I know that, to some people, I may seem mad, wheeling up and down and around a parking lot and singing torch songs. But there were no people, and the priest was in the rectory, and I did not care if he heard me; he is a priest, and must be merciful about things more serious than someone singing off-key. It amused me to imagine watching this from the height of a hunting hawk: the nursing home, and downhill from it the church, and the singing man on wheels speeding down and turning right and passing the front of the church, then pushing uphill to the tree. Safety was not the only reason I chose the church parking lot for laps; I did not want anyone to hear me.

The people who heard me arrived in cars a quarter of an hour after I started my laps. They parked near the rectory and gathered at its rear, by the open door of the garage. In the garage are steps to the basement, and at ten o'clock these people would go down there for a meeting. But now they stood talking, men and women, most of them drinking coffee from styrofoam cups, and smoking. I sang softly as I pushed past them, up the hill, and did not look at their faces. If I looked at their faces I would not sing. At the tree I looked up the hill at the three women sitting outside the nursing home, then turned right and sang loudly again and wheeled past the back of the church. All of us were receiving sensual and soothing pleasures: the workers at the nursing home, smoking; the alcoholics drinking coffee and smoking; me pushing and singing, after eating the body of Christ. At the end of the parking lot I turned downhill and steered as the chair rolled fast; to my left were houses, and across the street was the high school football stadium, but not the school, which is in another part of town.

When I came around the church and went up between it and the rectory, I stopped singing and looked at the alcoholics. I felt an affinity for them and believed that, because of their own pain and their desire to mend, they did not see me as an aberrant singer on wheels, but as a man also trying to mend. That was in their faces. They all watched me going by; some of the men greeted me; women smiled and looked. I said: "How y'all doing?" and went up the hill, sweating. I stopped at my car and unlocked the passenger door and drank water. A small gray bus with the engine in front, like a school bus for only a few children,

38

came up the driveway between the rectory and the church. It turned left and stopped and teenage girls and boys got out, some lit cigarettes, and they all walked down to the gathering of alcoholics. I pushed away from my car and went up to the tree and turned.

Going down the hill toward the street, I saw a man on the sidewalk, to my left; he was walking at a quick pace toward the church. His overcoat was unbuttoned, and he wore a coat and white shirt and tie; he had lost hair above his brow, and something about his face made me feel that he did not work in an office. I turned to roll in front of the church; he was walking parallel to me, thirty feet away, and he looked at me. I stopped singing. He was glaring, and I felt a soft rush of fear under my heart, and a readying of myself. He raised his right arm and his middle finger and yelled: "Fuck *God.*"

He was looking at the church, walking fast, his finger up. My fear changed; for a moment I expected a response: the sky suddenly dark gray, thunder, lightning. He yelled it again. We were both opposite the church door, and there was no fear in me now; I wondered if any of the alcoholics or if the priest in the rectory were frightened or offended. He yelled again, his finger up; his anger was pure and fascinating. By now I knew he was unsound. We passed the church, and I turned and pushed upward, looking at him over my left shoulder. He kept his finger up as he passed the rectory, still yelling. I moved past the alcoholics watching him; some smiled at me, and I smiled. As I pushed to the top of the parking lot, I looked up at the nursing home. The workers had gone inside. I sang, and laughed as I rolled past the rear of the church, seeing all of us: the roofs of the church and rectory, and the alcoholics talking and smoking, and me singing and sweating in the wheelchair, and the man in the suit and tie, with his finger up as far as he could reach. On that morning under a blue November sky, it was beautiful to see and hear such belief: Fuck *God.*

I wrote the story in four days; it is very short, and I knew before starting it that it was coming like grace to me, and I could receive it or bungle it, but I could not hold it at bay; and if I were not able to receive it with an open heart and, with concentration, write it on paper, it would come anyway, and pass through me and through my room to dissipate in the air, and it might not come back. That is why I prayed to Kennedy. It was strange, in those four days, to become one with the woman in the story, and the evil she chose, and the ecstasy it gave her and me. I called the story "The Last Moon," and in December I wrote

39

it again, and in January I wrote it again. I did not look at it for days between drafts, and worked at not thinking about it, because it was hot and I was hot, and we both needed to cool, so I could see it clearly enough to take words away from it. But in January it was done, which truly means I had done all I can ever do with it, and it became something that lived apart from me. I started another story, and in a few weeks "The Last Moon" was a memory, much like meeting someone while you are traveling, and you eat and drink and talk with this person, feel even love, and then you go home with the memory and it does not matter to you whether you ever see the person again.

That winter, snow fell and fell and froze and stayed on the ground. The church parking lot was ploughed often, but a coating of snow remained, and all winter I did not push my chair around the church. I live on a steep hill, and each time the snow stopped falling a friend ploughed it, then I paid young men to come in a pickup truck and shovel sand onto the driveway. A friend shoveled my ramps and spread rock salt on them and chipped away the ice on top of the railings I use to pull myself upward to the house. Most days that winter I did not go to mass; I could have gone, on many days, but waking in the morning and thinking of cold air and of rolling on the packed, thin layer of snow and ice blunted the frail edge of my desire to leave my warm bed, and I lay in it.

One of the regulars at daily mass is a pretty blond woman in her thirties. On a cold and gray spring morning I drove to the church, and a seventy-eight-year-old man walked from his car to talk to me while I lowered my chair. I knew his age because once I asked him how old Jack Kennedy would be if he were still alive, and he said: Same as me: seventy-eight. On that morning in spring, after the winter snow, I got into my chair, and the blond drove into the parking lot and stopped. We looked at her. She walked past us to the church and smiled and said good morning, and we did, and she went through the door I use. The man shook his head, grinning. He said: "If I were ten minutes younger."

Two days later he was standing outside when I drove to the church. The sky was still gray, the air cold. As I lowered my chair and got the armrest and seat cushion and leg rest from the back seat, I watched him. He was looking at the sky, at the green hill in front of the nursing home, at trees near the parking lot. I got into my chair, and he looked at me and said: "I'm looking for a robin."

40

I told him I had seen one this week, on my lawn.

Today is a Friday in early September, it is not autumn yet, but the air is cool and rain falls and in the rain I see winter coming, snow and ice on my ramps and driveway, on roads and parking lots and sidewalks, snowbanks pushed by ploughs to curbs, blocking the curb-cuts I use in my chair; and the long dark nights. While this September rain falls I want to be held, loved; but this morning I woke too late to go to mass. I have learned rarely to worry about my work, and not to write it in my mind without a pen in my hand and paper in front of me. But I have not learned to live this way, so I sit in September, listening to rain, glancing up from the page at it, feeling the cool air coming through my windows and open glass door, and I feel the sorrow of a season that has not come. This morning the sky was blue, and if I had gotten out of bed and gone to mass, I would not feel this sorrow now; it would be there, but as a shadow, among other shadows of pain; the trees that cast these shadows are mortality and failures in love, in faith, in hope; and if I had this morning received the Eucharist, all of these would be small shapes and shadows surrounded by light.

I go to mass because the Eucharist is there. Before the priest raises the disk of unleavened bread and the chalice of wine and consecrates them and they become Christ, the Eucharist is there in the tabernacle. When it is time for us to receive Communion, the priest will go to the tabernacle and take from it the consecrated hosts to give to us. But the Eucharist is not only there in the tabernacle. I can feel it as I roll into the church. It fills the church. If the church had no walls, the Eucharist would fill the parking lot, the rectory, the nursing home, the football stadium. And the church has no walls, and the Eucharist fills the women smoking outside the nursing home; and the alcoholics waiting to gather, but already they are gathered, as they are gathered when they are apart; fills the man cursing God from the isolation of his mind; fills the old man watching a woman, and looking for robins. When I am enclosed by the walls and roof and floor, and the prayers and duration of mass, I see this, and feel it; and when the priest places the host in the palm of my hand, I put it in my mouth and taste and chew and swallow the intimacy of God.

Nominated by David Jauss

THE CRY

by J. ALLYN ROSSER

from THE GEORGIA REVIEW

A busy sky: the birds have turned
their scratchy radios up so loud
at different stations, I've discerned
at least a dozen songs around.
There is one more I listen for,
the way a dog suspends his nap
to whump his tail and whine and sigh:
three arcing notes that overlap
in mind (or was it four?) each cry
I can identify, I listen for.
Bull crickets chafe their noon stick-legs
for all the lady crickets' pleasure.
A bit of trailing cobweb snags
the fence that fences off the pasture
I can't cross to listen for
the cry I heard in my mid-youth
that my stick-brain chafes to recall:
anthem for whatever truth
I knew before I knew it all,
when I heard what I listen for—
too vivid to have been designed
by a lonely child's inventive ear
or to leave me now, at dusk, resigned;
so sweet it can compete, each year,
with what I hear. I listen for
what matched the match with World I made

back then. What frightened off that bird
or silences it when I'm here?
Some secret unsworn? An oath?
It used to aim my self-lost cry
straight from that alder tree's tall shade,
and matched me Why for Why, for Why
was all we answered for; for both
served both as query and reply.

Nominated by Richard Jackson, William Olsen, Stanley Lindberg

CRIB

by KAY RYAN

from THE PARIS REVIEW

From the Greek for
woven or *plaited,*
which quickly translated
to *basket.* Whence the verb
crib, which meant *to filch*
under cover of wicker
anything—some liquor,
a cutlet.
For we want to make off
with things that are not
our own. There is a pleasure
theft brings, a vitality
to the home.
Cribbed objects or answers
keep their guilty shimmer
forever, have you noticed?
Yet religions downplay this.
Note, for instance, in our
annual rehearsals of innocence,
the substitution of *manger* for *crib*—
as if we ever deserved that baby,
or thought we did.

Nominated by Stephen Corey, Jane Hirshfield

THE SLAUGHTERHOUSE

fiction by KAREN HALVORSEN SCHRECK

from LITERAL LATTÉ

ALTHOUGH YOU MAY find this hard to believe, I was once a little girl, and terribly discontent. My bones ached with it, my desires pointing like fingers in all directions. For instance, the year I visited the slaughterhouse, I longed for another name. Mother and Father had called me for a flower, Rose, the flower of their youth. But I knew enough about fairy tales to know that a Rose is always dark like blood drawn from hands torn by thorns. I wanted to be a Lily—a Lily fair as snow, fair like you and the other women I first thought of as beautiful.

Like me, you were born in the upper reaches of Wisconsin, on that idyllic farm surrounded by Mother's Danish relatives. But your birth was as complicated as mine was simple. The story goes that while a three-day blizzard howled, Mother's cold deepened into pneumonia. She coughed until blood and phlegm ran down her chin and throat and stained the white pillowcases. Then the sheets were stained with her water, breaking one month early, and her labor began. She was too weak to scream, but her whimpers and whispered hallucinations seeped through the house like smoke. Every hour or so, an uncle saddled a horse and stumbled toward his memory of a road, only to return with his eyes frozen shut. Finally the storm lifted, and the two strongest men made their way to Luck, the nearest town. It took them hours to find the doctor, and when they did, he was woozy from the whiskey he'd slugged to soothe his own hacking cough. They brought him home anyway, for their sister-in-law was in convulsions now, her heavy body heaving on the bed, at times so bowed it seemed her spine might snap like the tree limbs breaking outside the windows of her room, borne down by the weight of the snow. They say her eyes were as blank as the sky.

When your bloody crown finally bloomed between her thighs, the doctor—sober now, perhaps too suddenly so—took the forceps from his black bag, locked them around the soft hollows of your temples, and pulled, drawing you from Mother's body and a scream from her raw throat, a jagged scream that tore the air so loudly and for so long, no one could tell that you weren't making a sound.

The doctor stood motionless for moments after the birth, as if transfixed by the cry issuing from his patient's mouth. Perhaps he also studied the delicate indentations in the blue skin shielding your skull, and just how tenderly these marks oozed red blood. It was Father who plucked you from his arms, lifted you up by the ankles, whacked your bloody bottom, stuck his fingers into your nostrils, down your throat, into your ears, scooping out anything that might obstruct your breathing, and finally turned in circles, spinning you in the air. Until (probably out of irritation more than anything else) you sighed. That's what they say: as if knowing we needed a sign, you uttered a single note of resignation, one tiny sigh and nothing more.

On this night, I found a lighted kerosene lamp, and sat down inside its dull yellow circle. I was four years old, and understood what was happening, although I couldn't translate it. They found me asleep, with my head on the kitchen table, my hands balled into fists. When they carried me to bed, someone touched my hand, and exclaimed at the chill, then opened my cold fingers and saw that the nails had gone violet. Back in the kitchen, they found the pattern I'd left on the windowpanes: my handprint replicated in the frost, crystals overlaying crystals in an intricate, mysterious system of shapes like leaves, honeycombs, flowers, and fossils regenerating; over and over again, my palm making a temporary home in this miniature garden of sharp angles, the glittering whorls of my fingerprints spiralling in the faint moonlight.

The next morning, the sun broke through the gray wall of sky, and thawed my handiwork and everything we'd assumed was fixed for months. Soon the only reminder of the storm was you, the still surface of your silence broken by spasms that shook your body. Everyone in the house searched for some means to calm you. Aunts bound you in strips of cloth; uncles ladeled whiskey and honey down your throat; Mother held you for days on end; Father danced a mirror before your

46

eyes; the minister prayed over your crib; and a specialist in St. Paul said it was all empty magic. The damage to your brain was final: you would be an invalid for life.

It would have been unfair to blame the doctor, who'd delivered more calves than children, and perhaps confused the two on the night of your birth; and so we said that no one was at fault, although we kept searching you for clues. With none to be found, this new world of green pastures and farmhouses became an old world for our parents. Within your first year, we'd packed our things, said good-bye, and moved to Chicago, there to find telephones, electricity, the Danish Baptist Church, and more than one doctor—the things our parents valued now, things that muted the unspeakable and tempered fate. We moved into our own house, with its leaded glass windows and icebox. Father became an interior decorator instead of a house painter, covering the walls of wealthy men's homes with flocked sheets of handmade cloth. He brought home samples, and Mother tacked them up on the walls of our front room. She often sat on the divan, and stared at them. I went to first grade in a room the size of the entire schoolhouse in Luck, Wisconsin; you grew bigger in your crib. But once a year, we left the city and the polio bred in its summer heat, and returned to what we had left behind, as mythic, now, to the family as they were to us.

The year I visited the slaughterhouse, you were seven and I was telling everyone that I wanted to be a Lily. We'd made a tradition of celebrating your birthday twice: once, in February in Chicago, and seven months later, at the farm. We waited until the end of the summer, when Father joined us. He'd arrive in the DeSoto, and stay for two nights—and one of them was always your party—then pack the car and drive us home again. This year, they pulled out the stops for your birthday, Sophy, delighting in the sounds you'd learned to make for 'yes'—sounds like little kisses. You kissed the air when someone offered you tiny bites of aebelskiver and chocolate raspberry cake. You managed to kiss the fingertips that held up a necklace of the colored glass you loved. You were passed from one embrace to the next. Consistently, your lips found a way to smile, and your blue eyes held as many charms; it was frequently exclaimed that they seemed to speak. You wore a yellow dress and calfskin dancing shoes, and your hair, which was the color and texture of milkweed, was curled and clipped back in a mother-of-pearl barrette. I saw how you took after this side of the family. And I heard the whispers: you were a miracle.

A gigantic oak tree stood in the far corner of the backyard, near the grape arbor and the chicken coops. It was the oldest tree on the property, and this summer, had provoked the family's concern, for it seemed to have been stricken by a blight. When your party peaked, and Father pulled out a bottle of cherry herring to begin the toasts, I ran to the oak, mounted the swing that hung from its strongest branch, and tried to touch my toes to aging leaves, curled dry and brown at the edges. Higher and higher I went, pumping my legs until the wind rushed in my ears, silencing the song they'd begun to sing for you. The branches creaked under my weight. Leaves rained around me. Sophy, back in Chicago, people stared at us when we walked the streets, and Father spent all his evenings with you in his arms, reading aloud from the Danish newspaper, his Bible, St. Augustine and James Fenimore Cooper, massaging circulation into your limbs. I knew better than to show what I felt for you, but how many days did Mother sense it, and scold me until she herself was in tears? Yet when other children scorned you, I defended your dignity with such furor that it might as well have been mine, you might as well have been me—my hands clenched around hunks of hair, red-faced girls and boys screaming in rage and pain. Indeed, I'd dreamed you were me, and I was you. I'd awake flailing, the sheets twisted around my limbs like the strips of cloth with which our aunts bound you as a baby, saliva pooling on my pillow, and the fading ghost of you (as me) standing over my bed, the expression on your face just the other side of discernible.

I heard my name through the rushing wind, and looked down from my heights. Richard stood at the base of the tree, the cousin nearest my age, who loathed me, as I loathed him, because of how often we were paired. "The Two R's," the adults called us; and especially this summer, the other children collected themselves into groups on either side of us: older and younger, teenagers and babies. "Rose," Richard was saying, "Rose, come here."

I leapt from the swing, followed Richard to the chicken yard, and watched him chase a hen into a frenzy of clucks and feathers. When he'd cornered it, he grabbed it by the neck and held it up like a trophy, but its wings beat the air so powerfully, that he dropped to his knees and clutched the bird against his thighs, crushing the fight out of it. "Get the axe," he shouted, "By the coop." I ran and found it there, propped against the side of the hen house. "OK," Richard said when I returned, "You hold the head."

"No," I said.

"Well, do you want to kill it?" His arms trembled with the bird's spasms. Its little black eyes glittered. Its beak was open, and it panted.

"No."

"Well, I can't do it by myself."

He was glaring at me now, and so I tried to remember how the most capable aunt stood, when she held a chicken down. I pressed the bird into the earth, bones napped beneath my hands. In the next moment, the axe whistled past my ear, there was a thunk, I blinked, and the chicken's head lay next to its body. The beak was open, the tongue a tiny dark triangle against the ground. Blood spurted between Richard and me; it seeped into the folds of my pale blue dress, but I didn't stand up or move away, for then I would have to lift my hands from the body which twitched beneath them. It might stand up and walk; the soul of it might emerge from the hole where its head had been and haunt us forever. I was trying to swallow this fear, which seemed to be solidifying into something substantial in my throat, when Richard laughed, a weak giggle with a hint of triumph. Then I laughed, and soon we were shaking, hysterical. By the time we quieted, the chicken had too. We covered the blood with dirt, stuffed the carcass into a feed bag, and headed for the woods.

There, we yanked out the feathers, now mucked with blood and grit, and plucked the quills as best we could. I insisted that we wash the prickly remains in a stream, and held it under water until the blood thinned, curling to the surface. These tasks were tedious, at best, and we were snapping at each other by the time we started to build a fire. Then we noticed that the sun was low on the horizon, in fact, above us the sky had turned the color of bruised fruit. Frantic now, we searched for dry twigs, leaves, shreds of bark, pine needles—anything to fuel the little flickers of flame we'd managed to ignite with Richard's box of matches, We skewered the chicken on a long stick, this in itself a clumsy trick, which involved Richard's pocket knife. Finally our meal hung between us over the fire, and all we had to do was wait. We waited for what seemed hours until the first drops of fat fell hissing onto the embers, and we cheered, our spirits briefly restored. We waited again. The woods were dark. Something was wrong, but I didn't know what. I looked at Richard to see if he'd noticed. He sniffed, I sniffed. Then his hand was to his nose, mine was over my mouth, and we were gagging. The stench that rose from the meat was beyond decay, beyond excrement, beyond anything we'd known. We'd forgotten to gut the chicken.

49

We threw the leaking carcass into the woods, and while I retched, Richard stamped out the fire. At home, everyone shrieked at the sight of us: at the blood caked in Richard's blond hair, the dried blood streaked on my arms, our clothes clotted with it and feathers. When they saw that we weren't hurt, they gave us whippings and sent us to bed. I lay awake for hours, my fingers testing the welts rising on my thighs, my empty stomach growling. I'd missed tasting your birthday cake.

The next day, our family headed back to Chicago, and on the way Father told Mother that he'd rented our house to strangers, and moved us into an apartment. Times were different, he said, with the Stock Market and all. Hearing this, Mother leaned across the front seat of the car, grabbed the steering wheel, and sent us careening off the road. Father slammed on the brakes, the wheels spat stones. The car stopped on the brink of the ditch. We sat in perfect silence, looking out through a veil of dust. When it dissipated, Mother got out, motioned for me to get out too, and then slipped into my place in the back seat. Standing in the dirt on the shoulder, I could see that she wanted to be next to you, Sophy. And you must have known that now you were free to cough—as all of us needed to, what with the dust lining our throats and nostrils. Only your coughs meant seizures, and soon Mother was holding you the way she'd been held during your delivery, and Father was on his knees, leaning over the seat, tearing through the picnic basket until he found a spoon, which he forced into your mouth, against your tongue. I looked in through the window like this was some kind of moving picture show. After a few minutes, you collapsed into sleep, your face wet with tears. Mother lifted wet strands of hair from your forehead; Father turned back around, started the car, and pulled the front door closed. Then he looked into the rearview mirror and saw me, still standing outside. He opened the door again. "Sorry," he said, shaking his head slightly as if jarring his memory into place. I slid in next to him, and in silence we drove the rest of the way to the new apartment.

The apartment was empty when we arrived; Father had rented our furniture as well. For several weeks, our voices and footsteps echoed through the rooms. To sleep we made pallets on the floor, and during meals, Father encouraged us to pretend we were Romans. "There are Romans downstairs, and they have a table," Mother replied. An Italian family lived beneath us, and the smell of garlic penetrated through our floorboards. Upstairs, the place was vacant for weeks, until one Saturday morning, when a man in a dark suit appeared, a roll of blankets under his arm, a young woman huddled at his side. We listened to them mount the stairs, enter the apartment, and echo—as we did—through empty rooms. For an hour, there was silence. Then they descended the stairs, got into their car and drove away. A few days later, a bed was delivered, and the next Saturday, the couple returned, without blankets. This time, we listened to the steady scraping of the iron frame against the floor.

Mother paced through the apartment in a rage. "They have furniture, even they—ours is no home, theirs is more home!" In moments of powerful emotion, she usually spoke Danish, but on this day she made her point in English. "Crazy, you are crazy, Jacob, to live like this. We cannot live like this. The girls cannot."

Father stood in the center of the dining room, looking around as if lost, as if directions might be written on the blank walls. He sank into a squat and rested his head in his hands. "Elizabeth. We are saving money."

"I do not ask for luxury. I ask for necessity. We did not come here to want."

That afternoon, Mother dropped a wad of bills into her handbag and led me out of the front door, casting a good-bye over her shoulder to Father, who sat on the floor in a patch of sunlight, you stretched out beside him, your head in his lap. We took the streetcar to Marshall Field's, marched to the furniture department, and ordered three beds, two dressers, a kitchen table and chairs, a mirror. Mother lingered over everything. She traced the carved details in a cherry wood armoire, trailed her hand across a mahogany china cabinet, fingered the gilt edges of a gold picture frame. She gazed at porcelain figurines, and I stared at the image of her, reflected back in plate glass cases. In "Fine Linens," she asked the sales clerk to show her napkins of Belgium lace. "But my dear," the clerk said. "Those are imported."

Mother looked up from the display. She opened her purse, drew out the pair of ivory gloves she usually wore on holidays, and slipped them on, adjusting them fingertip by fingertip. She stared at the clerk until the woman looked away, her spectacles glinting. "But my dear," Mother said, her voice low and measured. "So am I." Then she grabbed my hand and whirled around, with me stumbling behind her as we headed for the door.

Outside in the rush of State Street, she stopped so suddenly that I fell against her. "Stand up straight," she said. "We're going to have dessert." And back inside and up the stairs we went, to Field's best

51

restaurant. We waited through a long line to sit down to a linen table-cloth, heavy silverware and cut-glass goblets. Dark walnut walls stretched up to a dark walnut ceiling from which hung crystal chandeliers. We ordered ice cream, then leaned back in the plush chairs.

Light flashed before I saw her, then light bulbs were popping all around us, applause resounding. For a few moments, I sat and blinked, dazzled, dark spots floating across my field of vision. When I could focus, a girl my age materialized, standing on a chair just like the one on which I sat. She turned in circles as she waved her delicate, plump hand. Her dress was resplendent, a pink cascade of ruffles, cinched at the waist with a red velvet bow. Nothing in the world compared to this dress, it took dominion everywhere. Everything rose up to it, transformed.

The girl was the child radio star of the hour. No one remembers her today, but at that moment, in that place, she was the face on every product from canned cling peaches to whitewall tires, the name on everyone's lips. I could practically taste her sweetness. Whenever I woke from bad dreams about you, Sophy, I comforted myself with the vision of her, twirling like a ballerina on the cushion of a plush green chair. For months I begged for a copy of her dress. Every time Mother went downtown to buy something else for the apartment, I lamented my wardrobe, reminded her of the star, described the cut of the bodice and the color of the ribbon. My baptism loomed in the Spring, and it was my only hope. On that day, my outside had to reflect the soul inside me, and surely Mother knew that nothing hanging in my closet could serve this purpose. In that dress, I could be a Lily.

The week before my baptism, I came home from school and found a package wrapped in rose-scented tissue paper lying on my bed. My hands went cold; they were trembling as I undid the string, but, yes, inside, neatly folded, was the dress I'd coveted. Gently, I held it up; true to form, the pink ruffles floated into place, the red velvet bow hung heavy from the satin belt loops stitched at the waist, the neckline dipped and narrowed to a graceful point like a heart. I stared at it for a minute, then spread it out on my bed, went and switched on the electric lamp. I hoped it would illuminate what I wanted to see. I knelt on the floor and put my face to the fabric, smelled it. In a moment, I'd unbuttoned my wool jumper and cotton shirt, let them drop on the floor, and pulled off my heavy shoes and thick stockings. Shivering, I lifted the dress over my head. It descended in a pink haze. I fumbled with the satin buttons and the bow and couldn't get them right. So I ran to find Mother.

Sophy, do you remember that afternoon, the sound of my bare feet pounding down the long hall's bare wooden floor, into the kitchen—pause, no Mother there—pound pound pound down the hall again, aha! a glimpse of Mother in your room. So I back-tracked, entered your room, laughing in a whirl of pink, and stopped short.

Mother sat on the bed, bowed over you, who trembled and twitched in a pink ruffled dress. Kissing the air. My pink ruffled dress—a duplicate. Mother looked up at me and smiled. "Are you happy?"

"Yes, thank you." I left the room and went to mine, took off the dress, and hung it in my closet. It dropped there, disheveled.

"Save it for Sunday," Mother called.

The next morning, my grade school class was going to visit the slaughterhouse. I'd told Father, and he'd expressed some surprise, but then shrugged and said, "I suppose they know what's good for you." He was already at work when I got up, and Mother was out early as well, pushing you in your rickety wheelchair to the market. So the apartment was empty while I washed my face, ate my toast, and put on my new pink dress. It was as simple as that. It hung on me as simple as that. I looked in the mirror for a transformation, but didn't find one.

Our class boarded a bus—this in itself an adventure, since most of us walked to school—and I sat down carefully in a seat near the front. The dress's ruffles were already wrinkled, and my hands worked over the fabric, trying to press it into place. During the ride, I imagined all eyes on me, even the teacher's, who lurched up and down the aisle, clutching at seats, swaying with turns, maintaining order with a swat of her hand. Her voice wove a net over our heads: "Stockyards . . . Packingtown . . . immigrants . . . millionaires and finest citizens . . . the future"—a vision that contained the vision I was having, of me rising like an angel, my hands raised in a blessing over my adoring classmates. "Look," someone said. Clouds of thick, black smoke bellowed before us. I recognized the smell. Or at least one layer of the smell. It was the odor of hot blood, flesh, and entrails, the odor of butchering I'd known that summer.

We filed out of the bus, and into the packinghouse, where we were greeted by a guide, an old, weary man who pulled balls of cotton from his ears when he said hello to our teacher, then immediately put them back in. Music floated through the entryway, a soothing melody, reasonable and decorous. "Mozart?" our teacher asked, but the man shrugged, pointing to his ears. When she gestured toward the radios lodged high in the four corners of the hall, he mouthed, "Oh," and said, loudly, "To welcome visitors in. And to let the workers know when they're back."

He led us past a display of packaged meats, each piece labeled, its cut carefully printed on a card. We went outside and climbed a flight of stairs to a wooden catwalk, which overlooked the stockyards. The pens seemed to stretch on for infinity; at a certain point the animals grew indistinct from each other, and became a shifting mass. He pointed to a corral just beneath us, against the wall of the packing-house. Inside it, a small group of cows stood in a circle, their noses touching, their breathing heavy, rhythmic. The wind carried the faint strains of the music we'd heard inside. Our teacher cleared her throat and reminded us about Orpheus, whose myth we'd studied earlier that winter. "See how music soothes the savage beast?" she said, then put her hand to her throat. "Or is it 'breast?'" I tasted smoke and my tongue went chalky.

A herder moved around the cows, nudging their gleaming, brown haunches with his stick. Suddenly a door swung open, and he lunged at one of the herd, cursing as he prodded it toward the building. When it disappeared inside, the door swung closed.

"The chute," the guide said. He sighed, turned away from the sight of the yards, and pushed his way through us. We followed him down the stairs, back into the building, through a set of metal swinging doors and out onto an observation platform.

At first, I couldn't breathe. The place seemed to boil with something other than air, something more like soup, thickened with rot. Animals bellowed, men shouted, metal clanged and rattled. Hulking, lumbering shapes solidified into carcasses swaying, hanging suspended from chains. These bore great incisions, from which rose pockets of steam. Inside, membranes shimmered over organs. Men moved through this forest of meat, waving their arms like they were casting spells, wielding knives with blades like small scythes, blades like narrow daggers, blades broad as swords. They'd make passes over what dangled before them, sharpen their knives, then perform the same motions again on another, their magic practiced, precise and intricate. Their dull eyes never seemed to blink, set fast in slack faces, and glistening yellow pieces of fat and a bright sheen of blood covered their skin and clothes—covered everything. At the last stroke, hides dropped down into the muck with the weight of wet rugs, leaving behind naked gleaming flesh.

I looked away from all this, down at an empty pen. A man walked toward the door beside it, which he flung open. A steer entered, careening through the slime, and the man held up a hammer, its handle as long as an axe's, its mallet a spike. He brought it down on the skull of the steer, the spike embedding there with a crack so loud, he might have been striking stone. The animal collapsed, shuddered, its broken head back, tongue slavering, the powerful muscles above its spine jerking. It rolled to the side as another animal entered and it all happened again—only this steer had caught the scent of death, he reared and took a lunge that carried him half over the fence. The man cursed the steer's mother, the children never to be sired, and landed a blow behind his ears. But this was not the right place. The animal took another leap forward, which tore his belly and left a jagged wound. Perhaps the cost of a hide so damaged would come out of the man's pay—perhaps that's why he went livid, veins thick as garden snakes pulsing in his neck, his spit budding at the corners of his mouth. He heaved the mallet high, then down with a groan, striking the animal between the shoulders. The steer pitched back, landed rolling in the blood and mud, and bellowed when the spike finally pierced his skull.

The man dropped his hammer on the ground and hunkered down, trying to catch his breath. He rested his head briefly on the broad, wet, shuddering flank of the steer.

"Children." Our teacher's voice trembled; it broke with something like laughter. "Let's not lose our leader."

We shuffled forward, toward the sound of the guide's voice, shouting above the din, "We use everything but the squeal." There was an abundance of squeals like screams. The man before us wore an apron furrowed with blood. He held a narrow knife. A pig spun by, upside down, glossy hooves flailing. One hind leg was hooked through a metal loop at the end of a chain. As it passed, the man darted forward and slit its throat. Blood black as oil gushed from the cut, pumping in bursts with the regularity of a heartbeat, hanging in arcs in the air.

Do you remember what Father read aloud from St. Augustine: when the blood runs out of an animal, the soul runs out too. I knew this meant that animals didn't go to heaven, but what about the souls, running for eternity?

The man looked up and saw us watching him. Rows of children on a fieldtrip. He paused. Light gleamed on his slick skin. He pulled something from the deep pocket of his apron, waited for the next soft throat, slit it, and lifted what he held—a cup—up to the cut to catch the spurt of blood. He turned to us. "Time to go," our teacher cried. I felt the press of bodies, smelled vomit, heard sobs and laughter. Then the man looked right at me—at the girl holding herself just so in her child star's dress—raised the cup in a toast, and drank.

Why is everyone breathing so loudly, I wondered. People, speaking too slowly, are fading away. We must be leaving; I am ready to leave as well.

But Sophy, in the next moment, I saw you there instead of the pig, caught up by one small foot, your hair and arms hanging down and swinging as gently as the tumbled ruffles of your pink dress, as gently as a pendulum; and I stood beside you, instead of the man, holding high a glass of cherry herring. I put it to my lips and drank until the sticky red stuff ran down my chin.

Was there a knife in my hand, was there a wound at your throat, would I be haunted by your soul? Finally home, I ran to my room, and shed the mess I wore, the dress falling to the floor like a rotting flower. Mother and Father were in the kitchen, shouting—their two languages skidding in and out of each other, a blur of voices translating money and ruin, the cost of a baptism dress. I found you on your bed, the muscles in your face still and beautiful in repose. I thought you were dead, and threw my body down beside you. But you opened your eyes and grinned, then frowned, garbling words you surely understood, your hands batting the air. I grabbed your arms and put them around my neck, and with a strength that jarred my breath, you pulled me to you, nestling my head beneath your chin. As if you'd been waiting, you held me there, kissing the place where a spike shatters the skull of a slaughtered calf.

Nominated by Literal Latté

DUKE AND ELLIS

fiction by DAVID TREUER

from LITTLE (GRAYWOLF PRESS)

THE NOVEMBER NIGHT we found young Donovan, the snow dropped hard and drifted tight around the reservation. It snows different on the rez than it does off. Maybe it's our cars: all broken down, held together with duct tape. Or maybe it's our houses, shacks, and tract housing, like out at Poverty. It fell hard and drifted tight. The flakes started down like the scraps of paper Ellis and me covered our bingo cards with, lighting over numbers and trees, blank spaces and wrecked-out cars, numbers we didn't have, empty fields. The more snow that fell the fewer the possibilities. Though we didn't know where it would land we knew one thing for sure: the coverings and flutter would never stay put like they do on bingo cards, which we liked to keep clean and square. Now with big casinos the bingo cards aren't cards anymore, they're newsprint. The dabbers soak through and it looks awful.

We've never used the dabbers they sell at the bingo hall. We didn't use the Tiddly-Winky red plastic chips either.

The night we found Donovan half-frozen, wrapped in a beat-up quilt, we had packed up our house and drove it into town from where we parked it at Poverty. Our house had a V-8, four wheels, maroon paint, rust, half a muffler, and everything we claimed as our own in the world. We live in our car; we talk there, eat, smoke, fuck, tell dirty jokes, smile, and lie. The Catalina is a good eleven feet long and wide enough to stretch out full on the seats. We can squeeze everybody who needs to be in with just enough extra room to pass a bottle or a smoke.

We could live in one of the cardboard excuses for a house at Poverty. They weren't even five years old by the time we drove from Sheboygan and parked down at the end of Poverty. Not even five years old and already two houses had burnt down and another split in two during a storm.

The other houses just grew old faster than we did and looked worse. There's only so many times you can call the RTC about broken windows, drains that don't drain, roofs that were shingled without tar paper under the shingles, and foundations laid over roots above the frost line so they buckle and heave in the spring and you feel like you're living right over a fault line. Only so many times you can use duct tape to fix the problem yourself unless it's an election year and they send a whole crew with orange vests on just to caulk a bead around the shower surround. Then it's a ceremony, like when Poverty was first built.

Back in the bush, where basswood and maple used to shoulder each other for a view of the lake, is where they decided to build Poverty in '65. Tucked away in a backwater bay near where the river whines into the lake, they poured kerosene on the two tar-paper shacks that leaned into the jack pine, and built the first housing tract on the reservation. No one remembers this except Jeannette, but the first house, before Poverty and even before the tar-paper shacks, was built by us, Ellis and me. It had sighed back into the ground years before, a rectangular lump in the weak soil. The tribal chairman was there when they opened Poverty up. So was the assistant secretary of the interior. He was there smiling into the sun, shaking hands to plug for Johnson's War on Poverty.

So we named it Poverty and people moved in for the novelty that wore off as fast as the paint did. They moved out as quick as the cheap frames squeaked on the shifting foundations and a new batch moved in just as the pipes burst in the first winter.

Poverty was a joke. So Ellis and I parked our car there, used Jeannette's bathroom, and never slept under one of those leaky roofs.

We built the first house where Poverty is now; me, Ellis, and Jeannette. That lump in the ground they bulldozed used to be made of logs, reservation pine we knocked to the ground while working for the logging company after we stole Jeannette from Iowa. Even though it was rez pine that we sweated over, nickled down, and helped skid out to the camps, even though it was technically our pine, we had to steal it log by log from the lumber company until we could build our shack.

At that time, before Poverty, there was a low rise where the river emptied into the lake, halfway between the logging camp and town. There were all kinds of trees; maple and basswood back from the lake, white and red pine up next to shore. Even though the path from the camp ran right by where we were building with contraband lumber we weren't too worried about being caught. It was 1923 and, since booze was illegal, no one was worrying about a few trees that fell off the skidder. It was hard to turn it around, the long wooden runners yoked to stubborn and ill-treated Clydesdales or oxen. No one looked back. When we dropped trees next to shore and came back with fewer than the others, they thought it was because we were Indians, fifteen years old and lazy.

We dragged them through the snow in the winter and floated them along the shore in the summer so that within a year we moved from the lean-to we were huddled in to our cabin. Jeannette was pregnant.

Our cabin. *Our* home. It was drafty so we plugged the cracks with moss. The roof only sloped a little so the water worked its way inside. The floor was dirt and the cold ate our feet away, but it was ours, and Jeannette was fourteen years old and pregnant.

Every day we got up and walked with our axes to where we were logging. Every day early we left her as she threw up and then got dressed to check the snares for rabbits. It's not like today when you can get in your car and be there. From where we sweated down the trees miles away we'd stop, huffing steam into the air and ask ourselves: Is she okay? Has she eaten? We leaned on our axes or sat on stumps and wondered as we gnawed on our frozen camp bread with cramped fingers. We couldn't be there, couldn't walk the snare line with her, or help her carry the commodities back from town.

We warned her not to go to town for them because people would see her. The priest would take her and sell her to those white women from Iowa again.

By the time spring rolled around she was too big to make the walk from town. There wasn't any snow, so we couldn't set snares. Jeannette was too weak to sugar by herself, and all the sugar maples around the lake had been cut down anyway. There was no way to get our commodities because Ellis and I had to fill a quota of trees every day. Instead, we stole what food we could from the camp. We stole what we could, but it was never enough. We could never steal enough flour, lard, and bacon to fed the four of us. There was only so much that could go unnoticed. We set snares for deer, but they were set too high,

59

or too low, or in the wrong place, and we went hungry. And hungrier. Now even when we were with Jeannette we worried about her. She fainted all the time, sweated when it was cold, and said she could feel the baby kicking her out of anger.

We came back from the bush one night and she was asleep.

We shook her.

"Jeannette. Jeannette."

Ellis used her name to try and wake her up. She only moaned and tried to roll over on the spruce boughs we had laid out for her on the floor. She was too far along to do anything more than twist from side to side, swearing at us to leave her alone.

We didn't know what to do. So the next day when we went out in the bush to cut, Ellis gave me his axe, took off his boots, and started to run to town. It was March and warm. The ice was creeping away from the lake edge. There was no snow. The ground was crisp with dead grass and leaves.

Jeannette was seven months pregnant with Ellis's child, or my child. I was using an axe to cut down 200-year-old pine and Ellis was running the ten miles to town barefoot so Jeannette wouldn't die or lose the child.

I stopped chopping after the first three trees and sharpened my axe. I took the rasp from my belt and filed the edge. My heart was slowing, the woods sounds coming slowly back. The sun was out and I was sweating through my shirt. I could feel the shudder of trees falling far away. I listened and thought I could hear the sound of Ellis's feet thumping down the path to town.

By midday I'd dropped twenty trees and I stopped again to chew on a stale piece of camp bread I'd stuck in my coat pocket. The others had moved off. I could barely feel the thump of trees hitting the ground. There wasn't any wind and the sweat dripped along my neck where it attracted blackflies and mosquitoes, out of place in March. Ellis had probably reached town a couple of hours ago. We didn't know where to go in town for help. All of the other Indians were as bad off as us. The white people—the agent, priest, bar owner, lumber wholesaler, railroad men, and surveyors—had no reason to care, nothing in it for them.

I closed my eyes and tried to imagine what it would look like if time went by a lot faster. If I stood on high ground and could see the trees being logged off in fast motion. If I looked toward our cabin and the trees fell away like dominoes I could see Jeannette. See if she woke up, if she lost the baby, or died. If I could just know something then it would be all right. I could cry or laugh or run. So I imagined hard, tried to melt the trees away, push the brush away and find the cabin. I couldn't. They kept springing up thicker, closer together. The bark kept on coming into focus, the scaly cracked-mud look of red-pine bark.

I chewed the bread and opened my eyes. Everything was the same. The downed trees and the trampled brush spread away from where I sat on a stump. The bugs still battered their way to where they haloed my sweaty head. My toes curled and uncurled in my boots, my fingers flexed and unflexed. I could hear the river spill over the dam miles away.

Ellis came back in the afternoon right after I'd crossed the river and walked the path down to the lake. His feet were swollen and cut, but his breathing was regular as he led the priest and the doctor into our cabin.

I leaned my axe against the cabin wall by the door and touched Ellis on the arm as he let them in. I held him there with the pressure of my fingers so he would look at me, so I could read there what he did or said to get him to help us. He gave me a quick look and shouldered past me into where they were kneeling by Jeannette. Ellis and I stood over them to the side, letting the sunlight up the interior so the doctor could see what he was doing.

Jeannette was still asleep. She moved and moaned a little as the doctor listened to her heart, took her temperature, and put his ear to her rounded stomach, catching the stutter of the little baby's heart.

The priest stood next to us.

"How far along?" he asked.

"Seven," we said, not taking our eyes off Jeannette.

"Who's the father," he asked.

"We are," we said.

He laughed.

"You both can't be the father," he chuckled. "Which one, really?"

We turned to look at him.

"Both," we said.

Maybe it was our look, the way we didn't smile or look down, toeing dust. He saw something in our identical eyes, our broad shoulders. We were only fifteen but we were already six feet tall and strong from chopping and sawing.

We looked back at Jeannette. The doctor was giving her a shot of something in her arm. He stood up and wiped his hands with a white kerchief.

"She won't die," he said. "She won't lose her baby either. But she has to eat."

"The agent will bring food tomorrow," the priest said. "He promised me."

The doctor packed his bag carefully and walked gingerly out of the cabin, followed by the priest.

We bent close and knelt, finally, where Jeannette slept soundly.

The agent came with a wagon the next day with three months of commodities: flour, lard, sugar, bacon, salt, yeast, raisins. Jeannette grew stronger. Her fever broke within a week and Ellis and I went back to cutting, letting our axes bite into something we could see and touch, knowing the trees were there and real.

When Jeannette gave birth to a little boy she was strong enough to do it with only me and Ellis to help. It was summer full, and the water in the lake was warm and calm. We figured the hard part was over. Two weeks after the baby was born the agent and the priest showed up in a wagon.

Jeannette sat on the ground in front of the cabin nursing the baby. Ellis and I were coming around the house with fresh spruce boughs for the floor.

"Are they bringing more food?" I asked Ellis.

He shrugged and dropped the spruce next to the front door and stuck his hatchet in his belt.

"Are you ready?" asked the priest.

"Ready for what?" I asked, looking at Ellis and Jeannette. Ellis ignored me and stood in front of her.

"Ready for what?" I repeated.

The priest was looking at Jeannette and the baby. The agent had his hands on his hips and looked from Ellis to me and back.

"That's the agreement," said the priest.

We didn't move.

"That's the deal," he said, trying to use smaller words.

"No deal," said Ellis.

I moved to the side next to Jeannette. She was glaring from under her hair, the baby sucking contentedly at her tit.

"We gave you the food, Ellis," said the agent. He shifted his weight onto one leg.

"No deal," said Ellis. "We'll give the food back."

"You ate it," said the agent, his voice rising, leaning into his words. Sweat dripped off his nose.

"We'll give up our next three months of food," said Ellis.

"But you agreed," the priest said earnestly. "You agreed," he said again, looking at the agent nervously, then back to Ellis.

"The baby's going to be Christian," said the priest.

And finally I understood; Ellis had agreed to give up the baby to the church for three months of food. Jeannette jumped up and moved toward the cabin.

"You ain't getting him," she hissed. "You come here? *You come here?*"

She was screaming and backing toward the cabin.

In a blur, the priest ran past Ellis and up to Jeannette. He grabbed her arm. She tried to jerk away from him, shielding the boy with her shoulders.

Ellis started toward him to tear the priest away from Jeannette, but the agent grabbed and held him from behind. Ellis was stronger but the agent was big and fat.

I stood between the two struggles looking back and forth until I saw the agent reaching for his gun. I took three steps and punched him as hard as I could at the base of his skull. His head snapped forward and his grip loosened on Ellis. I turned and ran toward the priest.

I was only three steps away, maybe four. So close. He jerked on Jeannette's arm again and she lost her grip on our baby, swaddled in the scraps of one of my flannel shirts.

Jeannette tried to grab for him but the priest still held her arms. The baby fell.

He was only two weeks old, so soft; his skull as tender as a turtle's egg. The dirt was hard-packed with rocks and wood chips.

I could've caught him if I'd moved faster, been just a little bit smarter.

But his head hit the ground. There wasn't any sound, though you'd think you'd hear something, some small rip, a crushing sound. But there was nothing. His fat little legs twitched. He tried to cry and then lay still, the scuffle dust settling on his fresh skin.

The priest let go of Jeannette and stumbled back, falling into a sitting position, his arms flopped loosely on his legs like he was begging for something.

Ellis screamed and pushed the agent away from him. He pulled the hatchet from his belt. Before I had time to call out he raised it up and buried it just above the agent's collarbone, deep into his neck. His head snapped back and blood spurted from his neck in a long arc. He fell on the ground and rolled and rolled. He gurgled and splashed around in his own blood, his arms lifting and smashing down, the fat of his stomach jiggling, his heels gouging the dirt. Then he quit moving too.

The priest just sat there. Ellis stood over the agent while he coughed and spat. I looked over at Jeannette. She was cradling our dead baby.

I kicked the priest.

"Run," I said.

He looked up at me, dazed.

"Run, you fucker!"

He jumped to his feet and took off, his robes flapping, his black-shoed feet spitting up dust as he disappeared in the trees along the lake.

I took the baby from Jeannette and wrapped him in my shirt. There was no weight to him at all as I set him in the darkened cabin.

That night, after burying our baby by the lake, we threw the agent in the wagon and unhitched the horse. We took the agent's gun and rode northeast along the lake until we hit the rail line and jumped a train heading to Superior, then Ashland and south to Sheboygan.

We didn't see Jeannette or our lake for thirty years. We didn't know that she had burned the cabin after we left, that they put her in jail so she'd tell them where we went. She never did, and we vowed never to live in a house again, never to give anything a hold over us, ever.

The night we found Donovan we up and drove our car to the parking lot of the community hall, which doubled as a bingo hall on Thursdays. This was 1968, years and years before they started building casinos, before high-stakes blackjack and video poker. The community center was a cinder-blocked, thinly-insulated, cheap-paneled, linoleum-tiled, one-room building. But the air was warm, heated with space heaters every few yards, thick with smoke and gossip, where jackets were tossed over plastic-backed chairs, where people slowly folded and unfolded tattered stories and new jokes. We left our home in the parking lot and crunched our way through the few inches of new snow that had already fallen by seven o'clock. Clenching our arms and pushing our hands across our chests to opposite pockets, we tried to beat the cold from our jackets. We hit the toes of our boots against the wall, but it was too cold for the snow to stick.

Opening the doors with numb hands, we went inside to gamble our government checks. We nodded our way past the others who were halfway through their first card. We squeaked down into two chairs in the back. Shifting our weight as much as we could, we made the plastic seats sing out against the metal.

A couple of heads turned.

"Excuse me," I said loudly. A couple more heads turned.

Ellis and I began to take off our coats. The cold, stiff cloth snapped loudly in the hush. Ellis pushed his chair back to work on loosening his boots. His chair screamed across the linoleum.

No one said anything but I could almost hear all the bingo players sigh in exasperation. Jeannette used to bingo with us when she lived in town at the old-age home. She went into the home just before she turned sixty. She only lived there a couple of years. She says that Celia put her in. Celia says that Jeannette wanted to go on her own. We think that it was too much for Jeannette to live at Poverty, to live in the tract housing slammed down over the cabin we built when we brought her back from Iowa. It was too much because the three of us used to live there and it was too much for her to live with Celia when Ellis and I were away. I say this because she moved back from retirement housing within a year of our return and just months after Celia got pregnant. She quit playing bingo with us and would lock her door at the old-age home when we came by. She said we embarrassed her.

Really it was because she never ever in her life bingoed. She was too impatient, even at sixty.

"B 3," she'd hiss. "B 3, god damn it!"

The caller drew out the ball.

"B 12," he said, glaring at her.

"Jesus," she said, snapping a Salem from her beaded cigarette case.

"Keep it down," I said. "We're trying to win some money here."

"You're the loud one," she said sideways, trying to keep her eyes on the caller.

"If you think I'm loud here you should hear my bed springs groan." Ellis snickered.

"You're too broke to even have a bed," she said. "You sleep in your car."

"That's true," I had to admit. "But that's only because I wore 'em out."

I was winning.

65

"Don't make me laugh," she said, frowning around her cigarette. "The only thing that's wore out is the joke you keep hid in your pants."

I was calm, as I leaned back in my chair.

"Well," I drawled, "you'd know. You're the one that did the wearing."

"That's it!" she raged, pushing her chair back. "I ain't ever playing bingo with you again."

She got up, whisked her purse off the table, and blew out the door.

She kept her promise. So the night we found Donovan we settled down in our chairs without her while the wind groaned around the building. Jeannette fretted over her pregnant daughter back at Poverty, and we laid our cards out.

The hum of the space heaters mixed with the rattle of the numbered Ping-Pong balls that tossed around and around in the plastic bowl. The coffeepot ticked away in the corner. No one talked, thinking of bingo, or of snow.

But the same wind that brought the snow and Donovan carried our luck away so that all we had left after our last card were the bits of paper we used. We tried to blot out the numbers but they showed through too much sometimes, not enough other times, and always in the wrong place.

We shouldered on our coats and stumbled through the snow out to the Catalina. Ellis was driving. He hunched himself around the wheel and squinted through the bottom of the windshield as we pulled out of the parking lot.

When enough snow blew off the windshield and we realized just how hard it was coming down, we were too far from the bingo hall to turn around. The snow drifted across the highway in long snaking lines and blew into the ditches on either side so we didn't know where the road ended and the woods began. Ellis was driving and he knew better than to stare into the snow. He knew he would be hypnotized by the flakes streaking toward the windshield so he searched for the white line on the shoulder, keeping his eyes away from the light. The ice lifted off the asphalt and into the air so it seemed the whole car was being driven clear into the white sky. Ellis drove with the right wheels in the softer snow of the ditch so we kept straight on our path. We had to go slow; the wind was tearing at the car, forcing its fingers into the cracks of the door, into the seam where the windshield meets the hood, through the door handles. Even with the heaters on, its breath mixed with ours and drove us further into our coats and boots, which we had

66

lifted from the winter giveaway at St. Mary's in late October. It pushed us further down in our seats and Ellis looked out from under his eyebrows just enough to see the white stretch in front of the headlights and his ears stuck up just enough above the turned-up collar of his coat so he could hear, faintly, the crunch of thicker snow under the right tires forcing a line in the powdered shoulder of the ditch.

It was like this, picking our way slowly toward Poverty, that we almost wrecked our home on the car parked along the side of the highway. The front end was buried in the deep drifts that completely covered the front bumper and crept up across the hood. It sloped into the ditch almost touching the tree line. The black bark was chipping off the jack pine in the wind and their cones were clenched tight, frozen solid. Even in the summer, in the heat of July, jack pinecones don't open. Spruce, red pine, and white pine will open for anyone and anything. When they sprout they grow tall, straight up. Jack pine are never like that. It takes a fire to open them, to curl back the flaps on the cone, so the trees can lay their seed. Sometimes the new trees grow straight, other times they grow crooked and wobbly. I've even seen them grow straight down with the roots sticking up in the air. You can never tell until they've grown.

Like the jack pine the car was held tight. It could have sprouted anything, growing in any direction. Stalled-out cars aren't strange, especially on the reservation, but there was something about the way the snow held and covered it that made me wonder. It was as if the snow and ice were trying to hide something, push it away until it was too late; too late to save anything inside or to track where it came from. Already the snow was over the tires. It would have been buried in another hour and the banks would have crawled past the door handles, then over the windows, the roof, and on, and on. The snow did keep on blowing over and down and piled deep around us until morning, but we found the car in time.

For a while, Ellis and I just sat there and stared at our find. We didn't get out; we just ate the wind as it tore around our car. Ellis stared ahead and I glanced around, first at the car and then into the sky and back again. Finally I jerked myself awake and pulled myself from the Catalina in a tumble, knee-deep in snow. There was someone in the car.

Ellis sat in the driver's seat and kept the engine of our home running as I fought my way over to the cocoon that could have held anything. It was tightly wrapped and it could have been a present sitting there, waiting to be claimed. It might have been an empty shell filled to the top with birch chalk, dust, and snow. A winning bingo card. Or bones and spirits could have come spilling from the doors. I didn't know, and that was my protection. I pulled on the door handle glazed with ice, but the door didn't open. It was frozen shut from the snow that edged in the cracks and froze when it met the heat inside. The ice caked the whole door, and it even attached itself underneath the handle, latching onto the paint.

I pulled my hand from the handle and the skin ripped from the pads of my fingers. My hand had frozen to the ice and my fingers were bloody and raw, left bare in the whip of the wind. I could feel them bleeding down past my jacket cuffs and I winced as I cupped them against the window, trying to peer inside. Ice froze across the plate glass and distorted everything I saw. It was like the glass they put in public bathroom windows, bubbled and waved, so all you see is vague shapes, like you're underwater, or real drunk. I breathed against the glass and rubbed away the ice with my clothed elbow but I didn't see the future in that stalled-out car.

What I did see was a jumble of rags in the front seat. They were quilts worn and wrapped into tatters of cloth. I hurried. The cold swept through the bottom of my coat and the open tops of my boots were filled with snow, numbing my shins where my sockless legs met the cuffs of my pants, which were too high to shut out the snow.

I leaned back and hit the window with my elbow. The window was so slick it sent me spinning away. I smashed again with my elbow; my arm went numb. Looking in again I thought I saw a small form on the front seat, curled deep into the rags. Strips of cloth were wrapped around a small head tucked away from where the wind crept in the door.

I ran back through the ridges of snow to the Catalina and opened the back door. I looked to where Ellis sat in the front seat. He was hunched over and the green lights from the dashboard lit up his face. He didn't even turn his head as the ice blew in through the open door as I searched around in the mess for the tire iron.

"Leave it be, Duke." I glanced up as my hand wrapped around the cold iron.

"Leave him in the car; let's go."

He guessed I found someone and he knew whoever it was would slip away if we left him there. His dreams would get fuzzier and he would die.

I lifted the iron out of the back seat and slammed the door, running back to the car in the ditch. I could see the plates were out of state, and there wasn't enough mud or dirt caked on them for it to be from any reservation. They were yellow Wisconsin plates, the decal next to the fender read Henderson's Cars, Madison. It was an Impala and even though the wheels were almost buried to the top I could see that they were worn smooth, probably never changed.

The cold iron stung my fingers where the skin had been ripped off, the iced metal stuck in the blood that coated my palms. My cheeks were already numb. I hefted the metal above my head with both hands, almost tipping back in the snow. I was dizzy and my ears burned from the constant wind.

Once. Twice. The glass crinkled and dropped down, splashing onto the door, into the snow, and covering the blanketed form with flashing bangles glittering in the headlights. I threw the iron in the snow without thinking and cleared the glass from the opening with my forearm. I found the tire iron later in the spring, a rusted patch against the dead grass.

Now I only thought of reaching through the open window. My arms broke more of the glass from the edges of the door and I slid my hands under the small bundle in the front seat. I pulled it toward me across the space and it slid easily: there was no weight to it at all.

Even as I took it in my arms and saw that it was a child, it remained light. So much like the long lines in the snow that took the road into itself. I hugged the body close to my chest as I struggled for breath and the energy to move toward where Ellis sat waiting. The way the snow crept over the car made me think of a sinking ship as I waded through the deepening snow to the warmth of our car just a few yards away.

I unwrapped what turned out to be a small boy as Ellis put the Catalina into gear and edged around the abandoned car, moving us back to Poverty. I expected him to be frozen stiff, covered only in a small quilt, brown corduroy pants, and a Dallas Cowboys sweatshirt.

Once I turned the heat up and took off the ragged quilt I was shocked by the feel of his skin; he was so hot to the touch that I had to take my hands away. I lost the tip of my little finger to the cold because of that night. My hands were numb to everything, but when I touched the four-year-old boy's head and rubbed his hands in mine, I didn't warm him. I burned my own hands.

We pulled into Celia's.

Celia's house was at the end of Poverty. It was almost identical to the other four houses, almost and not exactly, because of us. Celia's

69

house was different. It wasn't that the pipes froze, they froze in all the houses. Nor the water stains in the pressed cardboard paneled ceiling, they all had that too. Her house at the end of Poverty wasn't yellow, well, almost not yellow. The metal siding *used* to be painted yellow. A sick yellow like fever or poison. But when her mother Jeannette had moved in after running away from the nursing home, Jeannette demanded a new color. She came puffing up to the door, only minutes after Ellis and I decided to park our car next door for good. Strange as it was, it never felt like coincidence. She stepped up to the front door and her shoulders sagged.

"Can't live in no nursing home. My own daughter's gonna let me rot in some place where I don't belong. I'm as healthy as I ever was." Truth was, Celia was pregnant with Little. Jeannette had her bags in her hand and she was flushed from having walked the seven miles from the old-age center. She took one look at the peeling yellow paint and the weeds up to the front step and shook her head.

"And I can't live in no piss-yellow house neither." She walked in and put her bags in the empty room reserved for boxes and old newspapers, for empty cans and children that hadn't been born yet.

So the next day Ellis and I drove into town and went to RJ's Hardware store. We checked out the whole place and then when the clerk was busy we stole four cans of paint. We grabbed the gallon cans that were closest to the door and ran them out to where the Catalina was still running in the parking lot. It must have been a funny sight, two seventy-year-old men running, bent over four cans of paint. We were charging like we were the Minnesota Vikings, carrying the ball across the goal line in the last ten seconds of the fourth quarter.

We didn't notice the color until we were driving back to Poverty, cackling about the slow-eyed store clerk, and arguing over which one of us was Joe Namath. Three cans were purple. The label on the side said "Lilac." This wasn't so bad, but the last can was labeled "Orange Flame."

There was nothing we could do. We couldn't let the paint go, and Jeannette couldn't live in her faded-canary, sun-bleached construction-paper, piss-yellow house.

So we did what any sensible Indians would do. We started painting the front of the house from the top down.

We did it all in one night so Jeannette would have a nice surprise in the morning. We had been afraid that she would wake up while we were painting, so during dinner we slipped a shot or two of Southern Comfort into her iced tea. As we painted we could hear her snoring straight through the walls. By three A.M., we got about two feet from the bottom when we ran out of Lilac. We couldn't just leave the rest yellow so we slathered on the remaining can of Flame.

It was too dark to step back and appreciate our work so we crept back to our home, me in the front seat and Ellis in the back, and went to sleep.

I woke up just after sunrise and looked over at Jeannette and Celia's house just as the sun hit our masterpiece. I jumped and woke Ellis from the back seat. I saw the front of the house catch on fire as the mid-June sun rose.

We stumbled out and scratched at the crusted corners of our eyes. The house wasn't on fire, but the border of orange below was slapped on with uneven strokes. There hadn't been enough paint to cover the yellow. It looked like orange and yellow flames licking up the sides of the house. We squinted closer and saw Jeannette standing in her nightgown of pink flannel. She stood on the front step with her hands on her hips and shook her head.

She saw us across the way, next to our Pontiac.

"Jesus Christ."

We stood straighter and quit smiling.

"Will you look at this house? Just look at it." She swung her head back to the Lilac and Flame.

"Were you boys drinking last night? This looks more like one of those whorehouses in Minneapolis you go to. This ain't no respectable-looking house, even for the reservation."

She spat on the ground.

"First I run away from the nursing home to a piss-yellow house. I wake up the next morning and I'm living in a brothel."

But I know she liked it 'cause later on she got some lilac cuttings and put them in a Ball jar on the front windowsill. Probably just for a little bit of color. At the time all she did was step up, wipe off her bunny slippers before she went inside, and pull the door hard enough to skip over the last catch where the metal stripping had come up off the linoleum.

It was through that door that we carried Donovan. We nearly dropped him as Jeannette jumped up from the game of old maid she was

71

playing by herself and rushed forward. We nearly dropped him. Our hands, numbed like they were, could barely juggle him from the car into the heat of the house.

"Watch out you fools," she snapped. "This ain't a bottle of whiskey."

We nodded. Jeannette had always been sharp. She knew a baby when she saw one.

We stood back as she laid him out on the kitchen table. I went over to the gas stove, and since it didn't have a pilot light I took out a blue-tip match and tried to strike it on the edge of the cast-iron inset of the front burner. My hands were frozen so hard I could barely hold the match between my two fingers. I struck once and completely missed. I tried again and skinned my knuckle on the ridge of metal right above the oven door. No blood came out, I just carved a white patch from my skin.

"Move over," Jeannette commanded. She pushed me away, lit the match with her thumbnail, and started the burner. She took a stick of commodity butter from the refrigerator and put it in a pan. She added sugar to it and set it on the stove until it dissolved into liquid. Then with a wooden spoon she stirred and lifted a gob of it out and over to the little boy's mouth. He sucked it in. It was the first move he had made. His mouth worked as he swallowed it. Jeannette gave him another spoonful.

My cheeks were raw and puffy red as the heat from the house warmed them. I could move my fingers better, but the missing pads burned when I pressed them against the flesh of my palm. I put the coffeepot—still half full from breakfast—back on the burner. Jeannette had taken the melted butter off the stove and put it next to Donovan's head. He moved some more and Jeannette rubbed his hands and feet. He cried and this woke Celia. She came shuffling out of the back room in a T-shirt and a pair of cream-colored long johns. Her eyes opened wide when she saw what was happening. She hadn't been much more than a zombie since Stan and Pick had left for Vietnam but she moved to her mother's side fast when she heard that baby cry.

Ellis and I sipped coffee as they worked. Rubbing, washing, feeding, singing, and clothing his body, they stood over him. My face became warm and I began to feel dizzy. The coffee roiled in my stomach and my hands could barely hold my cup. The room spun and I figured it must have been from going cold-warm, warm-cold all night. I put the cup I was holding down while Celia and Jeannette worked over the child and Ellis stood over them. I had nothing to do. Ellis just watched,

72

gradually moving closer until he stood directly behind Celia, towering over her in the lamplight. He put his hand on her shoulder and peered down at the little boy. There was nothing for me, nothing for me in that house. I walked to the door.

I grabbed the extension cord and the space heater from the wood box. No one moved and the lights went dim and flared again as I turned on the heater.

Opening the door I carried it out to the car, the red coils of wire glowed, marking my path red as I fought my way to the Catalina where I fell asleep alone under the wash of the snow piling flake by flake over the hood.

Nominated by Graywolf Press

FIRST SEX

by RICHARD TAYSON

from PRAIRIE SCHOONER

When we found your father's *Playboys,*
we went into your room and touched
the glossy tanned breasts of the naked
woman on the beach, you pressed
her unblemished skin against the milk-
white flesh of your twelve-year-old
body, I kissed my virginal
lips to your lips, and your father
walked in. I don't remember, now,
who had his pants down or who was
lying like a seed in the center
of the photos leafed around him,
all I remember is your father
stood in the doorway, shapely
as God, bearded, big-stomached, right
fist clenched, he wanted to eat us.
Yes, I tell you, fathers eat their sons.
I closed my eyes and waited for him to
tear away my best friend's leg or
carve a rib bone from his
untouched chest, I heard
the voice of my father:
*Are you a girl? Do you know what evil
is? Are you a girl?*
Are you? But my body proved I was
not a girl, if God

was about to send the flood
waters up over us, I must be
Satan, the spermatozoa hatching like
polliwogs in the twin fishbowls
of my testicles, and the kiss
I wanted even then, the work of Satan.
Your father began yelling in his deep
male voice, the earth of your room
shook, I
opened my eyes and thought he would
hit us with the bed or
bury us beneath a wall or two,
but he gave us one final look
which branded us for life and slammed
the door behind him: we were forever
separate from God, father, son, holy
spirit, we faced each other
in the dark and entered manhood.

Nominated by Prairie Schooner

BRUCE SPRINGSTEEN
AND THE STORY OF US

by HOPE EDELMAN

from THE IOWA REVIEW

THE FIRST TIME I HEARD a Bruce Springsteen song performed live was in 1979, when I was in the tenth grade and Larry Weinberger and A.J. DeStefano stood in our high school parking lot shouting all the words to "Thunder Road" from start to finish, zipping right through that tune at fast-forward speed. Eyes squeezed shut into brief black hyphens, shoulders pumping to an imaginary drumbeat, they sang to an audience of ten or twelve sophomores sprawled against the hoods of their parents' old cars, their red and green and blue looseleaf binders strewn right side up and upside down like blackjack hands along the pavement at their feet.

This was October, the second month of the school year, and the time between 3:40 P.M. and dinner was still a flat landscape of vast and open hours. A single cigarette slowly made its way around the circle, passed between the tight Vs of fingers and held just long enough for each of us to blow a smoke ring for effect. Across the parking lot, students called to each other by last name ("Yo, Speee-VAK!"), car doors slammed, engines revved like short-lived lawn mowers. Larry and A.J. finished their song and started on "Jungleland," pausing after "The Magic Rat drove his sleek machine over the Jersey state line" just long enough to allow:

"Into Rockland County!"

"The Ramapough Inn!"

"Yo mama's backyard!"

"Hey! Your sister's bedroom, *asshole.*"

We all knew the words to Springsteen's songs, and we knew, first-hand, most of the places they described. Some of them practically were in our parents' backyards. We were living in New York, just over the New Jersey border in the tiny towns that dot the bottom of the state map like scattered flecks of black pepper, a county filled with minor suburbs most frequently described by their relative position to somewhere else: thirty-three miles northwest of Manhattan, less than a one-hour drive from two international airports, and a half tank of gas north of the Jersey shore.

Springsteen Country, our bumper stickers read, though most of us took thick black magic markers and crossed out the second R. Springsteen County was far more accurate for a place where high school principals considered "Jungleland" appropriate music to play over the homeroom P.A. system; where parents routinely dropped off their children in front of Ticketron offices fortified with sleeping bags and pastrami sandwiches, returning the next morning to carpool them to school; and where sixteen-year-olds held parties in empty parking lots on heavy, humid, late-summer nights, where they sat on the hoods of cars and swirled beer around in the can, listening to Springsteen sing about a barefoot girl on the hood of a Dodge drinking warm beer in the soft summer rain. It was enough to make you wonder where the scene ended and the song began, or if there really were a difference, at all.

Those were our years of music, back when we still could find simple, one-step answers to life's most complex problems in the lyrics of the songs we sang, back when a deejay's mellifluous voice could still smooth out all the rough edges of a day. In those years, the late '70s and early '80s, we plucked our role models from the FM dial—Bruce Springsteen, John Cougar, Joan Jett, a cast list of sensitive survivors, underdogs with good intentions, minor idols who neatly met our critical adolescent need to constantly feel wronged without ever actually *doing* anything wrong, and we aligned our frustrations with the lyrical mini-dramas scripted for us in advance. Our mythology was created and recycled, and recycled and recycled, every day.

Though we liked to imagine ourselves as the kind of characters that peopled Springsteen's songs—he was, after all, *writing about us*—the fit was never quite right. We had pretty much the same anxieties, but the socioeconomics were all wrong. He sang of working-class kids stuck in dead-end towns who grabbed their girlfriends by the wrists, leapt into their rebuilt '69 Chevys and peeled out of town in search of their futures. Our hometown was an upper-middle-class suburb where a college education was more an expectation than an exercise in free will. Most of us would grow up to become just what our parents had planned, and to do just as they had done. *Doctor, lawyer, C.P.A.* But in the time we had before our decisions became too intractable to erase, we were free to try on and shrug off whatever clothing best fit our erratic moods. Even the most intelligent, even the most affluent among us had visions of a utopia free of parents, P.E. teachers, and pop quizzes. Springsteen offered us his version of that place, his promises surrounding us like audio wallpaper—hogging the airwaves on our car radios, piped into our homerooms, pumped into every store in our local indoor shopping mall, encircling us with songs of hot desire and escape.

This was 1978, 1979, and in the magazine interviews we passed from desk to desk in social studies class Springsteen told us he would never change, would never, essentially, grow up. His was a world of perpetual adolescence, an eternal seventeen. "I couldn't bring up kids," he told *Rolling Stone.* "I couldn't handle it. I mean, it's too heavy, it's too much. . . . I just don't see why people get married. It's so strange. I guess it's a nice track, but not for me."

Back then, like us, Springsteen was still living among his history, shuffling along the Asbury Park boardwalk with his hands jammed down deep in the front pockets of his jeans but his eyes fixed on the gulls that dipped and cawed on the horizon. He held tight to the Jersey towns where he began, always swore he'd never forget the people or the place, but he also knew where he wanted to go, and his duality pervaded his songs like a restless, wanton motif. His lyrics told us precisely what we wanted to hear: that when the pressures of adulthood started squeezing us too tight we could just peel out, leaving skid marks as our contemptuous farewell, and his music could, in the course of only three minutes, transform a solitary harmonica wail into a full band battle cry, the cymbals crashing *one, two, three* like a bedroom door slamming shut over and over again.

But I'm talking early Springsteen here, vintage Springsteen, those pre-1980 songs that put you in a fast car and took you on a one-way ride through images that came quick and fast as lightning, no time to bother with a chorus you could return to and repeat when you lost your place in the stream of consciousness lyrics that rambled on and on like Kerouac sentences in search of a period. The songs that gave you hope there was a simpler, gentler world out there somewhere, and that the happiness missing from your own backyard could be found in the next town. This was back before he cut his hair short and sprouted biceps, back when the guitar chords still came down angry and loud and an unshaven, scrawny Springsteen rooted himself behind the mike with a guitar pressed tight against his groin, his shoulders and neck twitching spastically in time with the beat. Back when you could still tell a lot about a man by the lyrics that he sang, and when you thought Bruce Springsteen knew a lot about you, as you lay alone on your twin bed with the door slammed shut and the hi-fi turned up to 9, listening to him play the piano introduction to "Jungleland" the way he did it every time, with his left hand firmly anchored in the bass chords as his right hand skittered maniacally up and down the soprano notes, flailing like a frantic fish, fluttering like wings.

When I met Jimmy T., I was seventeen and still a virgin, and three weeks later I was neither anymore. We did it for the first time on a Saturday afternoon in his lumpy double bed underneath guitars that hung suspended from a ceiling rack like electric pots and pans. He had a chair jammed under the doorknob and WPLJ turned up loud enough to mask our noise, and sometimes when the radio hit a bass note, a guitar string buzzed above my head. Two hours of songs must have played that afternoon, but the only one I remember is Springsteen's "Hungry Heart," because as soon as he heard the opening chords Jimmy T. started to hum and thrust in rhythm to the song. *Got a wife and kids in Baltimore Jack, I went out for a ride and I never went back.* Jimmy T. assured me that losing his virginity at age thirteen made him eminently qualified to relieve me of mine without unnecessary pain or pomp. He was right, on both counts, but I was disappointed nonetheless. I'd been prepared for several unsuccessful attempts, searing pain, and the kind of hysterical bleeding Sylvia Plath had described in *The Bell Jar.* The ease of it made me wonder, at first, if we'd done it right.

I was the last among his friends to lose it but the first among mine, and when I left his parents' house I drove straight to my friend Jody's, walked down the hall to her room, sat down carefully on her white-ruffled canopy bed, and started to cry.

"Holy shit . . ." she whispered, and when I nodded she threw her arms around my chest and hugged me, hard.

"Holy shit!" she shouted, bouncing her butt up and down on the bed. "Holy shit! Tell me what it's like!"

What was it like? What was any of it like? Like one long manic car ride on an open stretch of road with a driver whose license had wisely been revoked. And I'm not talking just about the sex part. It was like that all the time with Jimmy T. He could get a whole room of people singing with no more than five words of encouragement and a chord on his guitar, and when we went to the movies he'd have met everyone in our row and even collected a phone number or two by the time I came back with the popcorn and Junior Mints. The intersection of a precocious intellect with a cool-guy delivery had him performing monologues about hypothetical conversations between Hitler, Santayana, and Christ ("So, the Nazi dude would have said to the Jewish dude, man . . . ") to his small group of smoking-section disciples during lunchtime, after he'd cut three classes that morning and had to beg his English teacher to give him a passing grade. His mother once told me his I.Q. was 145, a fact I found suspicious considering he'd never learned how to spell.

Jimmy T. Just look at his name. James Anthony Spinelli was the full version, but he wouldn't answer to James or Jim and he always included the T. For Tony. When I reminded him that his middle name was Anthony, and shouldn't he then be Jimmy A.? he gave me a crooked half-smile and raised his open palms in a shrug. I told him Jimmy T. sounded like a name he got from a fourth-grade teacher with too many Jimmys in one class, and he laughed and created a list of last names he might have had, had this been true: Tortoni, Turino, Testarossa. Jimmy Traviata at your service, he'd say, opening the car door for me with a flourish of the wrist and a bow. Jimmy Tortellini here to escort you to Spanish class. My mother would have called him a man with presence, like Frank Sinatra or Tom Jones. The kind of man, she said, who can take your heart away.

Jimmy T., I'm certain, would have considered this a compliment. In fact, if it'd been on paper, he probably would have tried to autograph it. At seventeen he already envisioned himself as a celebrity of sorts, with an existence worth chronicling as it unfolded. Write the story of us, he used to say, assigning the task to me, because I was the one who would conform to the rules of grammar and could spell. But he was the storyteller among us, the one with the elaborate narratives of drag races and secret meetings with record executives, and of playing his guitar in smoky SRO bars where audiences lifted their brown beer bottles and shouted for more. Stories I would have immediately thought unbelievable had they not been told with such authority, such grace. Write the story of us, he would say, the "us" squeezing implied chapters between its two characters, but when I tried I could never get past our first, unremarkable conversation at a party in a cheap motel room at the New Jersey shore. The people who appeared on my pages were insipid and one-dimensional, nothing at all like the characters we aspired to be, and my efforts turned into crumpled wads of paper I tossed against his bedroom walls.

I spent most of my after-school hours between those walls, preferring to close a bedroom door against the silence of Jimmy T.'s house than against the disorder of my own. This was 1982. The summer before, my mother had died of cancer, quickly and unexpectedly, leaving my father to care for three children, ages seventeen, fourteen, and nine. When we returned from the hospital he looked at us and blinked quizzically, as if to ask, Have we met? and I realized for the first time how fragile a balance life must be, if it can be tipped so swiftly, so dramatically and irrevocably by the force of a single event. Only after my mother was gone did I understand she'd been the only adhesive that had held us all together, and as the empty Scotch bottles multiplied on the kitchen counter my father began to spout increasingly weird and existential rhetoric about how the individual is more important than the unit, and how we all must learn to fend for ourselves. I'm doing just *fine,* thank you, he hollered when he found me one evening pouring honey-colored streams of alcohol down the avocado kitchen sink. And I don't need *you* or anyone *else* to tell me how to live my life. Then don't you tell me how to live mine, I screamed back in a defensive panic, and he yelled *Fine!* and I yelled *Fine!* and everything, perhaps, would have been just fine, except that very soon I began to feel like a tiny, solitary satellite orbiting way out there, connected to nothing and no one, even after my father apologized and sent me on vacation to Florida to show how much he really meant it. I just smiled and kept saying everything was fine.

That was the fall I became obsessed with J.D. Salinger, read each of his books four times and began to quote esoteric Zen koans at wholly inappropriate cafeteria moments, and for an entire week that winter I ate nothing but ice cream and wore nothing but black. When teachers kept me after class to ask how I was doing, I said, with great conviction, I am doing just fine. But when you're out there spinning solo, it's only a matter of time before you get close enough to someone else's gravitational pull. That spring, Jimmy T. came trucking across the dirt-brown motel room carpet, black curls flapping and motorcycle boots clomping with each step, to sit next to me on the orange bedspread. He was a senior with a fast car, a reputation, and a Fender Stratocaster electric guitar. I didn't dare say anything as plebian as hello.

Our first, unremarkable conversation: He said So, and I said So, and he said Hope? and I said Jimmy T., and he said Yeah, and I said Yeah, and he said Cigarette? and pulled a pack from his back pocket, and I said Match? and pulled a book from mine, and he said Thanks, and I said Thanks, and he said Shit! I know you can use words with more than one syllable because I see you walking out of that AP English class every day.

It didn't take me much to fall in love at seventeen—the graceful arc of a smooth-shaven jaw, the smell of freshly washed hair, the sound of a telephone ringing at precisely the moment of the promised call. After Jimmy T. and I returned from the beach that Sunday, we intertwined our fingers and we held on tight. Two weeks later, we were officially in love.

We spent every afternoon together, in his bedroom at the top of the stairs. Jimmy T. played songs he said he'd written for me, on the beat-up acoustic guitar he'd bought with birthday money when he was twelve. He and his friend George had written a song on it they'd sold to a record label the previous year, a tune Jimmy T. played for me over and over again as I sat cross-legged on his bed. We kept the curtains drawn. His room was dark and womblike, like a tight hug, and far re-moved from the bright yellow-and-green pep of my own. The verve of my bedroom had become a hypocrisy in my father's house, where dust had settled on the living room tables and a television droned con-stantly in the background to give the illusion of discourse. The down-stairs bedroom that once had been my sanctuary from mother-daughter strife had transformed into something foreign and surreal. I'd grown much older than seventeen that year, but every time I walked into my room the geometric mobiles and kitten posters along its perimeter told me I'd once been that age, and not so very long ago.

Jimmy T.'s room, on the other hand, was testimony to postmodern teenage chaos: stereo components and recording equipment stacked schizophrenically against the walls; cassette and eight-track tapes scat-tered like loose change across the floor; Muppet dolls hanging in nooses from the ceiling; six-year-old posters of Bruce Springsteen taped to the sliding closet doors; and pages and pages of handwritten sheet music layered like onion skin on top of his dresser, desk, and bed. Jimmy T. was working on a project, he said, a big one that the record company was anxiously waiting to see. It would take him another two years, he said, maybe three. He couldn't reveal its content yet, but he said it had the potential to change the world. Three years, maybe four. He didn't think the world could wait much longer than that.

He'd chosen music as his medium, he said, because it was the most influential, *the most powerful* forum for widespread philosophical reform, our last-gasp hope to save our youth from an impending spiritual decline, and he was certain he'd be the one who'd one day use his guitar to make the difference that mattered. But he'd have to get moving soon, he said, seeing as how he was already certain he wouldn't live past forty.

"I mean, shit," he said. "Look at Springsteen. He's already pushing thirty-five. All right, the man's a genius, he's changed my life, but how many years does he really have left? Okay, I'm seventeen now, right? So say I take off at twenty, maybe twenty-one. Can you *imagine* how much I'd get done if I got started then?"

He told me this the night we met, as we walked along the beach before dawn. It was no surprise that our conversation quickly skidded into music, one of the few common denominators that fused the three distinct groups—Italians, Blacks, and Jews—that comprised our high school student body. In English class that year we all read Shakespeare and Keats, but our real poets were the ones whose song lyrics we carefully copied onto our spiral notebook covers. When our teacher asked three students to bring in their favorite poems for the class to interpret the next day, Elisa Colavito showed up with the lyrics to "Born to Run." It was worth every five-paragraph essay we had to write that year to see Mrs. Bluestein squint at the blackboard, trying to scan and analyze *Just wrap your legs round these velvet rims, and strap your hands 'cross my engines.*

My yearbook is filled with hand-scribbled verses like these, all the Jackson Browne and James Taylor and Bruce Springsteen aphorisms we reached for in moments of passion or distress. *I don't know how to tell you all just how crazy this life feels. Close your eyes and think of me, and soon I will be there. Baby, we were born to run.* They were the greatest hits of pre-packaged sentiment, providing me with words that sounded like what I thought I was supposed to feel. I had no blueprint for emotion, no adult I trusted to tell me what I should do with my mother's winter coats, or how to feel when I heard my siblings

83

crying alone in their rooms, or what to say to a father who drank himself to sleep each night. In the absence of any real guidance or experience, Jackson Browne's advice to hold on and hold out was as good as any I could divine on my own.

Discussing music our first night together gave Jimmy T. a convenient chance to introduce his favorite topic—Bruce Springsteen—and engage in open idolatry, which he did at every available moment. By our senior year, Jimmy T. had recreated himself almost entirely in the musician's late '70s image, adopting the appearance (long, dark hair, faded jeans, half smile), the voice (a gravelly just-got-outa-bed-and-smoked-a-packa-Marlboro grumble), the transportation ('69 Chevy with a 396, and a motorcycle, no license), and the look (chin down, eyes up, head tilted slightly to one side) we saw on album covers and in music magazine photo spreads. Jimmy T. wasn't content to merely listen to the man; he actually wanted to *be* him. Which meant that I, in turn, got to be his Wendy-Annie-Rosie-Mary-Janey, his co-pilot in passion and impulse. It gave me a clear persona, straightforward and well-defined. The first time we walked hand-in-hand between the rows of metal lockers, I metamorphosed from the girl whose mother had died of cancer last year into the girl who was dating Jimmy T.— the girl who rode tandem and helmetless on his motorcycle, the girl who didn't care about safety or the law. I'd been waiting all year for someone to hand me a costume that fit so well.

It wasn't a bad deal. After all, the scenery changed every day and I never had to drive.

There are two kinds of men, my mother told me when I was sixteen: the ones who need you, and the ones who need you to need *them*. I eyed my father closely the year after she died, looking for some kind of clue about him, but his actions were too inconsistent, his silence too enigmatic, to help me decide either way. From across the kitchen I watched him, a big, awkward man with a woman's apron tied around his waist, carefully measuring ingredients into a microwaveable casserole dish as his glass of Scotch and soda sweated droplets onto the counter at his side. He insisted on cooking every night, but after dinner he retreated to his room where he fell asleep, snoring loudly, by nine. "He *has* to go to bed this early, so he can wake up for work at five," my sister insisted, in that horrible "Don't FUCK with me . . . please?" tone we all mastered that year. But I knew that sometimes in the middle of the night she went to stand outside our father's room, listening for his breathing, and when

84

she didn't hear it she opened the door a crack just to make sure she saw his chest rise and fall. I knew, because sometimes when I came in late at night I went to check for it, too.

Jimmy T. and I worked out a system: Lying on my bed downstairs, I waited until the last floorboard creaked above my head before I dialed his number. I let it ring only once, hanging up before either of his parents could get to the phone. When I heard his engine idling in the street I climbed out my sub-basement window, crawled across three feet of slippery bark chips and rough shrubs and then sprinted across the lawn to the Chevy's passenger door. I held my breath until the moment when the cool metal door handle connected with my palm, that concrete smack of arrival, exhaling with relief as I landed with a soft thud in his vinyl passenger seat.

We navigated the back roads after midnight, with a Springsteen tape in the cassette deck and a Mexican blanket folded on the back seat. Night was when we made our mark. "Welcome to my beaudoir," Jimmy T. liked to say, gesturing toward the open blanket as I unzipped my jeans. "Would Madame like a mint on her pillow, or perhaps the services of a personal valet?"

We fucked behind a grade school, right beside the jungle gym. We fucked in the backyards of kids we were certain hated us at school. We fucked in a park, in a parking lot, and on a dock along the Hudson River while three geese fought it out over half a bagel. It's a miracle we never got caught. We learned how to be quick about it. Maybe that's why.

Jimmy T. always sang along with the tape as he drove me back to my father's house. He had a pretty good voice, on-key with a slight Jell-O quiver when he held onto the low notes and a scratch against the back wall of his throat when he reached for the high ones. It was a tight match to Springsteen's, and when he sang with the tape I had to listen hard to distinguish between the two. Jimmy T. drove with his left hand on top of the steering wheel and his right hand resting against the back of my neck. The damp summer breeze carried the scents of lawn clippings and moist tree bark through the open windows and into our hair. Sometimes I had to fight the urge to slide my left sneaker on top of Jimmy T.'s right one and press the accelerator to the floor. This was my fantasy: the two of us speeding deeper and deeper into the woods, with his right arm across my shoulders and my left palm resting against his thigh, like a couple in a tiny, private theater with a windshield as our screen.

I knew other girls like me in high school who saw their boyfriends as their saviors, turning to them for the nurturing and attention they couldn't get from home. We were everywhere, holding on to our textbooks with one hand and our boyfriends' belt loops with the other as we maneuvered through the halls; scratching their names into our arm skin with safety pins during study hall, making little love tattoos; sitting knee-to-knee in Planned Parenthood conference rooms while a counselor named Joe waved flat-spring diaphragms and Pill packets in the air as he talked about "shared responsibility." Outside in the waiting room, another group sat clutching their bouquets of ten dollar bills, waiting to file in. There were so many of us, so many rooms of women, all waiting to be saved.

When Jimmy T. and I were juniors, the year before we met, his best friend Billy D'Angelo died. The local newspaper reported it as an accident, no other victims involved. It happened in late May, just a few weeks before Billy would have graduated. I'd known Billy from fifth-period lunch, when we sometimes stood in the same circle in the smoking section outside with our shoulders hunched together to protect our matches from the wind. It was no secret that his grades hadn't been good enough to get him into any college, or that his parents were beginning to turn up the volume about enlisting in the military. "The fucking *army*, man," he said, flicking his cigarette butt into the grass. "Like I'm really going to cut my hair and do pushups. Right."

Wild Billy, his friends called him, after Springsteen's song "Spirit in the Night." *Crazy Janey and her mission man, were back in the alley trading hands, 'Long came Wild Billy with his friend G-man, all duded up for Saturday night.* It's sort of a lonely song, about old friends and drugs and a single night's attempt to get away from it all, but Billy didn't seem to mind the name.

I didn't know Billy all that well, but up until the time he died I still believed the universe was a largely benevolent place run by a judicious management. In this cosmos of my imagination, people didn't die young. My mother was still alive, and though she'd been diagnosed with breast cancer the previous spring, it hadn't yet occurred to me that she might actually do something as radical as *die*. Her own optimism blanketed the family with a false security, allowing us to believe we could all go on living just as we always had, treating cancer and chemotherapy as temporary boarders on a month-to-month lease.

Before Billy died, death was more than just an abstraction to me. It was damn near incomprehensible. When it caught up with him, it caught up with me, too, and I was left struggling to understand the insidious speed and finality of it. One day Billy was cupping his hand around a lit match, trying to light a cigarette in the wind, and the next he was gone, a quenched flame. For the first few days after he died, I kept half-expecting him to sidle up next to me outdoors with an unlit Marlboro dangling from his mouth. I just couldn't wrap my mind around the idea that someone who'd always been there could suddenly be so . . . well, *nowhere,* as far as I could see.

The accident—which is what we were calling it then—had happened on a Saturday night, in a state park about fifteen miles north of town. Jimmy T. and Billy and their crowd of high school friends used to go up there after dark and race cars on the narrow roads that hugged the mountain curves. Billy had convinced Jimmy T., don't ask me how, to lend him his '65 Mustang for the ride. Kimmy Rinaldi, Billy's unofficial fiancée, pulled him over to the gravel shoulder and pleaded with him not to race. Afterward she said she'd just had a bad feeling about that night. Not bad like you were on an airplane and suddenly thought it might be on its way down, she told me, but bad enough to say something, you know? Billy told her not to worry, popped a quick, dry kiss against her mouth, and caught the key ring Jimmy T. tossed his way with a quick twist of his wrist.

What happened next happened quickly. Moments after the two cars squealed off, everyone jogged up the road to see beyond the first bend. Jimmy T. was the first to arrive, just in time to see the Mustang take a sharp right turn off the edge of the road and to hear the sickening crash and thump of metal against granite and bark as the steep forest rejected the car all the way down the mountain's side.

Jimmy T. took off running to where the other driver stood, already out of his car, pounding its roof with a bruised fist and crying without tears. *Crying without tears,* they said. "I don't get it, man. He was on the *inside.* I don't *get* it man. I don't get it." A couple more people ran over, and there was a bunch of noise and some crying, and a lot of spinning around without any real direction before someone decided it would probably be a good idea to call the cops. When Kimmy finally realized what had happened, she started screaming Billy's name, over and over again. It took three people to hold her back, to keep her from going over the edge after him.

The funeral was six days later, in a church around the corner from our school. A wave of students outfitted in tan poly-blend suits and white peasant skirts left after third period that day, all absences excused. After the service, Jimmy T. and some other friends paid their respects to Mrs. D'Angelo and told her how they hoped she'd have "Wild Billy" engraved somewhere on the headstone. They said they knew Billy would have wanted it that way. She was very kind and courteous and said Bill had been so lucky to have had friends as nice as them, but when the stone went up a few weeks later, it read *William Christopher D'Angelo, Beloved Son and Brother, 1963–1981,* and nothing more.

The story of Billy's death quickly became a dark legend told and retold up and down the hallways of our school, increasing in macabre and explicit detail until even those who'd been there couldn't separate the imaginary from the real. The car did a complete flip as it went over the cliff, or was it two, or three? Billy had called out "Kimmy!" as he went down, or was it "Jimmy!" or "Why me?!" Overnight, Billy became our romantic hero, the boy who'd died at the same fast speed at which he'd lived. Never mind that he'd really spent most of his days red-eyed and only marginally coherent in the smoking area outside. Never mind that his car left no skid marks. In myth you have no mortal limits. You can do anything. You can become a god.

I didn't really know Jimmy T. before the crash. His friends later told me that watching it had changed him, but they couldn't explain quite how. It made him more . . . reckless, they said, gazing toward the ceiling as if adjectives grow between fluorescent lights. More . . . unpredictable. More . . . well, just *weirder,* you know?

Yes, I wanted to say. Yes. It's easy to pinpoint the effects of a positive change, harder—unless they're clearly pathological—to recognize those that stem from a loss. Those are our tiny secrets, the runaway pieces of psyche we bury under thick layers of silence and defense. We say we're managing. We say we're doing fine. We say we don't need help and people believe us, because they want to believe us, even when our actions clearly say the opposite is true.

It took me almost a month after our first weekend at the beach to tell Jimmy T. about my mother, though of course he'd known the story all along. Everyone did, by then. I tried to pass it off matter-of-factly in the car one night—"My mother died last year, you know?"—but before I could even finish the sentence I'd begun to cry. It was still that close to the surface. He pulled into the nearest driveway and held me tight, my hands trapped between his chest and my face. He pulled them away and kissed my eyes, licking my tears like a cat. "Shh," he said. "Don't cry. Jimmy T. is here."

That night was the only night he ever talked with me about Billy dying. He told me his version of the crash story from beginning to end: about the good-luck butt slap he gave Billy before he got into the Mustang; the way Billy drove off with his fist thrust out the open window and northwest into the air; and how for one crazy moment, when he first saw the car leave the ledge, he thought it might sprout wings and fly.

If only he hadn't given Billy the keys, Jimmy T. whispered. If only Kimmy had complained a little more. If only he'd been driving the car, Jimmy T. said, and that's when he started to cry, a loud, dry, keening sound like an animal left alone too long. I pulled his head to my shoulder and rocked him, my cheek against his hair. There are times when loss will bind you tighter than happiness or humor or music ever can.

College, Jimmy T. said, was just a place where all the problems of the world masqueraded as department names, but I might as well go anyway. "Someone's got to help me undo all the damage that's been done, and they'll take us more seriously if you have a college degree," he explained. Before I'd even met Jimmy T. I'd been accepted at a school in Illinois, and throughout the summer my departure date hung over us like a heavy Great Plains sky. As August merged into September, Jimmy T. still wasn't sure what he'd do in the fall. Maybe take some courses at the community college in town: philosophy, or religion, or poetry or film. He once casually mentioned coming to Chicago with me. My evasive "Yeah . . ." surprised us both, and told him not to offer again. We both knew he was only grasping for a plan as he watched his previously reliable audience begin to disperse, moving on to college, the military, and jobs in other states.

This hadn't been the promise. The promise had been that we'd stay young together, follow our dreams, and one day land on the cover of *Newsweek* or *Rolling Stone*. It hadn't accounted for the powerful force that smoothly propels upper-middle-class kids out of high school and into whatever it is they're expected to do next.

We'd counted on Springsteen, at least, to keep his original vow, but even he couldn't sustain it forever. With the release of *Nebraska* in the fall of 1982, he made the sudden transition from the prophet of one generation's rhapsody to the chronicler of another's demise. The album was a veritable avalanche of fractured dreams, filled with stories of plant shutdowns, home foreclosures, and debtors driven to desperate means.

Springsteen was just describing the times, I suppose, but they weren't my times anymore. The first time I listened to *Nebraska* and heard *Everything dies, baby that's a fact, but maybe everything that dies someday comes back,* was the first time I'd ever listened to a Bruce Springsteen song and thought, You are wrong. You are so completely wrong.

The night before I left for college, I tacked a calendar on Jimmy T.'s bedroom wall and counted off the days until I'd be home for Thanksgiving break. "Seventy-four," I told him with manufactured optimism as he sat sullenly on the edge of the bed, wrists dangling between his knees. "When you wake up in the morning, it'll be only seventy-three."

"I know how to subtract."

Overnight, I had become the traitor, he the betrayed. "Don't leave me," I pleaded, as I held onto him at the door.

"What?" he said. "You're the one who's getting on the plane without me."

Which I did, in the middle of September, on a direct flight to Chicago from New York. The first friend I made in my dorm became my closest one that year, a prep school graduate from Massachusetts with Mayflower ancestry and an album collection filled with Joni Mitchell, Johnathan Edwards, and Neil Young. "Bruce Springsteen?" she asked, scrunching up her nose in thought. And then, after a pause, "Isn't he that short guy from New Jersey?" By the second week of school, I'd buried all my cassette tapes in the bottom of a desk drawer. It's frighteningly easy to abandon the familiar when you discover it might be cliché.

Jimmy T. mailed me a letter in late September saying he couldn't contact me again until Halloween, because he was going on the road with his new band. So you can imagine my surprise when, in mid-October, I returned from an anthropology class on a Thursday afternoon and found him sitting alone in the first floor lounge of my dormitory, his black leather jacket with the chrome zippers at odd angles hopelessly out of place in the sea of Izod sweaters and wool peacoats from Peck & Peck. He looked like a page from one short story ripped out and used as the bookmark in another, and when I first saw him I pulled my books into my chest and took a step back. He understood that step, he told me later. Hey! he said. Jimmy T. is no fool.

90

I didn't know exactly what pushed—or pulled—me back into the protective pocket of the glassed-in entryway. All I knew was in that moment after I instinctively withdrew, I suddenly understood something about relationships, something important. I understood there was a third kind of man my mother never told me about, the kind who *you* need, regardless of how he feels about you. The kind who offers you shelter when no one else even knows how to open a damn umbrella. The kind you can love but can never stay with for long, because the reason you ran to him in the first place was to gather the strength you needed to leave.

Jimmy T. stayed with me in Chicago for three days. We argued the whole time. We apologized in harmony, and then we argued some more. He wanted me to come back with him. I wanted him to leave alone. He wrote prose poems and taped them to my mirror when I was in class. *The Chicago wind blows back your hair, you're living your art, your part. Long camel hair and scarf.* We couldn't get past metaphor. "My axe has broken strings," he told me late one night, and I asked him to please for God's sake just drop the poetry and get to the point.

Our conversation, at the end: He said I came here to ask you to do something with me, and I said What? and he said But now I see you won't, and I said *What?* and he said I can't tell you, exactly, but it has to do with a quest I can't fulfill alone, and I said Please. *Please* would you just tell me what you mean. And he said All right, but you can't tell anyone, you swear? So I swore, and he nodded, and then he told me, very simply, that he was the Second Coming of Christ.

After he'd gotten back on the plane alone, after I'd called his mother from the pay phone at O'Hare, after the iceberg in my stomach finally began to thaw, I spent long nights wondering about the role I'd played in all this. Could I have prevented it somehow? Could I have been the cause? As the letters addressed to Jimmy T. came back marked "Return to Sender" in an angry scrawl, I lay on my bed and stared at the ceiling, looking for the words that would help me understand.

I was lying like this in my dorm room one night with the clock radio tuned in to Chicago's WXRT when I heard the first few bars of Jimmy T.'s song, the one he and his friend George had sold to the record company, come through on the air. I lay very still, barely breathing, trying to identify whose voice was singing the familiar words. I didn't dare move, too afraid I'd miss the end of the song and the name of the band.

I had to wait through two more songs before the deejay returned " . . . and before that we heard the Greg Kihn Band," he said, as the music faded away. "Doing a remake of an old Bruce Springsteen tune."

Somewhere in the distance, I imagine, an engine revved and purred. Somewhere far beyond my reach, another boy shifted into high gear and pressed the pedal to the floor, believing he could sail on and on into the night.

Nominated by The Iowa Review

ONE STORY

by DEAN YOUNG

from THE THREEPENNY REVIEW

In one story, the coyote sings us into being.
The self is either a single arrow shot
into the sun or a long, squiggly thing
wet at one end. If someone were
to rip the roof off and look down on us,
we'd look like lice on a tribal mask.
Now Lorca, there was a poet. The disordered
strength of the curved water, he wrote
shortly before he was shot in the head.
Maybe distorted. We know he held hands
with a school teacher, also shot, and how
the last hour he was sure he'd be shot
and sure he'd be released. At the last moment,
Van Gogh slashed crows across the wheat field.
Winter is scary enough but to follow it with Spring . . .
God must be demented, he must spend a lot of time
out in the cosmic downpour. I mean what
would you do if you had to create Beauty?
I'm afraid I'd start screaming, the most irksome
forms of insects coming from my mouth. I'm afraid
I'd come up with Death. On my desk
is a paperweight, a copse of glass flowers inside.
The last few months my father amassed a collection
of paperweights. He knew he was going to disappear.
Finally my mother said, Take a couple.
I don't think I have the proper papers to weight.

The other is a pewter frog.
It was May, I was 19, writing a paper
on Hamlet for a professor who'd hang himself.
I remember the funeral director asking
my sister and me if we wanted to see my father
one last time. I thought for a moment
it was a serious offer. But he was talking about
a corpse. A corpse in make-up. But this year,
I will get it right, I will stare at a single branch
for all of May. I will know what it's going through
at least on the fructifying surface. In May
he bought a yellow suit he wore just once.
In May I will listen to the bark whimper and split,
the blossoms blink from sleep. I will
haunt the town I've haunted for years,
turning the corner of Sixth and
Grant, seeing myself just ahead
in that ratty jean jacket, sleeve ripped
to fit over the cast. A few pains remain,
become formalized, enacted in dance
but I'm careful not to catch myself. He might
want to get me high in the middle of the day.
I might have work to do, I might be going to the ash
I planted over my dead cat years back
behind the garden where Nancy lost the ring
my father made from a quarter during the war.
She will be sobbing, searching among the infant tomatoes.
It's okay, I will say and she will nod and vanish.
It's all right, I will say and my cat will cease
mewing beneath the earth.

Nominated by Ralph Angel, Richard Jackson, James Harms, Patricia Henley, Joyce Carol Oates, William Olsen, Donald Revell, David Rivard, David Wojahn

DAILY AFFIRMATIONS

fiction by ERIN MCGRAW

from THE GEORGIA REVIEW

A WEEK BEFORE FLYING back to my parents' house for Christmas, my suitcases were already packed. I knew that packing early was an unproductive habit, discouraging me from living in the moment, but by three o'clock one sleepless morning my self-control had ebbed and I hauled out the suitcases for the plain relief of doing something.

It was December 8th, and I had been focusing my support group on families and the holidays since September, talking about strategies, battle. "You're going to be on the front lines. How will you defend yourselves when the choppers start coming in?" I suggested that they take home one another's telephone numbers as well as talismans to carry or wear. Myself, I packed two books of affirmations, the cassettes from the seminars I had led the summer before, and my favorite button—the one I liked to wear to workshops. It showed a stick figure tugging at a huge barbell, and it said LIGHTEN UP.

Thinking about what lay ahead, I pinned the button to my coat. My mother, who insisted on going to daily Mass, had just broken her ankle on a slick spot outside the church, so she would be bedridden—*helpless* was her word—for three months. When I talked to my father on the phone, he said she was making the whole ordeal worse than it had to be: "She won't use the crutches. She talks like nobody's ever been in pain before." I had to fight down my impulse to talk about honoring her pain, which he wouldn't have paid any attention to. Anyway, as long as I was in my own apartment, it was their issue, not mine.

After I finished packing I wandered into the kitchen and flicked open the freezer. I could catalogue every item in it, including the mousse cake left over from dinner with Jon in November. Binge eating in the middle of the night was another behavior I tried to avoid; it channeled into every old complex that had wrecked my twenties. I thought about this, then fished out the cake and went to the cupboard for peanut butter and bread.

In *Returning to the Body* I wrote a chapter called "Eating For Two" about this exact phenomenon. That chapter roped almost as much attention as the ones on sex, and for months after the book came out I fielded phone calls from women who wanted to confess their late-night eating. One woman wept and admitted that she'd eaten a stick of butter like a candy bar. We talked for half an hour, and before she hung up she gave me permission to use her story in my next book. I was already at work on it, a follow-up that my publisher wanted to call *Into the Light*. My suitcases were stuffed with notes, a computer, and the transcripts of fifty workshops. My theory was that by writing while I was home I could distance myself from my past and—a bonus—allow my parents to see the woman I had become.

I tucked a third book of affirmations into my purse. Trips home always courted danger; one step into my mother's kitchen and my whole new life would start to waver and float. I'd found it useful to talk in sessions about the dream I had when I was home—how a warm, dark current pulled me farther and farther from shore. When I described it, every head in the room nodded.

After I finished the cake I crossed my legs, relaxed my shoulders, and closed my eyes. I inhaled to the count of five and began that day's affirmation: *Today I will acknowledge that healing is a lengthy process, and I will give myself permission to take my time.*

I took thirty deep breaths and shifted on the couch, easing my pants at the waist where they bit. This was the fifth night in a row I had dipped into the Skippy. Peanut butter was itself a danger sign—hadn't I counseled clients to purge their cupboards before Thanksgiving?—but my resolve was shrinking the closer in time I got to my parents. A dull recklessness had set in; I was sleeping through the alarm in the mornings, too, skipping exercise classes, and not telling Jon about any of it. He was fond of reminding me that as an adult I had choices. *He* wasn't the one going to visit his parents. "We've learned to avoid the holidays," he said when I asked him. "Damage containment."

After the flight landed in Los Angeles and I shuffled to the terminal behind a grim man carrying an enormous plush kangaroo, the first

96

thing I saw was my father, waving hugely, grinning and hooting like a Texan. Usually it was my mother who stood leaning against the low restraining gate. She was nearsighted but never could find glasses that pleased her, so she would crane over the gate and peer at every passenger until she found me. Dad would be waiting in the car outside, avoiding the parking lot where, my mother had once read, over a hundred muggings occurred every year. But now here was my father, whooping at me, calling my nickname, which only my family used.

"Tracy. Tracybug! Hey, sight for sore eyes," he said, trying to grab me with one arm, my bag with the other.

"Hi, Dad," I said into his shoulder. "Hey, yourself."

"You don't know how glad I am to see you," he said, letting me step back so he could look at me. He was beaming.

"It's funny to see you here without Mom."

"Everything's going to feel different," he said. "We've had McDonald's for dinner the last four nights."

"What, you forgot how to scramble eggs?"

"Your mother won't let me in the kitchen. She thinks I'll ruin her frying pans. But now that you're home, we've got her over a barrel. What say, halibut tonight?"

"Mom doesn't like fish," I said.

"I know," Dad said, wiggling his eyebrows, "but I do." He threw his arm around me again and squeezed. "It's good to have you home, Trace. You look good. Cornfed."

"I've been very busy," I said. I started down the corridor toward Baggage Claim—it was time to get moving, and Dad looked like he was ready to stand there all day. "You can't imagine all the conferences, and then small-group work. And my publisher wants the new book by June."

"Don't count on having much of your own life. This is your mother we're talking about."

I turned back to look at him. He was holding his mouth in a sour smirk, watching me. Usually it took a little longer before he started coaxing me to join in the chorus of his gripes. "You need to be generous with her now," I said. "This sort of challenge can be a good thing— a time of real growth. She's just discovering her own new needs."

"Me too," Dad said. "My need is to get her to quit complaining. When Monsignor called last night she talked to him as if her leg had fallen off. After she hung up she cried and reminded me that faith can move mountains."

I closed my eyes for a second. I'd heard about her faith all my life and hadn't seen it move so much as a note card. Then I told him, "We can fry some potatoes with the halibut—that's always nice. If you have any apples on hand, I'll make a pie."

"Now you're talking," Dad said.

We stopped at the big Thriftimart on the way home and bought seven bags of groceries; whenever I stopped to look at an item he put it in the basket. "I don't know what we have," he shrugged, collecting cornmeal, tortillas, vanilla. By the time we got home it was nearly four, the sun low. I tried to pull my snug jacket tighter against the sharp ocean wind. Dad unlocked the door, then gestured me in with a courtly sweep of his arm, and so I was the first one to see my mother crumpled at the bottom of the stairs.

"I was sure you'd been in an accident," she said. "I told myself you would never take so long to get home unless you were in an accident." She turned and I could see how she had tucked the leg without the cast underneath her to keep warm. I could also see the urine puddled on the back of her robe. "If you understood the pain I'm in you would have been home sooner."

"Mom, I'm sorry," I said, dropping the bag of groceries and squatting, letting her shoulder rest against me.

"Of course you are," she said.

Dad trudged up from the garage with the suitcases, muttering as he always did about how I must have packed bricks. When he saw my mother on the floor he sighed. "For Pete's sake!" he said, setting down the suitcases and bending to lift her up.

"I was trying to get to the bathroom," she said. "You were gone so long." I had never heard this flutter in my mother's voice before; it made her sound dreamy and mild.

"Why do you think the doctor gave you crutches?" Dad said.

"They hurt. You think it's easy, but it's not."

"You're working hard to keep it complicated, I'll give you that," he said, letting her lean on him as she steadied herself on her good foot. "This is quite a homecoming for our daughter."

"Don't worry about me," I said with idiotic brightness. "I'm tough."

My mother glanced at me and twisted her mouth. "I'm not weak. But I could never have believed the pain."

"Now that we've shared that, Mother, let's get you cleaned up," Dad said, steadying her hips while she awkwardly hopped ahead of him.

"Then you can come down and talk to Tracy. She's going to make dinner for us."

"A blessing," my mother said, breathing hard. Dad turned and winked at me, and I rolled my eyes despite my best intentions.

When I finally got Jon on the phone I told him, "It's like trying to skirt quicksand." I'd been home four days. "One foot is always being sucked in."

"This is your opportunity to work on detachment," Jon said.

"I *am* detached, dammit! She talks about God's will, Dad tells her he's sick of her whining, and I try to yell over the fray for timeouts."

"You can only take responsibility for yourself." His voice was hushed and choppy, and I could picture him nodding, waving his hands to hurry me along. His wife was probably in the next room.

"It's such a relief to talk to you," I told him, my voice sticky and wheedling. "Something solid."

"The holidays are a difficult period for everyone," he said. "We're set up to relive the traumas of our youth."

"We've got the mother lode here," I muttered, but he was still talking, reminding me not to let others define my reality for me. I didn't have a chance to tell him about watching Bob Hope on TV the night before. When I had stood up to bring in some cookies, I'd seen my mother's face covered in tears. "It hurts. It's like something gnawing with sharp teeth," she said when I touched her shoulder.

"For God's sake, Mother, why didn't you say something?"

"I didn't want to bother you," she said.

Now Jon was saying something about openness to life's richness. "I'm open, all right," I told him. "I'm taking in every morsel that my rich new life provides me."

Dad came down to the kitchen every night after the news, when I liked to have a snack. "At least you can get some sleep," he would say, breaking off a piece of whatever I was fixing. "She lies there and just moans—in case I forget for one second the torment she's in."

It was so hard to resist. Already I had found myself telling him about washing her hair, when she started screaming because I'd let shampoo seep into the corner of her eye. She pushed me out of the way and hobbled back to bed, soapy water streaming down her neck. "Fastest I've seen her move since I got home," I told Dad.

"Good to know something can make her jump," he said. "She lies in that bed like she wants to make a career of it."

Now that I was home, Mother was making more of an effort to get up, but her lurching progress exhausted her. She collapsed into chairs and sat, pinched and silent, for fifteen minutes before she could gather herself to speak, her suffering face a mask of accusation. I trudged downstairs later every morning and lost whole afternoons to elaborate recipes that called for stacks of phyllo and jasmine rice.

"I really would prefer plain chicken," she kept saying from the armchair we rolled into the kitchen for her. "Rich food doesn't agree with me."

"We're trying some new things," I said, enjoying myself. Every time I suggested a menu, Dad headed to the grocery store—I had never cooked better. With his encouragement I tried chicken stuffed with chestnuts, then chocolate-mint torte. Mom picked at all of it. "Good for the holidays," I said when I served the cashew-rolled tenderloin that, left over, made such good sandwiches. "I never eat this way at home."

In the mornings I stared helplessly at my computer screen. The chapter about coping strategies was only sketched out, so every morning I reviewed my thick stack of notes and case histories, but I couldn't manage to boil them down to the punchy, practical style my publisher liked. After a half-hour of twisting on the chair, I would go to call Jon.

I knew my relationship with him was not ideal, but it was a far cry from the terrible entanglements of my twenties. "More affairs than I could count. As long as men were unavailable—emotionally, maritally, fiscally, or physically—I was game," I wrote in the first book. That confession had been crucial to my recovery; it took all the courage I had to publish it. After the book was included in an article about recovery literature in *Newsweek*, my brother Patrick, who used to drive me wild by calling me Saint Tracy when I was a pious ten-year-old, sent a furious letter addressed to Slut Tracy. I brought it to the next session I facilitated, as an example of how families can stand in the way of our growth.

My parents never mentioned the book at all. I waited until two weeks after the *Newsweek* article, then finally asked whether they had seen it. Jon held my hand while I made the call.

"I'm not going to read your book. It doesn't seem like something I'd like," said my mother. "We're both very proud of you."

I didn't bring it up again. When Jon reminded me that issues unaddressed are issues unresolved, I flash my LIGHTEN UP button and told him to take it one day at a time.

Now I typed: *Health isn't a goal like a high-jump record. Life throws us curves.* I sighed and wiped it out. There was a tap at the door, and then Dad opened it a crack to look in at me. "Just making sure you were off the phone," he said.

"Never was on it. Couldn't get through."

"You've sure been trying."

"You monitoring my calls?"

"Now, now. Your mother frets. She thinks your publisher should be the one paying for long distance."

"I'm not calling my publisher," I said. "I'm calling my collaborator."

"Collaborator. Sounds like World War II." He raised his eyebrows at me; he wanted me to play, but I swiveled back to the keyboard.

"I'll shave my head and you can parade me through the streets," I said.

"I'll leave that to your mother. Who wants you to wash her hair this afternoon. Apparently she's recovered from your last assault."

I quickly typed: *We who seek and strive are heroes. If we really understood the powers we struggle against, we would never even try.* I saved it, turned off the computer and said, "Tell her majesty I'm on my way." I pushed back from the computer so hard my chair screed and stuttered on the wood floor.

After I'd been home a week, I had floated well out to sea. I sat at my computer from nine to twelve and buried myself in cooking all afternoon. My mother joined me when I came downstairs, so my sautéing and mincing stopped whenever she needed more pillows, or a sip of grapefruit juice, or—the most frequent—help in hobbling to the bathroom. Sometimes she sat at the table and phoned one of my brothers, then handed off the phone to me. "Well," said James, the one closest to me in age. "Doing your bit for family. Finding stories to tell for another book?"

"I'm working on it," I said evenly.

"Myself, I thought the first book was plenty."

"That was about opening the door. This one is about starting the journey."

"Mary's fine, and the twins are great," he said. "They've got almost all their teeth."

"You should bring them out to visit. Mom tells me all the time how she wishes you'd let her dote on them." That was the kind of meanness I wouldn't have stooped to a month before, but I was tired now

101

from treading water. Jon hadn't answered the phone since the first call. When I took time out to read my affirmations, they felt absurdly childish, chipper as Norman Vincent Peale, and it took an exhausting act of faith to bother opening the book at all.

"It's good to see you and your brothers talking," Mom would say after I hung up. "A close family is one of the graces I pray for every day."

This was an opening volley, but there was no way I could have known. All that time with idle hands and a throbbing ankle had allowed her to conceive a campaign. She launched it on Christmas day, after we came home from Mass, which had left us undone. She had winced and gasped the whole short ride, then redirected Dad three times inside the church so her wheelchair could be out of the way but she could still see the priest.

After the service she held court outside in the thin December sunshine, and it took a half-hour to wheel her away from the people who pressed their cheeks to hers and told her how she never left their prayers for a minute. "And see," my mother kept saying, grabbing my hand, "my daughter is home." I smiled while they nodded coolly at me. Clearly they had read the book. *I have nothing to apologize for,* I wanted to say. But they didn't talk to me, and by the time we came back home I felt as if I'd been flayed.

"I can't tell you the good it does me to go to Mass," my mother uttered faintly, her head resting against the chair back. "I miss it so."

"Until that ankle heals, God's just going to have to understand," Dad said.

"The Mass is a comfort," she said.

"You certainly are popular," I said. "It looked like you knew everybody there."

"We have a community."

"Now that people know what's happened to you, I'm sure they'll call," I said. "You won't feel so cut off."

"It's not the same," she said, twisting fretfully and waving her hand as if she would reach over the length of her cast and rub it herself. Dad and I watched her for a second, then I went over and rested her foot on my lap while I got to work. She went on: "The new priest, Father Jim, he gives such good sermons—even on weekdays. You wouldn't believe."

"What are you angling for, Mother?" Dad asked.

"Nothing. I'm not *angling for* anything."

"That's good," he said. "Because Trace and I have got our hands full here."

"I just think," she said, "it would be nice if you two went to Mass together during the week. It would be a nice sharing time for you. And you could tell me what Father Jim said."

I kept rubbing and shot a look at my mother's face, which was serene as the Madonna's. "Mary Grace," Dad said, "you're out of your mind."

"I don't know why you say that. I think it's a good idea."

"Tracy and I are not going to start getting up at five-thirty to go off to Mass for you. I can't believe the wild hairs you get."

"I don't see any reason that you should speak for our daughter," my mother said, trying to hike herself up in the chair. "She's perfectly capable of speaking her own mind."

I was bent over her foot, still rubbing away. "I write in the mornings," I said.

"You could manage a half-hour for Mass. It would probably help your writing."

"I don't think so," I said without looking up.

She yanked her foot away from me, swinging the cast out so hard it jerked off my lap and crashed to the floor. "So you won't even consider it? Both of you just too busy to do this simple thing for me." She sniffed hard and tried to clamp her mouth. "It's a small enough favor, God knows."

"Not everyone shares your sense of priorities, Mother," Dad said.

"You've made that perfectly clear," she said. I reached down to hoist her leg back up, but she snapped, "Just leave it alone. I wouldn't dream of putting you out."

"Don't jump all over the girl," Dad said. "You're making a federal case here. It isn't that important."

"I'm glad. I'm certainly glad to know that what I want isn't that important."

"Oh, for Christ's sake, Mary Grace, lighten up."

"I wish you wouldn't swear in front of Tracy."

"She's heard worse," he said.

"I'll go," I said. I was clenching and unclenching my hands, trying to control my breathing. I didn't look at either one of them. "Maybe I'll find something I can use in my book."

"No," my mother said, jerking her chin. "I don't want you to go now."

"Tracy, sweetheart, you can't just give in," Dad said.

I stood up. "I can't stand listening to you two. When did you start going for blood? You never used to fight like this."

Dad shook his head and sighed. "Always. But you didn't notice what you didn't want to see."

"You had your head in the clouds," my mother nodded.

"Things are different now," I said, and went into the kitchen. I had made brownies and icebox bars the day before, from recipes in my mother's oldest cookbook. I put a handful on a plate and then headed for the stairs and my room, but Mother called me back.

"You know," she said, "Doris Dilworth started going to daily Mass when she began her diet last year, and she was finally able to lose the weight and keep it off. Isn't that interesting? You could use a story like that in your book."

"You really don't know when to stop, do you?"

"I don't know what you're talking about," she said, starting to tear up again. "I just made a suggestion."

"Well, I've got a suggestion for you. Next time you're checking in with God and asking for graces, try asking for the grace to know when to shut the fuck up," I cried as I tore up the stairs.

Jon wasn't home when I called, and he wasn't home half an hour later. Grimly, I settled in for a siege, picking up the phone every twenty minutes. He would have to answer eventually. He and his wife were staying home for the holidays, taking the chance to spend time with their sons. I used his private number, which rang only in his home office. All afternoon and into the evening it rang.

At intervals I went downstairs to snack. Neighbors had been dropping by with cookies and fruitcake; the kitchen counter was crowded with fancy plates, and Mom held court in the living room. Once I ran into my father, who said, "You've been slaving away ever since you got here. What say I go out and pick up some Mexican tonight?" I shrugged, nodded. If he opened the refrigerator he would see enough leftovers piled up to see us into the new year.

I didn't get Jon until after eleven—after one, Chicago time. "I've been trying to reach you all day," I said when he picked up the phone.

"We went ice skating, and then we picked out a tree."

"How nice. Around here it's cruise missiles."

"You're giving in. This is how they win. What good is all your hard work if you don't hold tight under fire?"

"Families aren't supposed to be battlegrounds," I spat.

"Well, they are," he said shortly. "But at least you ought to be getting some good material."

"As a matter of fact, I'm not," I said. "My parents have staged a battle to the death, and my mother has bullied me into daily Mass."

"She can't make you do anything," he said, and I thought that finally he'd said something my mother would agree with. Even as irritated as I was, I was swayed by the heavy, creamy fall of his voice. "You're the only one responsible for your decisions."

"Listen, I got them to stop carping at each other for two minutes."

"Holidays. They should give out operator's licenses," he said. A moment's silence shimmered between us, a rare thing. "Is there anyone there you can talk to?"

"Jon, I'm talking to you."

"When you're in a bottom you need lots of support."

"Good. Support me. Did you tell your wife about the apartment?"

"I told you I don't want to bring it up until after New Year's."

The glittering silence descended again, and I pictured the lines of telephone wire between us shivering. "Look," I said. "I'm having a hard time. Things here are terrible. I need to know that you miss me."

"Of course I do."

"Try sounding like you mean it."

"I do. Of course. But remember," he said, "some needs can't be filled by another person." I could hear the wheels of his desk chair rolling over the floor, and I pictured a woman standing in the doorway of his office. "Some needs it's up to you to find a way to fill."

"Thanks, Jon. Good support. I'll be sure to call again," I said.

"It'll be easier when you come home. You'll remember who you really are. You'll reclaim your new life."

"If my old life lets me," I said.

I groped down the stairs the next morning at quarter to six, stuffing my shirt into my pants. Mom always put on a skirt to go to church, but if God were expecting me this early, He could accustom His all-seeing eyes to pants. Which, too tight, hurt.

Dad was already in the kitchen, dressed and glaring at the front page. "I didn't think you were going," I said.

"Once you gave in I didn't have any choice," he sighed. "What the hell. Let's go out to the Belgian waffle place afterwards. Salvage something out of this."

"What about Mom?" I said.

"I walked her to the bathroom at two, three, four-thirty and five-thirty-seven. If she's not dry as the Sahara, she can hold it." He fished in his pocket and tossed me the car keys. His night vision had gotten dicey, and the sky was still licorice black. "Let's go."

We didn't talk at all on the drive over, and had to grope our way into the tiny chapel where daily Mass was held. A dozen women were already yawning and waiting in sweatsuits and stretch pants, none of them under sixty. They swung their heads up together like deer when we slipped in; Dad and I took the folding chairs by the door. Everyone was close enough to touch.

When the priest walked in without any fanfare, the women rustled to their feet, and he smiled at them, a sweetly generous smile. "Let's begin," he murmured, and crossed himself. The women pitched into prayer with wonderful precision, none of them even bothering to glance at the missalettes. I tried to imagine coming here every morning in the dark, reciting prayers by heart, and then going home to make breakfast. It felt utterly peculiar.

"What do you make of that?" I asked Dad when we were back out in the chilly black air.

"I managed to nod off twice, which is about as much rest as I get sleeping with your mother these days."

"Don't tell her that. She'll count it as a victory."

When we got to the car I turned up both the heat and the radio, and we sang along to "The Lion Sleeps Tonight" all the way to the restaurant. A waitress with eyes that looked like they'd been set in with a wood-burning kit seated us without a word. Dad glanced at the menu, put it aside, and cleared his throat while I was looking at the strawberry waffles. He fiddled with his napkin, folding it into a little pup tent next to his fork until I looked up again. "You know, you're going to have to talk to your mother," he said.

"I'll pay attention to the sermon tomorrow. I'll take notes."

"Not that," he said. "You were pretty hard on her yesterday. She takes these things to heart."

I frowned at him. "She's got to learn to back off."

Dad smiled unhappily and picked up his spoon, trying to catch his reflection in its bowl. "She doesn't realize sometimes. She loses track. But Honey, she cried all night."

"Shit." I closed my eyes. "I lost my temper. I'm not perfect." I looked up; he was nodding, and my anger started to swell again. "We do everything she wants. You say so yourself. Why else are we going to church in the middle of the night?"

"You don't get it, Trace. You'll be gone in a week. When James told her not to come out after his babies were born, she cried every day for a month. She loves you all."

"So who are you trying to help here? You want me to go do a case study on her dieting friend to get her off your back?"

"She thinks you'd be happier if you were thinner. You *are* pretty big, Honey."

I folded the menu closed and shook out my napkin so it had no wrinkles. My stomach growled. I knew I had the words to respond to him; I had a whole speech. But the speech had drifted away, and there was only a table separating me from my father. It wasn't enough.

"Displacement?" I said. That didn't sound right.

"Not funny, Tracy."

"I'm not trying to be funny."

"I don't need your psychoanalysis," he said sharply.

"We're a long way from the couch. I'm just wondering what it means when a father avoids his wife by trying to win over his daughter."

He flattened his hand on the table. "I said *don't* condescend to me."

"Well then, *don't* intrude in my life."

"I'm so far from intruding, I can barely even see you," he snarled. "If I was going to start intruding, I might take your telephone away. I might ask why you're the one doing the calling, and why you don't mention his name to your mother, who would like to know. I could lock up the sugar and butter and feed you lettuce."

"I made the food you told me you liked," I said behind clenched teeth. "I'll be happy to make salads for you in the future. Better yet, I'll hand over the lettuce. You can make dinner to your own exacting standards."

The blank-eyed waitress materialized next to us and stood tapping her order pad. "Just coffee," Dad said, glancing at her. "I can't eat this early."

I opened the menu and pointed to a photo of three waffles mortared by thick layers of whipped cream with blueberries. "That," I said. "And coffee." The air in the restaurant was warm and sweet, full of low laughter and the scrape of cutlery on heavy plates. I was so hungry the images wobbled before me.

"That ought to help things," Dad said after the waitress turned away. "Good choice."

107

"We came to a waffle restaurant. I ordered waffles."

"Nothing I say makes any difference to you, does it?"

"I'm an adult. I have to make my own decisions."

"You make some piss-poor ones."

"Impressive talk from a man who's spent fifty years arguing with his wife."

Dad leaned across the table. "At least I married the person I sleep with. At least I don't have to plead with her to talk to me."

"No," I said. "You save the pleading for me."

Dad stared at me, then stood up. "You know what your mother says? She says evil takes good and makes it look bad. I *know* you, no matter what you think." He spun around and walked out. When the waitress came back I nodded at his place, as if he were going to be back in a minute, and I went ahead and ate my breakfast. Even though the berries were lost in the gummy syrup and the coffee was faintly burned, I ate every scrap and wiped the plate to get the juice. When I finished my cup of coffee, I drank Dad's.

Tiptoeing into the chapel by myself the next morning I still felt clumsy and shy, but the chair by the door was open and the quiet warmth of the room was comforting. I had joined my parents for TV the night before, apologizing at the first station break. They nodded, and I went up early to bed. When I left, I heard my mother sigh.

I folded my hands now and watched the faces around me—they were uniformly peaceful, as if bread were on the rise in every one of their kitchens. I couldn't imagine my mother wearing such a look. Patrick used to do imitations called "Mom at Mass": preoccupied, muttering, ticking off mysterious lists on his fingers, while James and I roared.

The side door opened and I looked up to see an ancient woman supported by a walker, wearing the shapeless polyester skirt and crepe-soled shoes of a nun. Two women near the door bounced up and guided her to a chair, one on each side, smiling and murmuring. They moved as if they had done this many, many times, waiting until the sister was secure in her chair before they moved her walker to the wall.

I kept staring at the nun, her faint hair coiled into a permanent that exposed rambling pathways of scalp. The way she tottered, she must have gotten up at three to make it to the chapel. Surely, I thought, the priest could have come to her. But when she had entered her face held the same calm, pleasant look as the other women's. If you came every morning, over enough years, did the calm come?

Abruptly tears began to well, and I couldn't stop them, although I knuckled my eyes hard. In fact, I started to cry harder, giving in, and had to bury my face in my hands to muffle the sniffling. After a minute I felt a hand rest on my shoulder. "There, now," a voice said. "There. Is it someone you're crying for?"

"My mother," I whispered, and though I didn't look up, I imagined the woman beside me nodding.

"No prayers are ever wasted," she said. "God hears you. He'll bring your mother to His side. He sends tears as a sign."

I glanced up then, blinking to see her mild face. "It's not that simple."

"I'll pray for her too," she said, smiling and patting my hand. I was saved from having to respond by the priest, who hurried through the door straightening his stole and inviting us to pray. Swiping my hand across my nose, I joined in the communal responses, feeling the tears stop and the sense of warm, liquid collapse drain away. I was back on dry land, beached on the shore of my recognizable life, where I stood uncomfortably waiting for Mass to end.

The old nun stayed seated through the opening prayers, but she swayed gamely to her feet during the intercessions. After the other women offered their personal supplications—"For my daughter Jenny," "For my cousin's surgery"—she said, her voice dry as a rusk, "God's peace to the believers." The prayer made me uneasy. I couldn't be sure what it meant, but the woman beside me shot up and cried "Amen" with a zeal that made me cringe, and the others echoed her. I craned, trying to see the nun's face—had she intended a call to arms? All I could see was her wavering stance, and then the unceremonious way she tipped over, dropping to her left like a carelessly balanced board.

The women were at her side instantly, straightening her legs, rubbing her hands and feet, and the priest was already moving toward her with the host. I stood watching from the back, caged between folding chairs, as out of place as an ungainly animal. The nun coughed once, tremendously, from the altar. At least she was alive. For the second time tears surged, and I groped to the door and felt my way out.

Ten minutes later I was still sitting in the cold car, listening to my breath shudder and catch. I felt chastised, slapped by some vast hand,

and I could stop crying only by focusing on what was directly in front of me: a spindly tree supported on three sides by wires. No leaves. Its branches made shadows like veins in the light from the church.

Going home was out of the question. Mom would ask about Mass, and I'd be helpless to control my ragged crying. Or Dad would shoot me an ironic look. I felt naked, skinned, lacking the barest boundary from the world. When my feet got cold enough to hurt, I started the car, but from the parking lot I turned right, away from East Gables.

Seventeen years had passed since I'd lived in California, but I drove with perfect memory. Jon had some expression about how adolescent knowledge is the hardest to lose. I felt more adolescent now than I had ever felt as a teenager—teary, shaken, driving because movement was soothing.

I turned onto Pacific, the first four-lane street I'd ever known. Windows were starting to light up; coffee-shop parking lots were half full, and a wobbly mechanical Santa on top of a computer store soundlessly waved and laughed. Four stoplights down was the rec center where I'd learned to swim. It had a flashy new sign out in front, listing classes and meetings for the holidays—Weight Watching In Fruitcake Season; Quik-stitch Quilting; Holidays Without Ho-ho-ho: Support Group. Surprisingly, lights were on throughout the building.

If I had been my mother, I would have called that sign the hand of God. I turned into the parking lot from the far lane. Even if the group wasn't a good one, I figured, there would be a coffeepot going in the back. The meeting was practically finished when I crept in—the leader, a shockingly thin woman with hair cut above her ears, was already reading from the closing statements. "We come together without fears or requirements," she read dully. "We allow each other our own needs. If you feel that you belong here, you belong."

The group was fairly large for so early in the morning—I counted twenty-two women listening in the circle. One, near the leader, was so frantic around the eyes and mouth she looked like she'd vibrate if you brushed her arm. "It is our faith that all pain is to be honored," the leader read. I knew all of this; I'd heard it hundreds of times, meeting after meeting, night after night. Sometimes two meetings a day, before I met Jon, when the loneliness was so sheer and bright I burned my fingertips with matches as a distraction. Next came call and response.

"Our experience—" the leader read.

"—is the center of our being," the group chanted back.

"Our responsibility—"

110

"—is our own healing."

I thought of my mother, her pursed lips and fussy fingers. With some shock, I realized that she would look right at home here.

"Happiness—"

"—is up to us."

"That's wrong, you know." I said to the woman beside me. She looked up with bloodshot eyes and shifted as if she might move, so I put my hand companionably on her arm. "I'm not criticizing. But if it was up to us we'd all be singing."

She stood up then, shaking off my hand like water, and scuttled to another chair in time for the next refrain.

"Honest," I said, standing now and speaking clearly, to be heard over the others. "I've written a book. I know what I'm talking about. Don't you all deserve sweet joy? I do. My mother does."

"Growth comes in knowledge—" the leader began, but the response was stammering and splintered as women turned to look at me and frown.

"Sure," I said, "but what does knowledge lead to? I know every bad habit I have, but I'm still sleeping with a married man. Every day for five years I've told myself I hold my own happiness, but I'm still coming to meetings like this." The group had fallen silent, the tense woman looking at me with a slack mouth. I took off my jacket and moved into the center of the circle, where I liked to stand when I directed groups. "We all want a map because we can't see the road. but there aren't any maps. There isn't a road."

"We all find our own path," said the leader, her voice quivering. "Only by working together can we find our individual paths. We've learned that this is the only answer."

Heads were nodding, but the women looked back to me, waiting for my response. I stood on a chair. "Aren't you listening? Individual paths is the same as no path. Every day is shapeless." As I spoke the welcome tears broke free again, crashing through seawalls and restraints. I couldn't wipe them away fast enough, so that looking at the group I sensed we were all held together by the warm, embracing water. "Listen! There's a new answer every day," I said. "I'm trying to tell you."

Nominated by Stephen Corey

JAPAN

by BILLY COLLINS

from THE GEORGIA REVIEW

Today I pass the time reading
a favorite haiku,
saying the few words over and over.

It feels like eating
the same small, perfect grape
again and again.

I walk through the house reciting it
and leave its letters falling
through the air of every room.

I stand by the big silence of the piano and say it.
I say it in front of a painting of the sea.
I tap out its rhythm on an empty shelf.

When the dog looks up at me,
I kneel down on the floor
and whisper it into each of his long white ears.

I listen to myself saying it,
then I say it without listening,
then I hear it without saying it.

It's the one about the one-ton
temple bell
with the moth sleeping on its surface,

and every time I say it, I feel the excruciating
pressure of the moth
on the surface of the iron bell.

When I say it at the window,
the bell is the world
and I am the moth resting there.

When I say it into the mirror,
I am the heavy bell
and the moth is life with its papery wings.

And later, when I say it to you in the dark,
you are the bell,
and I am the tongue of the bell, ringing you,

and the moth has flown
from its line
and moves like a hinge in the air above our bed.

Nominated by Linda Bierds, Marianne Boruch, Philip Levine

DARK AGE: WHY JOHNNY CAN'T DISSENT

by TOM FRANK

from THE BAFFLER

I. Wealth Against Commonwealth Revisited

> It was, indeed, the Age of Information, but information was
> not the precursor to knowledge; it was the tool of salesmen.
> —Earl Shorris, *A Nation of Salesmen*

In the United States, where political "change" means further enriching the already wealthy, and where political "dialogue" is an elaborate charade that excludes dangerous and difficult topics from public consideration, one must look to the literature of business to find serious talk about national affairs. Here, in publications like the *Wall Street Journal, Advertising Age,* and the steady stream of millennial tracts about the latest leadership practices, is where one hears the undisguised voice of the nation's ruling class grappling with the weighty affairs of state, raised in anguish over foreign competition, strategizing against its foes, proselytizing passionately for the latest management faiths, intoxicated with the golden promise of radical new marketing techniques. The jowly platitudes about "bipartisanship," "consensus," or "the center" that make up political commentary are thankfully absent: here all is philosophical *realpolitik*, the open recognition that the world belongs to the ruthless, the radical, the destroyer of all that has gone before.

114

The great earth-stopping subject these days in business literature is the fantastic growth of the culture industry. The nation is advancing from the clunking tailfin-and-ranch-house economy of the 1950s into a golden new hyper-consumerism, where ever-accelerating style and attitude fuel ever-more rapidly churning cycles of obsolescence; where the mall has long since replaced the office or the factory at the center of American life; where citizens are referred to as consumers; and where buying things is now believed to provide the sort of existential satisfaction that things like, say, going to church once did. And culture, once the bane of the philistine man of commerce, stands at the heart of this vital new America. No longer can any serious executive regard TV, movies, magazines, and radio as simple "entertainment," as frivolous leisure-time fun: writing, music, and art are no longer conceivable as free expressions arising from the daily experience of a people. These are the economic dynamos of the new age, the economically crucial tools by which the public is informed of the latest offerings, enchanted by packaged bliss, instructed in the arcane pleasures of the new, taught to be good citizens, and brought warmly into the consuming fold. Every leader of business now knows that the nation's health is measured not by production of cars and corn but by the strength of its culture industry. Nightly business programs routinely discuss the latest box-office receipts with the utmost gravity; France is threatened with trade war over its protectionist cinema policy; the *Wall Street Journal* publishes long special reports on what used to be naively called "the entertainment industry."

The shift has been a gigantic one, altering even the way we appreciate the world around us. Those things we used to read about in the quaintly eccentric books of post-structuralist theory have become facts of everyday life, the triumph of "the image" over "reality" promoted from "fascinating abstraction" to a simple matter of "profit and loss." We have entered what the trade papers joyfully call the "Information Age," in which culture is the proper province of responsible executives, the minutiae that were once pondered by professors and garret-bound poets having become as closely scrutinized as daily stock prices.

Guided as ever by that all-knowing invisible hand, the business "community" has reacted to the new state of affairs in an entirely predictable manner, rapidly erecting a Culture Trust of four or five companies (This just in! Spielberg and Geffen have started their own studio! That makes six!) whose assorted vice-presidents now supervise almost every aspect of American public expression. Business ideologists speculate wildly about the potential for "synergy" when "content providers" join forces with "delivery systems." Time-Warner unites the nation's foremost mass-cultural institutions under one corporate roof; Sony now produces the movies and recordings you need to make your Sony appliances go; a host of conglomerates battle over Paramount, then over CBS; Disney casts about for its own TV network; Rupert Murdoch acquires an international publishing and broadcasting empire bringing him cultural power undreamed of by bush-leaguers like William Randolph Hearst. Culture can now be delivered cleanly and efficiently from creator to consumer, without the static or potential for interference posed by such vestiges of antiquity as bolshevik authors, strange-minded artists, local accents, or stubborn anomalies like that crotchety old editor in the MCI "Gramercy Press" commercials who doesn't know how to work his voice-mail. The entire process of cultural production is being modernized overnight, brought at long last out of the nineteenth century and placed in the hands of dutiful business interests.

With the consolidation of the Information Age has come a new class of executives, a consumerist elite who deal not in production and triplicate forms, but in images. Management theorist and pseudo-historian Peter Drucker calls them "Knowledge Workers," Secretary of Labor Robert Reich has dubbed them "symbolic analysts," but the term applied to them by the nation's highest-ranking ass-kisser, *Vanity Fair*, in its recent "Special Report" on the handful of luminous fabulosities who head up the Culture Trust, seems more appropriate: "The New Establishment." Learn to revere them, the magazine wetly counsels its readers, for they are the new Captains of Industry, the Titans of the future, "a buccaneering breed of entrepreneurs and visionaries, men and women from the entertainment, communications, and computer industries, whose ambitions and influence have made America the one true superpower of the Information Age." As Americans were once taught to regard the colossal plunderings of Rockefellers and Carnegies with patriotic pride, we are now told to be thankful for this "New Establishment": it is, after all, due to figures like Murdoch, Geffen, Eisner, and Turner (memorize these names, kids) that the nation has been rescued from the dead end of "military-industrial supremacy" and restored to the path of righteousness, "emerging as an information-and-entertainment superpower." These great men have struggled their way to the top, not just to corner the wheat market, buy up all the railroads between here and New York, or

116

bribe the odd state legislature, but to fabricate the materials with which the world thinks.

As its products steadily become the nation's chief export, the Culture Trust further rationalizes its operations through vertical integration, ensuring its access to the eternal new that drives the machine by invading the sanctum of every possible avant-garde. Responsible business newspapers print feature stories on the nation's hippest neighborhoods, how to navigate them and what treasures might be found there. Sober TV programs air segments on the colorful world of "zines"; ad agencies hire young scenesters to penetrate and report back on the latest "underground" doings. Starry-eyed college students are signed up as unpaid representatives of record conglomerates, eager to push product, make connections, and gain valuable experience on the lower rungs of the corporate ladder; while music talent scouts, rare creatures once, are seen everywhere prospecting for the cultural fuel that only straight-off-the-street 'tude can provide. Believing blithely in the fabled democracy of the marketplace, the objects of this cultural speculation are only too happy to cooperate, never quite realizing that the only reliable path to wealth in the "entertainment" business starts with a Harvard MBA.

And as every aspect of American cultural production is brought safely into the fold, business texts crow proudly of the new technologies which promise to complete the circle of corporate domination. The delivery of such eagerly-awaited gloriosities as "interactive media" and "virtual reality," it is hoped, will open vast uncharted regions of private life to business colonization, will reorganize human relations generally around an indispensable corporate intermediary. Business writers understand that the great promise of the Information Age is not that average consumers will soon wake up to the splendor of 100 high-res channels, but that every imaginable type of human relationship can now be reduced to digital and incorporated into the glowing televisual nexus—brought to you by Pepsico, of course. What reformed adman Earl Shorris has written of the early promise of TV may finally be accomplished in the near future: "Reality did not cease to exist, of course, but much of what people understood as reality, including virtually all of the commercial world, was mediated by television. It was as if a salesman had been placed between Americans and life." TV is no longer merely "entertainment," it is on the verge of becoming the ineluctable center of human consciousness, the site of every sort of exchange. As the Information Revolution proceeds the

117

myths, assumptions, and folklores of business become the common language of humanity; business culture becomes human culture. Working and consuming from our houses, wired happily into what *Harper's* magazine has called the "electronic hive," we will each be corporate subjects—consumers and providers of "content"—as surely as were the hapless industrial proletarians of the last century.

Granted, few things in recent memory have been as over-promoted as "synergy" and the "information superhighway." But for all the hollow boosterism, for all the anglo-tincted squealings of that child on TV who equates MCI with God, the changes are real and they are vast, unimaginable. As Richard Turner wrote recently in the *Wall Street Journal,* "Don't let all the blather fool you, because this much *is* clear: A sea change is coming in communications, information and entertainment. And in some measure, it's already here."

The most intriguing aspect of these developments is not the unprecedented magnitude of cultural power being amassed by American business, but the singular imbalance between the size of the change and the comparative silence of protesting voices. Certainly the putatively 'conservative' politics of the nation's powerful Right does not include suspicion of vast cultural upheavals like this one, provided that responsible business interests are safely in charge (one can imagine their outrage were the government to assume comparable powers). From mainstream journals that dare to allow themselves an opinion, the only view one is likely to hear is the ecstatic proclamation that the rise of the Culture Trust heralds, perversely, a newfound cultural democracy. Not only are the guys who are taking charge of the American cultural economy a bunch of existential individualists—what with their jet airplanes, fabulous homes, virtual offices, and muscular celebrity friends—but the system they're setting up will allow each one of us to be exotic, VR game-playing rebels as well. With computers we'll be able to talk to people who are far away! And with the miracle of "interactive," it is believed, we will at last be able to talk back to those big media guys. "Consumers will be constructing what they're getting," chirps *Vanity Fair.* "Yesterday, we changed the channel; today we hit the remote; tomorrow, we'll reprogram our agents/filters," sings *Wired* magazine, in between the latest cyber-advertising and little editorial epiphanies about the most expensive new consumer goods. "We'll interact with advertising where once we only watched; we'll seek out advertising where once we avoided it." Since letters to the editor can now be electronic, it seems, the obvious and unavoidable dangers that come with rearranging human life around the cultural needs of business are, well, insignificant. Since "democracy" means having more consumer choices, and information technology will vastly increase the power of our channel changers, hey presto! More democracy!

The Baffler humbly asks anyone who believes this argument—that business is building as costly a system as "interactive" in order to *reduce* its power over viewers—to contrast the hastiness with which the Culture Trust is bringing this particular technology to market with the strange (and strangely unremarked) unavailability of consumer CD-recording technology (which *is* available to "professional" radio engineers and such-like), devices which, if accessible to everyone, would forever ground the soaring prices of Microsoft shares as well as David Geffen's much-admired private jet.

But still one is surprised by the quiet. Years ago Americans viewed similar instances of such rapid and complete concentration of economic power into so few hands with alarm. Democratic sensibilities were offended by the prospect of an entire region's or class's impoverishment for the benefit of a small ring of companies. Corporate arrogance invariably bred the outraged (and varied) political responses of Populism, Progressivism, Anarcho-Syndicalism, and the New Deal.

Today, of course, the situation is very different, and very strange. No social group is more audibly or visibly 'radical' than artists, musicians, and writers, and with the rise of the Culture Trust capitalism seems to have elevated these malcontents to positions of power and responsibility. And just think of the results: now we are sold cars by an army of earringed, dreadlocked, goateed, tattooed, and guitar-bearing rebels rather than the lab-coated authority figures of the past. But even while we live in a time in which ostentatious displays of rebellion are celebrated and admired as much as the building of grandiose imitations of Versailles and the burning of hundred-dollar-bills were once, we are constantly reminded of their meaninglessness, their irrelevance to questions of actual power. For all our radical soda pops, our alternative lifestyles, and the uninhibited howls of our hamburger stands, we seem to have no problem with the fact of business control over every aspect of public expression. Even as we proclaim ourselves a nation of credit-limit rebels, prepared to drive our Saabs "in the face of convention," we are incapable of raising even the feeblest material challenge to business's assumption of near-absolute cultural power. We are

119

left, glassy-eyed and numb, to choose between the various corporate accounts of media takeovers.

This is not to imply that no one has noticed the dangers of the Information Revolution or that direct assaults on the aesthetic and economic basis of the Culture Trust have not taken place. It is to point out, simply, that the dominant intellectual tendency of our time—in a strange complement to the prevalence of ersatz rebellion everywhere on TV—is to confront not the power of the media but those who dare to criticize it.

In academia, where proclamations of "cultural radicalism" are routine, we observe the consolidation of "Cultural Studies," a pedagogy that seems tailor-made for the intellectual needs of the Culture Trust. Beginning with the inoffensive observation that an audience's reception of a given culture-product is important and unpredictable, Cultural Studies proceeds to assert that the facts of corporate cultural production are therefore utterly irrelevant, that David Geffen and Madonna are exactly as cool as *Vanity Fair* says they are (but for different reasons, dude), and to devise new ways to apply the label "elitist" to people who don't like TV. Its rise to prominence, as Herbert Schiller noted a while ago, coincides perfectly with Information Revolution, both temporally and ideologically:

> The power of the Western cultural industries is more concentrated and formidable than ever; their outputs are more voluminous and widely circulated; and the transnational corporate system is totally dependent upon information flows. Yet the prevailing interpretation sees media power as highly overrated and its international impact minimal. . . . Its usefulness to existing power is obvious.

Rock music is a case in point: though Cultural Studies is overwhelmingly concerned with what is called "The Popular," a thorough reading of its leading books, journals, and anthologies turns up few references to *independent* rock music ("punk rock," by the way, is understood to have been a curious phenomenon of the late 70s that vanished soon afterwards) or non-corporate publications like, say, *Forced Exposure* or *Maximum Rocknroll*. Although these are "popular" works in the true sense of the word, they tend to take far too hostile a view of the Culture Trust—the only "reading," apparently, that "the people" aren't supposed to undertake. Therefore, they might as well not exist. Only corporate culture deserves to be considered, lauded over and over again for the ways in which this sitcom empowers that subaltern, this rock video questions that hierarchy. This blindness towards anything but the products of the Culture Trust makes the prognosis of one of its academic opponents more apt:

> Globalisation . . . means that (high added-value) cultural production is increasingly important to advanced economies so that an increased proportion of jobs are found in the cultural sector. Cultural studies prepares students for these jobs. It also prepares them to become good consumers of increasingly sophisticated cultural industries.

To judge TV programs from the top down by some rigid, pre-existing standard, Cultural Studies argues, is a serious intellectual offense. But just a mention of the more critical media theories of, for example, the Frankfurt School, is enough to send these self-proclaimed avatars of popular resistance into a fury of denunciation. Suddenly a different system of values seems to apply. Here one finds no finenesses of "negotiated readings," no hints of that liberating potential just beneath the text's surface: that *particular* reading is not OK; those who denounce the offerings of the Culture Trust are just plain *wrong*.

II. Serious Attitude Adjustment: The Rise of Corporate Antinomianism

The public be damned! I work for my stockholders.
—William H. Vanderbilt, 1879

Break the rules. Stand apart. Keep your head. Go with your heart.
—TV commercial for Vanderbilt perfume, 1994

The American economy may be undergoing the most dramatic shifts in this century, but for the past thirty years people in music, art, and culture generally have had a fixed, precise notion of what's wrong with American life and the ways in which the responsible powers are to be confronted. It is a preconception shared by almost every magazine, newspaper, TV host, and rock star across the "alternative" spectrum. And it is the obsolescence and exhaustion of this idea of cultural dissent that accounts for our singular inability to confront the mind-boggling dangers of the Information Age.

The patron saints of the countercultural idea, which for convenience is what we'll call this now-standard way of understanding power and resistance, are, of course, the Beats, whose frenzied style and merry alienation still maintain a powerful grip on the American imagination. Even forty years after the publication of *On The Road*, the works of Kerouac, Ginsberg, and Burroughs remain the *sine qua non* of dissidence, the model for aspiring poets, rock stars, or indeed anyone who feels vaguely artistic or alienated—in other words, for everyone. That frenzied sensibility of pure experience, life on the edge, immediate gratification, and total freedom from moral restraint which the Beats first propounded back in those heady days when suddenly everyone could have their own TV and powerful V-8, has stuck with us through all the intervening years and become something of a permanent American aesthetic, an official style of the consumer society. Go to any poetry reading in New York or Chicago and you can see a string of junior Kerouacs go through the routine, "upsetting cultural hierarchies" by pushing themselves to the limit, straining for that beautiful gasp as the nonexistent bourgeoisie recoils in shock, struggling to recapture that gorgeous moment of original vice when Allen Ginsberg first read "Howl" in 1955. The Gap may have since claimed Ginsberg and *USA Today* may run feature stories about the brilliance of Kerouac, but here the rebel race continues, with ever-heightening shit-references calculated to scare Jesse Helms, talk about sex and smack that is supposed to bring the electricity of real life, and ever-more determined defiance of the repressive rules and mores of the American 1950s—rules and mores which by now we know only from movies.

The verdict of the Beats is the centerpiece of the countercultural idea to which we still ascribe such revolutionary potential: the paramount ailment of our society is *conformity*, a malady that has variously been described as over-organization, bureaucracy, homogeneity, hierarchy, logocentrism, technocracy, the Combine, the Apollonian. We all know what it is and what it does. It transforms humanity into "organization man," into "the man in the gray flannel suit." It is "Moloch whose mind is pure machinery," the "incomprehensible prison" that consumes "brains and imagination." It is artifice, starched shirts, tailfins, carefully mowed lawns and always, always the consciousness of impending nuclear destruction. It is a stiff, militaristic order that seeks to suppress instinct, to forbid sex and pleasure, to deny basic human impulses and individuality, to enforce through a rigid uniformity a meaningless plastic consumerism.

As this half of the countercultural idea originated during the 1950s, it is appropriate that the evils of conformity are most conveniently summarized with images of 1950s suburban correctness. You know, that land of church-goers, tailfins, red-scares, smiling white people, lines of commuters, sedate music, sexual repression. An America of uptight patriarchs, friendly cops, buttoned-down collars, B-47s, and deference to authority—the America of such backward-looking creatures as Jerry Falwell. Constantly appearing as a symbol of arch-evil in advertising and movies, it is an image we find easy to evoke. Picking up at random a recent *Utne Reader,* for example, one finds an article which seeks to question the alternativeness of coffee by reminding the reader of its popularity during that cursed decade: "According to history—or sitcom reruns—" the author writes, "the '50s were when Dad tanked up first thing in the morning with a pot of java, which set him on his jaunty way to a job that siphoned away his lifeblood in exchange for lifelong employment, a two-car garage, and Mom's charge card." The correct response: What a nightmare! I'll be sure to get my coffee at a hip place like Starbuck's.

The ways in which this system are to be resisted are equally well understood and agreed-upon. The Establishment demands homogeneity; we revolt by embracing diverse, individual lifestyles. It demands self-denial and rigid adherence to convention; we revolt through immediate gratification, instinct uninhibited, and liberation of the libido and the appetites. Few have put it more bluntly than Jerry Rubin did in 1970, "Amerika says: Don't! The yippies say: Do It!" The countercultural idea is hostile to any law and every establishment. "Whenever we see a rule, we must break it," Rubin continued. "Only by breaking rules do we discover who we are." Above all rebellion consists of a sort of Nietzschean *antinomianism*, an automatic questioning of rules, a rejection of whatever social prescriptions we've happened to inherit. Do Your Own Thing is the whole of the law.

But one hardly has to go to a poetry reading to see the countercultural idea acted out, for its frenzied ecstasies have long since become the official aesthetic of consumer society, the monotheme of mass culture as well as adversarial culture. Turn on the TV and there it is instantly: the unending drama of Consumer Unbound and in search of an ever-heightened good time, the inescapable rock 'n' roll soundtrack, dreadlocks and ponytails bounding into Taco Bells, a drunken, camera-swinging epiphany of tennis shoes, outlaw soda pops, and mind-bending dandruff shampoos. For corporate America no longer speaks in the voice of oppressive order that it did when Ginsberg moaned in 1956 that *Time* magazine was

> always telling me about responsibility. Businessmen are serious. Movie producers are serious. Everybody's serious but me.

Today nobody wants to appear serious. Fox, Disney, and Time/Warner, the nation's economic standard-bearers, are also now the ultimate leaders of the Ginsbergian search for kicks upon kicks. Corporate America is not an oppressor but a sponsor of fun, provider of lifestyle accoutrements, facilitator of carnival, trusted ally of the people, our slang-speaking partner in the search for that ever-more apocalyptic orgasm. The countercultural idea has become capitalist orthodoxy, its hunger for transgression upon transgression, change for the sake of change, now perfectly suited to an economic-cultural regime that runs on ever-faster cyclings of the new; its taste for self-fulfillment and its intolerance for the confines of tradition now permitting vast latitude in consuming practices and lifestyle experimentation.

For consumerism is no longer about "conformity" but about "difference." Advertising teaches us not in the ways of puritanical self-denial (a bizarre notion on the face of it), but in orgiastic, never-ending self-fulfillment. It counsels not rigid adherence to the tastes of the herd but vigilant and constantly-updated individualism. We consume not to fit in, but to prove, on the surface at least, that we are rock 'n' roll rebels, each one of us as rule-breaking and hierarchy-defying as our heroes of the 60s, who now pitch cars, shoes, and beer. This imperative of endless difference, not that dread "conformity," is the genius at the heart of American capitalism, the eternal fleeing from "sameness" that gives us a thirst for the New and satiates it with such achievements of civilization as the infinite brands of identical cola, the myriad colors and irrepressible variety of the cigarette rack at 7-11.

Capitalism has changed dramatically since the 1950s, but our understanding of how it is to be resisted hasn't budged. As existential rebellion has become the more or less official style of Information Age capitalism, so has the countercultural notion of a static, repressive Establishment grown hopelessly obsolete. However the basic impulses of the countercultural idea may (and that's a big "may") have disturbed a nation lost in Cold War darkness, they are today in fundamental agreement with the basic tenets of Information Age business theory. So close are they, in fact, that it has become impossible to understand the countercultural idea as anything more than the self-justifying ideology of the new dominant class that has arisen since the 1960s, the cultural means by which this group has proven itself ever so much better skilled than its slow-moving, security-minded forebears at adapting to the accelerated, always-changing consumerism of today. The anointed cultural opponents of capitalism are now capitalism's ideologues.

The two come together in perfect synchronization in a figure like Camille Paglia whose annoying ravings are grounded in the absolutely non-controversial ideas of the golden Sixties. According to Paglia, American business is still exactly what it was believed to have been in that beloved decade, that is, "puritanical and desensualized." Its great opponents are, of course, liberated figures like "the beatniks", Bob Dylan, and the Beatles (needless to say, while Paglia proclaims herself a great fan of rock music, bands like Shellac, Slant 6, and the Subhumans never appear as recipients of her praise). Culture is, quite simply, a binary battle between the repressive Apollonian order of capitalism and the Dionysian impulses of the counterculture. Paglia thus validates the central official myth of the "Information Age," for rebellion makes no sense without repression; we must remain forever convinced of capitalism's fundamental hostility to pleasure in order to consume capitalism's rebel products as avidly as we do. It comes as little surprise when, after criticizing the "Apollonian capitalist machine" in her new book, Paglia applauds American mass culture (in that same random issue of *Utne Reader*), the pre-eminent product of that "capitalist machine," as a "third great eruption" of a Dionysian "paganism." For her, as for most other designated dissidents, there is no contradiction between replaying the standard critique of capitalist conformity and repressiveness and then endorsing its rebel products—for Paglia the car culture and Madonna—as the obvious solution: the Culture Trust offers both Establishment and Resistance in one convenient package. The only question that remains is why Paglia has not yet landed an endorsement contract from a soda pop or automobile manufacturer.

Other legendary exponents of the countercultural idea have been more fortunate. William S. Burroughs, for example, appears in a television spot for the Nike corporation. But so openly does the commercial flaunt the confluence of capital and counterculture that it has aroused considerable criticism. Writing in the *Village Voice,* Leslie Savan wonders what it means when a Beat goes bad. The contradiction between Burroughs's writings and the faceless corporate entity for which he is now pushing product is so vast, she believes, that one can do little more than marvel at the digestive powers of capital. "Now the realization that *nothing* threatens the system has freed advertising to exploit even the most marginal elements of society," Savan observes. "In fact, being hip is no longer quite enough—better the pitchman be 'underground.'" While Burroughs's manager insists, as all future Cultural Studies treatments of the ad will also insist, that Burroughs's presence makes the commercial "deeply subversive"—"I hate to repeat the usual mantra, but you know, homosexual drug addict, manslaughter, accidental homicide"—Savan wonders whether, in fact, it is Burroughs who has been assimilated by corporate America. "The problem comes," she writes, "in how easily any idea, deed, or image can become part of the sponsored world."

The most startling revelation to emerge from the Burroughs/Nike partnership is not that corporate America has overwhelmed its cultural foes or that Burroughs can somehow remain "subversive" through it all, but the complete lack of dissonance between the two sides. Of course Burroughs is not "subversive," but neither has he "sold out": his ravings are no longer appreciably different from the official folklore of American business. As expertly as he once bayoneted American proprieties, as stridently as he once proclaimed himself beyond the laws of man and God, Burroughs is today a respected ideologue of the Information Age. His writings are boardroom favorites, his dark nihilistic burpings the happy homilies of the new corporate faith.

For with the assumption of power by Drucker's and Reich's new class has come an entirely new ideology of business, a way of justifying and exercising power that has absolutely nothing to do with the "conformity" and the "establishment" so vilified by the countercultural idea. The management theorists and "leadership" charlatans of the Information Age don't waste their time prattling about hierarchy and regulation, but about disorder, chaos, and the meaninglessness of inherited rules. With its reorganization around Information, capitalism has developed a new mythology, a sort of *corporate antinomianism* according to which the breaking of rules and the elimination of rigid corporate structure have become the central article of faith for millions of aspiring executives. As the members of new class are, after all, children of the 1960s, it is a faith that is almost indistinguishable from the countercultural idea. The wisdom of the Grateful Dead seems as natural a business philosophy to them as did the orthodoxies of the past to their gray-flannelled predecessors.

Dropping *Naked Lunch* and picking up *Thriving on Chaos,* a best-selling management text written in 1987 by Tom Peters, the most popular business writer of the past decade, one finds more philosophical similarities than one would expect from two manifestos of, respectively, dissident culture and business culture. If anything, Peters's proclamation of disorder is, by virtue of its hard statistics, bleaker and more nightmarish than Burroughs's. For this popular lecturer such once-blithe topics as competitiveness and pop psychology there is nothing, absolutely nothing, that is certain. His world is one in which the corporate wisdom of the past is meaningless, established customs are ridiculous, and "rules" are some sort of curse, a remnant of the foolish 50s that exist to be defied, not obeyed. The book's oft-repeated catch-phrase is "A World Turned Upside Down," and at one point Peters launches into an liturgy of doubt that would have made T. S. Eliot proud:

> So we don't know from day to day the price of energy or money. We don't know whether protection and default will close borders, making a mess of global sourcing and trade alike, or whether global financing will open things up further. We don't know whether merging or de-merging makes more sense, and we have no idea who will be partners with whom tomorrow or next week, let alone next month.

Peters's answer is summed up in what may be the book's most overused term, "Revolution!" "To meet the demands of the fast-changing competitive scene," he counsels, "we must simply learn to love change as much as we have hated it in the past." He advises businessmen to become Robespierres of routine, to demand of their underlings, "'What have you changed lately?,' 'How fast are you changing?,' and 'Are you pursuing bold enough change goals?'" "Revolution," of course, means for Peters the same thing it did to Burroughs and Ginsberg, Presley and the Stones in their heyday: breaking rules, pissing off the suits, shocking the bean-counters: "Actively and publicly hail defiance of the rules, many of which you doubtless labored mightily to

127

construct in the first place." Peters even suggests that his readers implement this hostility to logocentrism in a carnivalesque celebration, drinking beer out in "the woods" and destroying "all the forms and rules and discontinued reports" and, "if you've got real nerve," a photocopier as well. He omits reading aloud from a volume of Burroughs or Kerouac, blasting the music of Presley or the Stones, but that's obvious.

This corporate antinomianism has become more emphatic in business texts since the appearance of *Thriving on Chaos*. Capitalism, at least as it is envisioned by the best-selling management handbooks, is no longer about enforcing Order, but destroying it. "Revolution," once the totemic catchphrase of the counterculture, has become the totemic catchphrase of boomer-as-capitalist. The back cover of *Thriving on Chaos* may have been emblazoned with the slogan, "RX: Revolution!", but this year's favorite business text, *Reengineering the Corporation,* is even more blunt, bearing the subtitle, "A Manifesto for Business Revolution." The Information Age businessman holds inherited ideas and traditional practices not in reverence, but in high suspicion. Even reason itself is now found to be an enemy of true competitiveness, an out-of-date faculty to be scrupulously avoided by conscientious managers. A 1990 book by Charles Handy entitled *The Age of Unreason* agrees with Peters that we inhabit a time in which "there can be no certainty" and suggests that readers engage in full-fledged epistemological revolution: "Thinking Upside Down," using new ways of "learning which can . . . be seen as disrespectful if not downright rebellious," methods of approaching problems that have "never been popular with the upholders of continuity and of the status quo." Three years later the authors of *Reengineering the Corporation* are ready to push this doctrine even further. Not only should we be suspicious of traditional practices, but we should cast out virtually everything learned over the past two centuries!

> Business reengineering means putting aside much of the received wisdom of two hundred years of industrial management. It means forgetting how work was done in the age of the mass market and deciding how it can best be done now. In business reengineering, old job titles and old organizational arrangements—departments, divisions, groups, and so on—cease to matter. They are artifacts of another age.

In advertising, where the new has always been pursued as a sort of holy grail, these calls to break rules and smash idols are made even more stridently. George Lois, one of the industry's brightest stars since the early 1960s (responsible, among other things, for the "I Want My MTV" campaign), explained his selling strategy in 1991 in terms of ever-escalating outrage and defiance. He describes himself reacting instinctively against established authority, challenging the conventional in every aspect of his professional life. "To push for a new solution," one of his book's sections is entitled, "start by saying no to conventional rules, traditions, and trends." Advertising, being "the art of breaking rules," follows a similar rebel path. Good ads are "inventive, irreverent, audacious"; they strive for what Lois calls "the seemingly outrageous." Good advertising should "stun" the consumer, as modern art was supposed to shock, by presenting her with an idea that upends her conventions of understanding. When Lois presents his work to clients, he expects it to "cause my listener to rock back in semi-shock." In an almost Futurist passage, Lois likens good advertising to "poison gas": "It should unhinge your nervous system. It should knock you out!" On the other hand, advertising that is created according to standard textbook rules is automatically bad: "Safe, conventional work is a ticket to oblivion," Lois observes. "Talented work is, *ipso facto,* unconventional."

As countercultural rebellion becomes corporate ideology, even the beloved Buddhism of the Beats has a place on the executive bookshelf. In *The Leader as Martial Artist* (1993) Arnold Mindell, "Ph.D.," advises men of commerce in the wise ways of the Tao, which he compares to "surfing the edge of a turbulent wave." For the Zen businessman the world is the same wildly chaotic place of opportunity that it is for the followers of Tom Peters, although an enlightened "leader" knows how to discern the "timespirits" at work behind the scenes:

> Change is . . . an incomprehensible, complex phenomenon;
> we have no way of knowing what creates change or when it
> is to occur. . . . Albert Einstein would cite the principle of
> nonlocality . . . ; C. G. Jung would speak of synchronicity,
> and Rupert Sheldrake of morphogenic resonance. We could
> just as easily call it chance, the Tao, or a miracle.

In terms Peters himself might use were he a more meditative sort of inspiration professional, Mindell explains that "the wise facilitator"

129

doesn't seek to prevent the inevitable and random clashes between "conflicting field spirits," but to anticipate such bouts of disorder and profit thereby. "Since agreement and antagonism are inevitable, the leadership position in a group should plan on being opposed or attacked," he writes. "Even a harmonious and balanced system must have a dynamic fluctuation between equilibrium and chaos if it is to grow." So c'mon, everybody! Angst and grow rich!

The American businessman is hardly the craven gray-flannel creature he is believed to have been back in the 1950s. He hasn't been for a long time. Today he decorates the walls of his office not with portraits of President Eisenhower and emblems of suburban order, but with images of extreme athletic daring, with sayings about "diversity" and "empowerment." He and his peers theorize their world not at the golf course, but in weepful corporate retreats at which he beats his tom-tom and envisions himself part of the great tradition of edge-livers, risk-takers, and ass-kickers. His world is powered not by sublimation and conformity, but by notions of "leadership" and defying the herd. And there is nothing this new enlightened species of businessman despises more than "rules" and "reason." This is a business philosophy, as the authors of *Reengineering the Corporation* note, that is directly descended from the antinomianism of the counterculture. "One of the t-shirt slogans of the sixties read, 'Question authority,'" they write. "Process owners might buy their reengineering team members the nineties version: 'Question assumptions.'"

The new businessman quite naturally gravitates to the slogans and sensibility of the rebel 60s to express his understanding of the new Information World. He is led by vanguard capitalists like the head of the CD-ROM pioneer Voyager, a former activist whose admiration of the Shining Path, as the *New York Times* notes, seems somehow appropriate amidst the current "information revolution." He speaks to his comrades through commercials like the recent one for "Warp," a type of IBM computer operating system, in which an electric guitar soundtrack and psychedelic video effects surround hip executives with earrings and hairdos who are visibly stunned by the product's gnarly'tude (It's a "totally cool way to run your computer," read the product's print ads). He understands the world through journals like *Advertising Age*, which illustrates the varied nature of contemporary "marketing" with a two-page array of such revolutionary items as "White guys with dreadlocks," "Tattoos," "Entertainers who only use a glyph," and "Crooners who sing with rockers." He is what sociologists Paul Leinberger and Bruce Tucker have called "The New Individualist," the new and improved manager whose arty worldview and creative hip derive directly from his formative 60s days. The one thing this new executive is definitely *not* is Organization Man, the hyper-rational counter of beans, attender of church, and wearer of stiff hats.

In television commercials, through which the new American businessman presents his visions and self-understanding to the public, perpetual revolution and the gospel of rule-breaking are the orthodoxy of the day. You only need to watch for a few minutes before you see one of these slogans and understand the grip of antinomianism over the corporate mind:

Sometimes You Gotta Break the Rules (Burger King)
If You Don't Like the Rules, Change Them (WXRT-FM)
The Rules Have Changed (Dodge)
The Art of Changing (Swatch)
There's no one way to do it. (Levi's)
This is different. Different is good. (Arby's)
Just Different From the Rest (Special Export beer)
The Line Has Been Crossed: The Revolutionary New
Supra (Toyota)
Resist the Usual (the slogan of *both* Clash Clear Malt and
Young & Rubicam—maybe they'll sue each other!)

In most, the commercial message is driven home with the now-standard iconography of the rebel: screaming guitars, whirling cameras, and startled old timers who, *The Baffler* predicts, will become an increasingly indispensable prop as consumers require ever-greater assurances that, Yes! You *are* a rebel! Just look at how offended they are!

The problem with cultural dissent in America isn't that it's been co-opted, absorbed, or ripped-off. Of course it's been all of these things. But the reason it has proven so hopelessly susceptible to such assaults is the same as the reason it has become so harmless in the first place, so toothless even before Mr. Geffen's boys discover it angsting away in some bar in Lawrence, Kansas: it is no longer any different from the official culture it's supposed to be subverting. The basic impulses of the countercultural idea, as descended from the holy Beats, are about as threatening to the new breed of antinomian businessmen as Anthony Robbins, selling success & how to achieve it on a late-night infomercial.

Our businessmen imagine themselves rebels, and our rebels sound more and more like ideologists of business. Nothing better demonstrates the impoverishment and terminal irrelevance of our inherited notions of cultural dissent than the doings of former punk rocker Henry Rollins. Maker of loutish, overbearing music and writer of high-school variety poetry, Rollins considers himself a bearer of the Beat tradition and no doubt imagines himself some sort of postmodern Ayn Rand, introducing us to the dark, hard side of life and the wild, chaotic underpinnings of American culture. Rollins strikes all the standard alienated poses of early twentieth-century American literature: he rails against over-civilization and yearns to "disconnect." His writings and lyrics veer back and forth between vague threats towards "weak" people who "bring me down" and blustery declarations of his weightlifting ability and physical prowess. As a reward he is celebrated as a rebel without peer by such arbiters of dissident culture as the *New York Times Magazine* and MTV. Most telling of all is Rollins's status as pre-eminent darling of *Details* magazine, a sort of periodical handbook for the young executive on the rise where rebellion has achieved a perfect synthesis with corporate ideology. In 1992 *Details* elevated Rollins to the status of "rock 'n' roll samurai," an "emblem . . . of a new masculinity" whose "enlightened honesty" is "a way of being that seems to flesh out many of the ideas expressed in contemporary culture and fashion." Early in 1994 the magazine consummated its relationship with Rollins by naming him "Man of the Year," printing a fawning story about his muscular worldview and decorating its cover with a photo in which Rollins displays his tattoos and rubs his chin in a thoughtful manner.

The message of the *Details* profiles is simple. Rollins is a role model for the struggling young businessman not only because of his music-product, but because of his excellent "self-styled identity," which he has cleverly derived from the same impeccable source that has made Japan the world-wide leader in the quality revolution: "The traditional samurai code," which "espouses the virtue of living in discipline and honor," and which has allowed both managers and consumers to "liberate . . . themselves from mundane consternations that inhibit a free and fearless lifestyle." Rollins's philosophy is described by *Details* in terms normally reserved for the breast-beating and soul-searching variety of motivational seminars: "Rather than lapse into anger, which isolates everyone, or retreat into ironic detachment—the easiest way for the incomplete to feel whole," the magazine dribbles, "—he triumphs over both, and the fruits of his triumph are the ability to engage the world without denying his needs." Although he derives it from the ascetic wisdom of the East rather than the unfashionable doctrines of Calvin, Rollins's rebel posture is identical to that fabled ethic of the small capitalist whose regimen of positive thinking and hard work will one day pay off. *Details* describes one of Rollins's songs, quite seriously, as "a self-motivational superforce, an anthem of empowerment," teaching lessons that any aspiring middle-manager must internalize. Elsewhere Iggy Pop, that great chronicler of the ambitionless life, praises Rollins as a "high achiever" who "wants to go somewhere." Rollins himself even seems to invite such an interpretation. His recent spoken-word account of touring with Black Flag, delivered in an unrelenting two-hour drill-instructor staccato, begins with the timeless bourgeois story of opportunity taken, of young Henry leaving the security of a "straight job," enlisting with a group of visionaries who were "the hardest working people I have ever seen," and learning "what hard work is all about." In the liner notes he speaks proudly of his Deming-esque dedication to quality, of how his bandmates "Delivered under pressure at incredible odds." When describing his relationship with his parents for the readers of *Details,* Rollins quickly cuts to the critical matter, the results that such dedication has brought: "Mom, Dad, I outgross both of you put together," a happy observation he repeats in his interview with the *New York Times Magazine.*

Despite the extreme hostility of punk rockers with which Rollins had to contend all through the 1980s, it is he (rather than a less hated figure like, say, Greg Sage) who has been chosen as the godfather of rock 'n' roll revolt. It is not difficult to see why. For Rollins the punk rock decade was but a lengthy seminar on leadership skills, thriving on chaos, and total quality management. Rollins's much-celebrated anger is the anger of the frustrated junior executive who finds obstacles on the way to the top. His discipline and determination are the automatic catechism of any small entrepreneur who's just finished brainwashing himself with the latest leadership and positive-thinking tracts; his poetry is the inspired verse of *21 Days to Unlimited Power* or *Let's Get Results, Not Excuses.* Henry Rollins is no more a threat to established power in America than was Dale Carnegie. And yet Rollins as king of the rebels—peerless and ultimate—is the message hammered home wherever photos of his growling visage appears. If you're unhappy with your lot, the Culture Trust tells us with each Rollins tale, if you feel you must rebel, take your cue from the most disgruntled guy of all: lift weights! work hard! meditate in your back yard! root out the weaknesses deep down inside yourself! But whatever you do, *don't* think about who controls power or how it is wielded.

The structure and thinking of American business have changed enormously in the years since our popular conceptions of its problems and abuses were formulated. In the meantime the mad frothings and jolly apolitical revolt of Beat, despite their vast popularity and insurgent air, have become powerless against a new regime that, one suspects, few of Beat's present-day admirers and practitioners feel any desire to study or understand. For today that beautiful countercultural idea, endorsed now by everyone from the surviving Beats to shampoo manufacturers, is more the official doctrine of corporate America than it is a program of resistance. What we understand as "dissent" does not subvert, does not challenge, does not even question the cultural faiths of Western business. What David Rieff wrote of the revolutionary pretentions of multiculturalism is equally true of the countercultural idea: "The more one reads in academic multiculturalist journals and in business publications, and the more one contrasts the speeches of CEOs and the speeches of noted multiculturalist academics, the more one is struck by the similarities in the way they view the world." What's happened is not co-optation or appropriation, but a simple and direct confluence of interest.

The people who staff the Combine aren't like Nurse Ratched. They aren't Frank Burns, they aren't the Church Lady, they aren't Dean Wormer from *Animal House,* they aren't those repressed old folks in the commercials who want to ban Tropicana Fruit Twisters. They're hipper than you can ever hope to be because *hip is their official ideology,* and they're always going to be there at the poetry reading to encourage your 'rebellion' with a hearty "right on, man!" before you even know they're in the auditorium. You can't outrun them, or even stay ahead of them for very long: it's their racetrack, and that's them waiting at the finish line to congratulate you on how *outrageous* your new style is, on how you *shocked* those stuffy prudes out in the heartland.

And if you really feel that rebel urge, if you really want to "break the rules," get yourself down to Decatur, Illinois, where the idea of social democracy is slowly being done to death. But be prepared to not see yourself on any TV, no matter how "interactive" it is.

III. Zomething Apocalyptic: The Culture of Forgetting

> "Temporal bandwidth" is the width of your present, your
> *now*. It is the familiar "Δt" considered as a dependent vari-
> able. The more you dwell in the past and in the future, the
> thicker your bandwidth, the more solid your persona. But
> the narrower your sense of Now, the more tenuous you are.
> It may get to where you're having trouble remembering
> what you were doing five minutes ago, or even—as
> Slothrop now—what you're doing *here*, at the base of this
> colossal curved embankment. . . .
>   —Thomas Pynchon, *Gravity's Rainbow*

Even in the shallowest public forums American cultural commen-
tators now seem to realize that we are living through what may be the
most dislocating period in a hundred years. Everyone recognizes, if
only dimly, that the old comfortable world is yielding to a new order,
an Information Age in which our thoughts (brand loyalties) and
dreams (brand aspirations) are as economically important as our labor
once was. The rise of the Culture Trust is just its most objectionable
public feature; on a different level it signals a shift that is at once cat-
aclysmic and unnoticeable, an economic change that deletes our abil-
ity to understand economic change. The cultural victory of business is
more than a simple matter of biased news broadcasts, an easily-made
case of factual misrepresentation: with the consolidation of the Infor-
mation Age culture itself—the fables and myths and ideas built up
over the centuries through a million varieties of experience, suffering,
and struggle—has become the province of business. As Neil Postman
observes, "Twenty years ago, the question, Does television shape cul-
ture or merely reflect it? held considerable interest for many scholars
and social critics. The question has largely disappeared as television
has gradually *become* our culture." And through the miraculous inter-
cession of the glowing box, business culture has become human cul-
ture; brand identity and the ravings of thinkers like Tom Peters have
effaced in a brilliant electronic flash the labor of thousands of years.
While they might carp sadly at its fringes, few critics have begun—or
desire—to comprehend the full magnitude of this change or to ex-
plore the vast implications of this transfer of cultural power.

Only the most unabashed partisans of business supremacy are will-
ing to boast openly about the deed they have done, to speak the name

of the great foe whose vanquishing now permits Western consumerism to stride the globe unchecked. Francis Fukuyama, the right's favorite pre-Limbaugh "intellectual," put it most plainly in a famous 1989 essay: business has *ended history*. Not just in the Hegelian sense, the simple victory dance over the corpse of the Soviet Union which was the essay's primary purpose, but in a philosophical way as well. While America's arms expenditures triumphed over the Red Menace, its comfortable consumer banalities triumphed everywhere over local and inherited culture, language, and ideas, literally ended people's ability to think historically. The visibility of Western consumer goods throughout the world signals the success of what Fukuyama hails as the combined Western effort "to create a truly universal consumer culture that has become both a symbol and an underpinning of the universal homogenous state." "Universal homogenous!" Glorious thing! And while Fukuyama readily admits that "The End of History" does not mean that all economic and social conflict has been resolved, that universal capitalism means universal happiness, he gloats that without the faculty of cultural memory our unhappiness, however grinding, just doesn't matter: people can no longer think about their social position in a manner that might lead to conflict, that might threaten Western business interests.

Americans have always been somewhat hostile to history. Visiting the new country in the mid-nineteenth century, Alexis de Tocqueville was deeply moved by its wilful rejection of the class rankings and tastes of the European past, by the settlers' tendency to forget the Old World and to abandon the ways of the countless generations before them. Casting off the dead weight of the ages has always been a favorite conceit of American writers less frightened by democracy than was the aristocratic de Tocqueville: deracination has in many ways been the centerpiece of the nation's self-understanding. The golden fable of opportunity—of an empty land where anyone could, like Jay Gatsby, remake himself unhindered by the artificial constraints of civilization—is, after all, the basic theme in the great American stories of immigration and western expansion. Even our atrocities obeyed this primal cultural impulse, this imperative to forget: slavery demanded a cultural uprooting of those who did not come to the New World willingly. But by and large our literature praises the power of the melting pot, celebrates the democracy of the frontier, sings the glories of getting out of the Old and into the Cold.

For American business, this suspicion of history is a longstanding article of faith. In the frequent denunciations of The Past voiced by the great Captains of Industry one finds not mere assimilationist longings, but profound disdain for any entangling traditions that could interfere with efficiency and restrict the absolute freedom of every individual to pillage every other individual. Henry Ford's famous outburst, "history is bunk," was a statement of fundamental business ideology, not merely a response to an immediate annoyance. According to the great capitalists' "practical" worldview, as Richard Hofstadter has noted, "The past was seen as despicably impractical and uninventive, simply and solely as something to be surmounted." In its quest for efficiency, the pre-Information business "community" set itself against the peculiar and backward-looking ways of tradition and human particularity in almost every way it could. Its hated time-motion studies aimed to suppress factory workers' humanity, transforming them into efficiency-maximized robots like the hapless line worker in Charlie Chaplin's *Modern Times*. Its glass-and-steel office towers were soulless machines for the paper-shuffling labor of its Organization Men, stripped of any concessions to human tastes and comfort; its suburbs and tenements sterile boxes for the propagation of obedient underlings.

Alongside the hyper-rational, hyper-efficient Organization envisioned by America's premier managers there also developed an emotional and religious conception of business practice, a cult of Positive Thinking that was even more hostile to cultural memory than was the dominant cult of Efficiency. In the writing of the Positive Thinkers anti-historicism reached a new plateau of sophistication: the annoyances of history and cultural particularity were not just to be over-paved, but *levelled,* reduced to a convenient flatness where every epoch was exactly like the present as far back as the eye could see. The economic struggle of daily life was and had *always been* a matter of individual men and God, a question of just how positively each up-and-coming entrepreneur could think, just how blindly he could pursue success. The cold statistics of the bureaucrats were ultimately insignificant, nor did social class or local economic conditions really matter: all you needed to succeed was a salesman's disposition and an open-faced readiness to work. All human history—and especially the doings of its big figures, favorites like Lincoln, Charlemagne, and Joan of Arc—could be understood as parables for the struggling executive of the twentieth century. The best known tract in this tradition, adman Bruce Barton's 1925 book

The Man Nobody Knows, examined the life of Jesus and distilled it down to a series of lessons in leadership, sociability, and the wisdom of teams. "They call it the 'spirit of modern business'; they suppose . . . that it is something very new," Barton wrote. "Jesus preached it more than nineteen hundred years ago." Theories of Efficiency may have wilfully ignored history, but Positive Thinking went them one better: for its believers the past was fundamentally identical to the now. Capitalism is the immutable way of God and nature, the unchanging condition of mankind. To wonder how things ever got to the sorry state they were was to engage in idle and even counter-productive conjecture (the social utility of such a doctrine becomes obvious when the economic facts of its heyday—the ugly depression of the 1930s—are taken into consideration): society *never* developed or changed, it simply produced a series of interesting executives and leaders from whose exploits we might learn a thing or two.

With the coming of the Age of Information this anti-historicism reaches its logical end, the simple credo of the Positive Thinkers having blossomed into a full-blown secular philosophy of economic antinomianism. Cause and effect is a meaningless illusion, the new business thinkers argue, for the Information Age is an "Age of Unreason," of instant, world-wide change and constant flux. Manage-ment theorists like Tom Peters insist that the world is mad, spinning chaotically out of control, and to remain profitable businessmen must become mad themselves, immersed totally in the present and intentionally ignorant of whatever developments have put us where we are. Never have a ruling class attacked the faculty of cultural memory as fiercely as in the theoretical handbooks of the Information Age: "How people and companies did things yesterday doesn't matter to the business reengineer," write the authors of 1994's ubiquitous management text, *Reengineering the Corporation.* The hero of the Information Age, according to its authors, is the businessman who is able to violate most violently, to separate himself most completely from both his own and his company's past—to *forget.* The virtue of forgetting is the book's essential message: its dust jacket carries this enticing legend: "Forget what you know about how business should work—most of it is wrong!" With total seriousness its authors recommend that businessmen adopt an epistemology of constant forgetting, of positive militancy against cultural memory. "At the heart of business reengineering," they write, "lies the notion of *discontinuous thinking*—identifying and abandoning the outdated rules and fundamental assumptions that underlie current business operations."

Unlike his Organization predecessors, who merely wanted to destroy annoying obstacles to efficiency like city blocks and the sleeping habits of laborers, the antinomian Information businessman dreams of what Russell Jacoby once called "social amnesia," a collective inability to recall who did what *yesterday,* never mind last year or last century. Overflying in glorious slow-mo a hundred ancient cultures in a day, travelling always in classic rock sound-tracked "Executive Class" lugzhury, the Information businessman—bold knight of unreason— seems to have attained that exalted state which postmodern theorists used to imagine themselves inhabiting alone. Freed from the gravitational pull of worldly history he floats deliriously on a rushing stream of detatched signifiers, the flotsam and jetsam of centuries of civilization become just so many shiny trinkets floating meaninglessly by, so many treats placed randomly on his tray table before he stows it safely away in upright and locked position.

In advertising, the flower of the Information Age, social amnesia is the pitch of the century, the great cultural dynamo of the new, the always-handy device by which even the most senseless products can be made to seem desirable and by which that gorgeously automatic disdain for the products of the past can be instantly summoned. But scoffing at the old just isn't enough anymore: reasoning itself, Madison Avenue now instructs us, is a stupid and backward thing, the pastime of oldsters who wear their trousers up around their armpits. The stuff for us is rule-breaking, perpetual rebellion against any attitude that might keep you from Crossing the Border, that might problematize your enjoyment of the the undulating and seamless drama of defiant cars and tie-dye fruit drinks, that might keep you from changing lifestyles just as soon as you get tired of your current one. "Why ask why," we are advised. "Just do it." (Hey! That's so mindlessly cool, it could be the motto for our twenty-something fakezine!) But the big prize for social amnesia has to go to the disgusting campaign for something called "OK Soda," with its idiot "coincidences" and pre-fab Gen-X cynico-cred: "Don't be fooled into thinking there has to be a reason for everything," reads the legend on cans of the loathsome liquid. For OK Soda, as for virtually every other product around which we make our lives, there is obviously no "reason" other than the glittering logic of the marketplace. The constant flux that supports us all, consumerism's endless piling of new upon new, can be bound by no tradition, reason, language, or order other than the simple mandates of ceaseless, directionless rebellion and change.

139

Turn from the business and "lifestyle" pages of your newspaper—all starstruck and dewy-eyed about the glorious 100-channel lifestyles of the future—to the think section, and you can watch the cultural progress of the Information Age: puzzled journalists note the appearance of an "anxious class," unemployed workers from a number of different industries made redundant by the latest developments in international finance. However obvious the causes of their predicament may be to the observer—in this case, Louis Uchitelle of the *New York Times*—this new disenfranchised class steadfastly refuses to acknowledge them. "While Americans are increasingly angry about their economic insecurity," Uchitelle writes, "neither business nor the forces that make companies so hard on workers are the targets of this anger. It is directed instead at government, immigrants and the poor, among others." This is class consciousness for a new century, human subjectivity tailor-made for the needs of business. The system's economic casualties cannot for the life of them figure out how they have been done, or by whom. Capital smugly enjoys the cultural proceeds, getting it both ways now: workers have truly become "human resources," fully disposable and yet ready and willing to turn their anger to the great project of making business even more powerful than it already is. You fire them, and they turn around and vote for your chosen politicians, who make it easier for you to fire even more of them.

Among media decision-makers themselves the curtailment of our historical attention span is assumed quite matter-of-factly, with what one imagines is a fair amount of pride, to be an accomlished fact. Thus the convention on 'objective' news programs of discussing events of last week or a few months ago as though they were dim memories of the distant, unenlightened past: mentions of Iraq must be prefaced by the reminder that the US was at war with that nation a few years ago; news from Somalia must begin by informing us that, quite recently, this country was occupied by American soldiers. Otherwise, it is understood, we just wouldn't remember: naturally we're too caught up in whatever the current patriotic frenzy is to recall those of the recent past. If we're lucky the logistical problems associated with this need to constantly remind viewers of what was once common knowledge may one day expand to the point where TV news becomes impossible altogether, with almost all of the 45-minute program devoted to telling us what country we live in, that other cities and nations exist, who our elected officials are, and so on. The only thing that will never require explaining, of course, is the glowing box itself, the central position it

140

occupies in our dwellings, and the reasons why we come back to stare at it, day after day.

No effective challenge to the rule of business can be mounted without solid grounding in precisely the sort of cultural memory that Information Capitalism, with its supersonic yuppie pan-nationalism and its worship of the instantaneous, has set itself out to destroy. Without memory we can scarcely understand our present—what strange forces in the dim past caused this agglomeration of seven million unhappy persons to be deposited here in the middle of a vast continent, clinging to the shores of this mysteriously polluted lake?—much less begin to confront the systematic depredations of the system that has made our lives so miserable. In contrast to American business's insistent denial of pastness, Richard Hofstadter continues,

> In Europe there has always existed a strong counter-tradition, both romantic and moralistic, against the ugliness of industrialism—a tradition carried on by figures as diverse as Goethe and Blake, Morris and Carlyle, Hugo and Chateaubriand, Ruskin and Scott. Such men counterposed to the machine a passion for language and locality, for antiquities and monuments, for natural beauty; they sustained a tradition of resistance to capitalist industrialism, of skepticism about the human consequences of industrial progress, of moral, esthetic, and humane revolt.

Without an understanding of particularity, of the economic *constructedness* of our lives, this kind of critical consciousness becomes impossible. All we can know is our own individual discomfort, our vague hankering for something else—an 'else' that can be easily defined away as a different product choice, a new lifestyle, a can of Sprite anti-soda, or a little rule-breaking at Burger King.

This century's technological advances are often described as victories over the primal facts of nature: hunger, cold, disease, distance, and time. But the wiring of every individual into the warm embrace of the multinational entertainment oligopoly is a conquest of a different sort, the crowning triumph of the market-place over humanity's unruly consciousness. The fact that the struggle has been a particularly long one—"timeless," even, is how it's referred to on dust jackets immemorial—does not alter the fact that business authorities seem to be on the verge of a spectacular and final victory. It is fitting that, as this century of horrors draws to a close, our masters rush to perfect the cultural equivalent of the atom bomb, to destroy once and for all our ability to appreciate horror. With no leader but the "invisible hand," with no elite but the mild and platitudinous Babbittry of the American hinterland, Western capitalism will soon accomplish what the century's more murderous tyrants, with all their poisonous calculation, could only dream of doing: effacing the cultural memory of entire nations. For there is no tradition, religion, or language to which business owes any allegiance greater than momentary convenience; nor does any tradition, religion, or language remain that can muster a serious challenge to its cultural authority. As David Rieff demonstrated so presciently last year, it is *capitalism,* not angry workers, unhappy youth, or impoverished colonial peoples, that is "the bull in the china shop of human history. The market economy, now global in scale, is by its nature corrosive of all established hierarchies and certainties. . . ."

When the twentieth century opened business was only one power among many, economically and culturally speaking, a dangerously expansive but more or less contained participant in a larger social framework. While it might mistreat workers, break unions, bribe editors, and buy congressmen, its larger claims and authority were limited by an array of countervailing powers. It does not require a rosy sentimental view of any past period to recognize that today there are no such countervailing forces. Not only is labor a toothless ghost, seemingly capable only of slowing its own demise, but there is no cultural power on earth—save maybe the quixotic imagination of each isolated "reader" of the corporate text[*]—that can stand independent from or intrude upon the smooth operation of capital. With its advanced poststructuralist powertrain, its six-barrel rock 'n' roll assimilator, and its turbocharged fiber-optic speed, multinational capital is able to run cultural circles around our ponderous old notions of democracy, leaving us no imaginable means through which the culture of business might be resisted, no vantage point from which "the public" might be addressed, no possible permutation of written English that might have an effect on the way people live, not even any way to address the subject with-

---

[*] Fukuyama's dismissal of Cultural Studies' basic argument about reception of Western culture products is significant: "For our purposes, it matters very little what strange thoughts occur to people in Albania or Burkina Faso. . . ." Not being "embodied in important social or political forces and movements," they just aren't "part of world history."

out lapsing into cliché. It's night in America, and we can feel ourselves slipping into a sleep from which we can't imagine ever waking.

Meanwhile the last twenty years have brought a palpable undoing of the American fabric, a physical and social decay so unspeakably vast, so enormously obscene that we can no longer gauge the destruction with words. We all know this: there it is every night on TV, there it is as you drive through the South Side on your way to work (thank God for the virtual office!). And yet it matters nothing, because we don't live in that America anymore: our home, as Jean Baudrillard snickered years ago, is *literally* the TV, the interactive wonder, the simulation that is so much more exciting, fulfilling, and convenient than any possible permutation of physical reality. We can do nothing but watch the world crumble because, our collective imagination being as much a construct of business necessity as the government's various trade agreements, we cannot imagine it being any other way. La Follette? Debs? IWW? That's a different world. When *we* say "Third Party," we mean a third *business* party.

Out here in the great flyover, ground zero of the Information Revolution, you can *feel* the world dissolving, everything from the hard verities of the industrial past to the urban geography beginning to melt away in the pale blue CRT fog. Our archetypes and ideas and visions and memories, the accumulation of centuries, are yielding as easily to corporate re-engineering as has our landscape, built and torn down and renamed and reshuffled, everything forgotten instantly and relegated overnight to the quaint land of sepia-tint. This year we'll live in beautiful Passiondale, just down the road from Cambry estates. Next year the noise and mud aren't so charming; wreck it down and move to a new box in a better fortified enclave: meaningless upon meaningless, stretching out across the infinitely malleable Illinois prairie, idiot fantasy after idiot fantasy tracing a senseless diagram of human gullibility and iron corporate will.

Even while we are happily dazed by the mall's panoply of choice, exhorted to indulge our taste for breaking rules, and deluged with all manner of useful "information," our collective mental universe is being radically circumscribed, enclosed within the tightest parameters of all time. In the third millennium there is to be no myth but the business myth, no individuality but the thirty or so professionally-accepted psychographic market niches, no diversity but the happy heteroglossia of the sitcom, no rebellion but the pre-programmed search for new kicks. Denunciation is becoming impossible: we will be able to achieve

143

no distance from business culture since we will no longer have a life, a history, a consciousness apart from it. It is making itself unspeakable, too big, too obvious, too vast, too horrifying, too much of a cliché to even begin addressing. A matter-of-fact disaster, like Rwanda, as natural as the supermarket, as resist-able as air. It is putting itself beyond our power of imagining because it has *become* our imagination, it has *become* our power to envision, and describe, and theorize, and resist.

Nominated by The Baffler

TWO GIRLS

by SUZANNE GARDINIER

from THE AMERICAN VOICE

       who come in the night whispering
Whose songs are too small to remember
Whose rest Whose gestures disappeared
To look for them without a sentence
To make a shelter for them here
One night dancer One firstlight singer
Who mark each lost nearness with tears
One torn cloth coat One pact unmended
Who warn in whispers fifty years
One who wants the word for morning
Two we think are here no longer
One who wants the word for footprint
Two girls tangled in the branches
One in smoke One in shadow
One from bridges One from snow

    Kaddish
The languages of wrists and ankles
Winter Soup Bread A woman's neck
Sealed train to suddenly an island
Here she who lay down her small flesh
This crow This star This metal bramble
This path where craft and bodies mesh
This night chimney This ditch This shamble
To manufacture smoke from breath
What you know of masks Of making
Forest clearing built of ashes

145

Nachtwache The word for footprint
All the songs you have forgotten
This ghost fury This disguise
Borrowed mouth and borrowed eyes

  at exactly 8:15 a.m. a thousand doves released from cages
    Mountain flanks Barley Delta bridges
    Salt river's movement in the heat
    Summer Daughter Breakfast Two fishes
    Shadows The language shadows speak
    A cricket Just before the brightness
    She who watches She who has seen
    Invention heralded by engines
    This labor's fruit This planned machine
    Straw umbrellas Coats of paper
    Temples choked with unclaimed ashes
    Thirst *Zenshō* The word for morning
    She who could not keep her skin on
    You who call her No Witness
    You who think she found her rest

              You
    Her hair smoothed back from fever forehead
    Her chill in nearness put away
    The fledgling kept The sapling guarded
    These two who knock with every rain
    Where there is warmth Where there is water
    The stamping songs of yesterday
    Two guardians Two raging daughters
    You who were taught another way
    You who think a word is useless
    You who mock and doubt your dreaming
    You who know dirt is not holy
    You who never were a child
    Archipelago Cistern
    You hungry You thirsty Turn

Nachtwache: nightwatchman
Zenshō: conflagration

Nominated by DeWitt Henry, Jane Miller, The American Voice

VENEXIA I

by CHARLES WRIGHT

from SHENANDOAH

Too much at first, too lavish—full moon
Jackhammering light-splints along the canal, gondola beaks
Blading the half-dark;
moon-spar; backwash backlit with moon-spark. . . .

Next morning, all's otherwise
With a slow, chill rainfall like ragweed
                         electric against the launch-lights,
Then grim-grained, then gray.
This is the water—watch landscape, the auto-da-fe.

Such small atrocities these days between the columns,
Such pale seductions and ravishments.
Boats slosh on the crushed canal, gulls hunch down, the
      weather rubs us away.
From here it's a long walk home.

Listen, Venice is death by drowning, everyone knows,
City of masks and minor frightfulness, October city
Twice-sunk in its own sad skin.
How silently the lagoon
                         covers our footsteps, how quickly.

Along the Zattere, the liners drift huge as clouds.
We husband our imperfections, our changes of tune.
When water comes for us, we take it into our arms—
What's left's affection, and that's our sin.

Nominated by Henry Carlile, Philip Levine

A MAN-TO-BE

fiction by HA JIN

from TRIQUARTERLY

At THE SPRING FESTIVAL Hao Nan was very happy, because a week before he had been engaged to Soo Yan, one of the pretty girls in Flag-Pole Village. She was tall and literate. By custom, the dowry would cost the Haos a fortune: eight silk quilts, four pairs of embroidered pillows, ten suits of outer clothes, five meters of woolen cloth, six pairs of leather shoes, four dozen nylon socks, a wristwatch, two thermos bottles, a sewing machine, a bicycle, a pair of hardwood chests. Yet Nan's parents were pleased by the engagement, for the Soos were a rich family in the village and Yan was the only daughter. The wedding was scheduled to take place on the Moon Day the next fall. Though the Haos didn't have much money left after the engagement feast, they were not worried. Since they had two marriageable daughters, they would be able to marry off at least one of them to get the cash for Nan's wedding.

It was the third day of the Spring Festival. Nan and four other young men were on duty at the office of the village militia. Because the educated youths from Dalian had returned home to spend the holiday season with their families in the city, the young villagers had to cover all the shifts. It was a good way of making ten work points—a full day's pay, so nobody complained. Besides, it was an easy job. For eight hours they didn't have to do anything except stay in the office and make one round through the village.

Outside, a few snowflakes were swirling like duck down around the red lanterns hung at every gate. The smell of gunpowder and incense lingered in the air. Firecrackers exploded now and then, mingled with

149

the music of a Beijing opera sent out by a loudspeaker. Inside the militia's office, the five men were a little bored, though they had plenty of corn liquor, roasted sunflower seeds, and candies with which to while away the time. They had been playing the poker game called Beat the Queen. Liu Daiheng and Mu Bing wanted to stop to play chess by themselves, but the others wouldn't let them. There was no fun if only three men drew the cards, and they wanted to crown two kings and beat two queens every time.

Slowly the door opened. To their surprise, Sang Zhu's bald head emerged, and then in came his small body and bowlegs. "Hello, k-k-Uncle Sang," Nan said with a clumsy smile, which revealed his canine teeth.

Without answering, Sang glared at Nan, who had almost blurted out his nickname Cuckold Sang. People called him that because his young wife, Shuling, often had affairs. It was said that she was a fox spirit and always ready to seduce a man. People thought that Sang, already in his fifties and almost twice his wife's age, must have been useless in bed. At least he didn't have sperm, or else Shuling would have given him a baby.

Sang was holding his felt hat. He looked tipsy, his baggy eyes bloodshot. "Uncle Sang," Wang Ming said, "take a seat." Without a word, Sang sat down and put his elbows on the table.

They needed a sixth person to play the game One Hundred Points. "Want to join us?" Nan asked.

"No poker, boys," Sang said. "Give me something to drink."

Yang Wei poured him a mug of corn liquor. "Here you are," he said, winking at the others.

"Good, this is what I need." Sang raised the mug to his lips and almost emptied it in one gulp. "I came here for serious business tonight."

"What is it?" Daiheng asked.

"I invite you boys over to fuck my wife," Sang said deliberately.

All the young men were taken aback, and the room suddenly turned quiet except for the sputtering of the coal stove. They looked at one another, not knowing how to respond.

"You're kidding, Uncle Sang," Daiheng said, after a short while.

"I mean it. She's hot all the time. I want you to give it to her enough tonight." Anger inflamed Sang's eyes.

Silence again fell in the room.

"Afraid to come, huh?" Sang asked, his sparse brows puckered up. A smile crumpled his sallow face.

"Sure, we'd like to come. Who wouldn't?" said Ming, who was a squad leader in the militia.

"Well, sometimes heaven does drop meat pies," Bing said, as if to himself.

"No, we shouldn't go," Nan cut in, scanning the others' faces with his narrow eyes gleaming. He turned to Sang and said, "It's all right to do it to your wife, Uncle Sang, but that could be dangerous to us." Turning to the others, he asked, "Remember what happened at the brickyard last summer? You fellas don't want to get into that kind of trouble, do you?"

His words dampened the heat in the air. For a moment even the squad leader, Wang Ming, and Liu Daiheng, the oldest of them, didn't know what to say. Everybody remained silent. What Nan had referred to was a case in which a prostitute had been screwed to death by a bunch of brickmakers. Of course, prostitution was banned in the new China, but there were always women selling their flesh on the sly. That woman went to the brickyard once a month and asked for five yuan a customer, which was a big price, equal to two days' pay earned by a brickmaker. That was why the men wouldn't let her off easily. They gave her the money but forced her to work without a stop. As they had planned, they kept her busy throughout the night, and even after she lost consciousness they went on mounting her. She died the next day. Then the police came and arrested all the men. Later three of them were sentenced to eight years in prison.

"Nan's right. I don't think we should go," Wei said at last.

"You're no man," Sang said with a sneer, stroking his beardless chin. "I invite you boys to share my wife, free of charge, but none of you dare come. Chickens!"

"Uncle Sang, if you want us to come," Daiheng said, "you ought to write a pledge."

"But I don't know how to write."

"Good idea. We can help you with that," Ming said.

"All right, you write and I'll put in my thumbprint."

Ming went to the desk, pulled a drawer, and took out a pen and a piece of paper. He sat down to work on the pledge.

Nan felt uneasy about the whole thing. How could a husband invite other men to have sex with his wife? he asked himself. I wouldn't.

Never. Shuling must've had an affair with someone lately and have been caught by Cuckold Sang. They must've had a big fight today.

Sang was dragging at his pipe silently. Sitting beside him, Bing was putting the poker cards back into the box.

"Here," Ming said, walking over with the paper, "listen carefully, Uncle Sang." Then he read aloud with his eyebrows flapping up like a pair of beetle wings:

> On the third eve of the Spring Festival, I, Sang Zhu, came to the Militia's Office and invited five young militiamen— Hao Nan, Liu Daiheng, Yang Wei, Mu Bing, and Wang Ming—to have sex with my wife Niu Shuling. By doing this, I mean to teach her a lesson so she will stop seducing other men and be a chaste woman in the future. If any physical damage is done to her in the process of the activity, none of the young men shall be responsible. I, Sang Zhu, the husband, will bear all consequences.
>
> The Pledger:
>
> Sang Zhu

Wei placed the ink-paste box on the desk. "Put in your thumbprint if you agree, Uncle Sang."

"All right." Sang pressed his ringworm-nailed thumb into the ink, took it out, blew on its pad, and stamped a scarlet smudge under his name. He wiped off the ink on the leg of his cotton-padded trousers, which were black but shiny with grease stains. Turning away from the table, he blew his nose; two lines of mucus landed on the dusty floor.

"Now, let's go," Ming said, and motioned to the others as though they were going off to bag a homeless dog, which they often did on night patrol.

Nan felt unhappy about the pledge, because Ming, the son of a bitch, had put Nan's name the first and his own name the last among the group, as if Nan had led them in this business. At least, it read that way on paper. He was merely a small soldier, whereas Ming was a leader.

The snow stopped, and the west wind was blowing and would have chilled them to the bones if they had not drunk a lot of liquor. Each of them was carrying a long flashlight, whose beam now stabbed into the darkness and now hit a treetop, sending sleeping birds on the wing.

They were eager to reach the Sangs', get hold of that loose woman, and overturn the rivers and seas in her. In raptures they couldn't help singing. They sang "I Am a soldier," "Return to My Mother's," "Our Navigation Depends on the Great Helmsman," "Without the Communist Party There Would Be No New China." In the distance, soundless firecrackers bloomed in the sky over Sea Watch Village. The white hills and fields seemed vaster than they were in daylight. The first quarter of the moon wandered slowly through clouds among a few stars. The night was clear and quiet except for the men's hoarse voices vibrating.

Nan followed the other men, singing, and he couldn't help imagining what it would feel like to embrace a woman and have her body under his own. He thought of girls in the village, and also of Soo Yan. Though they were engaged, he had never touched her, not even her hand. This was an opportunity to learn how to handle a woman.

They entered Sang's yard. A dark shadow lashed about on the moonlit ground and startled Ming and Daiheng, who were at the front of the group. Then a wolfhound burst out barking at them. "Stop it!" Sang shouted. "You beast that doesn't know who owns you. Stop it!"

The dog ran away toward the haystack, scared by the beams of the flashlights scraping its body. The yard was almost empty except for a line of colorful washing, frozen and sheeny, swaying in the wind like landed kites tied up by children. Ming tapped on a pink shirt, which was apparently Shuling's, and said, "It smells so delicious. Why no red on this, Old Sang? She's too young for menopause, isn't she?"

They broke out laughing.

Sang's little stone house had a thatched roof. Entering it, they put their two rifles behind the door. An oil lamp was burning on the dining table on the brick bed, but nobody was in. Finding no woman, the men began swearing and said they were disappointed. Sang searched everywhere in the house, but there was no trace of his wife. "Shu—ling—" he cried to the outside. Only the hiss of the wind answered.

"Old Sang, what does this mean?" Daiheng asked. "What do you have in mind exactly?"

"I want you to do it to my wife."

"But where is she?" Bing asked.

"I don't know. You boys wait. I'm sure she'll be back soon."

Sang's eyes were filled with rage. Obviously he didn't expect to see an empty house either. He took a large bowl of boiled pork and a platter of stewed turnips from the kitchen and placed them on the table. They climbed on the brick bed and started eating the dishes and drinking the liquor they had brought along.

"It's too cold," Wei said, referring to the food.

"Yes," Ming said. "Let's have something warm, Old Sang. We have work to do."

"You must treat us well," Bing said, "or else we won't leave tonight. This is our home now."

"All right, all right, you boys don't go crazy. I'm going to cook you a soup, a good one."

Sang and Daiheng went to the kitchen, lighting the stove and cutting pickled cabbages and fat pork. In the village Daiheng was well known as a good cook, so he did the work naturally.

"Don't be stingy. Put in some dried shrimps," Wei shouted at the men in the kitchen.

"All right, we will," Sang yelled back.

Nan remained silent meanwhile. He didn't like the tasteless meat and just kept smoking Sang's Glory cigarettes and cracking roasted melon seeds. In the kitchen the bellows started squeaking.

Ming and Wei were playing a finger-guessing game, which Nan and Bing didn't know how to play but were eager to learn. Nan moved closer, watching their hands changing shapes deftly under the oil lamp and listening to them chanting aloud:

> A small chair has square legs,
> A little myna has a pointed bill.
> It's time you eat spider eggs,
> Drink pee and gulp swill.
>
> Five heads,
> Six fortunes,
> Three stars,
> Eight gods,
> Nine cups—

"Got you!" Ming yelled at Wei. Pointing at a mug filled with liquor, he ordered, "Drink this."

They hadn't finished the second round when Daiheng and Sang rushed in. "She's here. She's here," Daiheng whispered, his voice in a flutter.

Before they could straighten up, Shuling stepped in, wearing a red scarf and puffing out warm air. She whisked the snowflakes off her shoulder with a pair of mittens and greeted the men. "Welcome," she said. She looked so fresh with her pink cheeks and permed hair. Her plump body swayed a little against the white door curtain, as if she didn't know whether she should stay in or go out.

"Well, well, well," Ming hummed.

"Where have you been?" Sang asked sharply, then went up to her and grabbed the front of her sky-blue jacket.

"I, I—let me go." She was struggling to free herself.

"I know where you were. With that pale-faced man again. Tell me, is that true or not?" Sang pulled her closer to himself. He referred to a young cadre on the work team which was investigating the graft and bribery among the leaders of the production brigade. Nan remembered seeing that man and Shuling together in the grocery store once.

"Let me go. You're hurting me," she begged, and turned to the others, her round eyes flashing with fear.

"You stinking skunk, always have an itch in your cunt!" Sang bellowed. "I want you to have it enough today, as a present for the Spring Festival. See, I have five men for you here. Every one of them is strong as a bull." His head tilted to the militia.

"No, don't. Please don't," she moaned with her hands held together before her chest.

"What are you waiting for, boys?" Sang shouted at the young men.

They all jumped up and went to hold her. "Brothers, don't do this to me," she wailed.

"Do it to her! Teach her a good lesson," her husband yelled.

They grabbed her limbs and carried her onto the brick bed. She struggled and even tried to kick and hit them, but like a tied sheep she couldn't move her legs and arms. Daiheng pinched her thigh as Ming was rubbing her breasts with his hand. "Not bad," Ming said, "not flabby at all."

"Oh, you hooligans. Let your grandma go. Ouch!"

With laughter, they placed her on the hard bed. She never stopped cursing, "All your ancestors will go to hell. Sons of asses . . . I'll tell your parents. . . . Your houses will be struck by thunderbolts! You'll die without a son. . . ."

Her curses only incensed the men. Bing rolled one end of her woolen scarf into a ball and thrust it into her mouth. Instantly she stopped making noises. Then Sang produced some ropes and tied her

155

hands to the legs of the dining table. Meanwhile, Wei and Nan, as they were told by Ming, were binding her feet to the beam that formed the edge of the bed.

They slipped their hands underneath her underclothes, kneading her breasts and rubbing her crotch. Then they ripped open her jacket, shirts, pants, and panties. Her partly naked body was squirming helplessly in the coppery light.

Daiheng took out five poker cards, from 1 to 5, mixed them and then put them on the bed. By turns they picked the cards. Wei had "5," Nan "4," Bing "3," Daiheng "2." As Ming got "1," he was to do it first.

"All right," Sang said calmly, "everything is fine. Now you boys enjoy yourselves." He raised the door curtain and went out.

Ming began to mount Shuling, saying, "I've good luck this year. Nan, little bridegroom, watch your elder brother carefully and learn how to do it."

Nan was wondering whether Daiheng had contrived a trick in dealing out those cards. How come both Ming and Daiheng had got ahead of the three younger men? But he didn't attend to his doubt for long, since soon Ming's lean body was wriggling violently on Shuling's. Having never seen such a scene, Nan felt giddy and short of breath, but he was also eager to experience it. They all watched intently. Meanwhile the woman kept her face away from them.

While Daiheng was on Shuling, biting her shoulders and making happy noises, Sang came in with a small enamel bowl in his hand. He climbed on the bed and placed it beside his wife's head. He clutched her hair and pulled her face over, and said, "Look at what's in the bowl." He picked up a bit of the red stuff with three fingers and let it trickle back into the bowl. "Chili powder. I'll give it to you. Wait, after they are done with you, I'll stuff you with it, to cure the itch in there for good."

His wife closed her eyes and shook her head slightly.

Bing, who was the third, obviously had no experience with a woman before. No sooner had he got on top of her than he came and gave up. He held his pants, looking painful as though having just swallowed a bowl of bitter liquid medicine. He coughed and blew his nose.

Now it was Nan's turn. He seemed bashful as he moved to that body. Though this was his first time, he felt himself having enough confidence. He straddled her and started unbuckling his pants. He looked down at her body, which reminded him of a huge frog, tied up, wait-

156

ing to be skinned for its legs. Looking up, he noticed that her ear was small and delicate. He grabbed her hair and pulled her face over to see closely what she looked like. She opened her eyes, which were full of sparkling tears and staring at him. He was surprised by the fierce eyes but could not help observing them. Somehow her eyes were changing—the hate and the fear were fading, and beneath their blurred surfaces loomed a kind of beauty and sadness that was bottomless. Nan started to fantasize, thinking of Soo Yan and other pretty girls in the village. Unconsciously he bent down and intended to kiss that pale face, which turned aside and spilled the tears. His head began swelling.

"What are you doing?" Daiheng shouted at Nan.

Suddenly a burst of barking broke out beyond the window. The wolfhound must have been chasing a fox or a leopard cat that had come to steal chickens. Wild growls and yelps filled the yard all at once.

"Oh!" Nan cried out. Something snapped in his body; a numbing pain passed along his spine and forced him off her. By instinct, he managed to get to his feet and rushed to the door, holding his pants with both hands. Cold sweat was dripping from his face.

Once in the outer room he dropped to his knees and began vomiting. In addition to the smell of the half-cooked cabbage soup in the cauldron, the room was instantly filled with the odor of alcohol, sour food, fermented candies, roasted melon seeds. His new cotton-padded shoes and new Dacron jacket and trousers were wet and soiled.

"Little Nan, come on!" Daiheng said. Putting his hand on Nan's head, he shook him twice.

"I'm scared. No more," Nan moaned, buckling his belt.

"Scared by a dog? Useless," Sang said, and restrained himself from giving Nan a kick.

"Come on, Nan. You must do it," Ming said. "You just lost your Yang. Go get on her and have it back. Or you've lost it for good, don't you know that?"

"No, no, I don't want to." Nan shook his head, groaning. "Leave me alone. I'm sick." He rubbed his eyes to get rid of the mist caused by the dizziness. His hands were slimy.

"Let that wimp do what he wants. Come back in," Sang said aloud, straddling the threshold.

They went in to enjoy themselves. "Ridiculous, scared by a dog," Wei said, giggling and scratching his scalp.

Holding the corner of the caldron range in the dark, Nan managed to stand up, and he staggered out into the windy night.

As Ming said, Nan lost his potency altogether. In fact, he lay in bed for two days after that night when he had walked home bareheaded through the flying snow. At first, he dared not tell his parents what had happened, but within a week the entire village knew Nan had been frightened by Sang's dog and had lost his Yang. His father scolded him a few times, while his mother wept in secret.

Two weeks later, the Soos returned to the Haos the Shanghai wristwatch and the Flying Dove bicycle, two major items of the dowry already in Yan's hands, saying Nan was no longer a normal man, so they wouldn't marry their daughter to him. Despite Mrs. Hao's imploring, the Soos refused to retain the expensive gifts. However, they did say that if Nan recovered within half a year they might reconsider the engagement.

For four months Nan had seen several doctors of Chinese medicine in town. They prescribed a lot of things to restore his manhood: ginseng roots, sea horses, angelica, gum dragon, deer antler, tiger bones, royal jelly, even a buck's penis, but nothing worked. His mother killed two old hens and stewed them with ginseng roots. Nan ate the powerful but almost inedible dish; the next day he had a bleeding nose and soon began losing his hair. His father cursed him, saying the Hao clan had never had such a nuisance. Indeed, after eating two or three slices of buck's penis, a normal man wouldn't be able to go out because of the erection, but nothing could help Nan. There was no remedy for such a jellyfish.

By now the villagers no longer counted Nan as a man. Lots of children would call out "Dog-Scared" when they ran into him. Though quite a few matchmakers visited the Haos, they all came for his sisters. Among all the unfilial things, the worst is childlessness. But what could Nan do? He used to think of poisoning Sang's wolfhound, but even that idea didn't interest him anymore. One afternoon, when he was on his way to the pig farm, that dog came to him, lashing its tail and wagging its tongue. He wanted to give it a kick, but he noticed Soo Yan walking two hundred meters away along the edge of the spinach field; so instead he threw his half-eaten corn cake to the dog, who picked it up and ran away. Nan watched the profile of that girl. She wore cream-colored clothes, her fiery gauze scarf waving in the breeze. With a short hoe on her shoulder, she looked like a red-crowned crane moving against the green field.

Nominated by Lloyd Schwartz

WHAT COMES FROM THE GROUND

fiction by WENDY DUTTON

from WITNESS

Y<small>OU KNOW HOW WHEN</small> you look back over your life and you see a day, a conversation, or maybe, as in my case, a single image that changed everything, not just in your life, but in the whole world? This is the story of how at the same time that my sister and I were left to run the farm, my dream-come-true was staring me in the face. It's hard even now when I am an adult to accept that the occupation I had picked out for myself in those days was not only unattainable, but ridiculous. I wanted to be an acrobat.

It's not that I was unrealistic. I did have true acrobatic talent. We had two acres of flat mowed grass leading up to the house. The lane was lined with fat maples, and I could do one-and-a-half back handsprings in the space of two trees. I could get quite a momentum going, then end in a half-twist just before the swampy part up by the road. That's where the abandoned log house stood, the original homestead, which, of course, my sister Clare and I believed to be thoroughly haunted.

Clare would spot me. That's what they call it when, her long white-blonde hair lashing at her face, Clare would run alongside me. Her flighty breath panted away while mine huffed heavy from tumbling. It's not like she could have broken any fall—she was so slight—but she did make me more careful for fear of it.

And actually my tumbling was just a way to compete with Clare's prettiness. Otherwise I was just Sue Shawn, more boy than girl and nothing to look at.

160

My father favored me because I somewhat lessened the blow of not only twins, but girl twins, a curse for any farmer who counted on boy children for chores and harvest, planting too. At least, that was the appearance of things when anyone could see we girls did the load of work, only it was hidden as women's work is.

My father was gangly, but not tall and with a rounder's chest. He had sunburned ears—I remember that—and sunburned hands to match his mean, slappy ways. Something of a cock crow, he was. Seemed about to fly off at any minute. And so I am glad he left before he could see his Sue Shawn outgrow him, for I am sure it would have enraged him. But you see what a jinxed beginning Clare and I had: we killed our mother being born, then grew up in what came to be called The Great Depression. By the time we turned fourteen, our father run off to fight Hitler and keep the world safe for democracy.

I remember my father, how he'd take us in the barn, empty by then, but still filled with the grassy smell of livestock. He'd go to the backside of the trough, stuck still with years-old hay, and he'd pull the old harness off its hook and put it round his neck and say real important like, "Girls, this here was my pop's from when in those days they farmed with horses."

We'd stare at him blankly, because he'd told the tale enough, how they came down from Minnesota or Michigan or some such watery country, came down, his father and his father's brother, looking to strike out on their own, looking to go back north their pockets full of southern coins, because in those days Indiana was the South.

He'd put that harness around his neck where it gulped him up like a big leather horseshoe, and he flared his nostrils and stomped his feet and neighed like a mad horse, and we laughed politely, nervous there in the dark barn. The corners scurried with mice, and maybe something bigger, and there were bats in the rafters. It was our number two most haunted place, but to our pop it was something else, like an empty theater.

Then he'd stop all of a sudden, remember us, and get his disgusted girl-child look. Like we couldn't possibly understand the beauty of it— farming with horses, two brothers, the heartland.

He'd brush right past us and head inside the house. We'd try to follow him, but stopped short just outside the barn. It was blinding to come into the light, even on a cloudy day. And we'd stand there blinking, holding hands, staring out across what was nothing but flat.

That was the view from one side of the farm anyway, the side that looked into Jackson County. The other side ran into Brown County, famous even then for its trees that broke into a riot of color come fall.

161

Of course, now people travel all over the state in RVs, but then they were lucky to have cars, so it was money people coming down, hot on the look-out for covered bridges and log cabins. Sometimes as a joke Clare and I would dress up in our parents' old clothes and sit beside our cabin, posing as local-yokel husband and wife, waving at the tourists driving slow past us.

That's what give us the idea, I suspect.

When our father left, we realized we had a farm to run and nothing to run it with but our wits. Here I'd been spending all my time tinkering in the old hen house and thinking on how I could advance my tumbling career. And Clare, she had grown into something of a startling beauty. Her hair that odd, washed-out color gave her the look of an angel, and she was so small I could ball her up in my arms, and that's just what I did every night. We'd sleep in the big bed, the bed we'd been born in and the bed our mother had died in, brass with tarnished balls and scratched spokes. We'd lie tangled together, and I'd kiss my dear Clare, kiss her all over until she stopped crying and shivering, and I'd rock her and love her like only I could.

We had neighbors, sure, but there were few who knew us well, most having made a point of steering clear of our pop. People in the country have a way of letting each other be. Could drive past your farm every day, wave even, but never know your first name. We watched each other, knew occasional stories, but that was about it.

It just became known that pop had gone off, and I, a short-haired, strapping youth, had risen up to take his place. They scarcely remembered Sue Shawn; I was so much the unfavored twin. I signed for our father with such confidence that folks seemed to decide to just let us alone. We weren't kids; but we weren't grown either.

It didn't take long for the little equipment we had to get repossessed, and I began to sell the land. Clare turned what was left into gardening, and her plot grew the size of five barns. She had this philosophy that a good garden should be equal parts vegetable and flower, a philosophy I still hold to. She set up a stand beside the old cabin. I oiled the cabin's logs and put fresh mortar between them to add to the charm, as if Clare weren't enough. Her produce, even way out there, sold well.

Was for Clare I auctioned off the back forty, to a Wyatt no less, the same ones plowed up the Grahams' family graveyard and just left the stones propped up against a tree. But with the money I bought Clare a horse, a palomino, her favorite kind since she was eight. We called

162

her Philomino, as a variation on her breed, and so there we were, back to farming with horses.

There never was better produce, plump with juice, shiny, vegetables with little hearts and souls all their own. And I think our garden grew so well because we were happy.

This was the mood all over the country during those war years, because everywhere you looked it was women. There was this kind of dare-devil feeling, like we better hurry up and milk what we could out of the world, because—as everyone kept saying—the men would be coming back soon. There already was a steady trickle of them, wounded and grim, silent as far as messengers go.

Our father left in the winter of '42. '43 and '44 were fair seasons, and things looked to be getting even better, though this would not turn out to be true.

It was the spring of '45 I came up with my greatest invention: Sue Shawn's Amazing Jumping Shoes. They were really boots with springs attached and a metal plate on the bottom. It was a cat's cradle of rubber bands on the inside made them bounce, and oh how they bounced. I'd get my gun and put on the jumping shoes and spring after rabbits, surprising the hell out of them. The shoes were good for hunting, but as you might guess, they were even better for tumbling.

The first thing I tried was a back handspring. The results were stupendous. I sprang through the air backwards and landed directly on my feet, my legs twanging, arms held straight in front. Perfect form was possible in those shoes. They were true tumbling innovation.

But Clare didn't like them. "What good are they for?" she questions me.

"They're for fun!" I instructed her.

"Fun." She curled her lip. It was like a foreign word to her, so bent was she on her garden and its upkeep.

"You wait," I challenged her. "These shoes are my future."

"Kids'd never buy them," she sniffed. "Their parents'd think they're unsafe."

"I could refine them. I could make them bounce higher or lower."

"Still," she said. She didn't believe in me. I can tell you it was a blow.

"Here I've helped you with your fool garden!" I roared. "Who bought you Philomino? Who pulled the plow after her? I've picked my fingers raw for you, and the least you can do is appreciate my shoes!"

This was our first big fight. It was a bad omen. We began to quarrel regularly, but always about little things—whether the milk was sour,

163

the corn seeds planted too high, the watermelon mounds not round enough. Underneath it all you could tell it was something else.

"I'll sell my shoes to circus clowns," I vowed. "I'll sell them to real acrobats. I'll make my fortune yet."

This, as it turned out, was not too far from the truth. Well, maybe not the fortune part, but the circus did come to Brown county, only it was an all-woman circus. They called themselves the Flying Women. Secretly they called themselves the Flying Widows, since more than half of them had lost their husbands in the war.

Chance Morton was one, a big woman, strong as any man, a champion spotter. There was Tiny (they all had nicknames like that), and Chance would throw her into the air, let her land on the trampoline and begin her flip-like-a-whip routine. Mama was another. She was one whose husband wasn't dead, but helped out, and she had five kids of her own who did most of the packing and hauling and assembly work. During the act, Mama's kids, schooled to be industrious like that, passed the hat, sold popcorn and penny candy, and also pick-pocketed some of the crowd, but only if they didn't clap.

Steady was another Flying Woman, named for her tightrope act, a real wonder to see, with a net held by Chance and three others following underneath her. She was like something you had seen in a dream when you were a kid, beautiful in her white lace bloomers, velvet waistcoat, and feather hat. When she was on the rope, swaying slightly, I would focus on the smallest parts of her, her toes, how they curled over in her ballet slippers, and her fingers, how they whitened on the pole she held sideways for balance.

They didn't have a tent; it was all open-air. They had been hired to perform at the Brown County State Park, which was fifty-some-odd acres and like a wonderland with all the men gone. During wartime women galloped on the riding trails—to hell with sidesaddle. And there was fishing and swimming and hiking in shorts. You would think during a state of emergency no one would visit a state park, but this was not necessarily true, especially with the Flying Women on hand. Clare and I, for example, rode Philomino twenty miles to see their first show.

Afterwards I waited by their painted truck.

"Look," I said to Chance. "I made something for you even before I met you. It's these. I call them Sue Shawn's Amazing Jumping shoes."

She turned them over in her hands. They were mannish hands like my own. I liked the looks of her, though she was twice my age. With her hair short and shoulders squared, it was like finding one of my own kind.

"They're good for tricks," I explained. "If you have skill. You can go ten, twelve feet off the ground. They're for acrobats only."

She was speechless really.

"Keep them," I urged her. "Try them out."

That evening the Flying Women came out to the farm. They came in their big jalopy truck, all except Mama and her family who were back at the campsite. The truck was painted with THE FLYING WOMEN in fat gold letters. The way Clare squinted at it, I could tell she thought it was trashing up the place with all its out-of-town flare, but it gave my heart a rise to see them coming up the lane, just as I'd nearly fallen over when I'd seen their show.

Now here The Flying Women were on my farm, and for the first time in my life I found myself popular. Chance had shown my shoes around, and I gave an additional demonstration. As I tumbled beside our maples, springing higher and higher into the air, I knew it was the performance of a lifetime. Chance asked me to join The Flying Women on the spot, and I quickly accepted.

Was then Clare got up from the porch swing where she'd been sitting without even swinging, and she slipped inside the house with the screen door banging behind her. I was mad at her—don't ask me to explain—but I didn't go after her. I looked over at that gaudy truck, and it's like I said: fate come calling.

There's one more thing to tell before I tell the end. It's how, in her own way, Clare said, "You go ahead and run off with a bunch of acrobats." It's how I heard her crying when she thought she was alone, and I came bounding up the stairs to find she was not alone at all. And she was naked, and he was naked, and he was on top of her, and he had a gunfire look, one I'd kill to keep away from her.

I had seen him at The Flying Women's show, one of the hollow men—you could just tell it. I remembered he had even spoken to Clare then, but I had been too entranced to give it any nevermind.

Now here he was on top of my twin, and like a fool all I could think was, "They'll never let it go on. The men will come back, and they will never allow women to tumble about in their bloomers."

I don't remember the rest, how he dressed himself and got out of there. Clare got up and stood in her slip at the window, studying the fields that weren't ours anymore. I never did talk about it. I left so she could dress.

On August sixth The Flying Women were scheduled to leave Brown County and head to the other side of the state where they had shows in the college towns, Greencastle and Lafayette. I planned to join the show then with my Sue Shawn's Amazing Jumping Shoes routine. I had been working on it every day while learning the trade, spotting and assembly and such. I worked for Clare in the mornings and evenings, to avoid the summer heat. But between us there was nothing but silence, and I expected the same on the day I left.

But on that day, Clare was a mess. She barred my path. She was weeping and sort of slapping herself across the face. She screamed, "All those babies! It was my fault!" I could see it was more than me what made her wail so.

"Stop it!" I commanded her, but nothing would stop her until I pushed her into a chair, and that stunned her but only for a minute before she was at it again. "We bombed the Japanese," she finally said, clear as could be.

"My God," I said. I knew it was true.

And Clare was saying, "It's my fault. I prayed all night for something to happen to make you stay on the farm. And now they've dropped this bomb, and killed all those people, just to end the war and make you stay."

She may have been hysterical, but she was right. We did drop the bomb. We did end the war. And I did not join The Flying Women.

I know what I'm about to say is a fake memory, because I know it is impossible. I am not even sure if the first part ever happened, but this is the way I see it. Clare and I were out in the field just beyond the garden, the fields we kept for Philomino, the last of our land. We were holding hands, because we weren't wearing our normal shoes; we were wearing Sue Shawn's amazing shoes, and Clare was afraid of falling. Rabbit-like, we slowly bounced, me schooling her in the ways of balance, managing the dirt clods.

Suddenly we stopped and looked to the horizon. There was a distant sound, a crash-and-boom all in one, but soft, and then silence. It was a clear white day with no breeze. What rose before us hadn't any color at first. It rose from the ground like a huge billowy mushroom, just as it had been described, just as you might imagine, though you would never guess it would be beautiful like that, a horrible beauty, distinctly man-made.

Nominated by Barbara Selfridge

SCORN

by CAROL FROST

from THE SOUTHERN REVIEW

She thought of no wilder delicacy than the starling eggs she
    fed him for breakfast,
and if he sat and ate like a farmhand and she hated him
    sometimes,
she knew it didn't matter: that whatever in the din of
    argument
was harshly spoken, something else was done, soothed and
    patted away.
When they were young the towering fierceness
of their differences had frightened her even as she longed for
    physical release.
Out of their mouths such curses; their hands huge, pointing,
    stabbing the air.
How had they *not* been wounded? And wounded they'd
    convalesced in the same rooms
and bed. When at last they knew everything without
    confiding—fears, stinks,
boiling hearts—they gave up themselves a little so that they
    might both love and scorn
each other, and they ate from each other's hands.

Nominated by Molly Bendall, Philip Booth, William Olsen, Michael Waters

THE LAST WHITE MAN IN BROOKLYN

by MICHAEL STEPHENS

from WITNESS

WHENEVER I VISIT Brooklyn, it makes me emotional. I don't mean paying a visit to some old or long-lost relative in Flatbush or Bay Ridge, but simply going *there*, to that ancestral, that interminable, that incestuous, platitudinous, vertiginous place. Walking or driving among its citizens and blocks, even casually going to Brooklyn does this to me. More accurately: it amazes me how emotional I get *afterward*. This time, though, I found my adrenaline pumping right there, a few blocks off that central juncture of the borough at Nostrand and Flatbush avenues, just off Brooklyn College. I had gone out there to read from my novel, *The Brooklyn Book of the Dead;* the turnout—three people showed—had been disappointing, but the paycheck was gratefully received. Afterward, though, walking across the campus, admiring the neo-Georgian buildings in a dense, early-spring fog and heavy rainfall, I had lunch with my friend Louis, a poet who teaches there and had invited me to read, and afterward, I went into the men's room to pee. Three white kids—they were probably no more than twenty years old—wearing leather jackets, though not looking too tough, were fooling and horsing around by the sinks. One of them wadded up a ball of wet paper towels, turning it into a giant spitball, and, unprovoked, hurled it with all his might at my head, hitting me. I could not go after them, schlong in hand, and had to finish peeing, and by the time I zipped up and rushed out, they were down the hall, laughing, and then

168

gone. I thought to myself, I'll be glad when I leave—get the hell out of here, though plenty of other times I have sought out Brooklyn, the closest thing I can imagine to a home, however long ago and short my stay was in East New York on the other side of Eastern Parkway. I realized, too, that people got killed in Brooklyn or, for that matter, anywhere else in New York City, for far less insulting behavior than what those three punks had proffered me. But what was I to do? Had they lingered—though I always, like everyone else in Brooklyn, talk a big game—would I have hit one of them? And is that the etiquette of the streets anymore? I mean, does anyone simply *fight?* Hurt pride, image on the line, a donnybrook breaks out, and afterward you shake hands and become best of friends over a beer. Well, I don't drink anymore and doubt, even if I did drink, that I'd want to quaff anything with those three morons. The protocol today would be to ice them, to whack them—to kill them dead. After all, the week before, someone got killed on the Brooklyn subway for looking at another passenger the wrong way. For *looking* at another person the *wrong* way! Perhaps, I thought, these three stooges were pledging for a fraternity. Or maybe one of them thought I was a teacher, or maybe I reminded one of them of his father. Anyhow, I had my check, and I was glad to go; saying goodbye to my friend Louis, I headed for the Number Two train, the last stop, Flatbush and Nostrand, the heart of Brooklyn.

I didn't see it when I got on the subway, but after a couple of stops when the car filled up with passengers, I noticed it then. I had been sitting there on the train, going into Manhattan, reading James Baldwin's *The Fire Next Time:* "If the concept of God has any validity or any use, it can only be to make us larger, freer, and more loving." His fiery prose sermon went on to warn white people of the black man's rage and indignation, not just now, but always, the sempiternal fire in the black belly, the seething images that ran through his head. Even God as we understood was white, and if He could not make blacks larger, freer, and more loving, Baldwin wrote, "then it is time we got rid of Him." Across from me, a group of stoned-out teenagers—probably newly out of high school classes since it was around three-thirty in the afternoon—mumbled about getting whitey. That's when I noticed that I was the only white man on the train. It was a standing-room-only car of black people shuttling underground through Brooklyn, mine and their ancestral turf, our once promised land. Later, I would wonder if Brooklyn made any of them as emotional as it made me; but there, right there on that train, I got nervous and even

169

scared, and as I get older, my fear does not simply manifest itself in a rapid heartbeat and jitteriness. When the fear took hold, I felt chemically sick. All my muscles seemed to turn to bones, and my bones became like frozen jelly; the pounding in my temples made me nauseous and dizzy, and I could feel my skin prickle and turn red. My palms dripped with sweat, and my lower back ached. I seemed to be almost hyperventilating. Besides everything else, the car rocked uncontrollably, sideways, and bucked up and down, lurching ahead, and the two motions, both of them highly unstable, made me sick to my stomach, so much so that I thought I might throw up any moment, but I did not. "Color is not a human or a personal reality," I read. "It is a political reality." I put the Baldwin essay away; his words created a sensory overload, though, oddly, being the only white man on the crowded subway car in Brooklyn made me understand—made me think I understood—what Baldwin felt like being the only black man in white restaurants and public places and work spaces. I thought I understood how uncomfortable he felt.

I know it is a truism of race relations that white people in the South—though considered more prejudiced than their Northern counterparts (at least in the old clichés)—had real interactions with their black neighbors, while in the North, we lived side by side, but really there were no human encounters. We did not eat together, hang out, kibitz, schmooze, go to the ball games together, or discuss politics or books or movies. Of course, like a lot of stereotypes, this one had some truth to it, and most of my white friends did not have any real black friends. Yet I had lived among black people since I was a child; they were my next door neighbors in Brooklyn, and my earliest, best friends were black boys on Macdougal Street in East New York. Still, when my family moved to Long Island, I can recall only one black family in our town, and though my friends and I—because their son was our age and a good athlete—played basketball with him at the playground, I don't recall his going to one party we attended. My friend Jimmy Farrell and I were considered weird by our white, Irish-Catholic friends because, still in our mid-teens, we used to drink in the black bars near the Roslyn train station, but, of course, this had more to do with juvenile alcoholism and getting served easily than it had to do with race relations. Yet I also remember that Jimmy had a "black" way of dancing at our Sunday church basement dances—a bottle of cheap wine drunk in the alleyway—that told me, at least that he was really into, truly ap-

170

preciated black culture, and that he thought it was just that—culture. But Jimmy Farrell died when he was in his early twenties, and other than he, I can't recall any friends with black sympathies until I dropped out of college and moved to the East Village, jazz clubs and drugs and after-hours bars. Still, over the years, I would be hard pressed to remember the last time a black friend came to my apartment for dinner. All that would change when I bottomed out on booze, wound up in rehab, got sober, and started attending 12-step meetings on the Upper West Side.

Not only do I live among black people, but I regularly see black people, have coffee with them in the morning, call them on the telephone, do favors for them—as they do for me—talk with them about our children, their schools, our former addictions. Nearly all the blacks I know are men my age and, like myself, in alcohol and drug recovery. We have an enormous amount of things in common, and even if some of them find that we are separated by our respective races—and I don't kid myself into thinking that some of them don't feel this way—race, at least in our relationships, is secondary to recovery and the community in which we find ourselves. Many of my black friends once hated whites, or, at least, certainly distrusted them, and maybe this was so until fairly recently, and the slightest off-color joke or irony or sense of humor can throw many of them back into old suspicions about whites. So I am aware of the tension, even amidst the camaraderie.

But riding on that subway train in the late afternoon from Brooklyn back to Manhattan was a whole other kind of experience in the history of my race relations. I never felt so white and scared simultaneously, even when I used to teach at Fordham University in the Bronx, and would take the subway north to Two-Hundred-and-Twenty-Fifth Street, and when the bus did not come, walk over to and up Kingsbridge Road, past Edgar Allan Poe's cottage, and finally to Fordham Road, a trek through one of the grittier landscapes in the urban world of New York City.

The next day I found myself writing a letter to my friend Hubert Selby Jr., the author of *Last Exit to Brooklyn;* Selby is my literary rabbi, a kind of mentor, and I've known him for more than twenty-five years. His books, to me, are the best that contemporary American literature gets, and, on a personal level, I admire the choices that Cubby—for that is what all his friends call him—made in his lifetime. While working on merchant ships as a teenager in the late 1940s, he contracted

171

tuberculosis, and spent several years in a hospital. He eventually lost one lung. During this period, mainly because of over-zealous doctors managing his pain, Cubby became a morphine—and then later on the streets a heroin addict. Plus, he had always been an alcoholic. But from those days until the present—he's in his late sixties now—he seems to live, survive, and flourish by pure will and spirituality, not by any choice of his racked body. Cubby was a heroin addict and alcoholic until the late Sixties, when he detoxed and got clean, first off the heroin, then a year or so later, the booze. This graduate from the streets of Bay Ridge and Red Hook and South Brooklyn *chose,* one day at a time, not to drink and drug. I often think that if Brooklyn kids—the really tough, shit-kicking, mean-assed, jive-talking, drug-snorting, fuck-the-system and up-your-ass, bad-attitude, school-dropout, chronically under-employed, low-self-esteemed, parentless, rootless, and cocky street kids want a role model, then they couldn't do better than Hubert Selby, this frail, though incredibly long-lasting and oddly durable street saint who, for the past thirty years, more or less, and on and off, has lived in Los Angeles, these days in West Hollywood, where he is the guru to a lot of young street kids, would-be and up-coming actors and directors and script writers, street poets and angry novelists, and even a few genuine superstars. That's what the streets of Brooklyn are able to produce.

But I'm only kidding myself because Cubby Selby is unique, a one-of-a-kind Brooklyn experience, and when he goes, there won't ever be another street guy quite like him. Still, I found myself trying to describe, in a letter to Cubby, what I felt that afternoon in the heart of Brooklyn, this land of my ancestors, for not too many blocks away in Holy Cross cemetery, just down the road from Flatbush and Nostrand, seven generations of my mother's family, all Brooklyn people, were buried, and going south on Flatbush Avenue, a bunch of them still live, refusing to give up their houses to anyone. They were from Brooklyn, and this was their home. I had to admire their foolish nostalgia, but the fact was, Brooklyn was no more Irish or Italian or, for that matter, any shade or disposition of white, than the North Shore of Long Island was a black enclave—except, of course, in pockets where the help for the Gatsby-like houses of Sands Point and Manhasset lived. Brooklyn had become the black capital of America, and though in the spring, summer, and fall, I regularly visited places like Coney Island, or even drove through the streets of East New York, oddly nostalgic over my horrible childhood there, my sense of being at home was a false one, because I had no more claim to Brooklyn than Custer had to the Indian territory, and probably the same fate awaited me that he got if I persisted in thinking that some part of Brooklyn was mine. It was not mine.

Brooklyn now belonged to young boys and girls without fathers and little motherly nurturing or love. They were angry kids without any elders to guide them, even if the role models, as often they were when I was growing up, were simply the neighborhood hoodlums as the actor/writer Chaz Palmintieri illustrated in his autobiographical movie, *A Bronx Tale*. Sometimes the local gangster can be a weird kind of stabilizing influence in a young life. If nothing else, you might learn, at least, how to survive on the streets. These kids, though, did not want to survive. In fact, they did not care if they died now or later; nothing in this life meant anything anyhow as witness the smirking faces of those young Coney Island boys from a gang called the X-Men off of Surf Avenue who commandeered a 42-year-old Russian woman from Brighton Beach, one community over, out jogging on the boardwalk, and dragging her off, a bunch of these boys, ages 14 to 18, raped her and beat her face and tried to destroy her life. My friend Philippe, with whom I walked the street of Manhattan, regularly photographed Coney Island, and over the past two years had befriended many of the X-Men, including a few of these kids, and though, when I went with him to Coney Island and realized how dangerous, at times, the place had become, this danger was always contrasted with the beautiful energy of the street and the majesty of the ocean a block or two away, and, as Philippe said, "These kids live in tenements with million dollar views . . ."

But the X-Men had no fathers or older brothers; they didn't have what we in Brooklyn call "rabbis." No elders even showed these poor, sorry kids how to commit crimes, how to make a getaway, how to do your business and slip away without a fingerprint, because, after all, the only crime that interested me as a kid was the kind you got away with, the bigger the better, not some douche-bag whack in the playground that sent you to jail for the rest of your life, but rather becoming a crime lord, the kind whose footprints disappeared in the sand the minute he walked away, so that nothing was ever traceable to this magnificent source, call him the godfather, the *capo di tutti capi*, the main man, the boss, or even the rebbe, the big rabbi in the sky; someone had to teach you how to do things and get away from their consequences. You were not born to kill cops; you were not made to spend the rest of your life in prison, even if you came from the ghetto, however poor your self-esteem and bad attitudes. Some of these older people showed you how to stay out of enough trouble not to do yourself in. But all of these older figures were gone; Brooklyn had been robbed of one generation showing a younger generation how to survive on the streets, and the results were people shooting each other on the subway for looking the wrong way and little boys raping Russian joggers on the boardwalk. There is no more hope left. That is how Brooklyn is these days.

A few days after my sojourn in Brooklyn I had breakfast with a lovely retired wiseguy from Mulberry Street, and he laughed when I told him about my trip to the outer borough. "Jesus Christ," he said "I can't believe it. What's the world coming to? Here you are an ex-boxer and the son of a Hell's Kitchen dockworker, and you are riding the subways in fear. Why?" But, of course, he knew why as well as I did. By the new rules, my ability to fight in the street was as worthless as hitting someone on the head with a foam cushion. The kids on the street had new rules; they all carried guns, and they would use those guns at the slightest provocation. I have no experience whatsoever with guns. My friend and I had learned how to survive in the city, and I had combined my street education with a literary one—my rabbis were all white-bearded writers now—to get by all these years on a minimum of acceptance and acknowledgment by the establishment, but each of us had survived in the city by the hand of elders, usually older men, though sometimes the kindness of a powerful woman. Bad men usually helped out bad boys, whereas the Brooklyn bad boys today—black and white as the spitball incident proved—got no help at all; they were on their own, had become freelancers by the time they had stepped from the cradle, and were only a few short steps away from the grave, whether they knew it or not.

Brooklyn used to make me angry, but that anger was the kind that fueled me to get ahead with my life, to try to accomplish something, if not the dreams my parents had for me or the ones my relatives presumed I deserved—in the military, working as a cop or fireman, becoming a priest or high school English teacher—then the ones I set for myself, those impossible literary ones which had taken a lifetime to achieve, though, really, I had not achieved them in any way that I had once dreamed, and, by general standards, I am a huge failure, because I am not regularly employed, am not tenured at some university, have never written a bestseller and/or a big film script. But if I'm not exactly satisfied, then neither am I disillusioned and ill-content; I am relatively content. I have been allowed to write my books, and though it usually is a struggle, eventually most everything I write gets published somewhere. I usually have enough money in my pocket for coffee and a muffin at the Greek diners and luncheonettes on Broadway after I see my friends in the morning; and I manage to make enough money to buy food and pay my rent.

Once, I probably was as angry as most of these Brooklyn street kids, but with that one important major difference: I did have a few adult figures in my life. Because, let's face it, this is not simply a racial matter—no matter how I felt on that subway train—but one of urban ecology. The poor die young; the poor kill each other. And, two major differences between myself and these youngbloods: guns and drugs. Most of them are probably—unlike myself at their age who went to boxing gyms to work out—in terrible physical condition. Crack breaks down the body; cocaine stresses out the heart; alcohol destroys the liver and brain cells. I should know because, like many of these Brooklyn kids, I tried to destroy myself this way, and failing that, finding some kind of spiritual light in my life, I came to believe in something else, I got help, I literally was saved. Yet I would be deceiving myself terribly if I believed that my miserable upbringing equalled or matched their miserable existences, because it did not; I did get some nurture, love, and rarely, some adulation. Teachers always admired my writing; sometimes I had a rare moment to excel at sports, boxing well or making jumpshots in machine-like perfection on the basketball court, or writing a poem for a literary magazine, not to mention women who adored me, as a child, teenager, and young adult.

You need to come to Brooklyn, whether at Nostrand and Flatbush or down in the tunnels on the Number Two train bound for Manhattan or over in Coney Island or across Eastern Parkway in East New York, Bushwick, Brownsville, or Bedford-Stuyvesant, to see how bereft of human nature some of these children in adult bodies are. That afternoon I sat in a subway car filled with them, some of them sitting, others standing, all of them hurt and angry and with big-time fuck-it attitudes, all of them jammed up and probably unaware of it. When you come from a dysfunctional neighborhood, there is no standard by which to measure your own aberrance, your own tortured psyche, your own angst—a word that is close to meaningless in a ghetto.

175

So I wrote a letter to my Brooklyn hero, Hubert Selby, my friend Cubby, a man twenty-five years sober, living all those years with one lung, diabetes, and an incurable hepatitis which old junkies get. But Cubby was—even if I thought so—no saint, and sometimes he was as crazy as any street kid in Brooklyn today. The last time I saw him, a year ago in West Hollywood, he sat in his studio apartment in one of those complexes you see in Grade-B movies, pastel and faux antique Mexicali by Southern California standards, the building full of sadness and broken dreams, and Selby smoked Camel filter cigarettes, upbeat and a great imaginer, listening to classical music on one of his several thousand CDs, staring across at an altar of various New Age trinkets, a rock crystal, a tiny Buddha, spiritual sands, colored glass, and a wall of Moroccan leather-bound tomes of great literary classics, and philosophized on the Great Void, and how he had mended his own life by giving up booze and heroin and by finding—goddamn it, why am I mincing these words?—by finding a spiritual center, a higher power, a God in his life, which he did then and still has today, so that Brooklyn or West Hollywood, Beirut or the moon, wherever he found himself, Cubby would live comfortably both inside and outside of himself.

In the letter, I told him about my trip to Brooklyn, about the reading, the giant spitball—were those stupid white boys even from Brooklyn or were they ghosts from the suburbs?—and I said to him, since I knew that he knew that Brooklyn was no Shangri-la, that people got killed for doing less than that at the juncture of Nostrand and Flatbush. My friend Louis, the poet who invited me to Brooklyn, told me a few days later, that sometimes he rode the subway back to the city so fearful that he could not read, and he would tell himself, yes, perhaps this is your time to die as some young punks talked about wanting to kill a cop or off a white poet/lecturer; and I told my friend Cubby, my mentor, my Brooklyn rabbi, that I read James Baldwin's essay *The Fire Next Time,* inhabiting this hypersensitive racial state with those charged words, and when I looked up, I saw, yes, that I was the last white man left in Brooklyn. It was both a lonely and spectacular feeling, kind of sweet and scary, though eventually it would become too terrifying to be anything but fearful incident, a hyperventilated blip in my life.

Black America had produced nearly all of my favorite musicians and singers—from James Brown to Thelonious Monk—and the only white musician who even came close to them was Glenn Gould playing Bach—and it was this music I listened to obsessively while I wrote my novel about Brooklyn, aware that the intention of my book was to il-

176

luminate the drift from Irish Brooklyn to black Brooklyn in East New York, and how dangerous and scary but somehow beautiful all that was. And there was James Baldwin, a favorite nonfiction writer—he was second only to Orwell in my mind, and only that because, even if at times he was more brilliant than Uncle George, as he was in "Notes of a Native Son" or *The Fire Next Time*, he was not as consistently good a stylist, and more important his honesty and compassion seemed to waffle, because Orwell, the consummate failure, never seemed to hate himself the way Baldwin sometimes did—the only one I was able to read over and over, year after year, and there I was again, forever reading that essay "Notes of a Native Son," which got me through my own Brooklyn father's Florida funeral the year before, and how Baldwin's combination of eloquence and anger, moral passion and social indignation, were the only literary spells which seemed to conjure my own boyhood in Brooklyn and later farther out on Long Island, the grandiosity and the low self-esteem, the poles that addicts and poor people (black and white) inhabited, his and my poor, his and my addicts. Also, I was in love with Baldwin's anger, fed on it like it was mother's milk.

When I thought of Baldwin, and how I thought of him as the great nonfiction prose writer of the American mid-century, the terror of that subway car turned into a magnificent—and spiritual—epiphany. The angry black faces seemed to inhabit a Rembrandt-like frieze; the grating of the subway wheels sounded like jazz cacophony; the smells of decay turned into mulch that would make the next things grow. Here was Brooklyn then, hyper-energized, forever angry and hurt, teeming and seething, dark and foreboding, and still home—even when it physically could no longer be home. It was where the next great American writer would come from, not Cubby Selby or James Baldwin, who, after all, was a black aristocrat from Harlem, but some angry writer from Brooklyn, black as coal, angry as the day is long, eyeing that lone honky on the Number Two train, wishing he had a gun to blow him away, but then deciding, fuck it, he'd write about this feeling when he got home; only I had to come to Brooklyn and go away from Brooklyn only sporadically, whereas Brooklyn was everywhere in his—although now that I think about it, maybe it is her—life, for her life was a constant reminder that the poor eat the poor while the rich live in Manhattan and in the suburbs; the poor attack the poor, while the others complain about them from far away; and the poor rob each other more than they rob the rich. Sometimes I think that she stared at me that very day at the midpoint of Brooklyn on that gray and sullen day where everyone's clothes were sodden with spring rain.

Nominated by Joyce Carol Oates

FACING INTO IT

by ELEANOR WILNER

from PRAIRIE SCHOONER

for Larry Levis

So it is here, then, after so long, and after all—
as the light turns in the leaves in the old golden
way of fall,
     as the small beasts dig to the place
at the roots where survival waits, cowardly crouching
in the dark,
     as the branches begin to stretch into winter,
freed of their cheerful burden of green, then

   it comes home, the flea-ridden bitch of desolation,
a thin dog with its ribs exposed like a lesson
in mathematics, in subtraction; it comes home, to find its bowl
empty—then the numberless
things for which to be grateful dissolve
like the steam from a fire just doused with water
on a day of overcast grays, a wash
of colors dull to begin with, then thinned
by a cold slanting rain—
      it is October, that season when Death
goes public, costumed, when the talking heads
on the tv screen float up smiling at the terrible
news, their skin alight with the same strange glow
fish give off when they have been dead a week or more,
as the gas company adds odor for warning
that the lines may be leaking, the smell of disaster

179

hanging, invisible, in the air, a moment
before you strike the match—

it is then, brother, that I think of you, of your Caravaggio,
of the head of Goliath swung by its hair,
wearing the artist's own weary expression;
his head, exhausted of everything but its desire
for that beautiful David he used to be; and I think
of all the boys walking the streets
each carrying the severed head of the man
he will become—and the way I bear it is
to think of you, grinning, riding high in the cart leaving
the scene, a pair of huge horses hauling the wagon,
a fine mist rising from their damp shoulders,
unconcerned with what hangs, nailed
to the museum walls—luckily
the fall of Icarus has nothing to do with them,
nor the ruined Goliath who fell like a forest,
nor the wretched Salomes with their blood-splattered
platters, nor the huge stone griffins sobbing
at the gates of Valhalla as the litters are carried past . . .

the dark eyes of the horses are opaque with wisdom,
their hoofs strike the pavements with such a musical decision,
the derisive curl of their lips is so like the mysterious
smile on the angel at Chartres, on Kuan Yin, on the dolphin,
as they pull the cart safe through the blizzards
of Main St., the snow slowly swallowing the signs
though the crossing light beckons—
a soft glowing green like some spectral Eden
in the blank white swirl of the storm.

The stallion neighs once, sends a warm cloud
of breath into the snow-filled air,
and the mare isn't scared yet—at least
she's still pulling. There's a barn out there
somewhere, as they plow through the light's
yellow aura of caution, its warm glow
foretelling what hides in the storm:

a stall full of gold, where the soul—
that magician—can wallow
and winter in straw.

Nominated by Marianne Boruch and Prairie Schooner

TAKE IT OR LEAVE IT

by ROBERT DANA

from THE KENYON REVIEW

I listen to her talk
about her 91-year-old
great-aunt up in Fay-
ette, who still bakes
her own apple pies,
the first her 9-year-
old son had ever tasted;
and of how the apples,
Wealthys, break down
sweetly, almost into
sauce, in the baking.
I tell her how much
I admire that rooted-
ness, that history,
and wish I had it; that
I know the apple, having
grown up in a town whose
ten thousand apple trees
I stole from. I don't
tell her what I will
tell you—that it's
taken me all this
time to come to myself,
and it's not pretty, not
perfect the way we dream
it might be when we're

young. Not even close.
It's creased and stringy
and strong; with a flavor
you probably won't like.
But take it or leave it,
it's what I've got.

Nominated by Kirby Williams

FANATICS

by ALAN SHAPIRO

from SOUTHWEST REVIEW

WHEN BILLY "THE KID" Lazarus called me to announce that he'd converted to Hasidic Judaism, I thought, okay, so Billy "the Kid" is now Billy "the Yid." What else is new? I wanted to see this fresh turn his life had taken as no different from the others: like his sudden craze for weightlifting in high school, for cars in college, like his brief stint as a Jew for Jesus the previous summer when he visited me and my first wife, Carol Ann, in Ireland. So what if Saul after an interlude of being Paul was Saul again, but in a purer way. Yet as I listened to him happily describe his life as a Lubavitcher, the long hours of study, the arduous yet joyous dedication it required, the heady sense of chosenness, the mystical connection to the Torah, to the Jews he lived among, to Yawveh Himself, his voice now inflected with the Yiddish intonations of our elders, I wondered if all his other passions weren't just so many dress rehearsals for this last big fling. Anyway, this was 1978, just after the mass suicide in Guyana of the followers of Jim Jones, whose cult, The People's Temple, had originated in San Francisco, just miles from where I was living at the time. Even more so than the rest of the country, the Bay area news was all abuzz with cults and sects, and the evils of fanatical devotion. There was nothing evangelical to Billy's faith in Jesus as his personal savior. He never tried to proselytize. He was quite happy to be the only one among his friends who wasn't damned. But Yawveh was a jealous God. And now, as a Lubavitcher Hasid, a member of the evangelical wing of Jewish Orthodoxy, wasn't Billy, or Shlomo as he now called himself, obligated to bring all Jews back into the fold? Wouldn't he be especially solicitous of me, his oldest friend?

My worst suspicions were confirmed when just before hanging up he mentioned that he'd be spending Chanukah with a fellow Lubavitcher whose parents lived in Oakland. He planned to visit me (just me, not me and Carol Ann), shortly after he arrived. And he prayed to *HaShem,* Blessed be his Name, that I would listen with an open mind to what he had to tell me.

Only after we hung up did I realize that Billy had done all the talking. Almost a year since we had seen each other, yet he never asked me how I was doing, what was new, how was Carol Ann. He'd always been extremely interested in my career. Though he himself had no artistic inclinations (in college he was a pre-med major), he'd always taken a kind of sentimental pleasure in my poetry, proud in an almost fatherly way that someone so close to him could do and succeed at what seemed so foreign to his interests. In the years I'd been at Stanford, first as a fellow in the writing program, then as a lecturer, he'd always made a point of asking me what I was working on, or if anything I'd written had appeared in magazines he might have heard of. He liked to brag about me to our old friends. But God apparently (being the jealous God He is) had claimed whatever interest Billy used to take in this side of my life. My wounded vanity aside, what troubled me most about our conversation was the sheer relief, the stainless steel serenity his voice possessed. How free his speech now seemed of that congenital yet touching urgency that used to make his words stumble and trip over one another in their hurry to get said, the sense anxiously running ahead of the sentences that often spilled out in a pell mell rush of fractured syntax, malaprops, and comically mixed metaphors. He once told me that he hated to be in a car that someone else was driving because he didn't like to put his life in someone else's foot's hand. He used to say things like "mea capo" for "mea culpa," "negligee" for "negligent" ("Hey, so, you know, so I was a little negligee, so sue me"), and he once bemoaned how he had squandered away his four years at college, adding, "For all *intensive* purposes I have no education." This new voice was clear, unstrained and eloquently simple. The sentences flowed from his tongue so gracefully they almost seemed to speak themselves.

The more I brooded on how differently he sounded, the more I could see Billy as he used to be not just in college and high school, but in grade school as well, and even earlier. As if in explanation of the person he'd become, I could see him in that third floor apartment he was raised in—the small flat made even smaller, more claustrophobic by his two stepsisters on whom his parents doted, his obese, often out of

185

work musician stepfather, and his mother who looked like a human thimble in her faded housedress, somehow both diminutive and dumpy at the same time, yet who compensated for her small size with titanic fury as she cooked and cleaned. Billy's biological father died in the Korean War. Since my father had been a mess sergeant during World War II and never killed anything but cows, I admired Billy for having a dead war hero for a dad. Even though he never knew him, Billy talked about his father all the time. He even carried around a crumpled photograph of him in uniform. Unlike his stepfather who mostly sat around the house all day picking on Billy, his "real" dad (that's how Billy would refer to him) had been brave, hard working, handsome, fun to be around, "a regular prince" he used to say, mimicking his mother. Billy's obsession with his "real" dad (not to mention that most of what the family lived on came directly from his "real" dad's army pension) must have fueled his stepfather's low-grade continuous hostility. In any event, he couldn't see Billy without complaining, Why can't you clean your room the way your sisters do? Why do you have to be so noisy? What are you made of, wood? Do I have to tell you everything a thousand times? Invariably, Billy would talk back, and the fight would escalate, his mother cleaning furiously all around her son and husband while they went on shouting at each other until her son was finally shut up in his room.

If you can call it a room. Just off the kitchen, windowless, no bigger than a jail cell, it had probably been a pantry once. One wall of it was brick. The room held nothing but a bed, a tiny dresser, and the baseball bat that Billy kept under the bed. More a pressure cooker than a room, in which for eighteen years Billy seemed to boil up more than grow up, jittery, high strung, breathless with angers and appetites, the small apartment and his room especially seemed to intensify by cramping. There he would steam and simmer for hours at a time, until he'd finally get the bat out and beat the brick wall with it, his terrible restlessness reflected in the thousands of tiny brick shards that were always peppering his sheets.

By the time he left home, his appetites and desires lived in his body the way his body had lived in the room. It was as if whatever limits, forms, proprieties, or expectations he encountered became another incarnation of the room itself, each impulse another bat to beat the brick wall with.

It saddens me to think that the very qualities I loved in Billy might have been the ones that most tormented him. His wild impulsiveness, his ever restless hunting after more and better, the edgy speed with which he gobbled up each pleasure as if some unseen hand were poised to snatch it from him if he didn't eat it quick—the very things that made him, in my eyes, fun and sometimes dangerous to be around—were, I see now, the very residue of thwarted need, ancient trauma.

Of course even back in college I knew that Billy was a problem to himself. But in those days, who wasn't? Seeing him through the lens of my timidity and inhibition, I envied his honesty, his courageous refusal to abide by codes of behavior I disparaged in superficial ways but was enthralled by in all the ways that mattered. As someone often paralyzed with self-consciousness and doubt, I found Billy's impetuosity exhilarating. If most of us, in theory anyway, were anarchists, abstract celebrants of openness and spontaneity, enemies of constraint and inhibition, Billy seemed to be the thing itself. And I admired him for it.

I remember early in my freshman year taking Billy to an open mike poetry reading in the student center. I at the time was too shy to read. But I was curious about the poetry the other campus poets wrote. Billy, the pre-med major, had no interest in anybody's poetry but mine. His over-heated nervous system, however, ill-equipped him for the concentration and discipline pre-med demanded. In fact, the grind itself aroused in him from the start the impulse to rebel, which was probably why he chose that onerous course of study in the first place. He was always on the verge of flunking out. That he managed not to, given how little he studied, was a measure of his natural ability. In any event, the more he fell behind in his studies, the more vulnerable he was to anything, even a poetry reading, that might distract him from the work he was supposed to do.

There were twenty or so kids in the room, a few genuinely attentive, but most just pretending to be, lending an ear to other people's poetry so other people in turn would lend an ear to them (with interest) when they got up to read. Each reader sat in a chair at the front of the room. The first poet gave a rather long introduction to his poem, saying, "I was walking back to my dorm from the library the other day and saw the sun setting, dropping down behind the tree tops and I realized now that I'm older and busier that I never stop to watch the sunset anymore, I never just go and groove on the moment like I used to when I was younger, so I went back to my room and wrote this poem." Then he started reading: "I was walking back to my dorm from the library the other day and saw the sun setting, dropping down behind the tree tops and I realized . . . " I remember another kid reading a sort of

Ashberian montage, full of abrupt shifts in tone and diction, ironic undercuttings and deflations. The end went something like this: "The almost misting of your violent nuance now at last drains you from the source they told me you could never find. So it is all weather, news, laughter, a dog barks, someone is eating yogurt, I wish I were dead, or fucking, I guess." Billy sat beside me like an engine whose idle had been set too high, with one knee trembling, one finger fiddling with his moustache, his big jaw twitching. The last reader was a cross between Rilke and Jug Head. His black beret, black shirt and trousers made his complexion seem paler and more ravaged than it was. I don't remember much about his poem except that it was long and hard to follow, an interminable smear of sensibility in which vagueness masqueraded as profundity. I thought it was terrific. I was so entranced by the way the poet swayed and chanted that I didn't notice till the poem was nearly over that Billy had crossed the room and was now standing right in front of the poet, looking down at him as he intoned the final lines: "I, too, have known the joys of rum. I have walked down what other men call sidewalks." The room was hushed. The bard looked up at Billy. Billy, smiling, stuck one finger up into the bard's nose, one finger nearly lifting him by the nostril off his chair. "Well, asshole," he said before he let him go, "I pick what other men call noses."

As we hurried from the room, all I could say was "Jesus!" Billy just shrugged. He seemed as startled as I was by what he'd done. That's how he always was after doing something outrageous, like a sobering drunk only dimly aware of what he might or might not have said the night before. He felt bad about embarrassing the poet. I said something encouraging like "Don't worry, Bill. By the turn of the century no one'll remember this had ever happened." Then, because he really did feel bad, I added, "Anyway, I guess it was a shitty poem, after all." He shook his head sadly. "Yeah, I know, but it wasn't just the poem, Al." But whatever else it was that made him do what he did he couldn't say.

Just as he couldn't say a few months later why he hurled the baseball through the plate glass window of the dining hall. We were playing catch in the quadrangle. It must have been around exam time for in my memory the quadrangle was entirely deserted, everyone else holed up cramming in their rooms or at the library, only me and Billy throwing the ball back and forth, each of us chanting hum baby lotta fire, lotta fire, as the other threw. The dining hall, too, was empty; only the tables and chairs nearest the massive window were visible within the gloom. After a half hour or so, I said I'd had enough, and threw the

188

ball to Billy and started back to the dorm. Billy was standing before the plate glass. He was flipping the ball in his hand, up and down, up and down, staring at his reflection as if admiring himself. I heard the shattering boom. The window was a panicky spiderweb of cracks around the jagged black hole where Billy's face had been. Billy just stood there, peering with a look of puzzlement into the shadowy room beyond the glass, at whatever it was his reflected face had been obscuring. "What are you crazy or something? You wanna get suspended?" But he just kept staring, oddly calm, at ease, as if a spring, that had been tightening inside him had suddenly sprung, though I could sense that it was already tightening again as I anxiously rehearsed the story we would tell, that it was all just an accident, that we were playing catch, that the ball just got away from us, and—"Al," he interrupted, "No problem. I'll handle it." Then he walked back toward the dorm, saying we probably ought to hit the books.

*

Billy looked pretty much as I expected him to look: fedora hat, full beard, black suit, white shirt unbuttoned at the collar. If I was somewhat ready, though, for his appearance, I was wholly unprepared for how he greeted Carol Ann. It had been only a year since he had spent two months working on her father's farm in Ireland. During his stay there, he and Carol Ann became good friends. With her long brown hair, pale skin, green eyes and slender figure made more shapely by the tightfitting clothes she liked to wear, Carol Ann was every Jewish mother's nightmare. Billy was drawn to women, any woman, with a kind of animal urgency he was unable to disguise. Some women were repelled by this, but some found it irresistible, enough anyway so that he always had a girlfriend. But the girlfriend he had on any given day never turned out to be the one he wanted. It almost seemed he was compelled to sleep with any and every woman who attracted him in order not to think about her anymore. In any event, whenever a pretty woman passed him in the street, especially the ones with other men, he'd stop dead in his tracks and gawk with such frank longing you'd think that she was paradise itself, and that without her he would hate his life. Carol Ann was charmed by his gruff directness. And he in turn was charmed by her gentle mockery of it. Their devotion to me made it safe for them to flirt and banter. And by the end of the summer they were pals. Or so Carol Ann thought.

Billy turned away as she came up to embrace him. He wouldn't look directly at her. She asked how his family was. Fine, he said—to me, as if I had asked the question. She asked him if he had seen a mutual friend of ours, and he said no, again to me, not her. Would he like something to eat or drink? No thanks, he replied, looking again in my direction as if an invisible harness strapped around his head were pulling it away from Carol Ann whenever she would speak. After a few minutes of this, visibly hurt and angry, she left the room. I asked him, what's up? How could he treat Carol Ann like that?

He ignored the question. Or rather he answered it by saying that the fate of the Jewish community as a whole, and beyond the Jewish community, of mankind itself, is tied to the particular fate of every individual Jew, believer and unbeliever alike. He talked about the 613 *mitzvot* (commandments), which govern every aspect, every moment, of a Hasid's life, and how a life lived according to the Law infuses everything—lovemaking, eating, even bodily functions—with holiness and joy. Billy *davened* as he talked, his upper body swaying back and forth as if in prayer, the way the old Jews used to in the Synagogue I went to as a child. The more I watched him, the more it seemed that the holy joy he felt (and I had no doubt that he felt it) was not a personal joy but the joy of personal extinction, the joy of the body transformed through ritual and unremitting discipline into a transpersonal vessel for the holy spirit, the living God. Wasn't that the purpose of the black suit, the ear locks, the beard, the teffillin the Hasid straps on the hand and forehead once a day—not just a way of saying that the self is this, not that, is Jew not gentile, Hasid not mere Jew, Lubavitcher Hasid not mere Hasid. But also a way of saying that the self has no identity except that corporate one. Not just a way of saying this transcendent unity has been achieved, but also a reminder that only with great and constant vigilance is it sustained, is it preserved. Implicit in the uniformity of dress and the ritual cirumspection of every single moment of the day is the recognition of anarchic appetite, unexpungeable violence, unbridled selfishness and egotism that require an equally violent or comprehensive set of rituals to be kept in line. Yawveh wouldn't be such a jealous God, if His children weren't so easily distracted. If we weren't so forgetful of His Word, He wouldn't need to repeat Himself so often, to remind us constantly to love "the Lord your God with all your heart, and with all your soul, and with all your might."

It was no surprise that Billy seemed most like his old self when he described the terrible and never ending struggle he endured to purify himself, to square his earthly nature with the heavenly rule of law. Sexual abstinence was especially difficult, he said. Since his conversion eight months earlier, he'd hardly so much as looked at a woman. In the Hasidic culture, unmarried women and men are carefully segregated. And what contact they do have is carefully monitored. Unlawful sexuality, even sexual thoughts or impulses of any kind are so proscribed that the Hasid guards against them even while he sleeps or prays. For instance, during prayers he wears a gartel, or belt, the purpose of which is to cordon off the upper, more spiritual part of the body from the lower, more earthly part, so that no profane thoughts might interrupt, contaminate his heavenly communion. Some yeshiva students (and Billy was one of them) sew shut the pockets to their pants so there'd be less temptation to masturbate while studying. It was also moving to hear Billy describe how embarrassing he found the jeering and taunts his dress and appearance usually elicited from people on the street. That he felt any mortification whatsoever only proved, he said, how entangled he still was in the snares of the ego, how far he had to go to reach the serene detachment and selfless devotion that genuine piety required.

If Billy was intent on extinguishing the ego, I in my life and work, at least from his point of view, was reveling in it. For Billy, there was no such thing as a career or the personal gratifications and excitements that a career entails. There was devotion to God, and the God-given Laws by which that devotion is achieved. The rest of life had value only insofar as it enabled or didn't interfere with that devotion. I was equally singleminded in my devotion to the art of poetry, and to establishing a life that would enable me to do the work I felt compelled to do. But to think that there was anything worth writing or reading that didn't glorify the Creator or the life that He demanded we, as Jews, should live, was to Billy's way of thinking at best deluded *chutzpah*, at worst unimaginable blasphemy.

I listened as Billy calmly, righteously, went on hammering away at everything on which my life was built. I wasn't angry or offended. Armed with my own unassailable pieties, I listened with superior, somewhat contemptuous amusement. For I, too (though I didn't recognize this then), was a true believer, and the faith I clung to with no less fervor not only had its sacred doctrine replete with clear and definitive prescriptions and proscriptions; it also had its spiritual leader. Billy's was Menachim Schneerson, the Rebbe of the Lubavitcher movement; mine was Yvor Winters, the late rebbe of the Stanford Creative Writing Program.

191

Winters had died in 1968, six years before I came to Stanford. But he was still very much a living presence to me and the other students in the writing program. As aspiring writers who had yet to publish (not for lack of trying), we identified with his outsider status in the literary world. Early in his career Winters had abandoned many of the modernist techniques and assumptions that had governed the work of his contemporaries and still governed to some extent much of the work of mine. His poetry and criticism (*In Defense of Reason* especially) were our sacred texts, our Torah and Talmud. Just as Billy believed that the Torah was not only the law of the Jewish people, but the cosmic law of the universe itself, so we believed that Winters' definitions and prescriptions were true not only for the poetry he wrote and admired, but for any poetry at all that aspired to be deathless and universal. By dividing all poets since the eighteenth century into sheep and goats, into those enlightened few whose procedures were essentially rational and metrical, and the unenlightened essentially romantic many for whom poetry was emotional release, immersion in irrational nature, Winters gave us, ignorant as we all were then, and insecure about our ignorance, a heady sense of mastery over everything we didn't know. We read the poets Winters recommended and ignored the ones he claimed provided only a dangerously incomplete account of what it means to be alive—dangerous because if you took the ideas seriously, if you put them to the test of experience, then you would either change your way of thinking and writing, as Winters had, or like Hart Crane, Sylvia Plath, and John Berryman go mad and kill yourself. That most poets of the irrational did not go mad or kill themselves only proved that they had isolated the poetry they wrote from the lives they led, trivializing both in the process. Like Crane, Plath and Berryman, we too had the courage of our convictions, but our convictions were life-enhancing, not life-threatening. For us, the acts of writing and reading had all the urgency of a morality play in which the self heroically confronts the brute facts of irrational nature and, in the confrontation, renews, strengthens, and extends the fragile boundary of human consciousness.

This is not to say we lived exemplary lives. Far from it. In the bars, in the streets, in one another's bedrooms, we caroused and rioted, while on the page we moralized about the dangers of excess. We lived like Rimbaud even while we wrote like Jonson. In fact, I sometimes wonder now if the almost magical power we ascribed to metrical control didn't in some way license and legitimize, not restrain, the chaos of the life. So long as our poems scanned, so long as we made rationally defensible statements, in meter, about what happened to us, so long as we believed that we had understood and mastered our experience, we were free to do whatever the hell we wanted.

I don't mean to condescend to who I was back then. Like new converts to any faith, I was more Wintersian than Winters himself, certainly more Wintersian than my teachers, Donald Davie and Kenneth Fields. But even that simplified Wintersianism was incredibly valuable. Through his anthology, *Quest For Reality*, which I read constantly, I was introduced to many wonderful poets I otherwise might not have read, poets like Fulke Greville, Frederick Goddard Tuckerman, Mina Loy, Elizabeth Daryush, Janet Lewis, and Edgar Bowers. Because I learned from Winters that great poems are written "one by one / And spaced by many years, each line an act / Through which few labor, which no men retract," I gave myself the freedom not to worry overmuch if this or that poem I was writing was even very good; even the bad poems were necessary preparations for the good ones up ahead, the good ones necessary for the great ones. As a result, I learned how to be patient and persistent, to go at my own pace. If my Wintersianism helped inflate my long term expectations for what I might achieve, at one and the same time it helped deflate my short term expectations so I could go on learning as I wrote. Even the more juvenile expressions of that enthusiasm were exhilarating and necessary. The circular logic that came with believing I was writing against the spirit of the age gave me what all young poets need, the stubborn arrogance to go on writing no matter how discouraging my prospects were, no matter how much the world (literary or otherwise) was telling me it had no need or interest in anything I wrote. Wasn't I in this respect like Billy too? For in the same way that persecution and suffering for the Hasid are a sign of divine election, of God's interest in his chosen few, so that the more he suffers, the more assured he is of his salvation, so I believed the health of poetry depended on the metrical poems I and my fellow students were writing in defiance of the barbarian, nonmetrical hordes. The very fact that we had trouble publishing our poems only confirmed their value. The more the literary world neglected us, the more convinced we were that only through our poems could the literary world be saved.

That afternoon I couldn't have acknowledged much less seen any of these similarities between me and Billy. My allegiance, after all, was to rational control, intellectual judgment, moderation of feeling—

qualities you couldn't have too much of, could you? Hasidism on the other hand, was the Jewish Orthodox equivalent of romantic excess. Moreover, didn't Hasidism and Romanticism both arise at roughly the same time in the mid- to-late eighteenth century? And like Romanticism in the arts, didn't the Hasidic movement favor energy over order, enthusiasm over learning, mystical release over rational control? Wasn't Hasidism pantheistic in its root assumption, that God was everywhere, in everything? And didn't the Hasid strive for dissolution into what Martin Buber calls "the everlasting unity"? Never mind that this is a highly distorted and reductive picture of both Hasidic mysticism and Romantic art, created by a highly distorted and reductive understanding of Yvor Winters. What this picture, though, enabled me to do was sit back and listen to Billy in a luxuriously condescending mood of pity.

Poor Billy, I thought, with his black suit, his arcane ritual observances, his dietary restrictions, his 613 laws, his new Old World voice—what did all this mean but that he now had turned upon himself, his body, his very being, the restless fury he once directed at his bedroom wall and, later on, at the conventions by which people tried to make him live. Wasn't he, at every moment of every day, hammering away at any impulse, desire, look or thought that didn't fit the impersonal mold of perfect piety? So what if he seemed happier, calmer, less edgy than I'd ever known him. He paid too steep a price for that serenity. All he'd done, I remember thinking, was exchange a universe of accident, surprise, doubt and adventure, for one in which nothing happens, no common cold, no massacre, no rape, no child abuse, not the slightest blink of an eye, that isn't tied directly to the Lord Our God, Lord of the Universe, blessed be His Name. Billy had escaped the bad dream of his independence and autonomy into the womb of *Yiddishkeit,* and what I imagined he had found there was what his family never gave: absolute unbreakable connection to the lives of others, a sense too that as a member of the tribe he had an absolute importance, that the very structure of the moral world depended on him and his devotions, his every action as a Jew. Thus, the very thing that extinguished his profane existence, the merely personal ego, at the same time greatly magnified his Jewish soul. But more than this, in Rebbe Schneerson didn't his new family also give him back his dead but perfect father? Didn't it give him back the opportunity to be the perfect son?

My pity, however, immediately turned to scorn when Billy began extolling Rebbe Schneerson's supernatural powers. He was telling me how the Rebbe, being more pious than others and therefore closer to

God, could work miracles through prayer. Billy knew of several people—a woman with breast cancer, a couple unable to conceive a child, a father whose son was straying from the faith—who after asking the Rebbe to intercede with God on their behalf, had soon found that their problems had been miraculously solved: the woman's cancer went into remission, the couple conceived, and the prodigal son came back into the fold.

"Billy," I said.

"Shlomo, please," he interrupted.

"Okay, Shlomo, you gotta be joking. I mean, you make the Rebbe sound like Jim Jones." I knew as soon as I had said it that the comparison was unfair. But as I mentioned earlier, Jones and his deluded followers had only recently imbibed their Dixie cups of poisoned Kool-Aid. I wanted to dramatize to Billy how irrational and superstitious he was being, how dangerous it was to deify a man. I quoted Montaigne's famous line about puritanical zeal: "They want to get out of themselves and escape from the man. That is madness: instead of turning into angels, they change into beasts." "How can you say such a thing?" is all he said, more wounded than offended. I stammered something back about the arrogance of thinking God would take a personal interest in your problems over anybody else's. What about the starving children in Biafra? I asked him. Did God ignore their prayers? What about the Holocaust? Didn't the Jews in Auschwitz pray? Were they punished because the Rebbe wasn't there to intercede for them?

"All that shows," he said now leaning toward me, pointing his finger like a gun directly at my temple,"is what can happen when a Jew neglects his Jewishness, when a Jew forgets."

"What are you saying, that Jews caused the Holocaust? that they deserved it?"

"Who knows why *HaShem*, may His name be praised, does what He does? All I'm saying is that it's no accident that the German Jews were assimilationists."

"You can't be serious." I said.

"No, Al, you, you're the one who can't be serious, living in ignorance like this . . . "

"I beg your pardon."

"Ignorance and filth. No better than a goy. Betraying your own people."

Both of us were standing now. I asked him who he thought "my people" were. I said I didn't have any "people," only individuals I loved, many of them the goys he hated. "We don't hate the *goyim*," he

195

said. "We even encourage Jewish women who turn out to be barren to divorce and marry goys, so they don't waste Jewish sperm." "Gosh," I sneered, "How ecumenical." He didn't come here, he said to be insulted. He came here as a *mitzvah* to me and to my parents because I was his oldest friend, because he couldn't stand to see me ruining my life. My marriage to Carol Ann was a sin against myself, my family, the Jewish community itself. And he hoped that someday, sooner than later, please God, I would come to my senses and put an end to this abomination. He said he would continue to pray for me. He said he would ask the Rebbe to pray for me. Since I obviously hated who I was, however, we had nothing else to say to each other. He went to the door. Then he abruptly turned around. He was holding out a dollar bill. It had been blessed by the Rebbe. Take it for good luck, he said, and give away another dollar bill to charity.

*

That was sixteen years ago. I have not heard from Billy or spoken to him since. Six years later, though, he visited my parents with his wife, a South African Jew, and their four young children. He spoke only Yiddish with my parents. He told them that his marriage had been arranged. He and his wife became engaged, he said, after spending only an hour or so in each other's company. After the wedding, they moved to South Africa where Billy became a Rabbi. He hoped that soon he and his family would be moving to Israel. He didn't ask about me, and my parents didn't offer any news. The news, however, surely would have pleased him. Carol Ann and I broke up a year or so after Billy's visit. Even at that time our marriage had been on rocky ground, though I didn't want to give Billy the satisfaction of knowing anything at all about our problems. She hated living in America, and I refused to live in Ireland. She missed her family, her four sisters especially, her homesickness made more acute by her complete dependence on me and my friends, all of whom of course were writers, for what community she had. At dinner parties, at bars, at any social functions, she often felt ignored or condescended to. "You're always talking shop," she'd frequently complain. "Listen," I'd joke back, "just be thankful we aren't gynecologists." Carol Ann was not amused. Her loneliness made her that much more impatient with what she called my fanatical devotion to poetry. I worked ten hours a day, seven days a week. Not wanting to let anything interfere with my daytime regimen of writing and reading, I balked whenever she would want us to do something together, just the two of us, go somewhere, have fun, relax. God forbid. She'd accuse me of caring more for poetry than I cared for her, which of course was true, though I denied it. Being with her, just living, ordinary life itself, was just a chore for me, she'd say, an obstacle, something to get out of the way so I could go back in good conscience to my desk. I told her it was poetry that kept me sane, that it was poetry that enabled me to be as loving to her as I was. Well if that's the case, she'd say, then maybe I should try some other form of writing because she didn't feel loved at all. Eventually she returned to Ireland, and we divorced.

I also had a more amicable parting of the ways from Yvor Winters. Around the time that Carol Ann and I split up, I began to feel constrained by the Wintersian injunction to "write little, do it well." To chisel every word of every poem as if in stone became, for me at least, a recipe for writer's block. What little I wrote, for all my patience and persistence, turned out to be pinched, narrow, bitten back. If not for Winters himself, then for many of his ardent followers, writing as if Ben Jonson were looking over their shoulder placed too great a burden on each and every line they wrote. Meter for them, moreover, seemed more a cage than a technique of discovery. And whereas Winters did in fact have a lion inside him that required caging, the poems by his epigones were lion cages holding pussycats. Around this time as well, I began to read many of the poets Winters dismissed or disapproved of: Wordsworth, Coleridge, Whitman, Williams (not just the few short lyrics Winters did admire), Eliot and Pound, and a host of more contemporary poets who were decidedly unWintersian: poets like Elizabeth Bishop, C. K. Williams, Frank Bidart, Jim McMichael, and Robert Pinsky (the last two, ironically, were students of Winters in the early sixties). And the more I read, the more impatient I became with what I felt was Winters' moralistic austerity of taste and judgment, his finicky rankings, his violent distrust of less rational, less rigorously orchestrated ways of writing. And unlike the neoformalists who were frequently invoking Winters' name, I no longer thought that accentual-syllabic meter was the only legitimate form of verse, the only road to genuine achievement.

Over the years, I've often thought of Billy. What would we say to each other if we saw each other now? I know I'd be no less uneasy with his absolutist thinking, his fundamentalism, his ironclad assurance of divine approval for everything he and his fellow Lubavitchers think and do. His total rejection of the secular world in favor of such a narrow and repressive orthodoxy still seems bizarre in the extreme. At the same time, when I think how transient my life has been, how often in the last sixteen years I've had to move, change jobs, rebuild a new life in a new place while the centrifugal pressure of professional commitments scatters old friends and family farther and farther from me, I can't help but envy Billy the fixed attachments that pervade his life. The image of a congregation worshipping together—freed from the daily drudgeries of getting and spending, from profane worries and ambitions and petty egotisms as they fix their minds as one mind upon sacred matters, ultimate mysteries, upon being itself—is an image I find more and more attractive. Though in my imagined congregation the men are not all wearing black, the women are not segregated, no longer does this act of worship seem, as it might have once, an image of irrational superstition but of reason, to quote Wordsworth, in its most exalted mood.

I have no doubt, too, that Billy would regard my life and work as pitiably flat and empty, rudderless in the most essential ways. At the same time, he would have to think his and the Rebbe's prayers on my behalf were answered, to some extent at least. A few years after leaving Stanford I remarried, this time to a Jew. We are not believers. We don't keep a kosher home. We don't observe the Sabbath. And we don't belong to any congregation. If we follow any of the 613 mitzvot, it's quite by accident. Moreover, as I was sixteen years ago, I'm no less obsessed with poetry, no less compelled to work and study every chance I get (which isn't all that much with two young children to take care of). But while I'm still prone to the feeling that ordinary life is an impediment to my real life as a writer, I have grown up enough to know that the feeling needs to be resisted, not indulged. I'd like to think that Billy would be relieved to know my wife and I are eager to give our kids a Jewish education of some kind or other, not just to teach them something about where they came from, who they are, but also to give them a defense against the sound bitten, crass, increasingly homogeneous mass distractions that pass for contemporary culture. I'd like to think that Billy would be pleased, if not entirely satisfied, with my spiritual development. But I know that he would not be pleased. For Billy, or rather Shlomo, anything less than complete commitment to the rigors of Hasidic faith, to each and every one of the 613 mitzvot, would be more contemptible than outright heresy, a more insidious betrayal. As a Hasid, he would view my emerging but still tempered sense of Jewishness as a shamelessly self-serving way of turning the most sacred matters into sacred fripperies designed to prettify an essentially secular existence. Because he thinks that being insufficiently Jewish is to make a mockery of what it means to be a Jew, because he couldn't ever be *entirely* satisfied with how I live my life, Shlomo would not be pleased at all. Shlomo would still be praying, angrier than ever, for my lost soul.

Nominated by Reginald Gibbons, Stuart Dischell, D. R. MacDonald, and The Southwest Review

BASIC ALGEBRA

by RICHARD JACKSON

from ATLANTA REVIEW

What does it matter if six is not seven?
Morning takes off its blindfold and the night
breaks into tiny roaches that scamper into
the crevices behind my refrigerator.
I refuse to pay such high prices for vegetables.
I don't feel any need to apologize for the number
of breaths I will take today. I have no
excuses for my age which has approached
the starting point of Zeno's paradox. Whenever
I see three at the supermarket, reaching
for more than he can hold, the legs and arms
of his clothes too short, he is distraught,
terribly distraught, that he is not eight.
Every number pretends to account
for more than itself. Therefore
the truth of every figure is a paradox.
Eight is the most sensual of numbers
writes Joachim of Avalon, platonic pimp
for the great Petrarch. When he pulls the chord,
the corporal at the howitzer has already
double checked his figures for elevation
though in the end he resorts to trial and error.
It was a mistake to keep this single knife in my heart
so long, but it is my knife, and my heart, too,
with its four distinct chambers. The only thing
that saves me is the certain fact that one is

not a number. It leans against the subway wall
afraid to go on. It listens to no one
and no one listens to it. I am going to
build a new nest for each of the birds in my throat.
For every kind thing you say, my father would
always tell me, a hundred kind things are
visited upon you. This is despite the fact
that someone somewhere is keeping
a second set of books about our lives.
Despite the number of howitzer shells
stockpiled inside our dreams.
None of this should enter our equation.
Maybe we should think of another number
besides ten which we can base our math upon.
Lately, despite the fact that some branches
refuse to offer a flower, despite the sky's
eating away at the horizon, I have been
thinking of eleven, which is also a lovely number.

Nominated by Marvin Bell, David Rivard

CAMO, DOPE & VIDEOTAPE

fiction by HAROLD JAFFE

from FICTION INTERNATIONAL

"*SLEEP IS LOVELY, death is better still,*
Not to have been born is of course the miracle."
"Sylvia Plath?" Shirl says.
"Naw," Earl says.
"Shirley MacLaine?"
"Sorry."
"Pound? Ezra Pound?"
"You've got to be kidding."
"This game gets on my nerves," Shirl says. "Let's cut."
"Where to?"
"There's a rave down on Mombasa. Dance your blues away."
"Lovely, except I don't have a thing to wear."
"Wear what you're wearing."
"Tenement T and jockeys?"
"Sure."
"The jocks aren't that, uh, fresh."
"Be a funky honky, Earl."
They go out, Earl in his funky jocks, tenement T and yellow patent leather mules, Shirl in her tattoos, black leather mini and Chicago Bulls cap turned sideways. He carries the Sony vidcam on a strap on his shoulder. On the way to the rave they run into a riot of cops working over a man they pulled from a Hyundai.

The man is brown. The 17 cops (Shirl counts them) are white. The cops are whacking him with their batons, kicking and stomping him with their black, thick cop shoes. Rockports, the majority of them. Rockport made a bid the NYPD couldn't resist. Plus, they're made in the USA.

When the beaten brown man's blood starts to spurt the assaulting cops skip away. See, if that spurting infected blood finds a cut or nick in an assaulting cop's neck, glove, or tricep and gets into his circuitry—forget it.

Four cops are confiscating the vidcams of anyone who videotapes the assault. Fuck that shit.

Shirl and Earl continue to walk, traipse, saunter, prance to the dance, or rave, on Mombasa.

Every once in a while Earl pauses to shoot vid. Shoots a seagull jabbing at the remains of a pigeon, flattened by a bus or truck in the middle of the street.

The gull jabs vigorously, looking up and around after every jab.

Shirl bites into a Baby Ruth.

Earl shoots a pair walking in their direction. The doll wears an olive drab bulletproof vest over a fuchsia silk sleeveless nightgown. Her head is shaved, she wears a gold ring in her nose and white Reebok shitkickers. The dude, barechested, is wearing Rolex tit clamps, baggy camo fatigues, mirror shades, a red stetson, and lilac high-heeled mules. He has delicate feet and knows it.

Earl shoots gutted buildings and a monster graffito which says: **LOVE OF CUNT.** He shoots a doll shooting vid. The doll is shooting a knot of near-naked homeless squatting around a rubbish fire.

One of the homeless plays the concertina.

Hey, look what's coming. A phalanx of vicious skinheads on rollerblades coursing through the street. They're barechested and tattooed and carry heavy chains and baseball bats. Their steel-tipped Doc Martens are tied around their necks. One of the skating skins, rear left, is shooting the others.

Earl, squatting, shoots the whole deal.

They get to the rave on Mombasa. It's in a warehouse, what used to be a warehouse. The music is loud, pulsing, percussive, lots of bass.

The theme of the rave is **Black Hole,** so most of the dancers are bare-assed, bending, thrusting, jiggling, spreading.

Earl takes off his funky jocks and flips them to the underwear dude.

Shirl takes off her panties and flips them to the underwear dude.

Shirl doesn't remove her black leather mini. Forms a line with other assfrees, dolls and dudes. They do a can-can routine.

An assfree standing on his head is selling Ecstasy.

Earl buys four hits, swallows two, hands the others to Shirl.

This is fast-acting, fast-fading X, and pretty soon the dancers are sexing: squatting, stretching, pumping on the filthy cement floor. Earl and Shirl do some muck in a X chain, which is a daisy chain fueled by Ecstasy.

What about zafe zex?

Yo, what they're doing is safe, Counselor. Low risk, maybe a little bit of medium risk. Fact is each and every strung-out assfree funk-punk at the Mombasa rave is intimately familiar with the Surgeon General's white paper on *AIDS and Abstinence*. Some even have key passages of the white paper inscribed on the inside of their eyelids. It's the last jolly news they see before falling asleep.

Later an assfree climbs onto one of the stanchions which support the strobe lights and pees on the dancers. A second assfree climbs onto another stanchion and pees down on the dancers. Soon whacked-out assfrees are climbing all over the warehouse, peeing on the dancers.

Well, the rave ends, as all delirium must, or so they say.

And now the underwear dude can't come up with Earl's jocks.

He's an old dude with a hearing device behind his ear.

Earl cuffs him across the brow, the hearing device pops free and skitters along the filthy cement floor.

"Sorry about that," Earl says. "But I get mad when old dudes lose my jocks."

The old dude hands Earl someone else's jocks.

Back at the condo, Shirl recites:
"The criminal injustice that deceives
And rules us, lays our corpses end on end."
"Poe?" Earl says.
"No."
"Rimbaud?"
"Who?"
"Rimbaud. Real name: Sly Stallone. He's a writer and philosopher besides being an actor and superstar."
"No."
"The X wore off," Earl says. "I'm not up anymore. You up?"

"No."

"Let's get up."

"Blue or pink?" Shirl says.

"Either. Both."

Shirl shakes some pills out of a container into her mouth, swigs Diet Pepsi from the bottle. Then she shakes some pills into Earl's fist and hands him the plastic bottle of Diet Pepsi.

They stick the vid he shot in the streets into the VCR and watch it while waiting for the up.

"Look at that doll shooting those near-naked homeless," Shirl says.

"Look at that near-naked homeless dude playing the concertina," Earl says.

"Isn't that a doll?"

"Yeah, you're right. She can really play that concertina."

"Isn't that an accordion?" Shirl says.

"No. Accordion is larger."

"I thought accordion was smaller."

"Hey, look at that vicious barechested, tattooed, skating skinhead shooting those vicious, barechested, tattooed, skating skinheads."

"What's he shooting, Earl?"

"Sony. KDX. Top of the line."

They watch the tape of the assfrees peeing down at the dancers in the Mombasa rave.

"Look at the equipment on that dude," Earl says.

"That's a doll with a garden hose tied to her hips, Earl."

"You're right. I think it's coming on, Shirl."

"Me too," Shirl says. "What do you want to do?"

"Dunno. We screw already?"

"Yeah. No. I can't remember."

"Let's spiff up and cut."

Over the funky jockeys that aren't his, Earl puts on Shirl's black leather mini. Removes his tenement T exposing his Rolex tit clamps. Puts on a Banana Republic stonewashed denim jacket braided with gull feathers, pigeon feathers, human hair, snakeskin, shell casings.

Shirl puts on a dyed-camo horsetail hairpiece, purple latex jump suit and yellow high-top canvas Nikes. Snatches the vidcam.

"How you feelin', Shirl?"

"Hot to trot. What's that noise?"

"That's the highpitched, dissonant whine of law and order, Shirl."

Earl's right. Halfway down the block from their condo is a zig-zag of cop cars, strobes rotating. Looks like they're working over someone on the pavement.

"I bet they're brutalizing a black or Latino gang member," Shirl says.

"Those gangs are real bad," Earl says. "With their drive-by shootings, drugging, pimping, they louse things up for the rest of us."

"They don't obey the English-only statute of this great state," Shirl says.

"They talk inner-city-jive-cholo talk," Earl says.

Shirl and Earl traipse away from the cop cars.

"Is that rain?" from Shirl.

"Naw. I just spit up in the air."

"Do it again, I'll shoot it."

Earl spits up in the air. Does it several times while Shirl, crouched on one knee, shoots it with the Sony.

They walk again. I mean: traipse.

"You up, Earl?"

"Kinda. I think I'm good for another twenty minutes, maybe."

"We need stronger shit."

"Hey, Shirl, look at the old doll."

An old woman with her drawers around her knees is squatting against a gutted building, hanging on to a rusted railing to keep from falling in her dung.

"Shoot her, Shirl."

Hell, Shirl is already on one knee shooting the squatting old woman. Walking again.

"We need stronger shit," Shirl says.

"I hear you," Earl says. " 'Cept where we gonna cop?"

"Good question."

"They don't mind us doin' weak and medium-weak shit," Earl says. "But we cop some good shit they'll bust us. Which means the joint. You know what the joint means, Shirl."

"Joint means heavy-duty time with zero parole."

"Why's that, Shirl?"

" 'Cause they privatized prisons, right?"

"Exactly. Your penal institution is the biggest growth industry there is. Hey, catch that tall dude, Shirl."

"Where?"

"Leaning against that yield sign. He's a long drink of water, ain't he? Looks like he's shooting ice."

Shirl turns, squats and shoots the dude leaning against the yield sign shooting ice.

Sudden loud whirring of choppers overhead. Two of them, sweeping low and someone yelling down through a bullhorn.

"They yelling at us, Earl?"

"I thing they're yelling at that dude shooting ice."

Sure enough, one chopper sweeps real low, drops a rope ladder and two chopper cops scamper down and leap into the street right near the dude shooting ice. Weird thing is the dude don't even seem to notice. Cops wearing rubber riot-gear snatch the dude, take his works, work him over a little bit, push him up the street. The choppers meanwhile have moved north toward Khartoum.

Shirl, squatting, is shooting the whole deal with her vidcam.

When it's over Earl and Shirl exchange a high five.

"Good shoot, Shirl."

"Yeah."

Walking again, they turn west at the pier fronting the lordly Hudson. The pier is boarded up, the sign says **No Entry—Danger,** but fuck that shit. Earl and Shirl slip through a gap in the fence and hear music, a banjo. Walk onto the crumbling pier where a cluster of young men are square dancing. When they get closer they see that the men aren't young but middle-aged and older. One is playing the banjo and six are gracefully do-si-do-ing. The men are all gay, and each has approximately the same fused expression on his face: wry irony, defiant pride, resignation.

Or so it seems to Earl who, grinning, watched them, and Shirl, who, kneeling, shot them.

Back at the condo, Shirl recites:
"*A virus eats the heart out of our sides,*
digs in and multiplies on our lost blood."
"Allen Ginsberg?" Earl says.
"Nope."
"Baudelaire?"
"Who?"
"Charles Baudelaire. French."
"No," Shirl says.
"Hang on," Earl says. "I think I can identify your quote. It was that Disney executive, at the site of the opening of that billion-dollar-plus Disney theme park near Paris. I caught this on CNN business news.

207

The Disney guy was a Rob Lowe lookalike with pulsing cheekbones. He was into this deal about how faggoty AIDS is destroying the virtuous lust for leisure."

"Did you say Rob Lowe lookalike?"

"Right."

"Did you say virtuous lust for leisure?"

"Right. Well, did I identify your quote?" Earl says. "And if I did, what do I get?"

"You identified my quote," Shirl says. "And what you're about to get is a face full of funk."

Nominated by Fiction International

FROM BASRA TO BETHLEHEM

fiction by TOM PAINE

from SEVEN DAYS

IT WAS UP THERE on the Kuwaiti-Saudi border back on Christmas eve, 1990. Right on the goddamn border. Saudis had a big sand berm 20 feet high that ran the whole border, and every thousand feet or so in the sand berm was a big concrete fortress we called the Alamo. Saudi border guards were in the Alamo in normal times to keep out the infidels. No sign of those Saudi fuckers now. Just a dozen Third Force reconnaissance marines, spitting chew on the sand rats' oriental rugs in the downstairs tea room of the Alamo, maybe thinking about you all back home holding hands around the Christmas tree singing hallelujah.

I was a clean-cut Burlington boy who joined the Marines to get money for college. I could run faster with a pack on my back than anyone else at boot camp that month, so they sent me off for recon training to be the best of the best and all I could be as the son of a tax-killed dairy farmer, whose land is now suburban homes you could park a B-52 in, and for which he got shit. Recon is an elite group of soldiers. We are the guys who get sent behind enemy lines to take a look-see around before the real action starts up. We have a 90 percent casualty rate during wartime, of which we are supposed to be proud.

My platoon was up there at the Kuwaiti-Saudi border on Christmas Eve, 1990. We called it being at the head of the spear, as there was nothing between us and the baddies. This was just before Desert

209

Storm, the 100-hour war, during what was called Desert Shield. Most people have forgotten the difference, just like they forget the details of the 1990 Super Bowl. We got better ratings, but still, nobody gives a shit, except it was a good show. Not like that Nam thing. Bad show. Bad feelings there. We were going to redeem ourselves on this one. Feel good again. Expose our superpower dick to the world.

Sergeant John Packer is one who doesn't remember what I remember—and what I don't want to remember as I sit here trying to hold a pen in my hand. He's more than dead, he's ashes and scorched bits of bone. Boom. Overkill for one single guy, but I guess they wanted to make sure. Merry Christmas, Sergeant Packer. Sorry about it, pal. Sergeant Packer got kaboomed by friendly fire from a Cobra helicopter. Whoops. Friendly fire. Sorry.

We were sitting around the old Saudi tea room that night, Christmas Eve, and most of the guys were cleaning their M-16s. Sergeant Packer was sitting next to me in one of the windows of the Alamo, the windows all blown out and stuffed with sandbags. He turned to me and gave me a bite of a chocolate bar. Somebody told me, I think it was Corporal Harvey, he didn't have any family. Packer hadn't ever talked to me, but he shared that candy bar, and then he started to sing "Silent Night." Every soldier looked up at him in that tea room. He had a beautiful voice. His regular voice was like he got a tonsillectomy with a buzz saw, but when he sang, it was this almost female thing, all high and sweet. Our captain, Captain Tolby, he looked up from where he was watching the RPV monitor, and said, "Shut the fuck up, Packer."

So that was where it started. Sergeant Packer, he didn't shut up. He just sang on and on and Captain Tolby, he watched him with the RPV monitor on his lap, and I thought he was going to stand up and ask him one more time, but instead he just smiled like a cat playing with a mouse. He laid this smile on Sergeant Packer, and you might have thought he had a change of heart, being that it was Christmas Eve, but the smile was more like *yea, asshole, you sing now, sing now while you can still sing*.

You say Captain Tolby couldn't know what was coming down, but I guess it depends what you believe is possible, what the whole thing was really about. Captain Tolby, no one knew much about him. He had just been assigned to us a day before Saddam went into Kuwait, and there was no explanation from Marine Expeditionary Force Headquarters why they replaced Captain Ord with him. Not like it was their place to explain shit to us, but Captain Ord was like family, and no one understood making a switch like that before a big action like Desert Shield.

But I will never forget that Cheshire cat smile that Captain Tolby laid on Sergeant Packer all through his angelic singing of "Silent Night" in the tea room of the Alamo on Christmas Eve 1990. I wish I could hear his voice now in this shit-ass North End apartment, but I can't. Just the sound of the jerk downstairs banging his kid's head against the wall. I've got a tape of Bing Crosby doing Christmas songs, but nothing can beat the voice of Sergeant Packer, sounds I can't hear anymore but remember as beyond beautiful. I understand now. I met the man.

You might be wondering if Sergeant Packer said anything to me as we sat there eating his candy bar on the Kuwaiti-Saudi border. He didn't say much, but I remember he got all philosophical when he was done singing and the Captain had stopped staring at him and smiling that *I know what you're up to* smile. Sergeant Packer was an ugly guy, nose all pocked and square like the handle of a .45. He was so ugly, when he first showed up in our recon platoon, which is a story in itself, we started calling something ugly *packer*. Yeah, he was that ugly. But he turned to me with a mouth full of chocolate after singing "Silent Night" and said, *"Is it still a war if nobody dies on one side?"*

I said, "What?" or "Huh?" I don't remember which, although I wish I remembered exactly, so I could get it down right. He asked the same question again, not getting pissed at all, and I expect I shook my head, as in those days thinking about things made me feel like a faggot.

Packer said, "I mean if thousands die on one side, and nobody at all dies on the other, is that still a *war*? Maybe we should have a new *word* for it?"

He was ugly, so I shook my head and ignored him. Remember, this is before Desert Storm, and we still thought maybe tens of thousands of us were going to die. I think he kept looking at me, so I said like I was pissed, "Nobody is fucking dead yet."

Sergeant Packer smiled, and he said almost in a whisper, "The dead are as good as dead." And then he flicked his chin at Captain Tolby as Tolby stared at the RPV. The RPV is this Remotely Piloted Vehicle— a mechanical bird with a camera in its guts. Captain Tolby was looking through the bird's eye at the Iraqi positions just over the line in Kuwait, behind the mined barrier plain. As I looked at the monitor I saw the mechanical bird was flying low over an Iraqi digging frantically into a sand dune, his tail up in the air. Captain Tolby mimed the Iraqi's frantic burrowing, laughed and laughed. Tolby was always laughing, always chilled out like he owned the world.

There's more you need to know about Sergeant Packer. The man wasn't one of us. This is some weird shit. We jumped on the C-131 in San Francisco to come to the Saudi, and there was this one sergeant in face paint. Everyone assumed someone else knew why he was jumping a ride to the Saudi with us, and Captain Tolby, he was looking at weapon manuals the whole way and laughing. No one noticed when he answered to the name of Sergeant Packer, but the thing is, *he wasn't our Sergeant Packer.* We figured it out in mid-flight, and he told Captain Tolby he *was* in fact Sergeant Packer, and then showed this stamped official T.A.D. order. That's *temporary additional duty* order. So there was some kind of computer screw-up, and we got this old Sergeant Packer, and our Sergeant Packer was who the hell knows where. You would think Captain Tolby would set it right when we landed, but when he found out he looked confused for only a moment, and then he had this look like *he understood everything,* like he had been waiting for this Sergeant Packer all his life, and he started laughing like a crazy fuck. He never reported the Sergeant Packer-Sergeant Packer screw-up. We kept the guy, even though he was from transportation—a rear job filled with dumbshits driving buses, so he wasn't exactly prepared for our sort of work.

So this brings us to the rest of the story. After Captain Tolby finished scaring the shit out of the Iraqis on the ground a couple of klicks north of us with his mechanical bird, he stood up and said, "Let's fucking celebrate Christmas." We all followed him up on the roof of the Alamo. It was pretty dark by then. We had a bunch of super-snooper night-vision scopes up there all in a row, and could look right over and see Iraqis beyond the mines and concertina wire of the barrier plain. When you looked through the scopes and looked at the minefield, the first thing you noticed were all the camel parts strewn all over. The Bedouins left them and the mines blew them up. So we were up on the roof, and Captain Tolby went chuckling over to the fun little Christmas toy known as the MULE. It stands for Multi-Utility-Laser-Engager. It's a plastic box with a laser beam inside.

One other thing I didn't tell you is that during the same day a team of four, including Sergeant Packer, had returned from an infiltration of Kuwait. They snuck across the mined barrier plain at night, and spent 48 hours a couple of miles in the Saddam-occupied badlands scoping things out. They came back with the coordinates for a lot of Iraqi installations and bunkers. I never thought we'd use the coordinates on Christmas Eve, but Captain Tolby had Corporal Fitch get on the communicator and order up an A-10 jet. Captain Tolby read in the coordinates of the Iraqi bunker for the pilot, and pointed the MULE laser beam from the top of our Alamo, got it all set to go, and then turned to Sergeant Packer.

The A-10 jet with its missiles was inbound toward the target, but somebody had to push the little red button, turn on the laser. The laser beam would guide the bombs from the jet to the target. Captain Tolby turned to Sergeant Packer, laughing, and asked him to do the honors. Told him it was like a video game. Sergeant Packer refused a direct order once, and refused again the next time the A-10 came around. Captain Tolby laughed like *he expected this the whole time.* He kept laughing and laughing. I can still hear him laughing.

It was then Corporal Branch saw the woman out there in the barrier plain through one of the night-vision scopes. We all went to a scope to look. She was coming through the fucking mine field. There had been a lot of Iraqi soldiers coming over to surrender before this, so it wasn't a big surprise in general, but this was a *female*. She was picking her way through the mine field step by step. Captain Tolby just grinned at her, like she was part of the great sweep of events. I turned around and Sergeant Packer was gone from the roof of the Alamo, and then we saw him making his way toward the woman through the minefield. And then the bad shit happened.

A Cobra helicopter came whacking in from the Persian Gulf, and Captain Tolby pointed to it and nodded like *now watch this shit.* The thing about the Cobra helicopter, it reads human heat on its thermal sights and destroys. The only way to avoid it is to lie down on the ground and pretzel into a non-human shape, so maybe you get read on the thermal scope as a plant or something non-human. So through the scopes we saw Sergeant Packer yelling to the woman and waving his arms like he was telling her to lie down, but of course she was freaked and just stood there.

So Packer started waving his arms at the incoming helo, which is sniffing towards the woman. Sergeant Packer takes out his .45 and starts waving that at the helo, then he starts firing, and the big whacking insect forgot the woman, who started running across the barrier plain. The helo greased Sergeant Packer with a TOW missile. Which as I said earlier was overkill. The woman came to the gate of the

Alamo, and then we saw she's got her arms around this baby in a little blanket. She's jabbering in Arabic. It isn't a dead baby, but *just the head and shoulders of her dead baby.* She walked from Basra in Iraq to show it to us. A note she carried said we killed thousands of her people with our bombing, our softening the bastards up for Desert Storm. We couldn't get the remains of her baby out of her arms that Christmas Eve, couldn't get a transport, so she stayed with us in the tea room all night jabbering and crying at us.

Captain Tolby never reported Sergeant Packer's getting greased. Said it never happened. Maybe this never happened either: Our third night in-country after the mobilization in the States but before we went up to the border, we were at Khafji, the first town just south of the Kuwaiti border in Saudi Arabia. There was a biological warning while we were eating chow. We pulled on our gas masks, and some of us, including myself, freaked and plunged the amalchloride antidote syringe into our thighs, thinking this was the end. It was then that Corporal Branch, in his gas mask, beckoned us outside. Coming down the street was this soldier on a camel like a fucking Bedouin. This soldier without a gas mask on a camel walked right past us and out into the desert. We all looked at each other, and one by one we took off our masks as the siren wailed on.

That soldier was Sergeant Packer, and now he's fucking gone. He came and now he's gone, and he couldn't do shit for nobody.

I got home and watched all the ticker-tape parades and instant replays of the great victory on the tube. My hands curl up with arthritis and they tell me it's my imagination. I had a kid with this great woman, and the kid was born with veins on the outside of his face, and they say it's unrelated to Desert Storm.

The man came and now he's gone. Merry Christmas to all.

Nominated by James Linville

BIG RUTHIE IMAGINES SEX WITHOUT PAIN

fiction by S.L. WISENBERG

from CHICAGO REVIEW

SHE IMAGINES IT THE WAY she tries to reconstruct dreams, really re-construct. Or builds an image while she is praying. She imagines a blue castle somewhere on high, many steps, a private room, fur rug, long mattress, white stucco walls, tiny windows. She imagines leaving her body. It frightens her. If she leaves her body, leaves it cavorting on the bed/fur rug/kitchen table (all is possible when there is sex without pain)—she may not get it back. Her body may just get up and walk away, without her, wash itself, apply blusher mascara lipstick, draw up her clothes around it, take her purse and go out to dinner. Big Ruthie herself will be left on the ceiling, staring down at the indentations on the mattress and rug, wishing she could reach down and take a book from a shelf. She does not now nor has she ever owned a fur rug. But when Big Ruthie achieves sex without pain, she will have a fluffy fur rug. Maybe two. White, which she'll send to the cleaners, when needed.

She imagines sex without pain: an end to feeling Ruben tear at her on his way inside, scuffing his feet so harshly at her door, unwitting, can't help himself, poor husband of hers.

She thinks there must be a name for it. She has looked it up in var-ious books and knows it is her fault. All she must do is relax. It was al-ways this way, since the honeymoon. Of course the first months she told herself it was the newness. She is so big on the outside, so wide of hip, ample of waist, how could this be—a cosmic joke?—this one

215

smallness where large, extra large would have smoothed out the wrinkles in her marriage bed? When all her clothes are size 18 plus elastic, why does this one part of her refuse to grow along with her? At first she thought, the membranes will stretch. Childbirth will widen. Heal and stretch, heal and stretch. But no. She has never healed, never quite healed. From anything. She carries all her scars from two childhood dog bites, from a particularly awful bee sting. I am marked, she thinks.

Ruben is the only lover she has ever had. "OK, God," Big Ruthie says, well into her thirty-fifth year, "I'm not asking for sex without ambivalence or sex without tiny splinters of anger/resentment. I am not even asking, as per usual, for a new body, a trade-in allowance from my ever-larger and larger layers of light cream mounds. I am not asking you to withdraw my namesake candy bar from the market, to wipe its red-and-white wrapper from the face of the earth. I have grown used to the teasing. It's become second nature, in fact. And I am not asking you to cause my avoirdupois, my spare tire and trunk to melt in one great heavenly glide from my home to Yours. I am only asking for a slight adjustment. One that I cannot change by diet alone. As if I have ever changed any part or shape of my body through diet. For once I am not asking You to give me something that just looks nice. Make me, O Lord, more internally accommodating." Big Ruthie, turning thirty-five, prays. Alone, in bed.

She is afraid.

She is afraid she will lose herself, her body will siphon out into Ruben's, the way the ancient Egyptians removed the brains of their dead through the nose. Ruthie wants to carve out an inner largeness, yet fears she will become ghostlike, as see-through as a negligee, an amoeba, one of those floaters you get in your eye that's the size of an inch worm. A transparent cell. Mitosis, meiosis. She will be divided and conquered. She imagines her skin as nothing more than a bag, a vacuum-cleaner bag, collapsing when you turn off the control. No sound, no motion, no commotion, all the wind sucked out of her. Still. A fat polar bear lying on the rug. Hibernating without end. No one will be able to wake Big Ruthie or move her in order to vacuum. No one.

She mentioned it once, timidly, to the Ob/Gyn man. He patted her on the knee. Mumbled about lubrication. Maybe the pain didn't really exist, Big Ruthie thought. Maybe it was her imagination and this was the intensity of feeling they talked about. But it is pain. It combines with that other feeling so that she wants it and doesn't want it, can't push this word away from her brain: Invaded. My husband is invading me. He makes her feel rough and red down there. As if he's made of sandpaper. Even with the lubricant they bought. It makes her want to cry and sometimes she does, afterward, turning her head away. How could her Ceci and Ellen fit through there and not her Ruben?

Still Big Ruthie imagines sex without pain, imagines freedom: f—ing out of doors. In picnic groves. She imagines longing for it during the day, as she vacuums, sweeps, wipes dishes, changes diapers, slices cheese for sandwiches, bathes her daughters, reads them stories. She imagines it like a tune from the radio trapped in her mind. It will overtake her, this sex without pain, this wanting, this sweet insistence. A rope will pull her to bed. Beds. Fur rugs. Rooftops. Forests, tree houses. She imagines doing it without thinking. Her family does nothing without thinking, worrying, wringing, twisting hands, with a spit and glance over the shoulder at the evil eye. At Lilith, strangler of children, Adam's first wife, who wanted to be on top. Who wanted sex without pain. Whenever she wanted.

Sometimes Ruthie begins. She might tickle Ruben. She might hope: This time, this time, because I started it, we will share one pure, smooth sweep, one glide a note a tune a long song, as sweet as pleasant as a kiss. She thinks, if she can conquer this, get over this obstacle, she of two children, a house and a husband—if she Big Ruthie can find her way to this sex without pain—then Ruben would be able to rope her, he would be able to lasso her from the next room, from across the house. She would rely on him, and on sex, on sex without pain. Then any man would be able, with a nod of his head, a wink of his eye, to pull her to him. Ruthie and Anyman with a fur rug, without a fur rug. Big Ruthie will advertise herself: a woman who has sex without pain. She will become a woman in a doorway, a large woman blocking a large doorway, foot behind her, against the wall, a thrust to her head, a toss, a wafting of her cigarette. Big Ruthie will start to smoke, before, after, and during.

Nothing will stop her. She will be expert. Till she can do it in her sleep. With her capable hands, with her ever-so-flexible back, front, sides, mouth. With the mailman, roofer, plumber; she could become the plumber's assistant, he, hers. She will go at it. She will not be ladylike. She will be a bad girl. She will swing on a swing in a good-time bar. She will become a good-time girl, wearing garters that show, no girdle at all, black lace stockings rounded by her thighs and calves, brassy perfume that trails her down the street. People will know: That is Big Ruthie's scent. She will have a trade-mark, a signature.

Big Ruthie, the good-time girl.

217

Fleshy Ruthie, the good-time girl.

Bigtime Ruthie, Twobit Ruthie.

Ruthie knows that other people have sex without pain. Men, for instance. Ruben. She has watched his eyes squint in concentrated delight. She herself sometimes cries out, the way he does, but she knows his is a pure kind of white kind of pleasure, while hers is dark, gray, troubled. It hurts on the outside just as he begins and moments later when he moves inside her. This was Eve's curse—not cramps, not childbirth, but this; hurts as much as what—as the times Ruben doesn't shave and he kisses her and leaves her cheeks and chin pink and rough for days. But this is worse.

But if she could have sex without pain—sex without secrets—she will have sex without fear, and without fear of sex without pain.

Then the thought of no sex at all will make her afraid, more than she is now of sex with pain, more than she is afraid of losing her body, more than she is afraid of never losing it, never being light.

Ruben said once she was insatiable. This is because she squirmed and writhed, wanting to savor everything, all the moments that led to the act, she wanted to forestall the act of sex with pain. When she has sex without pain, she will go on forever, single-minded of purpose. One-track mind. She is afraid she will forget everything—will forget the multiplication table, the rule i before e, to take vitamins, when to add bleach, how to can fruit, drive, run a PTA meeting using *Robert's Rules of Order*, bind newspapers for the Scouts' paper drives, change diapers, speak Yiddish, follow along in the Hebrew, sing the Adom Olam, make round ground balls of things: gefilte fish, matzo balls. Ruthie will become a performing trickster, a one-note gal, one-trick pony, performing this sex without pain, her back arching like a circus artist on a trapeze, a girl in a bar in the French Quarter. "You cannot contain yourself," Ruben will say, turning aside. She will feel as if she is overflowing the cups of her bra. Her body will fill the streets. People will say, "That Ruthie sure wants it."

She tries to avoid it. So does Ruben. They are sleepy. Or the children keep them awake, worrying. There is less and less time for it. When they travel and stay in hotels, the girls stay in the room with them, to save money for sightseeing. Ruben still kisses her, in the morning and when he comes home from work, after he removes his hat.

But if she and Ruben could have sex without pain—there would be no dinner for him waiting hot and ready at the table. Big Ruthie would ignore all her duties. She would become captive to it. Body twitching.

Wet. Rivulets. She would no longer be in control. No longer in the driver's seat, but in back—necking, petting, dress up, flounces up, panties down or on the dash, devil-may-care, a hand on her—"Sorry, officer, we had just stopped to look for—" "We were on our way home, must have fallen asleep—"

Sex would become like chocolate fudge. Like lemon-meringue pie. Like pearls shimmering under a chandelier. Or Van Gogh close enough to see the paint lines. Blue-gray clouds after a rainstorm. Loveliness. Would Big Ruthie ever sleep?

Big Ruthie's life will become a dream, a dream of those blue castles with long mattresses she will lie across, will f— in, far away, will never ever come back from, the place high on the improbable hill of sex without pain, the impossible land of sex without pain.

There in the castle she will find the Messiah himself. He too is insatiable. She will welcome him inside her. She will long for him, miss his rhythms when he departs her body. Up there in his castle, she will keep him from descending to do his duty for at least another forty years. In his land of sex without pain, she and he will tarry.

Nominated by Maureen Seaton

DESCENDING

by DAVE SMITH

from THE KENYON REVIEW

Remember that tinfoil day at the beach descending
on water the color of slate, the man descending,
just a bald head like an emptied melon descending
god knows where, same day a shy girl-child descending
with doll and bike to darkness where, descending
the hill with dump truck visor down, sun descending,
a father squints just once and the years descending
ever now spin him like a pump's flush-pipe descending
to pure waters he can never reach and, descending,
what of wings flamed gold, dusk's godly glow descending,
heron, tattered, wearied, news-heavy head descending,
that's left by hunters to float all night, descending
as they do into sleep, the earth clean, just descending?
Where, and with whom, are those we've seen descending?

Nominated by David Baker, Philip Booth, Stephen Dunn

CRABCAKE

by JAMES ALAN MCPHERSON

from DOUBLETAKE

SEVERAL WEEKS AFTER the call from Elizabeth McIntosh, and my response to it, the letter from Mr. Herbert Butler arrives.

> Dear Mr. McPherson,
> I am doing fine. I want to thank you for
> your card, letter and kindness during (my)
> the loss of my beloved Channie. She is with
> the Lord now . . .

Mr. Butler has crossed out the initial "my," his personal claim to Mrs. Channie Washington, and has instead generalized her death into a significance greater than his own loss.

His use of "the" implies acceptance.

I am glad that Mr. Butler is in this frame of mind. I am glad that he is open to acceptance of loss. I have clear fee simple in the house he now occupies. Mr. Butler was never the official tenant. Mrs. Washington was the person who sent the monthly rent. Although she never signed an agreement, there existed an essential understanding between the two of us. Mr. Butler was always in the background of our private, unwritten contract, as he was always in the background of her monthly letters to me. I have no bond with him.

I have decided to sell the house. I now intend to take the profits I have been avoiding all these years, and be rid of my last connection with Baltimore. A friend in Washington, D.C., has already put me in contact with a real estate agent in Baltimore, and this woman has already made an appointment to see me. I have already begun preparing, by the time his letter arrives, just what I will say to Mr. Butler: For almost eighteen years, I have not made one cent of profit on this house. I have carried it, almost on my back, at great loss. You must remember that when I purchased this house back in 1976, I lowered the rent to eighty-six dollars a month. Over the years, I have raised it only enough to cover the rise in property taxes. After seventeen years, the rent is still only two hundred dollars a month. Repairs, fire insurance, ground rents—all these additional expenses I have paid for, over all these years, out of my own pocket. Now I am tired of, and can no longer afford, so many scattered responsibilities. I must cut my losses now and try to consolidate. You, Mr. Butler, will have to go. But there are homes for senior citizens, with nurses on call and with organized activities for elderly people. Meals will be regular, healthy, and free. I have already checked into them for you. There will be a private telephone by each bed, free heat and electricity, family and visitors can come and go freely at almost any hour. In such well-cared for places, the furnaces always work in winter. Mr. Butler, you will be more comfortable, and maybe happy, in such a new home. Now, in this old place, you have nothing but memories to comfort you, or to haunt you. The change I am suggesting is probably, when you really think about it, a good thing. You should take some time and think carefully about it, Mr. Butler. I am not setting a deadline for you to go.

My plan now is to work on this speech and make it right.

It is essential that Mr. Butler understand my point of view. I am no longer affluent enough, or arrogant enough, to do for anyone else what the state could more easily afford to do. I do not plan to be ruthless. I will only disclose my intentions to Mr. Butler. The real estate agent, Ms. Gayle Wilson, will handle the hard part. As soon as she finds a buyer, she can handle the eviction. I will not have to get involved. No one could possibly blame me. I have already done more than enough for them. Their needs have become infinite, while my own surplus has shrunk. Mr. Butler will have to see the motif in my narration. It is the old story. Perhaps Mrs. Washington's death was, paradoxically, heaven-sent to bring the story to its end. Both Mr. Butler and I agree that she must be in heaven now. It may well be that the end her death brought to the story was her final letter to me.

Over close to eighteen years, I calculate, Mrs. Washington must have sent me almost 208 letters with her rent checks.

I remember some of them.

I go through the boxes of letters received this year and find several from her. I inspect them and see now, for the first time, that the very last letter, sent the first week in this month, is not even in her hand-writing. I sense this, but take care to check this last letter against the handwriting in the one that arrived with the September rent. This one is in Mrs. Washington's hand. It is her uneven writing, her flow of sentences without periods. I read it carefully and notice something unfamiliar. She has written "Dear James Family" instead of her usual "Dear James and Family." Also, there is a line that is completely new, something I have never seen before in any of her monthly letters. This new line is: "I will close my letter but not our love . . . " This new language seems strange. It suggests an intimacy that has never existed between us. It also suggests a finality that frightens me.

Mrs. Washington seemed to have known, back in early September, that she was about to die.

But I dismiss this thought. Besides, her profession of unending love is inappropriate. Mrs. Washington did not know me in that way. She knew only a few facts about my life. She knew that I once lived on Barclay Street in Baltimore, two blocks away from the house in which she lived. She knew that I made my living as a teacher. She knew that I was married, She knew that I moved from Baltimore to Virginia, and she knew that after two years I moved to New Haven. She knew that I moved back to Virginia for two more years. And she knew that I moved then to Iowa. Her monthly rent checks and letters followed me to these new addresses. I never wrote back to her and offered any more details about my life. I did visit her in Baltimore, from time to time, to see about her and the needs of the house. But for almost eighteen years the facts of my own life have been kept from her, while the facts of her life have been hidden from me by the standard phrases in her monthly letters. These phrases have not varied in 208 months: "Everything is fine." "Thank The Good Lord" "May God bless you all." "May God be with you all." "Thank the Good Lord For every thing." I wonder what the new owner would think about the letters wrapped around her monthly rent checks, if Mrs. Washington were still alive to write them. Then I think about its future sale.

Then I begin to remember the sweating, hungry heat of the crowd.

I begin to remember.

I begin to imagine and remember.

An Old Portrait in Black and White, July 1976

Two elderly black people, a man and a woman, sit on a porch in a tarnished metal swing. It is the porch of a run-down, redbrick rowhouse. The swing, under their weight, is straining against the rusty chains suspending it and swaying back and forth. The two people are sitting in the swing on the porch of 3114 Barclay Street in Baltimore. It is a weekday but they seem dressed in their Sunday best. The woman wears a white necklace and matching white earbobs. She is smiling as if it were indeed Sunday morning and she is lost in the sermon of a church. An other-worldly serenity, or perhaps a childish inability to appreciate finely textured reality, is in her smile. She looks wide-eyed from behind large spectator eyeglasses. But the man looks, from a distance, sheepish and embarrassed. He wears a gray touring cap pulled down close to his eyes. His belly rises up from behind his belt. There is a this-worldly awareness in his fat brown face. Other people, white, move through and out of the screen door of the house. They slide behind the couple on the swing, jostling windows, knocking on the fragile woodframes, scraping new rednesses into the worn bricks. Others move up and down the gray concrete steps or mill about on the sidewalk. A white auctioneer is standing on the top cement step speaking rapidly and abstractedly to all questioning newcomers. His dead eyes always focus on a space above their heads. He has the ritual assurance, the slow, sure movements, of a priest. Parked and double-parked along Barclay Street, glistening in the wet, hot morning sunlight, are tail-fin Cadillacs, wide-reared Buicks, Oldsmobiles, Fords, and Chevrolets—the nests of middle-class army ants. From a distance, from across Barclay Street, the entire scene, with the house at its center, seems too restless to be real life. It looks speeded up in time, like an animated cartoon. Framed as the slow-moving backdrop of such relentless restlessness, the two black people seem frozen in time. They look like stage props, brought by mistake onto the wrong movie set.

An awareness of this error seems to be in the old man's face. The old woman seems to see secret amusements in the show. As the priestly auctioneer opens the bidding, time seems to flow backwards, as if a hidden director now realizes his mistake in the staging of the scene. *This is not Barclay Street,* something is reminding. It is a public square in Virginia, South Carolina, Georgia. It is 1676, 1776, 1876, *not* 1976. The relentlessness of the ritual has only temporarily sucked open black holes into the flow of time, opening a portal into a finished past that has come alive again and oozed out and forward, into the future. Soon it will move back to where it was freeze-framed dead. Something in the air assures this coming correction of the scenery. This is why the two black people are so passive. This is why the white auctioneer seems so abstracted. The milling crowd, too, is restless for correction. The weight of ritual has pushed their roles too far back in time. *The portal into the past must close.* All—the crowd included—have found unholy meaning in the slipshod staging of this moment. All are look-ing from far back into what will be and from the here and now back on what was only *then* inevitable. The reflections in the life-linked mir-ror belie all notions of age and elevation and change. Time is not a cir-cle. What was was, before *was* was?-the answer to the puzzle *should not be* "is." No matter that in Virginia, South Carolina, and Georgia such people always wore their best clothes, *someone,* at a distance from the crowd, thinks. This is not Virginia or Georgia or South Car-olina. It is 1976. It is the celebration of the Bicentennial. *Someone* moves from the other side of Barclay Street and through the lines of cars and into the crowd. He moves close just as the auctioneer opens the bidding. It is anger that now makes his voice heard above all the others. It is arrogance, too, *but also something else,* that causes him to make a stand within the circling centuries on the hot morning side-walk. *What was that thing? What became of that something else?* The white auctioneer chants his mass. It is anger, and also arrogance, that causes *someone* to match each bid and raise by five hundred dollars. The blood sport flowing through the crowd begins to slow and ebb. Its forward motion is arrested by a single collective thought: this *must be* some trick, some sly rhetoric left over from the public bluster of the past decade. Time can prove promiscuous on such hot days. *But what if there is no bluff and the price keeps rising?* The collective voice falls into weak and individualized efforts at continuing combat. The heat in their blood begins to flow backward, into the past, while time hurries forward first to apologize and then to make its correction. The white auctioneer points disinterestedly and mouths the sacred incantation: "*Sold!*" The circle breaks. The black hole closes. The mirror looking out and in from hell is cracked. Time flows like clockwork, forward, while the crowd mills. Those who are most nimble speed off first in their cars toward the next house on the list. The auctioneer holds his hand out for a cash deposit. The balance is to be secured by mortgage in three days. He keeps his hand held out, like a kindly priest reclaiming the chalice from a slow communicant. *This is my body. This is my blood.* Now someone walks up onto the porch and kisses the forehead of the old black woman on the swing. She says, *someone remembers now* that she said, "You must be from up *there!*" The woman, close up, looks even more serene and on vacation from this world. The old man seems ashamed. But the woman seems to be smiling for both of them. Someone says to her, *not to him,* "You won't have to move now. You can live here for as long as you want. No matter what you are paying now, the new rent will be eighty-six dollars a month." The view, facing Barclay Street from the old porch, is now unobstructed. The last of the wide-reared cars, the habitats of army ants, are leaving. It is a wet, hot, summer morning in Baltimore, July 1976. The auctioneer, in his short-sleeved shirt, is sweating while he waits on the top cement step, away from the comfort of the porch.

I recollect now that day and that time.

It was not a public square in Virginia, South Carolina, or Georgia in any of the other centuries. It was Baltimore,in 1976. The time moved forward then, not backward. Nor did it circle round. The only time made sacred was the three days' deadline for payment imposed under force of law by the auctioneer. The news was not about ships reaching ports with fresh slave stock. It was about inflation, gasoline shortages. It was about oil-rich Arabs buying up the Sea Islands. It was about money and the lack of it and the fear of everything that made people afraid. I do not like to remember that time.

But while I am planning my trip, I remember the good things that I liked.

I liked Baltimore in summers and in winters. I liked the old harbor, the way it was before it was gentrified with shops and lights for the benefit of tourists. I liked to watch the boats and ships out on the water. I liked the old, worn bricks in certain streets, the ancient buildings, the squares with their statues, and the abundance of seafood from Chesapeake Bay. These aspects of Baltimore remind me of Savannah, where I grew up. There is a certain little square, I think on

Monument Street in Baltimore, with a metal statue and cobblestone that reminds me of Pulaski Square in Savannah. When I lived in Baltimore, I liked to walk through the neighborhoods and watch people sitting on the steps of their narrow rowhouses to escape the summer heat. On hot summer mornings, in both cities, people wash down the steps of their houses and let them dry in the hot sunlight. The heat in both cities, because of their proximity to water, is humid and wet. People in Baltimore, like those in Savannah, accept sweat as an unfortunate incident of summer. In both cities, the early mornings and the early evenings are the best times for walking. People in both places are most polite during those cool and special times of the day.

The soul of Baltimore, for me, is the old Lexington Market on Lexington and Eutaw Streets. It is a kind of warehouse off the downtown section that is crowded with little shops and concession stands, many of them selling crabcakes and other seafood. In this almost open-air market, all sections of Baltimore meet and breathe in common the moist aromas of fresh shrimp, oysters, crabs, every possible Atlantic Ocean fish, a variety of fruits, vegetables, and fresh meats. I remember oyster bars, where people stand and eat raw oysters after spicing them with condiments. I remember the refrigerated display cases featuring, among many other choices, row after row of uncooked crabcakes. These are a very special delicacy, made Maryland-style. The basic recipe is a mixture of crabmeat (fresh lump, blue, backfin, or special) and eggs, bread crumbs, Worcestershire sauce, fresh parsley, mayonnaise, baking powder, salt, and a variety of spices. This mixture, after being caked in the bread crumbs, is deep-fat fried, drained, and served while moist and hot and brown. All crabcakes are good, but Maryland crabcakes have special ingredients, or spices, not found in those crabcakes made according to the recipes of other regions.

Unlike in Savannah, in Baltimore they have soft, white, wet, clinging snow during the winter months. It seldom gets cold enough for the snow to freeze, so it remains white and clear and fluffy in the bright winter sunlight. I liked that. I liked the way the white, sun-melting snow would slide lazily and waterily off the skeletal branches of high-reaching trees and *plop* wetly on anything beneath the boughs. In Savannah, during the winter months, we got only cold rain. Still, I did not mind walking in it, as long as I was warm and dry and walking very quickly. I consider the number eighty-six lucky for me. It was the number of my old newspaper route, my very first job, when I was a boy in Savannah. I used to walk that route six days a week, in the sweaty summer heat and in the cold winter rains, with my papers. I used to take a personal interest in the lives and health of all my customers along that route. I used to be sympathetic to their excuses for not having the money to pay their paper bills. I tried my best to have compassion for them. I believed, then, that everything would eventually even out.

I have always considered eighty-six my lucky number.

The Natural Facts of Death and Life in Baltimore, November 1993

I fly from Iowa into New York, then rent a car at the Newark Airport, in order to avoid the traffic of the city, and drive south on Interstate 95. It is late fall in the East, and all the bright, crisp, red and brown and green and gold colors have bled from the sparse stretches of trees lining the interstate. The last brown leaves are wilting and falling in the warm morning breezes, and the cars around me seem to be navigating at unnatural speeds, all heading homeward from the sadness of the fall. Then I realize that the pace of eastern interstate traffic is too fast for my driving skills, which have become settled now into the slow and easy habits of country roads. Neither do I have, any longer, personal investments in the landscape. I can no longer remember, or care about, where I was going to, or where I was returning from, when I parked at the official rest stops in New Jersey, Pennsylvania, Delaware, on my way up and down this road. My polarities have now become strictly east and west.

I am told, when I arrive at the office, that my own agent, Ms. Gayle Wilson, has been detained. While I wait for her, I listen to an elderly, extremely muscular black man who is flirting with the young receptionist at her desk. He has just retired, and is now about to close on a house, his first in a lifetime of working. He talks about the kindness of the Jewish woman who has sold it to him. He brags about the new appliances he has purchased. I think, while I listen to him talk, This is what our struggle has been about all along. That man, this late in his life, has become renewed by the ethic that exists in ownership. This has always been the certified way people show that they have moved up in life. It is what the society offers, and it is enough for most people. *What did I have against it all these years?* The man is joyous, flirting with the young black woman. He is no longer a laborer. He is now an owner. He is now her equal. He now has a house, new appliances, and is on the lookout for a companion who would want to share the castle of his dreams. *It has always been as simple as that.* I have not observed the styles of black people in many years. The kindly flirtation between the two of them reminds me of something familiar that I have almost forgotten. It seems to be something about language being secondary to the way it is used. The forgotten thing is about the nuances of sounds that only employ words as ballast for the flight of pitch and intonation. It is the pitch, and the intonation, that carries *meaning.* I had forgotten this.

Ms. Gayle Wilson, my agent, comes into the office. She is a very tall, very attractive black woman in formal dress. "I've just come from a funeral at my church," she tells me. "It was a close friend who died and I was an usher." We sit down and get to business. She hands me her brochure. It says she is active in the affairs of her church, her community, and in the organizations related to her business. She tells me, "I know of someone who is buying up houses out in that area. We can probably make a sale today. I'll call him up right now." She picks up her telephone, dials a number, and the ringing is answered immediately. She says, "Mr. Lee, I told you about that house coming up for sale out on Barclay? The owner is in my office right now. Good. Can you meet us over there in half an hour? Fine." She hangs up and says to me, "I think Mr. Lee will buy the house from you right away. He's a speculator. He buys up old houses and then fixes them for resale. He said he would meet us over there in half an hour."

She leaves the office to tell the receptionist where we will be.

A car crash calls my attention to the busy street outside the plate glass window of Ms. Wilson's office. Other people, including Ms. Wilson, rush out the front door. A speeding car has side-swiped another car, and this car has been knocked off the street, across the sidewalk and the narrow lawn, and into the brown wooden fence surrounding the real estate office. The driver's side of the car has caved in. The windshield glass is broken, cracked into white webs. Some men, white passersby and store clerks, are trying to ease the passenger out of the collapsed car. The passenger is an elderly woman, white, who seems to be in a daze. She wobbles like a rubber doll as they handle her. Her thin, vanilla-white hair is scattered on her head. I cannot see any blood. But the car seems totaled.

It is only an accident on the busy suburban street. But I watch the men crowd around the old woman. More and more of them come.

There seems to be among them a desperate hunger to be helpful. The men, in their numbers, seem to be trying to make up for something. Although all their efforts are not needed, more and more men come from the service station across the street to push the car away from the wooden fence. There seems to be among them almost a lust for participation in some kindly, communal action.

Ms. Gayle Wilson comes back into her office.

I tell her that I think, now, that it would be inappropriate for her and Mr. Lee to meet me at the house. I say that first I must pay my respects to Mr. Butler.

Ms. Wilson agrees that this is the proper thing. She talks about the work she does in her church, about her love for rhyming poetry, about this afternoon's funeral, about the accident outside. We watch the crowd of men pushing the caved-in car away from the wooden fence, out of our view from the office window. The old woman has already been taken away. There has not been the sound of a siren or the lights of an ambulance. I assume that the crowd of men has grabbed this opportunity, too.

Ms. Wilson writes out detailed directions for my drive back into the city and over to Barclay Street.

I promise to call her from Iowa in a few days.

Barclay is a right turn off Thirty-third Street, one block before Greenmount. You are careful to not look at the house on the corner you once rented. You drive straight to 3114, two blocks to the right of Thirty-third, and park. The street is making a resurgence. There is a new neighborhood store, and several of the houses have been refurbished and are up for sale. Careful sanding has restored old blood to their red bricks. They seem freshly painted, too, waiting confidently for occupants. This seems to you a good sign. Life here is poised for movement, when spring comes. But there is the same rusty, white-spotted swing on the porch at 3114 Barclay. It is empty, speckled with peeling paint, and seems ancient. You do not pause to look at it. You knock, and a young black man opens the door. He invites you into the over-warm living room. Mr. Butler sits in his usual place: to the right of the door, in his old armchair, against the window. He wears his gray touring cap. He looks tired and old. His voice is only a croak. You shake his hand but do not hold his hand, or look long at him. Mr. Butler says to the young man, "This is the landlord. He came here from Iowa." The

230

young man, who has resumed his place on the sofa, answers, "Yes, sir." He is sitting in Mrs. Washington's place at the right end of the sofa, almost side by side with Mr. Butler. The television is turned to a late afternoon game show. The room is over-warm and dusty, but still retains a feeling that is familiar.

The young man's name is Eric. He seems to be about sixteen or seventeen.

You express your sympathies to Mr. Butler and to Eric. Eric keeps nodding and saying to you "Yes, sir." You do not want this formality. You miss Mrs. Washington's otherworldly good cheer. You miss her smile, You miss her saying "The landlord come. Yes in*deed!* He come all the way from *Ioway!* Thank the Good Lord. Yes, yes in*deed!*" But her voice does not come, except in memory. Eric says, "My Daddy left my Mama when I was born. My Mama is Elizabeth McIntosh, my Aunt Channie's niece. Aunt Channie raised me while my Mama worked. She was Mama, Daddy, Aunt, Uncle, parents, and grandparents to me. Yes, sir. I miss her. I come over here every evening and sit with Mr. Herbert. I don't know how he lives, sir, now that my Aunt Channie is gone."

You ask Eric if you can inspect the house. Eric asks Mr. Butler for his permission. The old man nods from his chair. Eric leads the tour. The small box of a basement contains only an old refrigerator and the ancient, red-rusted furnace. It is the old friend you have been nursing over all these years. It is so old it embarrasses you. "Why did she never mention the true condition of the furnace?" you ask Eric. He says, "My Aunt Channie didn't like to throw away nothing that could be fixed, sir. And she never liked to bother nobody. I gave her that refrigerator over there myself, because her old one was so bad." He leads you back up the loose, sagging basement steps to the dining room, where he shows you the cot where Mr. Butler sleeps. He is much too weak, Eric says, to climb the steps to the second floor. Eric leads the way up them. The top floor has three bedrooms and a bath. One of the bedrooms is obviously used by an occasional boarder. Another, Eric tells you, remains empty and ready as a place for guests. For an instant this seems to you a very extravagant gesture for a person in poverty. Then you recollect the dusty picture of Jesus, about to knock, on the wall above the television. Here you almost laugh. Eric opens, and closes very quickly, the door to Mrs. Washington's bedroom. In the brief illumination of light, you can see her bed, made up, with its pillow in place, waiting.

All of the ceilings in the rooms upstairs are cracked and peeling. You ask Eric why she never asked for repairs. He says, again, that she did not like to bother anybody with her problems. He says "sir" once more. The two of you go downstairs again, through the kitchen, and out onto the back porch. Its boards are broken and split. The wood is soft from age and weather. Eric says that Mr. Butler fell recently here. The twisted old tree still bends over the porch at an ugly angle, as if poised to grow confidently through the broken wooden porch and into the house. The bent tree, with its roots encased in concrete, seems to be nature's revenge on the illusionary order of city life. You suddenly say to Eric, "Please don't keep calling me 'sir.'" He says, "But I *always* say 'sir' to older people."

This also reminds you of something old.

Elizabeth McIntosh, Eric's mother, comes into the house then. Mrs. Washington was her mother's sister, she tells you. She talks freely about her Aunt Channie's life. Mrs. Washington had been married once, but had no children. She had come to Baltimore from a rural community in South Carolina. She had worked as a short-order cook in several restaurants around the city, until bad health caused her to retire. She was, of course, a churchwoman. "She loved you," Elizabeth says. "She considered you part of the family. She always wrote a letter to you to send with the rent check. Even when she was sick in bed, she insisted on dictating the letters to me. She kept saying, 'You *have* to write it. I *always* send a letter with my check.'"

You ask Elizabeth to send you, in Iowa, a copy of Mrs. Washington's funeral program.

You tell Mr. Butler, watching from his armchair, that everything will be fine.

You call Eric back to the back porch and tell him that the needed repairs will be made.

Eric says, "Yes,sir."

When you go back into the living room, you sit in Mrs. Washington's place on the sofa, before Eric can get to it. You sit there. You look at the game show on the television, and at the picture on the wall behind it. You ask Elizabeth whether Mrs. Washington ever prayed.

"Almost every hour of every day," Elizabeth answers.

You still sit there. You watch a few minutes of television with Mr. Butler. Then, for some reason, you ask the three of them to pray for you.

Then you want to see again, as quickly as possible, the brown stubble left, after fall harvest, in the rolling, open fields of Iowa.

But you still drive around the area until the streets begin to connect again in your memory. You are trying hard now to remember the other things you still have to do. You will have to find a short way back to the interstate, heading north. While driving, you look for your favorite bookstore on Greenmount. It is gone. So is the movie theater that was once several doors away. So is the Chinese restaurant. But the Enoch Pratt Library branch on Thirty-third and Barclay is still there. You decide that you do not have time to drive past the stadium. You will have to hurry, to better negotiate the early evening traffic collecting near Interstate 95, heading north. But you do stop, impulsively, at the liquor store on Greenmount, not for any purchase but just to see another familiar place. Old memories are returning now. But the yelling Jewish owners are gone. The new owners seem to be Koreans. Black clerks still do the busy work.

Now the connection you have been waiting for is suddenly made. You can now remember the route from here to the Lexington Market. You can remember the names of streets from here to there. Your plan now is to get some crabcakes, and find some way to keep them fresh enough to survive the trip back to Iowa. You will need ice and a plastic cooler. And you will need luck in shipping the plastic cooler on two different flights. There is an element of madness in this plan, but it also contains a certain boldness that you have not felt in many years. You determine to do it.

To get to the Lexington Market from Greenmount Avenue, you must turn left onto Thirty-third Street and head south. At the point where Thirty-third intersects St. Paul, you should take another left. The buildings and campuslands of Johns Hopkins should be at a distance as you turn left onto St. Paul. You should follow St. Paul Street south all the way downtown, pass the more stately rowhouses on both left and right, pass the shops and bars and restaurants near North Avenue, the mostly black section of St. Paul, pass Penn Station, and go all the way to the traffic circle on Monument Street, the old street with cobblestones and a bronze statue of Washington at the center of the circle, like those they have in the squares in Savannah. The other landmark here is the Walters Gallery. You should pass Monument Street and keep going down St. Paul. You are now approaching the downtown section of Baltimore. Here the buildings become taller and newer. The traffic becomes much more concentrated and the people walk with much greater purpose. On your left, just off the corner of Charles Street, should be the old building where your painter friend has a loft. Just beyond Charles, the buildings become mostly commercial. The lights of the harbor should be invisible in the distance, farther down St. Paul. On Franklin Street, you should take a right. Several blocks down, the main branch of the Enoch Pratt Library should appear on your left. Go several blocks beyond the Enoch Pratt, then turn left onto Eutaw. This is near the street of the Lexington Market. Find parking wherever you can.

The Threat of Downsizing at the Soul of the City

We find that the market has not changed that much after all these years. There are now some upscale boutiques and displays, and Korean families now run some of the produce stands and shops. But the old oyster bars are still there, as are the high, narrow tables where people add condiments to their oysters and stand while eating them raw. We breathe in the same familiar smells of fresh fish, flowers, fruits, vegetables, and raw meats. We see the same familiar mixture of peoples, from all segments of the city, blending one accord of accents into the commercial mass.

All of the seafood stands display crabcakes. Rather than waste time, we decide on those displayed in the showcase of just one stand. The most appealing, and the most expensive, are the lump crabcakes, made up in round, crumb-coated balls. They swell up out of their trays like overfed bellies. The other crabcakes on display—backfin, special, regular—are less expensive and therefore less attractive. The black woman standing beside us is also deciding. She is partisan to the lumps. "Them's the best ones," she says. "They taste best just out the pan. But all these other crabcakes is just as good." We decide on two lump crabcakes, to be eaten now, and a dozen regulars packed in ice to go.

Behind the counter of the stand, three black teenage boys in white aprons and white paper hats are filling orders. Behind them, at the stove, an elderly black woman lowers and raises webbed metal trays of crabcakes and French fries into deep frying pits of hot bubbling oil. Around the counter people lean, as if at communion, waiting for their hot orders to come. The woman and the boys seem to us essential to the operation. They set the standard of taste. The owner, or the manager, a white man, hovers near the cash register, giving orders in an unfamiliar accent. Then we remember that this is Baltimore, where the musical pitch of the South meets and smothers the gruffness of Germanic habits.

We are savvy enough to say that we are a tourist from out in Iowa, have heard good things about Maryland crabcakes, and want to take a dozen of them back home. We will need a dozen of the regulars, uncooked and packed in ice, to go, and two of the lump, cooked to eat now. The boy who takes our order communicates the problem to the owner. He comes up to the counter and says, "There ain't no way you can keep them fresh, even in ice, if you're drivin' such a distance." We respond that we are flying out of New York tomorrow afternoon, and that only enough ice is needed to keep the crabcakes fresh long enough, this evening, to drive into New York. There they can be frozen in the apartment of a friend. From New York, tomorrow, it will only be a four-hour flight to Iowa. Much like the mail. As an incentive, we add that people in Iowa seldom taste fresh Maryland crabcakes and that a desire to share a delicacy is at the basis of this gift. But in order to remain a gift, we say, it is essential that the crabcakes keep moving. If they lose refrigeration before New York, they will have to be eaten there. They will then become a simple meal. But if they should survive the trip into the city, and are frozen quickly, and then, tomorrow, survive again the two separate flights into Iowa—if the gift keeps moving at the same speed as it thaws—then, with luck, it can be shared with friends in Iowa tomorrow evening, along with the last of the harvested corn. Our plan, we say, is to ensure that some good part of Maryland will take up residency in the memories of friends in Iowa. We say again: It is essential that the gift keep moving. If it stops moving at any point before it can be given, the crabcakes will thaw quickly and lose the basic intention of their identity. They *must,* therefore, be shared with Iowa friends to remain essentially what they are. But to ensure this they must be kept moving. Once they stop moving, short of their goal, they will become just another meal. The action of the original intention will have then been defeated. To avoid this fate for them, we *must* have lots of ice. Fresh ice, if it is needed, might be found along the interstate heading back to Newark. We want now to risk this chance.

The manager becomes suspicious that we are mad. But we also sense that it is his bottom-line business to sell. Our request, or our outlandish demand, upsets the Teutonic order of his scale of values. To him, and to his black workers, the calculation of air time is as distant from the imagination as the lonely status of the "I" in uppercase. Perhaps he sees unrelenting cornfields in his imagination, or a bleak world of perpetual pork. Perhaps it is this that arouses his sympathy, and his skills. He gives orders to the black boy waiting at the counter. The boy nods politely, but cautiously, while he listens, his slow-moving eyes seeing the details of a radical plan. We enlist him deeper into our designs by ordering two lump crabcakes, deep-fat fried, to be eaten now, while we wait. This is the familiar thing. He passes the order to the black woman, the short-order cook, frying at the stove.

We are satisfied now that something that can be shown will be brought back from Baltimore into Iowa. We have been, and *are,* of both places. The balance between them that was disrupted has now been temporarily restored. But, while waiting, we become bothered by our lack of decisiveness, by the steady weakening of our initial strong resolve. A muscular "I" in the uppercase drove into Baltimore, but a fragmented self, crowded now into the lowercase, will be driving out. We worry over this problem when our steaming crabcakes come and we eat them at the counter. They are delicious. This is the body and blood that had been lost. This is the content of the cup that was long quested for. *It restoreth our soul.* We eat them, though, without the ketchup from the counter. The red would only spoil the delicate browns of their color. We savor what is already there in them. The taste and texture and wetness take us back many years, back to our original appetite for crabcakes. *This* is the body. *That* is the blood. "I bring you news of one who died and has returned. If Winter comes, can Spring be far behind?"

We think that this is the hidden basis of all belief.

But as we now consume the remaining crabcake, the missing part of us begins to reclaim its old, accustomed place. It says to us we have become sentimental about Mrs. Washington and her scant facts. She died. We have carried her above and beyond all expectation before she died. We have taken losses. We are reminded, now, that we should follow through on our original plan to sell the house immediately. Earlier today, we recollect, we almost became responsible again for its taxes and repairs. The two hundred dollars each month that will come now from Mr. Butler will barely cover the taxes. We should have come *here first,* to the Lexington Market, to satisfy our renewed appetite for Maryland crabcakes. We have done that now, even though in the wrong order of visits. But we can take comfort in the fact that Ms. Gayle Wilson, the real estate agent, is still available. She will maintain the business sense we need to rely on now. Our house can still be sold. Repairs will only enhance its value on the market, we are reminded. In the end, the house will have much more curbside appeal. It has never before had this, except during impersonal auctions. We are remembering now that it has been sentimentality, and that alone, that has undermined our purpose. The entire day has been a series of impersonal assaults on the muscularity of our self-standing "I." *I resent this.* It has taken us many, many years to move upward from the lowercase, and it has taken only one day for our *I* to be undermined into a wilderness of scattered, self-defeating selves. We sense that Eric has had something to do with this development. *I* should not have allowed him to continue saying *"Yes, sir. Yes, sir."* His subtle plea implied elderliness, and therefore liens of loyalty. We recollect now that these were snares, set to pull us down into the confusions of the lowercase. We recollect Eric's voice now, with no hint of a muscular "I" in it, chanting its leveling litany: *"My Aunt Channie was like Daddy, Mama, Grandmother, Grandfather, Aunt, and Uncle to me. Yes, sir. Yes, sir. Now that my Aunt Channie is dead, I come over every evening and sit with Mr. Herbert."* Eric has an "I" that is employed for only limited purposes. It would not know what to do if it became dislodged from the clutch of fealty. We follow this thread, and re-collect into it the new language in Mrs. Washington's last letter. *Dear James Family.* Another subtle assault against the self-standing of our uppercase. Even Mr. Butler had been uncomfortable in claiming the autonomy of personal loss for himself. He generalized his pain. Those were the traps, we are reminded now, that pulled our purposeful "I" down into the lowercase. This is why we are now who we are *now.* This is the source of our present mood of indecision. We decide, now finished with our crabcakes, that the only solution is to say the final goodbye that was originally intended.

Our dozen regular crabcakes are ready. The manager puts them proudly on display. They have been wrapped tightly in foil. The foil package has been wrapped inside layers of plastic bags. There is a layer of ice in each plastic bag. There are three plastic bags, each containing a layer of crushed ice, cooling the crabcakes. We pay our bill. The owner says, "Now we ain't go'n guarantee the ice will last till New York. But we done our best to get you there." Then he whispers to the black boy who is making change. The young man goes away then returns with a large soft drink, ice-cold, in a plastic cup. "One for the road. A gift," the manager says. Both of them take a mysterious pleasure in offering the liquid to us.

It is the impulse beneath the boosterism that contains the mystery.

Our drive to Interstate 95, heading north, is easier from the Lexington Street area. We drive much more comfortably now, inside the flow of early evening traffic. We plan ahead to the bus from Newark into the city, and the short cab ride from Port Authority to the friend's apartment on Riverside Drive. This friend is Japanese, and we think we should offer some of the crabcakes as a gift. The crabcakes will be cool by then, and a few might benefit from the changed intention. They might reach a much more healthy end as a commodity, or as a souvenir brought back from travel. The Japanese are great lovers of souvenirs. The presentation of one is considered a prologue to each meeting. It is not the quality of the gift, they say, but the purity of the intention behind it that is considered sacred. But then the apostate "I" of the scattered self reminds us that we are still stuck in lower-case, moving now from one small village-sense into another: We had thought *they* would be left behind us now, in the city. But even here, speeding purposefully through the evening traffic of Walt Whitman's south New Jersey, we find ourselves still de-selfing. We are still stuck in the village mode of mind.

We pull ourselves into full registration and *vote* with unanimity.

It is determined, once again, that our plan should remain the original one. All twelve crabcakes will be left overnight in the friend's freezer. After ten or so hours there, they should be frozen solid. By tomorrow afternoon, when we begin our flight, the crabcakes should still be fresh. They will fly next to us on the airplane, like express-mailed letters. All baggage will arrive together, *recollected,* from the separation caused by the two flights. When the brown, harvested cornfields are seen, we will know that we are *home.* All of us, the friends included, will have a feast. Once the gift is put into motion again, around the dinner table, the lure of de-selfing will have abated, and the other parts of us that have been scattered can be reclaimed.

Our "I" will be at home again, and can make its best decisions unfettered by the chains of ancient memories, is the thought that is kept fixed as we drive north.

But once at home again, beyond the welcome of the brown, harvested Iowa cornfields, there is a sudden decision to refreeze the crabcakes.

The Rescue of a Self from the Snares of the Past

There is hard work involved in relocating a respectable batch of the letters. They must be looked for in boxes of old letters, papers, magazines, bills, that have been stored over the years in various corners of the basement. They must be put into a pile on the dining-room table and reread. It is here that an initial intuition proves to be the correct one. The letters report few facts. They never vary in their language and in their focus. Nor do they ever mention the rent checks that accompany them. I find enough of the letters to pinpoint the dates of several repairs on the old furnace, one replacement of electric wiring, one occasion of work on leaking water pipes. These have been the only emergencies. The costs of the smaller repairs are always deducted from the rent. The receipts are always enclosed. These occasions are the only ones for news about reality. All other letters say almost the same ritual things: "Everything is fine," "God bless you and the family," "Thank the Good Lord," "By By." I realize now how accustomed *I* have become to these monthly reports on the nonfacts of life. Still, over the years they have become a respite of some kind. They have been monthly reminders of the insubstantial elements comprising even the most permanent of things.

But as I continue reading through the letters, my mature instincts keep reminding me that no human being is this simple. No human being could be *only* the repetition of the same old assertions from one month to the next. I do not expect a secret life in Mrs. Washington, but I find myself needing something more to mourn. It may be that the years have taught me to be untrusting of what once seemed simple, uncomplicated, pure. My mind has grown used to being vigilant. I have learned that things that seem to be *are not* what they seem to be. The thing that seems most like itself has, most likely, been calculated to seem to be that way. There is always something hidden. There is always that extra fact. I continue reading through the letters, all that I can find, for the clue that will lead to the private intuition, which in turn, in time, will merge with a larger and expanding reality, and give rise to the experience of truth. This is the metaphysic of detectives during times of universalized corruption. It is also the refuge of cynics. I cannot truly move against Mr. Butler until the self-interested action can be rationalized in terms of some hidden fact. This is, after all, the way of the world. It is the art of self-interested, savage discovery.

239

The funeral program, sent from Baltimore by Elizabeth McIntosh, arrives at my home a week after me. I let the letter sit, unopened, for several days, before reviewing the folded sheet. It is called a home-going service for Channie Washington. A faded picture of her is below this title. She looks the way I first saw her on the porch. She looks dressed for church on Sunday morning. Her funeral had taken place on October 26th, at the Second Antioch Baptist Church, 3123 Barclay Street, in Baltimore. Her church, like her family, was only a few doors away. The obituary recites the basic facts of her life.

Channie Washington, daughter of the late Cornellius and Annie Gibson, was born on January 29, 1915, in Hartsville, South Carolina. She departed this life on October 21, 1993, after a brief illness.

She received her education in the Darlington County Public Schools, in South Carolina.

Channie was married to the late Issac Washington.

At a young age, she moved to Baltimore, Maryland.

Later, she became a member of the Second Antioch Baptist Church. She served faithfully as a Missionary.

She worked at several restaurants, as a Short Order Cook, until she retired.

She loved to cook and enjoyed having her family and friends on Sundays, for her big meals.

Channie was a loveable and well-liked person. She loved her family and could never say no to anyone in need. She will be greatly missed.

She leaves to cherish her memory: her long-time beloved companion, Herbert Butler; two sisters, Mrs. Olivia Allen and Mrs. Rebecca Hankins of Norfolk, Virginia; eleven nieces; twelve nephews; fifteen great nieces; sixteen great nephews; fifteen great great nieces and nephews; and a host of other relatives and friends.

240

God saw the road was getting rough
   The hills were hard to climb;
He gently closed her loving eyes
   And whispered, "Peace Be Thine."
Her weary nights are passed
Her ever patient, worn out frame
   Has found sweet rest at last.
          Humbly Submitted,
          The Family

The opening hymn was "What a Friend We Have in Jesus."

There were remarks, a solo, a reading of the obituary, by the various sisters and brothers of Mrs. Washington's church.

It comes to me, now, that Mrs. Washington had never been alone on that porch when I first saw her. For all her life, she had been an intimate part of something much larger than herself. She had not really needed my help. My old friend, the teacher, had been right all along. I might have passed by the scene, and nothing tragic would have happened to her. She might have been allowed by the new owner to remain in the house. She might have moved in with one of her two sisters, or with one of her many nieces or nephews. Her church might have found another place for her. The welfare people, if all else had failed, might have moved both her and Mr. Butler into a state-supported retirement home, where their lives might have been much more protected and pleasant during these last seventeen years. My old mentor had been right all along. I had taken upon myself, in a publically arrogant way, a responsibility that was not my own. Now the needed fact begins to emerge in outline.

I had grown drunk on an infatuation with my own sense of "goodness" and had employed Mrs. Washington, and also Mr. Butler, as a prop for the background of the self-display I had wanted, then, to dramatize. I had challenged the white men in the crowd, inspired by motives I had rationalized into a higher sense of things, when I had, all along, been an actual member of the crowd. "Father, I am not like these other men. I pray ten times a day, I give tithes in the synagogue, I minister to widows and orphans, I . . . "

The fact comes clearly to me then: a value is not a value as long as it depends for its existence on a comparison to something else.

241

Then I remember a something else. It is a something else recollected from a time much longer ago than Baltimore. This memory merges with Mr. Herbert Butler and Elizabeth McIntosh, and with the young man named Eric. He was just a baby, two or three porches away on Barclay Street, when I first bought the house. I think to myself, What if she had been forced to move away and had not been available to Eric, during those years, after his father abandoned him and his mother went to work? How different would Eric's life be now if Mrs. Washington had not been there?

I think about this additional fact.

I think, again, that time *must* be a cycle because this fact brings me back, back, back to my *self*.

I *re-collect* what there was in Eric that had made me so uncomfortable.

Now I remember. Now I remember it all.

> Get my little sister, Sandy, and my big brother, Ray
> Buy a big old wagon, just to haul us all away.
> Live out in the country, with the mountains high
> Never will come back here, 'till the day I die.
> O,Baltimore, *ain't* it hard to live? Just to *live?*

"Baltimore," Randy Newman

Eric Abstracted and Recombined

When running away you always found that first pit stop. Your plans have been fueled by fear, by aloneness, by questions the answers to which no one seems to know because no one is *really* there. You are far past fantasy now, young adolescent, pushing with passion against all that does not push back. Nothing does. No one is there who has time to care. You are feeling the freedom to test yourself against something larger than yourself, something familiar at first, something gentle that will still push back. This becomes the place of the pit stop in your plans for running away. You always go there first, to the environs of the familiar, to gather strength for this first solo flight out into the world. This familiar foreign place is always on the outskirts of this woman's voice. She is a few doors down the block, a few blocks distant, the other side of town. Her house is a safe place to stop during the first part of your flight. She stands over you, looking down. She says things

242

like "Come in, boy. Take a load off your mind." She says, "Come on in and rest your feets." The renegotiation usually began in this ritual way. She is too old to be a bitch and much too far removed from this world to be a ho'. She is not the mammy of folklore. In the distant past of her life she had made the same mistakes you are inviting. You are not "black male" to her, but blood. She cares about the special ways it flows. She knew your father before he was your father, and your mother before the girlish dreams in her died. It is not her fault they have been taken from you by life. Unlike you, she long ago learned to expect not much good from it. She knows that you must learn to do the same. Her life has been a preparation for the worst, and her small joys derive from anything less. It is life's hard lesson, this special peace that is past all understanding, and she will take her time in teaching it. But just now she protects you from the central mystery she has learned to master. She does not yet want to instruct in the quiet joy she has located on the ebb of unrelieving pain. This will be life's lesson, not her own. She cooks. She seems always to be at home. Her place is where you pause to get your bearings for the road. Her familiar name, the name you call her, always has two sounds, preceded by "Aunt." They represent her as solid and without pretension. "Chi-na." "Beu-lah." "Gus-sie." "Ma-ry." "Chan-nie." She is the external aunt of archetype, not the mammy. Hers is the first outside model of finished woman you explore. She has lost all belief in even the most pedestrian possibilities of the self-standing "I" and has learned to live carefully inside a populated "we." She is the fountainhead, the base at the whisk of the broom that keeps the "we," the "us," collected. You are one of the straws about to stray. You feel safe running away as far as her house, for a pause at this pit stop, because you know there is fellow-feeling kept in unlimited supply for you there. But she still makes you feel uncomfortable. She has no material proof for her belief in God, but believes anyway. This increases her mystery. She has learned to see miracles in small, comic things: it is not too hot or too cold, a cool breeze comes through the window, the old furnace still operates all through winter. She also irritates you by giving all credit to "The Man Upstairs," to "The Good Lord," even when she can clearly see the causal physics involved. You want to teach her what you are learning in the streets, from radio, from television. But you also take secret comfort in the fact that her higher world, the one above your frustrations in this one, is viewed by her as under the strict control of a good *Man.* You would not want to be as burdened as *He* is, but at the same

243

time you are glad that He is there. He is the only Man, so far as you can see, to whom she defers. She talks always of His will. Because she is on such intimate terms with Him, you never consider that this man is white, or female. Her manner assures you that the world where He lives is beyond all such concerns. This man has to do only with things that are ultimate. He lists lies. He watches sparrows. He knows all secrets. There are no private plans that will not come to light. This man already knows why you are running. While she talks and looks at you, you begin to believe that she knows, too. Coming here always seems to cause a reconstruction. Maybe today, after all, you will not leave the comfort of her house. But tomorrow, or the next time, you will not come here first. You will just continue down the road. When she sees you again, years from now, you will be worldly, a grown man, with all the things you worry about not having now. You will pay her back for the meal she is giving you. You will bring back solid, seeable proofs that The Man Upstairs is much too busy with the flights of sparrows to see into the hidden corners you have found. The proofs you will bring back will be from fairyland, from Jacksonville, from the New York she has never seen. They might come, much more quickly, from the crack house just several blocks away, where other boys your age are already making money. Boys much younger than yourself have already made their own miracle. They have abstracted the assembly line from McDonald's, and sell, with a smart efficiency that you admire, small plastic bags of crack to white people from the suburbs who drive by. One, some boy you know personally and admire, Bro' or Dupe or Home, takes the orders; one, farther on, collects money; and the third boy, at the end of the block, just by the corner, delivers the plastic sandwich bags, the very ones that used to hold your lunch at school, to the eager white hand reaching out the window of the car. You have been invited to become part of this process, to stand at one end of the McDonald's line or at the other. It looks easy. Sometimes, in your bed at night, in the quiet and the darkness, you can imagine such an assembly line stretching *down* southward, from Savannah, into Jacksonville, Miami, Tampa, or *up* from Baltimoe, north, like in the old stories to Dover, Philly, Newark, New York, New Haven, Hartford, and Boston. *Phillymeyork.* With yourself at either end of the line taking McDonald's orders or delivering white dust. *Phillymeyork. Cowboys and silver dollars.* Meanwhile, now, she is talking at the child who is leaving you, in a language that no longer fits the way things are. Maybe tomorrow, or sometime soon, you will be going all the way. But for now, with the food and considering the time of day . . . and considering her sparrows and the ever-watching eyes she apparently looks into and sees through . . . *In later years,* close friends will tell you that in moments of frustration you tend to say *"Oh Lord!"* You will think back on the source of this, trying to remember. It is somehow connected, you recollect, with firm intentions that have come unglued. It will be connected with memories that are embarrassing. This Lord you petition will somehow have to do with the old dream of money, and with memories of fellow-feeling and food, and also with the natural flow of sympathy. But you are a man now and no longer think much about childhood. Still, you will begin to *recollect* a tired black woman, who stood in her doorway between the lures of the streets and you. She was one of your first loves. Inside her door you always felt a degree of safety, the sense of which has now been lost. But these recollections of dependency now threaten to intrude upon your present self-possession. You are self-made, in the terms of, and in the view of, the principalities and powers of *this* world. You know no other Lord beyond yourself. Besides, you say to those who heard your voice reaching, it would be crazy to call into the empty air for help. The voice that was heard was not your own. It possibly slipped out from the locked travel trunks of another time. It was a simple error in articulation . . . *But for now, here inside this house, in this beforetime,* all appeals to the other world belong to her. You confess to her, while eating, your fear that the holes in your world cannot be fixed. You do not expect her to understand. She does not understand. But at the same time she is there, has always been there, just to listen. It is enough while she feeds you, while she talks in her private language. She cooks the things she likes best that you do not like. You eat them anyway. She talks, selectively, about her own early life, in her own Old Country. She tells stories about the old-fashioned time in the old-fashioned place. She says things like "Take the bitter with the sweet." She says things like "Catch more flies with honey than with vinegar." But her language does not enter into the sore spots of *your* problems. It is only a meaningless counterthrust of words that obscures *your own specifics.* She always finds ways to turn you away from yourself, away from the life-and-death issues that first stalled you at her door. You had come to her for just a hint of understanding. You wait long for this, but it never comes. You eat the meal and decide to not come back again. But you always do come back, each time you make fresh steps toward that better world beyond her door. Her home is the secret pit stop you visit first,

245

for food, for fuel, before continuing on up the road. You know that you could get there much more quickly if she were not there. But she is always there, like the police squad cars, like the ticket agent in the toll booth at the entrance to the interstate, who has already memorized the exact price of travel up or down the road. She warns you to be careful and to watch your speed. She inspires you to slow down. She becomes the counterthrust to your full-forward. Sometimes she seems to be the bitch your older friends have learned to moan about. You think she will always be in your path, like a stoplight frozen forever on blood red. But one day, quite suddenly, she is not. You grieve some, but soon find the loss is less important than the life ahead of you. She can be forgotten. You still retain a mother, and a growing lease on life. At her funeral, you take comfort in reciting, in line with her beliefs, that the two of you will meet again. You *move on* in your own life, not really remembering much, until one day it happens. *You see her.* The armies of the world have massed to remove her from her house. The crowd does not know the importance of the place to her, *or to you.* They see only something that is free-floating above the ground, obsolete, old. They see a run-down rowhouse. You see a temple. It is the place where she *must be* for those times when you run away. The crowd does not understand this house's history. It cannot contemplate that something larger is involved. "*My Aunt Chan-nie-Chi-na-Beu-lah-Gus-sie-Ma-ry* must *be there for me.*" Her house is your one refuge from the world. In that place your "I" is a less troubled "we." She has always lived a few doors down the street, a few blocks away, a rapid run across the back-dirt lanes of town. You have grown used to dropping in and sitting. She has always been your rock of ages, who lifted you *up* above all undertows. You do not worry as long as she is there. But the crowd cannot see this always unfinished business. It threatens the unseeable self that has always lived between the two of you. It is cutting a connection that cannot be encased in reason. You cannot tell it that you have come to pause here, and eat your meal, before continuing down or up the road. Perhaps you can say that you *must* sit evenings with Mr. Herbert. Tell the crowd *anything* that will *make it go away . . . !*

I understand now why I claimed Eric's place on the sofa: The source of the bond we share was in that special seat.

I had sensed this *something*, almost eighteen years ago, during my walk that sweaty July morning.

246

After exploring up and down both coasts, *I* had circled back *home*.

Now I search again for the *nonfacts* in Mrs. Washington's last letter, the one sent in September, with the meaning of its new language suddenly clarified.

"Dear James Family": She was drawing me closer in, *claiming*.

"Only a few lines to let you hear from us": *Deselfing*.

"I am doing much better now": *Deselfing*.

"Mr. Butler is fine": *Beloved*.

"Give the family our love": *Consideration, same monthly basis*.

"I will close my letter but not our love": *"My" ends, "Our" lives on. Offer*.

"May God Bless you all with much love and Happiness": *Source of future surplus, to back offer*.

"By By": *Extra understanding concealed in formulaic signature*.

"Channie Washington and Herbert": *Lifelong tenants*.

In the new ways I am now sensing beyond thinking thoughts, this last letter is Mrs. Channie Washington's last will and testament.

I can read the nonfacts now. She has drawn me into her family. She has affirmed the stability of the present *status quo*. The declaration of her family's love stretching far into the future is her offer of consideration for something. It seems to be the kiting of the present circumstance against the surplus of some future time. There is a promise of abundant giving to balance something given of my own.

That is the way it has been for almost eighteen years.

Now I read back from the nonfacts and reconstruct the facts. Because she knew she was dying, Mrs. Washington was looking out for her family. She was intent on sheltering her beloved. She was deeply skilled in the uses of the intimate non-language of black people, the language that only employed words as ballast and sound. Because the money rent she paid had never been sufficient, she had grown used to sending what compensation she could. Now she was offering, from the surplus she expected, the same rate of extra compensation far into the future. Mrs. Washington was stationed in future time, looking back on the now, making her usual spiritual adjustment in her monthly rent.

This nonlanguage was her offer to lock me in, as the landlord of her home, at the usual rate of payment, for many years to come. Mrs.

Washington was offering a renewal of our old spiritual contract, locating future rent adjustments in the only source of surplus she knew. She had touched the most ultimate expression of kiting.

There was no will in the world sufficient to compete with the power of this offer. Mrs. Washington had always *known better*.

It is only now that I unfreeze my crabcakes and begin to eat them. Now I do not worry about their freshness, or about how they taste. Now they represent only a secret signature, the symbolic acceptance of an offer.

Nominated by Eileen Pollack

A RENTED HOUSE IN THE COUNTRY

by JAMES REISS

from RHETORIC REVIEW

Nail a bushel basket without a bottom
to the inside wall of a barn converted
into a garage and do lay-ups when the parked
Ford leaves its stall. Say you are big
for your age, but gawky, a bean pole whose hook
shots swish through a makeshift hoop. Say
you pivot and dribble on splintering planks

while upstairs in the locked loft under
a floorboard a canvas bagful of tax forms and cancelled
checks tells how the landlord ducked and dodged
to save his Cadillac from the IRS
before he scored years in the slammer—his candy factory
out back, a green tarpaper shack that sprawled
over an acre, was his front for a smuggling operation
stung by T-men in the Truman administration.

Now that your father has converted one of its ramshackle
storage rooms into an artist's studio,
say his unfinished still life of bananas
and a coconut big as a basketball is sweet
as Batista's regime. Say all the cane sugar

249

in rum and moonshine, all the impastoed icing
on life's cake, are something you can taste

while you study your father's footsteps as he pivots
to gain perspective, then leaps at the canvas
with his palette knife when he adds a palmetto
bush and a man in a panama hat to the new scene
on his easel—for hours he has been painting
an adobe farm house with a trapdoor,
a barnyard with chickens and a burro that belongs
to the boy who lives there. Say that boy is you.

Nominated by Linda Bierds, Stuart Dischell, David St. John

UTTAR PRADESH

by AUGUST KLEINZAHLER

from CHICAGO REVIEW

You were dozing over Uttar Pradesh
well after the shadows of Annapurna
swept across the big plane's starboard wing,

dreaming a peevish little dream
of Stinky Phil, your playground tormentor
from fifty years before, his red earmuffs

and curious cigar voice vivid as the tapioca
you used to gag on at the end of Thursday lunch,
when the captain's serene, patriarchal voice

suggested you buckle up, moments before
the plane jumped then yawed in an air pocket
and dropped five-hundred feet, Oh, shit,

there goes the Parcheesi board and what's left
of a very bold Shiraz. Melissa
purses her lips in the compact mirror,

turns a quarter left, then right a tad,
scowls at her mascara and snaps it shuts with a sigh.
You are the preeminent colorist

of your era. Some would suggest a fraud
with your grand chevelure of white hair and cape.
Mother would certainly not disagree,

but here you are again, crossing continents,
six miles above the petty quarrels,
the tossed green salads and car wrecks

to receive yet another prize, a ribbon,
a princely sum in a foreign capital
and a spread on the Sunday culture page.

How very far away now seem your student days:
happy, hungry, cooking up manifestoes—
turpentine, pussy, stale cigarette smoke.

It was evident from the start. It screamed
at you from billboards, fabric shops, museums;
and no one else saw it, no one but you.

Amazing. Then half a lifetime to execute it
in paint. What a long time with one idea.
But still, it was a doozy, put you

in the art books and kept you there for life.
There will be a car waiting when you arrive.
Kremer is visiting with the Philharmonic

and will do the Sibelius, your favorite.
You recall meeting him some years ago
at a dinner in—Cologne, I think it was.

An intense young man, but very pleasant.
Right, now you remember the evening,
the lugubrious molding and burgundy drapes . . .

Ah, yes, and a most memorable Hasenpfeffer.

Nominated by David Wojahn, Chicago Review

NEANDERTHAL TONGUES

fiction by RANBIR SIDHU

from THE GEORGIA REVIEW

I CAN TRACE IT back that far. It was Ismail's death that revealed the grammar of the landscape, that allowed me to understand the meaning of the flat desert plain as it fell into the disorder of the badlands.

In Ethiopia, inland from the slim ribbon of beach along the Red Sea, the land rises to a high levee of mountains that hoard what little rain comes down. A desert plain flattens the continent before it splits and falls into the Great Rift. It is there—a realm of gullies and valleys of infinite variation yet linked by a communal disarray—that the world is pulling apart.

I am dead, and below me water shuffles into darkness. Contrary to superstition, in which the dead become universal—no up, no down, just a bland everything—there is a below me, as there is an above me, and a me. I have not seen any land—only the wreckage of the plane, fragments of burnt and twisted wing, seat cushions, their springs popping out, the aftermath of what could have been a victory parade: torn barf bags like confetti, magazines, newspapers, boarding passes, passports. And sometimes the dead on the parade route, or at least pieces of them, their limbs, their eyes. I am better at knowing the bones, the small fragments of zygomatic arch, the lumbar vertebrae, shattered.

*

I had been in Ethiopia with Ismail. It was the only expedition I ever led. I had been teaching at Michigan for two years, and previously, as a graduate student in physical anthropology, I had worked on surveys in Pakistan and Kenya.

We were a small team. I had been denied NSF funding; I was a new professor, and though my thesis had been published, it was far from groundbreaking. I was as yet unproven. Only those students who managed to get travel grants on their own were able to accompany me. There were five of us, and a cook. Three were graduate students from Michigan: Bill, Ellen, and Steve.

Ismail was the only Ethiopian among us. He was going to start as one of my graduate students the following term, and we met him in Addis Ababa. We had planned a preliminary mapping of an area in the north, along the eastern rim of the Great Rift, a bare reconnaissance of the badlands whose thick fingers extended to the far horizon. A team of petroleum geologists who traveled through the area two years earlier had collected fossil mammal remains that suggested the region had exposed layers almost two million years old.

That first night in the desert found us all marveling at the stars, our blanket, at the stillness of a universe that had retracted from us only to show its distant splendor. The cook's heavy breath as he turned the goat on its spit, the fire bursting open the night—I remember the smells, the sounds. We had argued about Binford and Isaac, about the significance of recent excavations. When the fire died down, we thought the stars might blind us.

The following day Ismail saw a thin string of smoke in the distance, rising like an exclamation, but the cook had laughed at the city boy. Those were just hunters, he said. Ismail said nothing. Only later did he tell me of the rumors of the widening war, of trouble in the north. I tried to reassure him. We would never have been given our permit had there been the possibility of trouble, I said. Ismail's eyes still reflected the horizon, though he never spoke of it again.

*

My father, Hukum, had told me about his village in India. I had never been to India. I was born one cold winter in New York, and in those first few weeks, my mother told me, the pipes had rattled in the apartment building until finally they broke. Water flooded the first floor and became ice, and the firemen used blowtorches to melt their way into our building. My father said that in India they gave names to the dark spaces between the stars. It was the darkness that was novel, scarce, that seemed brilliant against so much light. Sometimes I would find my father late at night in the living room, the lights all off, only the clock glowing on the VCR. He would say that it was such a relief, this darkness, this not being able to see. Only years later did I learn what it was he was hoping not to see.

*

My body spreads every day, the currents and horizon of cold waves pushing me in different directions. One hour, one part of me is warmed by the red breaking of dawn, while another still misses the recent evening. Soon night and day will be eternal, dawn and sunset constants from which I will never be free. Sharks tear at pieces of me, at the water snake of my intestine, the sweet of my testicle, and I think I make out distant screams—faraway terrors, growing closer. One eyeball sinks to the ocean floor and is caught up in the warm currents of an underwater volcano.

Immediately after the explosion, when my body was blown into—how many? I don't know—maybe a hundred thousand, maybe a million fragments, I had the illusion that I was everywhere at once. That is, that every part of me—every smallest fragment, from the lengths of my femurs to the stray spots of blood suddenly red, diluting—was connected. Not in the physical sense, the way a body is naturally connected, but through our senses. It is hard to find a correct pronoun for the experience—we, us, I, it? In those seconds I saw everything that every part of me saw, experienced everything from all the diverse views that a splintered body possesses. I was, I think, at one with all the elements of my body for the first time. For a few brief seconds, I understood them all and understood their sudden and enlarging fear—my own fear—as within moments our consciousness began to deflate.

It lasted only seconds, as though we were living in the aftermath of a camera flash, slowly fading, the light dimming. I lost touch with the lines of my veins, the fragments of appendix, the small bones of the hand, the drowning balls of spit and urine.

*

The expedition was almost over. We had found no evidence of hominid remains, but many of the fossils we did recover suggested that in future seasons, with a larger team and more intensive surveys, this area could prove fruitful. Ismail and I were walking. The high sun hid our shadows under our feet. When we came to the last gully his face was weary and sweat glinted off his skin like jewels. I'll take this side, I said, you that. He nodded. He had been distracted all morning, said he had heard a gunshot in the night. But on the two-way radio back into town, there was no news of any trouble. There were the regular skirmishes farther north of us, but nothing where we were.

We'll finish in three days, I said, and then you'll fly with us to the States. He smiled at this, and I let the weight of my body pull me down into a gully, showering the air with fine white dust. Up on the ridge-line, he was watching me. I saw his silhouette, hesitant. In a week, I shouted up, Michigan!

Superbowl and McDonald's! Ismail shouted back. His body slid down into the next gully over.

An hour later, I was halfway along the cleavage of this ancient wound, finding nothing visible, when I heard his scream and the shouts of strange voices. Then Ismail again, his throat scrabbling for air.

*

When my parents moved to New York, my father already spoke English well, though haltingly. My mother's English, she told me, was poor, and she was excited at the possibility of improving it. She wanted both of them to take ESL classes at City College, but my father refused to listen to the idea. He said that they (meaning *him*, according to my mother) spoke English more than well enough to get by. He said they would both take classes in Esperanto, which—my father claimed— was the language of the future; in a decade, everyone would be speaking it. It was language, he told my mother, that had ripped India apart, thrown it into the pool of communal violence. How can a country persist—a world even—where people cannot speak to each other? This was his argument.

All this was when my mother was pregnant with me. Years later she told me she almost took his head off with her fist. It was the pregnancy, the sudden mood swings, the new country. She was furious. She slammed her fist into his face, knocking him down onto the carpet, bloodying his nose.

See! he shouted from where he lay on the floor. Until we all speak one language, we will always fight.

256

All argument fled my mother with that single blow. She was not a violent person and was shocked at herself. It was not the weight of my father's belief but of her own violence that persuaded her to go along with him and learn Esperanto before she mastered English. When I was still small, I remember her voice, sometimes late at night, singing me songs and nursery rhymes in a language I barely remember, a language I have never since heard anyone else speak.

Still, she did stand firm on one point. She made sure I was never forced to speak that language. I learned English and Hindi instead, and only those few words of Esperanto that I picked up sometimes from the two of them. It was a strange household, all of us speaking different languages. My father clung to Esperanto, my mother to Hindi, and I managed a patois of those two and English. It was the farthest thing from my father's dream of a common language that I can imagine.

One night, I remember, they were arguing—both shouting in Esperanto. I must have been five at the time. I can see them clearly, the small shelf of books behind my father, the black-and-white TV flickering, the smell of milk on the stove in the kitchen. I don't know *what* they were saying to each other, but it was the last night my mother ever spoke Esperanto in the house. At one point my father was about to hit her. I could see his hand forming a fist. Just at that moment, my mother let out a scream—the only time I ever heard her scream, a scream in no language I knew. It wasn't a Hindi scream or an English scream—I have heard those—and I cannot imagine that it was an Esperanto scream, because I cannot believe that my mother would resort to so foreign a language at such a moment. It was something else entirely, and it stopped my father's fist midair. Stunned, he stood motionless for a moment—then his body slumped, relaxed, and he put his arms around my mother, talking softly in Hindi.

*

Three men surrounded Ismail, all shouting, all with rifles. I had scrambled up and over the thigh of rock that separated our two small valleys, dirt catching under my nails, my breath suddenly hard. They wore torn jeans, old, beaten athletic shoes, and dirty T-shirts. Thick ammo belts hung across their chests, as though they were old-time bandits. I watched as one used the butt of his rifle as a bat, smashing it against Ismail's head. Ismail fell to the ground, screaming, a small puddle of blood forming on the dry desert surface.

257

Who the fuck are you? I shouted down, and suddenly the three faces turned to acknowledge me, their mouths rigid and tense. I heard the action of a rifle click. I was stiff with fear. I wanted to run, to scramble back down into the hot gully I had emerged from, to abandon Ismail right there to his murderers. I didn't see the one who aimed at me, but I heard the gunshot and felt my body suddenly thrown back, tumbling down into the white of the gully, dust in my mouth, the taste of blood. I screamed.

I lay there in a ball. I remembered my mother's scream that night. I remember it now. The clouds have cut away the stars from me, and a storm is heading in this direction, already tossing parts of me around, viciously. My mother's long-ago scream had seemed incomprehensible, as though something ancient were shouting through her. But when I heard Ismail's—and heard my own echoing through my skull—I began to understand the origin of that scream. I lay at the bottom of the gully, shaking, terrified. I knew already that Ismail would be killed, but I didn't know why. I didn't move to help him. Instead, I thought about the taste of blood and viewed the blueness of the sky, my only companion, as a glove strangling me.

At the camp, Steve, one of my graduate students who had been briefly in medical school, dressed my shoulder wound. Bill was slowly packing up the camp. I saw Ellen standing in the distance. She was looking out to the horizon, in the direction where the jeep had raced, carrying Ismail. She shouted over to me, her arm pointing at the far-away sky. I followed the line of her finger and saw the black specks of vultures swirling and dipping like mosquitoes over a stagnant pool.

When Bill had finished packing the two Land Rovers, we followed the distant shadow of the vultures. The cook was also gone, with all his belongings. Ellen said that when she ran back to the camp on hearing the gunshots, the cook and the other jeep were missing. We were all silent. My shoulder was burning, and I asked myself why I hadn't tried harder to stop them. They had guns, and they were willing to use them, but . . . What if I had been a different person, able to subdue the kidnappers with the sound of my voice? What if all it took were the right level of voice, the right determination? Instead I had lain at the bottom of that hole, shaking with fear, and comforted by the taste of my own blood, as though that were proof I had tried.

*

258

More than once I have come across the heads of my fellow passengers. Most often they were unrecognizable, only fragments—it was only many years of having studied anatomy and osteology that allowed me to see them as human heads at all. But some I did recognize. There was the stewardess who spilled coffee onto my lap when we hit a pocket of sudden turbulence. There was the large man who grabbed the last copy of *Scientific American* just as I was reaching for it. There was the blown-apart face of the child who sat behind me, constantly kicking at the back of my seat. It floated past me, or maybe I floated past it—it is so hard to tell now who is moving, who is stationary.

*

When finally we found Ismail's body, it was covered by a black scab of vultures picking at what little meat was left. Ellen jumped out of the Land Rover, a small revolver in her hand, firing into the air. Even when the birds had scattered, she tried to shoot at them, as though the vultures were somehow at fault. When the gun was empty, I saw the tears on her face. None of us had cried up to then. We did not want to admit what had happened, but Ismail's face had been slashed open with a knife and his chest made pulp by countless bullet holes.

In the days after we learned that Ismail's father was an assistant secretary in the Defense Ministry. His father told us he hadn't known that his Ismail had traveled north, that he would never have allowed it. He was shouting at his dead son's body, beating the collapsed chest with his fists. Perhaps Ismail had thought he would be safe among Americans, perhaps he was seduced too easily by the fact that he too would soon be an American.

His scream still haunts me. I never returned to Ethiopia. I found I couldn't continue my research there, or on anything that was connected to that summer. I kept returning to the picture of Ismail's body lying in the hot sun, the white of the sand become red.

I spent my days thinking about Ismail's scream. Looking back on it now with the blueness of the midday sky above me (somewhere I can hear parts of me, far off, saying something or maybe only mumbling, but I don't understand), I realize it was the same sky in Ethiopia when I had huddled in a ball, terrified. I had felt almost like an animal, like something that can no longer think but only grunts and scratches through the day. Was this what Ismail felt when they first appeared, guns pointing? Or when they pulled him away, his feet dragging on the old desert? Or when they finally took out knives and slashed open his face and emptied their rifles into his chest? The two of us had had language stripped from our mouths and were left with only antediluvian tongues. As though we were dogs, beaten, our barks become low whimpers.

Over a year later I received a small Neanderthal hyoid that had recently been excavated in Spain. The hyoid is a small U-shaped bone that sits behind the jaw, above the larynx and thyroid, and attaches to the tongue. It remains the only articulation we anthropologists have to the beginnings of language. The one shipped to me—small, delicate, packed in among layers of rough blue toilet paper and a cocoon of bubble wrap—was the first and only Neanderthal hyoid ever excavated. The excavators themselves were not interested in it, except to note it in their publication, so I had asked if I could be allowed to study it in further detail. Up to that point my career had been spent tracing the evolutionary paths of early hominids. Examining a Neanderthal hyoid presented something of a challenge.

I needed something new in any case. After Ethiopia, I found myself growing numb to my previous research, which seemed somehow empty, lacking meaning. I thought of my father, who had searched for a universal language and, later, for all languages. I began to understand why he had done those things that I had once found so strange and disturbing in the years before his death.

I traced the muscle attachments on the rough surface of the bone. It was a cold winter in Michigan, and my office heat was always failing. Huddled in sweater and overcoat, I sat cramped over the desk, a bright table lamp illuminating the bone's shadowed detail. I followed the slight rises and depressions, examining the bone under various magnifications. I compared it with human hyoids, and also with chimp and gorilla hyoids. I measured every point on it, every angle and distance. I carried out statistical analyses of the surface area covered by the various attachments for ligaments and muscles. I thought that, however slowly, I was beginning to understand something of the bone, of how it might be related to those first human grunts and mumblings, that finally I might be unearthing the lowest deposits of language, the first words themselves.

*

I have decided that I will try to find the other parts of me. I can no longer count time, and ever since those first seconds when my body was all and then diminished, I have been losing pieces of me slowly, losing contact, as though the many fragments of myself were slowly disappearing from the radar screen of my consciousness. This scares me. Each time a fragment disappears—that sudden moment of loss, as though a limb were cut off—every part shudders. If it does not stop soon, I will lose touch with every part of us, with everything.

I must start systematically. I must map the vectors of the explosion and see how widely scattered the original wreckage was. I need information on current strengths, on wind speeds, on local storms and weather patterns. I need to know what parts of us are likely to have sunk to the bottom, and what parts are likely still to be floating, bobbing toward some distant shore.

This is not easy. I have tried to use the aid of dolphins. They are intelligent, and with their sonar, they might easily be able to locate many of my parts. But they do not understand me. When I get one close enough to shout at it, it approaches, nudges me quizzically, but then moves on, having lost all interest. I have tried with the sea birds that occasionally fly past. Sometimes I see them picking at the scraps of flesh that dot this ocean now, as though it were all a single vast carcass. But the birds are equally estranged by my calling out to them. They quickly take flight, their wings flapping nervously. And all the time, I am drifting further and further apart. Soon, I will be scattered across the globe. Soon, my pleadings will be heard by the birds in the Amazon and fish choking in the Thames, by fisherman off the Red Sea coast, by the stone faces on Easter Island. Somebody must hear, somebody must understand.

*

My colleagues laughed when I first told them about my ideas. They all thought I was joking. I suppose it would seem funny at first, strange at least to someone who has not studied the evidence. But it was all there. I felt confident I could back up my claims with scientific evidence.

Ellen came in to see me one day. She was then finishing her PhD, and I could see the frown of concern on her face. She was determined. She said the work I was doing was crazy, it was useless. That ever since Ethiopia, I had lost it.

261

How can you possibly hope—she was almost shouting, her hand stabbing the air—to reconstruct a language from a stupid hyoid? If nothing else, what kind of sample size is one hyoid? She looked again as she had that day when she jumped out of the jeep, her face contorted in loss and anger, the small gun in her fist, firing into the air.

I let her go on. I knew she was worried about her reputation. If it got out—and it no doubt already had—that her advisor was a crackpot, her chances of ever getting a job would quickly crumble beneath her. I sympathized, but I knew then—as I know even more strongly now—that I was right, that my work would be vindicated. If only I could have been given a chance to present the evidence.

I tried to reassure Ellen. I tried to downplay my claims, to tell her that what she had been hearing were exaggerations, that it wasn't a language I was trying to reconstruct but rather the level of cognitive and linguistic potential. This wasn't true. I had reconstructed the language, but I wanted to wait until I had an opportunity to present my evidence to my colleagues in a proper environment. Ellen left, still worried I could tell, although she smiled as she walked out. But she was right. It was Ismail who had started it all.

The language I had reconstructed was one of grunts and squawks, of deep aspirated vocalizations, of long growls. I learned all this from the hyoid, from how the muscles and ligaments had been attached, how the tongue had to have moved. In my office, alone, I practiced those sounds, slowly trying to get my mouth to form such strange and distant voices. I was sure I had them, because in them I detected that ancient sound I had heard in Ismail's scream: the sound of an atavistic fear, the fear of *everything*. Alone, at night, making sure no one loitered in nearby corridors, I would let out that scream, as though I too had become a Neanderthal facing something so terrible it defied comprehension. I did not know exactly what it was, but I knew the sound, the scream that gave birth to everything.

*

This ocean feels endless. The first time I walked out across the badlands in Ethiopia, I imagined that I had finally found the meaning of desolation. But I would return to those badlands in a fast second. If only I had been scattered by the vultures, become a fossil myself. But here, all this water, and I can find no part of me that makes sense anymore. When I found my lower jaw, some teeth still intact, it was jabbering incomprehensibly. I was glad when the current pushed it away, its squawks fading among the growling waves. I am afraid now that I might find the other parts of what is no longer me, no longer comprehensible.

*

The last I heard of my father was a letter from a neighbor of his in the cramped tenement where he had lived during those final years of his life. It was a brief note telling of my father's death. He had had some last words for me, but the neighbor hadn't understood the language.

I had known he was dying of cancer. I visited him once in those years when he told me what he had never been able to tell my mother. It had been some years since I had seen him. After my mother left him, he hid from us, refusing ever to give us a current address. All we knew of him were the monthly checks sent dutifully. Finally, we received a letter from a friend of his, saying he had asked me to come to see him. My mother was not mentioned.

He lay in a confining, single bed in a small one-bedroom apartment in Greenwich Village. There was a pleasant view from the window, and on the roof, he said, was a lush, well-watered garden. The room was full of language books—books on Arabic and Swahili, Kazakh, and Uzbek, Urdu and Sinhalese, and many, many more. He looked so much older than I ever remembered. A thick comforter covered his thin body. I made the two of us tea and sat down on a chair by the bed to listen to whatever he wanted to tell me. I had no questions for him.

It was because of the Esperanto classes he and my mother had taken that she left him. She couldn't take his obsession with that crazy language anymore, and one day she had packed what she could into three large suitcases and hailed a taxi to her cousin's house in Flushing. My father told me now that she had never understood why he wanted them both to learn Esperanto. It may have seemed a little foolish—especially now that only a few decades after its birth, it was already a dead language—but he had had a reason.

He said that one night, when he was six—perhaps seven, he no longer knew—the whole village was awake, and the night had become a carnival. It was summer, those weeks before the monsoon broke the spell of heat and sweat that made such thick, airless nights. My father didn't know why the people were out. It was no special festival, no holy occasion. Not even the Sikhs in the village seemed to be celebrating

263

any holy day. He went from person to person asking, Why, Babuji? but no one would answer, saying only, Go play with your brothers.

The year, he said, was 1947. The month before, many of his friends had left the village. When India and Pakistan, born as twins, began their sibling rivalry, Muslims were fleeing west across the border while Hindus and Sikhs came east. Those who didn't leave—or were too slow, or were caught (whether at night or in the daytime) on the roads or on the trains—were often killed by whoever was at hand, by whatever weapon was the quickest and most bloody. All the Muslim children he had played with were gone. Where is Sharif? he had asked his mother. Where is Hasan? But she wouldn't answer. Go outside and play now, baccha, was all she said. He had walked over to their houses, but they were deserted. Everything was gone, the doors smashed down, the small fences broken.

Then had come the night that resembled a carnival. Everyone in the village—those that were left, the Hindu and Sikh families—stood in nervous clusters close by the railway tracks that passes through the village. The women brought out sweets and drinks for their husbands and fathers, and the men told jokes, laughed, fell into sudden, uneasy silences. Some were carrying guns, others short blades or kitchen knives, and others just sticks, spears, clubs. The children played war around their parents' feet. My father battled his friend with a twig, shouting loud, pretending he was Arjuna, always victorious.

When he first heard the distant pant of the train, the vibrations resonating along the tracks, there was sudden silence. Somewhere far off, my father heard a voice. Everyone began to move back from the tracks. Someone tugged at his hand, pulling him along, Go home now, go to sleep, they had said. But my father stayed, hiding first among all the legs, then behind the tall wheel of a cart.

No lights were on the train that finally approached. Before he could make out anything more than its shadow and starlight catching the clouds of steam, there was a shattering explosion. The sky lit up, the stars momentarily hidden. The train buckled, was hurled from the tracks. The night filled with screams. The crowd surged forward, waving sticks and knives, guns setting the darkness on fire. My father said he could make out little, could barely see what was happening. All he heard was the screaming, the shouts, the sounds of clubs battering at bodies.

Hours later, in the hot dawn, the ground was a red swamp of blood. Much of the crowd was still there when my father appeared, tired, from his hiding place. There were bodies all around him, beaten, knifed, shot. A hand grabbed his ankle. He recognized the face—it was the father of one of his friends, a Muslim, who had left the village only a week before. There was a knife wound across his face, and his chest was soaked in blood. My father screamed.

*

I was flying to Delhi when the bomb exploded. I had boarded my connection in New York. I was to give a paper on my research in the incipient language of early humans at the conference on the archaeology of Aryan races and their precursors. My paper was only tangentially related, but it was the only meeting that had accepted my synopsis. When I was transferring planes I thought about my father and the last time I had seen him in his apartment.

In that room, he said that he had once thought Esperanto the only hope. If only people could learn a common language—anything, even Latin, he had laughed hoarsely. He knew he was wrong to have pushed it on my mother. He wished he had told her what he had seen, but he never had. The blood that lapped up against the railway tracks was more than he could tell her in any language.

But without a common language, what hope is there? he asked me. I placed my hand on his wrist, surprised to find how little flesh was left. It was almost all bone. With his other hand, he waved weakly around the room, motioning to the piles of books. These past years, he said, I've been trying to learn every language. I thought that if the world doesn't learn one, I will learn them all.

*

I do not know who set the bomb. No doubt some group claimed responsibility. The Tamils or Sikhs or Biharis, or maybe the Hezbollah or Kurds or Greek Cypriots or the Red Army Faction or the Libyans or Welsh nationalists or the Basque or Puerto Ricans. It doesn't matter much to the dead. I do know I was standing up—I had wanted to get an article out of my briefcase in the overhead compartment. I clicked the hatch open, held out my arm in case anything should fall, reached inside for the handle of my briefcase. That was the last thing I remember. Seconds later I was scattered across the Atlantic Ocean by the force of the explosion.

265

I once told my father that I was studying anthropology at Chicago, that I would soon finish my PhD, and that one day I hoped to lead expeditions in Ethiopia or Kenya. He had smiled at this. Anthropology, he said, isn't all bad.

I've floated so far out that there is nothing on all sides of me except water and sky. I can no longer see any wreckage from the plane. I have no notion of how long it has been—days, months, years. I am all alone. I hear no other part of me, only the sound of the waves, sometimes the wind. I no longer hope to find the other parts of me. Some time ago, I heard my own voice. I was arguing with my right knee, which had floated by. We were both saying the same things, exactly the same, but all I heard were grunts and mumblings carrying an old sensation, a fear in both our voices. I so much wanted to know what part of my body I was. As we floated apart, I thought of my father, who had wanted desperately to understand everyone. And those last words of his. Incomprehensible.

Nominated by Judith Ortiz Cofer, C.E. Poverman, The Georgia Review

JERRY'S KID

fiction by ROBERT SCHIRMER

from WITNESS

I WOULD LIKE TO speak on behalf of my son," the father said. "That's not necessary," I told him.

"No," he said. "It is. Every word is necessary."

It was 3:30 a.m. and I had been asked to sit with the family. The hospital was short-handed, this was Labor Day weekend, and when cutting to the bone of the matter, what did I have in my life that was more pressing?

A doctor actually asked me this, a pale, old man whose lesioned skin cast an odor like soft fruit. The sad truth was, I couldn't answer him.

The family were parents to the boy who held up a Quik-Mart on the L-section of highway that connected the yellow fields of throat-high corn to the town lumber yards and smokestacks. Seventeen, face shining with doped-up glory, the boy had waited until the store was free of truck drivers and marginals and quarreling lovers who couldn't find their way on the map, then he thrust a gun at the cash clerk's temple and said, "I've got a bullet here just waiting to set up house."

Only the clerk packed a gun, too, in a side-drawer he kept always open. He was Fully Prepared, he told me later, when I first arrived on the scene with Len, my partner, and we clamored into the store with our oxygen and tubes and stretcher . . . he was Fully Prepared for the moment any fucked-up someone busted into *his* store and tried to make off with *his* life.

"Yes," I said. I was the first to kneel beside the boy sprawled across the tiles, both hands clutching his heart, which had slipped outside the hole in his chest. I ran my fingers through the boy's sweating hair. This

267

situation had me stumped. I was a paramedic, not Christ. The blood was everywhere—pooled over the tiles, settled beneath the beef jerky and magazine racks, stained across potato chip and cigarette cartons. Drops of it had already bloomed across the front of my uniform. If I were Christ—and I couldn't help thinking this—the spilled blood would be wine now, and instead of his own choking tongue, the boy's mouth would be filled with bread, rich whole bread I had conjured out of nothing more than my own desire to change things. Inside my head I would hear music and parables, not static. I couldn't let go of these thoughts.

"Jesus," Len said, shaking a blanket over the boy's body, covering his face and the silver gun lying beside him. "This one's a scene."

I folded the blanket back down around the boy's neck. "He's not dead," I said. Len stared in bafflement and located the pulse in his own throat. He had only one more year before retirement.

"My father owned a home furnishings store," the clerk said. He was rearranging items on a rack—packets of gum, spotted jelly beans, licorice sticks, red and black. I nodded and, with Len's help, hoisted the boy onto the stretcher. He was heavy to lift, but once in our arms, so very light I envied him such weightlessness. The boy mumbled to the angels I was certain had already descended upon the room. I could see them, or nearly, aglow around us, shouldering me out. "He knew the names of his customers," the clerk continued. "He sold rugs and velvet armchairs, he sold them sofa cushions and weed killer for their gardens."

The clerk was not a bad man. He had his business, his memories. As Len and I carried the broken boy out the door, the clerk cried after us, desperately, "What's your hurry?"

Now I stood on assignment in the echoing hospital hall with the boy's father, waiting to hear his son's fate. The clerk, I was certain, was telling his father's story to the police by now. Len had gone home, and the boy's mother had wandered off somewhere. I drank lukewarm coffee from a styrofoam cup and watched as the father stared out the window, breathing barely onto the glass where his fingertips lightly rested. Outside there was nothing much to see but lampposts, lighted windows, vacant buildings. For a moment I saw the giant shadow of something moving, and imagined a helicopter rising out of the darkness, or a prehistoric bird someone had forgotten to tell me about, but in the end it was just a billboard of the Marlboro Man, shivering in the wind to the joys of nicotine.

"He would never have pulled the trigger." The father turned to face me with this watershed.

"All right."

"No. I know you've heard this before. A man of your profession, the things you must have heard. All the excuses. But my boy . . . "

The father groped for the precise words. I couldn't look him in the face because it was unlike any I'd stared into before. Grief, regret, rage, denial, too many emotions to name were jumbled together, competing for expression, so that his face looked constantly in flux. I was looking right at him and I could not have told you the shape of his head, for example, or the color of his hair or his eyes. How could eyes be expected to hold such fevered emotion and color too?

"I don't care what you think of me," he said. "But you must not judge him as a son. He was a good boy. He didn't mistreat us."

"I wasn't thinking in any way about him as a son," I said.

"A boy picks up a gun, you think he means to use it? You think that's what he means?"

"I'm not a father."

"Guns, knives, what ends up in a boy's hand, that's not the point. It's not what's *real*. The real him." The father's eyes seemed to be burning down to some base element—liquid mercury, quicksilver. "Even a good boy, a first-rate son, will do these things, he will hold these objects, destructive things in his hands, a test of some kind, a challenge maybe, but it's not what he *means* to be doing—"

The father stopped for nothing more than a rattling breath, which I suppose fanned the flame inside him. "So don't tell me he meant to steal, he needed that money, hell, I have money, my wife and I would have given him the money, anything he wanted with all of our hands—"

"I believe you," I said.

The father struck me once in the jaw, hard enough to land me at his feet. I lay in surrender for a moment across the cool tiles, surveying the angles of the world from this position. I felt shot up with Novocaine, everything drugged and out of reach, not such an unpleasant feeling. The father leaned over. I thought he would drop across me like a sawed tree.

"Now you're sorry!" Veins popped out in his neck, those stinging eyes. "Now aren't you sorry?"

I stood up and walked away from him. I might as well have shot the boy myself, the way I was feeling. I had seen men on fire before, racing away from an exploding railcar as if they believed they still had a chance. Children sawed out of twisted car wrecks were placed in my arms, in their delirium mistaking me for a parent carrying them off to sleep. "Night," they breathed out of their swollen mouths and tried to turn over. And there were the old women with broken hips and collarbones and femurs, who mumbled gratitude as I lifted them off their floors or bathtubs or even the blue ice in the back yards of their lonely, unheated homes.

I'd seen good things, too, of course, and occasionally a wonderful thing. Once I saw a man and woman so frenzied with passion they danced atop a moving streetcar in a rainstorm while stripping away their office wear. Tie, blazer, shirt, nylons, all were cast down over the rails where the car had just been. The woman kicked off a shoe and it spiralled into my hands, I don't remember many things better than this.

My secret: during a rainstorm, I often open my window and hold the shoe out until it's filled. I drink from the woman's heel. You can't find water that good beneath your feet or at the crest of a mountain.

In this state, I wandered in to the TV lounge. I didn't realize until I was seated that a woman occupied the far end of the sofa. She was maybe forty and sat erect, unflinching, something beautifully numb about her, yet she clutched the sofa arm like she was spinning in a cup on an amusement park ride, and her mascara was streaked. I saw so much of the dying boy in her drawn face that I didn't feel the need for introductions. She stared at the Labor Day Telethon on TV. No one distinct was doing their act at four in the morning, because who would be awake enough to notice them? A fat woman who looked obliquely like she had once been a casual celebrity sang the high notes of some Broadway show tune. Applause was followed by a plea for donations. The telethon, we were reminded, fought a disease that rendered children motionless, digesting bone and muscle down to putty. I studied the phone volunteers in the background—smiling and drowsy-eyed, young and old—searching for someone I may have serviced once who was now doing well.

"Amazing, isn't it, how many people are up at four in the morning, willing to lend a hand?" I said. I could not feel my teeth or bottom lip. We were alone in the room except for an old woman in a far corner chair, squeezing medicated drops into her eyes.

"I don't know any of them," the mother said. She looked over at me. "Your lip's swollen."

"Your husband hit me."

"Yes, he would. Uniforms don't mean much to him. They've become the enemy." She looked as if she were fully ready to say more or fully ready to stand and go to him, but she ended up doing neither. She turned back to the TV. A boy in a wheelchair was brandished onto the stage, head a paperweight his wilting neck could not hold. While the boy struggled to articulate his name, the host brushed hair off the boy's forehead and managed a teary smile. The fat woman clasped her hands to her chest and nodded, yes, yes. "Well," the mother said. "Do you suppose those two rented the emotions along with the suits?"

"They mean well," I said. "Their hearts are in the right place," I added after a silence. Then this seemed like exactly the wrong thing to have said, so I let the silence alone after that.

"I don't know," she said vaguely. Her hands sought her own throat, stroked her veins, her collarbone, and for a moment I thought she meant to claw herself, until I understood she was moving more from exhaustion than panic. "I've known three children who have died over the past two years," she continued. "Can you imagine? Three. One was a friend of Tom's. Naturally I've *read* about dozens more in the papers. Not one has died from this disease, not one. Do you think I've missed something?"

Tom. This was the first I'd heard the boy's name spoken. At the bottom of the TV a list of donor names ran like ticker tape. Tom Gibbons passed over the screen, E. Gaylord, $40. I imagined this Tom with his wife and two children. He was up so late or so early because his own son had the flu or maybe a cold and Tom Gibbons had to feed his boy children's aspirin and talk him back to sleep. He called in his donation on a whim, because he'd turned on the TV for a few moments, saw the boy in a wheelchair, and thought, *Children's aspirin can't make the crippled children walk.* $40 was the price for banishing forever from his mind the image of a boy deteriorating in a chair, freeing Tom Gibbons to concentrate once again on the small comforts of his own son's minor, passing virus.

"I will tell you this," the mother continued. "One of Tom's friends had a heart attack. When he was twelve—*they* were twelve—he swam across a pool, and when he stepped out into the breeze, he dropped on the ground in a seizure. This was not the friend who died. The doctors said it was heredity, this heart attack, but his parents' hearts were strong as racehorses."

By now I had run out of things to even pretend to say.

"The point is, of course, that when Tom came to me later, and asked how he could tell if *he* was getting a heart attack, how would he know the signs, do you know how I answered him?"

271

"No," I said.

"Neither do I. For the life of me, I can't . . . I was probably busy doing something else. In the back garden, maybe. There was sun. Wasps. He probably waited for a minute and then walked away."

Down the hall, Tom's father began screaming. It was a sound of grief so terrible it bordered on rapture, a sound that could turn lives around and begin them again in a new place. I thought, *I should not hear this,* and yet I listened, even with relief. We knew what it meant without anyone's explanation. I turned to the mother as the reality of this moment struck her and lodged deep; she bowed slowly inward, wrapping her arms around herself as if she were her own child. All the while she did not tear her eyes from the TV. A drum rolled. The dollar signs flipped over into the next million. Bright lights flashed, the fat woman jumped up and down and wept. The host embraced her, the two swaying mightily above the displaced boy, who stared out from the screen upon us all. "Shame," the mother said.

Nominated by Witness

HAPPINESS: A MANIFESTO

by MARILYN CHIN

from ZYZZYVA

So, THE SUN SHINES, through the jacaranda trees; the purple flowers opening, opening imperceptibly. And it is only Charles and me, Charles and the feeling of him inside me. And that strong angle of descent, the visage of his pink, fleshy torso; starting from his sinewy neck down past his swollen, yet hard clavicle down to his groin. His beauty, his male beauty, is a feeling that I know; it is not anything that I could sum up, pontificate on, illuminate via a terse and explosive gender discussion with my radical women friends: on our "mindful" level, in the great dialectic of things, he shall always be the hegemonist/ oppressor/invader. The imperialist other who keeps us dissatisfied and yearning. As politically correct as I am, in that verbal bliss of the university, despite my own personal contentment, I continue the usual feminist dyed-in-the-wool diatribe against male domination: jeer at the Hemingway specialist down the hall with his love of spare, laconic fishing lore or Moby-Dick reduced to a male partriarchal writer's swollen cock, too large to be conquered in one sitting.

Yet this woman of the world secretly goes home and lives for a simpler love—somebody to look over the beaujolais and say, "Darling, the pasta is superb." That wonderful combination of garlic and x-tra x-tra virgin olive oil, that pungent tang of fresh roma tomatoes and, of course, the secret three fingers of green chilies, preserved in vinegar à la Charles. . . . Naked under his rococo apron, he would hum Debussy and meander in our small connubial kitchen, strutting all that love he harbors in his beautiful heart. He is the softer part of my "double consciousness." When I cross his threshold, I kick off my sensible

273

shoes, slither into my silky, sequined skin, lie back like some self-appointed goddess. And all weekend long, the birds are chirruping and the sea is savagely beautiful. And we would feast and fuck, feast and fuck, breaking all the ideological barriers until Monday morning. . . .

When the cold slap of "conviction" jars me awake and I put on that postcolonial/scruffy tweed jacket and on to the local Southern California state university to teach Introduction to American Ethnic Literature and I, the infernal goddess—with hanks of black unruly hair, thick wire-rimmed spectacles, brown sensible shoes—I shall represent all the oppressed female intellectuals of the Third World. I shall begin each day by reminding these spoiled blond surfing children that their fore-fathers were slave owners, their grandfathers were Chinamen killers, their fathers were patriarchal pigs . . . their boyfriends were possible rapists . . . their presidents were institutional criminals, their police force—a testosterone parade with nightsticks and battering rams.

And this month, in my office I call "the tenth orifice," I shall secretly preside over meetings with five powerful women litigators to initiate Project Alpha. We shall try to find a loophole in the university law code to get rid of fraternities forever. Those hellholes that suck up decent, malleable young men and turn them into opportunistic, money-grubbing, women-raping, racist, war-mongering, hegemonist Republicans! We have dubbed our secret society "The Nutcracker Suite." At least two of us are black belts in some exotic martial art form. I, naturally, fancy Wing Chun, a close-range form invented by a very small Chinese woman, 4 feet tall, 85 pounds. The idea is to move closer to the opponent, that is, two inches from his chest in a decep-tive embrace-gesture—and then, powww, a quick fist up the nose. He would see stars and a burst of rainbows before a panoramic blackness gripped him.

Meanwhile, the 5 o'clock bell chimes. My shoulders shrink back to normal size, and a smile spreads across my face, a pinkness blossoms, and I am hungry and wet and thinking about my love—how wonder-ful it would be to have his beautiful penis within me. I want him, this instant, as I am writing my last memo of the day, an endearing note via e-mail to my chairman:

Dear Chairman George Washington Franklin Hancock:
Your memo of yesterday, regarding reinstituting the canon
as a mainstay of our literature department, disturbs us
greatly; it rings of fascism, reactionary racism, and sexism,

274

and we, The Nutcracker Suite, demand that you enlighten
us as to your true intentions . . .

(Secretly, I still adore some of the dead male writers; they are like a
rich opium I snort behind closed doors. Inhaling goopy lines of Keats
is an onerous addiction I acquired during graduate school. I get turned
on to his poetic death-rattle: the sputum coagulating in his frail lungs,
his coughing hacking blood while he woos in that great European epis-
tolary tradition . . . and, ooh, how a lugubrious love-sonnet to Fanny
makes me sticky.)

Now back to my paltry memo and to that great tradition of memo-
invective. And right on the word "intentions"—I guess the im-
pingement is upon the absent modifiers of "good" or "bad"—and the
word "bad" conjures up many a wonderful fucking vignette involving
Charles and myself. . . .

One particularly succulent episode occurred in my tenth orifice,
during a sudden California earthquake delivered by the gods. Charles
and I spent that most glorious October morning fornicating on my
desk. I remember the elaborate maneuvering. First, we had to remove
my computer and laser printer and place them gracefully on the floor,
unstack and restack my present research on a Cantonese women
colony—silkworm breeders who collectively swore to be celibate. Al-
though it has not been thoroughly documented, the entire colony of 8,000
(plus silkworm breeders and mulberry-tree attendants) were known to
be militant lesbians. I went to this village in 1988 and taped oral his-
tories of these women's daily lives. To my dismay, the research turned
out to be boring narratives on horticulture, and on fish emulsion/
peatmoss/nitrates; human fertilizer/humus; and mandibles of caterpil-
lars . . . all subjects lacking in metaphorical interest. There were no
fructifying double entendres to be found. I just couldn't pry them
open to talk about their lives. The project bored me and I soon aban-
doned it—20 audiotapes/historical books/copiously noted and all—to
collect dust on the nethercorner of my giant power desk.

Now, when Charles and I finally moved this dinosaur off—oh the
dusty spines and femurs—paper clips, notecards galore—for a morn-
ing of naughty, insolent, remarkable romping, and I had worn that in-
valuable red thong with a slit on my woolly aperture and my love
slipped comfortably in . . . his halberd slightly irritating my entry—he
was biting my ear, uttering the most salacious dreams in all of the west-
ern empire. In my tenth orifice, we traveled the world. He was the

tour-guide, whispering in my ear, in French and Hebrew and various hybrid argots, offering all kinds of delectable treats; half-naked mulatto boys on the beach of Pago Pago; in and out and astride of the Leaning Tower of Pisa; in and out and astride the capsule of Gemini; betwixt and between the coffins of that gilded boy Tut and Chin Shih Huang-ti. OOOOOhhh baby, he murmured, OOhh Bathsheba, OOhh Lesbia, OOhh Mary Magdalena. OOhh the tundras, the prairies. Ohhh the furrows of the Dead Sea. How he plowed me backward and forward and forward, until I couldn't remember my race, my color, my destiny. . . . Gender studies were now rendered moot or just the name of some dusty journal printed in Indiana. My post-colonial position in the world at this moment was supine. And now as his finger was focusing on my ninth aperture, his penis was fulfilling my tenth, and his tongue was deeply spelunking in my fifth and most cavernous enterprise . . .

Suddenly, he said something terribly appalling: "I am fucking you now in the bathroom of your grandmother's Hong Kong flat." I finally balked. Now there are forbidden avenues, fruits that should be left unplucked, frocks to be left unsullied. "Oh, all right, all right, forget that last narrative about the bathroom of your grandmother's Hong Kong flat. How about in the callaloo of your father's giant wok? Yes, that is wonderful, that is a way to get back at him for abandoning your mother, for making you peel ten thousand shrimps in his restaurant in the summer of 1969." We know it is the end of the Confucian world order when filial piety meets the erogenous zone.

Then he whispered, "In the heavens. We are now fucking in the heavens." I said, "I can't. I just happen to be a leftist, radical, feminist, Marxist Chinese American separatist who believes in God. She would not approve." He continued, rocking me back and forth, in and out; the metal desk under my ass felt cold.

The cultural anthropologist next door pounded, "Hey, hey, what in hell are you doing? Hanging pictures? Fucking again, Ms. Asian American Poet!" And I let Charles harpoon me, as I howled my humpback-whale mating call.

Against our throbbing and pounding and the abstract melody of a busy campus in rain. Against the murmuring of our most verboten fantasies. Against the zen of willful subversion, we fucked. A distant telephone rang in the dark corridor. Nearby, my colleague, Dr. So-and-so Smith, was having a loud confrontation with an enraged Pocahontas. "You gave me a B, you pig," we heard her say. And suddenly, in slow motion, the giant metal shelf cradling the A through Z of major and minor female literary genius starting toppling: Alcott, Aidoo, Bradstreet, Aphra Behn (sadly unopened), and both Brontës as stout bookends, Browning (Liz, not Bob), Bishop (collected), and Mama Gwendolyn Brooks (fraught with Christmas greetings), Cather and Cixous, Chopin (Kate, not the pianist), Dickinson, Doolittle, Eliot (George, not Tom), Hooks and Hurston and Hong-Kingston, Jordan (Oh sister river!), Li (not Po, but Ch'ing Chao), Lessing (lots of her), Lowell (Amy's embarrassing Chinoiserie . . . well, better than Robert's iambic doldrums), Minh-Ha (alphabetized incorrectly) and Mew, McCullers poised with cigarette, Rhys, Rossetti, Rich (lots of her), Gerty, Gerty down to Stein and Soujourner: Truth is truth is truth . . . Silko and Mary Shelley . . . rolled off the shelves like tongues of the twisted sea . . . down past Wheatley, Wordsworth (a small pamphlet of Dorothy's) . . . down to Untermeyer (ughh, how did that mangy anthology get there?) . . . down to yet another misplaced minor male poet named Zukofsky (got that for Christmas from some pedantic L=A=N=G=U=A=G=E poet). The shelves came tumbling down. Oh Mother Jericho, what a historic occasion; how appropriately synchronized with our orgasmic paroxysms! The walls waved. The earth grimaced a giant gaping chasm. We stayed attached, cock and cunt, two multi-limbed creatures, fucking for dear life.

Nominated by ZYZZYVA

TIME AND SPACE

by IRA SADOFF

from THE AMERICAN POETRY REVIEW

I made her cry in public. They were singing, uproariously,
nine of them, all couples, save my wife,
dabbing her cheek with a handkerchief. Our betrayals

had been mutual, deleterious, densely textured,
less suggestive of Diana than Orestes. Then I'd left.
But they made no allusion to that schism, love, so

their happy faces must have seemed to her like prisms
of Cézanne's. The meal was all fable and deflection,
a melody sung off-key. Still, there was no denying it,

the shifting chairs, sudden coughs, subjects changing
with great alacrity. Across the water I heard no sirens
sing, though the harp of veins and arteries surely

had been plucked, reddening her stricken face. If only
art could make our stories larger. Dear friends
spared me the news. Years later, a thoughtless stranger told me.

Nominated by Michael Collier, Arthur Vogelsang

THE SECRET NATURE OF THE MECHANICAL RABBIT

fiction by PINCKNEY BENEDICT

from THE JOURNAL

THE GIRL WHO RESPONDS to Buddy Gunn's knock is young, maybe sixteen, maybe not even that old: the age of Buddy's little sister. She is wearing a thin cotton tee-shirt, and Buddy has a difficult time keeping his eyes off her chest. She stands on the other side of the screen door, her posture easy, indolent, as his gaze travels up to her narrow, small-featured face, then back again to her willowy body. She offers him no greeting.

Her tee-shirt is the color of old ivory from the many washings it's been through, a man's short sleeved undershirt. Buddy has on a sweatshirt that advertises a dog-racing track in the next county over. A cartoon rendering of a whipcord-thin greyhound decorates his shirtfront. The greyhound wears sunglasses as it streaks along, its ears pinned with speed to the sides of its long sleek head.

The girl rests a hand on her hip. She is on to me, Buddy thinks. And he thinks, Damn, and at the same time, Good for her.

"You want something," the girl says, and she folds her arms. Buddy breaks into a grin. The smile feels false to him, fixed, uncomfortable. He has seen beauty pageant contestants concoct much the same expression for the television cameras. He puts it on at each new door, hoping that it makes him look friendly, trustworthy, sincere. The girl does not return his smile through the brown doorscreen. "The whelps?" she asks him.

Buddy clears his throat. "Yes'm," he says, very polite. "I come about the whelps, as you say. I seen your ad in yesterday's classifieds." *Free to a good home 5 puppies bordercollie mix 6 wks old 3 boys 2 girls. Very cute, good with kids.* The clipping, along with numerous others more or less like it, is back in the van, in a green cardboard folder. The folder is beginning to tear along its spine. Soon it will be time to get a new one.

The ads have been gleaned from half a dozen newspapers in Shawnee and the surrounding counties. It is Buddy Gunn's job to respond to them. This is the first house he has visited today, but there are many leads in the folder, enough to occupy him for the next couple three days at least. Enough to occupy both him and his partner Willard, who sits hulking behind the wheel of the green Ford Econoline van in the driveway. Willard is large and hairy and unappealing, and he knows to stay with the van.

People are often uncomfortable when Willard is nearby. It is all the hair that turns them off, Buddy believes. The stuff sprouts weedlike from Willard's skin, it grows in stiff dark patches from the backs of his hands, his neck. It protrudes from his ears and from the moist wells of his nostrils. The hair that mats his arms and legs and shoulders is as thick and rank as a bear's pelt. Willard is strong and accommodating, but he is also terrifying to behold, like some forest creature that has risen up on its hind legs and wants to chat.

The girl glances at the van, and Buddy says quickly, "My brother." He immediately regrets the invention, imagining that the girl knows it for a lie. He cannot think why he might have said what he did. He has no reason to explain Willard to her.

There aren't any vehicles besides the van in the driveway, and that is a good sign. It means the girl is in all likelihood alone. The bitch that dropped the puppies no doubt belongs to her, and it is her chore to fob the little dogs off on people who want pets. The house is set well away from the paved state road, sitting aslant the points of the compass on a small lot in the midst of a yet-to-be constructed subdivision.

The footers of six or seven other houses have been set down and poured close by, and lots are staked off among the stunted fruit trees that dot the landscape. Stacks of boards lie near the footers, a lumberyard's worth of boards covered in leafy creeper. The boards on top are weathering, while those underneath them soften with rot. The house from which the girl peers at Buddy is old, idiosyncratic, ramshackle. It must have been the original farmhouse, he thinks, when this place was an orchard.

The girl unlatches the door. At first Buddy imagines that he is meant to come in, and there is a momentary embarrassing struggle between them as she endeavors to emerge from the house, he to enter. His hand brushes her arm, the door bashes him in the chest. He steps away in order to let her through.

"The puppies are in back," she says, and sets off at a brisk pace around the house, not looking to see whether he is following. She wears denim cutoffs that fit loosely around her slim waist. Her feet are bare and tough with callous, and she does not flinch or stumble as she strides over the variety of hard objects—bottle caps, the shards of a broken flower pot, bits of gleaming quartz gravel—that stud the dirt of the yard.

Still not looking at him, the girl says, "We'll have to get them away from the mother somehow." And Buddy thinks to himself, Bingo.

Buddy works for a man named Terry Robinson, whom everybody knows as Little Pig. They call him that because his nose turns upward so that you can see unpleasantly far into it and his cheeks are round and red and fat. Little Pig doesn't mind the nickname. He thinks it's funny, and sometimes he grunts and squeals in such a realistic swinish way that it makes Buddy uncomfortable.

Occasionally Little Pig will bump against Buddy with his head, shrieking like a boar hog. Buddy pushes him away at such times, jokingly at first and then more roughly as Little Pig keeps it up, squealing more and butting harder. Often, they end up shoving each other around the metal prefab shed that serves as Little Pig's workplace, Buddy using his hands, Little Pig using his head and shoulders and his thick, muscular torso.

Willard laughs like a wild man whenever Little Pig takes on so. Willard thinks Little Pig is a card, a regular caution. Buddy, on the other hand, would like to quit working for Little Pig. If he ever gets the chance to go back to work at the dog-racing track, back to the job he has lost, he will leave. Buddy loves the dog track, the pungent animal smell of it and the constant racket of excitement, the colorful shower of discarded tickets at the end of a race. He also loves the quiet, deserted feel of the place at the end of a long day of racing.

And he loves the dogs, the fleet greyhounds with their long arched necks and graceful heads and almond-shaped eyes, eyes that survey their surroundings utterly without expression: no greed, no affection, no surprise or dismay. Eyes that look only for the mechanical rabbit that leads the hustling pack around the oval of the dirt track, eyes that constantly search after the lure, even from within the steel crates where the greyhounds spend their time between races. Their training is almost unbearable to Buddy in its perfection. But a racing dog must never manage to catch the rabbit. It is a thing Buddy learned early on at the greyhound track, and he has not forgotten it. Once a dog catches the rabbit, it knows it for a fake and it will never race again.

Buddy feels sure he'll go back to work with the greyhounds one day, when the tracks are doing better, when the owners can afford more help. Until that day comes he will work for Little Pig. Little Pig owns a fighting dog that he has named Monster, and Monster keeps Little Pig's enterprise afloat with its astonishing prowess in the dog pit. Buddy Gunn has known a lot of dogs in his life, and Monster is hands down the worst dog that Buddy has ever seen; or the best. Monster is a savage, a remorseless killer.

Monster lives alone in a hutch of plywood and chicken wire, and it never makes a sound of any kind. Little Pig says its silence is proof of its lineage, its priceless dingo blood. It is this Australian heritage that makes the dog such a furious fighter, according to Little Pig. The dogs they have in the Australian desert are much tougher than regular American dogs, he says, and it's expensive to get the few imports in the U.S. to stand stud.

Little Pig has waited for years to get himself a dingo, and even then what he owns is in reality only a half-breed. Its mother was a thick-pelted fighting bitch named Queen Generator from up in the hills of the western end of the county. Monster's father, a nameless full-breed dingo, came to rut her in a covered pickup truck with Kentucky plates. Queen G, who all her life had been a death-dealer that never showed fear, was pushed shivering into the dark foul-smelling space under the truck cap, and the tailgate raised and latched behind her.

The dingo's owner leaned casually against the rear of the pickup and rolled himself a cigarette. He didn't offer the sack of strong-smelling tobacco to Little Pig. "You're going to have one hell of a litter there," he said, while Little Pig strained to see through the dark-tinted glass of the truck cap's windows. "If she lives through it."

"You should have heard the sound," Little Pig frequently tells Buddy and Willard. "It was like he was *killing* her in there!" It excites Little Pig to talk about the conception of his champion, his darling. Queen Generator was gashed and bleeding when she emerged from under the truck cap some time later. Both her ears had been bitten through.

When Monster builds a reputation for itself, as it has begun to in lo-cal fights, Little Pig stands to make a pile of money breeding it. He fig-ures to put a fiberglass cap on his own truck and go roving from place to place. Even quarter-dingo whelps are costly and hard to get. "We're going straight to the top together," he tells Buddy and Willard, mean-ing of course himself and Monster. He gives the impression that when he gets there, to the top, he will have left people like Buddy and Willard far behind.

Buddy and Willard procure puppies for Monster, to whet its ap-petite for battle. They feed the puppies to it in the days preceding a bout, getting its bloodlust stirred up. "A dog's got to make a hundred kills for every time it steps into the fighting pit," Little Pig tells them. "It's just like shoveling coal into a furnace, like stoking a boiler. The dog has to get a taste for blood. It has to kill without hesitating for a moment, an instant."

Monster never hesitates. It kills whatever they give it. They handle it with thick leather gauntlets and stout wooden poles.

When it was little, they gave it cats, several of them at a time sealed up together in a battered canvas bag. After a few months of that, Mon-ster graduated to puppies. As it turns out, puppies are easier to get than cats. In the spring, Buddy and Willard can easily fill the van in a few hours. Sometimes they manage to nab a half-grown dog, or a full-grown one, when they see it wandering along the berm, nose to the scattered gravel and hot dust, looking for roadkill. Little Pig especially likes them to bring in old dogs, with their weak jaws and crumbling teeth, because he knows they will not somehow accidentally injure his Monster.

The girl in the tee-shirt curses when she finds the bitch and puppies gone. A cardboard carton, half-filled with soiled towels, sits against the wall of the house, sheltered from the sun. The girl stirs the nest of tow-els with the toes of her right foot, as though she might dislodge a pup from the musty folds. "She's gone in under the house," the girl says. "It's a crawl space that she likes for nursing."

The girl's face is a long oval, her skin fine-pored and clear. Her hair is newly washed, and the scent of the soap she uses, like the crushed petals of wildflowers, carries faintly to Buddy. He can imagine push-ing his face into that hair, drinking in the fresh stinging smell of it. She gestures at the opening of the crawlspace, not far from the carton.

"You want me to go in after them?" Buddy asks.

The girl looks him over. "No," she says, "I'm littler than you. I'll go."
She drops to her knees and slips easily beneath the house. Buddy examines her rear end and her smooth flanks, the taut lines of her legs, half-ashamed of himself and his lewd thoughts but unable to look away. She and your sister probably go to school together, he tells himself. Maybe they share some classes. Maybe they are good friends.

He does not want other men to examine his sister in this covetous way, though he knows they do. He has not been able to resist the impulse himself at times. She is strikingly good-looking, his little sister, tall and lean and high-strung. In the family they call her Baby. She is like a racing dog, he thinks, a thoroughbred. He knows that, with dogs, it is acceptable to mate parents with offspring, but never brother with sister, the breed goes down quickly whenever that sort of thing starts happening.

The girl vanishes up to her trim ankles in the crawlspace. He can hear the sound of her voice. She speaks in a low, soothing tone to the bitch. He makes an effort to understand what she says, but her words come to him only as nonsense syllables.

A moment later she scoots backward out into the open again, blinking in the sunlight. A cobweb has caught in her hair, and her knees and elbows are smudged with black earth. The dirt makes her look like a child. Crouching, she holds out a couple of puppies toward Buddy, one in each hand. They are both males, small spotted dogs struggling and grunting, each one caught by the scruff of its neck. Their rear legs kick uselessly at the air. "What do you think?" the girl asks. She rises to her feet, still extending the puppies. The bitch appears briefly at the crawlspace opening, pokes her muzzle out into the light before retreating.

"They're fat ones," Buddy says. "Is it only these two? I thought there was more." He is disappointed at the meagerness of the haul.

"Just two left is all," the girl tells him. She is silent for a moment. "My Pop was flushing out his car radiator the other day, and he spilled some antifreeze on the driveway. The other pups got into the puddle, the two little girls and the one other boy."

Buddy guesses from the terms she uses for the puppies, *girl,* and *boy,* that she is the one who wrote the newspaper advertisement. *Free to a good home.* He can imagine her composing the lines, sitting at the kitchen table with the stub of a pencil caught in her fist, her face fierce with concentration as she looks to find the right words, words that will somehow, magically, secure her dogs a future. He has seen his sister Baby look so as she labors over her schoolwork.

The girl continues, "They lapped it up like they couldn't get enough of it. It took them a while to die from it, but they did die in the end. These ones here were the only two that didn't get any."

Buddy nods. "They sure do like that antifreeze, dogs. It's sugary to the taste," he says, "like syrup."

"Pop says it shouldn't ought to bother me. He says he'd of had to drown them pretty soon in any case. He says nobody's going to want to take them, and he won't have a pack of worthless hounds growing up around here. He says that's the way trash lives, surrounded by a tribe of mutts." Her voice is low and bitter. She puts the pups on the ground in front of her. They immediately set to work sniffing her bare toes and licking her feet. Their attentions cause her to giggle and kick at them gently.

"It's not so bad, drowning," Buddy tells her. "They say it's just like going to sleep." He thinks he may not have that exactly right, but he wants to provide some small comfort to the girl. He has to remind himself that he is not planning to give these puppies a good home. Soon, a day or two from now at the most, he is going to watch these puppies die.

The girl gestures at them. "So," she says, "do you want one of them? Which?"

Buddy hesitates. "Which? I'll take them both."

"All right," the girl says. She picks up the whelps again, gripping them around their pudgy bellies this time, and hands them to Buddy. They whine in identical voices as he takes them. He holds them against his chest, and the larger of the two nips at his chin with its needle-sharp teeth. "He likes you," the girl says. The smaller pup sits quietly. Its flesh is unhealthily warm against Buddy's hand, and he can feel its heart beating away inside its ribcage. The puppy's pulse seems impossibly fast, like the heartbeat of a bird.

"This one looks sick, don't it," the girl says, indicating the small pup. Its eyes are glassy. "It might be the distemper. Do you still want it?" She sounds almost hopeful that he will return the puppy to her. Buddy doesn't answer. He heads around the house, back to Willard and the van. The girl follows.

Behind them, the bitch emerges cautiously from beneath the house. She is an unsightly spotted dog, like the puppies, with a fringe of long silky hair along her low-hanging belly. She watches after Buddy and the girl until they are out of sight, and then she settles into the carton once again, rearranging the disheveled mass of towels to suit her slight solitary form.

When Monster entered the pit for its first fight, nobody in the watching crowd had any idea what to expect. The dog ambled about, its wedge-shaped, crocodile's head held low. It looked almost comical, with its undershot jaw and greasy, nondescript coat, its powerful forequarters and weak-looking hind end. It snuffed the air absently, nonchalant, and appeared to have no idea where it was or what it might be expected to do there. Buddy waited. A couple of fellows behind him speculated about what sort of a dog this new one might be, or whether it was even properly a dog at all.

"Tear him up," Little Pig said, almost inaudibly. "Tear him up." He was twitching with excitement. He had waited a long time for this night, Buddy realized, perhaps all of his life. His small close-set eyes were fixed on Monster's blocky, smoke-colored form as it drifted around the periphery of the ring. It occurred to Buddy to wonder what Little Pig would do if Monster were to meet defeat; if Monster were to be badly wounded, to be killed. For an instant he felt something like sympathy for Little Pig, or kinship with him.

A long moment passed before Monster's eyes lit on the opponent dog, which was a tough little pitbull variety from the Shawnee County highlands, a veteran fighter. Monster's stance grew rigid, and its eyes seemed first to darken and then to blaze with angry light. Its lips drew back in a frozen, silent grimace, revealing the serrated rows of its teeth, its lustrous black gums. Buddy felt terror steal over him, as though it were he trapped in the confines of the pit with the terrible half-dingo, the basilisk, and not the hapless pitbull. Monster's hackles stood, the hair stiff as iron spikes between its hunched shoulders and along the ridge of its sloping back. It took several short, hopping steps toward the pitbull, which gamely, naively, swung to face it.

By Little Pig's stopwatch, it took Monster two minutes and seventeen seconds to swarm over and destroy the pitbull. In short order it broke the more experienced dog's front legs and then its spine. By the time the horrified owner of the pitbull thought to throw in the towel, it was too late for him to salvage his dog. The dingo had to be driven back from the body by the use of electrified cattle prods, even then refusing to be humbled. Monster stood facing the prods, mutely daring them, lashing out again and again at the hands that held them, the fingers, until Little Pig took the foaming dog up in his arms and, whispering endearments into its ear, carted it away from the ring.

"Listen," the girl says as they near the van. Buddy has his puppies now and he is loath to stop and talk. The girl's tone won't permit his ignoring her, though, so he slows his pace, finally halting altogether when she does. Her mouth is distorted, her lips drawn down and quivering, and he is surprised to realize how close she is to crying. He hopes that she will be able to control herself. She has her back to the van, facing him, and she is unable to see Willard, who mouths silent words of congratulation at Buddy and gives him a thumbs-up. He sweeps the girl's body with his gaze, and Buddy feels a sudden irrational fury at his friend: at the hairiness of him, his inhuman size and appearance, his pitiable ugliness.

"A woman called me on the phone yesterday," the girl says. "She told me she planned to call everybody that was advertising puppies in the paper. She said she was calling to give me a warning."

"A warning?" Buddy's mouth is dry. This is what it is like to be found out, he thinks. He has been waiting for the day when someone, some authority, anyone, will stop him in what he is doing. Lately he has not felt so sure that the day is coming.

The girl continues. "This woman said it was a couple of men going around the countryside gathering up the puppies they see in the paper. They work for a laboratory, and they use the dogs in their experiments. They try out different chemical products on them to see if they'll die. I thought it was a joke at first, but after a while of listening I didn't think that anymore. She sounded like she knew what she was talking about."

Buddy considers. "I believe I've heard of those fellows you're talking about," he says.

"And you're not them. You and your brother." The girl indicates Willard and the van with a nod of her head.

"No," Buddy assures her. The fixed grin is back in its place. "No, we're not." He joggles the puppies up and down, one in each hand, and they cry out. He resettles them against his chest.

"I guess you wouldn't want a sick dog if you were," the girl says. "Not for science experiments and all." For a moment she looks directly into his eyes, and the strain on her face is easy for him to read: the strain of wanting to believe what he has told her, the strain of being unable to believe it. She knows where these two little dogs of hers are headed, he suddenly realizes, or if she does not know exactly, then she has a pretty strong idea. The realization repels him, and he turns from her, goes to the van, throws open the sliding cargo door. Heat spills from the dark interior of the vehicle, and with it the musk of earlier cargoes of vanished dogs, a heady ghost-reek.

The numerous wire cages that Buddy keeps inside the van are plain to see. He throws open the gate of the smallest, pushes the puppies in, and secures it again. The weaker puppy, the sick one, sprawls on the floor of the cage, oversize paws extended, tail stretched out limply behind. The other, larger puppy stumbles over it, seeking a comfortable place to lie down. Buddy slams the van door on the sight of them before he turns.

The girl is gone. She has disappeared back into the weathered house, or around it perhaps, to the place where the bitch lies curled in its cardboard box. Buddy wonders briefly what the girl has seen, what she makes of the thing he has allowed her to see: all the empty cages stacked one atop another; the cages that will most assuredly be full by evening.

This is Buddy Gunn's most vivid memory. He stands at the edge of a shallow ditch in the center of a large hayfield, and the ditch is full of dead racing dogs. The farmer who owns the field stands in the ditch among the bodies of the greyhounds, his rubber hipboots covered to midthigh with white caustic lime, a four-tined manure fork in his hand. His son sits in the cab of a rumbling endloader, ready to tip a bucketful of earth onto the sprawled corpses. Buddy has hauled the bodies of the dogs to the field in the covered bed of a ten-wheel dumptruck.

The farmer comes toward Buddy, clambering out of the ditch like a figure in a dream, waving the manure fork, shouting. "What are you standing around gawking at?" he demanded to know. "What is it you think you're looking at downt here, boy?"

Buddy doesn't know why the farmer seems so angry. He's been looking at the greyhounds, of course. What else is there to see out in the expanse of the empty rolling meadow? What but the long clay-sided cut into the carpet of newly mown timothy grass. What but the dogs.

So many of them, he thinks, still taking in the branchlike tangle of impossibly slender legs, the jumble of heads and ears and whip tails. The farmer breathes heavily beside him, no longer speaking. The eyes of the dogs: open, closed, half-shuttered, wholly inscrutable.

He knew before this, of course, that they killed the dogs at the end of their racing lives. Knew the owners bludgeoned them, shot them, poisoned them, and the thought has troubled him; but so many. Until this moment he has been unable to imagine them in their proper numbers. So many.

"Nice ass," Willard says of the girl when Buddy climbs into the passenger seat. He backs carefully out of the rutted gravel driveway, mindful of the van's long wheelbase and its clumsy handling. He spent five years working in a slaughterhouse before this, lugging carcasses from place to place like a packmule in the frigid meat lockers, and the job that they are doing seems almost too easy to him. He is terribly happy to be working for Little Pig. He genuinely likes Little Pig. There is no air-conditioner in the van, but that's okay with Willard. He is sweating. Droplets of perspiration catch in the hair that covers him and shine there like jewels, like pearls.

"You're nothing but an animal, Willard," Buddy tells him. "Just a God-damned hairy beast."

"I know you are," Willard says, chortling good-naturedly, "but what am I?" He thinks Buddy is in a bantering mood.

"No, I'm wrong about that," Buddy says to him. "You're not even an animal. Calling you an animal is giving you extra credit. It's like an insult to the animals." He sees the hurt starting to register in Willard's mild eyes, and that only serves to make him angrier. "I don't believe—" He searches for words. "I don't believe I could even tell you what kind of a thing you might genuinely be."

"I know you are," Willard says. He realizes that it's not a funny thing to say, realizes now that it wasn't funny the first time, but it's the best that he can do. He continues helplessly to speak. "I know you are," he says yet again. "But what am I?"

Buddy fingers the doorlatch on Monster's hutch, but he does not open it. Not yet. He flicks the catch once with his forefinger, twice, a third time. It makes a high-pitched musical sound when he strikes it. He is alone in the shed; Willard has departed in the van, driven away without speaking after off-loading the day's take. Little Pig hardly ever shows up before eight in the evening, and that is two hours off yet. Plenty of time.

In his right hand Buddy holds a gallon jug of antifreeze. The jug is more than half full. He retrieved it from the trunk of his aging Chevy Malibu not long after Willard drove off, and he's been standing this way since. He can see Monster's tin waterdish just inside the door of the hutch. There is only a finger or so of tepid water in the bottom.

289

Monster is probably thirsty. Buddy pictures himself pushing the latch up, swinging open the door, tilting the jug, directing the thick greenish stream of ethylene glycol into the dish, where it glitters like seawater. He pictures himself using the flat of his hand, shoving the waterdish deeper into the noisome confines of the hutch, back to the place where Monster reclines, glaring resentfully at him.

The pups in the surrounding cages make a terrible racket. It is late in the day and they are hungry. Perhaps, Buddy thinks, he will feed them, after he has poisoned the dingo.

Right now it is fear, he knows, that paralyzes him, that keeps him from lifting the latch and pouring out the sweet lethal stuff. Curiously, though, he finds that, with every intake of his breath, every breath laden with the stifling odors of the trapped dogs that look down on him from all sides, his fear is waning. His thoughts are taken up instead with a single question: How much antifreeze, to make sure of Monster's death?

He'll come to the answer soon enough, he thinks, for there is no one to stop him in this act. No one, apparently, to stop him in anything he might care to do. His fear recedes continually before him, it pulls itself away like the feverish sheet of an outgoing tide. He discovers himself calm, and eager to see what exactly the fear will leave behind it, what desires, what neglected cairns of small anonymous bones. In the moment before he opens Monster's cage, curiosity alone animates Buddy Gunn. It consumes him. It draws him irresistibly on.

Nominated by Laura Kasischke

THE REVISIONIST

fiction by HELEN SCHULMAN

from THE PARIS REVIEW

IT HAD BEEN A hundred years since Hershleder had taken in a late af-
ternoon movie, a hundred years since he had gone to the movies by
himself. It was 5:45. There was a 6:15 train Hershleder could still make.
But why give in, why not not do something as inevitable as being home
on time for dinner? At heart he was a rebel. Hershleder walked up the
avenue to Kips Bay. There, there was a movie house. He could enter
the theater in daylight. When was the last time he had done that—gone
from a dazzling summer afternoon, when the air was visible and every-
thing looked like it was in a comic book, only magnified, broken down
into a sea of shimmering dots—into the dark, cool mouth of a movie
theater? It was a dry July day. It was hot out. Who cared what was play-
ing? Porno. Action. Comedy. All Hershleder wanted was to give him-
self over to something.

He was drawn to the box office as if the gum-chewing bored girl be-
hind the counter was dispensing pharmaceutical cocaine and he was
still a young and reckless intern—the kind he had always planned on
being, the kind Hershleder was only in his dreams. She had big hair.
Brown, sprayed and teased into wings. She had a dark mole beneath
her pink lips on the left-hand side of her face. It looked like the period
that marks a dotted quarter in musical notation. She was a beautiful
girl in an interesting way. Which means if the light were right (which
it wasn't quite then), if she held her chin at a particular angle (which
she didn't, her chin was in a constant seesaw on account of the gum)
when she laughed or when she forgot about pulling her lips over her
teeth (which were long and fine and, at the most reductive—canine)
she was a lovely, cubist vision.

Hershleder bought two tickets from this young girl. He bought two tickets out of force of habit. He entered the building, passed the two tickets toward the ticket taker and realized that he was alone.

Back at the box office, the girl wouldn't grant Hershleder a refund. She said: "It's a done deal, doll." But she smiled at him.

Hershleder gave the extra ticket to a bag lady who sat under the marquee where the sidewalk was slightly more shaded than the street, where the open and close of the glass doors to the air-conditioned theater provided the nearest thing to an ocean breeze that she would feel on this, her final face.

Hershleder the blind, Hershleder the dumb—oblivious to the thrill of a beautiful big-haired girl's lyrical smile, a smile a musician could sight-read and play. Blind and stuck with an extra ticket, Hershleder gave it away to the old lady. He wasn't a bad guy, really. Hadn't the old woman once been somebody's baby? Wasn't it possible, also, that she was still somebody's mother? Were there ever two more exalted roles in this human theater? This woman had risen to the pinnacle of her being; and she'd fallen. She suffered from La Tourrette. Hershleder held the glass door open for her; he'd been well raised by his own mother, a woman with a deep residing respect for the elderly.

"Bastard," said the old lady, smiling shyly. "Cocksucker."

Hershleder smiled back at her. Here was someone who spoke his language. Hadn't he seen a thousand and one patients like her before?

"Fucking Nazi prick," the woman said, her voice trailing low as she struggled to gain control of herself. Her face screwed up in the concentration; she wrestled with her inner, truer self. "Faggot," she said through clenched teeth; she bowed her head now, trying to direct her voice back into her chest. The next word came out like an exhalation of smoke, in a puff, a whisper: "Motherfucker."

The old lady looked up at Hershleder from beneath hooded lids— in her eyes was a lifetime of expressions unfortunately not held back, of words unleashed, epithets unfettered—there was a locker room of vile language in her head, but her face seemed apologetic. When Hershleder met her gaze, she fluttered her lashes, morse-coding like the quadriplegic on Ward A, then turned and shuffled away from him.

•

It was delicious inside the theater. Cold enough for Hershleder to take off his jacket and lay it flat like a blanket across his chest. His hand

292

wandered across his crotch, stroked his belly. In the flirtation of film light, Hershleder felt himself up under the curtain of his jacket. There were a couple of teenagers in the back of the house who talked throughout the movie, but what did Hershleder care? It was dark, there was music. Stray popcorn crunched beneath his feet. A side-door opened, and he got high off the smell of marijuana wafting on a cross breeze. An old man dozed in an end seat across the aisle. A beautiful girl on screen displayed a beautiful private birthmark. A bare-chested man rolled on top of her, drowning Hershleder's view. Above war planes flew, bombs dropped, the girl moaned, fire, fire fire. Something was burning. On screen? Off screen? The exit sign was the reddest thing he'd ever seen. It glowed on the outskirts of his peripheral vision. Time passed in a solid leap, as in sleep, in a coma. When the lights came up, Hershleder was drowsily aware that much had happened to him—but what? Couldn't the real world have jumped forward at the rate of onscreen time in quantum leaps of event and tragedy and years? The movies, like rockets hurtling a guy through space.

•

Grand Central Station

Hershleder waited for information. On the south wall was a huge photo essay, Kodak's, presenting the glories of India. A half-naked child, his brown outstretched hand, an empty bowl, his smile radiant. A bony cow. A swirl of sari, a lovely face, a red dot like a jewel amidst the light filigree of a happy forehead. A blown-up piece of poori: a bread cloud. The Taj Mahal . . . *In All Its Splendor.*

The lobby of Bellevue looked something like this. The women in their saris, the homeless beggars, the drug addicts that punctuated the station like restless exclamation marks. Inge, his chief lab technician, had told him that at the hospital, in the ground floor women's bathrooms, mothers bathed their babies in the sinks. Hershleder could believe this. There, like here, was a place to come in out of the cold, the rain, the heat.

The signboard fluttered its black lids, each train announcement inched its way up another slot. Hershleder's would depart from Track 11. There was time for half a dozen oysters at the Oyster Bar. He headed out past Zaro's Bakery, the bagels and the brioche, the pies of mile-high lemon frosting. Cholesterol—how it could slather the arteries with silken ecstasy! (Hershleder had to watch himself. Oysters

293

would do the trick—in more ways than one. What was that old joke . . . the rules of turning forty: never waste an erection, never trust a fart.) He hung a left, down the curved, close passageway—the tunnel that felt like an inner tube, an underground track without the track, an alimentary canal, a cool stone vagina. Vagrants sagged against the walls, sprawled beneath the archways. There was a souvenir stand. A book store. A florist! Daisies, bright white for Itty, beckoned from earthenware vases. This was a must-stop on his future trek to Track 11. The passageway smelled like a pet store. The horrible inevitable decay of everything biological, the waste, the waste! Hershleder did a little shocked pas de bourrée over a pretzel of human shit, three toe-steps, as lacy as a dancer's.

•

They slid down easily, those Wellfleets, Blue Points. Hershleder leaned against the polished wood and ordered another half dozen. Not liquid, not solid—a fixed transitional state. A second beer. So what if he missed his train? There would always be another. Death and taxes. Conrail and Erie Lackawanna. The fact that oysters made him horny.

They slid down cold and wet. Peppery. Hershleder wasn't one to skimp on hot sauce. The shell against his upper lip was blue and smooth, his lower lip touched lichen or was it coral? Pinstripes made up his panorama. The other slurpers were all like him. Commuters. Men who traveled to and from their wives, their children, "the Office." Men with secret lives in a foreign land: the city. Men who got off on eating oysters, who delayed going home by having yet another round of drinks. They all stood in a row at the bar the way they would stand at a row of urinals. Each in his private world. "Aaach," said Hershleder, and tipped another briny shell to his lips. His mouth was flooded by ocean.

Delays, delays. A lifetime full of delays. Hershleder the procrastinator, the putter-offer. Hershleder of the term papers started the night before, the grant proposals typed once into the computer, the postmarks fudged by the hospital's friendly postmaster. He was the kind of man to leave things to the last minute, to torture himself every moment that he did not attend to what needed attending to, his tasks, but also the type always to get them done. While in his heart he lusted after irresponsibility, he was never bad enough. Chicken-shit. A loser.

Hershleder's neighbor at the bar was reading *The New York Times.*

"Hey, Mister," said Hershleder, sounding like he was seven. "Would you mind letting me look at the C section?" Now he spoke like a gynecologist.

The neighbor slid the paper over without even glancing up.

Hershleder turned to the book review.

David Josephson. His old pal from college. A picture of the sucker. A picture; why a picture? Hershleder thought. It wasn't even Josephson's book. He was just a translator, that schlep was.

Josephson had not fared well over time, although to be fair, the reproduction was kind of grainy. A hook nose. A high forehead. He still looked brainy. That forehead hung over his eyes like an awning at a fancy club. Hershleder read the article for himself.

> A 1,032-page study of the Nazi gas chambers has been published. . . . The study is by Jacques LeClerc, a chemist who began his work doubting that the Holocaust even took place. . . . The book, written in French, (translated by that bald rat Josephson!) . . . presents as proof, based entirely on technical analysis of the camps, that the Holocaust was every bit as monstrous and sweeping as survivors have said. . . . It is also a personal story of a scientific discovery during which, as Mr. LeClerc writes in a postscript, he was converted from "revisionist" to "exterminationist."

Exterminationist. What a hell of an appellative. Hershleder shook his head, in public, at the Oyster Bar, at no one in particular. Exterminationist. Is that what he himself was? His beloved mother, Adela Hershleder, just a child, along with her sister and her mother, her father recently dead of typhus, smuggled out of Germany on Kristallnacht. His mother's mother lost six brothers and sisters in Hitler's crematoria. And the friends, the extended family, even the neighbors they didn't like—all gone, gone. Hershleder's grandfather Chaim and his grandfather's brother, Abe, came to this country from Austria as refugees after World War I, the sole survivors of the sweeping tragedies of Europe that did away with their entire extended family.

And *heerre* . . . was Hershleder, the beneficiary of all that compounded survival; Hershleder the educated, the privileged, the beloved, the doctor! Hershleder the first generation New York Jew, Hershleder the bar mitzvahed, the assimilated, Hershleder with the shiksa wife, the children raised on Christmas, bacon in their breakfast, mayonnaise spread across their Wonder Bread, the daughter who once asked him if calling a person a Jew was really just another way to insult him.

He was lucky; his ancestors were not. What could you do? Isn't this the crux of it all (the history of civilization): those of us who are lucky juxtaposed against those of us who are not?

Mindy and Lori, his sisters, married with children, each active in her own temple, one out on Long Island, one on the Upper West Side. Irv, his father, retired now, remarried now, donating his time to the Jewish Home for the Blind. Were they any more Jewish than he was? Wasn't it true, what his own mother had told him, that what mattered in life was not religion per se, but that one strived to be a good person?

Wasn't he, Hershleder—the researcher and, on Tuesdays and Thursdays, the healer (albeit a reluctant one), the father, the husband, the lawn mower, the moviegoer (he did show that bag lady a good time), the friend to Josephson (at least in theory)—a good person? My God, thought Hershleder, just imagine being this chemist, this LeClerc, having the courage to disprove the very tenets upon which you've built your life. But Hershleder knew this kind, he had seen them before: LeClerc's accomplishments were probably less about bravery than they were about obsessive compulsion: LeClerc was probably a man who practiced a strict adherence to facts, to science. After all, Hershleder had spent much of his adult life doing research. You let the data make the decisions for you. You record what you observe. You synthesize, yes, you interpret; but you don't theorize, create out of your own imagination needs and desires. He knew him, LeClerc, LeClerc the compulsive, the truth-teller. They were alike these two men, rational, exact, methodical. Science was their true religion. Not the ephemeral mumbo jumbo of politicians, philosophers, poets.

Hershleder and LeClerc: they told the truth, when they were able, when it stared them in the face.

Hershleder folded up the paper and left it on the counter, its owner, his neighbor, having vanished in the direction of the New Haven Line some time ago. Paid up and exited the comforts of the Oyster Bar and headed out into the festering subterranean world. He stopped at the florist to pick up those daisies, two dozen, a field of them, a free-floating urban meadow. He held the bouquet like a cheerleader's pom-pom in his hands.

"Daisies are wildflowers," said the florist when he wrapped them up, those hothouses posies, in a crinkly paper cone. What did he think, that Hershleder was a poster child? He'd been to summer camp, away to college. Didn't he live in the suburbs and have a wife who cultivated daisies of her own? Daisies smell awful, but their faces are so sunny and bright, so fresh, so clean, petals as white as laundry detergent.

As he made his way to Track 11, Hershleder had a musical association: "Daisy, Daisy, give me your answer true." He had a poetic association: "She love me, she love me not." He had a visual association: the daisy stickers on the leaded glass windows that faced his yard, the plastic daisy treads that his mother had stuck to the bottom of his bathtub so that he, Hershleder, her precious boy-child, the third born and most prized, wouldn't slip, hit his head and drown. The big bright patent-leather daisies that dressed the thong of his own daughter's dress-up sandals. The golden yolk, the pinky white of Itty's eyes when she'd been crying.

Hershleder walked through the vaulted, starred, amphitheater of Grand Central Station with a sensual garden, his human history, flowering bitterly in his hands.

•

"Smoke," hissed a young man in a black concert T-shirt. "Thai stick, dust, coke." The young man stood outside Track 11. Hershleder saw this dealer there, this corrupter of the young and not so young, this drug pusher, almost every day for months and months. Hershleder nodded at him, started down the ramp to the train tracks, then stopped. He had been a good boy. At Bronx Science he had smoked pot, at Cornell he'd done magic mushrooms once in a while at a Dead show—then usually spent the rest of the night in the bathroom throwing up. For the most part, he'd played it safe; a little blow on prom night or some graduation, but no acid, no ups, no downs, (well, that wasn't true, there were bennies in med school, valiums after), no needles in my arm, no track marks. No long velvety nights of swirling hazy rock songs. Drugwise, he was practically a virgin. Hadn't this gone on long enough?

Hershleder backtracked up the ramp.

"How much?" asked Hershleder.

"For what?" said Mr. Black Concert T-Shirt.

For what? For what?

"Heroin?" asked Hershleder, with hope.

Mr. Black Concert T-Shirt looked away in disgust.

"Pot?" asked Hershleder, humbly, in his place.

"Smoke," hissed the young man, "Thai stick, dust, coke."

297

"Thai stick," said Hershleder. Decisively. "Thai fucking stick," said Hershleder the reckless, the bon vivant.

And then, even though he was in danger of missing his train (again) Hershleder went back into the lobby of the station and officially bought cigarettes. He bought Merit Ultra Lights, thought better of it, backtracked to the kiosk and traded the Merits for a pack of Salems.

•

The john was small enough that if you were to sit your knees would be in your armpits and your elbows in your ears. Hershleder and his daisies floated in a cloud of smoke, mentholated, Asiatic (the Thai stick). The chemical smell of toilets on trains and airplanes permeated all that steam. The resultant odor was strong enough to etherize an elephant, but Hershleder the rebel was nose-blind to it. He was wasted.

The MetroNorth rumbled through the tunnel. Outside the scenery was so familiar Hershleder had it memorized. First the rude surprise of 125th Street, all those broken windows, empty eye holes, the flash of graffiti, of murals, loud paint. The decals of curtains and cozy cats curled up on cheery sills pasted to crumbling bricked-up tenements, the urban renewal. Then onward, the Bronx, Riverdale, Spuyten, Duyvil. The scramble of weedy green, the lumber yards, factories, houses that line the train tracks in the suburbs. At night, all of this would be in shadow; what he'd see would be the advertisements for *Cats*, for Big Mac attacks, for Newport cigarettes; usually of a man gleefully dumping a bucket of something over an equally gleeful woman's head. The lonely maid still in uniform waiting for the train to carry her home two towns away. A couple of emasculated teenagers without driver's licenses. A spaced-out commuter who had stumbled off at the wrong station. Hershleder knew this route by heart.

In the train car itself, there was always the risk of running into one of his neighbors, or worse yet the aging parents of a chum from college. Better to hang out in that safe smoky toilet pondering the meaning of life, his humble existence. He was stoned for the first time in years. Drunken synapse fired awkwardly to drunken synapse. His edges were rounded, his reflexes dulled. The ghosts that lived inside him spiraled around in concentric circles. Hershleder's interior buzzed. His head hung heavy off his neck, rested in the field of daisies. A petal went up his nose, pollen dusted his mouth. He couldn't really think at all—he was full to the brim with nothing.

It was perfect.

"Laaarchmont," cried the lock-jawed conductor. "Laaarchmont," ruining everything.

·

Hershleder lit up a cigarette and coughed up a chunk of lung. Larchmont. The Station. A mile and half from Casa Hershleder, a mile and half from Itty and the kids, a mile and half from his home and future heart failures. His eyes roved the Park and Ride. Had he driven his car this morning or had Itty dropped him off at the train? Had he called for a cab, hitched a ride with a neighbor? Where was that beat-up Mazda? His most recent history dissolved like a photograph in water, a dream upon awakening, a computer screen when the power suddenly shuts down. It receded from his inner vision. Must have been the weed . . . It really knocked him out.

Good shit, thought Hershleder.

He decided to walk. What was a mile and half? He was in the prime of his life. Besides, Hershleder couldn't arrive home like this, stoned, in front of his innocent children, his loving wife. A long stroll would surely be enough to sober him; it would be a head-clearing, emotional cup of coffee.

Larchmont. Westchester, New York. One curvy road segueing into another. A dearth of street lights. The Tudor houses loomed like haunted mansions. They sat so large on their tiny lots, they swelled over their property lines the way a stout man's waist swells above his belt. A yuppie dog, a Dalmatian, nosed its way across a lawn and accompanied Hershleder's shuffling gait. Hershleder would have reached down to pat its spotty head if he could have, but his arms were too full of daisies. He made a mental note to give in to Itty; she'd been begging him to agree to get a pup for the kids. There had been dogs when Hershleder was a child. Three of them. At different times. He had had a mother who couldn't say no to anything. He had had a mother who was completely overwhelmed. The longest a dog had lasted in their home had been about a year; Mrs. Hershleder kept giving those dogs away. Three dogs, three children. Was there some wish fulfillment involved in casting them aside? His favorite one had been

299

called Snoopy. A beagle. His sister Mindy, that original thinker, had been the one to name her.

Hershleder remembered coming home from camp one summer to find that Snoopy was missing. His mother had sworn up and down that she had given the dog to a farm, a farm in western Pennsylvania. Much better for the dog, said Mrs. Hershleder, than being cooped up in some tiny apartment. Better for the dog, thought Hershleder now, some twenty-eight years later, better for the dog! What about me, a dogless boy cooped up in some tiny apartment! But his mother was dead, she was dead; there was no use raging at a dead mother. Hershleder the motherless, the dogless, walked the streets of Larchmont. His buzz was beginning to wear off.

Why neurology? Mrs. Hershleder had asked. How about a little pediatrics? Gynecology? Family practice? Dovidil, don't make the same mistakes I made, a life devoted to half-lives, a life frozen in motion. But Hershleder had been drawn to the chronic ward. Paralysis, coma. He could not stand to watch a patient suffer, the kick and sweat, the scream of life battling stupidly for continuation. If he had to deal with people—and wasn't that what a doctor does, a doctor deals with people—he preferred people in a vegetative state, he preferred them non-cognizant. What had attracted him in the first place had been the literature, the questions: what was death? What was life, after all? Did the answers to these lie, as Hershleder believed, not in the heart but in the brain? He liked to deal in inquiries; he didn't like to deal in statements. It was natural then that he'd be turned on by research. Books and libraries, the heady smell of ink on paper. He'd been the kind of boy who had always volunteered in school to run off things for the teacher. He'd stand close to the Rexograph machine, getting giddy, greedily inhaling those toxic vapors. He'd walk back slowly to his classroom, his nose buried deep in a pile of freshly printed pages.

Hershleder was not taken with the delivering of babies, the spreading of legs, the searching speculum, the bloody afterbirth like a display of raw ground meat. But the brain, the brain, that fluted, folded mushroom, that lovely intricate web of thought and tissue and talent and dysfunction, of arteries and order. The delicate weave of neurons, that thrilling spinal cord. All that communication, all those nerves sending and receiving orders. A regular switchboard. Music for his mind.

A jogger passed him on the right, his gait strong and steady. Hershleder's Dalmatian abandoned him for the runner.

300

Hershleder turned down Fairweather Drive. He stepped over a discarded red tricycle. He noticed that the Fishmans had a blue Jag in their carport. The Fishman boy was his own boy's nemesis. Charlie Fishman could run faster, hit harder. No matter that Hershleder's own boy could speak in numbers—a = 1 b = 2, for example, when Hershleder arrived home at night the kid said:"8-9 4-1-4" (translation: Hi Dad!)—the kid was practically a savant, a genius! So what, the Fishman boy could kick harder, draw blood faster in a fight. Could Charlie Fishman bring tears to his own father's eyes by saying "9 12-15-22-5 25-15-21" when Fishman's father tucked him in at night? (Even though it had taken Hershleder seven minutes and a pad and pencil to decode the obvious.) Charlie Fishman had just beaten out Hershleder's Jonathan for the lead in the second-grade play. The Fishman father was a famous nephrologist. He commuted to New Haven every morning on the highway, shooting like a star in that blue Jag out of the neighborhood, against the traffic, in the opposite direction. Hershleder admired the Jag from afar. It was a blue blue. It glowed royally against the darkness.

The jogger passed him again, on the right. The Dalmatian loped after the runner, his spotted tongue hanging from his mouth. The jogger must have circled around the long circuitous block in record time. A powerful mother-fucker. Bearded. And young. Younger than Hershleder. The jogger had a ponytail. It sailed in the current of his own making. His legs were strong and bare. Ropey, tendoned. From where he stood, Hershleder admired them. Then he moved himself up the block to his own stone Tudor.

Casa Hershleder. It was written in fake Spanish tile on the front walk, a gift from his sisters. Hershleder walked up the slate steps and hesitated on his own front porch. Sometimes it felt like only an act of courage that could get him to turn the knob and go inside. So much tumult awaited. Various children: on their marks, getting set, ready to run, to hurl themselves into his arms. Itty, in this weather all soft and steamed and plumped—dressed in an undulation of circling Indian shmatas—hungry for connection, attention, the conversation of a living, breathing adult. Itty, with tiny clumps of clay still lodged like bird eggs in the curly red nest of her hair. Itty with the silt on her arms, the gray slip-like slippers on her bare feet. Itty, his wife, the potter.

By this point, the daisies were half-dead. They'd wilted in the heat. Hershleder lay them in a pile on his front shrub then lowered himself onto a slate step seat. If he angled his vision past the O'Keefe's mock turret, he would surely see some stars.

The steam of summer nights, the sticky breath of the trees and their exhalation of oxygen, the buzz of the mosquitoes and the cicadas, the sweaty breeze, the rubbing of his suit legs against his thighs. The moon above the O'Keefe's turret was high, high, high.

The jogger came around again. Angled right and headed up the Hershleder walk. His face was flushed with all that good clean high-octane blood that is the result of honest American exertion. He looked young—far younger than Hershleder, but hadn't Hershleder noted this before? Must be wanting to know the time, or in need of a glass of water, a bathroom, a phone, Hershleder thought. The jogger was jogging right towards him.

In a leap of blind and indiscriminate affection the Dalmatian bounded past the runner and collided with Hershleder's head, his body, his lap. David was stunned for a second, then revived by the wet slap of the dog's tongue. He was showered with love and saliva. "Hey," said Hershleder. "Hey there, Buster. Watch it." Hershleder fended off the beast by petting him, by bowing under to all that animal emotion. The Dalmatian wagged the bottom half of his spinal column like a dissected worm would, it had a life all its own. His tail beat the air like a wire whisk. His tongue was soft and moist as an internal organ. "Hey, Buster, down." Hershleder's arms were full of dog.

The jogger jogged right past them. He wiped his feet on Hershleder's welcome mat. He opened Hershleder's door and entered Hershleder's house. He closed Hershleder's door behind him. There was a click of the lock Hershleder had installed himself. That old bolt sliding into that old socket.

What was going on? What was going on around here?

Buster was in love. He took to Hershleder like a bitch in heat, this same fancy mutt that had abandoned him earlier for the runner. A fickle fellow, thought Hershleder, a familiar fickle fellow.

"Hey," said Hershleder. "Hey," he called out. But it was too late. The runner had already disappeared inside his house.

The night was blue. The lawns deep blue-green, the asphalt blue-black, the trees almost purple. Jaundiced yellow light, like flames on an electric menorah, glowed from the Teretsky's leaded windows. At the Coen's, from the second floor family room, a T.V. flickered like a weak pulse. Most of the neighborhood was dark. Dark, hot, blue and yellow. Throbbing like a bruise.

A car backfired in the distance. Buster took off like a shot.

Hershleder sat on his front step feeling used. He was like a college girl left in the middle of a one-night stand. The dog's breath was still hot upon his face. His clothes were damp and wrinkled. The smell of faded passion clung to him. His hair—what was left of it—felt matted. He'd been discarded. Thrown-over. What could he do?

Stand up, storm into the house, demand: What's the meaning of this intrusion? Call the cops? Were Itty and the kids safe inside, locked up with that handsome, half-crazed stranger? Was it a local boy, home on vacation from college, an art student perhaps, hanging around to glean some of his wife's infinite and irresistible knowledge? The possibilities were endless. Hershleder contemplated the endless possibilities for a while.

Surely, he should right himself, climb his own steps, turn his key in his lock, at least ring his own bell, as it were. Surely, Hershleder should do something to claim what was his: "If I am not for me, who will be for me? If I am not for mine, who will be for mine?" Surely, he should stop quoting, stop questioning, and get on with the messy thrill of homeownership. After all, his wife, his children were inside.

The jogger was inside.

Hershleder and LeClerc, they told the truth when it stared them in the face. In the face! Which was almost enough but wasn't enough, right then at that exact and awful moment to stop him, the truth wasn't, not from taking his old key out of his pocket and jamming it again and again at a lock it could not possibly ever fit. Which wasn't enough, this unyielding frustration, to stop him from ringing the bell, again and again, waking his children, disturbing his neighbors. Which wasn't enough to stop him, the confusion, the shouting that ensued, that led Itty *his* wife to say: "Please, Sweetheart," to the jogger (Please, Sweetheart!) and usher him aside, that pony-tailed bearded athlete who was far, far younger than Hershleder had ever been, younger than was biologically possible.

She sat on the slate steps, Itty, her knees spread, the Indian shmata pulled discreetly down between them. She ran her silt-stained hands through her dusty strawberry cloud of hair. There were dark, dirty half-moons beneath her broken fingernails. She was golden eyed and frustrated and terribly pained. She was beautiful, Itty, at her best really when she was most perplexed, her expression forming and re-forming like a kaleidoscope of puzzled and passionate emotion, when she patiently and for the thousandth time explained to him, Dr. David

Hershleder, M.D., that this was no longer his home, that the locks had been changed for this very reason. He had to stop coming around here, upsetting her, upsetting the children, that it was time, it was time, Dave, to take a good look at himself; when all Hershleder was capable of looking at was her, was Itty, dusty, plump and sweaty, sexy-sexy Itty, his wife, his wife, sitting with him on the stoop of his house in his neighborhood, while his children cowered inside.

Until finally, exhausted, (Hershleder had exhausted her) Itty threatened to call the police if he did not move, and it was her tiredness, her sheer collapsibility that forced Hershleder to his feet—for wasn't being tired one thing Itty went on and on about that Hershleder could finally relate to—that pushed him to see the truth, to assess the available data and to head out alone and ashamed and apologetic to his suburban slip of a sidewalk, down the mile and half back to the station to catch the commuter rail that would take him to the city and to the medical student housing he'd wrangled out of the hospital, away from everything he'd built, everything he knew and could count on, out into everything unknown, unreliable and yet to be invented.

Nominated by The Paris Review

LOST

fiction by PETER GORDON

from GLIMMER TRAIN

IT WAS PAST NOON when the lieutenant saw the village.

He waved the cracked binoculars around, over the rickety hillside huts, serpentine ditches, mounds of crystallized animal dung, dark slabs of sleeping dogs. The whole thing seemed to cling to the mountainside like a burr. The main dirt road of the village rose up like a ribbon of gray smoke, splintering off near the top into dozens of tiny veins. Along the edges tall brown grass bent in the mild morning winds. Corporal Velasco and the others wanted to advance to the crest and check it out for themselves, but the lieutenant kept waving them back with vigorous hand shoos. Goddamn them—they were constantly putting him in the position of having to invent homemade signs and signals, so low was their military intelligence and so amateurish their sense of decorum.

To reach the village, they moved up a cruelly rising rocky path, the lieutenant trailing them, stoically watching their moldy green backs and breathing in their veil of dust. He saw them claw blindly at the shoulder straps of their bulging brown rucksacks. They palmed their thighs, pushing down with each forward thrust, an attempt to keep their rubbery legs working. They shook their shoulders to shift the pressure point, to roll it to any other place but where it was. They leaned forward, dipping their heads as though into a wall of wind.

They'd been marching on and off for five days now, soldiering pain—the pain that begins in the shoulder blades and spreads like a line of fire to the spine and sides, settles under the ribs, screams across the groin. One enemy was the irresistible urge to stop and have your joints lock up; the other was "soroche," altitude sickness, mountain madness. Right now they were floating at about four thousand meters, in air as light and transparent as the gossamer wings of the angel of death.

They covered a distance of five or so kilometers start to finish by the lieutenant's loose estimation—executing a final wide arc across three finger streams and through a mountain meadow of tall green stalks, the prickly bulbs of which rose up ominously to their throats—and reached the little village in a complicated web of late afternoon sunshine.

The villagers, seeing the advancing army, had gathered at the base of the settlement. Campesinos stood armed with crude homemade lances. The women were in wide-brimmed hats with red bands, big skirts with frilly waistcoats, rainbow kerchiefs, dark hairy sweaters. The men wore sandals, rope belts, poncho-like shirts, hats, and loose cloth trousers that fell only to their shins. Children scattered on the peripheries, some sitting on stones the size of craters, some crouched behind adults. Out in front stood the village mayor, a spindly spidery brown-skinned old man, long-nosed, high-necked, almost birdlike. His lance had a telltale blue string tied near the top.

"Velasco!" the lieutenant coarsely called out.

Velasco appeared, his sweat-stained green shirt untucked, one boot with a long untied lace trailing on the ground. It pissed the lieutenant off that the Indians up here didn't speak Spanish, and he didn't give a flying fuck about who was there first, who was native and who wasn't; this was the goddamn twentieth century, nearly the twenty-first, and some things should be givens. It also burned his ass that his official translator (and second in command) was a raw recruit who had done prison time for petty larceny. The level of trust hovered right around ground zero.

The army was turning to pure shit before his eyes.

"Ask him," the lieutenant said impatiently. "Ask him when was the last time the terrorists came through."

Velasco grimaced hard with his eyes closed. Half-Indian himself, he had a big dark face, kinky, curly hair, and a high rumpled forehead mottled with moles. His Indian words came slowly, unsteadily. As he listened to the mayor's answer, a smirk threatened to break out across his lips. "He says many nights ago. In the dark. Like bats."

"How many of them were there?"

Here the mayor seemed to be counting in his head. "Maybe twenty," Velasco translated. "Some of them kept to the shadows. Didn't dare show their faces."

The mayor walked over to the side of the road and pointed to a ditch. The lieutenant reluctantly followed. Cones of earth, like high

306

anthills, formed a little row along the spine of the culvert. One two three four five graves. The lieutenant lit a cigarette and squinted at the sun burning freely over the shit-brown mountains. A familiar feeling washed over him briefly, like a flash flood. Not grief or anger or despair over the inhumanity of it all—just a sharp pang of annoyance, the harbinger of a bad mood.

"So what's he got under there? Men? Women? Cats?"

Velasco had to have the mayor repeat his answer several times, and then he stayed mute for a few seconds.

"The rebels called the whole village into a big circle," Velasco said, his oversized hands describing the scene. "They accused everybody of being army sympathizers and committing crimes against the people's revolution, and then they picked out the biggest tallest boys and shot them once each in the head."

The mayor interrupted, causing Velasco to stumble. "Now he's telling me their names. You want to know their names, Lieutenant?"

The lieutenant looked at Velasco, at the mayor's moving mouth, at the makeshift graves, at the horseshoe of frightened villagers pressing in upon each other as though for warmth.

At the end of his monotonal roll call of the dead, the mayor smiled. Velasco smiled, too. "He says today is a great day for his village. Today, the national army has come."

The lieutenant couldn't decide which pair of eyes to settle on—Velasco's or the mayor's. One was lying. Probably both of them were.

"Ask him why they didn't kill him." Killing the mayor was standard practice up here in the high sierra. Usually the mayor and his family were symbolically executed in a public ceremony, after a crudely performed "people's trial." Most towns and villages they stumbled upon, the mayor was already eliminated, and for perfectly understandable reasons nobody ever seemed to want to take his place.

"He says he doesn't know why. He was ready to die for his people."

The lieutenant sent a thin line of spit through his front teeth. "Tell him he's full of shit."

Velasco shrugged and grinned stupidly. He moved his feet back and forth in the dirt in an awkward attempt to make the moment pass.

Silence followed. Faint whistle of wind coming across the valley below. Way up high, streamers of bluish sunlight glinted off the snow peaks.

"Tell him my soldiers are hungry. Tell him he needs to feed us. And ask him where we can sleep tonight."

The mayor tipped his lance as soon as he understood the requests. Velasco's voice, wearing out a little, rose in pitch as he tried to keep up. "There's a row of empty huts over there. He says to take any of them, as many as you want. He wants you to have his hut, lieutenant. It's the biggest one. He would consider it an honor."

The lieutenant frowned and scratched the side of his face. He was unshaven and licey and constipated and covered in raspberry-red rashes and more than that, he was completely unimpressed—he just wanted them to know that. He didn't give a fuck about being honored. You honor the dead. He flicked his wrist to wave the mayor off, but the old man just stood there gazing at him expectantly.

"Lieutenant, I think he wants to say something else to you."

The mayor's high dark cheeks radiated in the sun, the browned skin so finely lined it appeared to be swirling around like a cyclone. The terrorists would be back to reclaim the town at some point in the near future, he said through Velasco. They always come back. If they see the army's been here they'll kill everyone; they'll say everyone's contaminated.

That's how they are. And he's too old to resist them. Look at his hands; look how they quake. And his people are too scared. They pray to the gods every night—they lay their animals down on the altars and wait on the bird of sacrifice. They pound gourds into the shape of suns. They cut themselves open and let the blood fall, drop by drop, into sacred vessels.

The mayor rattled on but after a while Velasco stopped translating and just let his big ugly spotted purple tongue hang out in exhaustion and amazement.

The lieutenant lit a cigarette and slowly blew fractured shapes of smoke out of his nose and mouth. Everybody's wounded eyes were on him. A baby sitting on a father's head reached out to him. A small boy in a white alpaca poncho held out his cupped hands to be filled with God knows what gifts. The lieutenant stood there, untouched, unmoved. What was he supposed to do—save the whole fucking mountain?

"Prepare to encamp," he called out. He gave very specific instructions to Velasco, for Velasco to pass on to the men.

Then he walked away, scratching his raw flaky head right down to the soft open sores on his scalp.

He lay on a straw mat in the mayor's spartan hut, on the hard dirt floor, surrounded by cracked stone walls crawling with dark brown roaches and delicate gray spiders. It was a low cane hut, supported by crooked posts, with a roof of reed matting covered with a layer of mud. A shithole. His rifle lay in a diagonal line across his lap. He left on his grungy camouflage fatigues, his pistol belt, and his harness. His boots and socks were kicked off; blisters the size of peanut shells inflamed both his big toes. Through the lopsided window, unevenly cut out of the rough stucco, he saw clouds drifting across a shimmering white mountain peak.

He'd posted half his men as sentries and ordered the other half to sleep. He could see the backs of the big square heads of the two men on post—Velasco and Zavala. They were all completely cut off up here and completely blind to the situation. That was the grace of having slow wits under your command—they couldn't recognize the hopelessness of their own circumstances; they thought it was only storm clouds moving in. Of course, they were second- or third-rate sentries. They were poor marksmen and their minds wandered off like balloons. And they botched assignments almost by rote. If he sent out one mini-patrol to recon an area, pretty soon he'd end up sending out a second patrol to look for the first one.

Now he'd gone and gotten all these losers lost. They were a splinter group now, splintered off from the larger regiment, itself a severed piece of the greater regional infantry battalion of the Fourth Military Region. Six nights ago, acting out a routing flanking number, the lieutenant catching orders from an asshole captain with a hole in his head you could see clear through, they'd stumbled straight into a line of snipers as they crossed the river. Retreating blindly under cover of darkness, losing contact with the mother lode, they'd tried to follow the flow of the river, but it kept breaking off, and each break seemed to bring with it a new tributary that meandered off with a mind of its own. They tried to keep the covenant—always keep the river on your right—but it seemed rivers bloomed everywhere. They slowly worked themselves in one direction, then another. They slept in a cave the first night, in a bed of a deserted, rusting army truck the next. They had no vehicles, no radio equipment, no cellulars, no nothing. On the third day, they hit a hailstorm where the stones metamorphosed into plates of ice which sliced up their faces and hands. They crossed treeless plains where the only vegetation were ugly shrubs with sticky myrtle-like leaves, probably poisonous.

Now they were incommunicado and lost—sort of. The lieutenant bravely kept up appearances. He pretended to read his maps. He seemed to be charting a certain inevitable course. But he had to admit, if only to himself, that his sense of where they were was not up to strict military standards.

By his reckless reckoning, they were somewhere in the thirty-third quadrant of the farthest sling of the sierra. They were within smelling distance of the jungle, and just this morning Zavala—a teenaged gangly boy with huge ears and distended nostrils—swore he caught the whiff of fresh orchids.

So here he was, after five years in the military academy, a year in spec school, two years in intelligence school, two years in the officer corps, eight months of special courses in counterterrorism and counterinsurgency, and nearly a year in the field—lost in the sierra with a bunch of harps. On his shirt collar, his rank insignia floated inside a raised patch in the shape of a tablet: two gold bars signifying the rank of 1st Lieutenant.

That's about all he knew for sure about himself anymore. That he was a lieutenant, that he was lost, and that he was beholden to certain souls, among those souls one fat boy, one slow boy, one skinny pubescent, and one silver-tongued thief.

He intoned a mechanical Jesus, Maria y Jose and crossed himself without relish.

His Catholicism was as lapsed as his faith in the army, which was one more ruin in a country of ruins. Soldiers had no talent for anything more but fucking and dying—and some of them couldn't even manage those acts without instruction or assistance. They paid his men a lousy forty-five U.S. dollars a month. Some months they paid no one, like they just forgot you were out there.

The idea of it all rolled around at his feet like a live grenade.

He yelled out to one of the sentries to get Velasco and have Velasco get the mayor, and he meant now, he meant right now, no stopping to admire the goddamn view along the way.

While he waited, he dumped his rucksack on the mat. Three M-26 hand grenades spilled out along with a sheaf of maps tied together with a string, loose ammo shells, two revolvers, salt tablets, an extra pair of socks, a can of tuna, bits of broken glass, nail clippers, a porno mag, a cannister of bug spray, and a small framed photograph of his wife, posed in a blue dress, against a red wall, looking out at him with a kind of rueful smile, as though she were aware of his unfolding fate even before he was.

It was like her letter said—you're free now.

He shook apart one of the mountain region topographical maps and stared at it uncomprehendingly. The maps were numbered one through sixteen—he was looking at number six, as though it mattered—and everything was the same boring texture, brown, wavy, and meaningless.

The thing was, they'd been getting reports from the capital over the last few months that the guerrilla war was flickering out, that what they were seeing now were the last gasps of it. It wouldn't be long before the sierra returned to its customary doldrums, ruled by the wind and the shattered stones of extinct cultures. Jesus God help him, he was going to miss it. He'd miss it all. The smell of gunpowder. The black music of a night march, the cold rain pounding on your poncho, invading your dreams. The innocent faces of his men daydreaming about their girlfriends' pearly titties one minute and bellycrawling in wild panic across a stony delta the next.

Even stark betrayal, even getting your own oily heart ripped out, like when your wife informs you in a badly scribbled letter that she's embarking on a new life, taking your child, your car, your cash. Somehow, he'd miss that, too.

"Hey, Lieutenant, you wanted us?" It was Velasco standing in the doorway—there was no door, just the illusion of one—with the mayor smiling dimly behind him.

The lieutenant didn't look up. It took more energy than he wanted to expend just to nod.

This time the mayor spoke directly to the lieutenant, Velasco's words following close behind. "He's asking if you like it here. In his house."

The lieutenant had to smile, he had no choice, Velasco was so freaking stupid it was practically awesome to behold. "I love it here, Velasco. I love it so much, I never want to leave."

The mayor lit up at Velasco's literal translation of the lieutenant's sentiments.

"Now see if you can get him to show us our location on one of these maps," the lieutenant said. "Because I'm looking at them and all I'm getting is a bad case of the woozies."

An exchange of words. A wobbly pause. "He doesn't understand, lieutenant. He doesn't even know what a map is."

The lieutenant tilted his head back and opened his mouth, as though to taste the droplets of desperation hanging in the air. From this fucked-up posture, he still managed to bang his fist over and over

311

against the wall, raising white dust. Velasco blinked. The mayor raised his forearm, as though to ward off actual blows.

The lieutenant slunk to a far corner of the hut and slid to the ground, his knees raised up, his head rolling between them. "Tell him we're moving out in the morning. Tell him to get some food and water ready for us."

Velasco translated. The old man took a few steps toward the lieutenant.

He started to talk; Velasco started to talk.

"He wants you to take the children," Velasco said. "He says the rebels will be back. They'll burn and destroy everything. The big children can carry the little ones in their arms. It won't be a problem. You'll see. You won't have to do anything. They'll follow you. They'll do whatever you say."

The lieutenant kept his head down.

The mayor's voice kept going, Velasco's like a shadow inside it. "He says he'll give you everything he has. His best animals. His sharpest knives. His gold. Take everything. He doesn't care."

"Tell him no," the lieutenant said quietly.

"He'll give you a woman. He'll give you any woman—you pick her out. She'll be yours."

The lieutenant closed his eyes and saw dancing red pinpricks. He saw his wife's wet red lips. When he looked up, the mayor was still mumbling, and Velasco was staring at him like a dumb dog.

"Maybe we could take some of them," Velasco said, speaking directly to him. "I could carry a baby in my sack. So could the others."

The lieutenant looked at him. He was too young to know anything. He was a kid—he was only twenty-one, an overgrown child more than anything else; you sometimes forget that. It went for the rest of them, too.

"Velasco, this is a goddamn war we're into here. We aren't a mission of mercy. We're not a fucking orphanage."

Velasco looked crushed. "The revolutionaries will be back as soon as we clear."

"That's because we got the dumbest revolutionaries in history," the lieutenant said, putting his face as close to Velasco's as he could get it. "Our revolutionaries are so fucking dumb, they can't read the fucking writing on the fucking wall. The revolution's dead. It's dead all over, only our rebels are too dumb to know it. One of these days, they're gonna figure it all out. But we can't save every pisshole village waiting for it to happen."

312

"He says they'll all die, Lieutenant. Every last one of them."

"It's them or us, Velasco. It's his people or mine." The lieutenant raised his hand, made a stop sign of it. "So why don't you just cut the shit and tell what the deal is."

Velasco translated. He spoke so softly, it was like the sound of air escaping a baby's lips. The old man listened without expression, heavy head cocked, wasted eyes set permanently on the lieutenant.

Night fell.

The new sentry shift was Benavides and Flores, practically backed up to each other on a rise, one looking east, one west. They barely passed muster as soldiers. Benavides was a big kid, a big target, one of those full fleshy boys a bullet would have a field day tearing into. Flores was short and scrawny, with wiry black hair, skin the color of slate, and a look of perpetual fear on his face you had to be careful not to mistake for alertness or intelligence.

They looked sleepily at the lieutenant when he appeared at the window of the hut, and Benavides gave him a long lazy wave.

Using his flashlight pen, which sometimes worked and sometimes didn't, the lieutenant wrote some things down in a small journal he'd been keeping since they set out from base two months before. Mostly, he'd written down their position, their route that day, their supplies, his sense of the weather patterns. This time he wrote the names of his men: Zavala, Flores, Benavides, Velasco. Next to each man, he jotted down a kind of unofficial commemoration. Zavala: stupid, hopeful, naive, a virgin. Flores: ratty, careful, always having trouble with his stomach. Benavides: fat shit, slow moving, slow to anger. Velasco: the Indian giver. This way, if they all got raked, his amateur obits might survive.

After that he wrapped himself in an itchy blanket, smoked one of his last cigarettes, and drifted in and out of sleep. He had a flash dream that kept getting cut short. In the dream, he was walking through a field of glass trees, and each tree he'd pass would shatter, and the more he tried to pick up the shards and pieces the more pieces would rain down on him.

Each time he woke, he looked out through his weird misshaped window at his sentries. They seemed to him like little boys playing at being soldiers. He was responsible for them; they were on his head.

Up at three hundred hours, he lay on his back and waited; he'd given Velasco orders to wake him at five hundred.

Right now, he had no strategy other than to retrace their route, lead them across the same rivulets and ravines dotted with the same dying

313

trees, over the same broken-down bridges, up and down the same killer hills.

The next time he opened his eyes, a figure was standing over him. He instantly reached for his pistol and cocked it, ready to fire at the middle of the face, because even if you stray left or right, you've still got a healthy head hit.

A familiar voice started up. It was only him again—the old man, the mayor, el alcalde. He was gesticulating madly. He was beyond agitation. He spat out words, he aimed and fired them. He kept repeating the same sounds over and over, like a mantra. Blah blah blah, he was like a dog barking or a crow cawing, that's how much sense he made to the lieutenant.

The lieutenant tried to settle him, tried pushing him back gently, but the old man kept coming at him.

Finally, the lieutenant backed out of the hut and called Flores over. He gripped the boy's shoulder. "How the fuck did he get in there? He just walks in to your commanding officer's quarters and you do what? You stand there? You count your toes?"

"I thought it was okay if it was him," Flores said quietly.

"Flores, you tell me how I'm gonna save your ass if you don't save mine."

"Sorry, lieutenant."

"Sorry, lieutenant," the lieutenant mimicked.

"Sorry, SIR."

The lieutenant slapped him on the temple—a little wake-up call—and went back inside the hut. By now, the mayor was half-sitting, half-reclining, his head tilted against the wall. He'd taken off his shirt, and slashes of red appeared like glowing streaks on his chest, arms, and stomach. His skin was like tissue paper, his sharp bones like sticks bobbing on the surface of a river.

His eyes were open wide and pulled downward, as though the irises had been stretched into long liquid lines.

He'd thrust the knife way up into his chest cavity so that all but the wooden handle carved with strange icons disappeared.

His blue string was wrapped around the barrel of the lieutenant's rifle, so it looked like it was growing there.

The lieutenant had Benavides and Flores wrap the body in a blanket, carry it to the common gravesite, and begin digging a hole. All the

314

time he was digging, Benavides was crying. Big retarded oaf, who was he crying for?

When they were done, the lieutenant told them they'd done good work; they'd made a proper burial of it.

"Should we stick in a cross?" Benavides asked.

"Shouldn't we go get someone?" Flores said. "His old lady or something?"

"You two assholes worry about the things you're supposed to worry about," the lieutenant said.

He ordered them to retake their post. He stood over the old man's paltry pile of loose dirt and lit a cigarette. Eventually, he paced along the edges of the gully, playing with the thought that for the first time in his life he had no one to report to. He was floating loose. He sat on the damp ground and watched the sky go from black to blue to bars of streaky purple to a frayed blanket of pale yellow.

When the sun started to rise for real, he saw Velasco walking up to him, shoeless, his shirt wrapped around his waist, his pantlegs rolled up to his knees. The lieutenant told him about the blue string.

"He was making you mayor," Velasco said.

"Fuck you," the lieutenant said. "You don't know shit."

They were standing in the eerie half-light of morning, above the road that led down and out from the village. All around them, the mountains were taking shape, as though being created anew by the invisible hands of God.

The villagers started gathering in clumps, and the lieutenant couldn't figure out whether they were banding together by family or gender or what.

"What the hell are they doing?" he said to Velasco, who seemed to be silently blessing the whole operation.

"They think they're coming with us," Velasco said.

There were maybe fifty villagers. If he let them come, they'd be slowed down to a crawl that invited ambush—but they'd give off the illusion of a larger force, their army burgeoning from five to fifty. Not that they'd be good guides. According to Velasco, the villagers knew nothing about local geography. None of them had ever wandered beyond the surrounding valley. Half of them had never even been off the mountain. But they'd heard the old ones tell stories; they knew fantastic things were out there, rivers and ruins and the stone visions of the ancient empire they were all descended from.

"You should talk to them," Velasco said. He'd gone and come back. He was dressed; his hair was slicked back.

The lieutenant looked down at his feet. Velasco got too close.

"You're their leader now."

The lieutenant waved his corporal away, like he was trying to make him disappear. But fucking Velasco was right—something had to happen here. The commanding officer had to do something.

So he stood on a wooden box, an upside-down empty crate made out of whittled sapling chunks.

Spread out in front of him were packs of animals—hobbled vicunas, stricken llamas, lame dogs, skeletal cats, their dull coats splotchy with disease. The rest were men, women, children, a riot of shadows thrown across the dirt road, peaked by the pointy tops of their pull-on hats with the dangling pom-poms. He felt like saying he'd take all the shadows with him, but their bodies had to stay behind.

Finally, he wiped his mouth and looked at Velasco. "Fuck it. They can come. I don't give a crap what they do."

He stepped down and perched on the edge of the crate. The cables in his neck seemed to snap; his head fell.

Then the corporal disappeared into the heart of the throng. He launched into a long, steady drone of unintelligible sounds. At one point, he walked back up to the lieutenant and said, "Now I'm warning them about leg cramps on a long march."

When Velasco was done, he returned with an older man who had one eye swollen shut and scarred over, the other eye cloudy and vague. "Lieutenant. This one says he knows the way. A day from here there's a road. If we find that road, we're cool."

The lieutenant's mouth crumpled.

A young boy came up to them. "The kid says we head that way. Two peaks over, there's a big village somewhere. A real town."

"Does anyone know where the goddamn river is?" the lieutenant said.

"We'll find it," Velasco declared.

The people milled about, advancing a few tentative steps toward him, as though honing in on his thoughts. The men had fat bundles secured by long poles, their narrow faces grim and grimy. The women were bundled up in endless layers of petticoats, leggings, scarves. Children kicked at stones or danced around the animals. Then there were his other three soldiers, off to one side, locked onto him, trying to read him.

The lieutenant turned his back on everyone and slowly made his way to the top of the first rise. They all looked up at him, squinting, shielding their eyes from the sun. He needed a minute here—one lousy minute. He needed to eliminate distractions and think. A scrawny dog approached him, stiffened, crouched down, and yapped away. Velasco called out to him. The sun passed behind a soiled silver cloud.

He studied the vast expanse of emptiness overhead. He gazed at the shapeless horizons, the barely perceptible trails. That was the thing about being as lost as this. There was only one thing you could do, only one way you could go.

Nominated by Glimmer Train

SPRING SNOW

by ARTHUR SZE

from HANGING LOOSE

A spring snow coincides with plum blossoms.
In a month, you will forget, then remember
when nine raven perched in the elm sway in wind.

I will remember when I brake to a stop,
and a hub cap rolls through the intersection.
An angry man grinds pepper onto his salad;

it is how you nail a tin amulet ear
into the lintel. If, in deep emotion, we are
possessed by the idea of possession,

we can never lose to recover what is ours.
Sounds of an abacus are amplified and condensed
to resemble sounds of hail on a tin roof,

but mind opens to the smell of lightning.
Bodies were vaporized to shadows by intense heat;
in memory people outline bodies on walls.

Nominated by Ha Jin

COWS, ARROGANCE, THE NATURES OF THINGS

by TRUDY DITTMAR

from THE NORTH AMERICAN REVIEW

W E WERE DRIVING a jeep trail through a wide velvet valley, a gray wall of the Absaroka Mountains before us, when rounding a bend we were stopped by a cluster of cows. Ambling along the muddy ribbon of ruts that was the road, they'd heard our engine and, wondering what was here now, they'd turned to meet us with big, impassive stares. The woman riding beside me did three things. She wrinkled up her face, stuck out her tongue and, putting her thumbs in her ears, waggled her fingers at the cows. "I hate you," she spat at them.

The woman was an environmentalist; she worked for a number of national organizations that were trying to save the Earth. I wondered: why would a woman who works on behalf of the natural world stick her tongue out at a cow?

I was no rancher, and I too call myself an environmentalist. Still, I'd lived on a ranch once, and I'd had some vivid scenes of cow life burned into me. "If this woman thinks cows are just a heap of shit and flies with no brains, I have things to teach her," I thought, a hackle rising here and there. Not that I didn't appreciate the issues that prompted her. The cows-are-the-enemy attitude, its sources, its political expediencies were all familiar to me. But comrade in arms or not, my passenger's gestures didn't sit well.

The contingent of anti-cow environmentalists my passenger belongs to aren't the only ones to malign cows, of course. Many others with less

319

righteous motives disparage cows in similar, sometimes more hostile, ways. Most of them aren't even aware that cows damage fragile land and water supplies through overgrazing; they just think cows are dumb. "Stupidest goddamned things you could ever hope to see," they will say. Sometimes even so-called animal lovers will do this. In the same breath they'll extol the virtues of the bison and trash the cow.

Maybe we think cows are stupid because they're such easy victims for us—something along the lines of Groucho Marx's quip that he wouldn't want to belong to any club that would accept him: if these creatures submit so easily to our manipulation, they must be lowly indeed. (A cowboy might legitimately argue that, detail by detail, this manipulation isn't so easy. But when you consider how thoroughly we dominate cows' lives birth to death—tampering with their bodies, determining when they breed and with whom, appropriating their offspring, governing even the hour and manner of the young steers' deaths, and all this by the hundreds of millions—with all due respect to the rigors of cowboying, I think you can say overall we control cows with relative ease.) We manipulate other animals too, of course. But cows seem so passive. Whatever we do to them, much of the time cows more or less just stand for it.

Or do they? In the case of many of the other animals we manipulate so thoroughly, we actually seem to get through to them. We succeed in "breaking" horses. We get dogs to acknowledge us as boss. We say this is a sign of their intelligence, and by a certain definition it may be—although the idea that responsiveness to our biddings is a measure of brain power seems pretty self-centered. The thing is, though, after a course of our training the dogs and a lot of the horses offer us a kind of adulation. They don't just do what we want, they do it willingly, often even eagerly. But cows, while they tolerate us, just don't let us get through to them that way. They may not resist our efforts at manipulation so doggedly, but neither do they ever really give us the nod of assent. *Okay, so you're going to herd us. You've got us beat from the start on this one—it's our genes' orders to bunch—so we'll go along, but don't expect a show of enthusiasm.* They haven't much choice but to do what we want, but they don't flatter us that they've bought the idea as a good one.

Whenever we get animals to do what we want them to, what we're really doing is exploiting genetic predispositions; it's the dog's pack-animal nature, for example, which dictates his compliant behavior—as long as we manage to establish ourselves as a substitute for that alpha dog he's genetically ordered to submit to, that is. As for beef cows, most have a docile nature—they've had docility bred into them—and for our benefit (more flesh: more meat) they've had a certain cumbersomeness bred into them too, so at this point in their human-guided evolution they're no longer built, psychologically or physically, for effective rebellion or self-defense. Exploiting these traits we've fostered in them, along with their natural bunching behavior, we round them up fairly easily with our dogs and horses and bullwhips and crowd them into corrals, and once they're in there they're ours to do with as we wish. And to an uninitiated viewer much of what we do once we've got them there might very well seem not just fearsome, but probably diabolical, and maybe a little perverted too.

The herd is a serious security factor for bovids. Some wild cattle will collectively attack even a deadly predator—Cape buffalo, for example, will attack a lion—and even blind, lame, or otherwise handicapped individuals can thrive in such a herd. Although domestic cattle may not be aggressive enough to enjoy such solid defense as this, their reliance on the group is nevertheless very strong, and once we've exploited their bunching instinct by herding them into our stockades, we turn around and exploit their psychological dependence on it by isolating them. We run cattle through narrow chutes, separating them from the group they see as their protection. Then we pierce their ears with plastic earrings, day-glo tags with ID numbers on them and fly tags infused with pesticide. We immobilize them in webs of rope or in metal vises called calf tables and burn our symbols into their flesh. We cut off their horns, or "burn" them off with caustic, and if they're male we cut off their testicles. Segregated from the herd and confined in our contraptions, there's nothing much they can do about it. Given their nature, once they're released the most cows can do is run off bleeding and bawling, to band together again and hope for the best until the next time we come for them. And if we're talking in terms of intelligence, what's dumb about any of this? If they don't stand a chance against us, why fight a losing battle? But at the same time, why give us an inch more than they have to give? Maybe by human reckoning cows aren't as smart as dogs or horses in some ways, but on this count they seem to have good sense. And a certain stolid, self-respecting integrity too.

What's more, whoever pays attention will notice that cows aren't less-than-animal at all. Let them loose and they'll find forage just about anywhere—from grasslands to desert to forest to tundra—which is part of the reason my environmentalist passenger stuck her

321

tongue out at them. They're so "animal," so much a part of Nature, that they can get by eating the poorest, coarsest grasses, the most pitiful shrubs—even bark when all else fails. And cold weather has to be extraordinarily cold to be a problem for the right breed of cow. The cow has a multi-part stomach and chews a cud, meaning it can store food only partially digested in the first stomach part—the rumen—bringing it up later at will to chew and prepare it for final digestion and assimilation in the other stomach parts. In some breeds the contents of the rumen ferments at 40 degrees Celsius, providing these cows with a central heating system so that they don't need to generate extra heat by shivering or eating more, despite temperatures as low as -18 degrees Celsius. And the calves of such breeds are astonishingly hardy. Even born in below-zero weather, the calf of a Hereford or an Angus is soon up and cavorting around like a fawn in the month of May. Other breeds (Brahman and Santa Gertrudis, to name two) do as well in extreme heat, relying on a fleshy hump, or a generous dewlap, or long drooping ears, or a flap of flesh beneath the belly known as the underline to radiate heat away. Some breeds work without fatigue even in extreme climatic conditions, and with little food. Not even lack of sleep need be a problem for cows; they sleep in bouts of two to eight minutes, often with a total of no more than one hour in twenty-four. They're tough customers, cows, with a physical endurance any animal would be proud to match.

So why do we think so little of cows?

Maybe it's because we eat them. It takes some introspection, a little spiritual digging and turning over of stones, to acknowledge the complex virtues of a creature you're going to kill for food. And juxtaposed with that other possible motive—that tinge of self-hatred, Groucho Marx style—maybe in part it's our vanity. On the one hand, we look down on cows because they're so easy to manipulate. On the other, we scorn them because we can't get much of a rise out of them. If this bugs us a little, we rationalize it by saying they're stupid, not intelligent enough to feel much of anything: just look at that dumb blank stare. Once again this interpretation is anthropocentric, and it overlooks an interesting fact about the nature of cows. Cows have a rigid facial musculature that *prevents* a range of expressions. A dog can signal hostility or aggression through its facial expression, but a bull can do so only through posture and movement. The cow's blank look doesn't necessarily denote affectlessness at all, but oblivious to the cow's

322

proper nature, we interpret it as impassivity. Cows don't have the sensitivity of other animals, we say. Horses are high-strung, skittish, highly emotional in our eyes, and dogs quiver with love and the desire to please, but cows just stand there, as if (as we'd have it) they don't feel anything. But let me tell you a couple of stories about cows.

It should be just dusk, but the snowstorm has turned it dark early. The snow is falling thickly and the light of the pole lamp is only a lavender smear at the edge of the corral. Beneath it a cow lies on her side in the cow muck. Up to this point the heat of the muck has been melting the snow, as has the cow's body heat, but the snow has begun to stick now and the cow's red hide is covering over with a veil of white. She has been lying here for almost three hours with the tips of two little hooves and the swollen tongue of a calf sticking out her hind end.

When the rancher and his son gave up trying to pull it and called the vet, the cow was still struggling to get the calf out. At that point she'd been in this condition an hour. The vet was an hour from the ranch, but when they phoned him he was out on a call and there was the snow, so it's taken him twice the usual time to get here.

The cow is a little Hereford, a first-year heifer. One of the bulls on the ranch is a Charolais, and she accidentally got bred by him. Charolais are big white cows, one of the largest breeds, and they throw big calves, and you shouldn't breed a Charolais to a first-year heifer because she's too small. Last summer, though, the Charolais bull broke out of the bullpen and got to this little heifer, and now she isn't able to pass this calf. She appears just about out of whatever it takes to get through it, when the vet's headlights appear through the snow's whirl.

The three men bend above the cow, working. They try to get her to her feet, but no dice. They yank at her legs and shove at her swollen sides, finally wrestling her onto a tarp. Her feet are tied at this point, the two front ones lashed together and the two rear, and ropes are twined through the grommets of the tarp, and the men strain at these ropes. Her legs in the air, the cow moos in low moans, as the men, slipping in the snow and mud against the weight of her, drag the cow-laden tarp through the door of a nearby log shed.

In the shed the cow lies upside down mooing weakly. The men hang droplights from the ridgepole, and keeping her on her back they spread her front and hind legs in opposite directions, tying them to opposite walls so she can't kick. Kneeling over her swollen belly holding something that looks like a fire extinguisher, the vet sprays her with antiseptic. The cow's eyes roll, the whites showing, and she lets out faint moans, ever-dwindling protests of pain and fear.

The vet cuts through one layer of tissue, then another. Suddenly a huge slick grey balloon with veins running through it comes popping up out of the slit, part of her large intestine pushing out as the cow pushes to pass her calf. The vet presses down on the balloon the way you press down kneading bread, pushing stubbornly until he finally gets it back in. Eventually, he gets to the uterus and cuts that.

The vet drags a huge white calf out of the cow's belly and flops it down onto a hay bale. The little bull's sides are heaving and in a few minutes he's trying to get to his feet, but no one pays any attention to him. The cow's moos have stopped, her breathing is highly irregular, and for now all attention is on her.

Meanwhile, a little white heifer, just three days old herself, has been intruding periodically through the side door of the shed. When the men were binding and dragging the cow, the little heifer and her mother were standing at the edge of the circle of the pole lamp's light watching, and since then, all through the birth, one problem there's been to contend with has been keeping this little heifer from nosing in. Squatting at the head of the cow, watching to learn how the vet does the Caesarean, the rancher has had to interrupt his study many times to shoo the tiny heifer back out the door. Now that the birth is over, she has nosed back in again to catch the tail end of the commotion and to see the new calf.

Finally the cow is again breathing regularly, and the vet is finishing up his ministrations. The newborn lies all shaking on his hay bale. "I'm just a limp little fella, ain't I?" says the rancher, standing over it. "Cain't get up, just a limp little fella," he says. Opposite him is the little white heifer, having finally made it through to where she wanted to be. Across the hay bale from the rancher she stands, unimpeded, licking the little bull like a mama cow.

After the long hard delivery the Hereford was traumatized. She wasn't to get up for a couple of days, and as often happens with a traumatized first-year heifer, she wouldn't accept her calf. It was the little white heifer who took care of him. While he assisted the vet during the Caesarean, the rancher's son was figuring he was going to have one more calf to bottle feed, but he got a welcome surprise. It turned out all he'd be responsible for was ensuring the calf got his colostrum, a substance in the mother's first milk that provides immunity against disease until the newborn produces its own antibodies. After that, when the little bull was up and wobbling around, the little heifer coaxed him outside the shed to meet her mama, and from that day on he nursed from her.

Contrary to how this might sound, it didn't happen on Christmas, and this is not a little Christmas tale. This is a random, ranch-life event that happened one day in March, and the curiosity and generosity of the calf who took the abandoned newborn home to supper is pretty much run-of-the-mill calf nature; i.e., this is part of the way cows are.

The cow issue's a problem, no doubt about it. I have no quarrel with anti-cow environmentalists on that. Look at all the questions surrounding the cow. In a world in which one fifth of the people go to bed hungry each night, how can we justify eating beef when the grain used to feed one person an eight-ounce steak could provide 40 people with a meal? And in a world of dwindling resources how can we afford the 2,500 gallons of water used to produce a one-pound steak, and how can we afford the billions of tons of topsoil eroded in growing crops to feed livestock, the greatest consumer of which by far is the cow? And it's not just the water required to raise the cow, it's the water that's polluted and wasted through overgrazing of riparian areas. And it's not just the land devoted to crops that go to feed cows, it's the land that's eroded and rendered useless through overgrazing by cows. And in a world in which the number of plant and animal species is rapidly shrinking, it's what would grow on that land if it weren't overgrazed and eroded and what could live off that land if it didn't have to compete with the cow. "Biological diversity is the key to the maintenance of the world as we know it," says Edward O. Wilson, foremost expert internationally on biodiversity. He's not alone in his opinion. It's widely held that, working hand in hand with over-population, the accelerating extinction of species is the most serious threat to the healthy perpetuation of the biosphere. Like the car issue and the plastic container issue, the cow issue's a problem, no doubt. But is the cow the real enemy?

The cow is a cause of the deterioration of our environment. That's one way of looking at it. But another way of looking at it is this: the cow is not a cause but an effect. Over eight thousand years ago we began to develop the cow as a resource, when we began to domesticate the wild aurochs in Europe and the Near East. These wild cattle were six to seven feet at the withers, lanky and fast and agile and fierce, a far cry from the modern cattle we've produced. Witness a traditional prize-winning

325

Hereford. Thick-necked and broad-headed, deep-shouldered and so short-legged you wonder he's able to move, led around a ring on a rope with a ribbon at his temple, he's the result of a selective breeding process as old as domestication, but which has accelerated enormously since the development of modern breeds began in Europe and the British Isles in the 1600s, even more rapidly since the mid-eighteenth century. We've bred cows to grow faster and produce leaner meat (Charolais) and we've bred cows to withstand subtropical heat and ticks (Santa Gertrudis) and we've bred cows to withstand rigorous winter climate (Angus) and we've bred cows for easy manageability (Hereford), and on and on, not even to mention dairy breeds.

In short, taking advantage of attributes inherent in their nature, among them their natural hardiness and adaptability, we've bred cows so we could raise as many as possible, as easily as possible, to produce the greatest amount of meat, and we've deposited them all over the globe wherever they could survive, which is just about anywhere—the easier and cheaper for us, the better. In doing so we've taken a neutral creation of Nature and made it a positive force for our survival (food, shoes, etc.); but at the same time, it turns out, we've made it into a negative force. At this point, cows are serious contributors to environmental degradation, yes. But we're their keepers and promoters, the overseers of their breeding (in the U.S. cows now outnumber people by more than four to one), and it's we who decide what they're given to gorge on in feedlots (20 pounds of grain a day for 90 days), and it's we who determine where they graze (fragile public lands, among other places) and how long they're allowed to do so on any given stretch of range (traditionally, convenience to the rancher has been a chief determinant here). So in a sense, like the car issue and the plastic container issue and the air conditioner issue, the cow issue is man-made.

At the same time, however, the cow has its own Nature-given place in the biological scheme of things. And it has a Nature-given core that we haven't touched. We breed Anguses and Herefords, and we breed out fierceness and agility and breed in bulk and manageability, and brand and castrate and de-horn to our hearts' content. Still cows depend on posture over countenance to express emotion. Still they seek refuge in the herd. If they suffer badly enough during calving they're traumatized by the suffering and will reject their offspring. If the rejected offspring's lucky, another of his kind befriends him, another mother of his kind gives him nourishment. Despite our manipulations, a cow has its own essential nature and it behaves, sometimes regardless of us, sometimes despite us, accordingly. And if we pay attention, we notice its nature exhibits a good deal of depth and complexity.

Let me tell you another story about cows:

In June, when calving was over, the rancher and his son moved the cows to summer pasture. Because their summer pasture was a good forty-five miles away and their only access to it for most of the way was along a highway, rather than drive the whole herd on horseback, the rancher and his son carted them there in the back of a truck. They'd round up twenty-five head and haul them away, then several hours later they'd come back and round up another twenty-five head, making trip after trip until the whole herd was moved. They took the cows as they got them, and cow-friends got separated, and many times cows got separated from their calves.

When a truckload arrived at summer pasture, the cows already there were scattered all over. They were up steep sagebrush hillsides, they were down by the stream in the cottonwood groves. As soon as they heard the truck, though, they came running. Lumbering down hillsides, udders and underlines and loose neck flesh swinging, cows came mooing, and the more nimble little calves came bawling all the way. They gathered around the truck to see who'd arrived this trip. A cow or calf would come skittering down the ramp and its mom or its kid or its buddy would lumber or cavort up to welcome it.

When unloading was finished, a lot of cows and calves still stood around the truck mooing and bawling, demanding to know where their mom was, or their kid or their buddy, complaining the truck hadn't brought her, calling her as if she were still inside the truck. And they came running to meet every truckload until whoever they were calling for, blood or buddy, had arrived.

Even if you liked cows all right, if you were human you probably couldn't help having been tinged with the old human attitude that cows are somehow less-than-animal, and so watching this scene you couldn't help being a little surprised by this show of camaraderie and loyalty of the cows reunited with friends and blood, and you couldn't help being struck by the plaintive mooing and bawling of the ones whose anticipation of such a reunion had been disappointed. This was so especially if you were ignorant of another essential fact of cow nature, or if, having once known it, you'd come to lose sight of that fact. Female cows spend their lives in small closed herds, "groups of stable composition organized on the basis of personal recognition," as one student of cow nature has put it, meaning that cows choose their friends. Especially if you didn't know this, or had forgotten, you couldn't help being struck pretty powerfully by the nature of the cows, and how there was a good deal more to it than you'd bothered to think about.

It wasn't just my passenger's particular attitude toward cows that didn't sit well with me that day in that valley below the Absarokas. It was something to ponder: It might be that in this particular case she'd lost sight of Nature. Brainwashed over time through human custom, maybe even an environmentalist can lose sight of the cow as a creature of Nature, lose sight of the Nature in things.

I think it starts with control. Controlling the cow, subverting it to our uses, we begin to ignore its nature. We simplify it in our minds to our own concept of it—a creature with just those traits that fulfill our purposes, nothing more—and we stop seeing the full, subtle nature of the cow. And the less we acknowledge its nature, the more control we believe we have over it—and the more right to control—and on in a spiral we go. For usually it seems that the more we think we control something, the less we respect it, and the less we respect it, the less capable we are of seeing it truly and the more we see it as a tool/appurtenance/resource of ours. We de-nature it in our minds.

This may be the story in the case of the cow, and the story reminds me of a lot of others in the history of our dealings with the Earth. With the aid of our often splendid technology, we cleared forests, hauled boulders and stumps, plowed virgin soil, shored up waters, cut deep into rocks to dig minerals, and when we were through it seemed to us we'd tamed the Earth. Of course those who lived intimately with the mines or the fields or the dammed-up waters knew the constant vigilance required to *keep* the Earth "tamed." But to humanity at large—in most advanced societies at least—such elements as soil and water and vegetation seemed essentially conquered, where we wanted them forevermore. We saw the Earth then as pastoral and obedient, forgot for the most part the dynamic, unruly, extravagant body of activity that it was, except as a character in our old stories of subduing it. It had been that, and we had dealt with it, but now what it had been it was no more.

Still, the earth continued to express and proclaim itself as it always had, dropping lots of clues of its activity along the way. When we dammed the big rivers, silting resulted (many U.S. reservoirs are now 50% or more filled with mud) and, denied their natural annual over-flowing of banks, rivers responded with erratic, uncontrollable floods. In response to overgrazing by domesticated animals, the exposed soil increased Earth's albedo; with more sunlight reflected away, the land cooled, causing the air overhead to cool too so that it didn't rise as it once had, and so clouds didn't form as they once had, and so rainfall decreased, and as rainfall decreased there was still less plant cover, and greater albedo—and on and on toward desertification things went. In response to our pesticides, the pests we wanted to cancel developed hardier strains, or if those pests were in fact canceled, the species they'd once preyed upon flourished unchecked, presenting new pestly problems to us. When we pumped our pollutants into the sky as if to float them up and away forever, they came back down to us in the rain, poisoning our reservoirs and secluded mountain lakes, our backyard gardens and the wilderness forests, sickening us and remote fish and trees indiscriminately.

You can fill books with this stuff: example after example of human-ity punching the lump out of one side of the pillow of Nature, only to find a new lump popping out on the other side. But although in Na-ture's time the Earth's expressions and proclamations are big and full of consequence, in time measured by human lifespans they're slow and small, the early intimations of their far-reaching impact often lost on us, and because we're stuck thinking Nature is where we want it, we don't notice the new lumps for a long time. Or, who knows, maybe somewhere down deep in an old buried wisdom we *do* sense the hints Nature drops, but at the stirring of a faint, sickening awareness that we have never subdued Nature really, that we're not independent of her as we thought, we panic and stick our heads in the sand.

Whatever our reasons and motives, for a long time we've done the Earth as we've done the cow: de-natured it in our minds. We've focused just on what we've been doing to the Earth, and because we've failed to acknowledge what the Earth itself has been doing, in our minds it's seemed not to resist. And the longer we've managed to ignore its reac-tions, the more we've felt lords of the Earth, rightfully in dominion, and as we've felt our power more and more, we've felt the Earth's nature less and less. And the less we've felt *its* nature, the more divorced we've be-come from our own nature, and the more divorced we've become from Nature, the more justified we've felt in tampering heedlessly, and the circle goes on. But just as the cow acts and reacts whether we notice or not, so does the Earth, and in spades. And while the behavior of cows might go largely unheeded forever, the Earth's reactions have accumulated to the point that even if we would resist seeing them, we cannot.

One more cow story comes in October, after the cows have been hauled back down from summer pasture and gathered at the ranch where the rancher can put his finger on them for the winter, where he can truck them their hay every morning and tend to calving when it starts in mid-winter, if they need help. It comes after another bout of trucking cattle, this time loading up the little steers and some of the little heifers and hauling them away for good.

The cows stayed off in the fields on the ranch in question. You never caught them down around the corrals or the barns. They were lucky to have a nice-sized river flowing through their ranch, gravelly willow bottoms, cottonwood groves to meander through, and lots of flat, irrigated green pasture, and sagebrush hills to meander up and down when the fancy struck them, too. They stayed off in this bounteous varied land, never came down to the jumble of log sheds and pole barns where the corrals and humans were except when they were driven there—for branding and injections and de-balling and other indignities.

But the night after the little steers were hauled off to market was an exception. The area among the sheds and barns was filled with cows that night. We drove down after dark to check that some new water lines down there hadn't frozen, and cows filled the roadway and the turn-around, and all the packed down spaces among the sheds and corrals and barns were filled with cows. They stood bawling in our headlights, relentlessly. They stuck their necks out at our oncoming truck, their mouths open at it, and until we were right upon them they stood their ground, not shrinking from the beams of electric light coming at them, undaunted by the engine sound they usually shied away from. All night off and on we would wake and hear them all down there bawling, calling their lost calves, protesting the loss of them.

"What if hell was that we had to endure the suffering we've inflicted on animals?" a friend once speculated to me. I recalled those cow faces market-day night, eyes unblinking, necks extended, their bawling mouths held out to the two rounds of light coming at them in the dark—mourning in the headlights, recklessly.

Ranchers can't afford to pay attention to the more complex sides of cows because they're going to slaughter them. The general public can't afford to pay too much attention to their living nature because we're going to eat them. Anti-cow environmentalists can't afford to pay too much attention to a cow's creaturely complexities because they're trying to abolish them. It's the way of Nature that one life form sacrifices another to its own needs, and it makes it more bearable to do that if you de-nature the life form to be sacrificed, make it less "living," less like you.

Probably the image of those cows in the headlights sums up, as powerfully as you'd ever need to, why we tend to de-nature what we would use and control. But it's an insidious tendency.

The environmental movement has come about in response to myriad acts of de-naturing, some vast, some minuscule. We've ignored, at best oversimplified, the physical and chemical properties of nonliving elements of Nature—behaved to a great degree as if land, water, and air were static, non-reactive, as if they didn't have a dynamic nature of their own. We've numbed, sometimes even blocked, our awareness of the complexities of many living creatures of Nature, among those complexities their life-given dignities and their similarities and connections with us. If environmentalists are fighting to remedy the effects of this tendency, shouldn't we strive to keep the natures of all things—cows as well as bison—steadily in view?

John Donne said no man is an island. As any biologist will tell us, neither is any other part of Nature. If we lose sight of the nature of any part of the Earth, we're inevitably losing sight of other parts of the web of Nature too, and when we lose sight of enough of the web, we lose sight of our own selves as well. If we lose sight of the nature of the cow enough to believe it's no more than our convenient idea of it, we're blind not just to the cow but to ourselves. If we see the cow's nature fully enough to discover what we share with the cow, however, we have a better sense of both of us. We have a better sense of who we all are and where we all stand.

If not for the sake of the cow itself and the other living creatures and their life-given dignities; if not for the sake of the Earth itself and the elegant, intricate, prodigious systems that make it work; if for none of the compelling, enriching, enlightening, uplifting aspects of the things of Nature which are worth our attention in their own right, then for

331

the reason that all these things are inexorably and quite consequentially *there,* sustaining the web which defines and sustains us ourselves, it seems we'd be wise to foster a world view that takes note of the nature of the cow.

Nothing is ever simple. There are many proposed solutions to the car issue, the plastic container issue, the air conditioner issue, and to the cow issue, too. Even if we leave the question of food supply apart entirely, the question of cow-related land damage alone generates solution theories and sub-issues galore. Some put their faith in raising grazing fees to protect federal lands from the devastation of overgrazing. Some advocate measures to eliminate the cattle industry entirely. Allan Savory, an ecologist who has spent a lifetime with his eye on both the natures of cows and of semi-arid ecosystems like certain ones in the American West, puts a paradoxical spin on things: he believes that, properly managed, cows are the way to restore those ecosystems to health.

Simplified, his reasoning is as follows: Such areas were traditionally populated by vast herds of plant-eating ungulates (bison, mule deer, bighorn sheep, pronghorns) which through their particular grazing habits and patterns promoted the biodiversity upon which the health of an ecosystem depends. When bunching to protect themselves from predators, these herds broke up the hard soil, working in nutritive plant litter, thereby promoting water retention and seed germination, which the concentration of their urine and dung then fertilized. The herd then moved on to avoid their own waste, not returning until it was absorbed, with the result that while the area got heavily grazed, individual plants didn't and so weren't killed but instead were stimulated to grow. Cows are ungulates too, and if our cow herds were wild, their grazing behavior would be similar to that of traditional herds. But since they aren't wild, and since the large wild herds are gone now, Savory has developed a process for managing cattle to simulate traditional grazing patterns, including a method of bunching cattle without the use of predators. He says that in the semi-arid ecosystems in question, the difference between the heavy and short grazing of traditional herds and the light and prolonged grazing of today (where cows eat plants down to the roots) is the difference between trailing 365 cows along an area for one day and trailing one cow along the same area for 365 days. The former rejuvenates the land; the latter reduces it to barren hardpan. Though in certain ecosystems (e.g., riparian zones and

332

humid areas of uniform rainfall and climate) resting damaged land will restore it to health, in these semi-arid ecosystems Savory says the land will *worsen* with rest—to ensure carbon cycling, it *needs* the action of herbivorous ungulates—and, at this point, cows are our best bet for restoring these ecosystems to health.

On the other hand, there are biologists who disagree with Savory, arguing that we don't know as much about these ecosystems as he thinks and that therefore his ideas aren't as solidly grounded as he makes out. Nothing is ever simple. There are theories on this issue and its solutions to make your head swim. The cow stories here, these reflections, offer no solutions to the man-made cow issue, and they are not intended to.

But it may not be beyond our nature to be able to keep the natures of things in view. It's not unprecedented. It's been a practice in primal cultures to honor the prey, the sacrifice/thing used, to ask its forgiveness, to keep sight of a shared livingness with it, and—whether plant, animal, mineral, water, or sky—to keep sight of shared origins with it and of comparable if different places in a shared scheme. Maybe this capacity for respectful attention to Nature is muffled in us somewhere yet, gasping faintly but still not asphyxiated.

Maybe you'll say, Yes *but:* you can't expect us to think as primal peoples have. We have the whole vast buffer of our technology between us and the tooth-and-claw fight for survival; they had the wolf at the door. Well, yes, *but:* maybe in a way we've come full circle now. Maybe the wolf is at the door again, or has been all along, and as our technologies are backfiring—as our efforts, however splendid, are suddenly failing to camouflage from us one wolf after another—maybe we're beginning to notice its howl again.

It's the nature of things, yes, that we—environmentalists included—sacrifice others to our needs. But with managing this aspect of our nature, as with all things, there are ways and there are ways. The way of respect and attention will help keep the web functioning. The way of ignoring and unattended arrogance will disrupt the web. It's been disrupted before, of course, about a dozen times, the most recent disruption putting an end to the dinosaurs. Now we have the power to do to our world the same thing that the giant meteor strike or the great volcanic eruption or whatever it was did to theirs. But we don't have the ultimate power. Nature, which does, will readjust the web again in the long run . . . In the long *long* run that human minds can't really grasp.

Calves are cows' lot in life. There's always a new one on the way. Sometimes in difficulty, a cow will have to have her calf pulled for her; usually she's a first-year heifer, green to the whole thing. She lies on her swollen side not knowing what's happening to her, while some human mucks around at her hind end with a thing that looks like a handyman jack with a motorcycle chain attached. Then, maybe in a flash of red pain, the pressure is broken, and the mechanical operation over, she's escaped this mysterious martyrdom; if she wants, she can flee. One heifer I remember, after such an experience, pulled herself up on her feet so fast you wouldn't have believed it. She took one bewildered look behind her at the wet bundle and the mess on the ground and ran like hell the other way.

"Where's your damn maternal instinct," the cowboy said. "She looks at the little sucker like it was no more'n a big shit she just took."

Her maternal instinct was inside her; further trauma excluded, it would come out next time around. But thus far this first-year heifer had had only a mysterious man-attended ordeal for experience with motherhood, and for the moment she'd been divorced by it from an ingredient of her nature.

In this final story there was once again a nursing mother nearby who took the new calf. But this story is not as romantic as the earlier one. No innocent little white intermediary, lacking experience of the world and acting solely on instinct, intervened. Just an average cow, in whom instinct was blended with a healthy exposure to the natures of things via several years' calving experience. She knew how to recognize a creature of her own when she saw it, and although the little wet heap wasn't that, she knew it was one of her kind. And seeing it abandoned, and already having one of her own to feed anyway, she came to lick the new calf, rescuing it from the peril a benighted mother had exposed it to.

Nominated by the North American Review

FLOOR STUDY

by MARTHA COLLINS

from FIELD

Sorry, kids, you messed
the exam: in *err* we trust,

in *er,* there's no ease in us
anymore, for any user.

And here's Li'l Miss Take
herself, she's crossed a line

she cannot see, a way-
ward vertical line, she says

there is no under under
where we are, just un-

swept dust. And is that it,
the what that bends

the fender, spills the milk,
burns the money, spoils

the work? Why is wrong
our right these days? Thank

you, it was nothing much
the same as nothing more—

In these bare scenes we love
to lose: she gives it up, he shuts

it down, and no one's left
to run the show, which goes

on under cover of some night
before we knew. We're down

to clean-slate work again.
Then it's a question of.

Nominated by Lloyd Schwartz, Field

GRIEVANCES AND GRIEFS BY ROBERT FROST

fiction by DANIEL STERN

from BOULEVARD

Blazing may sunshine, but only through windows; floor to ceiling windows with the world well seen, but still windows between them and the sun.

"How can we both live in this bed?" Volya asks. "What a crazy idea."

"Only one of us is going to what you call live in this bed."

"None of your gallows humor," she says. "It hurts when I laugh. But you can see how difficult it's going to be."

"You can get out of bed when you want to. Go out into the world, flirt with men in the sunny streets."

"I can't go anywhere yet, so you shouldn't tease me. Weeks, he said, maybe months."

"That's what mine told me, too. It's mostly a matter of how many weeks or months. In some matters, quantity is everything."

The electronic timer on the endtable rings its *brrrrrrr*. Mickey reaches over and shuts it off.

"And there's going to be that sound all the time."

"Gargrrrlll."

"What?"

Mickey finishes swallowing his pills with the last splat of water in the glass. Spread all around them on the bed is the debris of a board game: Flight and Fancies, dice, cards, the delicately balanced board.

"I said you should try not to be so sensitive to sounds."

She turns towards him very carefully. Her elegant legs with their muscular curves of calves are significantly longer than his. With a touch of scorn she says, "I am a dancer. Was. I am trained to respond to sound."

"You mean music, not sound."

"Hegel says music is the Ur sound, buried already in ordinary squeaks and rings of life."

"If I didn't know that you were such an extraordinary lay you would sound like a stuffed intellectual."

"You have a vulgar streak I didn't see before. Anyway, a person could be both, no? But I am not."

"They gave you Hegel at that school in Moscow?"

"They didn't give. I found. And don't patronize my youth. Or Russia. They're the same thing. What's it like out today?"

He closes his eyes and imagines the pools of sunshine on Sixth Avenue, the bicycles chained to parking meters, the sun dazzling the eyes of the pedigreed dogs in the window of the pet shop on the Northeast corner.

"Sunny and warm," he tells her. "The tourists from the upper West Side and Montclair, New Jersey will be strolling on West 10th street."

"More patronizing. You just envy them because they're out and you're in." Volya smiles, a touch of malice. It is radiance when that superb rictus takes her unawares. You could light up Times Square at night with that smile.

"Don't *you*?" he says. "Wouldn't it be wonderful to get out of this bed, dress up, *sportif,* and take the air in a tobacco trance."

"No quotes," she says. "Michael, you promised."

"How about your Hegel?"

"That was my life, autobiography, not quoting. We have to tell each other—*things*. I counted up last night, it's only been twelve weeks, married for four. We've hardly met."

It is Mickey's turn to smile. "That's right." He turns towards her side of the bed, grazes his hand over her small peaked breasts. "Tell me," Mickey says. "Do you come here often?"

While Mickey is shaving—no matter how weak he feels he still insists on shaving every day, standing up, holding onto the bathroom sink—Bobby comes in to clear away the breakfast dishes.

"Bobby," Volya asks, "Why is Michael so sharp to me, so difficult these days? He was never that way before."

"You haven't had much of a before. But maybe it's because you're both trapped in that bed. Except that yours is a temporary trap called arthritis, a virus, whatever; his is a deep, dark trap called cancer. You'll be out of that bed in weeks, months at the worst. He's not getting out. That could make a person a little edgy."

"Yes," she says.

Bobby hesitates in the doorway, juggling the breakfast trays. "You knew it when you married him, right?"

"I guess so," she says. "Still—."

Bobby says, "You mean there's knowing and there's knowing?"

She half-opens a smile; very low voltage.

It was never supposed to come to this. It was never supposed to come to anything. They'd met in a welter of metal braces, rubber tubing. She'd come forward to meet him with some sort of electronic device in her hand ready to make him strong again, ready to undo the harm the 'problem' had already done, to his bones, his joints, his ligaments. He never called it anything but the 'problem.' It was his way of reducing it to manageable proportions. The thing itself was all-powerful, in charge of life and death. But a 'problem' was something you dealt with, a 'problem' was something you might solve.

Stretching him on the rack, forcing him to pull more weight than he could have pulled before, she told him how dangerous that way of thinking was.

"Pull," she said softly. "Harder, but slowly. The slower you do your exercises the better they build the strength."

Wheezing but playful with her, he asked. "Do you think I'll still be able to make the beast with two backs?"

"Pulllll," she intoned. "That is a quote. Shakespeare. Don't make conversation with quotes. Make your own."

"I mean—considering my 'problem'. . . . "

"Where I come from when you call something what it's not, everybody lives a lie. It's disgusting!"

"Moscow?"

"Leningrad. Now St. Petersburg."

"*Now?*" He tried to make her smile. He could always seduce his actresses, his actors, his designers, everybody.

She obliged and the smile blew him away. Day and night were included in that face, dark and subtle in repose, brilliant under the stretch of one of her many different smiles. She was an unexpected side effect of treatment.

"It's called St. Petersburg—now and then," she said. "Every fifty years or so. You can rest for one hundred and twenty seconds."

"You mean two minutes."

"You're not directing this production. I said one hundred and twenty seconds. You can wipe your sweat with this."

She slung a towel over his shoulder and walked away on astonishing legs.

Now, she asks, a challenge: "What would you do, exactly, if we could keep on making what you charmingly call 'the beast with two backs'? What that's fresh and new?"

"Ha," he rises to the bait. "None of your old world we've-seen-it-all cynicism! I can think of a thousand positions with no echoes of lovers from life or literature."

She leans carefully but elegantly on a slender forearm. "Start with one," she says.

Mickey has been challenged before—hundreds of actresses calling down from the stage into the darkness of the orchestra, asking for a precise example to back up an instruction or interpretation. He doesn't miss a beat. "I would make love to you in a car—"

"Ha! Big deal! Every teenager in the world . . . "

"—In a car, in the front seat, during an automatic car wash—the great golem of the machine-brushes whipping across the windows and windshield while we—"

"Michael, that's not a *position*."

"No but it would be thrilling, it would be extraordinary."

"Okay, it would be unusual. But positions!"

Now Mickey allows himself a little thinking time. In a formal, announcing voice, he says: "The Porcupine Position."

"The what?"

"No *interruptus* please. In this position the man and woman circle each other very carefully, touching each other only on the smooth insides of surfaces; they never lose control even at the end."

Volya was laughing. Her laughter did not move Mickey the way her smiles did. It was healthy laughter but not luminous. "Then how do they ever get to the end?"

340

"The usual way—or ways. And if it's successful, no skin is pierced. You've heard of blood lust. This position is bloodless lust."

Brrrr. The bedside reminder rang its bloodless reminder: medicine-time. Pills swallowed, invention resumed.

"Okay," he says. "The Rodeo Position."

"The *what?*"

"Rodeo. In this position, the woman tries to run out of the bedroom, the man lassos her with a lariat—"

"What is lary-at?"

"It's a rope with a loop tied in it to catch a steer or a calf usually. But this is an adaptation for sexual purposes."

Her clear blue eyes open wide. "I am to be steer or calf?"

"You don't care for that position. Then how about this one: the Professor Position. In this position the woman lies in bed naked, reading a book, preferably literary criticism. The man lies next to her, also naked, and caresses her, then makes love, complete passionate love to her; she continues reading until they are both finished. Afterwards, he smokes a cigarette and gives her a spot quiz about the book she was reading."

"You're crazy." But she gets the idea and turns on a 300 watt grin.

The late morning turns bad. Volya cannot find a place to lie without hurting. She's afraid to stand. She phones the doctor and gets his service who asks her if it's an emergency. She says no it's not an emergency, changes her mind, yes, it's a terrible emergency, hangs up and tries not to breathe. If the entire universe is still perhaps she will feel no pain. Also, it has come and gone swiftly in the past, so it is always accompanied by hope.

"Michael," she says. "Let's trade."

"What."

"I'll take your 'problem'. You take mine."

He pretends to think carefully about her offer. "I don't know," he says. "I wouldn't mind the extra years—but I don't take pain too well."

"Yes, but you would have years to learn."

"True."

SHE: (Extending her hand) Deal?

HE: (Shaking her hand) Deal!

SHE: Will you miss me?

HE: Like crazy! In between spasms of pain, mind you.

SHE: I miss you, already.

HE: Not fair. I'm still here. Remember Caligula at the end being stabbed by the members of his court, shouting in between the knife thrusts: "I'm still here." I did a production in St. Paul, Minnesota one February. Snowed in. Only one person in the audience—a man who doesn't take off his coat or snowy hat all during the performance. Kenneth Haig playing Caligula. When Ken is being stabbed and calls out "I'm still here," the guy stands up and says, "Well, I'm not," and exits.

Volya looks at him coolly.

"This really happened?"

"Well, no actually. It was a company joke. You have to do something when you're snowed in with twenty actors in St. Paul. God, how will I ever learn what makes a Russian woman laugh?"

To make up for his deception he caresses her, promisingly, a gliding hand closer to pay dirt than he's come in days, uncertain as he is certain that his 'problem' will allow him to deliver on any promise. She lays her head on his shoulder, eyes half-closed, breathing through her mouth. But the doctor returns her emergency call at that moment and advises an increase in the Percodan. Then Bobby comes in with lunch. Just to drive him crazy Mickey tells him about the trade deal. He looks at them with despair.

"When are you guys going to grow up?" he says.

Bobby is twenty-four, black or rather dusty brown, but already very grown up; Caucasian features, a Jamaican mother and a Jewish father, he pointed out to Mickey when applying for the job as his assistant. He could convincingly play any role, white, black, green, he'd said, not limited to traditional casting. He wanted to work closely with a director like Mickey Stamos—and there was no director like Mickey, only the man, himself, the man who created mad, ambitious projects: the man who revived Sartre's "Kean," who mounted a twelve hour adaptation of "Thus Spake Zarathustra." The man whose hallmark as a director was that he could make comedy out of anything.

Bobby got the job and Mickey was promptly confined to bed. The 'problem' had arrived and Bob went from being devoted theatrical acolyte to nursemaid, script-reader, bill-payer, project researcher, prescription-filler and cook. He was happy, but there would be no acting roles, traditional or otherwise, until the 'problem' resolved itself. What gave him the most trouble was watching Mickey make comedy out of what was happening to him.

By the time Bobby returned to clear away the lunch trays it had turned stormy out, the sun obscured by swirling clouds, spring rain threatening.

"Bobby," Volya says, "We are newlyweds. Suppose we want to make love? I mean you bounce in and out without knocking or anything."

"I assumed that was out. I mean I thought you were in this great *doleur*. From now on I'll knock," Bobby says. He balances trays, privacies, egos. Also, he has a little French to put on display having played Molière, having played Racine. Right now, it's Robert Frost who is his anxious concern.

He lingers.

"Yes?" Volya says, slightly imperious, as if the sex in question might commence on the instant.

But Bobby is talking to Mickey. When two people are in bed it's sometimes hard to know who's being addressed. The beast with four legs.

"I think I may have the Frost poem you need for the close of the show."

"Great," Michael half sat up in bed. "What do you think? Birches: *One could do worse than be a swinger of birches,* Or, here: *Good fences make good neighbors . . .* " Michael the actor, on-stage at age six with his famous father, is on-stage once more, intoning in bed, an audience of two will do.

"Well, no. I don't think one of the war horses is a great idea. You need something fresh, something the audience doesn't know. But one that still will pack a punch."

"Ah." Mickey subsides, but Volya rises. "I don't think you're doing Michael a favor—by going on with the charade of a new play." (She pronounced it a la Russe, Mik-ai-el, had dismissed the nickname, early on. 'Mickey, a name for a boy not a man.') "What is the matter with both of you?"

"Charade?" Mickey may be still acting. It's difficult to know. "Do you know what I went through to get the rights from the Frost estate?"

Exasperated, Volya shifts suddenly towards Mickey. A distortion of pain crosses her face. "But you are bedridden . . . you are—"

Bobby freezes, trays in hand, trying not to look at Mickey. Volya has almost said the unsayable. But he underestimates Mickey's *sang froid* in the face of the 'problem'.

"Anyway, lying down or standing up, I am going to produce 'Frost!' But I'm still not happy with the title. 'Frost!' It sounds like a Christmas musical for children, not a biographical play about a great poet. What do you think, Volya?"

She turns away, giving up on him for the moment. It was something she'd been doing a lot of since the impulsive marriage less than a month ago. Mickey was the first patient she had ever gone out with or slept with, let alone married, and Volya was convinced that she was being punished by whatever Gods were in charge of professional conduct. They'd begun with Shakespeare-In-The-Park: a production of *Othello*—where Iago had spoken to them of the beast with two backs. From there they'd progressed to long dinners and longer adolescent-style groping sessions.

"You're as nervous as I am," she'd murmured against his chest one night. "It is your famous 'problem', yes?"

Three times a week he continued to arrive at physiotherapy, to be stretched on the rack in the name of strength, in the name of restoring health. When it all began to feel too weird to her, she suggested they stop going out or that he find another physiotherapist.

Instead they fled to City Hall to be married. When her courage failed her, on the trip downtown, Mickey held her hand in a tight grasp.

"It's instant citizenship. Think of it that way," he'd said.

"Instant widow," she said, already teary.

"I'll leave exact instructions about how to invest the estate. Being a widow is a better job than being a physiotherapist."

"I like being a physiotherapist."

"Then you can do both." He had more arguments, more wit than she had strength to resist. They continued their ride to City Hall. It was the only possible end to the roller coaster ride they were on. The 'problem' did not intrude itself on their honeymoon, which was a trip to Brighton Beach, Little Odessa, the signs in Cyrillic, Russian songs blaring from loudspeakers outside records stores—"It's the closest thing to meeting your family," Mickey told her. Bobby came along for the night club trip and left them at a hotel near the boardwalk where all went well that night and continued well, through his first pre-production days of "Frost!" though by then he needed a cane to help him navigate and the necessary retreat to the bed was only a few weeks away.

Nevertheless, things continued well for the next two weeks, until Volya's virus hit, collapsing her down several unseen steps to the Ladies Room during a rehearsal. It turned out to be a peculiar virus which aggravates incipient arthritic conditions.

"But I have always been a healthy horse," she told the doctor. She lied, of course. It was the bone pain which had made her give up be-

344

ing a dancer, which had turned her, instead, to the ballet of ropes and chrome and the stretching of other people's muscles.

"Many dancers have arthritis without knowing it. They sort of hurt in their bones all the time, anyway, so they don't find out—until they have to. That's the bad news."

"I understand," Volya said, grim.

The doctor was young, smiling, lighthearted. "No, no," he said. "That's a joke. You're supposed to ask about the good news."

"I don't understand American jokes."

"The good news is, these viruses are self-limiting. Three weeks, eight weeks, two or three months. Then they go away."

She cheered up, considerably, after hearing this. "We will call it my 'problem'," she told Mickey, needling him with confidence now that her fear was diminished.

"Don't push your luck," Mickey had said and plunged into "Frost!" with a vengeance, a stream of visitors arriving at bedside with set designs in hand, with contracts to sign, with production schedules.

"If you cast Hal Holbrook or James Whitmore as Frost I'm quitting," Bobby said.

"What's your choice," Mickey said. "Sidney Poitier? Morgan Freeman?"

"I don't need somebody black, just somebody fresh."

Hence Foster Lanier, a young actor fresh from Yale Drama School, having spouted a stream of bona fides—a touring company of "Streetcar," fresh from playing "Salesman" at Seattle Rep, now standing near the doorway of the enormous bedroom, and in the middle of reading, in a rich and ripe southern accent, the poem Bobby had discovered for the opening and closing of the play:

> . . . I can but wonder whence
> I get the lasting sense
> of so much warmth and light.
> If my mistrust is right
> It may be altogether
> From one day's perfect weather,
> When starting clear at dawn
> The day swept clearly on . . .

It may have been the strangest audition setting in the history of the theater. Mickey, wearing a paisley robe, propped up in bed on a mass of pillows, notebook on his lap, reading glasses dangling from a red cord around his neck, Volya next to him, listening attentively, trying not to look embarrassed, and Bobby, on a folding chair near the bathroom, clipboard in hand.

When the young man finished his reading, his voice strained, his cheeks flushed red, Mickey said, softly, "Foster, you're from the south, aren't you? Robert Frost was Mister New England."

"Mobile," he said, "But ah can alter mah diction. Ah've done it before."

The silence in the room was deadly. Surprising everyone, herself, too, Volya broke it.

"My mother saw Robert Frost. Before I was born. In Moscow."

Quickly, Bobby stood. "We have your phone numbers," he said. "Thanks for coming to read."

"The service can always find me," the actor said, and when he was gone Volya turned on the two men.

"I never would dream you had such bad character, such bad faith."

"What?" Mickey was all innocence. "What do you mean?"

"You lead people on. That boy thinks he has a chance for a part in a play that will happen."

"So?"

She ran blood into her cheeks much like the actor had. "You are making promises you have no intention of keeping."

Bobby had left the room, as soon as he saw the trouble coming. He was good at exits.

"Darling," Mickey said. "I know what you mean. But there's always a chance of a swan song. It's only a seven week rehearsal period. I didn't know your mother saw Robert Frost."

She went from a rage to a sulk, swiftly. "He was on a tour; Khrushchev made it possible for Americans to come and everybody loves Robert Frost in Russia. She stood in line for four hours to get in to hear. She was very happy."

"I love learning things about you," Mickey said. "Everything's new."

She kissed him, quickly. "I am your swan song, is it not?"

"It is," he said. "And don't forget, swans mate for life."

"This," she said and smiled, "will not be too hard in our case."

He moved back to work, his old life-saving habit. "What did you think of the 'Happiness' poem? Is it the right one?"

"I liked the lines, 'O stormy, stormy world, the days you were not swirled around . . .'"

But she told him she needed to read it, slowly, to herself, and then out loud. She told him of reading poems and essays by Frost in school

346

and at home. One essay in particular had been very important to her. Her English was not quite up to it, but it was something to do with grief and grievance—she couldn't recall the name.

He tossed the fat, red-covered paperback of poems and prose to her. "Read it and weep," he said. "I'm going to the bathroom." They had not yet reached the total confinement stage, what Mickey called the bedpan-humor stage of their gallows humor situation. He could still navigate to the bathroom and back.

Volya riffled through the pages and found sentences, bits and pieces. She was looking for two key words she remembered. As if need were magic she found them swiftly:

But for me, Frost wrote, *I don't like grievances . . . What I like is griefs . . . Grievances are a form of impatience. Griefs are a form of patience . . . Grievances are something that can be remedied, and griefs are irremediable . . .*

Having held off tears and fear with equal strength, Volya was not prepared for the power of the simple word 'grief'. English was not her language, but she had learned it as a child, had liked its song. Now a few English words were shaking her bed-solid poise, threatening tears. *. . . there is solid satisfaction in a sadness that is not just a fishing for ministry and consolation. Give us immedicable woes—woes that nothing can be done for—woes flat and final.*

Some of the words were hopeless for her to understand, but she got the sense, in all its bright and clever darkness. Mickey returned from the bathroom and caught the glistening in the corners of her eyes. He eased himself into the bed and turned to look for the words which had brought the first hint of tears he'd ever seen in Volya. Quickly she flipped the book shut.

"Can't I see?" he asked.

"No," she said. "Not yet."

The game was called Flights and Fancies, a knock-off of Dungeons and Dragons, only less mystical. When a player was trapped there were 'flights' prepared for escape. But you also needed 'fancies', imaginings, chosen by a throw of the dice. It was a board game and used dice and you could play it in bed, so Mickey had become a bit addicted to it. Volya could take it or leave it and Bobby was restless. He had been pressed into service by Mickey, when he wanted to get back to work.

Mickey, normally the High Priest of Work said, "Play is everything."

"I thought *the* play was the thing."

"Please," Mickey admonished him. "Volya does not trust men who use literary quotations in their conversation."

"Volya doesn't trust me, anyway."

"You think not?" Mickey was interested. He moved a counter and opened up an avenue for flight. "Why do you think?"

"Because I'm bad for you. I encourage your delusions."

"Like what?"

At this Bobby packed in the game. "Okay, I'll be in the office, trying to get our playwright up here to discuss one of your delusions, this afternoon. Our production of his play."

"Don't make it too late," Mickey said.

"He gets tired in the afternoon," Volya told Bobby.

"Don't ever talk in front of me as if I'm not here," Mickey said, perhaps the first testy thing he'd ever said to Volya. "I'm still here."

"And you're still my Caligula," she smiled and he laughed out loud and started to kiss her. From the roiling skies beyond the window thunder cracked the air.

"Some spring," Bobby muttered as rain smashed against the bedroom windows.

"Listen to you," Volya said, "You can go where you want. If I don't get away from these walls and these sheets soon, out into the air, I'll go crazy."

Mickey climbed out of bed. "Jesus, every time I hear the rain I have to pee. Just like a child."

While he is in the bathroom, Bobby tries to enlist Volya's support for the poem he wants.

"It has this weird title."

"Which?"

"Happiness Makes Up In Height What It Lacks For Length."

"Yes," she said. "Weird."

"It's just the poet wondering out loud about having the sense, for his whole life, of a world full of sunlight and brightness, when for so much of the time he remembers it being swirled around with clouds, stormy, dark."

"That's all?" Volya asked.

"Then he decides, maybe it's just from the memory of one perfect day, when he and his lover, his wife, his friend, I don't know which, when they walked out together for one whole day of perfect sunshine and clear skies."

Volya thought for a moment. "I don't like it when you explain poetry. I have to read it." She examined Bobby's smooth brown face, closely. "Tell me, Bobby, why is it so important that this poem is to be picked for the play?"

"Oh, God." He sat himself down on the rumpled bed. "The playwright is set on it. Mickey wanted one of the famous poems, the ones kids learn in school, and I don't want him getting all upset, getting into a fight, making himself sick." He looked across the bed at Volya. "Did your mother really see Robert Frost?" he asked.

The playwright, Harold Howe, was short and round, passionate.

"You need a scene to dramatize the poem, if we're going to use it as our closing." He waved his one free hand, the other hand hefting the book of Frost poems. "Look," he said. "It's Frost at the very end, the old, white-haired prophet, the sacred icon, dying." Harold Howe read:

> O stormy, stormy world,
> The days you were not swirled
> Around with mist and cloud,
> Or wrapped as in a shroud,
> And the sun's brilliant ball
> Was not in part or all
> Obscured from mortal view—
> Were days so very few . . .

Mickey broke into the pause. "Will the audience be able to hold onto the sense of it, Harold?"

"Sure. It's just an old man looking back on a dark and stormy life—that's what the audience will register. Don't forget they'll be seeing a failing Frost, almost at the end." He ploughed ahead, a man who had spent a life convincing directors, producers, lyricists, composers.

> I can but wonder whence
> I get the lasting sense
> Of so much warmth and light.
> If my mistrust is right
> It may be altogether
> From one day's perfect weather . . .

349

"That, right there, that's the central wonder of it," Harold Howe was like a teacher, book in hand, two of his students in bed, and one sitting on an easy chair taking notes. "The memory of one day's perfect clear weather ransoming a whole life. To produce the effect of clarity there are three 'clears' in three consecutive lines."

When starting clear at dawn
The day swept clearly on
To finish clear at eve.
I verily believe
My fair impression may
Be all from that one day.

"Then getting out of his sickbed to walk—with only the shade of his wife, to whom he'd been so cruel, for one perfect day from sun-up to sunset. Then he comes home and dies." Harold Howe closed the book. "Happiness makes up in height what it lacks in length." He turned to face Mickey directly.

"It's a beauty," Mickey said. "I admit that, Harold. But it has archaic words like verily and whence."

Harold Howe was quick on his feet. "That just gives it the classic feel. Underlines the idea that Frost was our Wordsworth."

Mickey's eyes were closed. Bobby said, "Volya, what do you think?"

She gave him a conspirator's smile. Not one of her dazzlers; veiled. "It's beautiful," she said. She seemed to have forgotten her irritation with delusions. "The whole idea is beautiful."

"How will we show the walk?" Mickey said, eyes still closed.

"Rear projection," Harold Howe said happily.

That night, as they prepared for sleep, Mickey complained, for the first time, about their confinement. "I'd like to be one of those tourists from New Jersey," he said, "soaking up the sunshine and buying stupid souvenirs, lamps that don't work when you get them home and t-shirts that say I Love New York, with a heart where the word love goes. Anything just to get out, not to be trapped."

Wind joined the rain and the window across from the bed rattled in its frame.

"Yes." She shook out a Percodan into her palm and poured the necessary water. "I have the same grievance. That is the right word?"

"The perfect word."

350

She swallowed the pill with a quick shake of her head and opened the Frost collection. "I found it here. I think this was the essay I read in the kitchen at home, when I was a kid."

She read, *I don't like grievances. What I like is griefs.*

He reached. "Let me see that."

She held the book away from him and kept reading. *Grievances are a form of impatience. Grief is a form of patience.* Mickey nodded, settling back on his pillow. "Right," he murmured. "I'm damned impatient with the room inside and the rain outside."

Give us immediate woes—woes that nothing can be done for—woes flat and final, she read.

"Was that what you were reading yesterday that got you a little teary?" It was not a question.

"Michael." Volya frowned. "What is im-medic-able?"

"Frost tells you: flat and final. Something there's no medicine for."

"Ah." She handed him the book. "But look—look what he says next."

Mickey read, *Woes flat and final. And then to play. The play's the thing. Play's the thing . . .*

He grinned shyly at her. "The old boy was a mind reader. There's got to be a place for this stuff in the play. I'll show it to Harold."

Volya lay back and clicked the room into darkness. "I think," she whispered, "He was playing with play—not *a* play, or *the* play. Just play."

She smoothed a lotion over those long dancer's legs and Mickey smelled walnuts.

"Are there nuts in that stuff?"

"It's called Forest Cream. Maybe."

Mickey lay listening to the wild rain for a moment, on the edge of a wonderful idea, and not just an idea—something to be done— something absolutely extraordinary, something about griefs and grievances, happiness and play, edging at his mind and even deeper, where his breath came from. But the Valium and the Percodan had both done their work and before he could grasp the idea, he joined Volya in sweet, medicated sleep.

Mickey wakes early, much earlier than usual. The digital clock gives red hours: 6:05 A.M. He is usually a slow waker. This morning he is alert at once. The vague notion of the night before is crystal clear. It is no longer an idea; it has become an action, a scheme, however crazy. The only question will be: can Volya handle it without too much pain, and will he be strong enough.

He reaches for the long cord Bobby has placed near him. A flood of sunlight bathes the room. The storm is past and the idea of spring is back. Volya is still asleep behind her sleep mask.

"Psssst, Volya." He touches her shoulder gently. She rolls towards him—a moan of pain comes, though she still sleeps. Then she reaches up and pushes the black, silk mask from her eyes, looks at him with eyes rimmed red from days of exhausting hurt.

"What, Michael, what?"

He tells her of the plan. They will leave the bed, they will leave the house, secretly, Bobby still asleep, all doctors far away; they will play in the fields of sunny streets, of green parks, walk, as carefully or carelessly as they could manage, as long as they could manage. They would forget pain, problems, grievances and griefs. They would have one day, acting out the Frost happiness poem, testing its truth.

Volya dressed very carefully, holding onto the bed as needed. She took a slow step; no real pain, yet. Maybe a quick twinge. Mickey had gotten ready in a flash, a director eager to prove his concept could work.

Outside the six steps of the stoop wait, the first challenge. Mickey feels a surge of weakness, but leans on Volya, feels stronger, quickly, perhaps because of the excitement of the risky adventure.

It was a day that would have been thrilling even if nothing was being tested. The sun floated among bunches of clouds, the colors all pure, cloud-white, sun-yellow, undiluted, unshaded. Someone had hosed the streets down in front of the fruit market on Sixth Avenue.

Now: what to do? A poodle sleeps in the window of the fancy pet shop on the corner. Past Boccigaluppi's Funeral Parlor, past gelato stands is the flower market, where Mickey buys Volya a gardenia, which she wears in her hair, but loses in the cab uptown to Central Park.

"What day is this?" she asks. "I lose track cooped up in that bedroom."

"Sunday," he says. "Central Park will be lively."

In the park the last few clouds vanish and the sun dominates the sky and the day; yet it is cool enough to walk comfortably.

A park bench is a danger; if they sat down would they have the strength to get up again? They walk on, feeling strong, feeling triumphant. Later, they felt safe enough to rest on a bench, Volya's head on his arm, as if they were on a date, or newlyweds, something as banal as that. At noon when the sun becomes a touch too relentless they try to stand in the shadow of a slender tree, but it gives little shade in that perfect sunshine, so they walk on. A child, the one they would probably never have, throws a ball at them and Volya actually bends, supple and swift, to pick it up and throw it back. She looks at Mickey, startled at herself and her luck: no pain. The Percodan rests safely in her purse, slung over her shoulder.

Once, concerned, Mickey suggests she take one, as prevention for pain. No, she does not want to dull the day; she'll gamble. But passing a public phone booth she grows concerned, they must call Bobby.

Bobby: My God, where are you? Are you all right?

Mickey: We're just out for a walk.

Bobby: A walk. But how about Volya—and you're not strong enough. Come back, now, for God's sake.

Mickey: See you later.

There is a band concert in the park, but at first the sunny joy they've taken for their own is beyond sound; it's as if the band's music is muffled and simply seeing the players move their hands and mouths in playing their instruments, a silent movie, gives Mickey and Volya pleasure.

For an instant Mickey feels the old weakness topple his balance, even though he is sitting on the grass. His head goes around or the sky, it's not clear which. But he sits up slowly and the sagging weakness is gone.

As they walk on, all of a sudden the sound of the music sweeps over them, something wonderfully silly by Von Suppe, the drum beat and the harmonies of the oboes and clarinets bring tears of happiness to Volya's eyes. She feels foolish.

Lunch was a hot dog and a coke from a wagon near the lake, where couples escaped from a Monet past, from a Seurat dream, rowed the waters. Afternoon tea was weak, lukewarm liquid in cardboard containers at the Zoo, some animal in the distance screaming pain or pleasure, hunger or boredom, the perfect sun lower in the sky, shadows now more available but less necessary.

Giddy with freedom but afraid that the day was shutting down around them, amid the cardboard containers and the crumbs of cake, they broke up the poem and fed it to each other, like children reading a favorite story over and over again, turning a meditation into prose of passionate conversation:

"I can but wonder whence I get the lasting sense of so much warmth and light . . . "

Volya replied, as if answering his question:

"It may be altogether from one day's perfect weather . . . My fair impression may be all from that one day . . . "

Mickey's voice trembled with fatigue. He scraped his chair along the stone closer to hers and leaned his head on her shoulder.

" . . . No shadow crossed but ours as through its blazing flowers we went from house to wood for change of solitude."

They knew better than to talk much, knew better than to discuss anything. It was enough to steal the words from Frost. And Mickey knew better than to wear any of his ironic masks. It occurred to him that it had been a day without irony, a day sprinkled with laughter but without jokes. There had been none of the sharp-edged by-play, the verbal fencing which had been the currency of their courtship. They were happy. It was enough.

"What a day," Volya muttered. There was now a throbbing pain in her right leg and in the small of her back. But she registered it as from a distance, the way the music had played behind a shield of sunlight. She did not mention the pain.

"Yes." Mickey sighed.

The sight of the prison-bedroom was as thrilling as the first sight of the open streets had been. Bobby helped them off with their clothes, alternately angry, or sulking, alternately frightened and relieved. He wanted to call the doctor, either doctor.

"No," Mickey said. "It's the most perfect Sunday afternoon since the beginning of the world. Let the doctors picnic with their families."

"Let them play golf." Volya giggled. Surreptitiously, she reached for the vial of Percodan.

"We have something important to tell you, Bobby." Mickey sounded a little drunk, exhaustion reaching his voice.

"Yes," Volya said.

"I'll be pleased to hear it once you're both back in bed."

They chanted it at him, one after the other. Mickey began.

"Happiness . . . "

" . . . Makes up . . . " Volya sang out.

"in height . . . "

" . . . What it lacks . . . " Mickey was short of breath and laughing now at the same time.

" . . . In length . . . "

"no—*for* length." Volya corrected him, pleased at a small success in English.

354

They collapsed on the bed laughing. Mickey desperately weak again, Volya trembling with pain, as Bobby performed his own chant above them: about anxiety, about calls to 911, about responsibility to others.

Happy and exhausted, they were too hopped up for sleep.

"I feel like I do after an opening," Mickey told her.

"Tired but wired."

"And I feel like when I passed an audition," Volya said. "Ready for more."

Silly with fatigue, Mickey made up a new game for them to play: a board game with no need of a board. The Frost Game, he named it, using the words she'd read to him. Instead of Dungeons and Dragons, instead of Flights and Fancies, it would be Grievances and Griefs.

"How do we play it?"

"The name tells you—you tell me a grievance and I match it with a grief. Then I do a grievance and you do a grief."

"How do we know the difference?"

"You told it to me from Frost. Grievances are impatient. Griefs are patient."

Volya spread lotion on her hands and arms; a walnut smell arrived in the air. She reached back and found a grievance—never a long reach.

"My mother wanted me to dance because my cousin Mira danced—and Mira was the daughter she really wanted."

"Pretty good," Mickey said. "Okay—a grief." Pause. "Griefs are harder." A longer pause. "My mother died when she was forty-three; a sad, funny woman. She never saw a play I directed."

"Poor lady," Volya said quietly.

"She was proud of me, anyway. Now I do a grievance. My first wife, Anna, the one I never talk about, she was always too busy to think about having a child. And by the time she slowed down enough, I didn't want it to be *her* child."

"No fair," Volya said. "That's a grief. Because now you have no children."

"How do we know?" Mickey threw a laugh. "You could be pregnant right now. But you're right. I wasted a good one." A beat. "Here's one—my father never thought what I did was worth a damn until the first hit I had. A crummy musical, but money talked. Now you."

This reach was harder for Volya, slower. "I left my home because life was so hard there, and my brother Mikhail . . . "

"I didn't know your brother had the same name as me."

"—He was doing drugs and drinking, so I took him with me to America, but he ran back home and left me alone in Brighton Beach."

"My God."

She produced a smile. "*Voila*," she said. "A grief."

"A grievance," he announced. "I don't have a real audience, a real public. They know Eisenstein, Chaplin, Reinhardt, they know Coppola, Scorcese. Nobody knows who I am except other directors."

"I married a man because I was confused and attracted and stupid in love and now he's leaving me."

"But I'm still here." Mickey said. "Anyway, which category is that?"

"Ha. You don't know your ass from a grief."

"I think maybe I do," he said. He waited and when he spoke he placed each word with slow care. "I thought there would be more time," he said. "I've been checking my watch every few minutes since I was a kid. But I always assumed there would be enough time. Dumb!"

She was tempted to pack the game in, then. But she took a breath and took her turn. "I mostly know dancers and so many are gay I'll probably never get married again."

His turn: "If dying is like lying down when you're as tired as I am maybe it won't be so bad."

Her turn: "Are you really saying truth about the famous 'problem'? And not even a complaint."

"A friend of mine says, never speak in euphemisms. It's to live a lie and it's what led to the fall of Communism. Anyway, I think I'm finished playing."

But Volya wasn't through. Forgetting that it was only a game, she barreled on into the disappointing past. She was to have danced Swan Lake at the Leningrad Ballet Academy graduation (it was still Leningrad then)—but old Kasakov, her teacher, he of the herring breath and the wandering hands was sleeping with Sonia, another dancer whose mother didn't watch her as closely as Volya's mother watched *her* daughter. Kasakov gave Sonia the part of the Dying Swan and broke Volya's teen-aged heart.

She threw off the covers and raised two long, perfect legs, scissoring them open and shut and said, with passion, her voice roughening, losing control, "My body promised me a career, a life as a dancer and then betrayed me."

He reached for her and hoped she wasn't crying, that his foolish game hadn't broken her down. "Oh, Mickey," she said. It was the first time she'd used his nickname, but he sure as hell was not going to call her attention to it.

"Come here," he said, snaking her along the sheets, her legs v-ing towards him, "Your body promised me a few things, too. You still owe me some, more than I'm ever going to have time to collect."

"You can't owe bodies," she said, serious. "But you can offer them."

"I accept," he said into her open lips, then opening thighs, mouths, everything, legs, hands and even eyes all moist, wide open, unprotected, generous.

"Mickey," she whispered, "Who won the game?"

"It's a tie," Mickey said. "That particular game is always a tie."

Afterwards, they lay long in the gathering darkness talking, remembering, until they could no longer see each other but could only hear each other's voice; husband and wife acquainted at last, telling their lives, swapping griefs and grievances until the grievances were gone and only grief was left and finally even grief was still.

Nominated by Carolyn Kizer, Robert Phillips, Boulevard

YOUNG MAN ON SIXTH AVENUE

fiction by MARK HALLIDAY

from CHICAGO REVIEW

H E WAS A YOUNG MAN in the big city. He was a young man in the biggest, the most overwhelming city—and he was not overwhelmed. For see, he strode across Fifth Avenue just before the light changed, and his head was up in the sharp New York wind and he was thriving upon the rock of Manhattan, in 1938. His legs were long and his legs were strong; there was no question about his legs; they were unmistakable in their length and strength; they were as bold and dependable as any American machine, moving him across Fifth just in time, his brown shoes attaining the sidewalk without any faltering, his gait unaware of the notion that legs might ever want to rest. Forty-ninth Street! He walked swiftly through the haste and blare, through the chilly exclamation points of taxis and trucks and people. He was a man! In America, '38, New York, two o'clock in the afternoon, sunlight chopping down between buildings, Forty-ninth Street. And his hair was so dark, almost black, and it had a natural wave in it recognized as a handsome feature by everyone, recognized universally, along with his dark blue eyes and strong jaw. Women saw him, they all had to see him, all the young women had to perceive him reaching the corner of Forty-ninth and Sixth, and they had to know he was a candidate. He knew they knew. He knew they knew he would *get* some of them, and he moved visibly tall with the tall potential of the not-finite twentieth-century getting that would be his inheritance; and young women who glanced at him on Sixth Avenue knew that he knew. They felt that they or their sisters would have to take him into account, and they touched their scarves a little nervously.

He was twenty-five years old, and this day in 1938 was the present. It was so obviously and totally the present, so unabashed and even garish with its presentness, beamingly right there right now like Rita Hayworth, all Sixth Avenue was in fact at two o'clock a thumping bright Rita Hayworth and the young man strode south irresistibly. If there was only one thing he knew, crossing Forty-eighth, it was that this day was the present, out of which uncounted glories could and must blossom—when?—in 1938, or in 1939, soon, or in the big brazen decade ahead, in 1940, soon; so he walked with fistfuls of futures that could happen in all his pockets.

And his wavy hair was so dark, almost black. And he knew the right restaurant for red roast beef, not too expensive. And in his head were some sharp ideas about Dreiser, and Thomas Wolfe, and John O'Hara.

On Forty-seventh between two buildings (buildings taller even than him) there was an unexpected zone of deep shade. He paused for half a second, and he shivered for some reason. Briskly then, briskly he moved ahead.

In the restaurant on Seventh Avenue he met his friend John for a witty late lunch. Everything was—the whole lunch was good. It was right. And what they said was both hilarious and notably well-informed. And then soon he was taking the stairs two at a time up to an office on Sixth for his interview. The powerful lady seemed to like his sincerity and the clarity of his eyes—a hard combination to beat!—and the even more powerful man in charge sized him up and saw the same things, and he got the job.

That job lasted three years, then came the War, then another job, then Judy, and the two kids, and a better job in Baltimore, and those years—those years. And those years. "Those years"—and the kids went to college with new typewriters. In the blue chair, with his work on his lapboard, after a pleasant dinner of macaroni and sausage and salad, he dozed off. Then he was sixty. Sixty? Then he rode back and forth on trains, Judy became ill, doctors offered opinions, commas were deceptive, Judy died. But the traffic on Coleytown Road next morning still moved casually too fast. And in a minute he was seventy-five and the phone rang with news that witty John of the great late lunches was dead. The house pulsed with silence.

Something undone? What? The thing that would have saved—what? Waking in the dark—maybe something unwritten, that would have made people say "*Yes* that's why you matter so much." Ideas about Wolfe. Dreiser. Or some lost point about John O'Hara.

Women see past him on the street in this pseudo-present and he feels they are so stupid and walks fierce for a minute but then his shoulders settle closer to his skeleton with the truth about these women: not especially stupid; only young. In this pseudo-present he blinks at a glimpse of that young man on Sixth Avenue, young man as if still out there in the exclamation of Sixth Avenue—that young man ready to stride across—but a taxi makes him step back to the curb, he'll have to wait a few more seconds, he can wait.

Nominated by Richard Jackson, Lloyd Schwartz, Eugene Stein

WINTER IN LOS ANGELES

fiction by TOM MCNEAL

from THE GETTYSBURG REVIEW

ALREADY MARCY has a bad feeling about what she has done and what she's about to do. She is awake, but pretending not to be, when Randall rises an hour before dawn. It's autumn in Nebraska, already cold. Randall's getting ready to go hunting, and for once in his life he's being quiet about it. He sounds almost like a prowler, in fact—the slow, cautious way he moves through the dark trailer-home, setting out his coat and gear, wrapping up sandwiches, feeling in the closet for a gun. When he steps outside, he sets the front door softly to behind him. There is a clinking sound as he eases open the metal kennel gate, and the tinkling of collars as the dogs cross the yard and bound into the truck. The truck door opens and closes, the engine starts and idles.

Marcy lies in bed and listens as the truck door opens again, and then the front door to their trailer. Randall moves slowly along the dark, narrow hallway toward their bedroom—under his boots, the trailer trembles slightly on its piers—then stops at the open door. Marcy is turned from him, but she can feel him there staring in. Finally he comes near and touches his hand to her neck. She doesn't move. When he speaks, his voice is gentler than usual. "Guess you know I'm sorry I hit you," he says. "I lay there in bed all night trying to figure out how I could've done that." A moment passes. "Marcy?"

She still doesn't move.

His voice is low and serious. "Well, I just want to say that I love you, no matter what. Even if I wanted to, that's something I couldn't ever change."

Marcy opens the one good eye and turns over in bed without speaking. They try to see each other in the darkness, but she can only guess

361

at what is in his face. It is a little while in fact before she can see that he's brought one of his long guns into the room with him. "What's that for?" she says. Her voice is sleepier, softer than she wants it.

"It's the wrong gun. I'm putting it back for something else." He forces a little laugh. "Shoulda turned on the light, I guess." She doesn't say anything. With three fingers she's carefully exploring the edges of the bad eye. He says, "If you want, Marcy, I won't go. I'll call Leo and tell him. . . . " This is a sticking point for Randall—lying is something he prides himself in not doing. "I'll tell him we both feel punk and I need to lay low."

"No," Marcy says, "it's nice to offer, but it wouldn't help that much."

"Truth is, I'd rather stay," he says and stands waiting. The silence lengthens. In the darkness his face seems like a sad, ghostly mask of his face. At last he says, "Okay, then, Marcy, Sugar. I'm going now."

He does. He goes, Randall and his dogs.

After he leaves, Marcy dresses and moves in a daze back and forth from the trailer to the car, not thinking, just taking what she can and piling it into the trunk and back seat. She keeps at it until the sky begins to lighten. Not too far off, a tractor cranks and starts. From somewhere the metallic sound of pigs rooting a creep feeder carries in the still cold air. Across the street, in another trailer, a light goes on. Marcy puts on her dark glasses. She doesn't write a note. She doesn't consider what more she ought to take. She gets into the old Mercury Cougar and slowly drives away from her home and hometown, her parents and her husband.

She drives east out of Goodnight, through Rushville and Gordon, toward Valentine, where, beyond her range of acquaintances, she will swing south, and then, when she hits I-80, turn the Mercury west, toward California.

Once she settles into the drive, a low-grade melancholy overtakes her. Old sights put her in mind of Randall, and old songs, so while she drives she listens instead to call-in shows, people with terrible sounding lives talking to announcers who in Marcy's opinion believe they have all the answers even though they pretend not to. Every now and then Marcy glances at the radio and says, "Well, that's one theory." Her favorite thing to say to a caller is "Join the club, Lady." But, once, when a woman doctor leaves a caller speechless by saying, "Look, Elaine, desires affect decisions and decisions have consequences and you have to take responsibility for those consequences," Marcy, on I-80 out of Cheyenne, can see nothing but the caved-in look of Randall's face when he comes home and finds her gone. What would he do? What in the world would he do? He would swallow it whole, she knew that. He would tell no one. Would answer not one question from one friend. He would swallow it whole and bear it alone. He would become one of those thin still men with gray eyes and stubbled beards and stained coats whose insides are not right, whose sadness makes a perfect nesting place for cancers.

It takes two days, driving like this, to make the desert. Late at night, she crests the Cajon pass and drops into the San Bernardino Valley, a vast blackness dotted with what seems like a million million shimmering lights. Marcy, in that jangly state of hope that sometimes comes from travel alone across wide-open spaces, sees each dot not as a light but as a person, a single person, suddenly come to life and made bright and brand-new. That is one moment. In the next, she wishes more than anything that Randall were here, too, so they could both start new.

On her first morning in LA, Marcy drives along Sunset Boulevard, past places she's only heard of—Frederick's, Grauman's, The Roxy, The Whiskey. To her surprise, there are frightening people everywhere. When a muscular man in black leather pants, no shirt, and lemon yellow hair glances at her license plate, steps out of the crosswalk and, leaning into her window, drawls, "Miss Nebraska, I'd like you to meet Mr. Peanut," Marcy winds up the window and doesn't lower it again until the street turns residential.

Farther on, in a normal-seeming commercial section of town, Marcy goes into the first realty she likes the looks of. It's a big, oddly formal office with thick gray carpet and, on each of the many white desks, a small vase of bright flowers that Marcy's never seen in Nebraska. She asks about rentals and gets passed around. The men in the office wear blazers and ties. The women go for skirt suits, a nice look, Marcy thinks, though it's hard to tell exactly because she doesn't want to take off her dark glasses.

One man in the office seems to change the way everyone else acts. He is a stiff, frail-seeming man in wire-rimmed spectacles, white shirt, and burgundy bow tie—the man, Marcy realizes, who is the source of the office's formality. A trim secretary follows behind as he goes through the office desk to desk, chatting briefly with different agents. Each stiffens slightly at his approach. "A rental, sir," the agent helping Marcy tells the man, and they pass on, the frail man, his secretary, and her perfume.

"Whew!" Marcy says in a low voice of the perfume, and in the same low voice the agent, still clacking away at his computer, says, "It's not that Mr. Realty likes it potent. It's that Mr. Realty's got no sense of smell."

Marcy laughs. In a funny, happy way, this is what, without ever having put a finger on it, she had wanted from Los Angeles. This fancy office. The muttering help. The frail, feared executive. Marcy keeps her eye on him. He's talking on the telephone while filling his briefcase with papers. When he looks her way, Marcy does something that surprises her. She tilts her head and combs her fingers through her long hair, a method of flirtation she developed in high school but which, here and now, seems suddenly klutzy. The man snaps closed his briefcase, hands the phone to his secretary, moves through the office in stiff strides, past Marcy and her agent. But he stops, turns back.

"Look, Miss," he says, "I know of a place that's not listed, a nicely old-fashioned studio. May I ask if you smoke?"

Marcy, looking up at him, knows this is the moment when anyone with an ounce of politeness would take off her sunglasses, but she doesn't. "No," she says.

"Pets?"

"Nope."

"Drugs?"

Marcy stifles a laugh. "Hardly."

The man asks a few more questions. His glasses are coke-bottle thick and, behind them, his eyes are hard to read. Quiet? he asks. Responsible? Employed, or soon will be? Marcy smiles and says yes to each.

For a moment she can almost hear him thinking her over. "Okay," he says, "why don't I just run you up there and show you the place."

The car they drive away in is white, enormous, and deeply quiet. "This is like driving in a new refrigerator," Marcy says, going for a joke, but the man merely responds by turning down the air conditioning. "Two stops to make," he says, almost to himself. With one hand he unsnaps the briefcase lying on the leather seat between them and brings out a roll of chocolate toffees. Before partaking himself, he offers one to Marcy, who wants to accept, but doesn't.

The first stop is at a place called Prestige Motors on Melrose Avenue. The man leaves Marcy in the car while he goes inside, where the salesmen treat him a lot like the people in the real estate office had. They smooth their clothes and work their faces into smiles. It's funny to watch. Also funny to watch is the way the man walks. He is so stiff that Marcy imagines that someone has just wound him up and pointed him her way. When he gets back in, she says, "That where you bought this car?"

He stares at the car agency. "This car is a little newer than those."

The man accelerates the car smoothly into traffic, and Marcy says, "You left me and your keys in the car."

He says nothing, makes a lane change, turns up a narrowing canyon road.

"I could've stolen this big, fancy, newer car of yours."

"It's part of my tenant screening process." A tiny smile seems to form on his lips. "You irrefutably passed." For the first time, Marcy senses something playful in the man's formality. And he has the right voice for it. Besides his brains and expensive clothes, it's the voice, Marcy decides, that's gotten this man up in the world. It is a clear, pure voice that goes into your ear in a ticklish way. Marcy gives him another look. Forty to forty-two, she decides. Marcy has just turned twenty-three.

Their second stop is at the man's home, perched on a cliff out among tall, slender, smooth-barked trees. Marcy waits in the car. As the realtor approaches his house, a male gardener very slightly picks up the pace of his clipping, but a woman in gardening clothes merely pushes back her dark red hair with the back of a hand and says something before she resumes puttering with the potted flowers along the walk. Marcy picks up the tube of toffees. *Callard & Bowser,* it says on the foiled outer wrap, *Made in Great Britain.* Inside, each toffee is neatly wrapped in wax paper. She slips one into her mouth, fiddles with the radio, then the car windows. They slide quietly down, and the car fills up with a pleasant menthol smell from the outside air. She asks about it when the man returns.

"Eucalyptus." He points to the tall trees.

The man drives slowly, the road spiraling upward. He starts to set the toffees back into his briefcase, but pauses to hold the roll out to Marcy. "Another?" he says, and she says, "Nope, one was fine."

A turn in the road affords a sudden, sweeping view of the city. The car slows just a little. "That's the way it used to be," he says. "You could see Catalina Island almost every day. It was a wide-open world then." He looks off into the haze. "One day, when I was ten or eleven, I walked into the Sav-On drugstore at Ventura and Laurel Canyon and found myself standing at the candy counter not far from a man who seemed dimly familiar. I was nearsighted even then, so, without much awareness I was even doing it, I began edging closer and closer to this man, squinting up at him until I was so close I could smell his heavy tobacco smell. At the exact moment that I realized that he was in fact Bela Lugosi, he curled his lip and issued a hissing sound that scared the pea-wadding out of me." A small, self-mocking chuckle slips from the realtor. "I hastily retired. But as I was climbing onto my bicycle, a clerk caught up to me with a box of Callard & Bowser Toffee. There was also a note, which I still possess, that said, 'With this gift Mr. Bela Lugosi wishes to commemorate the pleasant occasion of your acquaintance.'"

The realtor glances at Marcy. "This reminds me that we haven't been formally introduced." He keeps his left hand on the wheel, short-arms his right toward her. "I'm Harmon Martin."

That was what the sign had said in front of the realty: *Harmon Martin's Mr. Realty.* Marcy decides to slip a small one by him. "Marcy Marlene Lockhardt," she says, "but everybody calls me Lena." Lockhardt is her maiden name and nobody in her lifetime has called her Lena.

Harmon Martin releases her hand, "Lena then," he says. More tall eucalyptus trees pass by, more snug bungalows. "So where are you from, Lena?"

Marcy considers lying about this, too, but worries that the man might've seen the plate on her Mercury. "Nebraska." She expects him maybe to ask what part of Nebraska, but he doesn't.

"I've been a lot of places," the man says, "but I've never been to Nebraska. In fact, I think of Nebraska as a kind of English-speaking foreign country. All that *swaggering* and *roping* and *branding*."

"They don't brand so much anymore," Marcy says. "Mostly they just tag their ears."

"Darn," Harmon Martin says softly. "No more hiss and sizzle."

"Not so much anyway," Marcy says.

They fall silent. Marcy leans out the window, stares up at the slender, smooth white trees, takes into her lungs this new, mentholated air.

After a while she says to the man, "Your wife's pretty."

He looks at her in surprise. "Yes, she is." Then, "How did you know she was my wife and not, let us say, a fetching Hollywood Hills gardener?"

Because she wasn't like all the others. She treated Harmon Martin like just another human being. "I could just tell," Marcy says, and as they drive along a fact presents itself like a utensil she has no use for, namely that if a woman wanted to get to Harmon Martin, the way to do it was to force him to imagine everything, and allow him to touch nothing.

Marcy loves the studio. It has hardwood floors, white walls and, beyond the parted French doors, an enamelled deck with solid siding. "For total privacy," Harmon Martin says in an abstracted voice, as if he's saying one thing and thinking another. She asks about rent, is shocked at how high the figure is. "You're kidding," she says.

"I know. It's a very good deal. The owner could get quite a lot more, but won't advertise. She's afraid of the riffraff." He gazes down the canyon toward the freeway. "You'll get a nice view at night."

She stares out.

"This is a Los Angeles address or Hollywood or what?"

"You're in the city of LA, but the mailing address is Hollywood." He glances at her. "Have you by any chance heard of Tom Hulce?"

"*Amadeus.*"

Harmon Martin seems pleased. "Yes. A good young actor, I'd say. He lived here nearly two years, until his salaries grew. He has a reputation, but he left the place neat as a pin."

Marcy knows she shouldn't take the apartment, but says she will. She takes out her folded cash, counts out the first two months' rent, and presents it to Harmon Martin, who, moving close as if to take it, instead reaches forward and gently slides off Marcy's sunglasses. In the change in his face, she sees what he sees: a swollen eye almost the color of eggplant with a yellowish subsurface. He slides the glasses back and steps away. "Who's the party responsible for this?"

Marcy answers quickly, as if there is only one answer. "A guy." She looks away. "My husband actually."

Harmon Martin makes a smile so small that Marcy wonders if she imagines it. "This isn't, I hope, an accepted form of husbandry out there in the hinterlands."

"No," Marcy says, pinkening a little, she isn't sure why. She also isn't sure what Harmon Martin is up to. He still hasn't taken the money.

"So is this imbecile husband going to be a problem?" he asks.

Marcy feels funny, letting this man call Randall an imbecile, which Randall is not, but she shakes her head certainly. "No," she says, "no problem whatsoever."

Marcy's new neighborhood, a curving line of smooth-plaster cottages nestled into the hillside, is as different from Nebraska as different

367

could be. She has painted the mailbox blue and nearly finished stencilling *L. Lockhardt* in yellow when a dog arrives, a small, bowlegged Doberman mix with a frisbee in his mouth. He drops it at her feet and looks up expectantly. She throws it, it wobbles off, the dog retrieves it. They do this several times. The dog's focus on the frisbee is absolute. Marcy can make him shake or nod his head by either waving the frisbee side to side or up and down. She kneels down, holds the frisbee overhead, and in a low voice says, "Will I find a job in television?"

The dog nods a slow yes.

"Will Randall find me?"

No.

"Will I find someone?"

An even more definite yes. Marcy laughs.

"Am I the fairest in the land?"

Yes.

Marcy laughs and tosses the frisbee a few more times, until it gets too slobbery to throw. The dog takes no offense. He merely picks up his toy and trots away, looking surprisingly businesslike. He knows what he wants and how to get it. He visits strangers, drops this plastic disc at their feet, and gives them the chance to make him happy. It seems so simple.

A few days later, Marcy sits in the sun on the private deck hugging her knees. She's come to LA with the idea of working in television, but the truth is, except for a friend's cousin who is an assistant director on *The New Price is Right,* and who, it turns out, left yesterday for Berlin, Marcy knows no one in LA. She thumbs through a *Variety* with her right eye closed. Something is still wrong with that eye. The shiner has healed, but the eye floats, feels unhinged. It weeps and blurs her vision.

She puts down the paper and doesn't know how many minutes have gone by when she realizes that, in this space of time, however long it's been, all she's done is look at her feet. There is so much *time* here. In Goodnight, there were tons of ways to keep yourself busy, but here it is like a vacation, except with all the fun drained away because there's no stop to it.

Somewhere a dog barks, but not the frisbee dog—she knows his bark by now. It is seventy-nine degrees, mid-November. Marcy lies back on her towel, closes her eyes, and tilts her face to meet the angle of the sun. What she wants is something in the television or movie business, not in acting or anything big. Just something that helps keep things going day to day.

She tells Harmon Martin this the next time he telephones, which he does fairly often. Just checking in on the newest leaseholder, he will say dryly. "Sure you wouldn't like to shoot a little higher?" he says today.

"Naw. I like to shoot at things I have a chance of hitting."

Harmon Martin makes a little humming sound, then says he'll do some asking around, see what he can turn up.

Thanksgiving Day, Marcy calls home and is swarmed over by questions. "Where are you?" her mother asks. "Are you okay? Do you have enough money? What're you doing? Are you coming home?"

"Not for a while yet," Marcy says, "but I'm fine, Mom. I am."

"But where—"

"Someplace warmer," Marcy says. "Has he been asking, do you know?"

"Not that I know of. His friend Leo was asking around for a while, but I don't know if that was on his own or for Randall."

Marcy doesn't know what to say. "Is Dad okay then?" she asks finally.

"He'll be better now, knowing you're okay. Provided you are."

"I am, Mom. I really am."

After a little silence, her mother says, "We heard he hit you."

Marcy doesn't say anything.

"Why would he want to do that?"

"He had it in his head that I was running around, Mom."

"But you weren't."

"Nope. But I couldn't convince him, he had it so much in his head."

This much is true, but the larger truth is that Marcy had concluded she'd married the wrong man. She didn't want to spend her life with an ingrown man who wouldn't be happy until she was ingrown, too. Marcy wanted out. And she needed Randall to give her a good enough reason to go, so she invented and told him a story instinctively shaped to organize his anger. At the moment Randall struck her, he was more surprised than she was. Marcy knows this. And for this entrapment of Randall's pitiful worst self, Marcy is beginning to believe, she can never be forgiven.

Marcy in a soft voice says, "So do you think Randall's doing okay?"

"I wouldn't know. He doesn't call and he hardly speaks when spoken to. He still goes to work, I guess, but he stays mostly now in Scottsbluff. People say he's hardly been at the trailer. It's a mess, they say."

A silence, then Marcy says, "I'll call soon, okay? I love you, and tell Dad I love him, too."

Later that day, Marcy cooks herself Thanksgiving dinner for one— a Cornish game hen, fresh peas, and a yam—then sits looking at it. She takes a few bites, wraps the rest in foil for the dog, and goes outside, but he's nowhere to be found. She climbs a winding set of public stairs to the top of a knoll where a public lawn is maintained, and where the dog lies sleeping. He stretches, wags his nubby tail. "Happy Thanksgiving," Marcy says as he greedily bolts the food. Marcy is gazing down at the city when—a slight shock—she realizes that from here there is a narrow line of downward sight to Harmon Martin's house. She stands looking into the brightly lighted kitchen where guests are milling. She can pick out Harmon Martin from among the men—he is mixing drinks, measuring things very carefully—but she can't be certain which of the women is his wife. From a distance, all of them look elegant, handsome, and happy.

Harmon Martin has lined up three job interviews for Marcy, all on the same day. "Trial by fire," he says. "But my advice is not to commit to anything. Say you have another offer pending, that you will tell them something definite within seventy-two hours."

"Three days."

"But you might say hours." His little smile. "In order to create the impression that your time units are small, compressed, and important."

The interviews are a nightmare. Marcy wears a simple beige-and-black dress that she hoped would seem elegant, but, she realizes, is made to be overlooked in. The men who interview her wear more color than she does. They ask questions like, What unique talents can you bring to this job? Marcy sweats, stammers, and introduces to the room the kind of awkwardness that infects others. At the final interview, the man breaks a long, horrible silence by picking up her application and reading through it. "What's KDUH?" he says finally.

"It's Channel 4 in northwest Nebraska." She daubs at her eye to keep the liquid in its pink sac from spilling down her cheek. "For about six months I read the weekend news."

"What's the ENG capacity there?" the man says and then, when he sees her confusion, says, "The electronic newsgathering capacity."

"Oh. I really don't know. I guess I should, but all I did was read the news." She pulls out another tissue from her purse.

Later, when Harmon Martin telephones to find out how the interviews went, Marcy says, "Not that great." She thinks about it and says, "Thinking about it makes me kind of tired."

"You might be wrong. You might be pleasantly surprised. But it doesn't matter. Those folks were flyweights, they couldn't carry your bags. So let's say we keep looking around until we find just the right fit."

The right fit, Marcy thinks. Fitting in. When she realizes she might begin to cry, she makes a quick excuse and says goodbye.

Another sunny day. Where she has come from, weather dictates activities and affects moods, and Marcy misses the little indicators. The smell of burning leaves, the creak of frozen porchboards, Randall carrying the fresh smell of winter with him into a warm room. But December in southern California is relentlessly green, leafy, and bright. There is only the changing angle of the sun as it streams onto the deck, where Marcy spends her afternoons reading and tanning.

Marcy has been offered a job. She can work as a cocktail waitress at a country-western place called The Palomino. Harmon Martin had nothing to do with this. Marcy saw the ad, called up, drove out to the valley. A woman looked her over the way a man would and said, "The one position is filled. But there's another in mid-January. Can you wait that long?"

Marcy said yes she could, but in truth she's not so sure about the job. The money would be good, and she wouldn't mind the get-up, but it seems so different out here. In Goodnight, she knew how to say no to men because she knew who they were and they knew who she was.

A crow glides past Marcy's deck. Marcy blinks, realizes she's been thinking of Randall. Of the tons of things she knows she shouldn't do, the one she knows she shouldn't do most of all is think about Randall, but she can't always help it. Usually she hopes Randall is with somebody, but today, a bad sign, she hopes he isn't. She sits down and writes Randall a long rushing letter full of explanation and questions and soft thoughts. Without reading it over, she seals it and means to walk it down the canyon to the mailbox before the last pickup, but when she opens the door, Harmon Martin is standing there about to knock. He hasn't saved her, not in any real sense, but when she awakens the next morning with the letter still in her purse, she will allow herself to think of it in almost that way.

Harmon Martin has come to the door because he has news. "Something quite remarkable." His little, self-knowing smile forms. "An interview, in January."

"Who with?" she says, but he merely winks. He's brought makings for what he calls "a celebratory gimlet." He mixes it precisely, savors his first sip. "Well," he says, seating himself. "I put in a word with a colleague. The colleague put in a word for me." He takes his handkerchief from his suit pocket, fogs and cleans his thick glasses, holds them to the light, gives them a finishing touch. He slides them on, looks beamingly at Marcy. "You have an interview on Tuesday, January 17th, 10:00 A.M., with Universal, for the position of personal secretary to Steven Spielberg."

Marcy stands frozen for a moment. "This isn't some kind of joke?"

"That's correct," Harmon Martin says. "It is not."

Marcy gives him a quick kiss on the cheek before walking about the apartment in a state of real agitation. "You did it," she says, as much to herself as to him and then, beside herself, she whoops, "*Hot chaw!*"—a phrase that makes Harmon Martin actually chuckle, a phrase that Marcy has never used before, a phrase that until now had been exclusively Randall's. She dances up to Harmon Martin, slips off his glasses, puts them on herself, keeps dancing. She takes his hand and, against his protests, pulls him up to dance. He moves mechanically for a minute or so, then retreats back to his chair. It's an endearing surprise, this rich man's embarrassment. When his blushing recedes, he makes a little smile. "I'm not much of a dancer," he says. "If I'd thought it was pertinent, I'd have told you sooner."

On Christmas morning, Marcy dials her old number in Nebraska, imagines the telephone on the coffee table in the living room of the trailer as it rings and rings. Finally she gives up and tries her parents' number. Her father answers on the second ring. "*Ha!*" he says when she says hello. "I *knew* it was you. It's the sixth time it's rung today, but this time I said to your mother, 'This one's her,' and, sure enough, here you are."

They talk amiably for a while, her father relying mostly on local crime stories to avoid touchy subjects. After telling about the stolen tractor discovered hidden in Raymond Fales's haymow, he says, "Okay, okay, I better give the phone to your mother before she turns blue."

372

"Hi, Polkadot," her mother says and, following a rush of questions, she takes a breath and says, "I was hoping you'd be home by now."

"I think I'm here to stay, Mom. The people are nice to me and I'm beginning to like it." Then, "Did you get my presents okay?"

Marcy has sent presents anonymously through a mail-order catalogue, a doe and fawn in a snow-globe for her mother and a set of nesting presidents for her father, who'd always taken pride in his ability to tick off all of them in order. To Randall she'd sent a pair of flannel boxer shorts in a duck-hunting pattern and a plaid electric blanket. She mentions this and her mother says, "I don't know that he'll receive those kindly."

"Why is that?" Marcy says. She can tell her mother is thinking something over. "What?"

"Oh, a story," her mother says.

"About him and somebody else?"

"No, but how would you feel about that?"

"Fine. I want him to be happy, is all I want."

"Well, I don't think he's so happy."

"What makes you say so?"

Another pause, then, "Well, the story, according to Flossie Boyles, is that about two weeks ago Randall took all your clothes out onto the carport by the trailer and heaped them up and burned them. Then he swept the ashes into a neat pile and put them in a Tupperware container and, the story goes, he consumes a teaspoon at a time by spreading it over his meals."

Marcy feels actually sickened. "Mom?"

"What, Polkadot?"

But Marcy catches herself. The story she was about to tell would've just played into her mother's hands. "I love you," she says, "and just tell Dad it's warm here and the people are nice to me and I miss him."

What she had thought to describe to her mother was the recurring dream she'd been having. In it, she brings Randall to the edge of a bluff overlooking the beach. They are both younger, in high school, happy, unsteady with laughter, trying to catch with their mouths black jelly beans they lob into the air. From the overhanging bluff face there is a steep, red-dirt channel, made by erosion, that is like a long chute down to the beach. There is sheer happiness in Randall's face when Marcy brings him to it. He plunges down at once, on the seat of his pants, whooping at first, but the moment he turns a corner, beyond Marcy's view, his voice stops and there are loud sickening thuds as his body bumps its way down the rocky slope. Marcy runs for the stairs, but cannot go down to look.

The first week of January, Marcy browses department stores for the right thing to wear to her interview (no luck) and reads everything about Steven Spielberg she can lay her hands on (the East Hampton inside-out barn in *Architectural Digest,* the money to Harvard for an extraterrestrial scanner in *Physics Today,* the rumors about Kate Capshaw in *People*). "Steven is boyish," says Richard Dreyfuss in *Life,*" and financially canny, but the word that really nails him is adventurous." In the background of one photograph, Marcy finds his secretary. She is dark-haired, too. Like his first wife. Like Amy Irving. Like Kate Capshaw.

The next morning Marcy spends seventy-five dollars on tinting her hair. "That color," she says to the hairdresser and points to a photograph of Kate Capshaw she's torn out of a magazine.

This is the first of two changes Marcy makes. The other is a molded leather eye patch she finds in a costume shop. It stops the double vision and the weeping, but she's not so sure about it. The first time she wears it outside the house, she turns away when a car passes. She whistles and before long the little bowlegged Doberman trots smartly around the corner carrying a new red frisbee. He drops it at her feet. She picks it up, holds it close to her head. "Shall I wear the eye patch?"

Yes.

No.

She tosses the frisbee into the empty street. It skips off the pavement and floats over the hillside. The dog leaps out into the air, disappears over the side. For a moment, time stands still, then the dog reappears, grinning around his red frisbee.

Whether she'll wear the eye patch, Marcy decides, will depend on the outfit she buys for the interview, but the days go by without finding the right thing. Finally, the day before the interview, she begins to cry in the dressing room of Bullocks Wilshire. Everything that looks good on the rack looks horrible on her. She takes off what she has on, goes to the most stylish saleswoman on the floor, and says, "I'm looking for something for a job interview at Universal, nice, but with a sense of adventure."

When Marcy arrives for the interview, she is directed to a large, tightly quiet room where about a dozen applicants are already waiting. Most of the women are wearing tasteful coat dresses in navy or cream, ex-

pensive but not too expensive. Marcy's outfit, she realizes, is just fool-
ish. A semi-safari look, the saleswoman had called it. A khaki skirt, a
Chinese peasant coat worn open to a tight, stretchy top in an orange
color the saleswoman called quince. With suede flats, long, dangly, cos-
tume-gold earrings, and a brimless red hat, the total was $625, more
money than Marcy had, so she opened an instant charge account.

"I heard the job was an aide to Steven Spielberg," Marcy says to the
woman closest to her.

Several of the women glance toward her. One of them, before turn-
ing just slightly away, says, "I hope you're right, Sweet Pea."

At a little past noon, Marcy is given a brief interview by a man—it
goes fine—and then is shown into a round, windowless room where
she is left alone. The walls are meant to be funny, Marcy guesses, but
they scare her a little. White Roman columns have been painted on
every wall and door, with dark vines trailing from one to the other.
Walking among the columns is an odd cast of creatures—browsing ze-
bras, penguins with parasols, grim-faced businessmen in bowler hats.
Two black chairs and a white, glass-topped table are the only furniture
in the room. Sitting on top of the table are a typewriter, a loud windup
clock, a telephone, and a shrink-wrapped leather book. She is staring
at the telephone when it rings. Marcy answers and a woman's voice
says, "Miss Lockhardt, kindly check Mr. Spielberg's daybook, confirm
for Lafcadio's and with Miss Wittenburg at CBS, cancel everything be-
tween 1:15 and 3:25, and if Mr. Wallace, White, or Wilson calls, advise
them that Mr. Spielberg will be out of the office until tomorrow."

Marcy does these things, politely and, as far as she knows, correctly.

Shortly thereafter, as if of its own, a door Marcy hadn't seen swings
open, cleanly sweeping out most of a Roman column. A woman rides
into the room on a wave of confidence and energy, gives her name as
Connie DeVrie, and, after a glance at Marcy's outfit, says, "What a *dra-
matic* coat!"

Connie DeVrie is wearing a dark, executive-looking skirt suit.

"First a five-minute typing test," she says and sets the clock.

The text concerns itself with the stress capacities of concrete. Mo-
ments after Marcy starts typing, the telephone rings. At the instant
that Marcy picks it up, Connie DeVrie suspends time on the test. "Mr.
Spielberg's office," Marcy says as briskly as she can.

A woman says, "Mr. Wade's office for Mr. Spielberg please."

Marcy, uncertain, says, "Your name again?" and the woman at the
other end hangs up without a word. Connie DeVrie starts time

running again and Marcy tries to concentrate on the typing. There are numbers and fractions everywhere. Marcy's fingers move unsurely over the top row of the keyboard. The last minute of the test, she tries to think up something worth saying to excuse her performance, but can't. She fights off the impulse to cry.

There are other tests, too, not quite as horrible, but almost.

When they're all completed, Connie DeVrie disappears through the swinging door, tests in hand. From the inner sanctum beyond the wall, Marcy can hear rich male laughter, and then laughter from men and women together, until finally the wall swings open again, but not completely. Connie DeVrie uses it like a shield, around which only her head appears. She says she'll call Marcy when all the interviews are completed and then, before Marcy can say a word, Connie DeVrie closes the door that wasn't a door.

When she returns to her bungalow, the dog is asleep on her stoop. The door is also ajar. Through the window she can see Harmon Martin in shirt sleeves, wearing an apron, standing at the kitchen sink washing spinach leaves one by one. Marcy, stepping inside, asks how he got in.

"Key," he says, with enough unconcern to annoy Marcy. He doesn't look at her. He nods toward the sinkful of carrot peelings. "You know if you keep eating nothing but carrots, you will actually turn yellow."

She thinks of telling him that the reason Howard Hawks wanted Lauren Bacall for *To Have and Have Not* was her yellow complexion, which looked good on film—it's the kind of story that interests Harmon Martin—but he turns and is brought up short.

"Good grief," he says.

He's never before seen the eye patch, the peasant coat, the quince-colored top. Marcy's shoulders drop. "I know, I know," she says.

He lays down the spinach leaves. "Look, Lena," he says, "I knew you were very attractive, but I didn't know that you could be so . . . fetching."

Marcy wonders if he's joking.

"I spoke to my colleague. He said the interview didn't work out so well. I was going to make you dinner as a way of . . . *condoling*, but, just for the record, whoever turned you down ought to have had his head examined."

Marcy stares at him. "You're not joking, are you?"

"We're going out, Lena Lockhardt. I'm taking you out. That much you owe me."

376

They go to a place called Sports. She orders crab and a flaming dessert. She enjoys every bite. "I'll pay my half," she says while he's sipping coffee. He smiles. Half, rounded off, is seventy-two dollars.

She pays it. She pays it so that after he drives her home, she can give him à quick kiss, say goodnight, and feel virtuous even while experiencing the strange pleasure of watching his appetite grow.

Last night Marcy worked her first shift at The Palomino. Joe Ely played, she made a couple of mistakes on drink orders, but still took home over ninety dollars. Except for a couple of unfunny remarks, it was okay, so this morning, a Saturday, Marcy feels just fine. She has gone out to sit in the sun on the deck, but as the sky clouds over she puts on a T-shirt and, a while later, sweat pants. When she hears Harmon Martin's peculiar knock on the door, she sings out, "It's unlocked! I'm out on the deck!"

He sets a grocery bag on the drainboard, slides open the door to the deck. "I've been wondering if you got mauled last night?"

She laughs. "No real bruises."

Harmon Martin regards her, then goes to the deck rail and looks out.

"Rain," she says. "Or would be if this was Nebraska."

He stares off. "It's coming up from the gulf. It's the kind that can really open up."

It's quiet except for the drone of an airplane. For the first time, Marcy wonders where Harmon Martin's wife thinks he is.

"Did I mention the hotel project we've begun in St. Martin?" he says, still looking off. "It's quite reckless, four hundred rooms, on the Dutch side." He turns around. "I have to go over there this week."

"How nice," Marcy says. It *does* sound nice, actually.

"Yes, well, I've been thinking," Harmon Martin says. "Do you remember the car dealership I went into the day I showed you this place?"

"The place with the old cars."

"*Vintage* cars, we call them, but yes. I own that agency. We sell pre-'68 Rollses, Mercedes, Porsches, Bentleys, and Bugattis that we bring over from Europe. We restore them to mint condition, guarantee them, and sell them as investment-quality classics, which they are."

Since when, Marcy wonders, does Harmon Martin fill her in on his work? "That's interesting," she says.

"There are three salesmen, but one will soon be leaving."

Marcy doesn't say anything.

He says, "What got me thinking were those clothes you wore the other night, the Asian coat and red top. Tasteful, but somewhat . . . *sportive*." He smiles his subdued smile. "I think you'd be, as they say, a selling fool."

On the freeway below, loose lines of traffic flow smoothly along.

Gently he says, "Six figures is not out of the question."

Marcy tries to keep her voice calm. "I don't know beans about cars."

"I'd be happy to teach you—history, horsepower, appreciation potential, that kind of thing." He snugs his glasses to the bridge of his nose. "Which is why I mention St. Martin. I'll have meetings, but there will be dead times. We could put them to use. Probably we'd just start with Mercedes and Bentleys for now, and work on the rest later on."

Marcy feels lightheaded. She needs to say something. "I never thought I was coming out to Hollywood to sell used cars," she says.

"*Vintage,*" he says, with his smile.

Then Harmon Martin half-closes his eyes, a few moments pass, and his lids slowly open. "Look, Lena," he says. "In a way it *is* part of the business. Take the day before yesterday. Alec Baldwin came in and used his American Express for a Porsche roadster, the '58 Super Speedster, eighteen thousand dollars. Last week Randy Quaid purchased a three-wheel Morgan. We sell to anybody, but it's amazing how many of the buyers are recognizable. Julie Newmar bought a '31 Bentley, and before he died Steve McQueen bought his 356 from us." Harmon Martin spreads his hands, looks at them, spreads them wider. His voice grows almost melodious. "Both of John Wayne's sons. Dwight Yoakam. Rita Moreno." It is a surprise and not a surprise, this new use of his fine, pure voice. Far away a car horn sounds. Harmon Martin slows his pace. "Fernando Lamas," he croons. "Whit Bissell . . . Strother Martin . . . John Cassavetes." Marcy grins dreamily. "Sterling Holloway . . . Elizabeth Ashley . . . Lou Diamond Phillips. . . . " One after another, the names, the dreamy, beautiful, expensive names, hover close by, floating, then on the updraft rise overhead.

"We'll need to leave by 4 P.M. Tuesday," Harmon Martin says. "You can pack light. We're building on the Dutch side, but staying on the French, where dress is informal, especially on the beach."

Slowly and with real effort Marcy brings the room back into focus. She has to say no, thanks but no thanks, and she has to say it now. Thanks but no thanks. Say it.

Harmon Martin is at the door, looking as lightheaded as Marcy feels, and then he is gone.

The storm takes hold that night and doesn't let go. The weatherman Marcy watches is called Dr. George by the cheery co-anchors. Dr. George runs a clip of two women in rain-drenched bikinis roller-skating in Santa Monica, then shoves his face muggingly into the camera and says that what we have here, folks, is a good old-fashioned gully whumper. Marcy spends the day reading and watching TV, eating popcorn and thinking of spending similar days when snow floated idly down in Nebraska. She puts on her swimming suit and stands on a stool to look at herself in the mirror. She tries it with the top off and actually laughs. If Harmon Martin thinks she'd go out on a public beach like that, he can think again. She wishes he would call so she could remember how his voice made her feel while he was saying those names, but he doesn't. By Sunday afternoon, whenever she looks at a clock, Marcy converts it to Nebraska time. That evening, for the first time since the storm moved in, she thinks of the dog. She opens the front door, calls into the sheets of slanting rain, but her voice is swallowed in the gurgling throat of the storm. Through the night she imagines hearing the dog scratching at the door, but when she shines a flashlight out, he isn't there. There is only the splash of water.

The storm is supposed to let up Tuesday morning, but doesn't. Marcy packs her suitcase in hopes that her feelings will catch up with her actions. She packs perfume, lingerie, diaphragm. But Harmon Martin's knock on the door makes her do something surprising. She slides the packed suitcase under the bed and opens another one on top, empty.

Harmon Martin shakes out his umbrella at the door and enters uncertainly. He doesn't seem completely surprised when Marcy leads him to the empty suitcase. "I'm not going," she says. He frets and coaxes, growing smaller by the minute. Beneath his linen jacket, he wears a pale pink long-sleeved shirt that seems to Marcy unpleasantly showy. While he walks stiffly about the room, he fusses with the pale pink cuffs, tugging them down on his too-thin wrists. When finally he sits down and pleads, Marcy says, "No. Once and for all, no."

Moments later, clouds outside part to a startling blue and the entire room lightens. Harmon Martin writes something down. "This is my home number. I'll be there another hour, in case you change your mind." He taps his glasses. "If my wife answers, just say, 'About the leak in the studio on Ione, tell Harmon never mind it's been fixed.'"

After he leaves, Marcy goes outside and is surprised that his car is actually gone. The sun glares down; vapor rises from the wet asphalt. Everywhere on the ground there are worms, and snails, and soaked

379

newspapers. People begin popping out of houses. From a distance, a dog barks, *her* dog, his sharp clear anxious barking. Marcy follows the sound down the hillside streets, along Ione, down finally to Cahuenga. In the traffic, the barking is lost, or perhaps it's stopped. Marcy keeps walking, farther from her studio, farther from Harmon Martin's house, taking deep breaths of the new clean air. In Goodnight, after a storm like this, there would be careful appraisal of crops and stock, but here there is nothing but a general sense of freedom after long constraint. Joggers appear. Bicycles whiz by. Music carries from open car windows.

The clearing, however, is a false one. The skies again turn dark, car windows slide up, fat raindrops spatter, and the sweep of windshield wipers begins again. Marcy, coatless, keeps walking, following the flood control channel, watching the water pour by, branches and bottles and plastic containers all rushing along on the fierce current.

It is from a bridge spanning the channel that she sees the dog. He is down below, to the right, in a muddy lot within the fence enclosing the channel, an area used to park orange government trucks, where neither the dog nor the group of boys surrounding him should be. The boys are bickering over whose turn it is to throw the frisbee next. When finally one of them throws it, the dog seems to skate above the mud, and to rise out of it for the long moment needed to pluck the frisbee from the air. Marcy can hear the boys' shrill voices. "*Whoa!* Check it out! This canine can *fly!*"

The cars splash past Marcy on the bridge, but the pedestrians and bicyclists have disappeared. The rain turns hard and finally the boys notice it, too. They hunch their shoulders, look up at the sky, and move toward their bikes. One, however, lags back and, as he sees the others mount their bikes, this last boy picks up the frisbee for one last throw.

What is this like? Like watching one of those TV nature shows and knowing that the snow rabbit or the lame gnu is going to get it and not turning the channel. Marcy wants to call out to the dog, to retrieve him from danger, but she doesn't. She stands mute as the boy turns toward the storm channel and without a moment's hesitation flicks the frisbee toward it. The dog races after the frisbee, pitches forward when the level ground gives way beneath him, then tumbles and skids down the concrete bank into the rushing current. His neck stretches up out of the water for a moment before he is swept away.

Marcy feels suddenly boneless. There are so many ways to act cowardly. There are just so many ways to do it. She could've yelled at that boy and saved the dog. She could've done that little bit. And she could've given Harmon Martin, a married man, nothing whatsoever to think about. And she could've told Randall that for reasons she didn't get and couldn't explain, she had to change her life or go crazy. She could've done that instead of telling him lies and making him hit her, making him feel and look to all of Goodnight like a brute. She could've done these things, if she were only not such a coward, and then besides saving that dog's life and saving Randall and Harmon Martin a lot of trouble, her life would now have more of the decency she always meant it to have. It was like that boy who threw the frisbee. That boy knew what that poor dog would do. Probably that boy would grow into someone worthless, and then the dog wouldn't matter. But it would matter if that boy somehow began to turn into somebody decent. Then his carelessness with that trusting dog would nibble away at him and he would learn that, no matter who said what to you, it was the kind of sin that only you who committed it could forgive yourself for, except that you never could unless you began scaling back your ideas of what makes a wrongful act. Marcy begins to walk. Water streams from her hair into her face. Her pant legs and sweater soak up the rain and grow heavy. She walks and walks, along Cahuenga, up the canyon toward Ione, past Harmon Martin's house, soaked through, not thinking, just walking in her own water world.

Marcy is at her gate when it dawns on her that the green Dodge pickup she has just passed seems familiar. Marcy turns and stares in disbelief. It is Randall's truck. The shadowy form slouched behind the steering wheel must then be Randall. Marcy moves toward him. In the truck bed there is a dark, wet canvas tarp roped over odd shapes that suggest furniture. Scattered on the dashboard are a seed cap, a road map, a box of Good & Plentys. A feeling of relief and perhaps even affection swells within Marcy. What kept you? she thinks of calling out when he rolls down the window, but he doesn't. He doesn't move at all, an indication, she guesses, of sullenness or mean satisfaction, and all at once Marcy has no real idea what she is feeling, what she will say. But she doesn't have to say anything. Behind the fogged windshield, behind the streaming rivulets of water, in a tightly closed cab that Marcy doesn't actually have to smell to know its wintry mingling of licorice and boot leather, coffee and flannel, Randall is fast asleep.

Nominated by Ehud Havazelet

FETISH

by LORETTA COLLINS

from TRIQUARTERLY

A shoe is valued highly if it is:

Placed in a man's hand.

Thrown into silhouette by a lamp.

Seen as an imprint in fresh snow.

*   *   *

I dig my heels in when I walk.
I grind my pumps down to the nails,
can't wait to wear them out,
just to get Woody to glue on taps.
When I pick up those red spikes with vinyl bows,
I'm going to put a whole lot of Estée Lauder
on my feet.
                    See, at Woody's Shoe Repair,
he gives your kid (whining mamma mamma,
shrieking like a jungle bird
while swinging on your purse) a dime
for jawbreakers; he shows you the heel,
shows how he worked it at the lathe.
Then he kneels and slips your sweaty shoe
right on your foot—says, "Only one way
to try it out," and waltzes you around
the shop. Holds your waist and gallops

you in circles until dust flies
up from Red Wings, Buster Browns no one ever
picked up. You want to ask
about newspaper clippings on the wall:
Woody in boxing trunks, his arm
around Ali, Leon Spinks;
Woody winning a boodle in the CA lottery
Big Spin. You want to ask
about the pink scar on his temple.
You really want to drag him off
into a back room full of shoe leather
and wear that man out. But you don't.
You paint your toenails Scarlet
Flamingo. And wear out your shoes. Save them
claim tickets for what's yours.

* * *

On her night off, Grandmother Kathryn dragged
the lawn chairs out. She propped up her feet.
It took pruning shears and all my weight
to cut through the yellow nail that stood
up like a wooden spoon from her big toe.
Thirty years back, while cutting out soles
at International Shoe Company in West Plains,
she'd dropped a shank on her foot.
She settled down after that.

* * *

We hit Carlsby, Nevada, after midnight,
nearly out of gas and the gas cap frozen up.
The woman at the pumps was locking up.
She said this wasn't any place for a gal
and her son to sleep in a truck.
She'd call her boyfriend to monkeywrench
the cap off.
                    Only one casino was lit
down the hill. For what I know, Carlsby's
a lovely place in early light,

383

vining clematis and hollyhocks shooting up
in great brakes around snug bungalows.
At midnight, though, it's wind and red dust
shuddering the truck, a train horn bleating,
and a tired man pulling tools out of his Nova,
plying the stubborn cap with a wrench.
He wore boxers and work shoes
full of so many small holes
that I saw his pale feet.

"Why do people live here?" I asked.
"Silver mining," she said.
"The big companies do pretty good."

She wore low-heeled pumps.

*   *   *

The first time we went to bed,
I wore a red-dragon kimono. His
was blue. Before we'd done it once,
he showed me all the positions
he'd like to try
in the book of Chinese erotic art:

Upside-down Clouds,

The Jade Stalk Knocks at the Door,

Penetrating the Cords of the Lute,

The Leaping White Tiger.

The ladies' feet curved like tiny pony hooves.
He said that connoisseurs
of bound feet could name fifty-eight
varieties: "Lotus Petal,"
"New Moon," "Gracious Salutation."

"The Golden Lotus" was reserved
for the smallest foot, three inches

at the most. We looked at pages
of Golden Lotuses in embroidered
silk baby boots. Then he showed me
how to raise my foot and bend
over until my hair swept the floor.

"What's this one called,
The Guppy Drowns in the Moat?"

"That's it.
Bend over."

            *   *   *

My friend, who had worked
at an orphanage in Honduras,
said to me:

I saw a child's shoe in the street.
When I picked it up, I saw the foot
was still in it.

After the police beat back
crowds from Rudolph Valentino's
wake, they found 28 shoes, umbrellas,
and torn sleeves in the streets.

            *   *   *

A shoe is valued highly if it is:

Placed on a man's lap.

Photographed in an alley.

Seen as an imprint in flesh.

Nominated by TriQuarterly

THE CATSKILLS REMEMBERED

by VIVIAN GORNICK

from THE THREEPENNY REVIEW

I HAVE NEVER been able to think of the old Catskills Mountains hotel circuit as the actual setting for all those Borscht Belt jokes. For me, a college student waitressing in the late Fifties, the Catskills was a wild place, dangerous and exciting, where all the beasts were predatory, none pacific. The years I spent working in those hotels were my introduction to the brutishness of function, the murderousness of fantasy, the isolation inflicted on all those living inside a world organized to provide pleasure. It's the isolation I've been thinking about lately—how remarkably present it was, crude and vibrant, there from the first moment of contact.

I walked into Stella Mercury's Employment agency one afternoon in the winter of my freshman year at City College. Four men sat playing cards with a greasy deck, chewing gum methodically, never looking up once. The woman at the desk, fat and lumpy with hard eyes and a voiceful of cigarette wheeze, said to me, "Where ya been?" and I rattled off a string of hotels. "Ya worked all those places," she said calmly. "Ain't the human body a mah-h-vellous thing, ya don't look old enough to have worked half of 'em." I stood there, ill with fear that on the one hand she'd throw me out on the other she'd give me a job, and assured her that I had. She knew I was lying, and I knew that she knew I was lying, but she wrote out a job ticket, anyway. Suddenly I felt lonely inside the lie, and I begged her with my eyes to acknowledge the truth between us. She didn't like that at all. Her own eyes grew even harder, and she refused me more than she had when I'd not revealed open need. She drew back with the ticket still in her hand. I snatched at it. She laughed a nasty laugh. And that was it, all of it, right there, two flights above Times Square, I was in the Mountains.

That first weekend in a large glittering hotel filled with garment district salesmen and midtown secretaries, weaving clumsily in and out of the vast kitchen all heat and acrimony (food flying, trays crashing, waiters cursing), I gripped the tray so hard all ten knuckles were white for days afterward, and every time I looked at them I recalled the astonishment I'd felt when a busboy at the station next to mine stuck out his fist to a guest who'd eaten three main dishes and said, "Want a knuckle sandwich?" But on Sunday night when I flung fifty single dollar bills on the kitchen table before my open-mouthed mother there was soft exultancy, and I knew I'd go back. Rising up inside this brash, moralistic working-class girl was the unexpected excitement of the first opportunity for greed.

I was eighteen years old, moving blind through hungers whose force I could not grasp. Unable to grasp what drove me, I walked around feeling stupid. Feeling stupid I became inept. Secretly, I welcomed going to the Mountains. I knew I could do this hard but simple thing. I could enter that pig-eyed glitter and snatch from it this soft, gorgeous, fleshy excitement of quick money. This I could master. This, I thought, had only to do with endurance; inexhaustible energy; and that I was burning up with.

The summer of my initiation I'd get a job, work two weeks, get fired. ("You're a waitress? I thought you said you were a waitress. What kinda waitress sets a table like that? Who you think you're kidding, girlie?") But by Labor Day I *was* a waitress, and a veteran of the first year. I had been inducted into an underclass elite, a world of self-selected Orwellian pariahs for whom survival was the only value.

At the first hotel an experienced waiter, attracted by my innocence, took me under his wing. In the Mountains, regardless of age or actual history, your first year you were a virgin and in every hotel there was always someone, sentimental as a gangster, to love a virgin. My patron

387

in this instance was a twenty-nine-year-old man who worked in the post office in winter and at this hotel in summer. He was a handsome vagrant, a cunning hustler, what I would come by the end of the summer to recognize as a "mountain rat."

One night a shot rang out in the sleeping darkness. Waiters and waitresses leaped up in the little barracks building we shared at the edge of the hotel grounds. Across the wide lawn, light filled the open doorway of one of the distant guest cottages. A man stood framed in the light, naked except for a jockstrap. Inside the barracks people began to laugh. It was my handsome protector. He'd been sleeping with a woman whose gambler husband had appeared unexpectedly on a Thursday night.

The next day he was fired. We took a final walk together. I fumbled for words. Why? I wanted to know. I knew he didn't like the woman, a diet-thin blonde twenty years older than himself. "Ah-h-h," my friend said wearily. "Doncha know nothing, kid? Doncha know what I am? I mean, whaddaya think I am?"

At the second hotel the headwaiter, a tall sweating man, began all his staff meetings with, "Boys and girls, the first thing to understand is, we are dealing here with animals." He stood in the dining-room doorway every morning holding what I took to be a glass of apple juice until I was told it was whiskey neat. "Good morning, Mrs. Levine," he'd nod affably, then turn to a busboy and mutter, "That Holland Tunnel whore." He rubbed my arm between his thumb and his forefinger when he hired me and said, "We'll take care of each other, right, kid?" I nodded, thinking it was his way of asking me to be a responsible worker. My obtuseness derailed him. When he fired me and my friend Marilyn because he caught us eating chocolate tarts behind an alcove in the dining room, he thundered at us, his voice hoarse with relief, "You are not now waitresses, you never were waitresses, you'll never *be* waitresses."

At the third hotel I had fifty dollars stolen from me at the end of a holiday weekend. Fifty dollars wasn't fifty dollars in the Mountains, it was blood money. My room was crowded with fellow workers, all silent as pallbearers. The door racketed open and Kennie, a busboy who was always late, burst into the room. "I heard you had money stolen!" he cried, his face stricken. I nodded wordlessly. Kennie turned, pulled the door shut, twisted his body about, raised his arm and banged his fist, sobbing, against the door. When I said, "What are *you* getting so excited about?" he shrieked at me, "Because you're a waitress and a human being! And I'm a busboy and a human being!" At the end of the summer, four more robberies having taken place, the thief was caught. It was Kennie.

At the fourth hotel the children's waiter was a dedicated womanizer. A flirtatious guest held out on him longer than usual, and one morning I saw this waiter urinate into a glass of orange juice, then serve it to the woman's child with the crooning injunction to drink it all up because it was so-o-o good.

At the fifth hotel I served a woman who was all bosom from neck to knee, with tiny feet daintily shod, smooth plump hands beautifully manicured, childish eyes in a painted face. When I brought her exactly-three-minute eggs to the table she said to me, "Open them for me, dear. The shells burn my hands." I turned away, to the station table against the wall, to perform in appropriate secrecy a task that told me for the first but certainly not the last time that here I was only an extension of my function. It was the Catskills, not early socialist teachings at my father's knee, that made me a Marxist.

One winter I worked weekends and Christmas at a famous hotel. This hotel had an enormous tiered dining room, and was run by one of the most feared headwaiters in the Mountains. The system here was that all newcomers began at the back of the dining room on the tier furthest from the kitchen. If your work met with favor you were moved steadily toward the center, closer to the kitchen doors and to the largest tips, which came not from the singles who were invariably placed in the back of the room but from the middle-aged manufacturers, club owners, and gangsters who occupied the tables in the central tiers, cutting a wide swath as though across a huge belly between the upper and lower ends of the dining room.

As the autumn wore on I advanced down the tiers. By Christmas I was nearly in the center of the room, at one of the best stations in the house. This meant my guests were now middle-aged married couples whose general appearance was characterized by blond bouffants, mink stoles, midnight-blue suits, and half-smoked cigars. These people ate prodigiously and tipped well.

That Christmas the hotel was packed and we worked twelve hours a day. The meals went on forever. By the end of the week we were dead on our feet but still running. On New Year's Eve at midnight we were to serve a full meal, the fourth of the day, but this was to be a banquet dinner—that is, a series of house-chosen dishes simply hauled out, course by course—and we looked forward to it. It signaled the end of

389

the holiday. The next morning the guests checked out and that night we'd all be home in our Bronx or Brooklyn apartments, our hard-earned cash piled on the kitchen table.

But a threatening atmosphere prevailed at the midnight meal from the moment the dining-room doors were flung open. I remember sky-blue sequined dresses and tight mouths, satin cummerbunds and hard-edged laughter, a lot of drunks on the vomitous verge. People darted everywhere and all at once, pushing to get at the central tables (no assigned seats tonight), as though, driven from one failed part of the evening to another, here, at last, they were going to get what should come through for them: a good table in the famous dining room during its New Year's Eve meal.

The kitchen was instantly affected: it picked up on atmosphere like an animal whose only survival equipment is hyper-alertness. A kind of panicky aggression seemed to overtake the entire staff. The orderly lines that had begun to form for the first appetizer broke almost immediately. People who had grown friendly, working together over these long winter weekends, now climbed over each other's backs to break into the line and grab at the small round dishes piled up on the huge steel tables.

I made my first trip into the kitchen, took in the scene before me, and froze. Then I took a deep breath, inserted myself into a line, held my own against hands and elbows pushing into my back and ribs, got my tray loaded and myself out the kitchen doors. I served the fruit cup quickly and, depending on my busboy to get the empties off the tables in time, made my anxious way back into the kitchen for the next course which, I'll not forget as long as I live, was chow mein. This time I thought violence was about to break out. All those people, trays, curses being flung about! And now I couldn't seem to take a deep breath: I remained motionless just inside the kitchen doors. Another waitress, a classmate from City College, grabbed my arm and whispered in my ear, "Skip the chow mein, they'll never know the difference. Go on to the next course, there's nobody on the line over there." My heart lifted, the darkness receded. I stared at her. Did we dare? Yes, she nodded grimly, and walked away. It didn't occur to either of us to consider that she, as it happened, had only drunken singles at her tables who of course wouldn't know the difference, but I had married couples who wanted everything that was coming to them.

I made my first mistake. I followed my classmate to the table with no line in front of it, loaded up on the cold fish, and fought my way out

390

the nearest kitchen door. Rapidly, I dealt out the little dishes to the men and women at my tables. When I had finished and was moving back to my station table and its now empty tray, a set of long red fingernails plucked at my upper arm. I looked down at a woman with coarse blond hair, blue eyelids surrounded by lines so deep they seemed carved, and a thin red mouth. "We didn't get the chow mein," she said to me.

My second mistake. "Chow mein?" I said. "What chow mein?" Still holding me, she pointed to the next table, where chow mein was being finished and the cold fish just beginning to be served. I looked at her. Words would not come. I broke loose, grabbed my tray, and dived into the kitchen.

I must have known I was in trouble, because I let myself be kicked about in the kitchen madness, wasting all sorts of time being climbed over before I got the next dish loaded onto my tray and inched myself, crab-like, through the swinging doors. As I approached my station I saw, standing beside the blond woman, the headwaiter, chewing a dead cigar and staring glumly in my direction. He beckoned me with one raised index finger.

I lowered my tray onto the station table and walked over to him. "Where's the chow mein?" he asked quietly, jerking his thumb back at my tables, across the head of the woman whose blue-lidded eyes never left his face. Her mouth was a slash of narrow red. Despair made me simple.

"I couldn't get to it," I said. "The kitchen is a madhouse. The line was impossible."

The headwaiter dropped his lower lip. His black eyes flickered into dangerous life, and his hand came up slowly to remove the cigar stub from between his teeth. "You couldn't get to it?" he said. "Did I hear you right? You said you couldn't get to it?" A few people at neighboring tables looked up.

"That's right," I said miserably.

And then he was yelling at me, "And you call yourself a waitress?"

A dozen heads swung around. The headwaiter quickly shut his mouth. He stared coldly at me, in his eyes the most extraordinary mixture of anger, excitement, and fear. Yes, fear. Frightened as I was, I saw that he too was afraid. Afraid of the blond woman who sat in her chair like a queen with the power of life and death in her, watching a minister do her awful bidding. His eyes kept darting toward her, as though to ask, All right? Enough? Will this do?

No, the unyielding face answered. Not enough. Not nearly enough.

"You're fired," the headwaiter said to me. "Serve your morning meal and clear out."

The blood seemed to leave my body in a single rush. For a moment I thought I was going to faint. Then I realized that tomorrow morning my regular guests would be back in these seats, most of them leaving after breakfast, and I, of course, would receive my full tips exactly as though none of this had happened. The headwaiter was not really punishing me. He knew it, and now I knew it. Only the blond woman didn't know it. She required my dismissal for the appeasement of her lousy life— her lined face, her hated husband, her disappointed New Year's Eve— and he, the headwaiter, was required to deliver it up to her.

For the first time I understood something about power. I stared into the degraded face of the headwaiter and saw that he was as trapped as I, caught up in a working life that required *someone's* humiliation at all times.

The summer I turned twenty-one I graduated both from City College and from the Catskills. It was an apotheosis that summer, that hotel. No one and nothing seemed small, simple, or real. The owners were embezzling the place, the headwaiter was on the take, the cook gave us food poisoning. The viciousness between busboys and waiters was more unrestrained than I had ever seen it, and the waitresses were re-quired to mingle—that is, show up in the casino at night and "dance" with the male guests, as the headwaiter leeringly put it.

The staff was filled with people I had worked with before, and two old friends were there as well: Marilyn of "you're not now waitresses" fame, and Ricky, the waitress who had advised me to forget the chow mein. We three roomed together in a tiny barracks room inside of which were jammed four cots, four small chests of drawers, two nar-row closets, and two rickety bedside tables.

The fourth bed in our room was occupied by Marie, a stranger to us in every way. From the moment I saw her sitting on the edge of her bed removing her stockings, as Marilyn and I came in from the first lunch meal of an early June weekend, I knew she was not like us. I knew it from the way she was taking off her stockings. Our hands would have torn quickly at the stocking, pulling it off in one swift ges-ture, hers moved slowly over leg and stocking together; the motion they made was one that prolonged the moment rather than telescoped it, the expression on her face sensual not concentrated.

She was tall and thin, one of those women with narrow shoulders, small breasts, a high waist and long legs who, even when she gains weight, looks slim: the kind of body that is never stylish, always alluring. Her hair, as unfashionable as her body, was a long red frizz that clung in Botticelli curls about her face and forehead and straggled down her back in a ragged ponytail. The eyes were large, the nose bony, the skin milk-white. Her mouth, easily her most distinctive feature, was long with deep creases in the lips. ("Ravaged" was the word that, with an unexpected thrill, came into my head). We all smoked, but she chain-smoked. Those lips came with a cigarette between them.

The three of us were twenty-one, Marie was twenty-five. We were students, she was an out-of-work actress. We were old hands in the Mountains, she was a novice. We lived at home with our working-class families, she came from a middle-class family with whom she had severed relations. Everything about her was an unknown. I could not imagine her before she came among us and I could not imagine her after she'd leave us. No, I take that back. It wasn't that I couldn't imagine her, it was that it didn't occur to me to imagine her.

In the Mountains only that which caused blunt outrage or open despair (bad tips, an intractable busboy, unhappy sex, a strained back) attracted deeper attention. If someone was not directly responsible for anger or misery, the instinct to speculate was not aroused. Like the dining-room furniture, the kitchen heat, or the heavy trays, people were simply "there," part of a vast set against which we moved without nuance or dimension.

The waiter at the station next to mine that summer was another social oddity: Vinnie Liebowitz, an ambitious pre-med student whose name wasn't Liebowitz at all, it was Lentino. But as Vinnie said, "Who could make out in the Catskills with a name like Lentino" and making out was what Vinnie was all about.

Vinnie was a smart, well-organized waiter who, while not expansive was not excessively guarded either. A once dedicated seducer of women, he had never been driven by the intense need to score that dominated all sexual transactions in the Mountains. He thought of himself as having a tender rather than a fierce appetite for the act of love.

In his second year in the Mountains Vinnie had met Carol, a girl whose conventional good looks matched his own to an uncanny extent: same chiseled features, same large brown eyes and dense black hair, same thin, self-regarding body. Vinnie had pursued Carol madly. She had expertly beckoned and avoided him. By the end of that summer they were engaged. The plan was to marry after Vinnie's first year in medical school.

Vinnie and Carol had not slept together, and were not going to until their wedding night. In this, the third summer of engagement, their passionate necking sessions had become regulated, and they found themselves absorbed by the more mature considerations of life, such as where they would make their future home (Brooklyn or Long Island), the kind of furniture they would have, number of babies, location of summer and winter vacations. Vinnie was sometimes baffled as to how it was that his life seemed settled at the age of twenty-two, but he was working-class from Brooklyn, and Carol was a princess from Forest Hills. Without her, he often said, he'd have spent the rest of his life pumping gas in Brownsville.

All this I knew because that summer Carol and her parents were guests at a hotel fifteen miles from ours where my boyfriend Danny was working as a busboy, and two or three times a week Vinnie (the only waiter with a car) drove over to see Carol and took me along. This boyfriend of mine was also a medical student, and a man of good-natured appetite as well. Danny loved sex, food, jazz, and memorizing medical textbooks. He also thought he loved me. And sometimes I thought the same. Together, we'd been meeting the needs of the moment for more than a year now.

The summer wore on in an exhaustion that came early and stayed late. By the end of July, young and healthy as we were, tiredness seemed to be dissolving collectively into all of us. People began to fall asleep sitting on the toilet, or standing on line in the kitchen, or taking a shower. One afternoon Marilyn got down on her hands and knees to retrieve a shoe that had been kicked under her cot: no sooner was her head parallel with the floor than her body forgot why it was there, and she fell asleep.

I don't think any of us ever felt lonely. Hot, angry, bored, weary yes, but lonely? No. Partly, it was that punishing physical labor precludes every kind of reflectiveness, including the one out of which loneliness arises; partly it was that we lived in a mob scene, and the absence of solitude obscures the issue. But even at the time neither condition seemed fully to explain our uniform disallowance of this particular emotion.

One morning at seven o'clock, as I was walking from the barracks to the kitchen door, I stopped to smell the air on the great hotel lawn.

The moment was lovely: clear and sensual. Buried in the early morning cool was the growing heat that would spread itself hour by hour across the sexy summer day. Suddenly I felt pierced to the heart. There were other ways to spend this day! Other lives to live, other people to be. I imagined myself standing in the same morning light somewhere else, under a great shade tree of a kind we didn't have in the Mountains. Beside me, on the grass, sat a group of strangers—graceful, beautiful, intelligent—animated by marvelous talk and laughter. They invited me to join them, even made a place for me on the grass. I longed to sit down. I felt that I *knew* these people, that I belonged among them. Suddenly and without warning, a space seemed to open between me and the image in my mind. The space lengthened into a road. It was clear that I would have to walk the road, step by step, to get to my people. The movie in my mind stopped running. I could not see myself on the road. I could not imagine the steps, taken one by one, that were necessary to close the gap between me and the people I was daydreaming. Inside, I began to congeal. Then all inner movement ceased. I stood on the lawn and stared at my own dumb longing. Desolation crowded in. I was lonely.

I remember that I wrenched myself then from the loneliness. It frightened me. I'd felt myself pitching forward, as though about to lose my balance. And balance, I knew, was everything. I looked around me at the lawn, the buildings, the parking lot, this small, tight world where function was all, and I had learned to operate supremely well (avoid gross humiliation and control the limits of surrender). All I had to do was look straight ahead, keep my mouth shut, and my balance intact. Life, I thought grimly, whatever its size or composition, depends on walking the straight and narrow of the moment. I turned away from my own daydream, and walked through the kitchen door.

Yet everything seemed harder than ever that summer. The tips were bad, the cook was a sadist, and we had to steal more meat, fruit, and milk than usual. The Mountains were always one long siege of vitamin deprivation. No one ever wanted to feed the help; the agony on an owner's face if his eye fell on a busboy drinking orange juice or eating a lamb chop was palpable. One night a waiter was fired because the maitre d' tore open his bulging shirt as he was leaving the dining-room and found two steaks lying flat against his chest. Six or eight of us watched from our stations. No one spoke, no one moved. What made things worse in this instance was that many of us knew the maitre d' was out to fire this waiter because he had refused to kick back.

The headwaiter was a Hungarian Jew with a despairing sense of class: life had dealt him a blow by making him end his working years in the Mountains. A vain handsome man, all brushed white hair, manicured hands, and sky-blue suits to match the color of his eyes, he perspired constantly and, if taken by surprise, his eyes rolled in his head. He often began staff meetings with a hysterical denunciation of these rumors about payoffs that his enemies (and don't think for a minute he didn't know who they were) were spreading. Most of us sat at these meetings genuinely baffled by such ravings, but some of us nodded our heads in vigorous sympathy for the injustices suffered by the sweating madman who paced the floor in front of us. Those of us who were baffled were indeed in the dark, those of us who were nodding were regularly handing over ten percent of our tips to be assured a full station each week.

In mid-August fifteen people came down with food poisoning. The huskiest waiters in the hotel were clutching their stomachs and heaving into their busboy's dish bins. One of them vomited all night, another was delirious for twelve hours, a third drooled up green bile. The barracks took on the hushed atmosphere of an epidemic ward. When we discovered that the source of the food poisoning had been a dinner made up of turkey wings the cook suspected of having gone bad, one of the waitresses broke. The cook had been making her life miserable, grabbing at her, taunting her, and now, her body racked with diarrhetic convulsion, she demanded and gained entry to the owner's office. He sat behind his desk. Beside him stood his son and the bell captain. The waitress began to speak. She told her story of weariness and harassment, and then described in detail how those poisoned were suffering. She demanded the dismissal of the cook. The owner stared into a space somewhere between her shoulder and the door. "Get this cunt outta here," he announced to the air. Stunned, the waitress allowed herself to be led, as though blind, from the office. In the barracks she told what had happened. Some of us were silent, some of us cursed, some turned quickly away. Needless to say, no one did anything.

My visits to Danny were, during these days, a consolation. I was grateful to him for providing me with a means of escape from the hotel. It was not only being with Danny that made going to see him important, it was everything about the visit itself—hurrying to get out of the dining room on the nights I knew we were traveling, climbing into Vinnie's car with the smell of summer stronger than when I was going nowhere, driving through the dark silent countryside behind the sweep of headlights beyond which the familiar daytime roads and hotels had become almost mysterious.

The night was invariably rich, dark, sweet, shot through with a kind of lit-from-within intensity. The smell of wet earth came up through grass, trees swayed in a warm wind, molecules of excitement gathered in the clear mountain air. Sitting close together on the front seat of his ten-year-old Chevy, Vinnie and I were both infected by the atmosphere.

Aroused in each other's presence, we hardly ever thought we were being aroused by each other, yet this closeness—which blossomed only on the ride out, never on the way back—began to accumulate a peculiar life. We never spoke of it, and certainly we did not bring it back with us to the hotel. Nonetheless, I felt its influence. Sometimes, something ordinary came into unexpected relief and then suddenly the familiar would seem threatening. I'd feel a shock to the system, and I'd find myself flashing on the ride out with Vinnie.

Take Marilyn and the butcher, for instance. This butcher, a good-looking ex-Marine, was a true primitive: murderous when crossed, slavishly loyal when done a good turn. In his lexicon Marilyn had done him a good turn by bestowing the gift of her virginity on him, and his devotion knew no bounds. He assured her daily he would steal and kill for her.

Marilyn, of course, had a hard time concentrating on Thomas's adoration as her virginity had been an obstacle to "getting on with it," and she was grateful to Tom for relieving her of its burdensomeness. The most hardened mountain rat participated in a fear of virginity, and every one of them had drawn back from the taint of Marilyn's purity. Thomas also had drawn back but she had been able to persuade him that her feeling for him was so deep it would be a sin not to. To this argument he finally assented, and thereafter treated Marilyn worshipfully, her capacity for such deep feeling, coupled with the contradictory reference to sin, having become confused in him with religious experience.

Thomas appeared regularly in our room after dinner and while Marilyn lay back on her bed, still in her work clothes, he would sit dreamily stroking her lower leg. As he did so the secret smile that seemed perpetually on Marilyn's mouth these days deepened and, beneath the dirty white uniform, a long delicate shudder moved visibly down the length of her beautiful midriff and flat belly. She had become sleek as a bird-eating cat since she'd begun making love, and almost as remote.

One afternoon I came into the room after the lunch meal, and saw the *Times* lying on Marilyn's bed. Surprised, as we never got the papers, I said, "Where'd this come from?" Marilyn followed my eyes to the bed. "Oh, Tom left it here this morning," she said. My eyebrows went up. "Thomas reads the *Times*?" I asked. Marilyn's face turned a dull red. "He does *now*," she said. Her eyes came up level with mine. We looked at each other for a long suspended moment. Then we both began to howl.

Suddenly I felt gripped with anxiety, and in my mind's eye I saw me and Vinnie riding through the night toward: who? what? I didn't know. But this, me and Marilyn laughing over Thomas, it frightened me. Something vicious here, something fearful and sacrificial. My heart pressed on my ribs.

Three weeks before Labor Day Vinnie and I climbed into the Chevy one night and took off. We'd been late getting out of the dining-room, and now Vinnie was driving fast. As he raced along the road he could drive in his sleep, I babbled at him a tale of dining-room fatigue having to do with a guest I'd spilled hot liquid on three meals in a row. The story had a point, and I was reaching it. Vinnie leaned forward over the wheel, his fine black eyebrows pressing closer together over the bridge of his thin straight nose, his wonderfully dark eyes narrowed with concentration. Just as I was about to deliver the punch line, the car swerved sharply to the right of the road and came to an abrupt halt.

Vinnie turned to me. Even in the dark I could see how white his face had become. His eyes were a film of misery. We stared at one another.

"I can't stand it anymore," he whispered.

"Stand what?" I whispered back.

"I want her," he moaned.

"Carol, you mean?"

"No. Marie!"

"Marie?" I repeated.

"Yes."

"Marie from our hotel?"

"Yes!"

"But you're engaged to Carol," I explained.

"I know!" he cried. "Don't you think I know that? Don't you think I say to myself every day and every night, 'You've got Carol. Carol who loves you, Carol who's a thousand times better-looking than she is, a thousand times sharper, nicer, more terrific in every way.' But it doesn't do any good. I want her. And it's tearing me apart!"

398

I could feel my eyes growing large in the dark. "How long has this been going on?" I asked, my voice nakedly curious.

"Weeks," he said, slumping back against the seat. He stared bleakly out the window. "It feels like years but I guess it's really only weeks."

"Does she know?"

"I'm not sure. I think so. But I'm not sure."

"You mean you've never said anything to her?"

"Christ, no. To begin with, I couldn't believe this was happening to me, and then" (the color was returning to his cheeks) "I was confused and ashamed. Jesus Christ. Marie! She's not good-looking, she's older than me, she's like no one I ever knew." His voice broke. "I mean sometimes she really looks like hell." He stopped talking. I waited. When he spoke again his voice was soft and steady. "I don't know how it started," he said. "One day I was just aware of her. Aware of her in the kitchen. Aware of her in the dining room. Aware of her in the barracks. Aware of her. Once we both reached into the silverware pail at the same time. My hand touched hers and I felt like I'd been burned. I was so surprised. I didn't know what it meant. After that I'd find myself looking for her in the dining room. And all this time I'm saying to myself, 'Vinnie, you crazy? What's goin' on here? Remember Carol? The girl you love? The girl you're gonna marry. The best-looking girl in the Mountains. What *is* this?' But it didn't do any good. Every day I'd find myself thinking about her. More and more. Not exactly thinking about her, just *feeling* her, feeling her presence, and then I couldn't take my eyes off her when she was anywhere near me." He struck his forehead with his balled-up right hand, and fell forward over the wheel. "She *must* know," he groaned. "I can't figure out how come everybody doesn't know. I feel like it's written all over my face all the time."

"It's not," I said dryly.

His long speech had given me time to absorb what he was saying but I, too, kept repeating to myself, "Marie? Carol is so beautiful, so right in every way. What has *Marie* got to do with anything?" I could not take it in. Handsome, pre-med Vinnie Liebowitz, with his life all mapped out, wanting Marie who in no way belonged. It was crazy, nuts, exciting. That was another thing I couldn't figure out: I was excited by Vinnie's confession of desire for Marie.

"I feel better for having told you," Vinnie smiled wanly. "You don't mind, do you? I mean, you're not sorry I told you, are you?"

"Of course not," I said briskly, not knowing what I felt. "But we'd better go now. They'll be waiting for us."

Vinnie's eyes clouded over and, nodding grimly, he started the car. We climbed back onto the road and in twenty minutes we were pulling into the driveway of Carol and Danny's hotel.

I remember lying in Danny's arms that night fantasizing about Vinnie and Marie. I saw them locked together, thrashing wildly, their faces contorted with pain, their bodies burning up with fever. My own body was so coiled with tension that Danny's pleasure was greatly heightened, and he suggested we might be falling in love anew. I said nothing. I could hardly hear his voice, my attention had wandered off so far from the man I was lying with. It was a relief, two hours later, to be back in the car where burning interest could be openly pursued. The ride home was spent with me pumping Vinnie about Marie, and Vinnie plunging eagerly into his tale of illicit desire.

After that night our rides took on new meaning. Vinnie's obsession had touched something secret in him, and a strain of wildness had flared in us both. When I had daydreamed my beautiful people, the clever ones, the ones I couldn't reach on my own, the fantasy had made me lonely but now, daydreaming Vinnie and Marie, there rose up in me a hunger so open and so acute it sent me into a trance. Reckless, sweet, compelling, it became a dream that settled in the groin. Vinnie's desire became all desire, his urgency all urgency, his necessity a drama we could, neither of us, get enough of. I felt released into complicity, about what I did not know. I only knew that the atmosphere inside the car had become rich with secrecy. He talked, and I fed him questions. My questions extended the obsession, deepened the drama. Some live, fluid movement went streaking through the furtive exchange. A wave of promise rose and fell in the speeding dark, and rose again. I wanted to go on riding it forever.

I could imagine for him what I could not imagine for myself, and often what I imagined felt alarming: hard, bright, insistent. This was the exact opposite of my lonely daydreams. This was all appetite and acquisition; what triggered everyone around me. It appalled and excited me. I remember once flashing on the woman who'd gotten me fired that long ago New Year's Eve. Suddenly I could feel her mean hungriness moving inside me. I wanted Vinnie to get what he wanted the way she had wanted to get . . . . what? What was it exactly that she *had* wanted to get? At this point my thoughts went fuzzy, but the feeling remained: hard and bright. The trance deepened. Nothing seemed to matter then, only that desire be gratified.

One night we got in the car and Vinnie said to me, "Talk to her."

I fell toward him as though I'd been slapped and had involuntarily jerked the wrong way. "What do you mean, talk to her? And say what?" He was silent, his handsome face white and drawn. "Tell her how I feel," he said. "I can't do it, I just can't do it. And you could. I mean, you're a girl, you live with her, you're sort of friends. You could explain it to her. Ask her to meet me after the meal tomorrow night. Just that. Nothing else. She's got nothing to be afraid of. Tell her that. I won't hurt her, I won't ask her to do anything she doesn't want to do. I just want to talk to her." He brightened up. "That's all," he repeated. "I just want to talk to her. She's got nothing to be afraid of. Nothing. I swear it."

My heart began to pound. I slept beside Marie every night but she was not as real to me in the flesh as she was here in the car, a conjured vision, the shared object of Vinnie's overexcited anguish. I stared at him. I yearned to remain as we were, locked together inside the night-time confessional of the car, and I think he did, too. I saw that he was afraid. Yet he was compelled to act: to move into consequence.

He lifted his head high in the darkened car, his eyes pinpoints of di-lated light, his jawline a throb of congested strain. Then his head dropped forward over his smooth, beautiful neck. Humbled by need, he was unbearably handsome.

"I'll talk to her," I said.

The next morning as we were stumbling around getting ready for breakfast I told Marie I'd like to talk to her after the meal. She looked quizzically at me, but I remained silent. "Sure," she said quietly. We each turned back into ourselves, finished dressing, and tore out of the room.

Four hours later Marie and I walked through the dining room doors together for the first time that summer, and headed wordlessly for the pool. This was a "singles" hotel; at ten-thirty in the morning, we knew, there would be no one lying on the painted concrete beside the chlorine-blue water. As we walked I glanced at Marie's bare legs. They were scruffy-looking, in need of a shave. For the thousandth time I thought, "Why her? Why does he want her?"

We sat down uneasily on the lower ends of two lounge chairs (we never used guest facilities), and faced each other across the black-and-white expanse of our morning uniforms. Marie seemed not tense but alert, her long narrow body waiting, her bony face a smooth mask.

Suddenly I was overcome with confusion. Why was I about to speak of intimate matters for one stranger with another stranger? I plunged in.

"I wanted to talk to you about Vinnie," I said crisply.

Marie's mouth tightened. Her hands, lying quietly against her thighs, now met in her lap and she twisted them together. "I knew it," she said, her voice soft with resignation.

"You *knew* it? How?"

"Come *on*," she said impatiently.

"He'd like to see you," I said righteously.

"No," she said. "I won't."

"You won't? What do you mean, you won't?" This I had never considered. "Why not? He just wants to see you. To talk. That's all. He just wants to talk to you."

"There's nothing to talk about."

"How can you say that? There's everything to talk about."

"Not as far as I'm concerned."

"For god's sake. He's suffering. Doesn't that mean anything to you?"

"No. Why should it?"

"It's *you* he wants!"

"No, he doesn't."

"What do you mean, he doesn't?"

"He doesn't know me at all," she said. "How can he want me? It's not *me* he wants."

"Who is it then?" I asked, stupefied.

"Don't you know anything?" she said softly. "It's never *you* they want."

She looked down at her hands. I looked out at the pool. The sun climbed high in the late morning sky. I felt drowsy. A warm yellow fog filled my head. Years seemed to pass.

Marie looked up. I looked over at her. My head cleared instantly. It was true, I knew nothing, but the anxiety in that face! I saw how isolated she was, alone inside the words she had just spoken. Not one of us could have said what she had said, and she knew it. My heart went out to her.

"I won't see him," she said. "That's final."

My heart came back to me. Vinnie! Handsome Vinnie wouldn't get what he wanted, needed, expected. And because of her! That *she* should deny *him*. I sat there cold, sluggish, belligerent.

"Besides," she said brightly (she had just remembered something useful), "I couldn't. Even if I wanted to. There's somebody else."

"Somebody else?" My eyes shot open. "Where? In the city?"

"No. Here."

"Here? Who is it?"

"Eddie," she said.

"Who's Eddie?" I said.

"The bell captain."

"The *bell* captain?" I said, and stared at her anew. The hierarchy of association was so strict in the Mountains that if you were a waiter you had nothing to do with chambermaids or bellhops. (Marilyn's affair with the butcher was a matter of desperate dispensation.)

"Yes," she said, face flushed, head at a defiant tilt.

I didn't know what to do next.

"Is he nice?" I asked idiotically.

"No," the laugh was short and sharp. "But we understand each other," she said evenly.

I turned away, and looked out again at the chemically colored water, the painted concrete, the striped deck chairs.

"It's all so disgusting," Marie said softly.

We rose without another word. I headed for the barracks, she headed for the side of the main building. For the first time I realized that she spent less time in the room between meals than any of the rest of us; Eddie lived just off the lobby.

That night Vinnie didn't see any of the people around him until he was crashing into them. I know he didn't remember his orders because his guests were yelling at him. Women who had loved him in the morning were now turning hurt, betrayed eyes on him as he forgot their special requests repeatedly, and their husbands, unmanned by the inability to control the quality of the service, threatened to become ugly. But Vinnie's gaze was fixed in space, his upper teeth nipping distractedly at his lower lip. No external threat could touch him. The next night he said he didn't feel well, and would not be going to see Carol as usual. He spoke with exaggerated politeness: he knew that he knew my name but for the moment it had escaped him.

Time began to expand and contract abnormally for days after that exchange, speeding up or slowing down for no discernible reason, as in a dream. In another minute the Labor Day weekend had arrived, and the season was about to end.

On Sunday, all day, the entire barracks seemed shrouded in a kind of convalescent inertness that contrasted strongly with the usual racketing about that went on from six in the morning until midnight. Abruptly, our agitation was ended. The summer had, all at once,

403

wound down with no resolution of the conflicts that had set the racket in motion. Neither explanation nor complaint was any longer to the point. We were all hanging on, waiting to get sprung.

The evening meal passed with less friendliness than ever before, many of us gone in spirit already. Faces were cool, guarded, remote; Vinnie's face, especially, was beyond reach. Our bodies, on the other hand, demonstrated a remarkable stylishness that night, arrived at with an energy fed, as never before, by the defensive cool. Trays were carried with the elegance of a dancer's control, the grace and skill of motion long ceremonialized. I had been right at eighteen: it would only take endurance. We were masters now, in possession of an art; behind the seamless skill, well behind it, our sealed-over young hearts. The survivors had achieved an awful beauty.

At eleven o'clock that night Ricky and I sat on our beds, talking quietly, the room half pulled apart with our just-begun packing. Outside our door hallway toilets flushed, sink faucets went on and off, rides were being arranged for. Suddenly, there was a muffled explosion against the wall behind our beds, and then everything was happening at once: the sound of furniture being flung, bodies thrown, a man's voice shouting, a woman's crying; waiters and waitresses running down the hall past the sinks nearly to the toilets, skidding to a stop, crowding into an open doorway, me and Ricky pushing forward with the rest; there inside, the chaos of cots half overturned, a bureau nearly pulled down, toilet things floating in the bedclothes as though on a shipwrecked sea, Vinnie in his black pants and sleeveless undershirt (muscles flexed, eyes glazed), and Marie, crouched in the far corner of the room, her uniform hanging in ripped shreds, clutching at her naked breasts, arms and neck covered with scratches already turning purple, her frizzy hair stringy with sweat, her crushed mouth twitching.

We all stood there: cold with curiosity. No one looked at Vinnie. Everyone stared at Marie. She was in solitary. Waves of emotion came off her: hot and silent. It was her loneliness she was sending out. Her wise, humiliated loneliness. ("It's never you they want.") We looked at her out of our flat, young faces without pity or regret. She sat there waiting. Her eyes flickered dully from one to another of us. They came to rest on me.

"You asked for it," I said, and turned away.

But I have continued to look at her, for years and years. Her bony, knowing face still floats past me as she sits crouched in memory, forever trapped in that room with me, her keeper in the doorway, standing there upon a ground of brutish innocence that in more than thirty years has not given way, only shifted position many times over, as I struggle ineptly to take in the meaning of her loneliness.

It was a world predicated on blind hunger: everything depended on the blindness. It took hard work to remain unknowing. Those of us who didn't manage it went into quarantine. Those of us who did required someone's humiliation at all times.

Nominated by Threepenny Review

STONE FLIGHT

by EAMON GRENNAN

from THE YALE REVIEW and SO IT GOES (Graywolf)

A piece of broken stone, granular granite, a constellation
of mica through its grey sky, one chalky pink band
splitting slabs of grey, it fits snug enough in the palm
of your hand. Toss it up and it falls, an arc saying *yes*
to gravity again, and saying in its one dunt of a word
when it falls with a thump on the soft path, *I'm here
to stay.* At a pinch, you might strip things down to this:
compact and heavy the pressure on your hand; the light arc
as if things weighed nothing, casting off; the apogee
and turn, catching a different kind of light; the steady,
at the speed of gravity, descent; and then that dull but
satisfying *thunk* to stop, its cluster of consonantal solids
allowing no air in, no qualifying second thought
as it lands like the one kiss to his scratchy cheek
at greeting or bedtime you'd give your father, or maybe
rolls an inch or two—depending on the chance of grit,
pebbles, the tilt of ground at this precise point
in the wide world, or the angle of itself it falls on. Not,
however, that *grunt* the condemned man makes
some fifty far-fetched seconds or so
after the injection has done our dirty work, the slump
of his head and just once that grunt as the body
realises its full stop, almost surprised. Nor yet the small
grunt of surprised satisfaction you've heard
when you're as deep inside and around one another
as you two can be, body bearing body away,

and you push, once, and flesh grunts with a right effort
that seems outside, beyond the two of you, something
old and liberated, a sort of joyous punctuation point
in the ravelling sentence that leaves you both as one
breathless wrap of skin and bone, your double weight
hardly anything as you kiss your way down and back
to your own selves, maybe rolling an inch or two
and then lie still, alive, in matter again, the tick of it
starting to fill the silence. But not that either—just a stone
that leaves your opened hand, lets go of you, ascends
to its proper pitch this once, and descends, kissing
gravity every inch, to hit the ground you picked it from
with hardly a thought, and staying there, mica stars
glittering in its granite firmament, a stone among stones
in the dust at a verge of meadowgrass and wild carrot.

Nominated by Linda Bierds, Ellen Wilbur

THE SLIP

by RACHEL HADAS

from ATLANTA REVIEW

Empty and trembling, haloed by absences,
whooshings, invisible leavetakings, finishes,
images, closure: departures so gracefully
practice their gestures that when they do happen,
dazzled with sunlight, distracted by darkness,
mercifully often we miss the event.
So many hours, days, weeks, years, and decades
spent-no, slathered and lavished and squandered-
ardently, avidly gazing at nothing,
pacing the pavement or peering round corners,
setting the table and sniffing the twilight,
sitting and gazing at edges, horizons,
preparing occasions that leave us exhausted,
recovering, staggering back to a climax.
Dramas of use, inanition, repletion!
and there all along, except not there forever,
was the beloved. The foreground? The background?
Thoughtful, impatient, affectionate, angry,
tired, distracted, preoccupied, human,
part of our lives past quotidian limits,
there all the while and yet not there forever.

Nominated by Marilyn Hacker

THE WEATHER IN HISTORY

fiction by DANIEL MELTZER

from VIGNETTE

HISTORY HAS NEGLECTED to note and few are therefore today aware that a heavy downpour was falling on Washington, D.C. on the night of April 14, 1865. The omission is significant because it was on this fateful date that Abraham Lincoln, sixteenth President of the United States of America, decided, unwisely, as we now accept, to attend, at Ford's Theatre, the heralded production of British dramatist Tom Taylor's witty comedy, *Our American Cousin*, with the popular actress Laura Keene in the starring role of Florence Trenchard.

Keene's role in "Cousin" was one of her most successful. But it could not begin to compare, on that tragic evening, with the role of the weather, whose ultimate and unforeseen impact on the lives of the key participants, their families and descendants, indeed on the future of the Republic, cannot be overstated.

The truth of the matter, as hindsight is our guide, is that the President should have stayed at home, as he'd been urged, and that John Wilkes Booth should have kept to his quarters as well. At the very least, both ought to have dressed more appropriately. A choice, in fact, of more suitable attire by either would almost certainly have changed history.

The day had been a glorious one in the nation's capital. The sun shone brilliantly through a cloudless sky from dawn nearly to dusk, symbolizing, one may have noted, the dawn of a bright new day after the long dark night of the horrible war just ended. Temperatures on the eve of the ides of what Eliot would, in a later century, so aptly characterize as the cruelest of months, were unseasonably and seductively temperate.

Late that afternoon, dismissing a poignant plea from the presumed neurotic and subsequently unmercifully maligned First Lady for her feverish husband to remain abed with the persistent upper respiratory infection that had kept him from his duties for the preceding two days, and responding instead to the heady essence of the early cherry blossoms wafting through his window from across the greening south lawn, the President impetuously flung off his hand-stitched quilt (presented to him the month preceding by the ladies of Peterborough, New Hampshire,) stood erect, if dizzily, in his night shirt, inhaled deeply the vernal perfume that had saturated his sickroom, and announced in a still-hoarse voice to the room, to his hand-kneading and furrowed-browed wife and to the capacious suite's only other occupant of the moment, a half-dozing male day-nurse on loan from the nearby military hospital, that he would go, that night, to the theatre.

*   *   *

The household was thrown into immediate confusion. First Lady Mary Todd Lincoln, emotionally ravaged by the many well-chronicled personal and political tragedies visited upon their long and troubled marriage, and concerned for her fatigued husband's precarious health, had earlier requested a supper tray of broth and boiled chicken breast to be brought to the President's room, had dismissed the livery for the night, and had notified the management of Ford's, with cordial regret, of Mr. Lincoln's unfortunate indisposition. Indeed, the State Box, festively festooned for the occasion with the Union flag and the Presidential Seal was, at the very moment of the Chief Executive's bedside pronouncement, in the process of having these formal adornments removed for storage, so as to return it to its more mundane state, in expectation of the house manager's brother-in law, a cabinet maker from Virginia, and his fiancee, a school-teacher, neither of whom had ever attended a theatrical presentation of this distinction before.

The couple's subsequent disappointment, after the somewhat elaborate arrangements involved in availing themselves of this windfall cultural opportunity, set the stage, as it were, for the eventual breakup

410

of their betrothal, for the cabinet maker's total political disillusionment and his indignant resignation from his local Republican Party club, his dismal descent into alcoholism, abandonment of a promising custom furniture business for a niggardly living as a repairer and refinisher and an eventual bitter alliance with a splinter group of reactionary revisionists who would malign, for decades to come, the reputation of our late, lamented President.

The teacher, who would suffer her first epileptic seizure two weeks later, was never to marry. She would take, also, an almost immediate aversion to all British writings for the stage, and go on to prejudice two generations of impressionable pupils against the literary products of such masters as Milton, Chaucer, Jonson, Marlowe, Beaumont and Fletcher as well as, of course, the Bard himself.

It would not be until well into the next century that an appreciation for the works of any of these fine minds would be publicly expressed on this side of the Atlantic.

*   *   *

The President's premature leap from his restorative rest was to prove no less unwise than his subsequent curt dismissal of the sage counsel of his reliable, rheumatic valet, one Jonathan Wilcox Appleby, whose sage sartorial selections had served the Commander in Chief so well at Gettysburg, Appomattox and countless other appearances and excursions which had previously exposed Mr. Lincoln to the caprices of the elements.

Appleby's knee was celebrated among the high command and held indispensable for its consistent accuracy in foretelling at least forty-eight hours of climatic expectations, and is justly immortalized in the President's own hand on the back of an early draft of his second inaugural address, for which occasion Appleby, in typically righteous opposition to the more conservative and often overcautious Mrs. Lincoln, lobbied strenuously and successfully against the President's wearing of his union suit to the dais.

Appleby had predicted that the temperature on that day would likely reach the seemingly impossible seventy degrees fahrenheit. The eventual high, recorded by one Frederick Steinmetz, a chemistry student and nephew of a congressman from Delaware, who witnessed the address and whose diary entry for that date was recently acquired by the Smithsonian Institution, was, in fact, sixty-two degrees. Close enough, and certainly warm enough for the then robust Commander in Chief to go without his long johns.

Appleby's own journal, a magnificent artifact of the age, with its watermarked, gilt-edged pages, concisely records his prognostication for the day from the previous evening:

> "One day of summer, yes. But back, I fear, to winter by dark and keep galoshes at the ready. Must get more liniment in the morning. Can barely walk."

*   *   *

Appleby vanished from the Capital within a week of the assassination, and lived out his remaining years in the considerably more beneficent climate of Window Rock, New Mexico, where he grew muttonchop whiskers, married a Navajo and operated a successful haberdashery and trading post under the name of Ben Durant until he died at the age of eighty-seven after being bitten by a rattle-snake while watching a Hopi rain dance at the Second Mesa just across the border in Arizona. A Scorpio, Appleby is frequently cited by historical astrologists as a classic example of the lurking water-borne perils that await those born under an earth-sign. You begin to see, then, how far-travelled are the ripples from the drops of rain that fell that day into the lives, not just of the President, but of all those surrounding and affected by him and by his whim to see a play when he was arguably not up to it and clearly experiencing a lapse in his otherwise sound judgement.

Entranced, then, by the balmy spring breezes billowing his curtains and stirred, perhaps, by his own somewhat (if only temporarily) restored vigor, the President bathed and dressed and joined Mrs. Lincoln for a hastily prepared dinner in the executive mansion's formal dining room.

A censored page from a letter sent to his brother in Provence, and recently acquired at an auction of the wine merchant's long-disputed estate in Mougin, discloses the profound discomfiture of White House Chef Gaston LeComte over the outcome of this uncharacteristically rushed dinner order. His offended professional pride is believed responsible for the omission from his anger-marinated missive of the details of the rush replacement menu he was obligated by the Presidential impulse to provide. And then, regretful for having so hastily written and dispatched the irretrievable correspondence that very evening, with its unfortunate and ungentlemanly outburst of Gallic temper which was directed, not just toward the thoughtless President, but at the perceived general lack of appreciation for carefully catered cuisine in "les colonies," as he called them, LeComte, racked with remorse, and assumed by contemporary graphologists to have been clinically manic-depressive, nobly took his own life within a fortnight of the assassination, never completing the compilation of favored White House recipes he had begun to catalog earlier that year. The forty-six year old Frenchman left a grieving widow and nine children under the age of fifteen, one of whom would grow up to be the poisoner of no fewer than twelve officers in the United States Navy during the Spanish American War.

But who, of course, could contemplate any of these consequences on that glorious, sunbathed morning that seemed so pregnant with promise?

And so, buoyed for the moment by the President's revitalized mobility and by the return of some color to his sorrowful, creased countenance, and as the inconsolable LeComte wept unashamedly into his apron in the executive mansion's kitchen, Mr. and Mrs. Lincoln set forth by carriage from the south portico for what both hoped would prove to be a diverting entertainment.

Feeling temporarily if deceptively robust as his body's defenses gained ground against its enemy virus, Mr. Lincoln declined the cape proffered him by the dutiful valet, gently rebuking his wife's plea that he accept it. The crucial rejection was recalled by the President's driver, William, "Wee Willie" Sullivan, in a talk to his daughter's third grade class four weeks later.

Sullivan's account was long held suspect, owing to his acknowledged resentment over having been discovered and summoned during his late-afternoon tryst that day with the Vice President's buxom chambermaid, Rosemond Burdette, in order to accommodate the President's caprice of the moment. Recalling Mr. and Mrs. Lincoln's conversation in the carriage en route to the theatre, Sullivan told the third-graders it consisted, largely, of references to the enormous deficits (in excess of two million dollars) incurred by the war, some talk of the looming challenges of reconstruction, a very brief and inconsequential argument over a problem with some White House redecorating ideas put forth by Mrs. Lincoln, mixed with and tempered by observations of the uncommonly temperate weather. The western sky, the diminutive driver told the open-faced children, held, at the outset of their ride, the promise of a brilliant sunset; a promise that however was, he noted, not to be fulfilled. By the time the slow-moving carriage, drawn by its two handsomely if hastily groomed black stallions, had arrived at Ford's Theatre, the winds had already shifted to the northerly direction and the descending orange ball in the west had vanished behind a rising, portentous dark gray partition.

Still in all, the driver reflected, The Great Emancipator, whose marked depression and disturbing seclusion during and following the final days of the war had been the talk of the Capital for weeks, seemed, on that particular evening at any rate, considerably less burdened. "Right rosy" were the words Sullivan's daughter Kate remembered him using to describe the President's mood, or perhaps his slightly feverish complexion, during the ride.

Mrs. Lincoln herself echoed that evaluation much later from her sanitorium bed, as revealed in only recently de-classified hospital records and notes. The President felt, she recited in a pathetic sing-song delivery, according to the hand-written hospital-chart notations, that "a new beginning is palpable in the air tonight." And his decision to honor the reservation at Ford's, she repeated, was a fully predictable product of his earlier articulated commitment to "go out among the people once more, that they should see us and take confidence from us."

*　*　*

The first drops of the evening April shower struck the President's deeply furrowed brow as he alit from his carriage at the entrance to Ford's Theatre. By all accounts, he paid them little notice as he acknowledged the attention of the other theatre goers. By the middle of the first act, members of the cast later reported, thunder was audible in the auditorium. A horseman assigned to the President's party, Corporal Ephraim Carmichael, was dispatched to ride, in the downpour, to the White House, for the President's wool cape. But Carmichael, delayed by the muddy going, would not return by intermission, and witnesses told of how the crushed corporal, tears and rain flowing together down his acne-scarred cheeks, draped the long, navy wool garment over the President's torso as it was carried past him from Ford's to the house across the street, where the Chief Executive would breathe his last.

414

Not having brought the warm outer garment along, then, the President was discouraged from taking the air on the landing to the rear of his box during the break following act one, which he reportedly enjoyed and during which he was seen to laugh at least twice. Ten minutes on the landing might not only have refreshed him. It would also, we may now conclude, likely have saved his life. For, had Mr. Lincoln or even one of his party taken the air at that interval, it would have been difficult not to take note of the unauthorized presence in the alleyway below of the errant thespian preparing to enter for his most historic role.

* * *

The familiar face of well-known actor John Wilkes Booth was camouflaged under false whiskers and concealed in shadow. He had arrived early, some twenty minutes before the end of the first act and was permitted, by a stagehand with whom he had worked in the past, to enter the alleyway. There he waited, wondering anxiously, no doubt, if he would be apprehended during the entre-acte. He needn't have worried. The capeless Chief Executive was discouraged from venturing outside the building during intermission and none in his party would be so discourteous as to step out without him.

Had it not rained, (as none but Appleby seem to have anticipated,) all might have been different. Booth likely would have been spotted and either arrested or, at the very least, chased from the scene to replan or, it might have been hoped, to reconsider entirely his fool's errand. Mr. Lincoln would have been spared to serve out his term and complete his memoirs. He wouldn't have even been at Ford's, of course, had the oncoming showers given some earlier indication of their approach. The frail First Lady, it can now be reasonably assumed, may have avoided the calamitous breakdown that was to darken her later years. The momentum of Lincoln's thoughtful reconstruction program might have been sustained and the nation might have been spared the regressive years of carpetbagging that marked the sluggish presidency of Andrew Johnson. Booth himself might even have redirected his anger and energies to more creative pursuits. And the career of his older brother Edwin, the country's pre-eminent tragedian of the day, certainly would not have collapsed as it did after it became known that he was sibling to the man who had killed the President.

John Wilkes' plan was far from watertight. As with his victim, the assassin's fatal error, it has been shown, also involved meteorological miscalculation. Shortly after he could hear, from within the playhouse, the muffled opening lines of the second act of *Our American Cousin*, (Mrs. Mountchessington's admonishment to the scatterbrained Augusta: "No, my dear Augusta, you must be very careful. I don't by any means want you to give up De Boots, his expectations are excellent,") Booth made his move. He slid from his cold, rain-soaked carriage seat and made his way to the staircase that led to the President's box, clutching carefully in his hand, under his own sodden cape, the loaded pistol he had selected and brought with him for the miserable deed to which he had pledged himself.

Halfway to the unlit staircase (its gaslight doused by rain,) Booth slogged ankle-deep through an invisible puddle, cursing both the weather and his own decision to wear his best buskins that night rather than his more practical riding boots. Theatricality prevailed over practicality in Booth's case, just as whim had overruled wisdom's in the President's. Both, it might be posited, were undone by nothing more than a change in the weather.

The accomplice who stood at hand with the getaway horse on which Booth would take his last gallop told his questioners afterward that the assassin's last words to him before he sped through the muddy streets were neither about his mad act in the theatre, nor were they about the war that had so embittered him or even the political motivations that had impelled him toward the suicidal mission. "Damn boots," he spat, the accomplice told his astonished interrogators.

Dragging a leg, his handsome face grimaced in pain, and cursing at his fate, Booth snatched the reins from the stagehand, threw the agreed twenty-dollars (in useless confederate bills, it turned out) into the mud, swung himself into the saddle, and was off, the storm inside the theatre now bursting out into the streets and alleyways as Booth's pursuers came after him.

Booth's boots, chosen for their dramatic and tragic associations, were his own fatal miscalculation, his hubric blunder, his actor's folly that doomed him, like Oedipus, that earlier bum-footed tragic figure, to his ultimate undoing. For, though sartorially correct in completing his dashing renegade's costume for the dastardly deed, complementing perfectly, as they did, the scarlet-tied black cape and the forearm-high black leather gloves chosen for the historic occasion, their slick soles, which had been so perfect for slinking through the roles at which

416

he had heretofore excelled, proved disastrous for Booth as they slid from beneath him on contact with the polished stage floor when the mad killer leaped from the stage-left box, after emptying his derringer into the head of the President.

The terrible pain Booth experienced from the simple fracture of his left instep must surely have colored his delivery of the line, "Sic Semper Tyrannis," which he had chosen to shout from the stage after he had done his deed. As this failed to register, he ad-libbed the more easily understood "Revenge for the South." Gasps and cries flew up from the stunned spectators as they discerned both the departure from the printed text and the sudden fuss in the State Box. By all accounts, Booth's leap, the fracture notwithstanding, was a stunner, even to an audience well inured to the melodramatic excesses of the day. Even the supremely composed Miss Keene, her own stage career hopelessly wrecked from her experience during this doomed engagement, was heard to comment years later that Booth seemed in especially rare form during his cameo, displaying, she offered, a concentration and tragic weight rarely encountered on the stage in that day. She never forgave him for upstaging her, however, and for choosing her production for his attention-grabbing "political hijinx," as one colleague reported her characterizing it.

But, while he managed to exit left as planned and depart the scene unmolested, the painful fracture Booth sustained brought him to interrupt his otherwise well-planned flight and detour slightly off-course so as to visit the unfortunate Dr. Samuel Mudd, a retired physician whose life would now also spiral ever downward, all because of the unexpected change in the weather that had caused the President to be where he otherwise should not have been, in the path of his assassin's bullet, had resulted in Booth's otherwise stageworthy footwear to fail him and now had contrived to provide the portentously-named practitioner with an unanticipated, unwanted and most unlucky patient on what otherwise should have been just another quiet night with his stamp collection. Compounding his sad position were the subsequent rejections by authorities, judge and jury of Dr. Mudd's earnest explanation, that his ministering to the lamed horseman who came to his door that rainy night was offered as nothing more than a faithful fulfillment of his obligations under the Hippocratic Oath and had in no way been prearranged or anticipated. The fact that Booth and Mudd had actually met casually by chance two weeks previous as he was out for a ride and the assassin-to-be was staking out his escape route, was

417

no help to the doomed doctor at his trial. How, further, could the devoted physician ever, in his wildest imagination, have predicted that his comprehensive collection of Confederate postage stamps, gathered and immaculately arranged in leather-bound albums in his study, would some day contribute, as evidence, to his indictment as accomplice before as well as after the fact.

We may note, with some relief, that all of the participants and victims of this awful occurence have long since returned to their maker or to dust or to wherever it is that any of us returns once all is said and done and sealed up in its earthly or cosmic finality. The curse of the day that altered, damaged or destroyed the lives of so many might have been assumed to have played itself well out by now, but for the apparent hard luck of Dr. Mudd's great-great-grandson, the mellifluous telejournalist Roger, who, as we know, was denied what he took to have been his rightful legacy as the presumed heir to the throne of the even more mellifluous Walter Cronkite. The elder network anchorman was replaced, of course, by the controversial, drawl-suppressing Texan. Mr. Rather, it may be argued, may himself never have risen to such heights had he not just happened to have been in the right place at just the moment when a certain hurricane veered unexpectedly, bringing furious winds and torrents of, yes, rain, in from the Gulf one summer's night.

Nominated by Kenneth Gangemi, and Vignette

A RELATION OF VARIOUS ACCIDENTS OBSERVABLE IN SOME ANIMALS INCLUDED IN VACUO

fiction by WILLIAM MONAHAN

from OLD CROW REVIEW

FROM THE VERY TIME *Torricelli* found out his First Experiment of *Mercury,* he had thoughts of including several *Animals* in the void space, to make Remarks upon their *Motion, Flight, Breathing,* and all other observable *Accidents:* But not then being provided with fit Instruments for this purpose, he was contented to perform what he was able to do: for small, and tender *Animals* oppressed by the *Mercury,* would be most commonly dead, or expiring; so that it would be hard to determine whether they had received more damage from the *Suffocation* of the *Mercury,* or from the want of the *Air.*

And either for this cause he forbore, or was deterred from attempting the *Experiment* in an open Vessel, misdoubting the sufficiency of the Apparatus to sustain the *air:* and besides, he was diverted soon from this *Invention* by other *Employments* which wholly took him up, that he had no time to apply himself to this, and give it a greater *perfection,* which it is probable he would have done, if a too hasty *Death* had not prevented him.

But we being satisfied, that the force of the Air was not so great that a Bladder well tyed down, was unable to withstand it, have always successfully made use of a Vessel open at both ends, as already hath been shewn, and as we have also done in these. Wherefore, we will now proceed to give an account of the Accidents observed in divers Animals included in this vessel; as follows.

An Horse-leech being kept *in vacuo* above an hour remained alive and well; freely moving herself, as if she had been in the *Air.*

The same did a snail; in both these, tho deprived of the Air we could observe nothing to argue it had any effect upon them.

Two *Grass-hopers* were for a quarter of an hour very lively, continually moving up, and down, but not leaping: upon the admission of the air they leaped away.

There are a sort of Flyes larger than ordinary, commonly called Moscone in *Italian,* that make a great Buzzing through the air with their Wings. One of these (which being shut up in the Vessel, continued to *buz* very vigorously) as soon the vacuum was made, fell down as if it had been dead: and the noise of its wings ceased. We presently gave it Air, wherupon it moved a little, but the Remedy was too late; for it was scarce taken out before it dyed.

A Lizard in vacuo quickly grew sick, and soon after closing her eyes, seemed to be dead: but perceiving a little swelling in the Thorax, between the Fore-legs, we agreed that we observed some Respiration, and we continued the Confinement for the space of six minutes: in which time it lost all breathing, and appeared Dead. We then admitted the air, which so recovered it, that presently the vessel being opened, she leaped out, and ran away. Catching the Lizard again, we Imprisoned it the second time, and in Ten Minutes, after some strainings as if poysoned, she vomited, and fell down quite dead in the glass. Dr. Chausible claimed that he heard a Squeek, but the rest of the Investigators did not.

Another little Lizard *in less time* suffered the same strainings, or Convulsions, in company with strange Distortions of the Mouth, and swelling of the Eyes, as if they would have started out of her head; she turned upon her back, and after a little gaping for breath, dyed. It was after observed that she had discharged something by the Mouth, and Anus; whence the Belly became flaccid and empty.

It was while we were engaged in the last experiment that we felt a trembling of the Earth, and then a loud Concussion. Running out of the House we saw a Footman cut in half by the Descent of a great Bell, which Encloased the Laboratory. Dr. Abbott fell upon his Knees and loudly implored his Maker for Assistance. Dr Chausible and Myself were sensible of no want of Air, but Dr Abbott in ten Minutes was unmeasurably puft up in every part.

Two great Bladders appeared upon the sides of his jaws, and vomiting up a great quantity of froth at his Mouth (which stood wide open, filled with his Tongue, and all the membranes, disformedly swelled, and blown up) in this posture he remained Motionless. Mr Skinner, as much swell'd as Dr Abbott, caft up a great deal of Froth, and other things at the Mouth: and in three minutes was found quite Dead. We observed a discharge of Guts at the Anus.

Dr Chausible propofed Spirits of Wine, which we Administered to Ourselves, Gold-finches at the same time Attacking Dr Chausible with many small Pecks, loud *screches*, and other signs of large Disfavour.

After some Interval, which did not pass pleasantly, a strange Young Man begged admittance to the Laboratory. He was Wigless and wore a suit of cloaths and a neck-cloth in no Fashion of which we were sensible and he spoke through his Nose in a peculiar Dialect of English, which we were able to understand only upon considerable Application of our Wits.

Taking some of our Spirits of Wine, and lighting a small white paper Tube which seemed to burn finest *Virginia,* he pleasurably Inhaled, crossed his legs, and enquired of us if we were so far interested in *Vacuums* as to Accompany him to a Good One he knew about.

We were in no position to Refuse. He clapt his Hands and said Vexillia regis prodeunt, and in a Trice we were sitting in Chairs of some base Metal in a square Room fabricated of large Bricks, in which a Young Woman with Spots was reading Dreadful fiction about her own supposed *Molestation* and Subsequent inability to Get Close. This went on for so long that Dr Chausible began to Figit and finally, with a great Look of mortal apology, winced, and loudly discharged gas from his bottom.

Nominated by Old Crow Review

CHRISTMAS TREE

by JAMES MERRILL

from POETRY

To be
Brought down at last
From the cold sighing mountain
Where I and the others
Had been fed, looked after, kept still,
Meant, I knew—of course I knew—
That it would be only a matter of weeks,
That there was nothing more to do.
Warmly they took me in, made much of me,
The point from the start was to keep my spirits up.
I could assent to that. For honestly,
It did help to be wound in jewels, to send
Their colors flashing forth from vents in the deep
Fragrant sables that cloaked me head to foot.
Over me they wove a spell of shining—
Purple and silver chains, eavesdripping tinsel,
Amulets, milagros: software of silver,
A heart, a little girl, a Model T,
Two staring eyes. Then angels, trumpets, BUD and BEA
(The children's names) in clownlike capitals,
Somewhere a music box whose tiny song
Played and replayed I ended before long
By loving. And in shadow behind me, a primitive IV
To keep the show going. Yes, yes, what lay ahead
Was clear: the stripping, the cold street, my chemicals
Plowed back into the Earth for lives to come—
No doubt a blessing, a harvest, but one that doesn't bear,
Now or ever, dwelling upon. To have grown so thin.
Needles and bone. The little boy's hands meeting
About my spine. The mother's voice: *Holding up wonderfully!*
No dread. No bitterness. The end beginning. Today's
Dusk room aglow
For the last time
With candlelight.
Faces love-lit,
Gifts underfoot.
Still to be so poised, so
Receptive. Still to recall, to praise.

Nominated by Sabrina Grogan

LOOKING IN A DEEPER LAIR: A TRIBUTE TO WALLACE STEGNER

by BARRY LOPEZ

from NORTHERN LIGHTS

THE PAST FEW WEEKS I have been thinking about a line of Brecht, from *Galileo,* I think: "Unhappy the land that requires heroes." I've been thinking about it because the tendency with a great person like Stegner—or Rachel Carson or Thomas Merton—is to see them as different from us, capable of lives we couldn't attempt. But this is not true. The complexities of their private lives, which we are not privy to, made them like us; and they expressed virtues of which we are capable. From a certain distance, Stegner—and Ms. Carson and the Trappist monk—were faithful. They did not break with their beliefs, they remained dedicated to something outside the self. As far as we know they never became the enemies of their souls or their memories.

Brecht's line can be read in two ways: a land requiring heroes must be a sorry place, or the emergence of heroes is a sign of trouble. Let me take the latter position. I believe Stegner saw the country, the American West in particular, as a troubled place, laid siege to not by greed alone but by venal imaginations and an insidious tendency to commodify its elements—its trees, its soil, its water. Giving this abuse an historical context, protesting its effects, and offering us a practical sort of hope, he was our great citizen-writer.

I don't know whether Stegner viewed with as much concern as I do an underlying cause of this trouble, but I would feel I was abandoning the esteem in which I hold him if I did not speak straight from the heart about it. What alarms and troubles me is woven tightly into the fabric of our culture, and it is apparent throughout the cultural West, from here to Buenos Aires and Amsterdam, even to Singapore.

Here's my perspective, and I ask your forbearance with its simplicity. When we founded our particular democracy, we built into its design a system of restraints so no traditional seat of tyranny could gain an upper hand. We called it "the balance of powers" among the judicial, executive, and legislative branches of government. Similarly, to guard against political intransigence and the growth of dynasties, we provided for regular elections and the individual vote. Today, the greater threat to individual freedom and dignity comes not from tyrannical government but—and, again, I ask your forbearance with a blunt and unparsed term—from capitalism.

Like every other human system, including religions, capitalism carries with it an intractable darkness. The difference for us is, though the effect of capitalism on our lives is at least as profound as that of government, we do not elect its officials; and a review of its policies, its plans for expansion, are, practically speaking, beyond the reach of the citizenry. The suggestion, in fact, of citizen review, to prevent the economic and social (let alone environmental) damage of which capitalistic enterprise is capable, is considered by many a threat to economic growth. Corporations, thoroughly integrated into public life but legally constituted as individuals, have a desire but no constitutional right to vote; they do vote, of course, through lobbyists, a pernicious system for corrupting and undemocratic influence.

Our modern predicament, the general malaise we share about our social prospects, grows out of the failure to check or balance a force this powerful. On the scale we practice capitalism, the markets for its products must expand significantly year by year if it is to survive. This doesn't mean, solely, that product advertising taps us more and more frequently on the shoulder, calling out to us from every flat surface, including our clothing; or that fashion now plays as prominent a role in shaping our society as ethics; or that our national landscape is continually shredded and polluted to produce, on any given day, another hundred distracting geegaws; or that obsolescence has become as much a part of a manufactured item as clay or metal once was. These are commonplace philosophical laments.

Something more disturbing, I think, lies in a deeper lair.

In Western societies, which patriotically support a system of economics promising mind-boggling material wealth to a few, competition is no longer seen as an occasional, useful good but as a desirable and indispensable constant. Unsettling questions which ethically astute business people are prone to raise about conducting business are now often dismissed as a failure of nerve, doubts of the unbelieving. With the failures of Communism, a system as cruel and appealing, we can see more clearly where the imperative to produce and acquire is pointing us.

We live in a country in which the rate of consumption must constantly increase. Our moderate birth rate expands that consumer base too slowly and in but one direction. The required rate of expansion can be attained only by creating more consumers from the existing population base, in short, by maintaining the high level of social disintegration we have grown to accept—divorce; the subdivision of an individual life into separate spheres of work, play, and home life; regular changes of address in pursuit of career goals; children living lives between and apart from their families. It means an inordinate emphasis on private ownership in preference to sharing and on the autonomy of individuals to do whatever they choose. It means a cynical promotion of individual thought and preference. And it means deliberately confusing the true line between mental health and true mental illness, for example, so that advertising that treats us as unfulfilled or unrewarded people will seem compassionate and knowledgeable in offering us emollients.

Perhaps the saddest aspect of this imperative to consume in the West is that we're asked to accept a piece of certifiable rubbish: more satisfaction is ultimately to be found in a product—a style of trouser, a personally tailored system of electronic communication, an exercise regimen, a career—than in another human being. We would be happier with a young, handsome stranger in Barbados for a week, it is implied, than in the company of someone we love and who loves us and to whom we feel responsible and obligated.

To an outsider, we would appear to be a race of people grown inept at human expression—making love, fixing dinner for someone, presenting an idea—without devices or accouterments to focus and enhance our meaning. To an outsider it might also appear that, psychologically if not actually, many of us live in isolation; and that separated from a continuous stream of stimulation derived from our purchases we become anxious.

What way is there out of this morass? If we read history, we know that on a smaller scale it was ever thus. We know that our measure as a people in the cultural West is, always, not what we have made but what we have imagined. And we know that the failure of a technology is as nothing compared with the failure of our imaginations. We know the way out of this. It is love—the Christian's agapé, tolerance of the Other, the compassion of the Bodhisattva, simple charity. It is the wisdom to accept rather than solve the intractable paradoxes of life.

On a practical level, we have to stop making things that sell and make things that help. We have to rediscover story—and music and the theatre and dance and painting and photography—as sources of renewal, not products, as the wellsprings of our dignity, our awareness. We have to discover, again, that our fate does not lie with government, or with capitalism, but with each other.

And we must rediscover a sense of humor. Laughter makes our straits no less dire but certainly more bearable, less tyrannizing. We need to joke that if the smoke-free building is a reality then the Musak-free building and the billboard-free neighborhood are close at hand, a virtual reality.

In my life I have had the privilege of traveling in several parts of the world with indigenous people. One of the lessons that has come from that experience is to understand the past not as a record of mistakes and imperfection but as a source of wisdom. We apply this so-called ancient but actually timeless wisdom repeatedly to the imperfections that dog us as a species—bad faith, self-aggrandizement, fundamentalisms. In this way we differ little from Aranda people in the Northern Territory, or Araucanians in Chile, Inuit on Ellesmere Island, or Kamba living in Nairobi. The repository of wisdom, in an oral culture or a literate culture like ours in the West, lies in story; that is to say, in what we tell each other that lasts. It is these stories, not the storytellers, who are indispensable. And if there are heroes among us it is the reader, I think, not the writer, who is heroic. If a writer should crystallize in a few stories, in a book, in public testimony, a way of seeing, a way of belief to which he or she tries to be faithful, its value lies not with the celebrity of the individual but with what the story or the book causes, with what the reader does.

I believe what we say in tribute to Stegner is thank you. Thank you for reminding us. Thank you for your faith. Thank you for historical perspective. Thank you for giving us to believe, as you did, that we have reason to hope because our fate does not lie with one man or one woman, with a few heroes, but with ourselves. And, day to day, one event to another, we are a determined, brave, and imaginative people.

Nominated by Rick Bass, C. E. Poverman, Pattiann Rogers

ALIENS

by KIM ADDONIZIO

from ALASKA QUARTERLY REVIEW

Now that you're finally happy
you notice how sad your friends are.
One calls you from a pay phone, crying.
Her husband has cancer; only a few months,
maybe less, before his body gives in.
She's tired all the time, can barely eat.
What can you say that will help her?
You yourself are ravenous.
You come so intensely with your new lover
you wonder if you've turned
into someone else. Maybe an alien
has taken over your body
in order to experience the good life
here on earth: dark rum and grapefruit juice,
fucking on the kitchen floor,
then showering together and going out
to eat and eat. When your friends call—
the woman drinking too much, the one who lost
her brother, the ex-lover whose right ear
went dead and then began buzzing—
the alien doesn't want to listen.
More food, it whines. *Fuck me again,*
it whispers, *and afterwards we'll go to the circus.*
The phone rings. *Don't answer it.*
You reach for a fat eclair,
bite into it while the room fills

with aliens—wandering, star-riddled creatures
who vibrate in the rapturous air,
longing to come down and join you,
looking for a place they can rest.

Nominated by Jim Daniels, Stuart Dybek, Diann Blakely Shoaf, Jim Simmerman

MERCY

fiction by SHARON SOLWITZ

from TRIQUARTERLY

SOMETIMES IN THE act of giving pleasure the hinge of my jaw'll catch, and I won't be able to open my mouth all the way. It doesn't happen when I talk or eat. Or yawn. Or get my teeth cleaned. It happens only in the event named above, and it hurts if I force it, and I can't always remember which way last time I wiggled to get free, and I recall instead the two men I saw once and never again, one of whom held my hair with one hand and pounded my face with the other, the side where the hinge of my jaw gets stuck now sometimes, till I was in the car with the door closed shut.

There was no pain. I remember that clearly, though it doesn't improve things. There was just the tiredness, the utter weakness a fish must feel, gills pulsing, pinned by a foot to the floor of the boat.

Gina had it worse though, Clark said, to make me feel better. Fifteen men on a beach in Mexico, fog so thick you couldn't see two feet in front. But you could hear her chanting, *om om om,* low and sweet like blowing into a seashell, Clark said. She was his *friend,* a traveling buddy, that's all—he stresses this. Someone had a gun. When the chanting stopped, Clark stepped toward the silence that had become a hole into which Gina was falling, and the gun waved him back. Get the foock from here, said the gun's bearer, or I blow your brains from your head! Clark, who was to become a professor of composition and rhetoric, repressed the impulse to say, It's get the fuck back or I'll blow your brains out. Feeling, among other things, crazy compassion for the guy who'd seen some but not enough American movies. Still the gun was multilingual. When the chanting started again Clark began shaking. Sometimes now, fifteen years later, he dreams his ineptitude, feet caught in cement or quicksand, no strength to save even himself. He wonders if he'll be able to rise to the necessary occasion if it's his lover in danger. Wonders if this is why he's thirty-eight right now with no lover.

When the man who picked us up outside of Binghamton stopped at Goody's Bar and Package Liquor, *I wanna check on my friend,* Lenny and I froze like deer in headlights. It was so late, so moonless dark, so far, still, from where we were heading, that we just held still on the cracked plastic of the front seat, staring out at the blank night beyond the windshield, till the man and his friend stood on opposite sides of the car—bookends, brackets, end-punctuation to our suburban Jewish English-major lives. I'll take shotgun, says the friend, and when Lenny doesn't budge, not from machismo but a failure to access the jargon, he pulls him out of the car. Let's go, Tama, Lenny says, his voice faint as a dog barking across town. But I start moving, I have my arms around my pack and a toe on the ground, about to shift my weight out the door back to my life forever, when the friend jumps in, and the car takes off with my feet sticking out. I feel with a spurt of dread one of my sandals coming off. Start to lose myself in the web of what it might symbolize.

Afterward, in the hotel we found in downtown Binghamton, Lenny told me how trying to call the police he forgot 911. It was a crazy thing, his mind was just not working, he had to ask at the 7-Eleven—he cried as he told me.

You don't have to feel guilty, I said generously. I was working on empathy, a step in my personal program of character development, feeling the feelings of the other. I had been a self-centered child, or so it was said. They could have killed you, I said to Lenny. You don't die from rape.

Lenny's guilt kept him up in our muggy hotel room, made him think about taking a martial-arts course, about seeing a counselor. It was 1978. Jimmy Carter was in office, though we didn't think about it. Disco screamed through the open window. We went over his responses in depth, from their origin in the American frontier ethic to his relationship with his blustery father.

Hey, thanks, Lenny said. But he looked at me as if I'd become someone else. To help him find his way back to me I described what he'd missed, the looks and personality of the driver's friend, not much older than us, hard and skinny, with army-short hair the color of his scalp.

Who in a book would be named something from the Bible but called by the name of an unattractive minor animal, Mink or Wolverine. Would swear every other word. To me he said over and over, Shut the fuck up. I had no idea I had been talking. I thrashed about, pulled at his fingers, trying to disengage without hurting him, as my mother said to do with my younger sister. Through the hotel window came someone's clear rage: I was better off before I met you!

Lenny said, You could have bitten his arm. Or stuck your fingers in his eyes.

Clearly, he wanted to break up with me.

Have mercy, I said.

The next morning we went back for my sandal—I knew the place more or less, and who'd want one shoe? But though we looked for an hour and found a woman's pointy-toed pump (leather uppers) there was nothing of mine.

My old socialist landlord, former union banker, was mugged, once, by a group of junior-high thugs who not only took his wallet but punched him in the stomach. For no reason. In bed a week, he blamed not the boys but the System (capitalism), which drains out all your human feeling, he said, rolling a piece of Generic bread into a finger to dip in the soup I'd brought him: Punks. I pity 'em.

Afterward Gina ran naked into the ocean, said it had passed through without touching her. I am not this body, she said to herself, my sister/alter ego. I've never met her in fact, but part of me aspires to her. A more devout Buddhist than I am a Jew, she has a system large enough to comprise what happened to her. Although her fingers trembled slightly, her face and voice, I imagine, were calm without the comfort of a boyfriend. The assault had failed to reach the radiant core of her.

I gave a pair of policemen the details of my assailants, including tone of voice, texture and smell of skin. I bought a baking-powder douche because baking powder cancels refrigerator odors and sounds cleaner than clean, no? But for me, for weeks afterward, though I'd upended my torso for quick and easy entry, it burned when I walked and when I peed, and kissing Lenny wasn't the same either. I used to love to smooch him, on the couch, in the car driving—I loved the smell of him, even when he hadn't brushed his teeth for a while. When school started in the fall we were planning to share an apartment. But afterward, with the pain gone so we could have sex again, we kissed only when he wanted to, not ever from my own impulse.

432

I think I'm angry, I remember saying.

With those guys! I don't blame you.

I don't know, I said, and he looked scared to death. I did not pursue the subject.

To be sure, nothing's resolved with "those guys," over whom in my dreams and daytime fantasies I wield the knife of castration. But they aren't only out of reach of my actual vengeance, they're out of my ken, Bad Guys, from nightmares and not daily life—no one I know.

I hugged Lenny. When school started, I studied somewhat harder than before. I did not become pregnant. Lenny and I very slowly became unacquainted. Like those Moslem men who cast out their violated wives and sisters, he felt I should have saved myself. (I might be wrong here.) At this moment I do not know where he is or what he is doing. His degree, I think, was in psychology.

I switched to European history, which I teach now (medieval and Renaissance) at a small-town branch of a state university. I publish infrequent articles. I'm writing a book about Christian saints. I'm married to a sweet and burly man who teaches social studies and coaches wrestling at the local high school, who'll protect me from marauders on the street. But when a male student cites an opinion with any ruffle of animosity I find it hard to disagree. *Now class, who can address what Richard is saying?* The area in which I feel utterly safe from harm is small and under assault, not only from people like the "guys" but something Lenny said a night or so after the event, *Tell me the truth, was there any, er, pleasure?* He was embarrassed. But he just had to know.

I want to beat on him—I think about that. To sock him in the mouth, the eye, watch it turn dark the next day. What kind of pleasure?, I'll scream. Is there pleasure for *you* being 100 percent at someone's mercy?

There was nothing but terror in the event—I've gone over it moment by moment looking for nuances, with friends, shrinks, and now husband Dan, though he's not big on nuances. He doesn't find power erotic at either pole. The sort of thinking that mixes good and evil he finds "sick." I sleep well in the absoluteness of his distinctions. And that he does not require oral sex. When I do it as a favor he seems to appreciate it.

Still, there's that weird boy at our son's summer camp, not so big himself, who likes to play with the little kids, the preschoolers, Mercy, it's called. In this game you take someone's thin wrist in your two hands and twist in opposite directions till the fragile chains of cells pull away from each other with a sensation that feels partly like ripping and partly like burning. It's supposed to stop when the victim yells Mercy! or maybe just a little later, this game of machismo, of personal grit in the face of pain, good practice, perhaps, for dissidents of repressive regimes who will not betray their comrades. But when I go to pick Noah up in the gym where the children wait for their rides, the weird kid is holding his arm, and Noah, who rarely cries from physical pain, has this blank look, as if the world has just opened its horrendous possibilities. What do you think you're doing! I hiss at the boy, and he puts his fingers in his ears. I hold him by the shoulders: If you ever touch him again, do you hear me?, if you put another hand on my son, I'm coming for you, do you hear what I'm saying, you think you know about pain but that's nothing compared to what I'll do to you!

Big talk. It bounces off his skull of some weird, impermeable fusion of lead, kryptonite and pure evil. He twists his fingers deeper in his ears, shuts his eyes. I give him a shake, not as hard as I'd like. In truth I want to kill this boy for making the world one shade darker for my child so full of light. This is a bad kid, I say to myself, with, obviously, problems at home. He has trouble controlling himself, the director says, seating him in a corner to wait for his mother who hasn't brought him up properly, as I turn to hide the fact of my shaking, from him, this sick child who'll shoot from towers if he doesn't get therapy soon and maybe even if he does, this demon boy from whom I must save my boy so utterly different from him.

But the next day when I poke my head in the door Noah is with him again. The two spring apart with identical expressions of rapturous guilt, as if caught in some complicit, consensual lovemaking.

In pain there is, or so I recall from childhood, a sexual element. I used to draw Prometheus on his rock, belly open to the beak and talons of Zeus's avenging vulture. And Joan at the stake, flames lapping the hem of her tattered dress (crayoned brown to resemble a sack). My fifth-grade teacher asked us once, seriously, was there anything we'd give our lives for? I loved this teacher. My sister and I played spy and counterspy, one or the other being captured by the Russians. *Confess!* she'd scream: *Would you rather be Red or Dead?*, further compressing my hand in the vise on my father's basement workbench. I remember a dark ecstatic quiver, not the sole province of male children.

The old pain/pleasure thing. Aside from God, that's the heart of it, and maybe even as big as God, at least people cry Jesus, cry Satan with the same blood urgency, seeking the pleasure of pain in hope of the same—we need a German word here—Ultimate-idea-feeling-of-light. I knew it once better than I do now, having set it down somewhere or stashed it in some inner pocket, incongruent with the work of becoming a grown-up citizen human being, what people do to keep their livers intact.

But in Roman Empire days, Julitta, a new Christian, saw her child murdered by a government official and rejoiced in his martyr's death. It's part legend, part fact: inextricable. Julitta is wealthy, noble, running from the Imperial law. Her son Cyricus, three, grown close to her body and soul over two years of hiding and wandering, bites the governor who's holding him, who hurls him off his lap and down steps the way you throw off a pesky kitten. The steps are hard gleaming marble. Julitta, rhapsodic in the Christian death of her toddler martyr, goes serenely to her own, which will be accompanied by torture. Mother and son saints, Julitta and little Cyricus.

It was 304 (date substantiated), with Diocletian fixated on the Christian Problem when he should have been securing his borders. More than the Huns he feared monotheism, the laser force of the One God overwhelming the wild crackling Olympian bonfire. But what is this drive to cast oneself into the bonfire? In Alexandria a Christian grandmother named Apollonia is beaten by members of an anti-Christian mob. Some of her teeth fall out. Renounce! someone cries, or it's the pyre for you! But when they light it she walks in of her own free will: Saint Apollonia.

With young Christian girls—virgins—sainthood was harder to come by. Moved perhaps by their youth or the beauty of a face, officials promised them their lives and more if they returned to the Imperial fold, sacrificed to Minerva, married a noble. Catherine is my favorite, high-born, beautiful and learned. Denying her faith she can marry the emperor. Both she rejects, instead converting fifty philosophers hired to best her in debate along with the empress she was to supplant. There are no documents to support any of these tales but they inspired medieval Christians including Joan of Arc. Beaten and left to die in prison, Saint Catherine is fed by a dove. The spiked wheel designed to end her life in torment falls to pieces as she's bound to it, its spikes injuring several spectators. She bends her head to the block, calling down blessings on those who'll remember her, ecstatically mirroring the agony of

Christ. Milk flows from her several veins and arteries. The instrument of torture that failed to harm her will be called the catherine wheel.

But at dusk when a tree or stop sign turns into the figure of a man I can't rise on the wings of her unimaginable suffering or ecstasy. Nor, in my self-defense class, can I strike the padded attacker with even half my strength. My blows have an element of caress. I am neither saint nor self-protector. My ego refuses either to die or prevail.

Don't think so much, says my instructor, herself a rape victim turned fierce with her message. You have the power to save your life.

I know that in theory.

You don't have to be a saint, says Dan.

If I were a saint I'd have forgiven them.

They're scum! Dan says.

That's what makes it so hard.

It's what separates the medieval mind from that of the Renaissance, I tell my students, the notion of there being two sides. It's the perspective from the mountaintop. Good-hearted, inept Jimmy Carter. What removes us from Catherine on one side and the Huns on the other, a sense of the unresolvable ambiguity of practically everything. I bear it like an illness.

My personal Huns had no such interior division. Resolute and fierce, they followed the rush of their blood to its culmination in act. If their minds held a self-image, it wasn't even as naughty boys but as executors of a primitive justice. The younger, the wolverine, kept calling me whore, as if rape were a punishment he was meting out for my promiscuity. Cornell—the name on my sweatshirt—'s a real cathouse!, he kept saying that. He went first, and after waiting patiently for his friend, slightly paunchy, limper of dick, to finish, he re-unzipped and said he wanted to do it again, not in the car but on the cool night asphalt of the empty lot we were parked in, and this time I was to show him how much I liked it.

Sometimes now I stop my car in bad neighborhoods, buy a Coke from a store outside of which stand dissolute teens trying to get up the energy to mug someone. As if this fifteen-year-old event is my primal scene, to be played and replayed till it comes out right or else covers over what in fact occurred, what I haven't detailed yet, not even to Dan.

But fifteen years ago my jaw was starting to hurt, something like a molar toothache, an augmenting pain with no end in sight. Then in the face of Wolverine's uncircumcised dick, his bullet-shaped, almost hairless head, I push panic to one sector. From the small area of mind that can still think and speak come words from some high-school play, sticky nauseous-sweet in the back of my throat: *You are a kind man. You're a good and merciful man.* Not to Wolverine but to the older, limper one. Prone on his backseat, I half raise my head, palms together in the Christian prayer position, though there's nothing Christian in what I am doing, no ideal to exalt, of faith or sexual purity, no one's life to save besides my own. I speak into his eyes, beseeching like Olive Oyl, like Pauline tied to the tracks: I've learned my lesson. I don't need to be hurt anymore, please, really I don't.

Kiss my hand, he says.

I do so.

Kiss my dick, says Wolverine.

I reach, but clumsily. He pulls back the flap of gentile skin.

Kiss it I said!

I lean farther forward, alert, blank—whoever I was in the past or might be in the future in a bubble rising up and up. Then Limp-dick grabs his buddy by the back of his shirt. Stop farting around, he says.

Keep your eyes off the plates, Wolverine says to me. One look back and we're coming for you!

Thank you, I say, once, so as not to seem ironic.

But I do not feel ironic. I feel unambiguous gratitude. Later I'll hate them for rubbing my face in the smallness and smarminess of my female power. But there on the pebbly asphalt of the parking lot I tremble with love for the limp one for thwarting his friend. Between his rear plate and my view in the approaching dawn he stands, his arms crossed like a genie from a bottle, like my hero-deliverer, my God in his mercy.

I'd rather be Red than dead, I say to myself. I'd rather be anything than dead.

I walk in my one shoe away down the road.

Nominated by TriQuarterly

THE DISSOLUTION OF THE WORLD

fiction by CAROLINE A. LANGSTON

from PLOUGHSHARES

June, 1973

Eᴀʀʟʏ ᴏɴ ᴛʜᴇ ᴍᴏʀɴɪɴɢ of Alice's wedding, when I was nine, I woke to hear the front door slamming into the quiet, and I got out of my bed and went to the window. Standing on tiptoes, feet bare against the floor planks chilled by the air conditioner, the breeze running up my nightgown, I held open a crack in the Venetian blinds and peered through to see my father stepping down the front porch stairs. In one hand he held *The Clarion Ledger*, still in its rubber bands, and with the other he clutched at the banister on account of the polio I knew he'd had as a child: under his trousers one leg was forever crooked, just slightly. He wore a coat and tie, as if he were going to work down at the insurance office, but it was Saturday. It was odd to me that he would be leaving then, only a few hours before the wedding at noon, ambling with a vague limp along the flagstone walk to the iron gate that creaked open onto Franklin Avenue.

Just then, I heard the front door again, and my mother rushed onto the porch after him, the hair she'd had done the day before tied up in a scarf and her jewel-toned caftan billowing. From the angle of my room, I could see her calling to him from the top of the stairs, her chin imploring and forward. I could hear nothing, though, could only see him glance back and mouth a word or two—perhaps her name, "Maybelle"—close the gate behind him, and continue down the sidewalk toward town. For a little while, my mother waited on the porch, arranging the folds of her caftan and looking after him forlornly, as if she thought he'd come back, but he didn't, and suddenly she flew inside again, as quickly as she had come out. Yet I stood still, and watched him growing smaller in the distance as Franklin Avenue bore downhill toward the courthouse and downtown, through an aisle of huge old clapboard houses shrouded in clusters of hydrangea bushes that were bursting forth in clusters of blue and pink blooms. At the bottom of the hill, my father would go to his office, I was sure, and I tried to imagine him behind his desk at the insurance agency on a Saturday, on this Saturday of Saturdays, when Alice was a bride and I was a brides-maid, I could form a picture of him sitting in the dark there, with the glowing red sign, *Car—Home—Health—Life*, blinking long shadows through the picture window onto the linoleum, and I held that scene in my mind until he disappeared from view, then scuttled out into the hall.

Stillness lay thick over the house, except for tiny voices from the television in the kitchen and the floorboards which creaked as I shuf-fled down the dark hall, pushing open all the closed doors to see who was about, and finding no one. Not Gill, Alice's fiancé from out in the county. I hadn't seen him since the night after she announced their en-gagement two weeks before, when he came to dinner and sat con-founded and awkward at the table, twisting his long, stringy ponytail in hand and mumbling "yes'm," and "no sir" to all questions. I did not much care for him.

But where was everybody else, I wanted to know, where were all the Memphis cousins who were supposed to be arriving? The year before, one of them had gotten married, one of the Rands, my mother's fam-ily. We had all gone up to Memphis, my parents, my brother, Rand, Al-ice, and I to see her in stiff white satin at the Second Presbyterian Church. At the reception CiCi ran about the country club with her husband carrying her train, exclaiming, "I'm so happy, y'all!" and tak-ing tiny sips of champagne out of glasses passed on trays by waiters. I had thought it brilliant, sneaking round the hundreds of guests and stealing four rice bags wrapped in tulle and ribbon which I fingered in the back seat of the car all the way back down toward home. My cousin had eight attendants who had worn wide-brimmed hats and carried nosegay carnations, which, abandoned on the tables at the reception, I had picked up and admired. "Now you will have one just like them," Mama had assured me over and over; it would match my bridesmaid's dress from Peter Fran's in Jackson that was waiting in plastic. How

439

many bouquets would be in the refrigerator? When would all the raucous day begin?

Light from the dining room chandelier burned down the hall, and I walked into it to find my mother settled now at the head of the long table, bent over addressing announcements. She did not see me, and I could see her teeth chewing upon her lower lip as she dashed off an address in her fine longhand, and put the finished envelope on the tottering pile before her. Announcements had to be sent the day of the wedding, she had explained, to all the people who wouldn't've been able to come in such a hurry. Then she had read out to me the section on them in the new edition of *Emily Post* she had bought on the day after we all found out Alice was getting married. "Mama," I braved the silence, "why come Daddy left?"

She seemed not to hear me, but instead ran a finger from a page of her tapestry address book to a name she was copying out on another envelope. My mother had a tendency to ignore questions that she did not think were appropriate for children to ask, and her children were always asking such questions. I stepped farther into the room and spoke again, this time asking, "Mama? Where're Alice and Rand?"

Again she didn't answer, only looked up, softening her face, and said, "Hallie." She stretched out her arms and drew me into the lap I knew I was too big to sit on anymore. At first I felt comforted, and clutched her around the neck with my bare arms, but then something did not feel right and filled me with unease. I could see in Mama's face how tired she was; she looked pale and veined and she hadn't put on her big eyelashes yet. Her arm was around me tightly. Once again, I tried starting over, "Well, where are all of them?"

Writing out an address, she did not look at me but replied with finality, "Daddy had to go to work for a little while; Alice is still asleep," and then, unsure, "Rand is . . . out somewhere."

"Then when are the cousins going to get here?" I was getting impatient.

"You know I told you yesterday that they were going to meet us at the church, be easier that way," she sighed over the satiny white box of announcements, then silenced me, "Now just wait on me for a little while and I'll help you get ready."

I fidgeted and caught at one of the announcements, pulling it out of the first envelope with our address embossed on the back, and the second one with its square of tissue beneath it, running my fingers over the engraving and reading:

440

Mr. and Mrs. William Exum East
have the honour to announce
the marriage of their daughter
Alice Honora
to
Mr. Gill Thrasher
Saturday, the ninth of June
nineteen-hundred and seventy-three
First Presbyterian Church
Anathoth, Mississippi

Then I looked around the dining room to see what Mama had done to it, for it had been off-limits all week. The reception was going to be in here, afterwards, with the table set up as a buffet, because the country club had been booked. Every last leaf had been added, and she had draped the table with her best damask linen cloth, but now this morning all was disorder: the stacks of announcements spilled haphazardly around the three-tier cake. On the sideboard she had stacked silverware brought home from the bank vault, next to the great punch bowl, which was hung round its rim with a dozen tiny cups and had fifths of rum stuffed in its hold for the planter's punch. My parents rarely drank, and so my mother had been excited about it, pulling out the recipe their cook had used when she was little. Mama had also set up card tables draped with lawn along the walls, which displayed the presents Alice had received; there were only a few, for in the short time, Alice had registered neither china pattern nor flatware. And through the open swinging door that led into the kitchen, I could see Vera—the maid who had raised Alice and Rand but by my time had retired to the new convalescent home on the edge of town—wearing the uniform she only wore for special occasions. She was standing at the counter arranging deviled eggs in circles on a tray, one eye on the small black and white television perched on the counter, which resounded loud and hollow through the room. She was older than I could imagine, but watching a dance show broadcast from Jackson called "Black Gold." When she finished the tray, she stepped shakily into the dining room and set it on the table edge, saying, "Here you go, Mrs. East," before she disappeared into the kitchen and the door swung shut behind her.

Every night my family had dinner at the table, my mother bringing our plates in full from the kitchen, and it was here that two things had happened. The first had been six months before, in the gray lull between Christmas and New Year's, when Alice had sat down one night in her usual chair next to the sideboard and announced, right after the blessing, "I don't think I want to go back to school this semester, after all." She smiled apologetically as she said it, as if she knew nothing could be more unexpected than this, and pushed a loose strand of blond hair out of her face. For a moment, everyone sat tense and glazed until Rand remarked shortly, "Well, where're you going to go?" He was only fifteen, but observed an orderly code of rules about what was and was not proper.

And Alice had replied, too easily, "I think I'm going to come home and live for a little while."

Diagonally across the table, my mother blanched and asked, "Is there something wrong, sweetheart?" worrying a napkin ring with her fingers. Alice shook her head slightly, as if only for her to see, and Mama visibly quieted. "All right, then," she pronounced. My father only looked sad; he was the first person in his family to graduate from college, and had all our lives told us if you didn't finish young, you didn't finish at all.

But when I thought about Alice back in town, I only felt horrified: In my mind the greatness of her senior year in high school, *last year*, suddenly crumpled in on itself; I blurted out, "You cain't! You cain't come back here!" while my mother leaned across the table and intoned, "Shh, shh, calm down now." People who had never amounted to much could stay in Anathoth without going to college, girls typing in the offices on Attorneys' Row and boys doing shifts up at the plant or the cotton compress. They were all around, but invisible. My sister, Alice, however, had shone, and was meant to carry her brilliance far before she brought it back to Franklin Avenue again, I thought. Her senior year at the Academy, she had sat in the back of a showroom Cadillac convertible as it wound around the edge of a new football field eked out of an acre of cotton land; it was halftime and she was grinning in my mother's mink stole, carrying a sheaf of roses and wearing a ribbon over her shoulder that spelled out, in glitter, "Demeter." She had been crowned queen of the Harvest Festival, and sat on a dais adorned with fruits and vegetables and cotton, her hair like corn silk. Later she had placed the roses in my arms, bending over and saying, "These are for you, Hallie," and I had glowed. Then after the game she had gone off to a party, and out of the window of the car, I had seen her sailing across the school parking lot with her tiara in hand and holding up the skirt of her brocaded silver dress that was luminous un-

442

der the streetlights. Mama caught sight of her then, and murmured into the dark well of the Impala, "Isn't she beautiful?" Peering over the top of the back seat, I had seen her give my father a look I don't think I ever saw again, a look completely open and full of pure gratitude. It was only the second class to be graduated from the colonnaded Academy that rose up brick-new on the road to Vicksburg, and here she walked with the authority of an empress.

Then she was graduated and went up to Oxford like my mother and father many years before, where she pledged the same sorority as my mother had. Every day during rush, she had called home and described for Mama the parties to which she had been, which houses she had liked and who she had met, as I listened in on the extension. "This boy is pouring champagne for me and I've never been so happy," she crowed to her on Bid Day, speaking of unfathomable knowledge I would have to wait to know.

But then something happened. All fall after that, whenever the phone rang, I ran into the hall from my television program to answer it, but only rarely was it Alice. As the months progressed, she had less and less to say, and there came into her voice an impatient edge: she was just fine, there were more parties than ever, could she speak to Mama, and was I behaving, anyway?

But in January, Alice did stay home, after the letter from the sorority arrived de-pledging her for such a low average, and a note from the housemother of the dormitory expressing doubts about the crowd she had gotten involved with. After I heard my parents whispering about the letter, I found it in my mother's secretary and read it, but could not relate it to the sister I knew: There had been evenings when she disappeared for hours and had to be let in the door by campus security in the small hours of the morning, and she had been visited by boys "who did not appear to attend the University."

"Now what do you suppose that means?" I heard my mother say to Daddy one evening. Nights, they sat in bed and read, the light from the nightstand shining down through the open door into my room; they were reading the letter again, I knew, but my father never answered her. It, like everything else, was passed over in perfect silence.

So the next Saturday, my parents hauled her belongings back from Oxford in Daddy's truck, and she took a job at the public library next to the courthouse, where there was nothing to do but stand behind the great oak reception desk all day long, reading magazines or propping her elbows on the counter and staring out the Palladian windows onto

443

Main Street. A couple of times, I dropped by there with Mama to visit, and one day Alice was not at her post. "She always takes too long a break, Miz East," the librarian, Miss Eloise, complained.

"It's 'cause that job is a drag," Alice replied when my mother timidly confronted her, but she kept on working. As winter passed she began to seem withdrawn, curiously dulled. She began to wear clothes I had not before seen, Empire dresses that trailed the floor and brown leather sandals with bells that jingled as she walked, wandering about the house aimlessly as if she were imprisoned, and smoking cigarettes at the kitchen table against Mama's raised brow. Sometimes after dinner she would escape in the Impala, and in the morning when my mother drove me to school, the car would smell of lake water. Rand was in tenth grade, and I had heard him mention once that there were parties, out on the levee, crowds of wild people camping against the dusk. These were the hippie rednecks with long hair who also hung out in the parking lot of the Big Barn Minit Mart that people said smoked drugs.

"You wouldn't believe who I've heard goes out there," he told Mama one day after school when they were watching *Somerset* in the sitting room, after he had told me to go away and I had lingered on the other side of the door. "Which ones of your friends' children," he added, but then she turned up the volume.

Often that spring my mother had Junior Auxiliary meetings, and Alice picked me up from fourth grade. One day close to Easter, when red buds were beginning to bloom, Alice drove up to the Academy with all four windows down, humming to herself, and when I got in the front and tossed my books into the back seat, she turned and said, "I have to go do something before we go home, okay?" She was barefooted and pressed her toes against the gas pedal, steering the wheel in the flat palms of her hands, and the wind blowing through the car smelled of sweet olive. She drove through town, climbing into the hills under trees hung with kudzu, heading for the fertilizer plant that burst forth at the top, overlooking all the delta. Silvery smokestacks thrust against the sky pouring white smoke and yellow sulfur. In the middle, an aluminum tower rose for a dozen stories, laced with pipes and threaded with stairs. A cooling tower, Daddy had once told me. Getting out, Alice went toward it, shouting up, "I'm here, come on!"

High on a catwalk was a man, with a blond ponytail sticking out of his hard hat, who leaned out over a rail. "Hang on jus' a minute, Alice!" he called out, and when I heard his unfamiliar voice speak her name, I became awakened and suspicious. He disappeared and I knew he was coming down; his footsteps rang on the metal staircase rungs. Then he emerged from the entrance, with his hard hat in one hand, and with the other he suddenly clasped her on the shoulder.

"Get in the back, Hallie, please?" she asked, and they got in the car and slammed the doors. "Oh, this is Gill," she said as she backed out onto the road.

He turned and gave me a look that was too immediately friendly, what my mother would call "familiar," and I mumbled hello.

"Guess your sister don't want to talk to me none," he said, and turned back around. Coming down from the hills, Alice took the by-pass that rounded town toward the delta and then went over the river bridge.

"We're going to take Gill home. His car is broken," she explained, and turned on the FM rock station from Jackson. On the other side of the river, she turned onto a county road that meandered along the levee, past a country store or two and a rusty, long-defunct gin. Then she pulled off onto a gravel driveway that ran in a long straight line back to a tiny frame house and a single cottonwood tree, where she cut the motor.

"Y'all'gn come in a while," he said, and I followed behind them with arms crossed as they went inside through the unlocked door. The house was filled with gray, empty light because there were no curtains on any of the windows except one, over which was tacked an old bed-spread. "Y'all sit down," he said, and Alice smiled at him, but there was hardly any furniture, only an armchair placed directly in front of a tele-vision set into which Alice plopped, a couple of side tables, and a chair that looked as if it were part of a dinette set which I didn't want to sit in because it looked dirty.

"You want a Coke?" he called at me from the kitchen doorway, to which I answered no. Then he came back in bearing two beers, one of which he gave to Alice, who did not, I noticed, ask for a glass. You were always supposed to ask for a glass.

He saw that I was still standing. "She don't want to sit down, eh?"

"Oh, Hallie," Alice said dismissively. My sister was transforming be-fore my eyes; she had already metamorphosed into something different than the dreamy princess who moped around our house on Franklin Avenue. Now she was serenely expectant, leaning back languidly in the armchair so that her short sundress came above her knees. The sweat from the beer can was running down her fingers in rivulets, and she was looking up at him. "Well, now," she pronounced. I sensed that they were waiting for something, and acquiesced, sitting down in the kitchen chair with my feet dangling stupidly above the floor.

He picked up a strange pipe off one of the side tables and began to pack something down in it with an index finger, then lit a sparking lighter to it and inhaled. Don't burn yourself, I thought, or maybe you should. Then Alice took the pipe from him and also inhaled as the scent like incense curled again into the room. Bewildered, I stared at an unplugged electric guitar leaning idle against an amplifier, whose silver logo I began to spell out to myself, trying to tune everything else out: *Fender.*

He saw me looking at it, picked up the guitar, and ran his fingers along the strings so that they made soft faint twangs. All of a sudden, he got down in my face, leaning toward me with the guitar in his arms, and said, "Aren't you going to smile at me?" At first I felt embarrassed, then stole a glance at him and saw he had the clearest green eyes, and for an instant before he turned away, I allowed myself to realize they were beautiful.

"Well," Alice said again into the silence, and got up from the chair. "We better go."

"I talk to you," he called from the open doorway as we walked back out to the car. "Thanks for the ride." All the way home, Alice said nothing, she had not even asked me not to tell, but I never would, anyhow, because no one would believe.

That afternoon became like an illusion, half-forgotten, and I had not thought of him at all until two weeks before, on a day that Alice came home late from the library. This was the second thing that had happened at the dining room table. Mama had entrusted me with collecting plates and Rand was asking could he be excused when Alice appeared in the doorway, her long, pale hands clasping the door jamb. For a second she stood very still, then announced, "Mama, Daddy, I'm going to get married to Gill Thrasher." He was coming over to meet them the very next night. The whole picture of him, that house and those green eyes, came crashing into my mind, and I yelled out, "Hunh? Hunh?" until I fell quiet when I heard my father's tone, "Be quiet, Hallie."

"Who Thrasher?" Daddy demanded, turning around in the chair at his end of the table to face her, while Mama clattered a spoon through her coffee.

There were a thousand Thrashers that farmed on parts and parcels of rented land, and he was one of them. "Gill Thrasher," Alice repeated hopefully, coloring, "from out in the county. He works at Chemical. I knew him," she paused for a second, "when I still went to the public schools."

Flushing red, Daddy glared wordless at her until my mother finally waved Rand and me out of the dining room and slid shut the heavy rosewood doors against us. We waited, not saying anything, sitting on the bottom of the staircase to see if it would truly happen, and in the quiet, I heard through the doors an awful, strangulated sound. It was my father crying. Then I could hear my father asking her questions, questions that began with her name, Alice, and trailed off, inaudible. Her voice would answer, a constant soft murmur, and I heard the clink of china, Mama sitting there nervously arranging the plates I had not finished stacking. When the doors reopened, Mama emerged briskly, and I could see my father stroking Alice's hand with his own, imploring, "You don't want another sin before God, do you? You think you can live with this Thrasher for the rest of your life in some shack back on a field?" then leaned close to her and whispered so I could barely hear, "Can't I just take you away for a while?"

"Daddy, really," she said impatiently, rising to follow my mother into the hall. She stopped to kneel before me and ask, "You'll be my bridesmaid, Hallie, won't you?" Yes, I mouthed nervously, just as Mama returned from the hall closet struggling under a powder-blue box uplifted in her arms. She set it on the hall table, pulling off the top that smelled of mothballs and unfolding a cloud of pastel tissue. Exhilarated, she drew out her wedding dress carefully, fingering seed pearls that sprinkled down the bodice and fluffing out a crinoline that rustled taffeta under the skirt. "Now if we can only let out the waistline a little, it will be perfect. And what should we do for Hallie?"

Through the doorway I saw that my father had laid his head down on the table, but Mama was smiling and excited. Rand sat listlessly beside me, and all I felt was confused. "Oh, don't make it such a bother, Mama," Alice cried out. "You always have to make everything a big deal." She ran up the stairs to her attic room, leaving my mother thinking furiously: two weeks for preparations.

Mama was finally finishing her preparations, writing out the last announcements and pulling them into a neat stack so that Vera could add more dishes to the table. I watched as she brought in crystal bowls of nuts, silver salvers of pink mint roses, ordering them around the great icing-festooned cake in the center, until the table was filled. "Thank you so much, Vera. Now go on and take you a rest for a while until

447

we're ready," my mother said, dismissing her back through the swinging door. Then she hoisted me off her lap and stood, "Now you. We have got to get you dressed and get your hair fixed." She was hurrying me to my room when footsteps fell behind us in the hall, and she called, "William?"

When she saw it was only Rand, swatting a tennis racket idly against his knee and holding the Impala keys in his other hand, she demanded, "Where have you been?"

"Been up at the Club," he shrugged. "Where'd Daddy go?"

She didn't answer but countered stiffly, "I had things for you to do. What came over you to run off today?"

I waited as he pointed up at the ceiling, indicating Alice's room, then spoke soft and volcanic, "She doesn't care, does she?"

My mother stood straight. "Alice was up late last night. As were you. You ought to know," she accused. Alice and Rand had come in late the night before from a rehearsal party that Gill's friends were giving them, even though there had been no rehearsal. It was at the Motel, I heard Alice tell Rand as they left, when they didn't know I was listening. I had fallen asleep visualizing it, the swimming pool glowing blue with underwater bulbs and all the doors around the motor court that winked a haze of pink, then green neon, filled with faceless friends. Later I woke hearing when the front door cracked open into the dark, hearing thudding steps and stifled giggles, knowing it was way after midnight, and now I peered at Rand to inspect him. "Mama, it wasn't all that late, all right?" he protested.

"Go get ready, you hear?" she answered, hustling me into my room by the shoulders and raising my nightgown over my head when I could have done it myself, but all I did was stand quiet. Mama pulled my dress from the chifforobe and buttoned me into it, dotted Swiss that fell to my ankles and a sash with ends that hung down my back, then I found stockings, new shoes from Vicksburg. In my parents' room I sat before Mama's dressing table as she coaxed my hair through her big silver brush, parting it sharply and plaiting it to the ends, which she tied with pink ribbon. Last, a single drop of Shalimar on my neck, and I sat while she stepped into a linen suit, took off her hair scarf, and spruced up the French twist with White Rain. At the dressing table, she put on eyelashes and liner, pinned on a tiny circlet of hat like no one did anymore, collected her pumps and handbag, then padded off into the hall in stocking feet, calling, "Rand? Rand?"

"Mama." I followed her. "Doesn't Alice got to get up now?" But she was not listening.

Rand returned with a loud green tie and his hair wet, which my mother combed to the sides with her fingers as I looked on. Except for his longish hair that brushed against the starched collar of his shirt in curly tendrils, he already looked older, polished, as neat and grave as my father's picture in the Phi Delt composite that hung in the hall, Daddy one tiny black and white square lost in the middle. As she arranged him, he frowned helplessly, resisting her hands, toeing his white bucks into the grooves between the long cypress floorboards. "This isn't going to take long, is it? There better not be a lot of people there, is what I say. I don't feel too well." So they had been drinking, I thought; that must have been the only reason he had gone.

"Listen," Mama stopped, her manicured hands outstretched and imperative, "we are all going to make the best of this."

Just then I saw my father on the porch, his features distorted into pieces by the panes of leaded glass in the front door, and he came inside with a look on his face as if he'd been dreaming. Mama focused on him, "Finally you are back! Your things are all laid out on the bed—" but he disregarded her, interrupting.

"I saw all your people down to the café, Maybelle." These were the Memphis cousins. "Drinking coffee and waiting all dressed up."

"William, they're going to meet us there."

"That's what they said." He looked at the floor.

I hung back in the hollow of the staircase curve, wondering how we were supposed to act: everyone was apart somehow, sunk in themselves. Alice. I held up my hem so as not to tread on it, and edged slowly and unnoticed up the stairs. The curiosity of our old family house was that the stairs didn't go anywhere, only to an attic under the roof peak. Our great-great-grandfather on the Rand side had built the house, and put them there "for decoration," Mama always said. But when Alice came home from Ole Miss, she moved into the attic, dragged up her things, and hung a motel "Do Not Disturb" sign on the knob of the battered door that closed shut at the top of the landing.

Slowly I pushed the door open, whispering, "Alice!" feeling for once older than she, getting her up on her own wedding day with everyone acting so strange. Alice had been very secretive about her room, and though I had been here a couple of times, today it seemed as if I were seeing it for the first time. Bare boards ran steep walls fifteen feet up into ceilings, and only two dormer windows shone thin bands of light across the floor. The windows were open because there was no air conditioner up here, only a huge box fan that droned noisily and swirled the stifling air into waves, which licked under the edges of wrinkled posters she had tacked all along the walls. On the floor, album covers were scattered next to a record player still spinning at the end of a side, its needle rasping in the run-out groove, over and over. And in the middle of the room stood Alice's bed, heaped high with clothes and covers. Alice lay lost among them.

I walked toward the bed and saw her asleep, tangled blond hair across bright paisley sheets, the wild pattern winding under and around her. Against the heat she had slept naked, and the covers and bedclothes trailed down to her waist. I felt embarrassed, thinking I should avert my eyes, but I was stunned still, seeing her tanned shoulders disappear into the whiteness of breasts that seemed swollen, more pendulous. Suddenly it came to me I knew what Mama, Daddy, Rand knew, the knowledge that I now saw had run like a current under the surface of the house. I stepped back, breathless and filled with shame, feeling myself an ignorant child. But I managed, piping up, "Alice, you got to get up now."

She stirred and, when she saw me, pulled up the sheet over her like it was nothing, smelling of smoke and spirits, mascara smudging her lashes. "Hallie Day," she said, pronouncing my full name as I stood rigid, not sure what to say.

At that moment Mama came yelling up the stairs, "Let's get you ready," and Alice stood up, draping the sheet around her like a robe, and loped off to the shower. Freed, I ran downstairs, took my bouquet from the refrigerator, and idled in the hall, picking restlessly at the tight knot of carnations and greenery. I remembered things I had heard adults say, of shotguns, and people counting up on their fingers how many months since the wedding to see if it was nine, and Alice seemed vulnerable to me now, as vulnerable as I, who could only wait for her to come down.

She appeared at the top of the staircase with Mama hovering behind her, crowing, "Here she is!" as Daddy and Rand walked in from the sitting room. Her hair hung across her shoulders like a curtain of light and her dress tumbled loose to the floor in yards and yards of white cotton gauze, its wide angel sleeves fluttering as she descended. She hesitated for a second, and in the silence I heard my father's foot heavy on the cypress planks, saw him limp slowly up the stairs in his

450

seersucker suit to meet her, his face fallen and sad but his eyes fixed on her as he took her hand and led her down, saying, "Well, come on now, we're late."

Rand jingled the keys to the Impala and opened the front door to step out, the humid air rushing in, then Mama murmured, "Your flowers, Alice. They're in the refrigerator."

But Alice said, "No, I want these," and walked out with a train of gauze behind her into the bright heat of June that spirited through the trees. Looping the gauze over an arm, she broke off a stem of hydrangeas from our bush and cradled it in her arms, even as the petals fell on her dress, scattered in her hair.

Mama called out, "Vera," who came out the door wearing an orchid corsage and got in the back seat of the car on the other side of Alice from me. Mama was in the front, squeezed up between Daddy and Rand, so that her elbow was in my face. The car seemed to move in slow motion down the hill, and I felt faintly ill.

"It's hot in here," Rand complained, but no one replied, because Daddy soon pulled the Impala up to the vestibule of the church, where a small crowd of people was waiting under the Gothic arches against the sun because we were late. The minute we opened the doors, my mother's friend Ticey Williamson clambered rapidly toward us, the panels of her long aqua chiffon dress shaking back and forth. My mother had asked her to "direct" the wedding. "Y'all hurry up," she ordered, marching us through all the people toward the sanctuary. "I have had Estelle playing the organ for a half an hour." As we moved through the cloister behind her, I noticed the piteous looks on the faces of the Memphis cousins and looked away, but beyond them was only a throng of unfamiliar people, loud and fidgeting, the Thrashers upon Thrashers I had imagined.

While we waited for everyone to resume their seats, we stood in the foyer, listening for the muddy chords of organ to swell. For a small moment, we seemed to share some kind of understanding, of having something to get done, but then Mrs. Williamson said, "Here," crooking Rand's arm around Mama's and pushing them through the doorway. "Now go."

Then it was my turn, and I trod down the aisle towards the giant, unadorned cross that hung over the altar, then turned my back as I had been told. All too soon, my father and Alice were following as everyone rose to their feet and admired, as her hair caught the light from the tinted windows and hydrangea petals fluttered to the floor in the wake

451

of her billowing white hem. In front of us all, Gill took her hand from Daddy, and as I looked again at his green eyes, I realized that it was not him, that he was not the reason we were sad. The reverend began speaking then, but though his words sounded urgent, they were unintelligible; they fell like soft rain on the ears of the people, who did not seem to be listening. Rand was inspecting all the Thrashers across the aisle, while my mother sat with her face perfectly composed, beaming at no one. It appeared as if my father might start crying again. Right then, I closed my eyes and, behind them, saw what I was feeling: the dull, empty dark that was bearing us away, each from one another.

Nominated by Rosellen Brown, Mary Peterson

BROWN DOG ANGEL

fiction by ANDREA JEYAVEERAN

from GLIMMER TRAIN

THESE LAST DAYS when she walks home after teaching at Grant Academy, a certain amount of dust gets in Chandi's mouth. Since this is the second dry season she's experienced in Lusaka, the dust isn't a surprise. It settles on her lips, on her tongue, and tastes a little bit like skin, as if she's just licked someone's palm and fingers. One night the week before her husband, Rohan, left Zambia for the States she did this, licked all the long fingers of his right hand, and he was so surprised he nearly fell out of bed.

She arrives at the house with her toes and sari hem turned the shade of ground cinnamon, and Joseph, the houseboy, meets her at the door. Duke still hasn't come back. Mild alarm widens Joseph's yellowed eyes because, in the last couple of months, roughly the amount of time that Rohan has been gone, dogs have been getting killed in the neighborhood. Guard dogs like Duke, mostly. Chandi won't let herself consider out loud that this fate has befallen their own Labrador, though. Instead, she tells Joseph not to worry. She tells him that Duke will come trotting home soon with his bent tail springing side to side. She won't let herself consider the possibility of harm out loud, but this morning even before Joseph and his wife, Marita, woke, Chandi went outside to look.

Usually, she gets up near six because this is the hour Mini has decided is the start of the day. She's so hungry in the morning that her crying sounds raw and desperate. When she feeds Mini this early, the pull at Chandi's skin feels more intense than it does later on in the afternoon or evening. She's groggy just after waking up and this is the first real sensation of the day, this hungry clutching. After feeding

453

Mini, Chandi always goes to fill up Duke's tin bowls with food and fresh water. He waits behind the house every morning, dusty, grass smelling, and with a surprisingly pink tongue draping out between his teeth at the sight of her.

This morning, the sun was only halfway up when Chandi went outside. The wild poinsettia bushes made unfamiliar shapes in the low light. Skinny leaves stuck to her bare heels as she walked around the jacaranda tree and looked toward the door of the servants' quarters where Joseph and Marita and their baby, Dola, were still sleeping.

Looking around, Chandi imagined Duke hiding somewhere near the house, chewing on a dead bird or a rat. He enjoys doing this for fun every once in a while, secretly batting around a dead animal in the dust and having a good gnaw on it. Last year, he ate most of a long-dead rat and was so sick that Chandi and Rohan had to rush him to the veterinarian while he vomited in the car.

As she stood there next to the tree in her caftan, two jacaranda petals fell to settle by her toes. Their purple-blue was as bright as the colored electric bulbs someone strung up at a barbecue she went to last weekend. The veterinarian who had treated Duke for the rat was also there, one of the few single British men that Chandi has met in Lusaka. Watching him that evening, she thought about university in London. She remembered the slight chill she had always complained about but had secretly come to like because it made her feel adventurous. Some days there, she had imagined herself an explorer wrapped in layers. The veterinarian reminded her of that city far more than British couples. She was single in London and so were all of her friends.

Now, in front of her, Joseph is still looking worried. Chandi shakes out her sari and tells him again that Duke will come home.

Nodding, he hands over the small bundle of today's post. She sits down in a calamander chair in the front room with the letters on her lap, twisting around to look for Marita, Mini, and Dola. Once in a while, when Chandi gets home after school and walks up to the door, Marita is in the front room, turned away, with Dola on one hip and Mini on the other. For a few seconds, Chandi can watch her baby held close against another woman, a stronger woman. The day after Marita had given birth to Dola, Rohan asked Joseph if they were ready to be picked up from the hospital, and he was told that they were already on their way. Marita had tied the baby on her back early that morning and set out to walk the eight miles back.

454

Chandi is sure that Marita would have been very quiet during her labor. While she was having Mini, Chandi was the only woman screaming in the large maternity hall. The sound pouring out of her ricocheted around the huge room and over the beds, while Zambian women pushed their babies into the world in silence. Eventually, Chandi fainted and, when she came to, she learned that tiny capillaries in her eyes had burst from the effort. The tiny wavy lines on both sides of her abdomen had grown.

As she stretches, the letters slide off her lap to scatter on the cement floor and Chandi sees an envelope from Rohan plastered with America-flag stamps. Right now, though, she feels too drained from walking to lean forward and grasp it and tear it open. If she wanted the lift after school, Joseph would come for her in the car. He offers every day. But since Rohan has left, she has walked every day with her zebra-skin purse hanging from her wrist and all the girls' papers tied into a stack with hairy string, tasting dust, while the wind works pieces of hair loose from her bun. Once, as she walked she closed her eyes, trying to follow a line as straight as she can draw on the chalkboard freehand for triangles and coordinate axes. The girls marvel at her lines, how straight they turn out without a ruler edge. But when Chandi stopped walking and opened her eyes, she was standing in the middle of the road with a Mercedes truck barreling toward her.

Rohan sends a letter every other week. Chandi has noticed that his handwriting is nice, smooth, and easy with English. He usually writes the same things: how much he misses them, descriptions of Connecticut, updates on hunting for a job. Even though it is a terrible year to find work, especially as an engineer, he has already had two interviews at a minting factory that makes commemorative coins for special events.

The work situation is bad here in Zambia, as well. The price of copper is down, and everything rides on this metal like expectations on an only child.

In today's letter, Rohan has included a slightly sticky photograph wrapped in the onionskin pages. A frozen lake fringed by trees, a dull balance of blue and brown, with his own tiny figure standing on the solid water, a little off-center. Chandi thinks the ice looks like a layer of whitened grease congealed over some kind of refrigerated food. Curry or soup, maybe. And then she thinks, reluctantly, of how well Rohan must be eating in Connecticut with his sister to cook for him.

He hasn't made any comparisons, but having eaten her food years ago in Madras, Chandi knows that Neela is the much better cook.

Rohan ends this letter reminding Chandi to keep Duke inside at night and asking whether or not Joseph has screened the windows yet. The last letter had these same reminders, but until two nights ago when Duke didn't come home, she was still letting him outside at night. He would get impossibly restless at dusk, whining toward the door as though the wood could hear him. Chandi understood this. He thought his chocolate fur blended in outside to make him invisible at the very last light. Dogs know the absence of fear, she thinks.

Joseph hasn't screened the windows yet simply because she hasn't asked him to. When she considers things such as screens, they seem like a waste of time and money, since she and Mini will be leaving Lusaka to join Rohan in a month and a half.

Through the open windows blurry white moths sometimes wander inside at night, their wings stuttering against framed family pictures and batik hangings. Over the breathing from Mini's cot, these trapped moths sound faint and anxious. *They are stupid, really,* Chandi thinks, *to not know by instinct the difference between inside and outside.* The dead ones she scoots under the refrigerator so that they can break down into white powder out of sight, or get eaten by other insects.

After supper, she tries to feed Mini, who twists and squirms. Grabbing one of Chandi's gold hoop earrings, she pulls so hard that Chandi thinks the lobe will rip before she manages to maneuver her head away. The problem is Duke's absence. Usually after supper, he folds down next to Mini's carry cot, close enough so that she can reach out and pull his ear or bump his nose with her fist. When Chandi and Rohan first brought Mini home from the hospital, Duke growled low in his throat for a day, but by the next morning, he had decided he was her guardian, refusing to budge from her side. "Behold Mini's personal angel and best friend," Rohan used to say at this amazing constancy.

Marita and Joseph will take fine care of Duke when she leaves for the States, Chandi thinks. If he comes back. Mini is drooling on her arm, almost asleep, and Chandi allows herself to hope, for the first time since he's been missing, that he's still alive. To not hope for this until now made the possibility of death seem ridiculous, because ignoring a negative possibility is the best and only way she knows to mock it.

The other dogs died sadly. Last month, the Hale's bread-white German shepherd was found curled loosely in its own blood, with glass shards from a heavy pickling jar catching the light in its fur. Chandi saw the dog on the street before they flung a bedsheet over it and took it away in a wheelbarrow. As she watched, she could smell something sour, something like rusted nails or an old dishrag. And two weeks ago, Mrs. Manicotwe's noisy Pomeranian got a bullet in the head, a third blackened hole of an eye. Against the calm, white face, the three together formed a perfect isosceles triangle.

Chandi closes her eyes and considers the way violence is slowly rising all around them, a cold tide crawling farther and farther up a shore, creeping fog in a northern city. Zambia is landlocked and peaceful, but the countries around it are not always. People bomb in South Africa or in Congo and then often jump the border into Zambia to hide themselves.

So far, here in Lusaka, the main problem is robbery. Cars are sometimes rolled out of their drives at night and never seen again. Chandi knows that their VW, at least, is safe because it's too stubborn and finicky for thieves to make off with. The image of black-clad men grunting and cursing, while trying to roll the car away, is amusing and comforting. After gently putting Mini in her cot, Chandi goes to bed, flung diagonally across both her and Rohan's spaces on the mattress. She drifts off thinking, not of the car, but of Duke. She imagines him at night, running loose and free with other dogs, nosing them lightly in delight. This is the sum of his life, what is behind him and also what will come. *The harmony of it,* she thinks.

On Saturday, Chandi asks Joseph to take her into town because she needs basmati rice, cloves, and ginger root from the Indian-import grocery. Several of these establishments have sprung up lately since there are now so many Indians in Lusaka.

Though it's unspoken, on the way back from the grocery Joseph takes a longer route and they both start looking for Duke. They look silently, separately combing roadsides and squinting to see under sisal bushes. Chandi steps on the edge of the twenty-pound rice sack by her feet as if it's a gas pedal and she can speed up the car. Long ago, she promised herself that one of the first things she'll do in Connecticut is learn to drive.

The sun burns into the crook of her arm, and her hair, fallen out of its loose braid, snaps around her head. When her eyes start to ache, she thinks, *We'll never find him like this, never.* An old longing is coming back to her. It's a hunger for places she has lived before Zambia, before being married. She won't see these places again for years and

457

years at least: the sweet, burning heat of South India, and London, where rain slicks the roads but doesn't turn everything to impossible mud the way it does here. During the last rainy season, the main roads were completely impassable. They went without sugar and flour for over two weeks.

"Joseph, let's go back now," she says abruptly.

When he glances at her, she catches a flash of exasperation, realizing that he was just warming up in this search.

But only two miles from the house, next to a row of casuarina trees, Chandi sees what appears at a glance to be a pile of dirt.

"Stop," she says, but Joseph is already braking the car so hard that they both slide forward and the bottles of spices clang in the back seat.

It's Duke. He is shrunken and dusty as they come toward him, stopping close and then inching closer. Joseph leans down, brushing his hand over the relief of Duke's ribs, scattering a crowd of twitching flies. Chandi shivers to think of how they must have tickled and bothered him while he couldn't move to shake them off. Or he might be numb, not noticing the prickle of fly legs, not caring. His tongue is white. It slips out of his mouth as they lift him, together. *So light,* Chandi thinks, dried-up and withering like an old cornstalk, but alive. His tail makes an unbelievable angle hanging down behind him, and she thinks of the motorcycle that ran over and broke it when he was a puppy. They had just brought him home with them, and Chandi wanted to spit and mutter words she had never used in her life because he was hurt, because they had allowed him to get hurt.

Joseph turns the car back toward town so that they can make it to the veterinarian's office before it closes, and Chandi sits in the back seat with Duke's shallow breath against her knees. She thinks of how Rohan is good in crises. He is equal parts emotional and in-control, which makes him feeling, but also calm. Chandi sometimes wishes that she were more like that, wishes that she could get anxious as he does because it's normal and human to be that way. Right now, she doesn't feel anxious for Duke, only sad and angry with herself.

When they fought the week before he left, Rohan had been more emotional than calm. He was upset that she wouldn't promise to have Joseph drive her everywhere—to barbecues, to buy food, to and from school. Everywhere, day or night. Something inside Chandi resisted. Everywhere seemed unreasonable and too much for Rohan to ask.

"You have no normal sort of caution!" he yelled at her, scrunching his hair with a fist and pulling at it. "Things are not so safe."

Chandi watched him and thought of how, at their wedding, she noticed that Rohan's brothers were all starting to lose their hair. Instead of concentrating on what her husband was telling her about normal caution, she remembered the brown sheen of scalps under the sun. "Don't do that; don't pull like that," she said.

He frowned then and said that she was spoiled. After a few more minutes, more quietly, he knelt in front of her. "Can you not please be reasonable in this?" He took her hand in his and tried to interlace their fingers.

But she wasn't able to smile and nod right then. Her fingers were limp so he ended up simply holding her hand for a minute. And later that night, trying to make peace, trying to be spontaneous, she had clutched his hand, licking it, tasting the dust of this country mingled with his own saltiness, and shocked him.

Duke's tail stirs slightly and a parallel sensation shifts inside her lungs, a swelling of various kinds of guilt that makes her want to crouch down beside him and say that she is sorry, over and over. For a moment she can't breathe properly, but the car stops in front of the veterinarian's and the sensation disappears.

Joseph opens the back door and they ease Duke out carefully. *Dying is not an option,* she thinks. To her, this animal isn't bound by normal constrictions, and this is partly why she persisted in allowing him outside at night. He is untouchable, the baby's best friend, their own perfect guard dog. Chandi knows, too, that if he doesn't mend it will be her fault and no one else's.

The veterinarian's name is Rufus Graves. He looks different today in the white light of the office than when she saw him at the barbecue last weekend. In this setting, he seems taller and slightly thicker in his neck and wrists, the thickness of certain kinds of athletes. He has been recruited to work here like herself, like Rohan, and so many other Indians, British, and South Africans who have been promised a work contract for two years or three and then relocation expenses to anywhere in the world paid when the time is up. Here they're professional people, needed to fill spaces left empty by native Zambians.

Chandi talks because Rufus Graves starts examining Duke in silence. She tells him that her visa has come through, finally, and that she is going to join her husband in the States soon. He nods, looking up from Duke every few moments. These quick flashes of dark iris draw her on, making her ramble as he continues checking and prodding. His fingers are blunt and large, not long and graceful like Rohan's. *A bowl could be made from this man's hands,* Chandi thinks. She smiles at the stray thought, a bowl of hands, and looks up to find him raising his pale eyebrows at her.

At the barbecue last week, she wanted to speak to him and ask where in England he was from, exactly, but didn't know how to approach him. Then, as she talked with other people, the urge passed. The British in town are forever barbecuing, and Chandi always goes and talks until only a few people are left. Before Rohan went ahead to the States, he came with her to the barbecues sometimes, but more often he would say that he didn't feel like standing around in the dark, eating too much and getting chubby. The first time he said this, Chandi realized immediately that it was an excuse, and that her husband was, in fact, very shy of crowds. It had made her feel warmly toward him.

Chandi looks at Rufus Grave's big ringless hand and thinks of pubs in London. Pubs and parties and traveling on the continent. She used to get aerograms from London friends often, telling her of marriages or a baby, sometimes a new job. Lately, she realizes, she hasn't been in touch with any of them.

"Poisoned," Rufus Graves finally announces. "Poor animals," he says, considering Duke lying still on the metal table. "I treated three other dogs poisoned this way in the last month." Gently, his hands stroke the ridges of skin over rib.

It's too terrible to think about poison in Duke's body, and Chandi can only stare at Rufus Graves, trying to locate some assurance in his features, but only seeing him. She knows that the large sideburns coming down on both sides of his face are called muttonchops. These, along with his meaty hands, are the distinguishing features she'll remember if, in the future, the veterinarian who treated Duke for poisoning is mentioned. Suddenly, she is conscious of her hair, tangled from the wind and hanging around her shoulders like strands of a kitchen mop.

Rufus Graves says that despite the dust, despite being skin and bones, Duke is a fine-looking dog.

When Chandi glances up, his eyes are on her, and she holds her breath for a moment. But then he looks down at Duke, saying, "His coat's a real coffee-bean color."

"It's goes a little red in bright sun," she says. "When he's not covered in dust."

"My favorite trousers are just this color."

She wants to laugh, suddenly, because they are talking about dog fur and trousers. She realizes how little she's felt like laughing at silly things since Rohan left. At night it's so quiet most of the time. She can hold her breath and hear the pulse inside herself. The only other sounds are Mini's breathing or the moths flickering, not the buzz of her husband's gentle snoring. She misses him most fiercely at night. The space of time when he dozed off and she was still awake is the thing she remembers. This is how she would like to be lulled asleep every night: hearing his breathing, sensing the warmth of his skin, and the rise and fall of his chest in the corner of her vision.

Of course, once in a while, noises she doesn't want to hear come through the open window—breaking glass, shouting, dogs barking wildly. During these moments, Chandi holds her thin pillow over her head and hums into it. Mini, thankfully, sleeps through like a bundled stone.

Joseph is standing in the middle of the tiny waiting area reading a wrinkled newspaper and whistling when Chandi and the vet come out of the examining office. They hold Duke gingerly and he sags, a soft bridge between them.

Mending turns out to be a frustrating process. Chandi has to feed Duke mashed liver twice a day and let him suck water from one of Mini's old bottles. After a week he doesn't look much better than when they found him at the roadside covered with flies. His tongue, at least, isn't ashy anymore, and his nose is damp again. Mini is sulky and bored with him because he rests there and ignores her gurgling.

Lying in bed tonight, Chandi sees Duke's body curling in front of her, the way a strip of burning paper curls, drying till it disintegrates into dusty powder like one of the old moths under the refrigerator in the kitchen. Duke will make handfuls of coffee-bean-colored dust, the kind she walks home through each day, and the wind will blow him all the way to a big-game park in Kenya to be stomped and kicked up in the wake of giraffes and impala.

Mini murmurs unintelligibly in her sleep, and Chandi wonders, briefly, if her daughter dreams yet and, if she does, if it's anything more than a confused jumble of human shapes and sounds. Her own dreams, lately, are only this.

Holding the pillow over her face, Chandi wills herself not to think about Duke moldering, and doesn't. But the silence feels deep, tunneled somehow, with no sleep inside.

Friday is her last day at Grant Academy, though she will be in the city for three more weeks yet. In the middle of class, the girls sing her the Zambian national anthem and "God Be with You." Their voices float and buoy Chandi, resonant in themselves, as though sitar strands are being plucked inside each round mouth. Standing in front of them does not feel final, but it is. It is the last time she will teach mathematics to them or to any classful of students because, in the States, she wants to become certified as an accountant. She's heard horrors about the American schooling system, how lacking it is in form and rigor, and knows she doesn't have the patience to endure it.

After singing, the girls give her two bunches of red flowers. They clap for her, as if she's a local celebrity among them. Often, in the last few months after school was over, several of them would gather outside the school building, throwing their books under the leaning palm tree. As they danced, their thin white blouses would pull loose from their navy skirts to show slices of back or stomachs. Chandi watched from a small distance, and, if they noticed, they didn't seem to mind a teacher looking on. Sometimes, they kicked off their shoes and the dust stirred up in small clouds around their naked ankles.

Now, after her final school day, no one is dancing. Chandi lingers a little, waiting for a few girls to throw down their books and gather, but they have all left. She remembers the way they move when they dance—these children who can't sit still for numbers—liquid and springy at once. The ease of animals is inside them. The same ease Duke finds jumping through elephant grass. At the state park, twenty minutes from the house, it grows uncut, sharp and high, taller than a man standing upright. She and Rohan used to take Duke to the park often. He has a routine, disappearing into the grass for a few minutes, pawing his way deep, and then jumping through like a deer in flying arcs and pauses. *To watch his abandon is moving,* Chandi thinks.

If Duke were a thin, brown-skinned girl with ashy knees, and if he were recovered, he would dance like the best of her students. He would sing to her with those same floating notes.

The next weekend, the Eakins announce a barbecue, and at first Chandi hesitates about going. She really should be staying at home these last evenings, packing things up and organizing. This is what she tells herself and then thinks that she sounds too much like Rohan.

She puts on a sari she's never worn in the two and a half years she's lived in this city. It's dark pink with a frieze of blue running around the bottom. The sari was her mother's, and this quality of silk is hard to find anymore, even at the best shops in Madras. As Joseph drives her over, she has a moment of doubt about the sari. It's too fancy for a bar-becue, really, but the decision has been made, and she shrugs her shoulders in the dark of the car.

In the garden behind the Eakin's house, big torches are lit. By the time Chandi arrives, about twenty other people are talking and eating, mostly British and one other Tamil couple Chandi knows. The hus-band, Mahil, is a mechanical engineer with NAM Board, just as Rohan was before his contract ended. His wife, Keran, eats a plum and asks Chandi where she got the sari as she reaches out a hand to finger it, telling her how much she will be missed when she leaves with the baby.

Chandi hardly listens. Smiling at Keran, she glances around, look-ing for Rufus Graves. She tells herself that she must talk to him about Duke, about the way she has followed instruction perfectly, mashed the liver till it was finer even than strained baby food, fed and cajoled him, gently forced the medicine down his throat. Though she has tried everything she can think of, he still isn't recovered or happy. Then she remembers the elephant grass. Nodding at something Keran says, Chandi thinks she will have to take Duke to the grass next week.

She isn't hungry and hardly eats anything as the evening moves on, though food keeps getting passed under her nose like a small tempta-tion, platters of crisp-looking chicken and lamb chops. She can't eat because her stomach feels quivery. The torches are burning low when she notices the veterinarian talking to someone next to a card table heaped with plates and a profusion of cutlery. She studies the width of his back, noticing how the corners of his shoulders move a little as he talks. This small observation seems both trivial and important to her, and she feels her stomach roil some more.

By the time she's able to make her way toward him half an hour later, the party is breaking up. It's after eleven, and she should telephone Joseph soon so he can come for her in the car. Rufus Graves smiles at her as he finishes off a chicken leg. In the orange glow, she watches him notice her immaculate hair, so different from the way it looked in his office. Putting the chicken bone aside, he asks about Duke.

"He seems sad," Chandi says. "And not much better. I don't know what to do for him."

"Time," Rufus Graves says. "You have to allow for time to help." His eyes are dark points in the lit whiteness of his face. "When something strikes, something big, you can't expect it and the remnant to just dis-appear without a kind of vigilance."

"Yes," Chandi says. *He is right,* she thinks. *You must watch the thing disappear and make it leave by your relentless waiting for it to go.* She swallows. "Well, I should leave. It's late."

"How will you get home?"

"Our houseboy will come," she says, watching Rufus Graves. The torch next to him burns out suddenly. The fireshine goes off his forehead, and she adds, "That, or someone here won't mind."

"Hmmm, someone here," he says. Then he smiles, raises his eyebrows, and after a second, Chandi smiles back weakly.

Before they leave, Rufus Graves picks up a leftover plate of chicken with a plastic wrapping over it and hands it to Chandi. "Take it; you didn't eat anything much."

The warmth of the meat rises up against her chest and chin. "How do you know?"

"I was monitoring."

Rufus Graves has a Morris Mini, either dark blue or black, Chandi can't tell in the dark. In India, she and Rohan drove a Mini, now the property of one of Rohan's brothers and also the origin of their daughter's nickname.

During the drive, they are mostly silent. Again, she wants to ask what part of England he's from, but the atmosphere in the car feels tense and uncertain, so she doesn't. Looking out the window, she thinks of his country. Stepping off the ship for the first time there, she wasn't nervous. She was eighteen and felt strong. The daring and risk of going to study in an alien place infused her with a feeling of overcoming without having begun. *This thing I'm doing,* she thought with wonder during her first days there. *This strange new place.*

Now, in the quiet of Rufus Graves's Mini, Chandi feels the tension inside her, inside the car, and thinks again. *This thing I'm doing,* but with fear, as well as wonder. She realizes that, except for Rohan and Joseph, she has never been alone in a car with a man. And now she is holding herself stiffly in the front seat beside this doctor who tends sick animals with carefully styled sideburns and a plaster on his index finger. She has just noticed the plaster, half wrapped around the fingernail. At the sight of it, she can't help herself wondering if he hurt himself operating on a dog or slicing vegetables for his lunch.

Intermittent yellow streetlights flash on the road now. From out of the corner of her eye, Chandi looks at the thick fingers wrapped around the steering wheel, thinking of the bowl they could make and all that they could hold inside them. She remembers, too, the way these fingers slid over Duke gently and thoughtfully, even after he diagnosed the problem, as if he just wanted to touch.

If only one of us would talk, Chandi thinks, closing her eyes. But she doesn't want to talk about any of the things she can think of. The silk of the hardly worn sari feels strange against her calves because she has forgotten to wear a slip. On her lap, the plate of chicken is still a warm pressure.

When he pulls up in front of her house Chandi fumbles with the door handle, bending back a fingernail.

"Here, wait, let me come 'round." Rufus Graves moves before she can say anything and opens her door, stepping back with a flourish as she gets out.

"You have this; I really shouldn't have taken it." She holds the plate toward him.

"No, you must have it. Come on, what's the harm?" he says, gently pushing it back against her.

Then they are walking up to the front door. Chandi notices the smokiness of her sari. She will have to have it cleaned, but much later. *Tonight,* she thinks, *when I unwind myself from it, it will pool on the floor and stay there till morning.* Closing her eyes, she imagines it, a sari crumpled on the floor in the bright sun and a forgotten plate of chicken covered with ants that have been crawling over it all night.

He touches her arm, and she flinches, but he doesn't remove his fingers. *Vigilance,* she thinks. *Wait for it to go; expect for it to go.* But against the skin on the inside of her elbow is the texture of Rufus Grave's plaster, and what she wants to do right now is to take this wounded finger into her mouth.

But as she turns toward him something breaks, a window shattered on another street, muted by distance, but loud enough. The suddenness and violence of it make them both jump. From inside, Duke starts barking so loudly that he will wake the world. If Mini were in the house, instead of at the servants' quarters with Marita and Joseph, she would be screaming by now from all the racket coming out of Duke's mouth.

"What lungs," Rufus Graves murmurs.

He laughs, *nervously,* Chandi thinks. As they stand there, someone's home is being invaded, the corners of it, the secret places. It's too far away to do anything about, but close enough to remind her of the situation that they live in. She touches the gold thali hanging around her neck, an anchor inside a heart she has worn every day of her married life.

Rufus Graves shifts beside her, waiting, she knows, for what she will say. He sighs impatiently, but still it's a dreamy sound that might have carried her away except for Duke's barking, a pure and unbroken line of sound in her ears. It is the sound of his recovery, she realizes. She will take him to the park tomorrow instead of next week. *Tomorrow*, she thinks, *early when the air feels unstirred.* And his body will be loose in the green blindness. If the blades wouldn't cut her face, she would follow him through.

Instead of dying down, the barking is louder now and harder. Something else is in it, though, and after a moment, Chandi imagines that she hears a note of grace for herself and for her weakness.

Rufus Graves's fingers have slipped away from her arm at some point, and in her hands, the plate of chicken has gone cold. When she holds it toward him now, he takes it. The exchange is silent. It's a gesture so final that she looks fully at him for the first time since leaving the company of other people, and his eyes held in the moonlight are stunned. She has to blink it away quickly, this sight, as she leaves him standing outside with the rest of her whole past.

Nominated by George Keithley

A WOOD NEAR ATHENS

by THOM GUNN

from THE PARIS REVIEW

1

The traveler struggles through a wood. He is lost.
The traveler is at home. He never left.
He seeks his way on the conflicting trails,
Scribbled with light.
              I have been this way before.

Think! the land here is wooded still all over.
An oak snatched Absalom by his bright hair.
The various trails of love had led him there,
The people's love, his father's, and self-love.

What if it does indeed come down to juices
And organs from whose friction we have framed
The obsession in which we live, obsession I call
The wood preceding us as we precede it?
We thought we lived in a garden, and looked around
To see that trees had risen on all sides.

2

It is ridiculous, ridiculous,
And it is our main meaning.

467

At some point
A biological necessity
Brought such a pressure on the human mind,
This concept floated from it—of a creator
Who made up matter, an imperfect world
Solely to have an object for his love.
Beautiful and ridiculous. We say:
Love makes the shoots leap from the blunted branches,
Love makes birds call, and maybe we are right.
Love then makes craning saplings crowd for light,
The weak being jostled off to shade and death.
Love makes the cuckoo heave its foster siblings
Out of the nest, to spatter on the ground.
For love has gouged a temporary hollow
Out of its baby-back, to help it kill.

But who did get it right? Ruth and Naomi,
Tearaway Romeo and Juliet,
Alyosha, Catherine Earnshaw, Jeffrey Dahmer?
They struggled through the thickets as they could.

A wedding entertainment about love
Was set one summer in a wood near Athens.
In paintings by Attila Richard Lukacs,
Cadets and skinheads, city-boys, young Spartans
Wait poised like ballet dancers in the wings
To join the balance of the corps in dances
Passion has planned. They that have power, or seem to,
They that have power to hurt, they are the constructs
Of their own longing, born on the edge of sleep,
Imperfectly understood.
                              Once a young man
Told me my panther made him think of one
His mother's boyfriend had on *his* forearm
—The first man he had sex with, at thirteen.
"Did she know about that?" I asked. He paused:
"I think so. Anyway, they were splitting up."

"Were you confused?"—"No, it was great," he said,
"The best thing that had ever happened to me."

And once, one looked above the wood and saw
A thousand angels making festival,
Each one distinct in brightness and in function,
Which was to choreograph the universe,
Meanwhile performing it. Their work was dance.
Together, wings outstretched, they sang and played
The intellect as powerhouse of love.

Nominated by Susan Wheeler, David Wojahn

DISORDER AND EARLY SORROW

by GEORGE PACKER

from DOUBLETAKE

In EARLY 1969 my father suffered a stroke that paralyzed his right side and left him a cripple who had difficulty speaking whole sentences. He was forty-three and about to leave his position as an academic administrator at Stanford to return to the rational world of teaching law. Throughout 1968 he had been battling sit-ins and fire-bombings at the university, while the country was torn apart by riots, assassinations, and the endless war in Vietnam. Out of these upheavals, the year ended with the election of Richard Nixon, the politician my father had hated all his life.

At the time of his stroke I was eight years old. I didn't know why my father got sick; I knew still less why students shouted at him on the campus radio, why the Democratic Convention in Chicago turned into a pitched battle as we watched on television, why the word *assassination* put such a spell on me. But I understood with a child's clarity that the world, which not long before had been a delightful place of caterpillars and basketball, was suddenly full of danger, that the adults had lost control and were helpless to protect me. Even then I sensed my father's fragility, not just in his body but in his manner of thinking and living—that his commitment to the life of reason stood no chance against the world going mad.

He was a liberal. He once called himself "a nineteenth-century liberal," but it would be more precise to say that he was a procedural,

470

civil-libertarian, John Stuart Mill, Adlai Stevenson, Eugene McCarthy liberal—and he believed in liberalism with a confidence that would be impossible to muster today. In 1968 this species was under assault from two directions: on its left, radical students denounced their teachers as apologists for imperialism or, even worse, irrelevant; on its right, the Nixon-Agnew backlash proclaimed it spoke against the elitists and for the great silent majority who wanted law and order. Between intolerable pressures and the rage of his own response, my father's brain, the instrument of his life's work, was flooded with blood from a burst vessel one night as he slept. He lived for three more years, struggling to walk again, thick of speech, increasingly despondent, until he committed suicide on December 6, 1972.

I never knew him well, and I spent the first twenty years after his death trying to escape the shadow of the man in the wheelchair. The face of his illness—pallor, the dark beard, the stammering mouth, and the deep black eyes that shone with fear—blotted out every other memory. Of the man who had studied, gone to war, practiced law, loved, married, fathered, taught, written, argued, and reasoned in the forty-three years before the stroke, I knew little and remembered nothing.

A few years ago, I found myself wondering about him again. All through the autumn of 1992, as the Democrats closed in on the presidency and conservatism finally looked defeated, I kept thinking about 1968, the year my father's liberalism collapsed. Six weeks after Clinton's victory, I took five moldy cardboard boxes down from my mother's garage and stayed up late every night for a week, reading through the papers my father had left behind. I didn't know what I was looking for—simple facts, evidence of the other life apart from the wheelchair and me, and the kind of life it had been. I suppose I was digging for an answer to the question buried under the intervening years: Why did it happen? And the related question, unanswerable when I asked it at eight and unanswerable now: Will it happen to me?

He was born in 1925, a meat inspector's son, removed by one immense step from his Jewish, Eastern European origins. He grew up a bookworm in various northeastern towns, outside of any cohesive community, which partly accounted for his inwardness. His politics became liberal and individualist instead of socialist and sectarian, refined by reading Mill at Yale instead of arguing with nineteen-year-old Stalinists at City College. In my father's vocabulary there was no trace of

471

Yiddish or its isms, no Coney Island or gefilte fish in his tribal memory. Despite the ritual bar mitzvah and the anti-Semitism he encountered at Yale and in the navy during World War II, he lacked not only religious belief but any sense of group identity or grievance or memory. He rushed into the embrace of the twentieth century carrying the texts of enlightenment. Both his parents died when he was still a young man; I only learned recently that his father, too, had been incapacitated by a stroke, for he never told me anything about either of his parents, nor was there a single picture of them in our house. They belonged to pre-history.

The past was not his personal or ancestral one, with its obscure roots among bottle dealers in the mud along the Polish-Russian border, but a tradition of thought that connected him to Aristotle and Locke and Madison and Dewey. My father's political hero was the darling of the intellectual class, the egghead from Illinois, Adlai Stevenson, for whom he worked in the 1952 campaign and of whom Saul Bellow later wrote in *Humboldt's Gift:* "If you could believe Humboldt (and I couldn't) Stevenson was Aristotle's great-souled man. In his administration cabinet members would quote Yeats and Joyce. The new Joint Chiefs would know Thucydides."

Humboldt and my father were on the wrong side of history. He received his political education amid the hysteria of McCarthyism and the bland all-Americanism of Eisenhower. "In politics I grew up a loser," he said years later. "Adlai Stevenson took my virginity—twice." When Eisenhower's vice-presidential nominee and attack dog, who had already destroyed the careers of previous opponents, insisted that he wasn't questioning Stevenson's loyalty while making him out to be at the very least a Communist dupe, Richard Nixon won my father's lifelong loathing. It was character more than ideology that made Nixon such a personal enemy: his contempt for fairness, his perversion of intellect, his elevation of power to the highest virtue. And in turn my father was exactly the sort of man Nixon hated most: an Ivy League Jewish liberal intellectual, a moralist in politics.

He had strong political beliefs but not a political temperament. In what he once called "the Faustian struggle between power and knowledge," he was tempted by the former but inclined toward the latter. His taste for the fray was undermined by his love of argument on the merits and ideas for their own sake. And something vulnerable in his character, a principled rigidity combined with a lack of resilience, made him unfit for the blows of the arena.

The first one came in 1955, when my father became a minor target of McCarthyism in its twilight. That year he was hired by Stanford Law School; at the same time, having defended loyalty security cases as a pro bono lawyer, he was given a grant by a civil liberties fund to study the testimony of Whittaker Chambers and other former Communists. For a solid month, a Washington radio commentator named Fulton Lewis Jr. raised the alarm that New York pinks were going to white-wash Alger Hiss, using a young foot soldier under the cover of the in-nocent palm-lined university out on the West Coast. Stanford's board of trustees, led by Herbert Hoover, tried to block the appointment, and it only went through under pressure from the law school faculty. My father became an academic, he later said, "under sort of false pre-tenses," with the reputation of a radical politico and the *bona fides* of a witch-hunt victim. And when, after years of research through two hundred thousand pages of testimony, *Ex-Communist Witnesses* ap-peared in 1962, it must have disappointed Fulton Lewis Jr. Far from vindicating Alger Hiss, my father concluded that Hiss had in all likeli-hood perjured himself. The stance was scrupulously objective: "As we now close the books on the Hiss case it must be with the conscious-ness that we have stopped far short of even so imperfect an approxi-mation of 'truth' as the processes of law permit." My father's life as a scholar, begun amid the muck of partisan politics, established itself on ground he held more sacred—the rational mind's ability to analyze fact and establish probability, if not truth itself, which belonged to Stalin-ists and Republicans.

He made his career on the West Coast, at a young university where local tradition was weak enough to allow for an experiment in the un-fettered mind. By the time my sister and I came along, California off-spring of a Jew in name only and a lapsed Southern Protestant, the air we breathed was bracingly pure secular humanism, clean of the low-land fog and smoke of any ethnicity or region or faith.

I always think of the early sixties as a golden age, though an essential feature of golden ages is that one remembers almost nothing about them: a dead orange cat buzzed by flies on a sidewalk remains my most vivid memory from the New Frontier and Great Society. Kennedy and Johnson were not exactly Aristotle's great-souled men, but they presided over an era of reform in which liberal intellectuals were no longer Stevensonian egghead pinkos and not yet Spiro Agnew's effete corps of impudent snobs. Instead, bringing knowledge and power into harmony, they were asked to put their minds at the service of social change. Whatever I've since discovered about the "best and the brightest," early Vietnam, the Kennedys' weakness on civil rights, the "other America," Cheever's suburban misery, and Sexton's mad house-wives, has made little impression on my sense that it was a wonderful time in America. Convictions that are personal and impressionistic have nothing to do with historical knowledge and are far stronger. It doesn't matter that some of the associations date from years later. To this day the word *cocktail,* the typeface of books circa 1964, the black-and-white pictures of serious forty-year-old men in black-rimmed glasses and thin ties, give me a feeling of extraordinary well-being: the world is in capable, grown-up hands. Good will prevail. LBJ is helping the Negroes in East Palo Alto, where my racially progressive parents have me enrolled for the summer at the Nairobi Day School.

It was also, in my personal mythology, the golden age for my family—the more so for how thoroughly my memories before 1968 have been wiped out. In color pictures my father looks tan and healthy in the California sun, his hair longer on top, with a black summertime goatee. Holding hands with his pregnant wife, standing outside the modernist house they built in 1960, cooing over his baby daughter, clutching his baby son in both arms, he is smiling as never in pictures before or since.

I depend on photographs because I have not one real memory of my father in his health. I can't see him walking; I can't see his right hand holding a drink; I can't hear his clear, measured voice. What I re-member are the things around him: his pipes on a circular pipe stand, and the pleasant sharp smell of tobacco; his blood-red shampoo and my sense of initiation into the mysteries of adulthood when he washed my towhead with it. However acerbic in public life, I am told he was a gentle, warm husband and father. He had no taste for domestic con-frontation. His most consuming moments came in the quiet of his study, with a book. Not the sort of cruelly absent father thirty-year-olds rediscover in therapy; but a benevolent, inward one, who left faint im-pressions that were erased as easily as footprints by the tide.

It didn't matter to me. I was in the middle of a splendid boyhood, on the country's most beautiful campus, in its most beautiful state. The red-tiled roofs, the smell of juniper and live oak in the foothills, the swarms of tadpoles that magically sprouted legs in a bog behind our house, the games of kick-the-can with other kids on our dead-end street in the long, long summer evenings—the scene of my childhood

474

was so idyllic that my whole adulthood seems like a corrective, even the decision to live in Boston's harsh climate.

As late as 1968 the picture holds. Home movies show my father, my sister, and me collecting starfish on an overcast beach. He's paler than in the earlier photos, and his body has thickened in the middle as if returning to boyhood plumpness. Never one to exercise much, he looks badly out of shape. His life has taken an irrevocable new course.

My father tasted power as a university administrator just as the breed was finding itself thrust into the role of crisis manager, crowd controller, target, even hostage. Ten years before he had been redbaited; now he was about to be cast as a "fascist." While he held his liberal ground, American politics jolted violently under his feet. In 1967 he tangled with David Harris—student body president and soon to be famous as a draft resister and Joan Baez's husband—over the selection of students to a committee chaired by my father that was embarking on a complete reconsideration of education at Stanford. Harris wanted representatives to be voted by the student legislature; my father argued for open applications for spots that would be chosen by the administration with the advice of student body officials. To the student radical, it was a question of democratic rights. To my father, it was a question of intellectual independence. "The Steering Committee should not be viewed as representing any constituencies or interests," he answered Harris in the student newspaper, the *Daily*. "The Study and those who are engaged in it would have no 'power' other than the persuasiveness of the ideas they put forward."

He was arguing against the very primacy of "interest" in debate and thought: what mattered was "critical intelligence." In the free marketplace of ideas, a disinterested sophomore could vanquish a disinterested dean. Now, of course, no enlightened person even pretends to believe in objectivity; everyone with a graduate degree knows that disinterest has been abolished and nothing exists except power and interest groups. But in 1967 the idea was up for grabs. And the tendency of student thought in 1967 was running against my father.

"Those who agree with Mr. Harris' reported exhortation in White Plaza that students should boycott the Study," he wrote in the *Daily* letter, "betray a preference for the irrationality of confrontation politics over the reasoned discussion of educational policies." From the beginning he refused to bury conflict under conciliatory euphemisms; he made himself a lightning rod. "I love flak," he said near the end of his life. "I thrive on it." But it wasn't true: his commitment to principle was firmer than his grip on life itself. My mother knew it, and when he became vice provost she feared disaster.

Throughout 1967 and 1968 he labored on the massive study of education, generating thousands of pages of recommendations from teachers and students on hundreds of subcommittees. He was responding to crisis the way he knew how, through "reasoned discussion," but at a punishing pace, trying to reform the university before it was pulled down from within or policed from without.

In May 1968, a week after the occupation of Columbia, hundreds of Stanford students, demanding changes in judicial policy, staged a sit-in. Two days later the faculty narrowly voted to grant most of their demands, including amnesty for them and previous demonstrators. My father drafted a letter of resignation: "The message is very clear and has already been understood by the students who celebrated their victory on Wednesday night: coercion pays. Confrontation politics will now become the daily routine of academic administrators. I want none of it." He never submitted the letter; instead, a few nights later he poured all his bitterness about what he saw as the faculty's betrayal into a speech. He was smoking a cigar and using it to gesture as scorn dripped from his words. "Procedure," he told the colleagues sitting before him who had ignored the judicial process and voted to give in, "is at the heart of all liberty."

A few months after the sit-in, in another speech, he reflected more dispassionately on the "cult of irrationality" among youth, "a penchant for the apocalyptic that is profoundly disturbing to those of us who have staked our lives on the proposition that progress in human affairs depends upon rationality and self-restraint." He offered "the joys and the frustrations of intellectual analysis" as "the best anodyne against existential despair."

But this was 1968—the year of Tet, assassinations, riots, Paris, Columbia, Chicago, George Wallace, the new Nixon. Over the summer a firebomb destroyed the office of Stanford's retiring president, and as a possible target our house was fitted with exterior floodlights and an emergency phone with a direct line to the police. Who could believe in rationality and self-restraint? Against existential despair and its fraternal twin, romantic primitivism, intellectual analysis was as weak as paper. And liberalism looked like the excuse of hypocrites who wanted to end the war but not the system that started it. As that year of apocalypse unfolded in a series of explosions, each stronger than the last, leaving the reasonable world in ruins, my father was battling his own existential despair. And it had become a matter of principle not to give in. To throw up his hands, surrender to madness, appease the student radicals, vote for the Peace and Freedom Party ticket, become a neo-con, weep, shout in rage, tear his hair—these would be to abandon rationality and restraint. It would be self-betrayal. In the face of an onslaught, he had to stiffen and clench. The burner was turned to a high flame, and the lid of his values pressed down on the boiling pot.

Nineteen sixty-eight was the year I discovered the wider world; it was the year I discovered politics. All but oblivious to my father's battles, barely aware of the turmoil less than a mile from our house, I became obsessed with the history of presidents and the ongoing presidential campaign. In the spring and summer, Eugene McCarthy became my first hero. I wore a campaign T-shirt three sizes too large, wrote letters of adoration and advice long after he had withdrawn into his famous sulk. Not coincidentally, he was my parents' candidate, too, heir to *their* hero Stevenson, dovish, witty—Nixon's opposite, flawed with a weak will. In a little essay I wrote about the looks of all the candidates, McCarthy became a benevolent protector touched with fatherly wisdom: "Eugene J. McCarthy has wavy gray hair. He has sad eyes but he is always happy. He has a nice smile. He has sort of long hair." As for the Republican nominee of 1968, I had fully absorbed my father's point of view: "Richard M. Nixon has big jaws. He has a long ski nose. He has a head shaped like a foot-ball."

I predicted victory for McCarthy. Everyone we knew was for him—how could he lose? The Chicago convention left me thunderstruck, unable to comprehend the unfairness of it. But accepting compromise as the price of politics, I transferred my loyalty to Humphrey. On election night I had to go to bed before the results were final. I woke up to the news of Nixon's razor-thin win and took my second blow in what was becoming a series that would last for most of a year. My parents blamed Humphrey's defeat on the liberals and radicals who had sat out the election or voted for Dick Gregory. Politics, with its personalities and drama, its thrilling styrofoam hats and delegate counts and campaign rallies in the Stanford basketball arena, had suddenly become a cause of intense pain. Like my father, I lost my virginity twice, but at eight I had no remedy.

477

In the shadow of all this precocious interest lay another kind of fascination: I was mesmerized by violence. The real drama of politics was death. The night of Robert Kennedy's murder I had a dream in which Eugene McCarthy was gunned down. It may be that my mother had woken me up to tell me about the shooting in Los Angeles and then I'd gone back to sleep with murder aboil in my unconscious. But in a sense I was already prepared for it.

In the way a younger child is frightened by monsters he can't get enough of, my political awakening was haunted by the assassinations of Lincoln and John Kennedy, then King and Robert Kennedy. I read about them in a state of absolute terror, going over every detail. In my parents' study there was a volume called *The Torch Is Passed,* a photographic narrative of the day of JFK's death put out by the Associated Press. This book became my dark secret. The knowledge that it existed, crimson and knife-thin on the shelf among world atlases, was enough to make me shudder whenever I was in the study alone—often enough, since I couldn't keep myself from staring at those black-and-white pictures that never lost their power to shock. The sunlit smile in the unbearable last moment, the blur of his hands clutching his throat, the shiny shoe sticking up over the seat. And later, Oswald under escort staring obliviously ahead as the stout figure of Jack Ruby rushes from the corner of the frame, snub-nose extended. In a home movie I'm dressed like Lincoln, black beard and coat and stove-pipe hat, sitting in a kitchen chair. Suddenly I mouth an explosion, grimace, and slump forward.

Apparently these horror films were rolling in my imagination throughout that year. My interest in presidential names and dates gave me a rational way to master events—I was my father's son after all—but disorder and death seeped into my mind and worked on me. How much did this have to do with the pressure my father was under? An eight-year-old's parents are very important furniture, heavily depended on yet barely noticed. McCarthy was much more vivid to me than my father—he had an existence separate from mine, while my father was the background against which my boyhood was played out. A quarter century later, I can see how the candidate became a stand-in and why his defeat wounded me so personally; how my parents' anxiety and the sense of siege in our house colored my new interest in the red of assassination. Throughout 1968 I was simultaneously out of it and acutely aware, protecting and exposing myself, struggling to handle what couldn't be handled. People and things changed form, good and evil filled a single dream, adults offered comfort but turned out to be helpless, intellect sharpened but so did terror. The world opened and I fell in.

In January of 1969 my father announced that he would leave his position as vice provost in June and return to teaching and writing. Two months earlier, his old nemesis had been elected president like an unkillable vampire returning from the grave; liberalism had crashed in flames. A week after the election, the Study of Education at Stanford that my father had led published its ten volumes of recommendations for reforming the university. A television crew came to film the troubles at Stanford: they interviewed my father in our living room while Whiskers, our Siamese cat, kept hopping on his lap in spite of my father's attempts to get rid of him. The interview captures my father as I imagine him wanting to be seen: criticizing students but also sympathizing with them, joking ironically, ranging over politics and education, rejecting both youthful nihilism and academic deadness, arguing for reform over revolution and for bringing thinking and feeling into balance, quoting "that really great humanist E. M. Forster who in *Howards End* said: 'Only connect the prose and the passion.'" And his voice—listening now to the tape, I have no memory of it, I can't recognize it as his: slightly nasal, measured, calm, and strong.

The program aired in April. My father watched it from his hospital bed, on a television that had been wheeled in by nurses. In mid-March, in the middle at the night, an artery wall on the left side of his brain had broken. At the hospital, an arteriogram probing the damaged vessel worsened the hemorrhage, causing another stroke that almost killed him. For a few days his life hung in the balance. And even when it began to seem that he would survive, the damage done was permanent: paralysis of the entire right side of his body. As he lay watching the articulate triumph of an earlier self, he couldn't speak.

He came home a stranger in a wheelchair. When he was still in the hospital I spoke to him on the phone: at the end of what couldn't be called a conversation he said, in a moaning, ghostly voice, "Good-bye." I said good-bye, relieved to get off the phone, but he echoed himself, and again, and each time I tried to get away this terrible new voice drifted from the receiver. "Good-bye. Good-bye."

Ramps went up outside our house and inside, long black ramps with rails. We ate at a folding card table in the family room where access was easier: low-cholesterol chicken and fish every night. His right arm hanging against his body, the useless hand curled rigid, my father brought the food to his mouth with his shaky left hand. His thoughts now reached his tongue and stuttered out thirty seconds too late. When his frustration was unendurable the curses exploded in thick choked stammers. Dinner became the sound of silverware.

The stroke put my father on my psychic map. From being remote, kind, reliable, and hardly a person at all, he became an indelible presence. I was aware of him all the time now, partly out of pity but mainly because I was afraid and careful to keep a distance. He seemed much less like a parent than a child, physically helpless, prone to sudden storms of anger or tears. Even when he learned to walk again, after heroic months of physical therapy, the metal brace that imprisoned his right leg, the ubiquitous cane, the clumsy rigid step, the electric golf cart he drove to school, the thick black beard he grew because shaving was so difficult and that soon began to gray—this strange new man never ceased to frighten and, I must confess, repel me. In pictures from the years after the stroke his eyes and mouth have a kind of vulnerable beauty that wasn't there before, with more feeling—warmth, desperation—as if the stream of blocked words was struggling to find a way out. But it wasn't beautiful to me then. I couldn't look him in the eye.

In the lifelong struggle of this most rational man to connect the prose and the passion, it was passion that ruled his last years.

My father and I are playing a military board game called Waterloo, in which divisions of troops are little chips that need to be stacked an inch or two high and moved from square to square. This game, our only source of father-son intimacy, seems designed to tax his mechanical skill to the limit, and from time to time he knocks over his troops or mine. Once, as he fumbles to stack the spilled chips, I notice that his French forces have crept a square closer to my Prussians. "You're cheating!" I tell him. How should he respond? Like a father, like his former self, coolly explaining the difference between trickery and mistakes and suggesting that I give him the benefit of reasonable doubt? With wisdom and restraint, acknowledging that his illness is hard on all of us, that we need to pull together as a family? No doubt he would like to, but his emotions begin their gallop and trample him underfoot. "No I'm not, god dammit!" The game is over: he tells me I've ruined it for him. Later, my mother draws me aside and wearily asks me to be more sensitive. "Your father is a great man," she says. "As great as Abraham Lincoln?" She nods, and I pretend to believe her.

I'm on a rooftop with two schoolfriends, passing around an illicit cigarette. Tom Gann is describing what he admires in his father, and Marc Larrey turns to me. "What do you admire your dad for?" A booby-trapped question, and before I can think of something he follows it up with another: "For being a crip?" I start to sniffle, less out of real grief than the idea that this is expected of me. What I mainly feel is the shame of the word, the truth. Later Tom Gann tells me, "I'd of hit him," and my shame doubles: my father is a crip, and I won't stand up for him.

My father, mother, sister, and I are at a restaurant, demonstrating to ourselves that we are still a family. My father asks my sister and me for a lunch date at the faculty club in a week or so: an unprecedented invitation, and we both hedge, mumbling about being busy. "Do you prefer your mother so god-damn much to me," he cries out, "that you won't even have lunch with me?" We try to mollify him, embarrassed that there might be a public scene, as if we aren't already conspicuous enough; and we both know it's true.

I am riding on an exercise bike that my father uses to build up his atrophied muscles. It runs on electricity, its handlebars attached to a metal stem that moves up and down at varying speeds. I try to get off with the machine still running and my heel catches between the stem and the seat, pinned there, the exercycle crushing my Achilles tendon. I cry to my father for help. He's sitting across the room, immobilized, stamping his cane in the futile effort to get up. My mother comes to my rescue. Years later, I impute to myself the worst of motives: a desire, even in the midst of terror, to show him his helplessness, fling it in his face, punish him for it. I'm aware of the kinder interpretation, that I simply wanted a father, but the guilt that colors all these memories won't allow me to be convinced.

I come home from the basketball playground one evening after dark in the last year of my father's life, to see my parents sitting on the other side of the glass doors in the lighted kitchen, wearing sunglasses. I know at once that they've been crying, which terrifies me, so that the sunglasses have the opposite effect my parents intended for them. Instead of disguising their despair, they make it horribly, almost comically apparent, like ill-fitting wigs. In this sense the gesture perfectly represents the way my family has attempted to survive the thing that blew our old life to pieces: we refer to it as little as possible, while every moment serves to remind us, so that this tragedy we live with all the time has charged the house with tension and driven each of us into the separate rooms of our isolation. In home movies post-stroke, we hardly look at one another.

For twenty years the stroke completely defined my father for me: he was nothing but impotent rage, desperate hope, misery, and a kind of vulnerable tenderness. But in the boxes of papers in my mother's garage I discovered a separate life. During the months when he was pedaling the exercycle and shuffling up the stairs he was also writing articles and volumes of letters. The blue onion-skin carbons are like facsimiles or ghosts of the life that seemed to have all but ended with the stroke. It was still going on, in private, in silence, on paper, away from the humiliations of conversation. And I knew nothing of it.

From a letter to a college friend: "Last spring, after I had quit being Vice Provost, I suffered a severe stroke, God knows whether as punishment or just as consequence. I am slowly but steadily recovering." The man I remember sounded nothing like that. The ironic stoicism is so superior to his paralysis, so determined to be unfettered by it, that I wonder if I knew him at all during those last years, and if, had I been able to recognize such a tone, we could have been father and son after all. Is it the letter or my memory that lies? Which man was he? Was he both at once?

I search his papers for signs of the gathering disaster. In his published work, which continued to appear steadily in the *New Republic* and the *New York Review of Books,* arguing against Nixon's crime policy or for the decriminalization of heroin, the voice is the same— sharp, reasonable, humane—but there's now a tendency to reach judgment without quite as patient an argument as before. And some of his letters, especially the later ones, seem out of control, crossing the line between tartness and incivility. "I have just yawned my way through your article," he begins a note to a sociology professor he apparently doesn't know; but to an old friend he writes, "Since I got sick, I've had so much hostility floating around that it affects my work. Of course, I don't want to be a gratuitously curmudgeonly fellow." And then there is a document titled "Notes on My Speech Therapy":

> After my stroke in 1969, I underwent speech therapy. The therapist was an inexperienced young lady who made up for her own lack of confidence by trying to assert herself in our relationship. Toward the end of our therapy, she insisted on giving me exercises in remembering series of

numbers. I objected strongly to this because I did not think that remembering series of numbers was at all relevant to my condition. She also gave me some exercises in spelling words. One of those sessions occasioned the following incident, in which she is represented by the letter C and myself by the letter P:

C: Spell "banister."
P: B-a-n-i-s-t-e-r.
C: That is wrong: it has two n's.
P: I disagree. Look it up in the dictionary.
C: Well, let's just go on.
    (The dictionary gives the spelling as "banister" with "bannister" as an occasional alternative.)
C: Spell "barrister."
P: "B-a-r-r-i-s-t-e-r." Would you like me to use it in a sentence?
C: Sure.
P: She broke her ankle sliding down a barrister.
C: That doesn't make sense to me.

I had remembered an old joke, which I used to get some revenge. The therapist did not understand that she had been one-upped. Shortly after this session, she phoned my wife and said that she would like to talk with her about my case. My wife, whom I had told about the preceding incident, went in and talked with the therapist, who complained that my attitude was not good. Shortly after this complaint, my wife and I decided to terminate the therapy.

The therapist did a competent job, but she struck out because she did not know how to "handle" me. That I would suppose was how she would put it. As a former patient, it still makes me bridle when therapists talk about "handling" people.

In the indignity of learning to speak again, he locked himself in a power struggle with poor C and outwitted her—to no avail. So he went home and told his wife, who at least provided a competent audience. Did she also want to tell him to let himself be "handled"—that these little contests were not going to heal his wounded mind? Later in the notes, he writes that a different speech therapist, along with a psychiatrist, "aided me to recover my self-confidence, to the point where I was able to speak extemporaneously before a large and critical audience." An impossible standard that would daunt someone in full possession of his faculties—the standard of his former self, the man he had seen on television as he lay paralyzed and speechless. He set himself tests he was bound to fail. In his letters he is forever recovering his self-confidence. Each recovery means that he has lost it again; each time he proclaims himself on the road to health there is a more desperate edge; each recovery betrays months of despondency that the letters don't describe. And no wonder—he couldn't bear to be what he was.

In 1971 we took a trip through Europe: five months on the road, from Sicily to Norway, never staying in one place longer than ten days, my father hobbling up countless church steps. A test set, I suppose, in a period of supreme self-confidence or supreme need; and he, we, failed it so miserably that within a month of our return my father tried for the first time to end his life. I was sitting at the kitchen table the morning paramedics wheeled him out of the house on a stretcher. His face was turned toward me: it had no color except in the lips. It looked to me like the face of a dead man—I thought he was dead. My sister and I were told that he'd had another stroke, and for years this story held a comfortable place in my narrative of his decline; at the time I even used it to excuse my delay in answering a friend's letters, though I knew that this was expedient and false. Yet when, twenty years later, I learned the truth—that the "mild stroke" was a suicide attempt—I wasn't surprised. It was as if I'd also known that all along, from the moment I saw his gray face on the stretcher: a face of annihilation beyond any medical condition. The truth of that sight stayed with me, existing unofficially alongside the other version. It was possible to "know" two contradictory things at once: one a rational explanation that made biological sense and was easy on memory, family history, the need for public accounting; the other unconscious, dark, connected to assassinations and a sense of disaster, to the death wish, an unshakeable conviction I didn't know I had.

We like to think that the second kind of knowledge is the "truth," yet I still find myself wondering whether I haven't misremembered what I learned two decades later: perhaps I have it wrong, there was no suicide attempt, I invented one to confirm an adult idea. This inability to accept one single version is bound up with my inability to give a final answer to the question of why this happened to him, which is also the question of who he was. Was he a man with a genetic flaw like a time bomb or fate that sooner or later had to destroy him? Or was there about him something rigid and fragile and remote, which, in the stress of events, released a hemorrhage that didn't have to flow and drove him to a decision he might have avoided if, for example, he had cooperated with *C* the speech therapist? Documentary evidence proves no more definitive than fallible memory. The old account is as tenacious as the new. The rational one handed down to me won't completely yield to the one I've pursued on my own.

In the spring of 1972 my father took on his last public battle. It was also the last spasm at Stanford of the years of sit-ins, firebombings, window smashing, and "Ho, Ho, Ho Chi Minh, NLF is gonna win!" The mass protests of the mid-late sixties had degenerated into the underground factions of the early seventies. The dance of death exhausted itself in its own feverish energy. Richard Nixon, after contributing generously to the slaughter in Southeast Asia, was finally withdrawing the troops, and his popularity was at its zenith. Liberalism headed toward its worst defeat ever in the person of its latest incarnation, George McGovern; a quarter century of liberals' status as believers in a despised minority creed had begun. And in this atmosphere of burnout and rancor, Stanford played out the last act in the drama that had contributed so much to my father's decline.

At the center of Stanford radicalism stood a young Melville scholar, former tactical air squadron pilot, and convert to revolution named H. Bruce Franklin. He was a particular type among New Left figures, the Stalinist-Maoist with tenure, equal parts commissar, outlaw, and nerd. After a faculty panel dismissed Franklin for inciting students to destruction of property, my father defended the decision in an article in *Commentary,* holding his breath through pages of careful legal reasoning and then letting it out at the end with a tremendous sigh of relief: "The Franklin era at Stanford is over. The apologist for violence at the University is gone. . . . There is now an insistence on rational discourse. Free inquiry and the other values of academic life have been affirmed."

The article led to a tangle in the letters column with no less than Alan Dershowitz, who had been visiting at Stanford during the Franklin hearing and had taken up his cause in the name of academic freedom. Two law professors, one at the beginning of his fame, the other near the end of his life, arguing in the old style, the fist of

485

polemic and passion gloved inside the claims of analysis. Four years earlier, the quarrel might have ended over our dinner table, neither side giving in but both perhaps giving a bit of ground and affirming mutual regard over a bottle of the wine my father collected. In 1972 there was no dinner. The conversation table had become a place of defeat and despair. Dershowitz's quick tongue would have been partnerless, and my father's frustration might have ruined the evening with an intemperate word and an ensuing bout of black depression.

As I weigh their arguments back and forth, all the while I have another response, which is to tell Dershowitz to lay off. "Leave him alone," I want to say, "he can't fight back," even though my father would never have asked such indulgence for himself nor given it to someone else in a matter of principle. Between the prose and the passion, the article's author and the trembling figure at our dinner table, the man I discovered in boxes of papers and the memory this discovery intruded on, I can find no connection. One of them emerges at least even after a round with Dershowitz; the other is down for the count.

"Look, when I feel threatened, I just get very conservative," he told an interviewer in that spring of 1972. "I've felt very threatened by what's gone on at the University—not in a personal sense, just institutionally."

The interview marked, in a sense, my father's last public appearance. He proposed it himself, during one of his periods of restored confidence—the very last one—and everything in it betrays the shakiness of the recovery, including the question he suggested for openers: "What's a crippled guy like you doing on our faculty?" "I've only just really recovered," he said. "I thought about everything, including suicide. I had a real period of depression, but I think I'm out of it now." The interviewer pressed him: "Do you feel that because of your stroke you had difficulty communicating with your children?" "For a while," my father answered, "but now I find that barrier's been overcome. Actually, I'm happier now than I think I ever was."

My mother had a phrase that, since I never heard it from anyone else, as a child I assumed was our family's own: "Whistling past the graveyard." In the interview everything seems out of balance: profane, vehement, even boastful, the public and private man come together in a combustible mix, the judgments of one set loose from restraint by the impulses of the other. In the following months he cast about for ways to keep the air in his balloon. He wrote an Op-Ed for the *New York Times* that was refused. He wrote to George McGovern's campaign manager with advice, offering himself as "idea man and occasional speech writer," and got no reply. He arranged to give a series of talks in Japan, traveling by himself. Then, at the end of the summer, he canceled the trip. He canceled other engagements and projects. He wrote to friends that his health had taken a bad turn; in one letter he spoke of being "frankly too damned depressed to do anything affirmative." He was losing altitude fast.

It must have been around this time, in the late summer or fall of 1972, that my parents called my sister and me into the family room. They had something important to tell us. "Your father can't work anymore," my mother said on his behalf, for he seemed unable to speak. They were trying to prepare us for the worst, but at that moment the words made no sense to me, since he was still driving himself to campus in his orange golf cart. At the same time, my parents' manner terrified me, and on some level I knew that this was the crash. I tried to buck him up, in a fatuous, let's-take-it-like-men way that makes me cringe at the memory. I thought this would be the brave, manly thing to do. I wanted desperately for *him* to be brave. My sister and I had been given a fact that was inexplicable, intolerable, and irremediable. Instead of my own grief, I felt an overwhelming desire to make my parents' go away. But they were saying that it wouldn't.

Throughout that fall I stayed out playing basketball as late as I could. In November Richard Nixon was re-elected in a landslide. On a Monday in December my father disappeared. Two evenings later, as I walked up to the patio with a basketball in my hands, I saw my mother through the kitchen window let the phone drop. Her knees buckled and I ran to catch her. In her arms I cried, for her more than for the news she'd just heard—that her husband had died of an overdose of sleeping pills in a San Francisco hotel room. I wanted physically to hold her up: one parent was gone, I couldn't lose the other. Then I went to my room and sat on my bed, where I began the process, doomed at the outset, of removing my life from the death and escaping catastrophe.

Six months before he died, my father wrote me a long letter, flawlessly typed and signed "Dad" in pencil in his left-handed, childlike scrawl. It was a letter about sex and growing up, and when I received it from him, with dread, for (as he pointed out at the start) I had been evading this topic for months, its contents embarrassed me deeply. I didn't throw it away, though. I read it once and then put it in a drawer beneath my school binders, and I didn't look at it again. It was never mentioned between us.

Throughout my adolescence I was aware of its hidden presence in my room. The drawer gave off an odor of shame: not just for the sentences about masturbation and the "homosexual phase," but because it contained my only personal token of my father and so became a repository for all the shame I felt about him, about myself, about the connection he had tried clumsily near the end to create between us, about its failure. Still, I didn't throw the letter away. It was, I knew, "important," more so as time went on, a rite of passage in my life, a reminder of his.

When I was searching through the cardboard boxes in my mother's garage, I found the letter. Reading it for the first time in twenty years I came across these sentences: "Some day, when you have had your share of experiences, you will find another person whose happiness is just as important to you as is your own. Only by practicing the art of giving pleasure and learning that giving it means that you too receive pleasure will you really grow up. Love, which to me can be identified with what I have been calling pleasure, is the thing that matters most in life."

It's with these lines that the letter ends. They came as a shock, for somehow I had managed to forget them completely. I remembered the letter as being full of sex; I remembered nothing of love, perhaps because at eleven I didn't grasp what the words meant, any more than I grasped my father's other life in articles and letters. It was as if he had appended them in the hope that I would reread them when I was older and that they would speak to me then.

Having tried for two decades to become someone other than my father's son, I now think about him all the time. Every year, I'm told, my face resembles his a little more, and I find myself mimicking gestures that I have no memory of being his. I have my cholesterol checked annually and wonder about a certain artery wall. And the famous legacy that suicides are supposed to leave their children seems to be my inheritance as well. For eighteen months in an African village when I was in my early twenties, killing myself seemed as easy and ordinary as shaving. The ordeal of resisting wore me out and I went back home six months early, but not before convincing myself, one strange night, that I was about to have a stroke and live out my father's fate where no one would know or be able to help. The belief became so strong that I had a village driver rush me to a provincial hospital, where a German doctor informed me that everything was normal except my mind. In retrospect the delusion seems comical; at the time it was frightening enough.

So in that unlikely tropical place, under a tin roof halfway around the world from Stanford's terra-cotta, I was instructed in the power of unreason and the spell of the past. I had my nervous breakdown, and moved on. The inheritance remains, will always remain.

My father shed his own—the family, the tribe, the sticky particulars of culture and place. Out in the golden West he lived in the sunlight of reason, trusting free man to solve his problems through the uses of mind. When the explosion came he had no fallback position and it hit him full in the face. Stricken, he was more available than he'd been, and at last he and I took notice of each other, but the hand held toward me was atrophied and curled. Love, "the thing that matters most in life," didn't have the power to save him. It was advice he couldn't live by—unless, by some dark logic, he decided that the happiness of others depended on his ceasing to exist. In either case, I wasn't consulted. "The only way to go through life," he wrote to me six months before he committed suicide, "is to find what work and love can mean. I'll devote another letter to work some day."

That day never came. Instead, the alternative scenarios crowd and clamor. If he had kept a picture of his parents on the wall. If he hadn't become vice provost. If we had stayed out of Vietnam. If he hadn't risen to the bait with David Harris in 1967 or the faculty in 1968. If he had spent more time with his children before the stroke. If I had been kinder. If he had taken up a hobby like left-handed painting. If he had had his breakdown at twenty-three like me. If he had only connected knowledge and power, love and work, reason and rage. If his only faith, the liberal faith in man and man's mind, had gone from time to time past the graveyard without whistling and silent before the power of irrationality and blood.

"It is love," wrote Thomas Mann, "not reason, that is stronger than death." My father's letter suggested another life we might have had. By then it was too late, and I buried the words in a drawer. Twenty years later, wanting the connection I'd always shunned, I went in search of him, only to end with a letter I'd had all along, and the charge to find the meaning of work and love, to affirm life over death without him.

Nominated by Sue Halpern

THE BUTTON BOX

by GRACE SCHULMAN

from WESTERN HUMANITIES REVIEW

A sea animal stalked its prey
slithering under her bed, and gorged
on buttons torn from castaways;
ever unsated, it grew large

until it became a deity
spewing out buttons in a fire
of brass for blazers, delft or ruby
for shirts—and dangerous. You'd hear

it snarl when the beds were being made.
It ate stray pins and shot out poison.
But mother, who stuffed its wooden frame,
scooped up waterfalls of suns,

enamel moons, clocks, cameos,
carved pinwheels, stars, tiny "Giottos,"
peacocks strutting out at sundown,
FDR's profile, flags of Britain,

steel helmets, each with a mission.
Mother sewed ballerinas set
in circles on your satin dress,
onyx buttons that would join

you, collar-to-hood, at graduation;
she would find in the creature's lair
"bones" of an army officer,
"pearls" of a war bride's dressing gown;

nights when the radio hissed *dive bombers*
my mother dreamed that she could right
the world again by making sure
you had your buttons, sewed on tight.

Nominated by Carol Muske, Arthur Smith

THE SHORTEST NIGHT

by W. S. MERWIN

from POETRY

All of us must have been asleep when it happened
    after the long day of summer and that steady
clarity without shadows that stayed on around us
    and appeared not to change or to fade when the sun
had gone and the red had drained from the sky and the single
    moment of chill had passed scarcely noticed across
the mown fields and the mauve valley where the colors were stopped
    and after the hush through which the ends of voices
made their way from their distances when the swallows
    had settled for the night and the notes of the cuckoo
echoed along the slope and the milking was finished
    and the calves and dogs were closed in the breath of the barns
and we had sat talking almost in whispers long past
    most bedtimes in the village and yet lights were not lit
we talked remembering how far each of us had come
    to be there as the trembling bats emerged from
the crevices in the wall above us and sailed out
    calling and we meant to stay up and see the night
at the moment when it turned with the calves all asleep
    by then and the dogs curled beside them and Edouard
and Esther both older than the century sleeping
    in another age and the children still sleeping
in the same bed and the hens down tight on their perches
    the stones sleeping in the garden walls and the leaves
sleeping in the sky where there was still light with the owls
    slipping by like shadows and the moles listening

the foxes listening the ears the feet some time there
    we must have forgotten what we had meant to stay
awake for and it all turned away when we were not
    looking I thought I had flown over the edge
of the world I could call to and that I was still flying
    and had to wake to learn whether the wings were real

Nominated by Richard Burgin, Stuart Dybek

MAD

fiction by JEWEL MOGAN

from ONTARIO REVIEW

THE DOG WAS at the gate, biting the air in snatches. The deaf child was watching. A stranger was coming.

Paquet. A dark man, a little old drunken, foul-mouthed tinker, he had turned up one blistering day the year the century turned, had walked upriver from New Orleans on the levee with a pack of pots and pans on his back.

Cassie! Cassie! The name tore out of her throat, bursting out as Unnnngh! and she clutched her apron pockets full of pecans as she ran, terrified. Cassandra, bent over in the pecan grove, straightened up and saw what was coming. "Hush, now. Hush. Umm!—Umph! Here come the devil own right ahm!" She hurried Baby Girl away and forgot about picking up pecans the day that Paquet came.

That wasn't his real name. Anybody who was extra small was a "Paquet," a small package. They might also have called him that because he had disembarked in New Orleans with Gus Wiegand years ago carrying only the bundle on his back. Or, perhaps, because he had come down the levee that day to the Wiegand place, emerged from the dense river haze one morning shouldering the clinking load of pots and pans that made him sound like a one-man band, wearing an ancient Russian sailor's cap, his dark skin underneath stretched like gut membrane over the bones of his face, sweat running into his yellowed mustache that drew flies, Sidonie said, because it was so filthy. Skin and bones, him, Sidonie said. Shiftless. No more to show than what he got off the boat with, and that was damn little. Had drunk it all up, him. Had his nerve to raise hell and expect more than four bits a day, which was not quite

494

what the canefield workers made. But handsome pay for the trifling things he did. And, besides, look how well the niggers behaved and didn't give any lip. Paquet gave everybody hell except Baby Girl.

Gustav just laughed him off, kept him on because of the old bond. Perhaps the old man had done him a favor in the new country, or on the way over. Whatever had been recognizable as human in Paquet, whatever Gus had seen in him at first and perhaps tried to retrieve, had died long ago, had been stomped out like his dead and unremembered youth by liquor, the language barrier, and ill-treatment. He was as expendable as two little nigger boys drowned in the river.

He had been nursemaid to the two Wiegand boys, and ever since they could speak they had made fun of his rags and his gibberish. With Baby Girl it was different. Once he made a pinwheel for her out of palmetto fronds, and she laughed spontaneously, to everyone's amazement. He answered her with "Son of a bitch!"—one of his few English phrases—losing his eyes in the wrinkles of his smile. At this the squirrel walking down a tree waved his tail at her, and trees clapped their hands this way and that. She let Paquet babble right in her face with his liquor breath, and she adored it, ever since he had leaned down and said to her in Hungarian, "Come! Don't hide!" His language made as much sense to her as English. And she knew something interesting was going to happen when he talked in her face. "Dumb can't sing but it can dance, eh child?" he would say to her in Hungarian. Then he would clap his hands, turn, and take solemn high steps, like some stern patriarch, blowing and puffing out his moustaches. She would follow the steps in time, clapping, squealing in delight.

Once in a great while, if she threw herself on the floor and held her breath long enough, she would be allowed to roam with him and the boys. While the boys ran ahead, she and Paquet would dawdle drunkenly in the pastures and woods while he unriddled nameless mysteries for her. His imagination overlaid hers with a bright patterned transparency. He pointed out everything to her, turned all the stones. At night on the back gallery they might investigate a June bug in a spinout under the lantern. In the grove they spied on the jay as he tracked an unsuspecting squirrel and methodically dug up his pecans. They surveyed villages of bee houses, watched the smokestacks of boats moving swiftly behind the levee. If she felt the blast of an approaching river boat, she grabbed at his hand for him to take her to see it.

She remembered the high steps he taught her and did them in front of her mirror. She had an inner loquacity. Not able to tell herself to

495

anyone, she talked to her other self in the mirror, making the shape of Paquet's name, the dog's name, and about fifty other things that she had noticed over and over on people's lips, like the sharp S of Sidonie, and the slack jaw of Gus. ("She'll talk when she's ready," Doctor De-Jean was still telling them.)

Now: She and her mother walking hand in hand across the cow pasture, through a back gate, and into the woods on a sun-speckled path where clematis vines snaked up the scrub oaks and luminous moss hung down, seeming to gather the light and glow from within. "Paquet! Awww, Paquet!" Sidonie called.

The girl wore a pinafore, black stockings, and ankle-high shoes. She swung a small tin pail by the handle. She shuffled slightly, dragging the heels of her high-strung shoes. She breathed noisily. Made odd sounds. "She gon' talk when she get ready," the loyal Cassie was still quoting, telling them what they wanted to hear, none of them believing it for a minute. "She be gettin' tired fallin' on the flo' squealing. When she fittin' like that, she be gettin' herself ready." When the child raged in primal wolf cries and unintelligible black curses of her own devising, Gus would lift his spadelike hands helplessly, chide his wife for being too indulgent with her and bringing on these fits. Sidonie, pepper-pot French, ignored him. She ran the house and its precincts—the pecan grove, kitchen garden, back lot, Paquet's woods—the way she saw fit. Cassie observed, "M'em Sidonie run the men and Miss Baby Girl run her. O, but she love that baby! Dress her up like a picture-book."

"Paquet!" Sidonie called again sharply as they approached a one-room shack. On its unpainted exterior wall of junk lumber, an orange board here or a blue one there caught flimsy tatters of sunlight. Under the one shuttered window, a great weathered red board from the side of a barn said AUGHT, the ghost of BLACK DRAUGHT. When they reached the wooden stoop, which was merely a sawed-off, upended tree trunk, the mother motioned to her child to wait, and took the pail from her, calling from a safe distance into the open doorframe once again, as one calls livestock, "Paquet! Awww, Paquet!"

While the mother gave him the wide berth of an unpredictable animal, the little girl was not afraid. After seven years, she and the man trusted each other, understood something of one another's exile. Now she was ten, not really a child, but dutifully holding her mother's hand when they went abroad together because it was what she had always done.

"Drunk!" Sidonie said disgustedly, and slid the pail inside the doorframe. She seldom addressed the girl directly but the girl generally

496

knew what her face was saying. "Sent word he had a fever. Couldn't go out this week." She talked to the air around Baby Girl. "You hellion! Come on here and get your dinner." Paquet should have been out in their woods now with her father and brothers and the others. He cooked for them when they were cutting down trees. They lived in a shack like this back in the woods for a long time when they were cutting down trees. Maybe he didn't go because their dog had bitten him.

Queenie. There had been the dog at the gate, then the dog of that dog, and then Queenie. All of them had always showed their teeth to Paquet. They hated him. Out on the edge of these woods she had seen Queenie bite Paquet. She believed that he had then shot the dog. He kept an old shotgun in his shack. After Queenie bit him, acting like a wild animal, leaping and slashing at him, he had run back to his cabin with Queenie behind him. She was missing now.

"I brought your dinner, you hear—" Sidonie heard a moan from inside. She put her hand briefly on Baby Girl's shoulder to anchor her in that spot, then stepped up into the shack with her skirts tightly furled. Oh, but, yes, he was reeking of liquor, and flung out on his greasy mattress. His face was flushed; he was stupefied, breathing hard. Old hellion.

Like the girl, he did not understand much of what Sidonie said, only how it looked on her face. And this time, he could barely make out her face.

That night Baby Girl, whose real name was Elise, but she didn't know it, thrashed around and around on her moss mattress. It had darked again. Every dark was the same: when your eyes closed you were not anything. So you never wanted to let your eyes close. Never.

Never see a child fight bedtime so. . . . Buttin' and scufflin' around. . . .

There was no air in or out of the mosquito bar. Not a breath. She struggled to see. The familiar was strange and oppressive. Her goose-feather pillow, blue-white in the night, the bars of her iron bed, the heavy furniture—except for her friendly open-armed rocker in the corner—seemed misshapen, monstrous. Even her favorite plissé gown felt heavy and damp around her body. The shutters, like the outside doors, were fastened but not locked against miasmas with their harmful influences. Closing the shutters also kept out bats and a few mosquitos, guarded the sleeper against the full moon, longing, and madness.

Even if she could have told them about Queenie's biting Paquet, she wouldn't have done it. They would take Queenie's part. They would accuse him of killing her, even if he hadn't. Baby Girl imagined that they might even run him off if they thought he had killed Queenie. They cared more for Queenie than they did for him. Baby Girl herself half-felt this way. She fiercely loved the mute, adoring animal. And where was poor Queenie now?

On the other hand, Queenie had attacked him first. Baby Girl felt both ways about it, and it was a very bad night for her. Good Queenie. Paquet, warm in her heart. She clapped her hands rhythmically in the dark, in a version of Pease Porridge Hot that he had taught her, and threw her palms out to meet his invisible ones. She rocked herself side to side in her customary way, then she drummed her head against the bedstead bars to make her eyes stay open.

She slept late into the morning in her wispy white nightdress that lay like a small collapsed cloud in the middle of the iron bed, as if she herself had evaporated in the night out of her dream-cloud. Cassandra, walking in upon her, tangled and lost in the gown and bedclothes and her own long hair, thought, "Angel." Her forehead was like her father's: stubborn with intimations of the fixed purpose that had driven him to the new world, but innocent and blank. Her eyes were deepset like her mother's, but when they were open they lacked Sidonie's sharp restless scan. They were empty of expression, fixed as in a daguerreotype.

"Come on, Angel, heist your wings!"

Her waking impression was of Cassandra touching her back lightly between the shoulder blades. She was irritated at this and threw her arms and legs around on the bed, rolling over, glaring at Cassandra and making angry-elephant noises. She was small but gangly, her limbs not nearly finished. Cassandra left her alone. "Miss Baby being quarrelsome this morning," she told Sidonie.

When she woke up again, she was feeling better. She and the black woman raised the mosquito bar and threw it over the top of its frame. Then they folded back one end of the pliant moss mattress, revealing the "springs" of the bed, the shuck mattress. The shuck mattress had to be fluffed every morning through openings in each end. After struggling for a while at one end, they moved to the other end, folded back the moss mattress, plunged their arms into the dusty shucks, worked out the bulges, reshuffling, pummeling, and smoothing out the shucks until the mattress was roughly symmetrical again, or at least, until the lumps were uniformly distributed. They did the same to her mother and father's mattress. They would have given her brothers' beds the same treatment as part of the morning routine, but the brothers had been away in the woods for almost a week now. She didn't miss the brothers. She didn't feel kin to them, never having seen the color of their eyes or their mouths moving at her.

She did not get dressed, testing the women. Her mother looked at her pointedly, ran her hands down her own muslin dress, looked again at her daughter. Baby Girl shook her head pleadingly and her mother humored her, since the men were gone. The child padded barefoot into the kitchen, stretching elaborately, and tried the new kitchen pump, pushing up on the big handle and then hanging from it, her feet off the floor, until it worked up and down easier, and clear, cold water began to gush into the sink. She washed her hands and face, and when it turned icy cold, drank some of the water. Sidonie herself fixed them something "simple," she said, *pain perdue,* for breakfast. She used a stale loaf. She cut it in thirds, then sliced it lengthwise, soaked it in beaten egg mixed with fresh cream, raw brown sugar, and vanilla, and fried the pieces in deep fat. It was freeing to her soul to have the men gone for a while. She and Cassie did not have to fry steaks and make a stock pot of grits every morning before dawn, or cook a big spread for dinner right on the heels of breakfast. She could tend to her little garden off the end of the kitchen gallery, catch up on her mending in the afternoons, sitting in the porch swing. She decided to ease her mind even more and forget Paquet, too, leave him to stew in his own stinking juice as long as it took. She would be switched if she'd bring him his dinner again, she thought, impaling a puffy golden chunk of bread with a two-tined fork as long as her forearm, and lifting it from the black Dutch oven.

Two days went by without a sighting of Paquet. Then two more. On the fourth evening, sewing on the back gallery before dusk, Sidonie wondered if he might be dead back there in the woods. Maybe he really did have a fever. People said that dengue fever—they called it breakbone—was spreading up the river. Maybe she should send for Doctor DeJean—he was a good fever doctor. Maybe he is dead of drinking back there, she kept thinking. Oh, he's slept off many a binge back there. Days at a time he'd be hung-over, full of rot gut. Maybe . . . she didn't know what to think. Queenie didn't show up either, even when Sidonie brought out her big dishpan and banged it with a wooden spoon, calling loudly to raise them, either one, man or beast.

"Paquet! Paquet! Queenie! Queenie! Queeeeenie!" Her shouts echoed back from the darkening woods. She must go see about him in the morning. She directed Cassandra to stay the night. "We'll go see about him as soon as it's daylight. Now, don't suck your cheeks in like that. I need you here. If they don't see a light in your cabin, they know you are here with me because the men, they gone."

"Yessum."

Hours later, as branches of trees scratched at the rising moon, an unusual sound pulled Sidonie from a deep well of sleep, up to consciousness. She wouldn't have heard it, probably, if her bedroom hadn't been across the hall from the kitchen, overlooking the back gallery. It came from the gallery, or, it seemed, under the gallery. It was a low, snarling kind of sound, and when she first heard it, she rose up in bed and called softly, "Queenie!" Again, harshly rolling sound, constant, from a throat that seemed not to be taking, not able to be taking breaths. "Queenie?"

She was only to her bedroom door when she heard him burst into the kitchen. It had to be Paquet. Even then, she was more angry than afraid, not especially wanting to wake Cassie. If he's drunk again . . . She had handled him in the past, she could handle him now.

The noises he was making! From the black hole of the hall she hurried into the moonlit kitchen. His back was to her. He was naked to the waist, staggering forward to the pump, and she noticed at once that he was thin, thin—his back was bony. She had one coherent thought—that she was not altogether relieved that he was not dead, after all—before he took hold of the pump handle and began to rave at it. The water came and he flung himself away from it, coughing out unintelligible words, hurling the kitchen chairs against the walls. She screamed for Cassandra. He turned to her, coughing, drawing air in great sucking, rasping breaths. Then she saw—O JesusGod, all on the sharp intake of breath—froth had gathered on his moustaches. Some had fallen in small puffs, moonlit on his naked chest. He grabbed at her as Cassandra pounded into the kitchen, snatching a broom as she came, warding him off for a moment.

"He's not drunk, Cassie! It's a fever. Or he's gone mad!" They turned and ran by instinct back to the girl's room. He ran too, easily got through the door right behind them. Baby Girl began making high squealing shrieks that drew him to her. Then she saw that it was Paquet. Making steps and clapping his hands? And laughing? Laughing, in the half-shuttered moonlight. He was biting at the air in snatches. She sat up dead still and watched him. Sidonie just managed to drag her from the bed as he threw himself on it and lay there convulsing and choking. She held her hand over her daughter's mouth. Cassandra and the mother looked over the girl's head into each other's faces, wild with the same thought. Rabid.

Cassandra had a mad stone in her cabin. Be no use going there to get it, she told herself. They done be bit up time I got back. She turned and ran back to the boys' bedroom, where she had been sleeping.

"Cassie, come back! Oh, God, don't leave me!"

She came back quickly, dragging a moss mattress. Sidonie grasped the other side of it and they lunged clumsily with it toward the man. He sprang up screaming, wrestling the mattress away, biting and clawing it, trying to climb over it. Their screams joined his on the other side as they threw themselves against the wall of the mattress, scarcely any less berserk than he, possessed with the energy of the berserk. They managed to drive him back onto the bed, against the wall, crouching behind the mattress. They pushed with all their strength and he suddenly gave way, crumpling down on the bed. They climbed on top, panting, still screaming, Sidonie calling for Gustav, as if he might hear her from the farthest woods, Baby Girl joining her high squeal to the man's agonized cries half-stifled under the mattress. Directly on top of him, the white woman and the black in their nightgowns grappled with him in the semi-darkness, clung to the thin mattress as to a liferaft on a heaving sea. He fought for his life. His spasmodic movements were like convolutions, from the sea-floor, of a great demonic worm attempting to surface. They grasped the iron bedstead, hooked their free hands under the siderails.

Suddenly they felt her strong wiry body on the bed. She pulled her mother's streaming hair, howling desperately, trying to loosen their hands. She jerked at the corner of the mattress where she knew his face was, and Sidonie beat her off with her fists. She fought her mother, leaped on her back like a savage. Sidonie threw her off violently to the floor. The girl made two more attempts to pull the women off the mattress. They held tight.

They did not know when he stopped struggling or when his last sounds, or Baby Girl's, ended. Sobbing and praying through the night, they didn't dare get off the bed until daylight, and Sidonie clung tight to the bed even after bright splinters of sunlight fell on the floor. It was Cassandra who threw a shawl over her nightgown at dawn and ran to the cabin road for someone to fetch the men home from the woods.

The girl awoke to the vibrations of feet around her. In the tumult no one thought of her. Her parents were distraught. To her brothers she was essentially invisible. She crawled to her rocker and huddled there in the corner of the room, rocking in a small steadying rhythm. Doctor DeJean, quickly summoned, confirmed the death. Hydrophobia, he said, without a doubt. When they made ready to remove the body, Gustav noticed his daughter, picked her up out of the rocker, and carried her out. She was long-limbed and stiff, like a dead body in his arms. She remained that way while Doctor DeJean gently disrobed her, gnawed at his moustache in suspense, and found no marks on her. "Elise is a fine brave girl."

They hauled her moss mattress and her shuck mattress, as well as the mattress with which they had smothered him, out to the back lot, soaked them with kerosene, and burned them. Doctor DeJean told them, "Queenie might have been the carrier of the disease. Or possibly it was a rabid squirrel or coon."

When he came back in two weeks to check her daughter again, Sidonie told him she despaired of explaining it. "You can't make Baby—Elise—understand," she said. "Why we did it. She sees everything like pictures on a wall. She doesn't understand before and after. I try to act it out, but she's not ready for it, and she screams and runs away. Terrified! Oh, I tend to her so! I keep her close and dress her pretty and cuddle her. But now she's so inside herself, she's turning away her head and pulling away from me. She hates me now."

She caught the doctor's sleeve. "Please, please, explain hydrophobia to her." Desperately, she tore a blank page from the back of Gustav's ledger and handed it to him. He took Gustav's rigid accounting pen and his ink pot, and lifted Elise to his lap at the dining room table. He drew pictures of a stick dog with a mad, vicious look on its face, biting a stick man. The mean-looking stick man, in turn, bit another stick man. All expired, became a pile of sticks. Elise stared at the little scene for a long time. Then she burst out crying—Unnnnngh!—swept the paper to the floor, hid her face between Doctor DeJean's vest and his tight black coat.

At night she dreamed of smothering and woke up gasping, but did not make a sound. She felt writhings under her new mattress. So she did not sleep on her bed now. The rest of the summer nights, she took her goosefeather pillow and quilt to the front gallery and slept out there under a makeshift mosquito bar. She became more inward, they all noticed. She ceased to make sounds. They never heard the trumpeting elephant or the old wolf cry that had stood equally for frustration, pain, or, occasionally, supreme delight. They did not hear her squeal.

Gustav thought, "She's growing up."

Her mother thought, "*Là bas*—out there on her sandbar—how can I explain it to her—" the *it* now grown to such imponderable proportions that she could hardly, for all her practicality, see the whole of it. "Will I ever be able to explain? And if I find a way, will it be too late?"

Nominated by H. E. Francis, Joyce Carol Oates, and Ontario Review

THE TALE OF A KITE

fiction by STEVE STERN

from DOUBLETAKE

I T's SAFE TO say that we Jews of North Main Street are a progressive people. I don't mean to suggest we have any patience with free-thinkers, like that crowd down at Thompson's Cafe; tolerant within limits, we're quick to let subversive elements know where they stand. Observant (within reason), we keep the Sabbath after our fashion, though the Saturday competition won't allow us to close our stores. We keep the holidays faithfully and are regular in attending our modest little synagogue on Market Square. But we're foremost an enterpris-ing bunch, proud of our contribution to the local economy. Even our second-hand shops contain up-to-date inventories, such as stylish au-tomobile capes for the ladies, astrakhan overcoats for gentlemen—and our jewelers, tailors, and watchmakers are famous all over town. Boss Crump and his heelers, who gave us a dispensation to stay open on Sundays, have declared more than once in our presence, "Our sheenies are good sheenies!" So you can imagine how it unsettles us to hear that Rabbi Shmelke, head of that gang of fanatics over on Auc-tion Street, has begun to fly.

We see him strolling by the river, if you can call it strolling. Because the old man, brittle as a dead leaf, doesn't so much walk as permit him-self to be dragged by disciples at either elbow. A mournful soul on a stick, that's Rabbi Shmelke; comes a big wind and his bones will be scattered to powder. His eyes above his foggy pince-nez are a rheumy residue in an otherwise parchment face, his beard (Ostrow calls it his "lunatic fringe") an ashen broom gnawed by mice. Living mostly on air and the strained generosity of in-laws, his followers are not much more

504

presentable. Recently transplanted from Shpink, some godforsaken Old World backwater that no doubt sent them packing, Shmelke and his band of crackpots are a royal embarrassment to our community.

Like I say, we citizens of Hebrew extraction set great store by our friendly relations with our Gentile neighbors. One thing we don't need is religious zealots poisoning the peaceable atmosphere. They're an eyesore and a liability, Shmelke's crew, a threat to our good name, seizing every least excuse to make a spectacle. They pray conspicuously in questionable attire, dance with their holy books in the street, their doddering leader, if he speaks at all, talking in riddles. No wonder we judge him to be frankly insane.

It's my own son Ziggy, the kaddish, who first brings me word of Shmelke's alleged levitation. Then it's a measure of his excitement that, in reporting what he's seen, he also reveals he's skipped Hebrew school to see it. This fact is as troubling to me as his claims for the Shpinker's airborne faculty, which I naturally discount. He's always been a good boy, Ziggy, quiet and obedient, if a little withdrawn, and it's unheard of that he should play truant from his Talmud Torah class. Not yet bar mitzvah'd, the kid has already begun to make himself useful around the store, and I look forward to the day he comes into the business as my partner—(I've got a sign made up in anticipation of the event: J. Zipper & Son, Spirits and Fine Wines.) So his conduct is distressing on several counts, not the least of which is how it shows the fanatics' adverse influence on our youth.

"Papa!" exclaims Ziggy, bursting through the door from the street—since when does Ziggy burst? "Papa, Rabbi Shmelke can fly!"

"Shah!" I bark. "Can't you see I'm with a customer?" This is my friend and colleague Harry Nussbaum, proprietor of Memphis Bridge Cigars, whose factory supports better than fifteen employees and is located right here on North Main. Peeling bills from a bankroll as thick as a bible, Nussbaum's in the process of purchasing a case of Passover wine. (From this don't conclude that I'm some exclusively kosher concern; I carry also your vintage clarets and sparkling burgundies, blended whiskies and sour mash for the yokels, brandies, cordials, brut champagnes—you name it.)

Nussbaum winces, clamping horsey teeth around an unlit cigar. "Shomething ought to be done about thosh people," he mutters, and I heartily concur. As respected men of commerce, we both belong to the executive board of the North Main Street Improvement Committee, which some say is like an Old Country kahal. We chafe at the association regarding ourselves rather as boosters, watchdogs for the welfare of our district. It's a responsibility we don't take lightly.

When Nussbaum leaves, I turn to Ziggy, his jaw still agape, eyes bugging from his outsize head. Not from my side of the family does he get such a head, bobbling in his turtleneck like a pumpkin in an eggcup. You'd think it was stuffed full of wishes and big ideas, Ziggy's head, though to my knowledge it remains largely vacant.

"You ought to be ashamed of yourself."

"But, Papa, I seen it." Breathless, he twists his academy cap in his hands. "We was on the roof and we peeped through the skylight. First he starts to pray, then all of a sudden his feet don't touch the floor . . . "

"I said, enough!"

Then right away I'm sorry I raised my voice. I should be sorry? But like I say, Ziggy has always been a pliant kid, kind of an amiable mediocrity. He's never needed much in the way of discipline, since he's seldom guilty of worse than picking his nose. Not what you'd call fanciful—where others dream, Ziggy merely sleeps—I'm puzzled he should wait till his twelfth year to carry such tales. I fear he's fallen in with a bad crowd.

Still, it bothers me that I've made him sulk. Between my son and me there have never been secrets—what's to keep secret?—and I don't like how my temper has stung him into furtiveness. But lest he should think I've relented, I'm quick to add, "And never let me hear you played hooky from Hebrew school again."

And that, for the time being, is that.

But at our weekly meeting of the Improvement Committee—to whose board I'm automatically appointed on account of my merchant's credentials—the issue comes up again. It seems that others of our children have conceived a fascination for the Shpinker screwballs, and as a consequence are becoming wayward in their habits. Even our chairman, Irving Ostrow of Ostrow's Men's Furnishings, in the tasteful showroom of which we are assembled—even his own son Hershel, known as an exemplary scholar, has lately been delinquent in his studies.

"He hangs around the Auction Street shtibl," says an incredulous Ostrow, referring to the Chasids' sanctuary above Klotwog's feed store. "I ask him why, and he tells me, like the mountains should tremble"—Ostrow pauses to sip his laxative tea—"'Papa,' he says, 'the Shpinker rebbe can fly.' 'Rebbe' he calls him, like an alter kocker!"

"Godhelpus!" we groan in one voice—Nussbaum, myself, Benny Rosen of Rosen's Delicatessen—having heard this particular rumor

506

once too often. We're all of a single mind in our distaste for such fictions—all save old Kaminsky, the synagogue beadle ("Come-insky" we call him for his greetings at the door to the shul), who keeps the minutes of our councils.

"Maybe the Shmelke, he puts on the children a spell," he suggests out of turn, which is the sort of hokum you'd expect from a beadle.

At length we resolve to nip the thing in the bud. We pass along our apprehensions to the courtly Rabbi Fein, who runs the religious school in the synagogue basement. At our urging he lets it be known from the pulpit that fraternizing with Chasids, who are after all no better than heretics, can be hazardous to the soul. He hints physical consequences as well, such as warts and blindness. After that nothing is heard for a while about the goings on in the little hall above the feed store.

What does persist, however, is a certain (what you might call) bohemianism that's begun to manifest itself among even the best of our young. Take for instance the owlish Hershel Ostrow: in what he no doubt supposes is a subtle affectation—though who does he think he's fooling?—he's taken to wearing his father's worn-out homburg; and Mindy Dreyfus, the jeweler's son, has assumed the Prince Albert coat his papa has kept in mothballs since his greenhorn days. A few of the older boys sport incipient beards like the characters who conspire to make bombs at Thompson's Cafe, where in my opinion they'd be better off. Even my Ziggy, whom we trust to get his own haircut, he talks Plott the barber into leaving the locks at his temples. He tries to hide them under his cap, which he's begun to wear in the house, though they spiral out like untended runners.

But it's not so much their outward signs of eccentricity as our children's increasing remoteness that gets under our skin. Even when they're present at meals or their after-school jobs, their minds seem to be elsewhere. This goes as well for Ziggy, never much of a noise to begin with, whose silence these days smacks more of wistful longing than merely having nothing to say.

"Mama," I frown at my wife Ethel, who's shuffling about the kitchen of our apartment over the liquor store. I'm enjoying her superb golden broth, afloat with eyes of fat that gleam beneath the gas lamp like a peacock's tail; but I nevertheless force a frown. "Mama, give a look on your son."

A good-natured, capable woman, my Ethel, with a figure like a brick mikveh, as they say, she seldom sits down at meals. She prefers to eat on the run, sampling critical spoonfuls as she scoots back and forth between the table and coal-burning range. At my suggestion, however, she pauses, pretending to have just noticed Ziggy, who's toying absently with his food.

"My son? You mean this one with the confetti over his ears?" She bends to tease his sidelocks, then straightens, shaking her head. "This one ain't mine. Mine the fairies must of carried him off and left this in his place." She ladles more soup into the bowl he's scarcely touched. "Hey, stranger, eat your knaidel."

Still his mother's boy, Ziggy is cajoled from his meditations into a grudging grin, which I fight hard against finding infectious. Surrendering, I sigh, "Mama, I think the ship you came over on is called the Ess Ess Mein Kind." Then I'm pleased enough with my joke that I repeat it, reaching across the table to help Ziggy bring the spoon to his mouth: "Eat, eat, my child!"

Comes the auspicious day of Mr. Crump's visit to North Main Street. This is the political boss's bimonthly progress, when he collects his thankyous (usually in the form of merchandise) from a grateful Jewish constituency. We have good reason to be grateful, since in exchange for votes and assorted spoils, the Red Snapper, as he's called, has waived the blue laws for our district. He also looks the other way with respect to child labor and the dry law that would have put yours truly out of business. Ordinarily Boss Crump and his entourage, including his hand-picked mayor du jour, like to tour the individual shops, receiving the tributes his shwartze valet shleps out to a waiting limousine. But today, tradition notwithstanding, we're drawn out of doors by the mild April weather, where we've put together a more formal welcome.

When the chrome-plated Belgian Minerva pulls to the curb, we're assembled in front of Ridblatt's Bakery on the corner of Jackson Avenue and North Main. Irving Ostrow is offering a brace of suits from his emporium, as solemnly as a fireman presenting a rescued child, while Benny Rosen appears to be wrestling a string of salamis. Harry Nussbaum renders up a bale of cigars, myself a case of schnapps, and Rabbi Fein a ready blessing along with his perennial bread and salt. Puffed and officious in his dual capacity as self-appointed ward heeler and committee chair, Ostrow has also prepared an address:

"We citizens of North Main Street pledge to be a feather in the fedora of Mayor Huey, I mean Blunt . . ." (because who can keep straight Mr. Crump's succession of puppet mayors?)

Behind us under the bakery awning, Mickey Panitz is ready to strike up his klezmer orchestra; igniting his flash powder, a photographer from *The Commercial Appeal* ducks beneath a black hood. Everyone (with the exception, of course, of the Shpinker zealots, who lack all civic pride) has turned out for the event, lending North Main Street a holiday feel. We bask in Boss Crump's approval, who salutes us with a touch to the rim of his rakish straw skimmer, his smile scattering a galaxy of freckles. This is why what happens next, behind the backs of our visitors, seems doubly shameful, violating as it does such a banner afternoon.

At first we tell ourselves we don't see what we see; we think, maybe a plume of smoke. But looks askance at one another confirm that, not only do we share the same hallucination, but that the hallucination gives every evidence of being real. Even from such a distance, it's hard to deny it: around the corner of the next block, something is emerging from the roof of the railroad tenement that houses the Shpinker shtibl. It's a wispy black-and-gray something that rises out of a propped-open skylight like vapor from an uncorked bottle. Escaping, it climbs into the cloudless sky and hovers over North Main Street, beard and belted caftan aflutter. There's a fur hat resembling the rotary brush of a chimney sweep, a pair of dunstockinged ankles (to one of which a rope is attached) as spindly as the handles on a scroll. Then it's clear that, risen above the telephone wires and trolley lines, above the water tanks, Rabbi Shmelke floats in a doleful ecstasy.

We begin talking anxiously and at cross-purposes about mutual understanding through public sanitation, and so forth. We crank hands left and right, while Mickey Panitz leads his band in a dirgelike rendition of "Dixie." In this way we keep our notables distracted until we can pack them off (photographer and all) in their sable limousine. Then, without once looking up again, we repair to Ostrow's Men's Furnishings and convene an extraordinary meeting of the Improvement Committee.

Shooting his sleeves to show flashy cufflinks, Ostrow submits a resolution: "I hereby resolve we dispatch to the Shpinkers a delegatz, with the ultimatum they should stop making a nuisance, which it's degrading already to decent citizens, or face a forceable outkicking from the neighborhood. All in agreement say oy."

The only dissenting voice is the one with no vote.

"Your honors know best"—this from Kaminsky, a greenhorn till his dying day—"but ain't it what you call a miracle, this flying rebbe?"

509

For such irrelevance we decide it also wouldn't hurt to find a new secretary.

En route across the road to the shtibl, in the company of my fellows, I give thanks for small blessings: at least my Ziggy was telling the truth about Shmelke. Though I'm thinking that, with truths like this, it's maybe better he should learn to lie.

We trudge up narrow stairs from the street, pound on a flimsy door, and are admitted by one of Shmelke's unwashed. The dim room lists slightly like the deck of a ship, tilted toward windows that glow from a half-light filtering through the lowered shades. There's a film of dust in the air that lends the graininess of a photogravure to the bearded men seated at the long table, swaying over God only knows what back-numbered lore. By the wall there's an ark stuffed with scrolls, a shelf of moldering books, spice boxes, tarnished candelabra, amulets against the evil eye.

It's all here, I think, all the blind superstition of our ancestors pre-served in amber. But how did it manage to follow us over an ocean to such a far-flung outpost as Tennessee? Let the goyim see a room like this, with a ram's horn in place of a clock on the wall, with the shnor-rers wrapped in their paraphernalia, mumbling hocus-pocus instead of being gainfully employed, and right away the rumors start. The yids are poisoning the water, pishing on communion wafers, murdering Christian children for their blood. Right away somebody's quoting the *Protocols of Zion*. A room like this, give or take one flying rebbe, can upset the delicate balance of the entire American enterprise.

Returned at least in body from the clouds, old Shmelke sits at the head of the table, dispensing his shopworn wisdom. An unlikely source of authority, he appears little more substantial than the lemon shaft pouring over him from the open skylight.

"It is permitted to consult with the guardian spirits of oil and eggs . . . ," he intones, pausing between syllables to suck on a piece of halvah; an "Ahhh" goes up from disciples who lean forward to catch any crumbs. "But sometimes the spirits give false answers." Another sadder but wiser "Ahhh."

When our eyes adjust to the murk, we notice that the ranks of the Shpinkers (who until now have scarcely numbered enough for a minyan) have swelled. They've been joined this afternoon, during Hebrew school hours no less, by a contingent of the sons of North Main Street, my own included. He's standing in his cockeyed acad-emy cap, scrunched between nodding Chasids on the rebbe's left side. To my horror, Ziggy, who's shown little enough aptitude for the things in this world, never mind the other, is also nodding to the beat of the band.

"Home!" I shout, finding myself in four-part harmony with the other committee members. Our outrage since entering having been compounded with interest, we won't be ignored anymore. But while some of the boys do indeed leave their places and make reluctantly for the door, others stand their ground. Among them is Ostrow's brainy son Hershel and my nebbish, that never before disobeyed.

Having turned toward us as one, the disciples look back to their tsadik, who God forbid should interrupt his discourse on our account. Then Hershel steps forth to confront us, a pincenez identical to Shmelke's perched on his nose. "You see," he explains in hushed tones, though nobody asked him, "figuratively speaking, the rebbe is climbing Jacob's Ladder. Each rung corresponds to a letter of Tetragrammaton, which in turn corresponds to a level of the soul . . ." And bubkes-bobkes, spouting the gibberish they must've brainwashed him into repeating. I look at Ostrow who's reaching for his heart pills.

Then who should pipe up but the pipsqueak himself, come around to tug at my sleeve. "Papa" like he can't decide whether he should plead or insist, "if they don't hold him down by the rope, Rabbi Shmelke can fly to paradise."

I can hardly believe this is my son. What did I do wrong that he should chase after moth-eaten yiddishe swamis? Did he ever want for anything? Didn't I take him on high holidays to a sensible synagogue, where I showed him how to mouth the prayers nobody remembers the meaning of? That is, if they ever knew. Haven't I guaranteed him the life the good Lord intends him for?

Not ordinarily combative, when the occasion calls for it I can speak my mind. To the papery old man whom I hold personally accountable, I ask point-blank, "What have you done to my child?"

Diverted at last from his table talk, Rabbi Shmelke cocks his tallowy head; he seems aware for perhaps the first time of the presence among his faithful of uninvited hangers-on.

"Gay avek!" he croaks at the remaining boys. "Go away." When nobody budges, he lifts a shaggy brow, shrugs his helplessness. Then he resumes in a voice like a violin strung with cobweb, "Allow me to tell you a story . . ."

"A story, a story!" The disciples wag their heads, all of them clearly idiots.

The rebbe commences some foolishness about how the patriarch Isaac's soul went on vacation while his body remained under his father's knife. Along with the others I find myself unable to stop listening, until I feel another tug at my sleeve.

"Papa," Ziggy is whispering, Adam's apple bobbing like a golf ball in a fountain, "they have to let him out the roof or he bumps his head on the ceiling."

"Do I know you?" I say, shaking him off. Then I abruptly turn on my heel and exit, swearing vengeance. I'm down the stairs and already crossing Auction Street, when I realize that my colleagues have joined me in my mortification. I suggest that drastic measures are in order, and as my anger has lent me an unaccustomed cachet, all say aye.

They agree there's not a minute to lose, since every day we become more estranged from our sons. (Or should I say sons and daughters, because you can't exclude old Kaminsky's orphaned granddaughter Ida, a wild girl with an unhealthy passion for books.)

But days pass and Rabbi Fein complains that even with the threat of his ruler, not to mention his assistant Nachum (whom the boys call Knock 'em), he can't keep his pupils in Hebrew class. Beyond our command now, our children are turning their backs on opportunity in favor of emulating certifiable cranks. They grow bolder, more and more of them exhibiting a freakish behavior they no longer make any pretense to conceal. For them rebellion is a costume party. They revel in the anomalous touch, some adopting muskrat caps (out of season) to approximate the Chasid's fur shtreimel. Milton Rosen wears a mackintosh that doubles for a caftan, the dumb Herman Wolf uses alphabet blocks for phylacteries. My own Ziggy has taken to picking his shirttails in ritual tassels.

He still turns up periodically for meals, silent affairs at which even Ethel is powerless to humor us. For his own good I lock him in his bedroom after dinner, but he climbs out the window, the little pisher, and scrambles down the fire escape. "Not from my side of the family does he get such a streak of defiance," I tell Ethel, who seems curiously resigned. "I think maybe comes the fairies to take him back again," she says, but am I worried? All right, so I'm worried, but I'm confident that, once the Shpinkers have been summarily dealt with, my son will return to the fold, tail between legs.

Still the problem remains: what precisely should we do? Time passes and the Shpinkers give no indication of developing a civic conscience; neither do they show any discretion when it comes to aiding

512

their blithering rebbe to fly. (If you want to dignify what he does as flying; because in midair he's as bent and deflated as he is on earth, so wilted you have to wonder if he even knows he's left the ground.) In response to their antics, those of us with any self-respect have stopped looking up.

Of course we have our spies, like Old Man Kaminsky who has nothing better to do than ogle the skies. He tells us that three times a day, morning, noon, and evening, rain or shine, and sometimes nonstop on Shabbos, Shmelke hovers above the chimneys. He marks us from a distance like some wizened dirigible, a sign designating our community as the haven of screwballs and extremists. We're told that instead of studying (a harmless enough endeavor in itself), the shiftless Shpinkers now spend their time testing various grades of rope. From the clothesline purchased at Hekkie's Hardware on Commerce Street, they've graduated to hawser obtained from steamboat chandlers down at the levee. They've taken to braiding lengths of rope, to splicing and paying them out through the skylight, so that Shmelke can float ever higher. Occasionally they might maneuver their rebbe in fishtails and cunning loop-the-loops, causing him to soar and dive; they might send him into electrical storms from which he returns with fluorescent bones. Sometimes, diminished to a mote, the old man disappears in the clouds, only to be reeled back carrying gifts—snuff boxes and kiddush cups made of alloys never seen on this planet before.

Or so says Old Man Kaminsky, whom we dismiss as having also fallen under Shmelke's mind control. We're thankful, in any case, that the Shpinkers now fly their tsadik high enough that he's ceased to be a serious distraction. (At first the yokels, come to town for the Saturday market, had mistaken him for an advertising ploy, their sons taking potshots with peashooters.) But out of sight isn't necessarily to say that the rebbe is out of mind, though we've gotten used to keeping our noses to the ground. We've begun to forget about him, to forget the problems with our young. Given the fundamental impossibility of the whole situation, we start to embrace the conviction that Shmelke's flights are pure fantasy.

Then Ziggy breaks his trancelike silence to drop a bombshell. "I'm studying for bar mitzvah with Rabbi Shmelke," he announces, as Ethel spoons more calf's foot jelly onto my plate. But while his voice issues the challenge, Ziggy's face, in the shadow of his academy cap, shows he's still testing the water.

Ethel's brisket, tender and savory as it is , sticks in my gorge. I want to tell him the tsadik's a figment of his imagination and let that be an end to it, but Ziggy's earnestness suggests the tactic won't work.

"What's wrong," I ask, clearing my throat with what emerges as a seismic roar, "ahemmm . . . what's wrong with Rabbi Fein?"

"He ain't as holy."

Directly the heartburn sets in. "And what's holy got to do with it?"

Ziggy looks at me as if my question is hardly deserving of an answer. Condescending to explain, however, he finds it necessary to dismount his high horse, doffing his cap to scratch his bulbous head. "Holy means, you know, like scare . . . I mean sacred."

"Unh-hnh," I say, folding my arms and biting my tongue. Now I'm the soul of patience, which makes him nervous.

"You know, *sacred,*" he reasserts, the emphasis for his own sake rather than mine.

"Ahhh," I nod in benign understanding, enjoying how his resolve begins to crack.

"That's right," pursues Ziggy, and tries again to fly in the face of my infernal tolerance, lacking wings, "like magic."

I'm still nodding, so he repeats himself in case I didn't hear.

"Oh sure, ma-a-agic," I reply, with the good humor of a parent introduced to his child's imaginary friend.

Flustered to the point of fighting back tears, Ziggy nevertheless refuses to surrender, retreating instead behind a wall of hostility. "You wouldn't know magic if it dumped a load on your head!"

You have to hand it to the kid, the way he persists in his folly; I never would have thought him capable of such high mishegoss. But when the admiration passes, I'm fit to be tied; I'm on my feet, jerking him by the scrawny shoulders, his head whipping back and forth until I think I'm maybe shaking it clear of humbug.

"I'll magic you!" I shout. "Who's your father anyway, that feeble-minded old scarecrow or me? Remember me, Jacob Zipper, that works like a dog so his son can be a person?" Then I see how he's staring daggers; you could puncture your conscience on such daggers, and so I pipe down.

I turn to Ethel cooling her backside against the hardwood icebox, an oven mitten pressed to her cheek. "So whose side are you on?" I appeal.

She gives me a look. "This is a contest already?"

But tempted as I am to make peace, I feel they've forced my hand; I cuff the boy's ear for good measure and tell my wife, "I don't know him anymore, he's not my son."

Understand, it's a tense time; the news from the Old Country is bad. In Kiev they've got a Jew on trial for blood libel, and over here folks are grumbling about swarms of Hebrews washing onto our shores. Some even blame the wreck of the *Titanic* on the fact that there were Guggenheims on board, and right next door in Georgia comes the lynching of Leo Frank. It's a climate created by ignorance, which will surely pass with the coming enlightened age—when our sons will have proved how indispensable we are. But in the meantime we must keep order in our own house.

At the next meeting of the North Main Street Improvement Committee I propose that the time is ripe to act.

Ostrow and the others stir peevishly, their hibernation disturbed. "Act? What act?" It seems they never heard of fanatics in our bosom or the corruption of our youth.

"Wake up!" I exhort them. "We got a problem!"

Slowly, scratching protuberant bellies and unshaven jaws, they begin to snap out of it; they swill sarsparilla, light cigars, overcoming a collective amnesia to ask what we should do.

"Am I the chairman?" I protest. "Ostrow's the chairman." But it's clear that my robust agitation has prompted them to look to me for leadership, and I'm damned if I don't feel equal to the test.

"Cut off the head from the body," I'm suddenly inspired to say, "and your monster is kaput."

At sundown the following evening the executive board of the Improvement Committee rounds the corner into Auction Street. There's a softness in the air, the stench of the river temporarily overwhelmed by the smell of potted chicken wafting from the windows over the shops. It's a pleasant evening for a stroll, but not for us, who must stay fixed on the critical business at hand. We're all of one mind, I tell myself, though yours truly has been elected to carry the hedge shears— donated for the deed by Hekkie Schatz of Hekkie's Hardware. Ostrow our titular chair, Nussbaum the treasurer, Benny Rosen the whatsit all have deferred the honor to me, by virtue of what is perceived as my greater indignation.

This time we don't knock but burst into the dusty shtibl. As it turns out our timing is perfect: a knot of disciples—it appears that several are needed to function as anchors—are uncoiling the rope beneath the open skylight. Rising into the lemon shaft (now turning primrose), his feet in their felt slippers arched like fins, Rabbi Shmelke chants the Amidah prayer:

"Baruch atoh Adonoy, blessed art Thou, our God and God of our Fathers . . ."

The Shpinkers start at our headlong entrance. Then gauging our intentions by the sharp implement I make no attempt to hide, they begin to reel their rebbe back in. My colleagues urge me to do something quick, but I'm frozen to the spot; though Shmelke's descending, I'm still struck with the wonder of having seen him rise. "Decease!" cries Ostrow, to no effect whatsoever; then he and the others shove me forward.

Still I dig in my heels. Disoriented, I have the sensation that the room is topsy-turvy; above is below and vice versa. Standing on the ceiling as the rebbe is hauled up from the depths, we're in danger of coming unglued, of tumbling headfirst through the skylight. I worry for our delinquent sons, who now outnumber the Shpinkers, and in their fantastic getups are almost indistinguishable from the original bunch. Among them, of course, is Ziggy, elflocks curling like bedsprings from under his cap, perched on a chair for the better view.

Then the room rights itself. Holding the handles of the hedge shears, I could say that I'm gripping the wings of a predatory bird, its mind independent of my own. I could say I only hang on for dear life, while it's the shears themselves that swoop forth to bite the rope in two. But the truth is, I do it of my own free will. And when the rope goes slack—think of a serpent when the swami stops playing his pipe—I thrill at the gasps that are exhaled ("Ahhh") all around. After which: quiet, as old Shmelke, still chanting, floats leisurely upward again, into the primrose light which is deepening to plum.

When he's out of sight, my Ziggy is the first to take the initiative—because that's the type of person we Zippers are. The pistol, he bolts for the open window followed by a frantic mob. I too am swept into the general exodus, finding myself somehow impelled over the sill out onto the fire escape. With the others I rush up the clattering stairs behind (incidentally) Ida Kaminsky, who's been hiding there to watch the proceedings. I reach the roof just in time to see my son, never an athletic boy—nor an impulsive or a headstrong or rebellious one, never to my knowledge any of these—I see him swarm up the slippery pane of the inclined skylight (which slams shut after) and leap for the rope. Whether he means to drag the old man down or hitch a ride, I can't say, but latched on to the dangling cord, he begins, with legs still cycling, to rise along with the crackpot saint.

Then uttering some complicated mystical war cry, Hershel Ostrow, holding onto his homburg, follows Ziggy's lead. With his free hand Hershel grabs my boy's kicking right foot, and I thank God when I see them losing altitude, but this is only temporary reversal. Because it seems that Rabbi Shmelke, handicaps notwithstanding, has only to warble louder, adjusting the pitch of his prayer to gain height. I console myself that if he continues ascending, the fragile old man will come apart in the sky; the boys will plummet beneath his disembodied leg. Or Ziggy, whose leap I don't believe in the first place, unable to endure the burden of his companion, will let go. I assure myself that none of this is happening.

From beside me the wild Ida Kaminsky has flung herself onto Hershel's ankle, her skirt flaring to show off bloomers—which make a nice ribbon for the tail of a human kite. But even with her the concatenation doesn't end: the shambling Sanford Nussbaum and Mindy Dreyfus, the halfwit Herman Wolf, Rabbi Fein's own pious Abie in his prayer shawl, Milton Rosen in his mackintosh, all take their turn. Eventually every bad seed of North Main Street is fastened to the chain of renegade children trailing in the wake of old Shmelke's ecstasy.

One of the rebbe's zealots, having mounted a chimney pot, makes a leap at the flying parade, but for him they're already out of reach. Then another tries and also fails. Is it because, in wanting to pull their tsadik back to earth, his followers are heavy with a ballast of desire? This seems perfectly logical to me, sharing as I do the Chasids' despair.

Which is why I shout "Ziggy, come back! All is forgiven!" and make to jump into the air. In that instant I imagine I grab hold and am carried aloft with the kids. The tin roofs, the trolley lines, the brand new electric streetlights in their five-globed lamps, swiftly recede, their incandescence humbled by the torched western sky. Across the river the sunset is more radiant than a red flare over a herring barrel, dripping sparks—all the brighter as it's soon to be extinguished by dark clouds swollen with history rolling in the east. Then just as we're about to sail beyond those clouds, I come back to myself, a stout man and no match for gravity.

Nominated by Steven Millhauser and Debra Spark

BABY MAKER

fiction by KARLA J. KUBAN

from THE LAUREL REVIEW

WHEN MONA ARRIVED for work that morning, a customer was waiting for her to open the store. "Hey, Jimbo," she said, letting him in.

Mona's Doughnuts was located on Jefferson Street, between the drug store and Radio Shack, across from Chet's boots. Two people worked for her: Grace and Grace's boyfriend, Juan; they had both dropped out of high school. Juan got there early to mix doughnut batter in the vat which stood on the kitchen floor. He had black, curly hair to his shoulders, and Mona made him wear it in an elastic net so that the ends were tucked neatly under. Grace wasn't there yet. She was at the doctor.

Mona walked briskly to the back, past Juan, and told him to spit out his gum. She went to the refrigerator and took out a carton of buttermilk. The back door opened and Grace burst in, her face flushed and damp, a T-shirt stretched across her pregnant stomach.

"Morning, Grace," Mona said. "How was your ultrasound?"

"It's a girl!" Grace said.

"Well! A girl," Mona said. She glanced at Grace's stomach, then at her face. "She's got all ten fingers and toes?"

"Every one," Grace said.

"Well, well," Mona said.

Grace had a boyish face and short blonde hair. Her bare legs, under the skirt, were spindly and pale. Grace lived in a trailer house with Juan. The trailer house had been Grace's parents', but her father was now dead, her mother in the state penitentiary for shooting him two years before.

A week ago Mona had brought an old rocking chair to Grace's trailer. Mona saw the bedroom where Juan and Grace slept. She saw the sheets printed in yellow daffodils, the covers strewn on the floor. She imagined the curve of their bodies together at night and wondered how they kissed, and if they tried to make a baby or if they just had a good time.

She'd thought of her own baby-making. She was always nervous, tight, conscious of slightly lifting her hips after whoever she was with was finished. She'd recently been to the doctor in Laramie, and the report had said she was probably infertile. The report hadn't said definitely, though, and until it did, she was going to keep trying.

Somebody up front called out for a dozen cinnamon apple doughnuts and Mona caught a glimpse of one of her regulars.

"Hold your horses, Merle," she said kindly, then went to a cupboard in the back, took out her purse, and pulled out two jars of vitamins. She handed them to Grace.

"Vitamins C and E," she said.

"They won't hurt the baby?" Grace asked.

"You'll need them to keep healthy," Mona said. "Now, put on your apron. Grab me some decaf packets. Juan, the flour bin needs filling." Mona caught his fleeting smile and it made her cringe.

Later in the afternoon, while Juan was out by the dumpster smoking a cigarette, Mona said to Grace, "Are you and Juan getting married?"

"Juan's not sure," Grace said.

"I see."

"The problem is, there was somebody else. It was only a one-night stand. I feel so guilty. Sometimes I wonder if Juan suspects. If you promise not to say anything to anybody, I can tell you."

Mona crossed her heart with a finger.

"Juan would leave me if he found out. It was John Braddock."

"Johnny Braddock? Why, how old is he, Grace? Fourteen? Aren't you robbing the cradle a little bit?"

"Not Johnny Braddock, Junior. John Braddock, Senior."

"Oh, Senior. Well. My. That is bad."

Then Juan came in the back door, blowing smoke through his nostrils.

"No smoking!" Mona shouted to him, and he muttered, then began rinsing coffee cups and stacking them in the dishwasher. "Tell him not to smoke in here," Mona said sternly to Grace. "And not to smoke around you, either."

Mona refilled a napkin dispenser at the far end of the counter, where two customers had left fifty-cent tips. She caught Grace's attention, then nodded in the quarters' direction. Grace said, "You sure?" and Mona said, "Go on." Grace made a little shivering sound as she picked them up and put them in her pocket.

"You feeling sick?" Mona asked.

"Just a little cold. Maybe we could turn the fan down."

"Don't you have a sweater?" Mona asked.

"I have one, but it's old and ugly and some moths got to it." She stood close to Mona and whispered, "I suppose I'll have to wait until the baby comes. To see if she looks like John or Juan. Then I'll have to make some decisions. I can't raise a baby alone. I've got to have some help."

Grace tailed Mona to the bins, where Mona plucked doughnuts and carefully placed them in a wax-lined bag. She paused, a doughnut in her hand, and looked hard into Grace's face. "Grace, a baby eats, drinks, gets diapered, then potty trained, and one day gets on a bus to go to school. It can't go naked. A child is something that stays with you the rest of your life. You've got to get this all worked out beforehand. You've got to get your ducks in order."

"Yes, well, I'm trying."

Mona whispered, "You have to have a plan. Every day I have a plan, and every week and month I meet certain goals, and every year and every five years. How do you think I got this place? Why do you think we're always full of customers, these booths filled, this counter so busy? Everything I have is because of careful consideration." She looked around and nodded her head at her customers as if, like roses, they had grown and bloomed with her nurturing. "We are reliable here. We open on time, we have a clean operation, and we are polite. Grace, this place started with a dream, and from there you plan, and of course you don't have a pot to spit in if you don't carry out the plans. I don't always get what I want, but look here, I get most of it."

Grace struck a roll of quarters on the counter's edge and peeled away the paper. "I don't have much," she said to Mona, "but what I have got, I'm thankful for."

"Well, be thankful your health is good," Mona said.

Throughout the day, Mona wiped up counter crumbs and took plates and cups to the kitchen to be washed. As each customer paid she said, "And have a very nice day." At times in the afternoon she studied something, a part of the wall, the light fixtures, lost in thought, her eyes fixed and gleaming as she planned.

In the late afternoon, as they were getting ready to close up, a trucker came in, his sixteen-wheeler stretched out across Mona's lot.

He said, "Is it okay, Ma'am, if I park her there for a minute? I'd like my coffee to go, sugar, no cream." He was tall as a house, thin as a branch, his eyes bright blue. He said, "Do you know where I can get a fried egg sandwich?"

Mona pushed the bangs off her forehead and, when she turned to pour him a cup of coffee, pinched both her cheeks to bring color into them. She thought she might go to the bathroom and brush her hair, but no, then she might lose him. She turned around and faced him with softened eyes.

"Let me show you," she said, taking off her apron and setting it on the counter. "Grace," she called out as she opened the door. "I'll be right back."

Mona and the trucker went outside. The truck was still running. Mona whispered in his ear, "Over there. Far end," she said as he climbed in.

They drove to the Wal-Mart parking lot and he stopped at the edge of the blacktop. He opened the glove compartment and took out a package of Trojans.

Good sign, Mona thought. A careful dude.

They got out of the truck and climbed in the small side door, where there was a bed wide enough for one. At first she was disappointed, but thought, then, that it might be okay because they were going to stack themselves up in there.

Inside the cubbyhole, as he leaned down to kiss her on the mouth, she smiled with satisfaction. He was the second trucker this week. He tore open the condom package but she put her hand over his. "That's okay," she said. "No disease on this end, and I'm protected." She grabbed his face and kissed him.

Mona lived in the country. Two miles out of town there was a cemetery in which her parents and sister were buried. They had died in a fire more than twenty years ago. She hadn't been to the cemetery for a while, and felt a pang of guilt as she sped past. She would take some carnations next week.

Out Mona's front window was a valley. Sharp shadows cut across it, and farther west she could see cliffs known as Sapphire Hill. The sun sat low and blackbirds looked like rocks in her yard.

From her living room, through binoculars, Mona saw her new next-door neighbor in the twilight. The man was about one hundred yards from her house, walking to the corral. This was land that had belonged to her friend, Smoky. Every night around eight the man came out of his house and walked half crouched to the center of the corral. There he fell to his knees, bowed his head, and sat cross-legged on the dirt. His thumb and forefinger formed an O, resting upon his knees, the other three fingers splayed in the air. An hour later he stood and went back into the house.

In the mornings he went out there, too. He mounted his pinto and cantered around the corral. Two braids hung down his back, bumping to the beat of his horse's hooves. She watched him with her binoculars, then took a shower and got ready for work.

She took a big purple sweater from her closet, and six lamb chops from the freezer. Warmth and good food were necessities. Why did Grace not own a decent sweater?

She drove to Grace's trailer and gave her the sweater and lamb chops, and noticed she was wearing a new pair of black patent leather shoes. What had she bought for the forthcoming child? There was no baby crib, no highchair. She didn't see a changing table.

"You shouldn't of brought all this," Grace said. "My gosh, you didn't have to go to all this trouble!"

She pulled the sweater on over her T-shirt. Mona noticed Grace's breasts, big and rolling, and she watched Grace move through the narrow hallway, then turn twice around to model the sweater. Her steps came from her full hips, not from her knees.

Grace said, "It fits perfectly!"

How could it not! Mona thought. It would have fit a buffalo.

"Did you tell Juan yet?" Mona asked. "About John? About the possibility?"

"Oh, no. Ssh. Not yet." She whispered, although Juan was long gone, making doughnut batter at the store.

Mona suddenly felt irritated, and pushed a fingernail into her arm. "If you want, I can help you take care of that baby. You're going to need some help."

"I'll always have Juan," Grace said. "But you'd be willing to sit for me sometimes? Like when we want to go out to a movie?"

She avoided looking at Grace. Life was not a movie. Life was a baby. Mona saw her face in the mirror against the wall. She hated to see herself. It was her there, and yet it was her here, and she was alone. She pushed her nail harder into the soft flesh of her arm, and came back into her body.

That night, she put on her Nikes and walked across her two acres to the house which had been Smoky's. Smoky had died the year before of pneumonia.

The pinto pricked his ears as she walked up to the front door and knocked. When the man answered, for a moment Mona could not speak. He was not so tall as she had thought, but big-chested and dark with black eyes. His eyelids were thick. She saw now that he was about forty, about her age.

"Hello," she said calmly. "I'm your neighbor, Mona. And you are?"

"Albert," he said without smiling. "Hello."

She wanted to glance past him into the two-room house, but his body was in front of the door. She'd never been in the house. Smoky had always come to hers, where they bounded into her bed.

"I live just over there," she pointed.

He nodded.

"Smoky was a friend of yours?"

"He was my uncle. My father's brother."

Then there was a long silence. He made her feel uncomfortable and unwanted. She looked helplessly at him. "I came to borrow an egg. Do you have one?" she said.

"Come in," he said, holding the door open, keeping one eye on her.

She stepped inside. A brass lamp with a pale, stained lamp shade stood in the corner. The lamp shade reminded her of Smoky's cowboy hat. After he died, she once felt his ghost behind her house. It was the spring before, as she was hanging blouses on the line. Her clothes lifted, flapped and billowed, then blew off the line, scattering across the sage. She wondered if the wind had taken her clothes or if it was Smoky. And if Smoky, why? Because, Mona thought, he knew Albert would be coming to that house. Smoky was jealous, sure that Albert would be the one to make a baby with her.

A large-paned window took the evening light. There was a small bathroom at the rear of the house, a fireplace, hot plate and teakettle. There was a gold refrigerator, a torn moth-green couch against the yellowed wall, a bureau missing knobs.

"Here you go," he said, handing her the egg, watching her all the while.

"Thank you." She took the egg in her palm, then closed her fingers around it. "I'm sorry about Smoky," she told him.

He nodded. "Where did you say you live?"

"Just over there."

She pointed, again, in the direction. She wanted to say, "Don't be a stranger now," but could feel his eyes on her. She noted the tapping of his foot, and guessed he wanted her out of there—the day was ending and he had his ritual—so she thanked him again, then left.

She went home and sat by her window, looking north to his property, but he did not come out right away. She looked about her house, thinking she did not live in lavish style; there was no baby grand piano, no rare book collection, no giant-screen television. Still, she lived with a kind of comfort. Everything she owned—her heated waterbed, a sterling silver gravy bowl, the Gorman prints—she had bought with her own money, money she had worked hard for.

Albert came from his front door, went through the gate, knelt, and sat in the corral. The sky clouded up and before Albert was finished with his sitting and praying and listening—maybe to drums inside his head—it began to rain. The pinto danced. Albert stayed fixed and Mona closed her eyes. She imagined a censer, incense like lilacs, a drumbeat, a bull, black against the gray rain, spinning around. Its feet fell upon the earth in perfect time as Albert walked through the gate, his back white in the rain, outlined sharply against the house.

Grace and Mona wiped down the counter stools with Lysol spray.

"People are pure pigs," Grace said vehemently.

Mona stepped back. "Is everything all right?"

"Oh, sure," Grace sighed.

"Did you tell Juan about John Braddock yet?"

"Shoot, no," she whispered, holding a finger to her mouth. "This morning before work we were trying to figure out how to pay the hospital bills when the baby comes. We figure it's going to come to twice what we've got in savings. Then, what if there's a problem? Like a heart defect."

"God forbid!" Mona said.

"Well, I know, but what if?" Grace said.

"You're right, you've got to think of such things," Mona said.

"You don't like to be a pessimist, you like to be a realist, and so you plan and get your ducks in a row," Grace said, standing next to the coffee machine with her cheek against the wall. "Juan sends some of his check home to his mother in Nogales. It's not easy to make ends meet."

Mona eyed Grace's stomach as Grace rubbed it with the flat of her hand.

"I might be able to help you some," said Mona. "I wouldn't do it for anybody but you. A baby's got to be cared for."

"How come you never had any babies, Mona?"

Mona tensed up, gazing down at Grace's patent leather shoes. This girl is too young, too irresponsible, too ignorant, Mona thought.

"I apologize. That's not my business," Grace said.

"I don't believe I can have children," Mona said abruptly.

"Oh, Mona," Grace said. "I'm sorry."

Mona's vision blurred and it went away altogether for a second, as if a bird had come down and plucked out her eyes. Her sight returned but she was left spinning.

"Excuse me," she said, moving to the kitchen. She poured herself a glass of water. Juan was glazing doughnuts. He smiled at her and she smiled back. She thought that some people smiled when they were angry, and his was that kind of smile. The more he smiled, the more angry she thought he must be. He was a decent employee. She knew that Juan was too lazy to look for another job. He didn't have the courage to steal, and after she scolded him, her words made a mark. If you wanted to make eye contact with him, you had to go around and face him directly. He was not a stupid boy. His girl was carrying a child that was not necessarily his, and Mona knew he might suspect it.

At twilight Albert didn't come out of his house. Mona sat with a thin spool of thread, winding and unwinding. There was a knock at the door.

"Who is it?" she said.

"Albert," came the voice.

He stood under the yellow floodlight with a dead duck slung over his arm. He placed it on her stoop, leaving it as a cat would leave a rodent. It was, in a way, disgusting. He reached into his pocket, lifted Mona's hand, turned it palm up, and sprinkled seeds into it. Then he walked off.

She put the seeds in a bowl. She plucked the bird, gutted it, and chopped it into quarters. She heated the oven to three twenty-five. She placed the meat in a casserole dish with rosemary and garlic, and surrounded it with leeks, then slid it in the oven. She picked up her phone and dialed.

"Hello, Albert?"

"Yes."

"Would you come over for some duck?"

He came back to her house, wearing stained chamois pants and beaded moccasins. He was bare on top. His hair was down, out of its braids, parted in the middle. The way he was looking at her, one brow arched high, the other sunk over his heavy eyelid, made her chilly with excitement.

They ate the meal, then went to the living room. He sat on the chair, she on the couch. He said, "Thank you for dinner. It reminds me of something my mother used to make."

"You going to get sentimental on me now?" Mona said.

"It just reminds me of her, that's all. We used to live outside of Grand Junction. In the summer you can find flax and buckwheat in the meadows. The flowers are larkspur and black-eyed Susan. Man, it's a beautiful place."

"What's your line of business, Albert?"

"I work at the railroad now. In Junction I planted trees. I worked the passes, mostly, you know? Climax, Monarch, Ouray, Wolf Creek."

She patted the couch. "Would you like to sit here? It's more comfortable."

He went there, but to the opposite end.

"What kind of seeds are those, that you gave me?" Mona asked.

"Mount Pima Indian farmers called them mystical. They're amaranth. The grain's full of lysine. I'll plant a crop of it next spring." He shifted around, facing her.

"What does lysine do?" she asked.

"Well," he said, "mostly it increases responsiveness to mercurial diuretics. I've got some calabash seeds, too. Do you know that tomato?" He moved closer, within two feet of her. "Calabash is just about the ugliest tomato in the world. Big bulbous lumps. Looks like somebody's skin falling through a sock. Oh, but it makes a rich spaghetti sauce."

"So you save seeds," she said.

"They're organic," he said. "Do you grow flowers? I've got purple morning glory. I can give you pink tomato seeds, if you garden. Do you know of the Havasupai tribe? Man, they grow ancient sunflowers."

His thigh was touching hers, and she was staring at his hair, black and thick and glossy. She reached forward and took a handful of his hair, slowly drawing his face toward hers. "Why do you like to collect all those seeds?" She kissed him on the mouth.

"I got seeds resistant to insect plagues."

She ran her tongue across the front of his teeth. He began unbuttoning her blouse.

He said, "There's this thing with big companies. They're buying all the little ones. Forcing hybrids."

526

Mona closed her eyes as tightly as she could. She saw her mind one hundred horses galloping through the valley, entering the river, snorting water out of their noses, legs pumping to the other side.

Mona woke to Albert's face just inches from her own. She gave a slight shriek. He smiled and lay back on his pillow, hands clasped behind his head. She was not happy that he was still there, but she couldn't just kick him out.

She hurried into the kitchen to boil some water. He came to her, wrapping his arms around her waist, his left temple against her right one. She remained stiff. He let go of her, turned, and went back into the bedroom. In a few minutes he came out wearing his pants and moccasins. Then he left.

She did not watch him ride that morning. She sat on the couch and read a little of yesterday's paper. In the stillness around her she could hear the clock, and she looked up at it. The black arms of the clock looked like heavy clubs, the big hand edging forward. So, she had taken from him. What was a little of that to Albert? Albert was like a sunflower whose seeds went away and grew in again.

She took a bath and toweled off, wiping between her legs. She wiped quickly there. How many times had she been with a man, taken a bath, and wiped herself there? She'd been with so many men. She sat down on the toilet seat and stared ahead, adding things up, realizing that her inability to get pregnant was not any man's fault. The sun came in her bathroom window and made rulers of light across her arms and legs.

That evening when Mona got home from work, there was a bouquet of sage, bluebells, and pink twinflowers on her doorstep. They were arranged in a milk carton filled with water. "I can't have this," she muttered, taking them inside. She would have to tell him to stop bringing gifts. She regretted getting to know someone who was so damn sensitive.

Just after supper there came a knock on the door. When she opened it, Grace tumbled into her arms. "Juan's mother is coming to live with us, and his two brothers and sister. We got the letter yesterday."

"You'll have built-in baby sitters," Mona said brightly.

Grace sniffled. "But I don't know for sure, you know. Maybe it was John Braddock who—maybe the baby's going to come out looking like him, too."

"Babies come out looking like pug dogs at first," Mona said.

"There was just Juan and me, and now, with the baby, there'll be seven in that trailer. I wish we could send his family to Guadalajara, where Juan's aunt lives. I wish we could send them there and help them out till they got jobs. Then they wouldn't have to come here at all. Do you know, Juan already got them jobs here at Montoya's poultry farm."

They went to the kitchen table, where Mona laid out a box of cookies and poured some juice. "You're a bright girl, Grace," Mona said. "You've got a good life ahead of you. Why, I like to think you'll get your GED, maybe even go on to college. But how are you going to do all that with a little one? Babies are expensive. Have a cookie, dear."

"We'll manage," Grace said, frowning, crossing her arms over her chest. Mona at once realized she had moved too fast. But she also took pride in the way she could turn these kinds of conversations around.

"Naturally, you'll manage. I'm just saying, there are so many factors here."

Grace looked stumped. "Factors like what?"

Mona got a piece of paper and drew a vertical line through the middle. She said, "You've got a baby here." She wrote "baby" on top of the left column. "That's the positive aspect. On the right, you've got a list of negatives. Money, sitters. Although Juan's mother and siblings would possibly sit. You've got your own time to think of. Newborns don't sleep all night. That's a fallacy." She wrote quickly. "And where will the baby sleep when all those relatives arrive on your doorstep?"

"In our room, of course. It's a baby," Grace said. "A baby."

"Did you know that there are adoption agencies that might even pay the hospital bills?"

"My baby, with another family?" She sat there, her hands spread upon her stomach. "Oh, I couldn't."

"I wonder what might happen if Juan or John Braddock's wife found out about this?"

Grace stopped chewing her cookie, then seemed to swallow it whole. "We don't know *for sure* if it's John's or Juan's yet." She eyed Mona. "And besides, how would they find out?"

"I know Braddock's wife. She's a kind woman. A Christian woman. Maybe you're in love with Braddock?"

"I certainly am not," Grace said, looking down. "I'm only in love with Juan. John Braddock was a mistake."

A knock came on the door. Mona opened it and Albert stood there, his hair falling loosely around his shoulders. He peered past Mona.

"Albert, this is Grace," Mona said.

The said hello to one another. Mona did not invite him in and she did not thank him for the flowers.

"Hey. How you doing? I made a bean casserole," he said. "Would you like to come over later?"

"We're way busy over here," Mona said. "Sorry."

He backed away from the door, then turned and walked off. She shook her head. "Strange," she muttered.

Mona went to the kitchen to boil a pot of water for tea. When she came back to the table, tears were falling down Grace's cheeks. Grace made no sound except that every once in a while she caught her breath.

"Oh, dear." Mona patted her on the hand. "I could loan you the money to help Juan's family in Guadalajara, until they find jobs. You could pay me back a little at a time."

"Would you?" Grace said.

At work, Mona heard Grace's patent leather shoes clicking across the floor. Grace came to where Mona was kneeling, in front of an open Wurlitzer juke box. "I called Randy at the hardware store like you asked, and he called his friend in Rock Springs. They're coming out next week to fix the juke box, and I hate to tell you what the minimum is."

"That's okay," Mona said. "We need to get it working. The customers depend on it." She closed the door, then stood and faced Grace, whose eyes were green as peas in the light, and unsteady.

There was only one customer in the shop. Mona had thought so many times how the place could quiet down when suddenly a whole slew would walk in, and how all life seemed rhythmic like this.

"Mona, I talked with Juan last night after I got home from your place. About your maybe loaning us a little money. You could take some out of our paychecks every week."

Mona cocked her head and stroked her chin. "The thing is," she said. "Oh, I feel so bad. I didn't think of it last night, but I've got to buy a new roof for my house before winter. I'm sorry."

"I see," Grace said.

"Eventually Juan's family will get their own place. For a while, though, whew, you're going to have one crowded house."

Grace's shoulders sagged, and she sighed. She looked to have a kind of misery that she had never before felt. She made a choking sound and Mona handed her a napkin.

Grace blew her nose and clutched the napkin, her knuckles white. "What if—oh."

"There are such things as consolidation loans," Mona said. "Do you know about those?"

"But what if—I know I couldn't possibly—" She looked up at Mona, her eyes red and full of tears. "Could you—"

Then there was a moment of silence, of feigned ignorance, as if Mona couldn't quite understand what Grace was about to ask; then, the sudden realization. "Oh, I don't know," Mona said imperiously. "I don't know."

"The baby could have a good life with you," Grace said.

"Well, now, that gets a little sticky. Lawyers. Adoption papers. Of course, I'd pay for all that, but have you thought about giving up your baby? How would Juan feel about this?"

She said, "Mona, would you want my baby?"

Mona went to the gas station to fill her tank. Albert pulled up and got out. He eyed Mona. He lifted the pump and said hello. She nodded and looked at the ground to avoid his eyes, then paid for her gas and left. She saw him in her rearview mirror, staring after her, his face lost and miserable, and she shivered.

She ate in town, then headed back to her house. The sun was going down to the right of her, swollen and red and ruddy. It hung in a pouch of clouds as if it might burn a hole through, and fell toward earth.

A half mile out of town, she heard something like a shot and called out, "Oh," felt her heart skip, and whirled around to see where the shot had come from. Her rear tire was thumping. She pulled over to the side of the road, got out, wiped her brow. She took the jack, the jack handle, and the spare out of the trunk. It was very quiet. Behind her and to the sides of her were only brown dirt and sage. She quickly changed the tire.

Dust rolled in the distance, and she could see Albert's truck coming up the road. She knew he would stop. He pulled alongside her and got out of the truck, grinning. She held the jack handle in front of her, close to her body.

He raised his hand and she raised the jack handle. He took it from her and threw it into the dirt. Her arm was in the same raised position when he got back into his truck. He put the truck in first, and quickly into second, blowing a cloud of dust into her face and onto her clothing.

She got into her car and drove on, glancing in her side mirror, thinking he could have doubled back; but instead saw herself, tired, and the words: *objects in mirror are closer than they appear.* She tried to shake Albert's image and thought of Grace, that Grace never knew the consequences of her actions and how they might affect her. Mona thought how she herself planned the store's coffee deliveries and the oil changes in her car. She thought of how she charted her cycles.

She passed the cemetery where her family was buried. She and her sister, Lucy, used to have races there. They used to sit, their backs against the headstones, writing diary entries. They read them aloud, laughing, or being frightened, or repulsed. If her sister hadn't died in the fire, Mona might have confided in her: I'm forty. I can't make my own baby.

She turned around and drove into the cemetery. She went to her family's headstones, barely able to read them in the waning light. A moon rose, but it was only half, and it was white and full of gloom. She lay down in the grass and looked south in the direction of her house. She closed her eyes and saw a horse dance across the sky, its hooves like quartz, the tail a trailing cloud, eyes bright northern stars.

She opened her eyes. In the distance she saw smoke. She saw it rise into the sky and cover the moon. She jumped up, tripped, and ran to the car.

But when she got home, her house was quiet, standing, the same as it had been that morning. She stood shaking outside her door, listening, breathing quickly, then holding her breath. She listened for crickets but could hear nothing.

Nominated by The Laurel Review

THE BRIDGE

fiction by DANIEL OROZCO

from STORY

I<small>T WAS TRADITION</small> on the bridge for each member of the paint crew to get a nickname. It was tradition that the name be pulled out of the air, and not really mean anything. It was just what you go by at work. But Baby's name was different. Baby's name was a special case.

Union Hall had sent him up when W. C. retired last summer. Although he'd been working high steel for a few years, Baby was young, about twenty-five, but looked younger. He was long and skinny, with wide hands that dangled by thin wrists from his too-short sleeves. He had a buzz-top haircut that made his ears stick out. His face got blotchy and pink in the sun. He was the youngest in Bulldog's crew by twenty years. His first day, when Bulldog brought him to the crew shack inside the south tower and introduced him around, you could see this boy sizing up the old-timers, calculating the age difference in his head and grinning about it. He tossed his gear into W. C.'s old locker and flopped on the bench next to it. He pulled out a Walkman and started fiddling with the earphones. And while the crew was getting down to first things first, discussing a nickname for him, he let out a phlegmy little snort and muttered, Well geez, just don't call me Kid. Then he turned on his Walkman, opened his mouth, and shut his eyes. Bulldog and the crew regarded him for a moment, this skinny, open-mouthed boy stretched out on W. C.'s bench, his big booted feet bouncing fitfully to the tinny scratching of music coming from his ears. The painters then returned to the matter at hand. They would not call him Kid. They would not call him Sonny or Junior, either. They would go one better. And with little discussion, they decided to veer from tradition just this once. And Baby's name was born.

Being new to bridge painting, Baby is still getting the hang of things, with his partner Whale telling him to check his harness, to yank on it at least a hundred times a day to make sure it's fast; to check that his boots are laced up because there's no tripping allowed, not up here, the first step is a killer; and to always attach his safety line, to clip it onto *any*thing and *every*thing. Baby listens, but under duress, rolling his eyes and muttering, Yeah, yeah, yeah, I got it, I got it, which sets Whale off. But Bulldog and the rest of them tell him to take it easy. They are old hands at this, they remind him. They are cautious and patient men, and Baby's just young, that's all. He'll learn to slow down, as each of them learned; he'll learn to get used to the steady and deliberate pace of their work, what Bulldog calls the Art of Painting a Bridge: degreasing a section of steel first; sandblasting and inspecting for corrosion; and after the iron crew's done replacing the corroded plates or rivets or whatever, blasting again; sealing the steel with primer one, and primer two the next day; then top coat one the day after that, and top coat two the day after that.

Whale doesn't like working with Baby, but he's partnered with him. So the two of them are under the roadbed, up inside the latticework. They go from the joists down, moving east-west along a row of crossbeams on the San Francisco side of the south tower. Whale is blasting rust out of a tight spot behind a tie brace, and Baby moves in to spray primer one, when suddenly his paint gun sputters and dies. He yanks off his noise helmet, shouts at Whale over the wind, and unclips his safety line to go look for the kink in his paint hose. Pissed off, Whale yells, Goddamnit, but it's muffled under his helmet. Baby clunks down the platform in his big spattered boots. His line trails behind him, the steel carabiner clip skittering along the platform grating.

He spots the trouble right away, at the east end, just over his head—a section of hose hung up between the power line and scaffold cable. He reaches up, stands on his toes, and leans out a little, his hips high against the railing. He grasps the hose, snaps it once, twice, three times until it clears. And just as he's turning around to give Whale the thumbs-up, a woman appears before him, inches from his face. She passes into and out of his view in less than two seconds. But in Baby's memory, she would be a woman floating, suspended in the flat light and the gray swirling mist.

The witnesses said she dived off the bridge headfirst. They said she was walking along when she suddenly dropped her book bag and scrambled onto the guardrail, balancing on the top rail for a moment, arms over her head, then bouncing once from bended knees and disappearing over the side. It happened so fast, according to one witness. It was a perfect five, according to another.

But her trajectory was poor. Too close to the bridge, her foot smashed against a beam, spinning her around and pointing her feet and legs downward. She was looking at Baby as she went past him, apparently just as surprised to see him as he was to see her. She was looking into his face, into his eyes, her arms upstretched, drawing him to her as she dropped away.

And wondering how you decide to remember what you remember, wondering why you retain the memory of one detail and not another, Baby would remember, running those two seconds over and over in his head, her hands reaching toward him, fingers splayed, and her left hand balling into a fist just before the fog swallowed her. He would remember a thick, dark green pullover sweater, and the rush of her fall bunching the green under her breasts, revealing a thin pale waist, and a fluttering white shirttail. He would remember bleached blue jeans with rips flapping at both knees, and basketball shoes—those red hightops that kids wear—and the redness of them arcing around, her legs and torso following as she twisted at the hips and straightened out, knifing into the bed of fog below. But what he could not remember was her face. Although he got a good look at her—at one point just about nose to nose, no more than six inches away—it was not a clear sustained image of her face that stayed with him, but a flashing one, shutter-clicking on and off, on and off in his head. He could not remember a single detail. Her eyes locked with his as she went past and down, and Baby could not—for the life of him, and however hard he tried—remember what color they were.

But he would remember hearing, in spite of the wind whistling in his ears, in spite of the roar of traffic, the locomotive clatter of tires over the expansion gaps in the roadbed above, in spite of the hysterical thunking of the air compressor in the machine shed directly over him—Baby would remember hearing, as she went past, a tiny sound, an *oof* or an *oops*, probably her reaction to her ankle shattering against the beam above less than a second before. It was a small muted grunt, a sound of minor exertion, of a small effort completed, the kind of sound that Baby had associated—before today—with plopping a heavy bag of groceries on the kitchen table, or getting up, woozy, after having squatted on his knees to zip up his boy's jacket.

Whale drops his gun and goes clomping down the platform after Baby, who stands frozen, leaning out and staring down, saying, Man oh man, man oh man oh man. He gets to Baby just as his knees buckle, and hooks his safety line first thing. He pulls him to his feet, pries his gloved fingers from around the railing, and walks him to the other end of the platform. He hangs on to Baby as he reels the scaffold back under the tower, too fast. The wet cables slip and squeal through their pulleys, and the platform travels in jolts and shudders until it slams finally into the deck with a reassuring clang. He unhooks their safety lines—Baby's first, then his own—and reaches out to clip them onto the ladder. He grabs a fistful of Baby's harness and eases him—limp and obedient—over the eighteen-inch gap between the scaffold gate and the ladder platform. He puts Baby's hands on the first rung. They brace themselves as they swing out; the gusts are always meaner on the west side of the bridge. The shifting winds grab at their parkas and yank at their safety lines, the yellow cords billowing out in twin arcs, then whipping at their backs and legs. They go one rung at a time, turtling up the ladder in an intimate embrace—Whale on top of Baby, belly to back, his mouth warm in Baby's ear, whispering, Nice and easy, Baby, over and over. That's it, Baby, nice and easy, nice and easy. Halfway up, they can hear the Coast Guard cutter below them, its engines revving and churning as it goes past, following the current out to sea.

They knock off a little early. In the parking lot, Baby leans against his car, smoking another cigarette, telling Whale and Bulldog and Gomer that he's okay, that he'll be driving home in a minute, just let him finish his cigarette, all right? Whale looks over at Gomer, then takes Baby's car keys and drives him home. Gomer follows in his car and gives Whale a ride back to the lot.

Suiting up in the crew shack the next morning, they ask him how he's doing, did he get any sleep, and he says, Yeah, he's okay. So they take this time, before morning shift starts, to talk about it a little bit, all of them needing to talk it out for a few minutes, each of them having encountered jumpers, with C.B. seeing two in one day once—just an hour apart—from his bosun's platform halfway up the north tower, first one speck, then another, going over the side and into the water, and C.B. not being able to do anything about it. And Whale taking hours to talk one out of it once, and her calling him a week later to thank him, then jumping a week after that. And Bulldog having rescued four different jumpers from up on the pedestrian walkway, but also losing three up there, one of them an old guy who stood shivering on the five-inch-wide ledge just outside the rail and seven feet below the walkway, shivering there all morning in his bathrobe and slippers, looking like he'd taken a wrong turn on a midnight run to the toilet; and after standing there thinking about it, changing his mind, and reaching through the guardrail for Bulldog's outstretched arm, brushing the tips of Bulldog's fingers before losing his footing.

But that's how it goes, Bulldog says, and he slaps his thighs and tells everybody to get a move on, it's time to paint a bridge.

At lunch, Baby is looking through the paper. He tells Gomer and C.B. and the rest of them how he hates the way they keep numbering jumpers. She was the 975th, and he wished they'd stop doing that. And when they're reeling in the scaffold for afternoon break, he turns to Whale and tells him—without Whale's asking—the worst thing about it was that he was the last person, the last living human being she saw before she died, and he couldn't even remember what she looked like, and he didn't need that, he really didn't.

And that's when Baby loses his noise helmet. It slips out from the crook of his arm, hits the scaffold railing, and lobs over the side. It being a clear day, they both follow the helmet all the way down, not saying anything, just leaning out and watching it, squinting their eyes from the sun reflecting off the surface of the bay, and hearing it fall, the cowl fluttering and snapping behind the headpiece, until the helmet hits with a loud sharp crack, like a gunshot. Not the sound of something hitting water at all.

At break, Baby's pretty upset. But Bulldog tells him not to sweat it, the first helmet's free. Yeah, Red says, but after that it costs you, and Red should know, having lost three helmets in his nineteen years. But Baby can't shut up about it. He goes on about the sound it made when it hit the water, about how amazing it is that from 220 feet up you can single out one fucking sound. He's worked up now. His voice is cracking, his face is redder than usual. They all look at him, then at each other, and Bulldog sits him down while the rest of them go out to work. Baby tells him he's sorry about the fucking helmet, he really is, and that it won't happen again. And that's when Bulldog tells him to go on home. Go home, he says, and kiss your wife. Take the rest of the day, Bulldog says, I'll clear it with the bridge captain, no sweat.

Everybody's suiting up for morning shift. It's a cold one today, with the only heat coming from the work lights strung across a low beam overhead. They climb quickly into long johns and wool shirts and sweaters and parkas. They drink their coffee, fingers of steam rising from open thermoses, curling up past the lights. They wolf down donuts that Red brought. Whale is picking through the box looking for an old-fashioned glaze, and C.B. is complaining to Red why he never gets those frosted sprinkled ones anymore, when Baby, who hasn't said a word since coming back, asks nobody in particular if he could maybe get a new nickname.

The painters all look at each other. Tradition says you don't change the nickname of a painter on the bridge. You just never do that. But on the other hand, it seems important to the boy. And sometimes you have to accommodate the members of your crew, because that's what keeps a paint crew together. They watch him sitting there, concentrating on relacing his boots, tying and untying them, saying, It's no big deal, really, it's just that I never liked the name you gave me, and I was just wondering.

So they take a few minutes before the morning shift to weigh this decision. Whale chews slowly on the last old-fashioned glaze. Bulldog pours himself another half-cup, and C.B. and Red both sit hunched over, coiling and uncoiling safety line. Gomer tips his chair back, dances it on its hind legs, and stares up past the work lights. The boy clears his throat, but Bulldog reaches out, touches his knee with two fingers, shakes his head. The boy falls silent. He looks over at Gomer rocking his chair with his head thrown back. He follows his gaze. Squinting past the lights, peering up into the dark, he listens to the gusts outside whistling through the tower above them.

Nominated by Michael Bendzela

THE NEWS

by RUTH STONE

from *SIMPLICITY* (PARIS PRESS)

What have you to say to that
contorted gunned-down pile of rags
in a road; possibly nameless
even to the one who throws it
on a cart and pushes it away.

The discarded *New York Times*
is wrapped around your garbage,
a now wet, on-the-scene still
from someone's news camera,
stained with scraps from your kitchen.

And whose illusion that woman running
with a child? Already struck,
the machine gun crossing the line
of her body yet she does not fall
although she is already dead—

her history written backward—
There is no time to weep
for her. This was once the snot of semen,
the dim blue globe of the egg
moving through the fallopian tube.
That single body casting itself into the future.

Nominated by Jane Cooper, Sharon Olds, Michael Waters

NOTE FOLDED THIRTEEN WAYS

by RICHARD GARCIA

from THE GREENSBORO REVIEW

When you speak to me I feel blood sliding
beneath my skin, and I remember my father.
I see him behind your eyes, as if I stared
into the past through the wrong end of a telescope.
He used to take me to cowboy bars and pass me off
as his girlfriend. I remember Old Spice aftershave,
Hank Williams's "I'm So Lonesome I Could Die," the two
of us slowly turning to that sad, ghostly waltz,
his smiling down at me, the envious glances of strangers.
Later, walking along a tree-lined street in the dark,
I would hold on to his left arm and let my right breast
brush against it with every other step
in a kind of marching rhythm. I wanted him all to myself.
Is that why I once snipped off my sister's braid while she slept?
Why, when he went away, I would take his letters to mother
from the mailbox and hide them under my mattress?
He used to call me his Little Femme Fatale, his Lady in Red.
"What I like best about you," he'd say to me,
"is that you're like me, capable of betrayal."
I used to fantasize we were sidekicks driving
across the country robbing banks in small towns,
that I would walk into a jail where he was being held,
me all innocent in a gingham dress, Mary-Jane shoes,

white stockings, pull a pistol out of a picnic basket
and set him free. I wrote *I always desire my teachers*
on a scrap of paper and slipped it into your notebook.
You will never know who wrote it. Even if you took me
in your arms you would not know because I would disappear,
lifted, completely taken up, enclosed into something large,
warm and feathery. I would be a country road that stretches
into the distance. You would be a dark cloud arched
over a white horizon, ragged at the edges, raining
streaks of black rain that never touch the ground.

Nominated by Alberto Rios, and The Greensboro Review

LOVE SONGS FOR THE SS

by MICHAEL KANIECKI

from THE KENYON REVIEW

I GO TO POLISH coffee shops alone, to be alone. Christine. Elka. Lillian. Jolanta. Only the ones with women's names will do. Screw Bruno and Leshko. Like my father and his father before me, I need a strong woman to protect me. To sit at her table and pout like a little boy.

At my father's mother's table I learned how to spell *Kanyetski* or *Kanicki* or *Kanecki;* that it means *horses* or *peacock* or *necessity;* that nothing in the world is black *or* white; and that I was Polish first and American second, that my real country is Polonia, an invisible country that went all over the world during the diaspora of the partitions and the emigrations and the deportations. I am the Polish border. It goes wherever I go and we were in this country now, hoping the United States would bomb Russia and we could all go home. My father and his brother had been in the American army during the war in the hope the United States would bomb Germany and we could all go home. Until World War II we were like most immigrants: we were here to make a lot of money, learn a few tricks, and then we could all go home.

Buszia Kaniecka taught me that we live with our dead.

I go to coffee shops so I won't have to talk and I won't have to listen. I sit by myself like my father sat in his mailman uniform. I drink one cup. Two cups. Three. I sit and smoke and get steamed up at everyone who isn't there, and especially at everyone who is.

I go there to have no name. To be Kaniecki. To see the stoney faces and hear the language I never understood, the language that sounds like dogs chewing chirping birds, even though I could say all the words. I go alone to feel at home, where the waitresses look at me like

541

I don't belong, where one time I told one about my favorite polka song and she said, "That is not really Polish."

I'm a fucking joke to these people. My dad's name was Staś, my cat is Zosia, and long ago I could pray. I didn't know what I was saying, but it was more beautiful that way. I understood the secrets of the secret language because I could see into the hearts of the speakers.

The waitresses all move away. They know I know them better than they thought any foreigner in this city could. They close their collars and move away saying, "That is not really Polish," and I say, "Oh, yes. This is."

I was sitting in one of the female coffee shops—evoking memories of my home with chicken soup, trading hateful love glances with the staff, listening with disgust to the high-pitched voices of the men—looking with embarrassment at all their hairlines just like mine. They were waiting for the napkin salesman.

The obviously non-Polish napkin salesman came in.

"What's the matter what's the matter!" two sentences at once.

The main Polish guy started very deliberately: "Two cartons, I don't understand . . ."

"One sentence at a time!" The salesman bit each word and spit it on the counter in front of the Polak. "One sentence at a time."

I cringed. The Polish guy stammered. I had seen this before. Polish people talking to non-Polish people. Always stammering, always feeling stupid, always thinking the other might be right, that he was smarter, that he probably *was* right—the eyes narrowing as the mouth opens . . . the brain . . . freezing, the jaw . . . locks. The instant the Pole's jaw locks he is lost. He comes from a people who have learned to shut up to stay alive.

A minute later it's over. The Polak is beaten, looking down at the counter, nodding, and the salesman is shrugging and smiling, magnanimous in victory, and is out the door.

This, I imagine, is how the Auschwitz convent deal was negotiated: the deal made in the mid-'80s to remove the convent, the one that reads like a confession of complicity in the atrocities and admits that our presence anywhere is an insult, even if it's where we died too.

The Polaks not only don't get the napkins, they agree to pay twice.

But I know these people. They don't intend to pay. They freeze like rabbits when the gun is trained on them, but once the priest or soldier or salesman goes, the terror leaves, the brain unlocks and begins to turn.

The Polak sits alone to be alone, where he won't have to speak or be spoken to and agree to anything stupid; hating everyone who isn't there, and especially everyone who is.

*

Me and my dad would take long drives, or else wait for everyone to fall asleep and we were the only survivors, watching late-night TV. We got excited when we saw Jan Murray.

"He's Polish," my dad would say. "Murray Janowski."

Of all of us, Daddy came closest to being an adult. He was the only one who'd ever gone away from Natrona, Pennsylvania, our town of European runaways, their children, and *their* children. He'd gone away once, to Europe; got shot and came back and everybody said, "See? Bad stuff happens when you leave Natrona."

We'd take long drives around the town. Angry drives around the steel mill, along the river, and into the farms. We hated rich people and distrusted the king. The world couldn't touch us in our Rambler protective bubble—only the wind with our windows down.

We'd drive past the bottle plant where Leon Czolgosz, the Polak who shot McKinley, had worked, and feel oddly proud. This was the '60s. Assassins were *in*. Oswald Schmoswald—Leon was a Natrona kid! He went to school with Buszia's brothers. Nice guy. Quiet. Not quiet enough. He should've never left Natrona.

That was the '60s. Natrona kids were coming home dead from the army. We were mad about this in the car. They shouldn't send Natrona kids away. When the engine shut off we'd get out of the car, and we'd keep our mouths shut about this.

The dead kids were my sister's friends.

My big sister, Teeta, was a local hunky high-school beauty queen. (All Slavs were called "hunkies," after Hungarians, who are not Slavs.) We opened the windows when she sprayed her hair. She'd whip out the SprayNet and we'd run like rats onto the lawn. It could even overcome the smell of cabbage cooking.

She was cool and dug Motown and English groups and made me dance while she played piano.

She hated Polaks. She said we were mean, and she chose to be Slovak like our mum. She was attracted to the elegance of the Hapsburg Court and never held it against them for handing the Slovaks over to the Hungarians so they'd have somebody to push around.

We called our Polish grandpap "Dziadzia." He'd deserted the czar's cavalry to come to America when he was sixteen and there was no Poland. He could be one mean Polak. I liked it when he yelled, but he scared hell out of Teeta. He had those kinds of eyes Polish people get when they get mad. Teeta called them "Dziadzia eyes." I liked my own looks best when I'd get "Dziadzia eyes."

Teeta works in an emergency room in Pittsburgh. She hates the drunken Polak out-of-work millworkers who beat each other up in South Side bars, who wake up and swing at her and swear while she's intubating them on the operating table.

"I like Slovaks best," she says. "And all the doctors are Jews."

My little sister, Tooie, just had a baby. My first niece or nephew. When I held her in my lap we laughed. I had seen this face before.

"Who are you?" I said. "Which one? Who did you used to be who left and now you're trying to sneak back in at children's prices? How many times has this face come to faces like ours? On Polish plains or in American houses that are too small? How many times has it been misunderstood and didn't understand?"

And the baby looked at me with "Dziadzia eyes."

*

Between 1939 and 1945 the Germans killed more than six million of thirty million people in Poland. One out of five. Half were Jews; half were Gentiles. Hitler's stated aim was the destruction of the Polish nation, a nation of mongrels in a place where Slavs, Asians, and Jews had bred like dogs with wayward Germans to produce pigs.

He stayed away from us when we had Pilsudski, benevolent socialist warrior dictator, who creamed the Russians and occupied the Corridor; protector of minorities and rival of the Church for the people's loyalty and affection. He held his family together with his Dziadzia eyes, and when they closed, his children went to bickering while the neighbors sneaked in.

The first to be killed were those who could be most quickly identified by their uniforms: soldiers, priests, aristocrats, and Jews. Next came civic leaders, artists, teachers, scientists, skilled laborers, and anyone else who could command any respect and might conceivably lead a rebellion.

The surviving mass of unskilled peasants and factory workers was forbidden to attend schools and was to be kept alive only as long as it

544

was needed to work in German war industries. Deprived of a "digni-fied" death, these Poles were left the life of humiliation and fear left to animals on a farm the butcher has visited.

The SS was the elite Nazi corps which included the Gestapo and the most fanatical fighting units. Their job was to institute Aryan racial policy while demonstrating its utter logic. They asked no mercy and they gave none, whether they were parachuting onto Allied tanks or grabbing babies by the ankles to swing against a wall. They enjoyed the Joy Division. They ran the camps. They wore all black with skull and crossbones on their caps and lightning bolt SS rune on their collars. In Poland they were the law. They followed the army, carrying out their executions in its wake.

When I was little, I made up one prayer, and I said it every night be-fore I went to sleep. I begged on my knees: "Lord, protect me from seeing and hearing things I don't want to see or hear." I still say this from time to time. Unfortunately, it doesn't cover feeling or smelling.

What was Jesus's ethnic group? In history he's a Jew. In paintings he's Italian. In the movies a Swede. Jesus is like us all. He's every bigot's dream and nightmare.

All Catholics are anti-Semitic. It's part of the deal. We learn it in the church and in the school next to the church. It's inherent to the Chris-tian movement—*we* are the chosen people now; they blew it by mur-dering Jesus. The best you can do is feel sorry for them. When you teach this to peasants who are regularly beaten and burned for not be-lieving, they tend to believe you, particularly when you forbid them to live among Jews and gain experience which might contradict what you scream at them from the pulpit.

*

My young Buszia took a job as maid to a Jewish family in Sierpć. They had something she had never heard of: a toilet inside the house. They gave her a room next to it.

One night they had a party for their friends. My grandmother lay awake in the dark, unable to sleep, listening to them. One by one, it seemed, she'd hear their footsteps in the hall come to her door, and stop. They would turn the knob, open the door, look in at her, quietly close the door, and leave.

After many instances of this, she started shaking under her skin. She lay completely still, trying to quell the riot happening inside her, but remembering stories she had heard. She started to sweat. Hard. Like a fever.

Again—footsteps . . . turn the knob . . . the door OPENED!

"Please!" She sat up. "Please don't *eat* me!" and she started to cry.

Her employers and other guests ran to her, curled and rocking in her bed. They asked her what was wrong.

"I know you want to eat me!" she sobbed.

They knew what she meant, but let her explain.

She had taken the job because they looked like nice people. Even if the stories were true about *some* Jews, they certainly could not be true about *them*. Or so she had thought until tonight, when each of the guests, it seemed, was being sent down the hall for a peek at the feast animal. What else could explain the ritual?

"They were looking for bathroom!"

My grandmother laughed when she told me this. She laughed so hard that she made no sound. Her eyes watered. A spasm rose from deep inside . . . it paralyzed her face and neck into the pantomime of a scream. It was hilarious.

She shook her head, shaking off the laugh. She flinched and got serious. She looked embarrassed and I looked away.

"People are stupid," she said. "They believe what you tell them."

She added, "Always work for Jews. Our people don't know how not to lose a business."

I told this story to a friend. She was horrified at how stupid my Buszia could have been. I told her to think of all the stupid things she believes about people from New Jersey.

All my life I've heard Polish people talk about something to watch out for called "the Jews," but none of them has ever named a Jew they actually knew who fit this description. They would know entire extended families, find out they were as likable or not as anyone else, conclude these were not like the other Jews, the *real* Jews, the abstract Jews, who stuck together and lived somewhere else, making it hard on us.

And laughing at us.

*

As a Pole, you are taught by history and social comment that you belong to an anti-Semitic people. It is treated like a genetic defect over which you have no control and can never be cured. You are told what Poles did or did not do to Jews, but the reasons are never examined.

Of all the Nazi-occupied countries, only Poland suffered an SS civil administration and experienced frequent executions of those who harbored Jews. The Germans weren't dumb. They didn't give you the chance to be a hero. They would hold a gun to your family's heads and ask, "Where are the Jews? Where is the Home Army?" The only heroism offered was "Who do you choose to murder?" And who would pick his sister over the neighbor, even a friend?

But we don't sympathize with Polaks because we are good and strong and honest and good and highly principled and good; we have earned our illusions through inexperience.

A friend of mine asked how could I. How could I have sympathy for people whose culture and training had not prepared them to do the obviously historically right thing?

Should I have countered with "Why did Jews turn Poles over to the Russians?" and begun another pathetic round about each side's betrayals, real and perceived, that didn't start and didn't end in 1939? Over half the names on the *Yad Vashem* belong to Polaks, but my friend strives for truth and needs to blame and cannot accept the portrait of a Poland as morally gray as a *Wehrmacht* uniform.

"I'm sentimental," I said, avoiding historical explanations. "But I could hold your parakeet near scalding water and get the name of every German on the block."

Of all the nations subjected to Nazi terror, nobody else was forced to see just how weak and low they could go; how stupid and scared and panicked they'd get when the jackboots hit the hall outside the door.

Historians tell the truth that Poles weren't really afraid of having their families killed because they conducted other underground activities also punishable by death. They seldom go a step further to admit the lie that it is easier to hide a gun or radio than a human being, that a gun or radio doesn't eat or shit or cry in the night when it is disassembled and hidden beneath floorboards.

All that rotten stuff the Poles did to Jews—oh, it happened. But if you don't try to understand why, it will happen again and there's no telling who the Poles will be next time.

And don't come up with that king of Denmark crap—"And the next morning they all came out of their houses wearing yellow stars." A Dane is a German who died and went to Valhalla. Try pulling that when you're an *Untermensch* Slav pig and they'll laugh about it for weeks at the secret police station.

World War II was long ago and far away and safe to judge. No one is dying of prejudice or fear or apathy here. Feel good. Pull the covers up to your chin and ask to be protected from seeing and hearing things you don't want to see or hear. I'm the one with the guilty stain—it's my name. And dream of all the signs in Berlin that said "Support Our Troops."

*

My most secret Polish fantasy is to be in a dark room in Warsaw with my Jewish girlfriend. We kiss like two apples taking bites out of each other. The curtains are closed and the world can't see, and I tell her what pigs my people are and she tells me what pigs her people are, and we run away to be Americans.

We get to America. God the Protestant stands with perfect posture behind his wall. Something is wrong. There is the blood of Indians and Africans all over everything. The air is black. The water is yellow. The trees are coughing up blood. It's amazing how anything stays white in a place like this.

We go back to our room in Warsaw. Our German lover enters. We are confused.

*

My dad was a Polish kid named Staś who changed his name to Chuck and became an American by playing baseball. *Constantly.* He loved anybody who could play: the Bucs, the Grays, the Sons of David sliding into second with their *peyes* flying. He'd look for games all day to watch or play. Everybody came out to see Chuckie Kaniecki pitch. Scouts sent letters. So did the draft board.

He traded his baseball spikes for infantry boots. He made sergeant and rode the *Queen Mary* to England. He waded through pieces of people at Normandy. He was in the nerve-wracking room-to-room fighting in Saint-Lô and Cherbourg. He jumped off a hedgerow and was blown out of the air in midleap by a German sniper. There were holes in his chest and back. His buddies on the other side of the hedge called his name. He couldn't answer. They left.

For a day and a night he passed between his dreams and his waking nightmare as American medics passed him up, refusing to waste time or medical supplies on someone they considered a goner. He tried not to breathe too deeply. That made the blood come faster up the well of the wounds, but he needed air, and the blood was out and gone before he could stop. It burned in the holes, then got so cold. He lay like a cup, trying not to spill himself.

As he lay there, he dreamed, or relived, the night he was cut off from his squad and found a farmhouse. He found a French girl and her little brother and sister inside. Their parents were dead under a blanket. American shells had killed them in the yard. He carried them back to the yard and dug a grave for them and buried them in the dark while their children cried and prayed to themselves so Germans would not hear.

As he lay there, he dreamed, or relived, staring into Corporal Sweeney's eyes as Sweeney, his last friend, had time enough to say "Chuck" and never stopped staring back while his brains leaked out of his ears.

As he lay there, he dreamed, or relived, ordering men to run across a street so that he and the others could see where the bullets were coming from until he could not send another man again and climbed the hedge himself.

As he drifted out of sleep back to the burning in his chest and back, he heard German voices. A heavy boot kicked him. He contracted like a slug expecting to be squished. They shot him with morphine and disinfected and bandaged the big holes, wasting valuable time and supplies they needed for their own flight away from the coast. They left him in suitable condition for his own people to pick him up—this time.

A medic shook his head, "We thought you were a goner."

This act of mercy took place in the middle of a week in which my young dad had seen that men were really bags of liquid—had himself sprayed a German's head all over a wall from three feet away.

In my house we thanked those Germans for not killing Daddy, and prayed that they had made it home to pray with their own families.

*

After a lifetime of kvetching about being a Polak, it was clear what had to be done. There was no Hitler, no Stalin, no Khrushchev, no Brezhnev . . . no excuse.

Would I melt when I crossed the line? Maybe I'd forget English, be given ill-fitting clothes and told to operate a lathe where my family would pick me up in twelve hours. Maybe I'd just fall to pieces, flesh slough off my bones, to be claimed and recycled by the soil as compost, which had so far eluded it. There would have to be danger—how

549

else could it be? Maybe I was making a mistake—I was screwing with Nature and Order and . . .

I took the night train east from Berlin—the path of the machines. The buzzing kept me nervous, like saws in the woods. I heard engines above me, beside me, in front of, behind me. I had gotten in the wrong line. I had the wrong helmet on. I was afraid I'd be discovered. *Ich spreche kein Deutsch,* so I kept my mouth shut. I was traveling with the power mowers, heading for the tall grass where my family slept.

Rattling in a box from Prussia to the East had been done many times under many circumstances, but it could never have been much more than this: rattling in a box from Prussia to the East. Men played cards. There could have been rifles in the corner.

The train crossed the line at midnight, and I could not close my mouth.

I stood alone in the narrow hall at the opened window. Polish air was in my face and hair. Cold. Hard. My face and hair made sense to me now. In a long, slow dawn standing still at the opened window.

The sun opened over dark green farms. They were wet like the eyes of the farmers I imagined waking up inside the uneven houses that looked like they'd been built by people from Natrona waking up to see a Kaniecki return to Poland for the first time.

I felt jittery like a boyfriend who'd spent all night out—the hardest night in his girlfriend's life—feeling guilty and afraid of the hell I deserved to hear only to hear: "Oh. You."

Like I'd never left.

A phrase started coming into focus along with the face of Leonard Nimoy, who is from Pittsburgh. It made me smile: I had come in search of ancient Natrona.

I went on a pilgrimage from Tarnów to Częstochowa to see the Black Madonna. The first 740 inmates of Auschwitz, Polish resistance fighters, were from Tarnów. Seven thousand of us walked 160 miles in nine days through woods and fields and villages. There were no billboards or magazines—no ads sticking ideas in our heads that we didn't want there, more horses than cars, thousand-year-old historical sites unpolluted by neon signs ("St. Make-a-Buck Motel," etc.) that you know would ruin these places in America.

We slept in barns and washed in rivers and told *real* Polish jokes with shaving cream on our faces, bent over pocket mirrors in barnyards surrounded by chickens and pigshit and ducks. Poland was a playground for me—once they were sure I wasn't German.

If you are German, they will make anything difficult for you that they possibly can. They have no rooms at empty hotels. They have never heard of that street in front of their house. The cost of this item rises at the sight of you.

"Wanda," the national name, is prized for little girls because of its wondrous airy sound—"Vaahn-daah"— and because it belonged to a princess who threw herself out a castle window rather than to marry a German.

They are angry. A lot of people are missing. They set the table for them every night and every night they put the plates away unused. Patience is wearing thin.

Everywhere I went I'd meet someone whose face smiled permanently from a joke told by a Nazi rifle butt, or who'd visited Germany as a young person in striped clothes, or remembered playing a game as a child, which was all the rage in Poland for six years—waking up in the dark to run to the woods to watch and see how bright a fire your village made.

"But," they'd say, "you should've seen what they did to the Jews!"

We marched in three loose columns, saturating a network of roads along a six-mile stretch. People stood in their yards and waved like we were heroes, and gave us food. We were billeted one group of 250 per village. We leapfrogged like all infantry: rear units wake at four; by seven you are passing the lead unit, now breaking camp. That night you will be the lead unit and sleep late tomorrow.

In the evening you are greeted in the farmyard by the farmer and his wife. They bow. He heats water. You use it to shave, then to wash your feet. (Always wash your feet. Let them breathe. Keep them clean and keep them wrapped and deal with blisters, cuts and corns.) She lays out a spread on a big farm table like you've only read about. Meats and stews and breads. The tomatoes are different and better than any you have ever had. The men eat first. Boys are next. Then the girls. The women disappear, taking over houses, and live as they please, God knows how.

We gather for jokes and songs around a fire. We walked back to our sleeping bags in pitch-black, flashlights in clusters on the lane. The men sleep on the floor of the barn; the boys in the loft. The girls are in the farmhouse, where Pani keeps them out of trouble. The women do as they please.

*

I am night blind and had to be led by my friend through the trees to a pit the villagers had dug for us to defecate in. I could hear grunting in the dark around me, beyond my vision. I dropped my pants. My friend held my hands as I bent my knees and leaned backwards, out over the pit. It is strange, afterwards, how you feel toward someone you depended on to keep you from falling in.

*

(August '44: Daddy lies dying during Warsaw's rising. Both are rebuilt. If you look closely, you can see there are cracks.)

My father traded infantry boots for mailman boots and dragged his fully disabled body around a twelve-mile route five days a week for the next thirty-nine years. When I was little, he was *our* mailman.

I was usually disturbed about something or other. I would be in the yard, hear him whistling one of his songs, blocks away sometimes if it was quiet enough, and run down the alley looking between houses until I found him in his powder-blue mailman suit, and we'd finish the route together.

Sometimes the pictures from the war would come back and he would go away to mental hospitals. I was conceived during a conjugal visit to one of those hospitals. After he died, my mother said he used to cry for me that I was the way I was, always crying and finding the sadness in everything, because I was made with shock-treated sperm.

When he and Mumma had their nightly fights, it was my job to run after Daddy and jump in the car so he wouldn't drive into a tree or into the river while the other kids stayed home and hugged Mumma and brought her Kleenex.

I was comfortable in the dark, front seat saying nothing, watching his tight lips and angry eyes focus on the road in front of us. Eventually he'd talk. I'd ask questions. We'd sing songs. Stop for coffee.

During the quiet parts of the ride, the idea formed in my head from a feeling in my chest and back that *I* was the German who had saved my dad. I had never made it home to Germany. Instead, I was killed just over the hedge a moment after we'd left him. My spirit went back to him, and we waited. I got into the American ambulance and I hovered over his head until the shock-treated sperm opened the egg and I ducked in after it.

When I was little and he'd be asleep on the couch without his shirt, I'd poke my finger in where the two big chunks had been taken out and say, "I'm sorry."

He named me for a statue in the mental hospital. After Saint Michael the Archangel, patron saint of cops, but favored by soldiers over Martin of Tours, their officially appointed advocate in the court of Heaven.

My mother was seventeen and a little scared when she married the twenty-four-year-old who had gotten too skinny and didn't seem to speak as much as people said he did before the war. Ten years later there were two little kids running around the house asking where he was. She would leave them to visit him in this place.

They sat together in the chapel in the hospital in the dark near the statue of a winged man in armor driving a spear into a snake. They sat apart in the same pew, his head full of pictures, her belly full of me.

"Who's that?" he said.

"Saint Michael," she said. "The Archangel."

"If it's a boy, let's name him after *him,* so he'll be stronger than me."

Michael is a sad angel. He threw Lucifer, his best friend, out of heaven to avoid getting into trouble with the boss. He is the patron saint of collaborators and should be pictured crying and cursing God for making him learn such horrible things about himself.

Sometimes I wish the Gestapo would come and arrest me. At least then I'd know I wasn't one of them.

*

We were walking to see our queen. Mary is the crowned ruler of Poland. Do you see how brilliant this is? What a masterful political maneuver? Do you see who is left out?

When your country is threatened or it doesn't exist, you name a supernatural creature head of state—someone who can't be kidnapped, killed, or blackmailed. She was crowned in 1711 during an episode of foreign meddling, then recrowned in 1911, during the Partitions. The pilgrimages were illegal, but as long as people crowded the trails and roads to Mary's castle at Jasna Gora, like blood to the heart of their comatose country, Poland was alive. It was *the* way to tell Protestant Prussians and Orthodox Russians "fuck off!" It was the civil disobedients' expression of nationalism ("We'll *sing* them the hell out of here!") These pilgrims were proud singers. They'd just sung the Russians out of their country. Church songs were their bullets and the war stories they shared. The kids did little routines, with hand gestures and such. Adults would wink—they knew the song, and the priests were the ringleaders.

I asked Father Richard (code name: Father Cutie Pie. He could have had any man or woman in our group) if he was comfortable with the Polish priest's role as pol.

"We are not political leaders," he said.

But on the morning we marched into Częstochowa, the day we woke up earlier than usual to put on the white we'd kept till now in bags, it was Ojciec Ryszard who broke out the Polish flags and passed out red and white ribbon. I've got pictures. We were Mary's army and we went to Jasna Gora, threw ourselves on the ground in a medieval gesture of fealty, rose, and passed in review.

I have been naive to think priests simply coerced Poles into piety. They pissed us off with their better food and the way they'd disappear for an hour or two and return somehow showered while we grew grungy, hot, and skunky, but they were *so damned charming*.

In the United States we think the priesthood is a place for losers, sickos. In Poland it's a good job. Priests are treated like rock stars. Girls surround them. They are the youngest, smartest, handsomest guys. The goofy ones have wit. They are not aloof. They were our happy camp counselors for 160 miles, and on the last night we picked them up and threw them high in the air. It was strange to see them help-less—they flap and flail like any fools.

There are forty-five thousand priests in a country of thirty million. My American companion, an ex-girlfriend who was the only other one among seven thousand who spoke English (I was able to communicate in a hastily learned Tonto-like Polish. It's amazing what you can do with a few hundred words in the present tense in a country that surely produces the world's best charades players) said I should stay and be-come a priest.

I like Jesus, but I can't swing with the sky god of the Christians and Jews. Too much thinly veiled penis worship. The whole thing goes wacky almost from the start with those lines about having dominion over . . . That's why Krakow smells like it's burning and redwoods are turning into picnic tables. There are other problems, too. (When asked why I was there, I wanted to say, "I am a gay man with AIDS who has come to Poland to perform abortions." But didn't.)

In Poland priests are a strangely revolutionary yet conservative class. When the country gets invaded, they're always the first to get knocked off. They are the ones who hid the baby, kept the dream alive during the Partitions and Soviet occupation. The fighting priests of Krakow turned back the Moslem Tartars, and Father Kordecki and the Kickass Monks of Jasna Gora beat back the Protestant Swedes in a battle that swelled the nationalist tide Sobieski rolled over the Turk at Vienna.

Only Pilsudski, among the devoutly secular, ever held emotional sway with the people that rivaled the Church.

*

My mother is Slovak, so we went to the Slovak church and school. Her family and her priest, Father Gbuca, did not like the idea of her marrying a Polak.

"They tortured our people," her mother, my grandmother explained, referring to incidents one to ten centuries old. "But you daddy was good Polak" because he let us go to the Slovak church and school.

(In Eastern Europe there is one thing you can be sure of: at one time or another somebody from the next valley killed one of your relatives with an ax. Strangers are trouble, and people who travel are up to no good—*watch the chickens.*)

Grandma had run away to Vienna when she was a girl. She found a job cleaning house for Jews. Her brother followed her. He banged on the door and threatened to turn them in as kidnappers if his sister didn't leave with him. The next time she ran away, she put an ocean between her and him. She wasn't sure if he could swim. Wet footprints on the porch would scare her. In America she cleaned houses for Jews and told us always to work for Jews—they know how not to lose a business, not like us.

Slovakia, unlike Poland, enjoyed its greatest independence in the last thousand years between 1939 and 1945. Monsignor Tíso had been given the choice of forming a Slovak government or accepting German occupation. It was a chance to get back at the Czechs, who tortured our people.

Slovakia was not occupied, one of my Slovak uncles explained, because "Hitler knew the Slovaks were the smartest Slavs and could take care of themselves.

"You . . ."

(me)

555

"... are Polish."

In the Slovak church everyone sat still—spines erect, hands at their sides, listening to Father Gbuca. They filed to communion in two orderly columns.

In the Polish church people turned and laughed openly at the priest. Altar boys made faces behind his back, and at communion time people crowded up to the railing like it was an airport baggage carousel. It was easy to see which group would be more offensive to Germans.

The Kaniecki kids were the captured Polaks at the Slovak school. Like our older brother and sister before us, my little sister and I went to the school where every morning you joined your class at mass in the old language.

One winter morning Father Gbuca was telling us a new story about some Jew torturing kidnapped communion wafers—this time *with a pin*. He was just getting to the part where the blood of Christ squirts the Jew in the eye and blinds him, when somebody whispered, causing Father Gbuca to glower at the third and fourth grades.

After church the nuns made us kneel in the snow until the whisperer confessed. I was in the fourth grade; my sister was in third. There was ice on the cement. My pants were wet, but at least I was wearing pants. My sister's knees were turning colors. Her lips were turning down. I knew she was trying not to cry.

Everybody knew it was Johnny Fendak who had been the whisperer. "Turn yourself in, Fendak," kids started saying.

My sister looked at me. "Michael, I'm cold."

"Fendak did it!" I yelled. "Everybody get up! It was Fendak!"

All the children stood, rubbing their knees, and Fendak was led away.

"Good work, Kaniecki," Sister John Thomas said. "You did what was best for the group."

"Oh, shut up, you Slovak jerk," I said. "This would never happen in a public school."

Sister John Thomas's imp, Sister Placid, lunged for my hair and yanked me out of line. "This one listens to Beatles!" she screeched. "You wanna hold my hand? You wanna hold my hand?"

I was taken to a room under the church were Johnny Fendak was kneeling. There was a smell of shit coming from his pants. His face was red and his eyes wide open, shocked red and open by nuns' fists and shouts. Neither of us had expected our mornings to come to this. They made me kneel and face the other way, away from Fendak, and left us alone while they called our mothers.

"I'm not sorry, Johnny," I said. "My sister was cold. She gets sick."

During Lent the whole school went to church on Fridays to pray the stations. There is a station of the cross wherein all good Catholics assure Jesus they would not have been like the Apostles and other Jews, who abandoned him to the Romans: wherein you even say you wish you could go back in time just to prove it to him.

Every time we got to that station I would stop reciting and look at Johnny Fendak. I'd think, "Who are they kidding?"

*

At home in bed at night with my brother in the unheated attic, we would watch our breath condense in the dark and pretend we were in Pawiak Prison, where the SS made members of the Polish Resistance stand outside naked in the freezing night and in the morning would feed them alive to their dogs.

We would see the sun coming up. Hear the dogs behind the door. See the door swing open. Their stupid eyes. Their stupid teeth. Wish all the dogs in the world were dead.

I would think of a photograph I had seen of a Polish boy and girl on the gallows, staring at each other as the ropes are being placed around their necks.

There is a second photograph of them, taken a few moments later.

*

I was a special Polish baby from the day I predicted Mill Mazeroski's home run that would win the 1960 World Series for the Pittsburgh Pirates.

"Dere home run king!" I pointed at the TV from my mother's lap as Maz stepped to the plate. When he hit the ball, she threw me into the air and I flew with the ball. We made our special magic there, the baby and the ball in the air together, sailing. Over the wall and over the hedge, freeing Pittsburgh and Poland and France from the New York Yankees.

*

I was the only male in my family subjected to a newly recommended post-war health practice for Gentiles: circumcision.

"It's a Jewish thing," the doctor said. "But it's a good idea. It's easier to clean."

Hmmmm . . . Penis of the Future: streamlined, modern, *American.*

After looking down at my skinned little weenie, it was difficult to look at my father and brother standing in the shower without thinking of them as animals. They resembled large dogs.

I am the son of a local sports legend whose career was cut short by German bullets, and the brother of a Saint Joe's varsity starter. From what I saw on TV, except for Sandy Koufax, Mike Epstein, Hank Greenberg, Red Holtzman, Sid Luckman, and a string of forgotten boxers (Slapsy Maxie Rosenbloom—?), there were very few Jewish athletes, while there seemed to be no end of Slavs pounding a ball or each other.

Playing team sports is the only acceptable way to distinguish yourself when your parents are peasants who turned into factory workers. To be educated and speak up is to be like the priests and aristocrats and Jews who think we are potatoes, and you don't want to look down on your family—do you?

"Promise you'll never like Shakespeare," Mumma pleaded, naming the emblem of the effeminate elite who despised us.

"You better never change your name," my father warned.

As the worst-ever football, baseball, and basketball player whose name ended with *ski,* I concluded that athletic ability resides in the foreskin. (This did not, however, explain my high-school girlfriend, who was a champion softball pitcher and used to play catch in the yard with my dad while I served refreshments.)

During a circumcision it's typical for the baby to scream or at least to cry. Except for me. Mumma said Doctor Fetchko made a couple of paring motions, and I looked up at him, and I smiled.

In this moment I embodied a necessary aspect of the Polish character, the flip side of Dziadzia eyes: Always smile at the guy with the knife.

*

When I was little, I drew pictures in school. One day the nuns told me I was very lucky. I would have to go to art school in Pittsburgh every Saturday morning at six thirty.

Pittsburgh—city of mystery, twenty-six miles and an hour and a half away by bus along a winding two-lane stretch of Route 28.

Pittsburgh—city of . . . not only Slavs, but . . . black people, Italians, Greeks, Germans, the dreaded Irish, and—*Jews,* who were rumored to fill the schools there.

"They run those schools!" my mother said. "That's how they get ahead. How could those nuns do this to you? They'll hate you because you're a Polak!"

A sickly feeling rose in my throat. I stopped eating with any kind of verve, like a condemned boy who only tasted himself now in his food. I took walks to the hill overlooking the big black steel mill and green Allegheny River.

I imagined myself being thrown into a pit of Jewish people, who I pictured as Zero Mostels and Barbra Streisands with fangs.

Saturday came.

We were packed like cattle onto the bus. Fumes from the engine filled my head. Just as I was ready to pass out, we arrived. Black smoke poured out of Carnegie Institute—and I saw them. I recognized them from TV . . . they looked just like *Murray Janowski!* I fell immediately in love with their noses, which were bigger and sharper than my ball of Play-Doh.

I came home wearing a Herzl Zion beanie.

"Don't wear that around your grandparents," Mumma warned.

Jeez. It wasn't a picture of Martin Luther.

My progressive attitudes were a luxury the rest of my family could not afford. I was, after all, a kid: young and secure from the world of jobs and draft deferments, having my way paid by them. The '60s were no use to my older brother and sister. We didn't have enough money for them to be hippies.

But I lived the insular life of the family artist, taking my grants of food and clothing, accepting the safety they provided, and using the leisure created by their work to articulate insults of their life-styles and beliefs. It was my duty to raise them above their ignorance.

Like any artist in a repressed society, I learned to disguise my insults as love songs.

My brother was always beating me up. Once I threw my fists at him. He caught them like Wiffle balls. I could never win. But I was never mad at him. His life was hard. Everybody called him ugly. He had to beat someone. And I would never tell. He was in enough trouble. I loved him. And I would never yell. I was the little brother of the world, and all its hurts could be healed if it just took them out on me.

Some people look around my town and see an oppressive mob. I see an oppressed mob. I see a field of choking flowers, sheared into conformity by a history of peasant fear. I made up my mind to avoid the clippers. I would grow above the rest, and when I did I could see the whole sad field.

You couldn't blame big-lipped Ronnie Richociewski. He cried like a baby when he realized "Lippy" was the name he'd be stuck with for the rest of his life. After that he made fun of kids with the best of them.

I pretended our house was Poland, and I was the ghettoized Jew. While others were whipped into work gangs downstairs, I, in my room, produced Marx, Freud. I'd read my history books, come down to dinner, stare at their faces and think, "Ooooohhhhhh."

A mailman and a drive-in movie snack-bar worker could barely afford four kids. We know not to ask for things. That would only make them yell. Then feel guilty, and look worried. Some months they looked extra worried. Six people in four rooms made a seventh a curse.

Most Catholic men in my father's position, observing the ban on contraception, turn to alcohol to quell surging hormones. But my dad was obsessively sober. He *never* drank. He seethed. And because he was a singer, he knew what my love songs really were.

"You're real deliberate," he said. "One of these days somebody's going to pop you one."

Every Saturday I found myself playfully defying history by running away from my Slavic ghetto to hide among the Jews.

I would wonder to myself, "What's the big deal! We're so much alike. I eat a lot of the same foods in my grandparents' kitchens as my Jewish friends do in theirs, since neither group can claim to have invented the animals or vegetables of Eastern Europe. I hear the same defeatist ironies and self-deprecating humor designed to beat the other guy to the punch. We're both overly sentimental and self-reverential. We're both incredibly cynical and self-loathing egomaniacs. We share a history of repression—by the many of the same despots, of being forced to conduct our cultures secretly, of having no state. . . .

Maybe that's the problem. People who are told they're ugly hate the mirror. We make each other think too deeply about ourselves and that, of course, is the reason *anybody* hates anybody else.

One day a Jewish girl I liked said to me, "Did you hear about the Polish toy?"

I shook my head.

"You wind it up, and it stinks."

I withered. I lost my Herzl Zion beanie.

I went home and ate meat and thought about her. "She'll never trust me. Maybe she's right. Maybe I shouldn't trust me. Wanting to be liked *is* an ulterior motive. Maybe the only honest thing to want is to be hated."

My big sister was home from the emergency room. She knew which ones among the unconscious were Polish without seeing their names. She knew them by their smell.

"They smell like us," she said.

I quit art school.

*

Daddy, I'm beginning to worry.

Did you hear the Polish joke? I would not help my neighbor to escape while the Gestapo held a gun to my sister's head and neither would you. They're saying it was a picnic and we lit the charcoal while Hitler poked the weenies.

Everyone has seen "Shoah" and nobody talks about the children of Zamość. You say "Warsaw Rising" and nobody knows you mean the big one in '44 when the city was demolished and two hundred thousand Gentiles died.

What about the Partisans?

Nobody knows about the Home Army's executions of Poles who extorted or turned in Jews. Nobody knows what the Home Army was, and they stop reading when they get to the part that says Polish Gentiles died in the camps and on the streets just because we weren't human either.

>Pig children.
>Pig children.
>What does it take?
>When will your voices sound sweet?
>They just don't like you.
>That's the way you'll always be,
>Polish pig.
>How do you keep a Polak occupied,
>Polish pig?
>How do you break his fingers,
>Polish pig?
>How many Polaks does it take to
>. . . alliterate?
>. . . collaborate?
>Pig babies.

Every day I put a rubber pig nose on, so I remember. Whoever wears the pig nose never forgets *who* makes him wear it. But everybody still calls him "pig."

Slavs and Jews. The SS would be pleased at all the infighting over who was the bigger victim. We are mongrels obsessed with pedigree.

*

I have made nigger jokes and I have made Jew jokes and I have made Polak and chink and spic jokes, and anybody who never made or laughed at a joke with a victim is nobody I know.

It's easy to make Auschwitz jokes or use it figuratively when it's only a word or an idea. It is often used by persons trying to sound alarms— "Holocaust" this, "Death Camp" that. (As in "AIDS is the Republicans' Auschwitz.")

But the fact of it closes your mouth. Its undeniable physicality disqualifies it from figurative use. This thing is beyond suspicion of being a conspiracy. There is no submerged intent here. It sticks brazenly out of the ground. As a member of the species that concocted this, you begin to fear what shape your reflection might take in a different kind of mirror. You feel an animal breathing close to your head. You turn and chase the thought away.

The day I spent alone at Auschwitz and Birkenau was a beautiful sunny day. Tall grass weirdly swirled and whipped like pudding or meringue. Sugary smell of the woods behind the selection platform and crematoria. The breeze like babies' hands brushed across my face.

It seemed all wrong. I should be here on a cold, dark day in obvious gloom. But it hit me—it happened here every day. Days like this one, too.

Everybody had told me to take flowers. I took a song instead.

I stood in the woods and sang my song for the ghosts. I stared at the selection platform through trees, seeing people running toward me on a day like today, getting shot in the back while I sang. Falling near me, crawling toward me, past me. SS men with pistols walking up behind them. Finishing my song.

I turned to look down the sweet, quiet path where the bodies were taken to be burned, limbs dangling lazily from carts.

A blast of wind smacked my face. How dare I think they needed my little song? "Here! Go! Take *it* and all the stupid flowers, too!"

You can step inside the gas chamber if you're not scared the door will close behind you. If you can get past the clawing, screaming people tearing at each other and the door, losing fingernails to get past you because the Germans chintzed on the Zyklon-B so it took twenty minutes.

If you are prone to feeling ghosts, you will feel them here. They are not at rest and they've been up for years. They don't want you in their barracks. They remember how you blocked the door of the gas chamber. They stare at you like something to chew and spit until you get the message.

Doors and shutters slam suddenly in the wind. I jump. "I'm sorry." (I hear someone saying this over and over. I find a child hiding behind a door in my mouth.)

I photographed the special little wall of matted fibers, like a guest mattress the Germans built and stood on end to keep bullets from ricocheting or chipping the neat brick wall behind it. It opened like a futon your friend would welcome you to sleep on while you were in town a few days.

Twenty thousand Polish Resistance members were shot against this bed. It absorbed them like dreams, along with the bullets; their souls were driven in and trapped inside this fiber limbo, pinned like insects with needles of lead. Their names read like the Natrona phone book. Many of my families' names are there.

I photographed the wall from where the Germans stood. It felt wrong. Then I went to the wall and said, "I'm sorry, please . . ." and I turned and quickly photographed the last thing twenty thousand people saw on earth, shitting their pants, before a train slammed into their heads, and stepped away before they could pull me into the wall, too.

I stare at that photograph. It is haunted. It clearly shows a line of invisible Germans.

I start to choke on numbers. The numbers make us cheap, and that was the point of this place's builders. There are no numbers other than the single thing they all become.

I feel stupid for ever arguing about who died here. For trying to make sure the Polaks and these with this kind of nose and those with that color hair get a fair shake from the undertaker.

You come here, and it's big, and it asks one question about one thing that can't be bickered about. And you realize there are only two kinds of people, and hope you are the right kind.

*

563

Once the older kids had left home, gotten married, and gotten jobs and houses, and only my little sister and I were home, my parents stopped fighting so much.

Instead of riding around in the car every night, me and my dad would go straight to the coffee shop and have a cup. Two. Three. It was as comfortable as the car seat, only now we'd stare *at* each other, smiling; admiring the similarity in size and shape of our heads, and stir sugar.

All my life, people—adults—had been coming up to me telling me what a great ballplayer my dad had been, what a thrill it used to be to see him play. I knew from our earliest days of watching late-night TV that my dad had always been a movie buff. He admired actors.

One day after I had reentered art as a famous local high-school actor, I told my dad:

"You know, I always wished I could do what you did—go out in front of people and do things that made them love you."

And he told me:

"You do something I always wished I could do. You get up in front of people and make them hate you."

Nominated by Joyce Carol Oates

A DOG WAS CRYING TO-NIGHT IN WICKLOW ALSO

by SEAMUS HEANEY

from POETRY

In memory of Donatus Nwoga

When human beings found out about death
They sent the dog to Chukwu with a message:
They wanted to be let back to the house of life.
They didn't want to end up lost forever
Like burnt wood disappearing into smoke
Or ashes that get blown away to nothing.
Instead, they saw their souls in a flock at twilight
Cawing and headed back for the same old roosts
And the same bright airs and wing-stretchings each morning.
Death would be like a night spent in the wood:
At first light they'd be back in the house of life.
(The dog was meant to tell all this to Chukwu.)

But death and human beings took second place
When he trotted off the path and started barking
At another dog in broad daylight just barking
Back at him from the far bank of a river.

And that is how the toad reached Chukwu first,
The toad who'd overheard in the beginning
What the dog was meant to tell. "Human beings," he said
(And here the toad was trusted absolutely),
"Human beings want death to last forever."

Then Chukwu saw the people's souls in birds
Coming towards him like black spots off the sunset
To a place where there would be neither roosts nor trees
Nor any way back to the house of life.
And his mind reddened and darkened all at once
And nothing that the dog would tell him later
Could change that vision. Great chiefs and great loves
In obliterated light, the toad in mud,
The dog crying out all night behind the corpse house.

Nominated by David Wojahn

ONE MOMENT ON TOP OF THE EARTH

by NAOMI SHIHAB NYE

from MID-AMERICAN REVIEW

For Palestine and for Israel

In February she was dying again, so he flew across the sea to be with her. Doctors came to the village. They listened and tapped and shook their heads. She's 105, they said. What can we do? She's leaving now. This is how some act when they're leaving. She would take no food or drink in her mouth. The family swabbed her dry lips with water night and day, and the time between. Nothing else. And the rooster next door still marked each morning though everything else was changing. Her son wrote three letters saying, Surely she will die tonight. She is so weak. Sometimes she knows who I am and sometimes she calls me by the name of her dead sister. She dreams of the dead ones and shakes her head. Fahima said, Don't you want to go be with them? and she said, I don't want to have anything to do with them. You go be with them if you like. Be my guest. We don't know what is best. We sit by her side all the time because she cries if we walk away. She feels it, even with her eyes shut. Her sight is gone. Surely she will die tonight.

Then someone else who loved her got on an airplane and flew across the sea. When she heard he was landing, she said, Bring me soup. The kind that is broth with nothing in it. They lit the flame. He came and sat behind her on the bed, where she wanted him to sit, so she could lean on him and soak him up. It was cold and they huddled together, everyone in one room telling any story five times and stretching it. Laughing in places besides ones which had seemed funny before. Laughing more because they were in that time of sadness that is fluid and soft. She who had almost been gone after no eating and drinking for twenty days was even laughing. And then she took the bread that was torn into small triangles, and the pressed oil, and the soft egg. She took the tiny glass of tea between her lips. She took the match and held it, pressed its tiny sulphuric head between her fingers so she could feel the roughness. Something shifted inside her eyes, so the shapes of people's faces came alive again. Who's that? she said about a woman from another village who had entered her room very quietly with someone else. She's lovely, but who is she? I never saw her before. And they were hiding inside themselves a tenderness about someone being so close to gone and then returning.

She wanted her hair to be washed and combed. She wanted no one arguing in her room or the courtyard outside. She wanted a piece of lamb meat grilled with fat dripping crispily out of it. She wanted a blue velvet dress and a black sweater. And they could see how part of being alive was wanting things again. And they sent someone to the store in the next town which was a difficult thing since you had to pass by many soldiers. And in all these years one had never smiled at them yet.

Then the two men from across the sea had to decide what to do next, which was fly away again, as usual. They wished they could take her with them but she, who had not even entered the Holy City for so long though it was less than an hour away, said yes and no so much about going, they knew she meant no. After 105 years. You could not blame her. Even though she wasn't walking anymore, this was definitely her floor. This voice calling from the tower of the little village mosque. This rich damp smell of the stones in the walls.

So they left and I came, on the very next day. We were keeping her busy. She said to me, *Marhabtein*—Hello Twice—which is what she always says instead of just Hello and our hands locked tightly together. Her back was still covered with sores, so she did not want to lie down. She wanted to eat whatever I had with me. Pralines studded with pecans, and chocolate cake. They said, Don't give her too much of that. If it's sweet, she'll just keep eating. She wanted cola, water and tea. She wanted the juice of an orange. She said to me, So how is everybody? Tell me about all of them. And I was stumbling in the tongue again, but somehow she has always understood me. They were laughing at how badly I stumbled and they were helping me. It was the day which has no seams in it at the end of a long chain of days, the golden charm. They were coming in to welcome me, Abu Ahmad with his black cloak and his cane and his son still in Australia, and my oldest cousin Fowzi the king of smiling, and Ribhia with her flock of children, and the children's children carrying sacks of chips now, it was the first year I ever saw them carrying chips, and Sabaa whose name means morning, and my cousin's husband the teller of jokes who was put in prison for nothing like everybody else, and the ones who always came whose names I pretended to know. We were eating and drinking and telling the stories. My grandmother told of a woman who was so delicate you could see the water trickling down her throat as she drank. I had brought her two new headscarves, but of course she only wanted the one that was around my neck. And I wouldn't give it to her. There was energy in teasing. I still smelled like an airplane and we held hands the whole time except when she was picking up crumbs from her blanket or holding something else to eat.

And then it was late and time for sleep. We would sleep in a room together, my grandmother, my aunt Fahima, my cousin Janan of the rosy cheeks, a strange woman, and I. It reminded me of a slumber party. They were putting on their long nightgowns and rewrapping their heads. I asked about the strange woman and they said she came to sleep here every night. Because sometimes in such an upsetting country when you have no man to sleep in the room with you, it feels safer to have an extra woman. She had a bad cold and was sleeping on the bed next to me. I covered my head against her hundred sneezes. I covered my head as my father covered his head when he was a young man and the bombs were blowing up the houses of his friends. I thought about my father and my husband here in this same room just a few days ago and could still feel them warming the corners. I listened to the women's bedtime talking and laughing from far away, as if it were rushing water, the two sleeping on the floor, my grandmother still sitting up in her bed—Lie down, they said to her, and she said, I'm not ready—and then I remembered how at 10 o'clock the evening news comes on in English from Jordan and I asked if we could uncover the television set which had stood all day in the corner like a patient animal no one noticed. It stood there on its four thin legs, waiting.

Janan fiddled with dials, voices crisscrossing borders more easily than people cross in this part of the world, and I heard English rolling by like a raft with its rich R's and I jumped on to it. *Today,* the newscaster said, *in the ravaged West Bank* . . . , and my ear stopped. I didn't even hear what had happened in this place where I was. Because I was thinking, Today, in this room full of women. In the village on the lip of a beautiful mountain. Today, between blossoming trees and white sheets. The news couldn't see into this room of glowing coals or the ones drinking tea and fluffing pillows who are invisible. And I, who had felt the violence inside myself many times more than once, though I was brought up not to be violent, though no one was ever violent with me in any way, I could not say what it was we all still had to learn, or how we would do it together. But I could tell of a woman who almost died who by summer would be climbing the steep stairs to her roof to look out over the fields once more. Who said one moment on top of the earth is better than a thousand moments under the earth. Who kept on living, again and again. And maybe an old country with many names could be that lucky too, someday, since at least it should have as much hope as invisible women and men.

Nominated by Philip Booth, Alberto Ríos

THE GHOST OF SOUL-MAKING

by MICHAEL S. HARPER

from CRAZYHORSE

> "On that day it was decreed who shall live and who shall die"
> —Yom Kippur prayer

> "Art in its ultimate always celebrates the victory."

The ghost appears in the dark of winter,
sometimes in the light of summer, in the light
of spring, confronts you behind the half-door
in the first shock of morning,
often after-hours, with bad memories to stunt
your day, whines in twilight, whines in the umbrella of trees.

He stands outside the locked doors, rain or shine;
he constructs the stuntwork of allegiances
in the form of students, in the form of the half-measure
of blankets—he comes to parade rest in the itch of frost
on the maple, on the cherry caught in the open field
of artillery; he remembers the battlefields of the democratic
order; he marks each accent through the gates of the orchard
singing in the cadences of books—
you remember books burned, a shattering of crystals,
prayers for now, and in the afterlife, Germany of the northern
lights of Kristallnacht, the ashes of synagogues.

The ghost turns to your mother as if he believed
in penance, in wages earned, in truth places these flowers

571

you have brought with your own hands,
irises certainly, and the dalmation rose,
whose fragrance calms every hunger in religious feast or fast.
Into her hands, these blossoms, her fragrant palms.
There is no wedding ring in the life of ghosts,
no sacred asp on the wrist in imperial cool,
but there is a bowl on the reception table,
offerings of Swiss black licorice.
On good days the bowl would entice the dream
of husband, children, and grandchildren;
on good days one could build a synagogue in one's own city,
call it *city of testimony, conscious city of words*.
In this precinct male and female, the ghost commences, the ghost
    disappears.

What of the lady in the half-door of the enlightenment:
tact, and a few scarves, a small indulgence for a frugal
woman; loyalty learned in the lost records of intricate relations:
how to remember, how to forget the priceless injuries
on a steno tablet, in the tenured cabinets of the files.
At birth, and before, the ghost taught understanding:
that no history is fully a record, for the food we will eat
is never sour on the tongue, lethal, or not, as a defenseless
scapegoat, the tongue turned over, as compost is turned over,
to sainthood which makes the palate sing. These are jewels
in the service of others; this is her song. She reaps
the great reward of praise, where answers do not answer,
when the self, unleashed from the delicate bottle,
wafts over the trees at sunrise and forgives the dusk.

—For Ruth Oppenheim

Nominated by Rita Dove, David Jauss, Sharon Olds

BELOW FOURTEENTH STREET

by GERALD STERN

from COLORADO REVIEW

Somewhere above Fourteenth he pulled up his shirt sleeves
the way he learned to do in Scotland. He found
two rubber bands and two feet of yellow string
in one of the metal baskets on Sixth. He smiled
at the color combinations but he was too stricken
to worry the way he used to. After he passed
Sam Goodys he opened his shirt. For thirty blocks
he thought of the upside-down bird; once he got
the name right he would stop in one of the restaurants
above Thirty-Fourth and write for an hour before
he went back down. Two girls wearing shorts
and yellow T-shirts made their fish faces and tried
their French on him. They wished he were dead, he ruined
their morning. Up in the sterile pear tree the bird
sang her heart out. She was a chickadee,
he was sure of that, and leaped to one perch
then to another and cleaned herself and chirped
a little more since it was the end of April
and it would never snow again. He sang
himself with his lips though there was a clicking heart
behind it and under the pear tree; across the street
from Blockbuster's there was such music, there were
so many pure complaints that when he whistled

to mark the ending, and to repeat, since who
could bear an ending, there was a quickening
and slackening in the blossoms—he even thought
he and the bird were working together, he even
waved to those girls—at least a gesture—he found
the harmony for that day, whatever you think
he was able to find his notes. He hugged
his ledger to himself—he carried a ledger—
and he adjusted his tie. When he turned left
into the forest, so to speak, those shoe stores
and ugly theatres and busy rag stores, he did
the rest of the trip in silence, that way he showed
respect for the dirt, though it was two feet down,
and for the stream that crossed there, maybe the west
side of Fifth, maybe in front of Fayvas,
and took his shoes and socks off so the muck
could bring life back into his arches and give him
back what he had lost. He put his shoes on,
he put his socks in his pocket, he tilted a stone
to see a snake, at least he thought so, and raced
past the sock store—that of all things—and past
the Moroccan cafe and up the forty-seven
steps to the right hand door beside the flutist,
she who played all day and kept her cat
in a harness, all the time looking for clover—
that's what he said—and when she opened the door
he talked about the clover, there was no life
without it, clover the rabbits needed, her cat
if there were clover would roll in her harness, clover,
in maybe a month would cover the lawns, it was
the flower closest to him, after the blooming,
after the exchange, their petals turn brown
and drop, like a skirt, it is ironic that clubs
are black when clover is white, the ace of clubs
is only a flower, he has hope and he has
three leaves in his ear, he said these things, she said
she missed the country, upstate New York, the flats
of Nebraska, but he had taken one of the leaves
and put it in his mouth and turned the bolt
twice to the right and turned the light on beside

the second refrigerator and opened the window
and found some music, Dvorak in Iowa,
a town near the Mississippi, Spillville, his cuff
like Dvorak's, already full of notes, the sound
the same, the state abounding in clover, Irma
putting her head underneath his hand, the straps
twisted around a chair but she was so tired
she had to sleep and she was so trusting she had
to purr, for this is the New World and the doors
are both open the way they should be and music
from one place is mixing with music from another,
a flute with a piano, a flute with a violin,
the cellos now taking over, the horns taking over,
hope going down the stairway, despair going up,
somewhere on that plaster the two meeting,
the man in the busy cuffs, the cat in the harness.

Nominated by Christopher Buckley, Sharon Olds, Carol Snow

SPECIAL MENTION

(The editors also wish to mention the following important works published by small presses last year. Listings are in no particular order.)

POETRY

On Censorship — Rodney Jones (New Orleans Review)
My Own Little Piece of Hollywood — James Harms (Missouri Review)
Body of Life — Elizabeth Alexander (Crab Orchard Review)
The Canary — Albert Goldbarth (Quarterly West)
Excavation Photo — David Wojahn (Green Mountains Review)
Orphic Rites — Edward Hirsch (Chicago Review)
Theft — William Dickey (Georgia Review)
Hornwork: Autumn Lamentation — Stanley Kunitz (American Poetry Review)
Time Problem — Brenda Hillman (Colorado Review)
Newcomer — Robert Pinsky (Salmagundi)
Self-portrait in Two Ages — Lucia Maria Perillo (Black Warrior Review)
The Blessing of the Throats — Debora Greger (Poetry)
Lifeline — Vijay Seshadri (Paris Review)
Bernini: Bacchanal: Faun Teased by Children — Margaret Ryan (Poetry)
Woman Friend — Alan Shapiro (TriQuarterly)
The Jumping Figure — E. C. Hinsey (Missouri Review)
Skowhegan Owl — Kenneth Rosen (Ascent)
Alba: Failure — Carl Phillips (Harvard Review)
Ant World: The Leaf Cutters — Richard Foerster (North Atlantic Review)
Seven White Butterflies — Mary Oliver (Shenandoah)
Calle Visión — Adrienne Rich (Agni)

576

ESSAYS

Up-and-Down Sun: Notes on the Sacred — Reg Saner (Georgia Review)

Welcome to My Country — Lauren Slater (Missouri Review)

Don't Touch the Poet — Lyman Gilmore (North Carolina Literary Review)

Deleting Childhood — Mary Ann Lieser (Plain)

The Mutable Past — Lewis Turco (Virginia Quarterly Review)

The Aquarium Fancier — Armand Schwerner (Pequod)

Herb: A Memoir — Alvin Greenberg (Antioch Review)

Walk on Water for Me — Lorian Hemingway (*A Different Angle*, Seal Press)

Eats with Lentricchia and Ozick — Gordon Lish (Salmagundi)

Zaniness — Daniel Harris (Salmagundi)

Straw, Feathers & Dust — Marvin Bell (AWP Chronicle)

For the Love of a Princess of Mars — Frederick Busch (Threepenny Review)

Puissance — Jane Smiley (Flyway)

Cultural Literacy and the Necessity of Invention — John P. Sisk (Shenandoah)

On Rarity and Mischance — Daniel Hall (Yale Review)

A History of Flat Stones — Stanley Crawford (Doubletake)

"El Barrio Alto" — Caroline Wright (International Quarterly)

Life With Medicine — Naomi Shihab Nye (Iowa Review)

Stein is Nice — Wayne Koestenbaum (Parnassus: Poetry In Review)

Into the Unknown to Find the New: Baudelaire's Voyage into the Twenty-First Century — Sherod Santos (American Poetry Review)

The Destruction of Poetic Habitat — Biddy Jenkinson (Southern Review)

The Poetry of Life and the Life of Poetry — David Mason (Hudson Review)

FICTION

Off Route 17 — Lauren MacIntyre (Shenandoah)
The Four A.M. Dream — Po Bronson (Fourteen Hills)
Light Opera — Lee Martin (Georgia Review)
The Mexican Maid — Alan Cheuse (Antioch Review)
Baby Girl — Fred. G. Leebron (TriQuarterly)
The Surrogate — Alix Kates Shulman (Green Mountains Review)

Intensive — Joyce Carol Oates (Gettysburg Review)
A.B.C. — David Huddle (Glimmer Train)
Forever — Jean Thompson (TriQuarterly)
Refuge — Lucy Honig (Doubletake)
House Fires — Nancy Reisman (Glimmer Train)
Skin Deep — T. M. McNally (Yale Review)
Meat Cove — D. R. MacDonald (Epoch)
Old River — Glenn Blake (American Short Fiction)
Etcetera Period — Ann Knox (*Late Summer Break*, Paper Mache Press)
Casual Water — Don Lee (New England Review)
Mrs. Calder & The Porno Man — Russell Chamberlain (Boulevard)
Nails — Paul Griner (Glimmer Train)
Pot o' Gold — Tricia Bauer (*Working Women*, Bridge Works Press)
Boys, Downstairs — Amber Dorko Stopper (Northwest Review)
A Wind From the Past — Francine Julian Clark (Negative Capability)
The Off Season — Joan Wickersham (Ploughshares)
The Incredible Appearing Man — Deborah Galyan (Missouri Review)
Can You Forgive Me — Molly Giles (Witness)
Landlocked — C. E. Poverman (Santa Monica Review)
Confession — Mark Wisniewski (Gulf Coast)
Zenobia — Gina Berriault (Threepenny Review)
Los Asesions — Eric Miles Williamson (Georgia Review)
The Birds — Hilton Als (Grand Street)
Mister Marvelous and The Margarine Men — Jeffrey Merrick (American Literary Review)
Wild Indians & Other Creatures — Adrian C. Louis (TriQuarterly)
The Dinosaurs — Frances Oliver (Antioch Review)
Fundamentals — Daniel Stolar (Doubletake)
Homage — Jonathan Veit (Missouri Review)
Salsipuedes, 1994 — Janet Peery (Shenandoah)
St. Tracy — Erin McGraw (Ascent)
Laissez-Faire — Marilyn Krysl (North American Review)
Almost Barcelona — Tracy Daugherty (Gettysburg Review)
The Dreaming — Brian Swann (Beliot Fiction Review)
The Cat and the Clown — Maura Stanton (TriQuarterly)
The Consul's Wife — Ranbir Sidhu (Other Voices)
Seven — Joe Tsujimoto (Bamboo Ridge)
Ysrael — Junot Diaz (Story)
The Cathedral of Tears — Bernardine Connelly (Story)
The Rich Man's House — Jean Thompson (Ontario Review)

Two Wings of a Bird — Philip Russell (Wascana Review)

California — Robley Wilson (Iowa Review)

The Chaste Desdemona — Katie Greenbaum (Literal Latté)

His Chorus — Christine Schutt (Alaska Quarterly Review)

Consent — C. J. Hribal (Witness)

Rembrandt of Skin — Stephen D. Gibson (Quarterly West)

Easter — May-lee Chai (Missouri Review)

Negro Progress — Anthony Grooms (*Trouble No More*, LA Questa Press)

Bluestown — Geoffrey Becker (*Dangerous Men*, University of Pittsburgh Press)

A Basket Full of Wallpaper — Colum McCann (Grand Street)

CONTRIBUTORS' NOTES

KIM ADDONIZIO is the author of two books from BOA Editions and a chapbook from Pennywhistle Press. She lives in San Francisco.

MARILYN CHIN has published books with Milkweed and Greenfield Review Press. She teaches at San Diego State.

BILLY COLLINS' third book, *The Art of Drowning,* was published by the University of Pittsburgh Press in 1995.

PINCKNEY BENEDICT received the Nelson Algren Award, a James Michener Fellowship and an award from the Bread Loaf Writer's Conference. He lives in West Virginia.

LORETTA COLLINS received an MFA from the Iowa Writers' Workshop. Her poems have been featured in *Black Warrior, Quarterly West, Missouri Review* and elsewhere.

MARTHA COLLINS won the Alice Fay DiCastagnola Award for her poetry collection, *A History of Small Life on A Windy Planet* (University of Georgia, 1993).

ROBERT DANA's latest book is *Hello, Stranger* (Anhinga, 1996). He was visiting poet at Stockholm University in 1996.

TRUDY DITTMAR lives in Dubois, Wyoming. Her work has appeared in *North Dakota Quarterly, High Plains Literary Review,* and elsewhere.

ANDRE DUBUS won the 1996 Rea Short Story Award. His books include *Broken Vessels* and *Dancing After Hours.*

WENDY DUTTON's work has appeared in *Frontiers* and *Threepenny Review.* She teaches in Oakland, California.

HOPE EDELMAN is the author of *Motherless Daughters*. She has taught at the University of Iowa, Northwestern University and the Fine Arts Work Center in Provincetown.

TOM FRANK is editor of *The Baffler*. He lives in Chicago.

CAROL FROST's books are *Pure* (1994) and *Venus and Don Juan* (1996) both from TriQuarterly Books. She teaches at Hartwick College.

RICHARD GARCIA is poet-in-residence at Childrens Hospital, Los Angeles, and the author of *The Flying Garcias* (University of Pittsburgh Press, 1993).

SUZANNE GARDINIER is at work on a novel, *The Seventh Generation*. She teaches at Sarah Lawrence.

PETER GORDON's fiction has been published in *Yale Review, North American Review*, and *The New Yorker*. He is at work on a novel.

VIVIAN GORNICK is the author of *Fierce Attachments* and other books. She lives in New York City.

EAMON GRENNAN's books include *As If It Matters* and *So It Goes*, both from Graywolf.

THOM GUNN's recent books are *The Man With Night Sweats, Collected Poems*, and *Shelf Life*. He lives in San Francisco.

RACHEL HADAS teaches at Rutgers and is the author of eleven books of poetry and criticism, most recently *The Double Legacy* (Faber and Faber, 1995).

MARK HALLIDAY teaches at Ohio University. His most recent book is *Tasker Street* (1992).

MICHAEL S. HARPER teaches at Brown University and is the author of numerous poetry collections.

SEAMUS HEANEY teaches at Harvard and Oxford. He won the 1995 Nobel Prize for Literature.

RICHARD JACKSON teaches at the University of Tennessee. His most recent book is *Alive All Day* (Cleveland State). He is a past poetry co-editor of this series.

HAROLD JAFFE is the author of five fiction collections and three novels. He is editor of *Fiction International*.

HA JIN grew up in mainland China and is the author of a story collection, *Ocean of Words* (Zoland, 1996) and two poetry collections.

MICHAEL KANIECKI is a writer/performer best known for his work in theater, music and film. He has earned a fellowship from the New York Foundation for the Arts and an Academy of American Poets prize.

KARLA KUBAN's first novel, *Marchlands,* will be published by Scribner soon. She lives in Taos, New Mexico.

AUGUST KLEINZAHLER lives in San Francisco. His most recent poetry collection was published by Farrar, Straus and Giroux.

CAROLINE LANGSTON lives in Yazoo City, Mississippi. She has just finished a novel, *The End of History.*

BARRY LOPEZ's *Arctic Dreams* won the National Book Award. His essay on Wallace Stegner is just out in a fine edition from Lone Goose Press, Eugene, Oregon.

BOBBIE ANN MASON's most recent novel is *Feather Crowns* (Harper, 1993) Her "Graveyard Day" appeared in *Pushcart Prize VIII.*

ERIN MCGRAW's second fiction collection, *Lies of the Saints,* is just out from Chronicle Books. *Ascent, Laurel Review, Georgia Review, Southern Review* and *Atlantic Monthly* have published her stories.

TOM MCNEAL has been a Stegner Fellow at Stanford University. His work has appeared in *Black Warrior, Epoch* and elsewhere.

JAMES ALAN MCPHERSON is the author of two story collections: *Hue and Cry* and *Elbow Room.*

DANIEL MELTZER lives in New York City and conducted a fiction workship at Chautauqua Institution in 1996.

JAMES MERRILL died on February 6, 1995. His last book was *A Scattering of Salts* (Knopf, 1995).

W. S. MERWIN lives in Háiku, Hawaii. He last appeared here in *Pushcart Prize XIX.* Knopf will issue *Vixen* soon.

JEWEL MOGAN's first short story collection, *Beyond Telling* (Ontario Review Press, 1995), won the Texas Institute of Letters Award. She lives in Lubbock, Texas.

WILLIAM MONAHAN has edited a magazine on Long Island, lived in New York City, and is now on the road.

NAOMI SHIHAB NYE lives in San Antonio and recently edited two anthologies for young readers. She has been featured in three previous *Pushcart Prize* editions.

DANIEL OROZCO lives in Seattle. His work has appeared in *Seattle Review, Story,* and *Best American Short Stories.*

TOM PAINE lives in Vermont. His stories have been picked by *Best New Stories from the South* and the O'Henry collection.

GEORGE PACKER is the author of *The Half Man,* a novel, and *The Village of Waiting,* a memoir.

JAMES REISS is the author of *The Parable of Fire* (1996) and other books. He is editor of Miami University Press in Ohio.

J. ALLYN ROSSER teaches at Ohio University and won the 1990 Morse Poetry Prize for her book, *Bright Moves.*

KAY RYAN is the author of three poetry collections. She lives in Fairfax, California. Her *Elephant Rocks* is just out from Grove/Atlantic.

IRA SADOFF is the author of two collections from David Godine. He lives in Hallowell, Maine.

ROBERT SCHIRMER won New York University's Bobst Award for Emerging Writers. His *Living With Strangers,* a story collection, was issued by NYU Press in 1992.

KAREN HALVORSEN SCHRECK teaches at Wheaton College. Her fiction has been featured in *Other Voices, Image, Private Arts, Quarter After Eight* and elsewhere.

GRACE SCHULMAN is poetry editor of *The Nation* and the 1996 recipient of New York University's Delmore Schwartz Memorial Award. She is a past poetry co-editor of *The Pushcart Prize* with Jon Galassi.

HELEN SCHULMAN teaches at Columbia University. She is the author of *Not a Free Show,* stories, and *Out of Time,* a novel.

ALAN SHAPIRO's most recent book of poetry is *Mixed Feelings* (University of Chicago). He teaches at the University of North Carolina.

RANBIR SIDHU holds a degree in anthropology and worked for several years as an archaeologist before earning an MFA in fiction at The University of Arizona. He lives in Concord, California.

DAVE SMITH is co-editor of *The Southern Review*. His poetry collections have been published by Louisiana State University Press, Bloodaxe Books, Ecco and Morrow.

SHARON SOLWITZ's first short story collection is forthcoming from Sarabande Books. She has received three Nelson Algren Awards.

MICHAEL STEPHENS is author of the novel, *The Brooklyn Book of the Dead* (Dalkey Archive, 1994) and winner of the AWP Award in nonfiction.

DANIEL STERN's collection *Twice Told Tales* was published by Norton. His work has also been selected by the O'Henry and *Best American Short Stories* collections.

GERALD STERN is a past *Pushcart Prize* poetry co-editor, with Carolyn Forché. He has been featured in six previous editions of this collection.

STEVE STERN's books include *Isaac and the Undertaker's Daughter*, and *Lazar Malkin Enters Heaven*.

RUTH STONE won the Whiting Award, the Delmore Schwartz Award and the Shelley Memorial Award. She teaches at SUNY, and lives in Vermont.

ARTHUR SZE has published five books of poetry, most recently *Archipelago* from Copper Canyon Press. He won the 1995 Lannan Literary Award and the 1996 Before Columbus American Book Award.

RICHARD TAYSON's next book is *Look Up For Yes* (Kodansha), his first nonfiction work. His poetry has appeared in *The Paris Review, Crazyhorse* and elsewhere.

DAVID TREUER is Ojibwe from the Leech Lake Reservation in Northern Minnesota, where he currently resides. *Little* (Graywolf), is his first novel, and won the 1996 Minnesota Book Award.

ELEANOR WILNER won the Juniper Poetry Prize and is the author of four books of poetry. She teaches at Warren Wilson College.

S. L. WISENBERG's work has been published in *Tikkun, Michigan Quarterly* and elsewhere. She lives in Chicago.

CHARLES WRIGHT's *Chickamauga* was published by Farrar, Straus and Giroux (1995). He teaches at The University of Virginia.

DEAN YOUNG is the author of *Beloved Infidel* and *Strike Anywhere*.

PRESSES FEATURED IN THE PUSHCART PRIZE EDITIONS SINCE 1976

Acts
Agni Review
Ahsahta Press
Ailanthus Press
Alaska Quarterly Review
Alcheringa/Ethnopoetics
Alice James Books
Ambergris
Amelia
American Literature
American PEN
American Poetry Review
American Scholar
American Short Fiction
The American Voice
Amicus Journal
Amnesty International
Anaesthesia Review
Another Chicago Magazine
Antaeus
Antietam Review
Antioch Review
Apalachee Quarterly
Aphra
Aralia Press
The Ark

Ascensius Press
Ascent
Aspen Leaves
Aspen Poetry Anthology
Assembling
Atlanta Review
The Baffler
Bamboo Ridge
Barlenmir House
Barnwood Press
The Bellingham Review
Bellowing Ark
Beloit Poetry Journal
Bennington Review
Bilingual Review
Black American Literature Forum
Black Rooster
Black Scholar
Black Sparrow
Black Warrior Review
Blackwells Press
Bloomsbury Review
Blue Cloud Quarterly
Blue Unicorn
Blue Wind Press
Bluefish

BOA Editions
Bomb
Bookslinger Editions
Boulevard
Boxspring
Bridges
Brown Journal of Arts
Burning Deck Press
Caliban
California Quarterly
Callaloo
Calliope
Calliopea Press
Canto
Capra Press
Carolina Quarterly
Caribbean Writer
Cedar Rock
Center
Chariton Review
Charnel House
Chelsea
Chicago Review
Chouteau Review
Chowder Review
Cimarron Review
Cincinnati Poetry Review
City Lights Books
Clown War
CoEvolution Quarterly
Cold Mountain Press
Colorado Review
Columbia: A Magazine of Poetry
    and Prose
Confluence Press
Confrontation
Conjunctions
Copper Canyon Press
Cosmic Information Agency
Crawl Out Your Window
Crazyhorse
Crescent Review
Cross Cultural Communications

Cross Currents
Cumberland Poetry Review
Curbstone Press
Cutbank
Dacotah Territory
Daedalus
Dalkey Archive Press
Decatur House
December
Denver Quarterly
DoubleTake
Domestic Crude
Dragon Gate Inc.
Dreamworks
Dryad Press
Duck Down Press
Durak
East River Anthology
Ellis Press
Empty Bowl
Epoch
Ergo!
Exquisite Corpse
Faultline
Fiction
Fiction Collective
Fiction International
Field
Fine Madness
Firebrand Books
Firelands Art Review
Five Fingers Review
Five Trees Press
The Formalist
Frontiers: A Journal of Women
    Studies
Gallimaufry
Genre
The Georgia Review
Gettysburg Review
Ghost Dance
Glimmer Train
Goddard Journal

David Godine, Publisher
Graham House Press
Grand Street
Granta
Graywolf Press
Green Mountains Review
Greensboro Review
Greenfield Review
Guardian Press
Gulf Coast
Hanging Loose
Hard Pressed
Harvard Review
Hayden's Ferry Review
Hermitage Press
Hills
Holmgangers Press
Holy Cow!
Home Planet News
Hudson Review
Hungry Mind Review
Icarus
Iguana Press
Indiana Review
Indiana Writes
Intermedia
Intro
Invisible City
Inwood Press
Iowa Review
Ironwood
Jam To-day
The Journal
The Kanchenjuga Press
Kansas Quarterly
Kayak
Kelsey Street Press
Kenyon Review
Latitudes Press
Laughing Waters Press
Laurel Review
L'Epervier Press
Liberation

Linquis
Literal Latté
The Literary Review
The Little Magazine
Living Hand Press
Living Poets Press
Logbridge-Rhodes
Louisville Review
Lowlands Review
Lucille
Lynx House Press
Magic Circle Press
Malahat Review
Mānoa
Manroot
Massachusetts Review
Mho & Mho Works
Micah Publications
Michigan Quarterly
Mid-American Review
Milkweed Editions
Milkweed Quarterly
The Minnesota Review
Mississippi Review
Mississippi Valley Review
Missouri Review
Montana Gothic
Montana Review
Montemora
Moon Pony Press
Mr. Cogito Press
MSS
Mulch Press
Nada Press
New America
New American Review
The New Criterion
New Delta Review
New Directions
New England Review
New England Review and Bread
    Loaf Quarterly
New Letters

New Virginia Review
New York Quarterly
New York University Press
Nimrod
North American Review
North Atlantic Books
North Dakota Quarterly
North Point Press
Northern Lights
Northwest Review
O. ARS
O·Blēk
Obsidian
Obsidian II
Oconee Review
October
Ohio Review
Old Crow Review
Ontario Review
Open Places
Orca Press
Orchises Press
Oxford Press
Oyez Press
Painted Bride Quarterly
Painted Hills Review
Paris Press
Paris Review
Parnassus: Poetry in Review
Partisan Review
Passages North
Penca Books
Pentagram
Penumbra Press
Pequod
Persea: An International Review
Pipedream Press
Pitcairn Press
Pitt Magazine
Ploughshares
Poet and Critic
Poetry
Poetry East

Poetry Ireland Review
Poetry Northwest
Poetry Now
Prairie Schooner
Prescott Street Press
Promise of Learnings
Provincetown Arts
Puerto Del Sol
Quarry West
The Quarterly
Quarterly West
Raccoon
Rainbow Press
Raritan: A Quarterly Review
Red Cedar Review
Red Clay Books
Red Dust Press
Red Earth Press
Release Press
Review of Contemporary Fiction
Revista Chicano-Riquena
Rhetoric Review
River Styx
Rowan Tree Press
Russian *Samizdat*
Salmagundi
San Marcos Press
Sea Pen Press and Paper Mill
Seal Press
Seamark Press
Seattle Review
Second Coming Press
Semiotext(e)
Seven Days
The Seventies Press
Sewanee Review
Shankpainter
Shantih
Sheep Meadow Press
Shenandoah
A Shout In the Street
Sibyl-Child Press
Side Show

Small Moon
The Smith
Some
The Sonora Review
Southern Poetry Review
Southern Review
Southwest Review
Spectrum
The Spirit That Moves Us
St. Andrews Press
Story
Story Quarterly
Streetfare Journal
Stuart Wright, Publisher
Sulfur
The Sun
Sun & Moon Press
Sun Press
Sunstone
Sycamore Review
Tar River Poetry
Teal Press
Telephone Books
Telescope
Temblor
Tendril
Texas Slough
The MacGuffin
13th Moon
THIS
Thorp Springs Press
Three Rivers Press
Threepenny Review
Thunder City Press
Thunder's Mouth Press
Tikkun

Tombouctou Books
Toothpaste Press
Transatlantic Review
TriQuarterly
Truck Press
Undine
Unicorn Press
University of Illinois Press
University of Massachusetts Press
University of Pittsburgh Press
Unmuzzled Ox
Unspeakable Visions of the Individual
Vagabond
Vignette
Virginia Quarterly
Volt
Wampeter Press
Washington Writers Workshop
Water Table
Western Humanities Review
Westigan Review
Wickwire Press
Willow Springs
Wilmore City
Witness
Word Beat Press
Word-Smith
Wormwood Review
Writers Forum
Xanadu
Yale Review
Yardbird Reader
Yarrow
Y'Bird
ZYZZYVA

CONTRIBUTING
SMALL PRESSES

(These presses made or received nominations for this edition of *The Pushcart Prize*. See the *International Directory of Little Magazines and Small Presses,* Dustbooks, P.O. Box 100, Paradise, CA 95967, for subscription rates, manuscript requirements and a complete international listing of small presses.)

A

Agni, Boston Univ., 236 Bay State Rd., Boston, MA 02215
Ahsahta Press, English Dept., Boise State Univ., Boise, ID 83725
Alaska Quarterly Review, Univ. of Alaska, 3211 Providence Dr., Anchorage, AK 99508
Alligator Juniper, Arts & Letters Prog., Prescott College, Prescott, AZ 86301
Alpha Beat Press, 31A Waterloo St., New Hope, PA 18938
AMC Publishing, P.O. Box 64185, Tucson, AZ 86301
Amaranth, P.O. Box 184, Trumbull, CT 06611
American Fiction, P.O. Box 229, MSU, Moorhead, MN 56563
American Letters & Commentary, 850 Park Ave., Ste. 5b, New York, NY 10021
American Literary Review, Univ. of North Texas, P.O. Box 13827, Denton, TX 76203
American Poetry Review, 1721 Walnut St., Philadelphia, PA 19103
The American Scholar, 1811 Q St., NW, Washington, DC 20009
The American Voice, 332 W. Broadway, Ste. 1215, Louisville, KY 40202
The Anderson Valley Advertiser, 12451 Anderson Valley Way, Boonville, CA 95415
Angel Flesh Press, P.O. Box 141123, Grand Rapids, MI 49514
Another Chicago Magazine, 3709 N. Kenmore, Chicago, IL 60613
Anterior Bitewing, Ltd., 993 Allspice Ave., Fenton, MO 63026
Antietam Review, 7 W, Franklin St., Hagerstown, MD 21740
Antioch Review, P.O. Box 148, Yellow Springs, OH 45387
Artful Dodge, English Dept., College of Wooster, Wooster, OH 44691
Arts Indiana, 47 S. Pennsylvania, Indianapolis, IN 46204
Ascent, P.O. Box 967, Urbana, IL 61801
Asian Pacific American Journal, 37 St. Marks Pl., New York, NY 10003
Atlanta Review, P.O. Box 8248, Atlanta, GA 30306
AURA Literary/Arts Review, P.O. Box 76, University Center, Birmingham, AL 35294
Avec, P.O. Box 1059, Penngrove, CA 94951

B

The Baffler, P.O. Box 378293, Chicago, IL 60637
Ballast, 2022 X Ave., Dysart, IA 52224
Bamboo Ridge Press, P.O. Box 61781, Honolulu, HI 96839
The Basement Magazine, 39 Setalcott Pl., Setauket, NY 11733
Bearhouse Publishing, Rte. 2, Box 94, Eureka Springs, AR 72632
Belletrist Review, 17 Farmington Ave., Ste. 290, Plainville, CT 06062
Bellowing Ark, P.O. Box 45637, Seattle, WA 98145
Beloit Poetry Journal, RFD 2, Box 154, Ellsworth, ME 04605
Bilingual Press, Hispanic Research Center, Arizona State Univ., Box 872702, Tempe, AZ 85287
Black Hammock Review, 1032 W. Robinson St., Orlando, FL 32805
Black River Review, 855 Mildred Ave., Lorcra, OH 44052
Black Warrior Review, P.O. Box 2936, Tuscaloosa, AL 35486
Block Publications, 1419 Chaplin St., Beloit, WI 53511
Blue Penny Quarterly, 7 Elliewood Ave., Charlottesville, VA 22903
BOA Editions, 260 East Ave., Rochester, NY 14601
Bone & Flesh, P.O. Box 349, Concord, NH 03302
Bottomfish, DeAnza College, 21250 Stevens Creek Blvd., Cupertino, CA 95014
Boulevard, Box 30386, Philadelphia, PA 19103
Bread & Butter Press, 1150 S. Glencoe St., Denver, CO 80222
Briar Cliff Review, Briar Cliff College, 3303 Rebecca St., Sioux City, IA 51104
Bridgeworks Publishing, Bridge Lane, Box 1798, Bridgehampton, NY 11932
Broken Shadow Publications, 472 44th St., Oakland, CA 94609
Brooklyn Review, English Dept., Brooklyn College, Brooklyn, NY 11210
Buffalo Spree Magazine, P.O. Box 38, Buffalo, NY 14226
Burning Deck, 71 Elmgrove Ave., Providence, RI 02906
Button Magazine, box 26, Lunenburg, MA 01462

C

Caesure, 110 S. Market, San Jose, CA 95113
Cafe Solo, 5146 Foothill Rd. Carpenteria, CA 93103
Calyx, P.O. Box B, Corvallis, OR 97339
The Camel Press, HC 80, Box 160, Big Cove Tannery, PA 17212
The Caribbean Writer, Univ. of Virgin Islands, RR02-Box 10,000, Kingshill, St. Croix, U.S. Virgin Islands, 00850
Carolina Quarterly, Greenlaw Hall, Univ. of North Carolina, Chapel Hill, NC 27499
Cerberus Books, 381 Casa Linda Plaza, Ste. 179, Dallas, TX 75218
The Chariton Review, N.E. Missouri State Univ., Kirksville, MO 63501
Chattahoochee Review, DeKalb College, Dunwoody, GA 30338
Chelsea, Box 773, Cooper Sta., New York, NY 10276
Chicago Review, Univ. of Chicago, 5801 S. Kenwood Ave., Chicago, IL 60637
Chicory Blue Press, East St., N., Goshen, CT 06756
Chimney Hill Press, 510 Grandview Ave., Valparaiso, IN 46383
Chiron Review, 522 E. South Ave., Saint John, KS 67576
Christopher Street, P.O. Box 1475, Church St. Sta., New York, NY 10008
Cimarron Review, 205 Merrill Hall, Oklahoma State Univ., Stillwater, OK 74078
Cincinnati Poetry Review, College of Mt. St. Joseph, 5701 Della Rd., Cincinnati, OH 45233
Cinco Puntos Press, 2709 Louisville, El Paso, TX 79930
Claritas Imprints, P.O. Box 629, Brookings, SD 57006
Cleveland State Univ. Press., Poetry Center, CSU, Cleveland, OH 44115
Coffee House Press, 27 N. 4th St., Minneapolis, MN 55401
Columbia, 404 Dodge Hall, Columbia Univ., New York, NY 10027

Common Boundary, 5272 River Rd., Ste. 650, Bethesda, MD 20816
The Compendium, P.O. Box 542327, Houston, TX 77254
Confluence, Box 336, Belpre, OH 45714
Confluence Press, Inc., Lewis-Clark State College, 500 8th Ave., Lewiston, ID 83501
Confrontation, English Dept., C.W. Post of L.I.U., Brookville, NY 11548
Conjunctions, Bard College, Annandale-on-Hudson, NY 12504
Controlled Burn, 10775 N. St. Helen Rd., Roscommon, MI 48653
Coracle Poetry, 1516 Euclid Ave., Berkeley, CA 94708
Coreopsis Books, 1384 Township Dr., Lawrenceville, GA 30243
Countermeasures, Humanities Dept., College of Santa Fe, Santa Fe, NM 87505
Crab Orchard Review, English Dept., Southern Illinois Univ., Carbondale, IL 62901
Crazyhorse, English Dept., Univ. of Arkansas, Little Rock, AR 72204
Creative Nonfiction, P.O. Box 81536, Pittsburgh, PA 15217
The Crescent Review, P.O. Box 15069, Chevy Chase, MD 20825
Cripes!, 514½ E. University Ave., Lafayette, LA 70503
Cross-Cultural Communications, 239 Wynsum Ave., Merrick, NY 11566
Cups, 475 Fifth Ave., New York, NY
CutBank, English Dept., Univ. of Montana, Missoula, MT 59812

D

Damascus Works, One East Univ. Parkway, #1101, Baltimore, MD 21218
John Daniel & Co., Publishers, Inc., P.O. Box 21922, Santa Barbara, CA 93121
Daughters of NYX, P.O. Box 1100, Stevenson, WA 98648
Defined Providence, P.O. Box 16143, Rumford, RI 02916
Dog River Review, see Trout Creek Press
Double-Entendre, 3941 Legacy Dr., #204–206A, Plano, TX 75023
Doublestar Press, 1718 Sherman Ave., Ste. 205, Evanston, IL 60201
DoubleTake, 1317 W. Pettigrew St., Durham, NC 27705

E

Edge City Review, 10912 Harpers Sq. Court, Reston, VA 22091
Eighth Mountain Press, 624 S.E. 29th Ave., Portland, OR 97214
Epoch, 251 Goldwin Smith Hall, Cornell Univ., Ithaca, NY 14853
Event, P.O. Box 2503, New Westminster, B.C. U3L 5B2, CANADA
Exit 13 Magazine, P.O. Box 423, Fanwood, NJ 07023
Exquisite Corpse, P.O. Box 25051, Baton Rouge, LA 70894

F

Faultline, P.O. Box 599-5960, Univ. of California, Irvine, CA 92716
Fiction International, English Dept., San Diego State Univ., 5500 Campanile Dr., San Diego, CA 92182
Fine Madness, P.O. Box 31138, Seattle, WA 98103
Firehole Press, P.O. Box 2196, Russellville, AR 72811
Fish Stories, 5412 N. Clark, South Ste., Chicago, IL 60640
The Florida Review, English Dept., Univ. of Central Florida, Orlando, FL 32816
Flyway, Iowa State Univ., Ames, IA 50011

Footwork: The Paterson Literary Review, One College Blvd., Paterson, NJ 07505
Forkroads, Box 150, Spencertown, NY 11975
The Formalist, 320 Hunter Dr., Evansville, IN 47711
4 A.M. Press, 1527 N. 36th St., Sheboygan, WI 53081
Four Way Books, P.O. Box 607, Marshfield, MA 02050
Fourteen Hills: The SFSU Review, San Francisco State Univ., San Francisco, CA 94132
Free Spirit Magazine, 107 Sterling Pl., Brooklyn, NY 11217

G

The Georgia Review, Univ. of Georgia, Athens, GA 30602
Gettysburg Review, Gettysburg College, Gettysburg, PA 17325
Ghost Planet Press, 7 Clark St., Calais, ME 04619
Glimmer Train, 812 SW Washington St., Ste. 1205, Portland, OR 97205
Graffiti Ragi, 5647 Oakman Blvd., Dearborn, MI 48124
Grand Street, 131 Varick St., Rm. 906, New York, NY 10013
Granite Review, 4 Main St., Eliot, ME 03903
Graywolf Press, 2402 University Ave., Ste. 203, St. Paul, MN 55114
Green Hills Literary Lantern, P.O. Box 375, Trenton, MO 64683
Green Mountains Review, Johnson State College, Johnson, VT 05656
Greensboro Review, English Dept., Univ. of North Carolina, Greensboro, NC 27412
Gulf Coast, English Dept., Univ. of Houston, Houston, TX 77204

H

Haight-Ashbury Literary Journal, 558 Joost Ave., San Francisco, CA 94127
Harvard Review, Harvard College Library, Cambridge, MA 02138
Hayden's Ferry Review, Box 871502, Arizona State Univ., Tempe, AZ 85287
High Desert Honey Co., 1742 Os Rd., Glade Park, CO 81523
High Plains Literary Review, 180 Adams St., Ste. 250, Denver, CO 80206
Hot Pepper Press, P.O. Box 39, Somerset, CA 95684
Hubbub, 5344 S.E. 38th Ave., Portland, OR 97202
The Hudson Review, 684 Park Ave., New York, NY 10021
Hummingwoman Press, P.O. Box 60352, Florence, MA 01060

I

The Ice Cube Press, 423 Highway One West, Box 18, Iowa City, IA 52246
The Iconoclast, 1675 Amazon Rd., Mohegan Lake, NY 10547
The Illinois Review, English Dept., Illinois State Univ., Normal, IL 61790
Indiana Review, 316 N. Jordan Ave., Indiana Univ., Bloomington, IN 47405
The Iowa Review, 308 EPB, Univ. of Iowa, Iowa City, IA 52242
Iowa Woman, P.O. Box 680, Iowa City, IA 52244

J

The James White Review, P.O. Box 3356, Traffic Sta., Minneapolis, MN 55403
Janes Alley Fine Press, 1420 Constellation Dr., Colorado Springs, CO 80906

The Journal, English Dept., Ohio State Univ., Columbus, OH 43210
Journal of New Jersey Poets, County College of Morris, 214 Center Grove Rd., Randolph, NJ
  07869

K

Kaimana, 509 University Ave., #902, Honolulu, HI 96826
Kalliope, Florida Community College, 3939 Roosevelt Blvd., Jacksonville, FL 32205
Kaya Production, 8 Harrison St., Ste. 3, 5th fl., New York, NY 10013
Kelsey Review, Mercer County Community College, P.O. Box B, Trenton, NJ 08690
Kelsey Street Press, 2718 Ninth St., Berkeley, CA 94710
Kent State University Press, Kent State Univ., Kent, OH 44242
Kenyon Review, Kenyon College Gambier, OH 43022
Kestrel, Fairmont State College, Fairmont, WV 26554
Kinesis, P.O. Box 4007, Whitefish, MT 59937
Kings Estate Press, 870 Kings Estate Rd., St. Augustine, FL 32086
Kiosk, SUNY, 308 Clenew Hall, Buffalo, NY 14260

L

Laureate Press, P.O. Box 450597, Surise, FL 33345
The Laurel Review, English Dept., Northwest Missouri State Univ., Maryville, MO 64468
The Ledge, 64-65 Cooper Ave, Glendale, NY 11385
Liberty Hall Poetry Review, P.O. Box 426967, San Francisco, CA 94142
Licking River Review, Nunn Dr., Highland Heights, KY 41099
LILT, Kansas City Art Institute, 4415 Warwick Blvd., Kansas City, MO 64111
Lips, P.O. Box 1345, Montclair, NJ 07042
Literal Latte, 61 East 8th St., Ste. 240, New York, NY 10003
Literary Renaissance, P.O. Box 3685, Louisville, KY 40201
The Literary Review, Fairleigh Dickinson Univ., 285 Madison Ave., Madison, NJ 07940
Lone Stars Magazine, 4219 Flinthill Dr., San Antonio, TX 78230
Los Angeles Review, P.O. Box 1858, Hollywood Sta., Los Angeles, CA 90078
the low twenties times, 221 Ave. A, #5, New York, NY 10009
Lynx Eye, 1880 Hill Dr., Los Angeles, CA 90041

M

The MacGuffin, Schoolcraft College, 18600 Haggerty Rd., Livonia, MI 48152
MagiCircle Press, P.O. Box 1123, Bozeman, MT 59771
Manic D Press, P.O. Box 410804, San Francisco, CA 94141
Manoa, English Dept. Univ. of Hawaii, Honolulu, HI 96822
Many Mountains Moving, 420 22nd St., Boulder, CO 80302
Massachusetts Review, Univ. of Massachusetts, Amherst, MA 01003
Maverick Press, Rte. 2, Box 4915, Eagle Pass, TX 78852
May Day Press, 9893 Georgetown Pike, Ste. 510, Great Falls, VA 22066
Mayapple Press, P.O. Box 5743, Saginaw, MI 48603
Mercury House, 785 Market St., Ste. 1500, San Francisco, CA 94103
Michigan Quarterly Review, Univ. of Michigan, 3032 Rackham Bldg., Ann Arbor, MI 48109
Mid-American Review, English Dept., Bowling Green State Univ., Bowling Green, OH 43403

Midland Review, 201 Morrill Hall, Oklahoma State Univ., Stillwater, OK 74075
Milkweek Editions, 430 First Ave. North, Ste. 400, Minneapolis, MN 55401
Mind in Motion, P.O. Box 1118, Apple Valley, CA 92307
Mississippi Review, Univ. of Southern Mississippi, Box 5144, Rattiesburg, MS 39406
Mississippi Valley Review, West Illinois Univ., 900 W. Adams St., Macomb, IL 61455
The Missouri Review, 1507 Hillcrest Hall, Univ., of Missouri, Columbia, MO 65211
Mockingbird, P.O. Box 761, Davis, CA 95617
Mostly Maine, P.O. Box 8805, Portland, ME 04104

N

The Nebraska Review, Writer's Workshop, Univ. of Nebraska, Omaha, NE 68182
Negative Capability, 62 Ridgelawn Dr. East, Mobile, AL 36608
New Letters, Univ. of Missouri, 5100 Rockhill Rd., Kansas City, MO 64110
New Orleans Review, Loyola Univ., Box 195, New Orleans, LA 70118
New Poets Series, Inc., 541 Piccadilly Rd., Baltimore, MD 21204
New Rivers Press, 420 N. 5th St., Minneapolis, MN 55401
The New York Quarterly, P.O. Box 693, Old Chelsea Sta., New York, NY 10113
Next Phase, 5A Green Meadow Dr., Nantucket Island, MA 02554
Nightshade Press, Ward Hill Rd. & Rte. 9, P.O. Box 76, Troy, ME 04987
Nimrod, Univ. of Tulsa, 600 S. College Ave., Tulsa, OK 74104
North American Review, Univ. of Northern Iowa, Cedar Falls, IA 50614
North Carolina Literary Review, English Dept., ECU, Greenville, NC 27858
North Dakota Quarterly, Univ. of North Dakota, Grand Forks, ND 58202
North Stone Review, D Sta., Box 14098, Minneapolis, MN 55414
Northern Lights, P.O. Box 8084, Missoula, MT 59807
Northwest Corridor, Beaver College, Glenside, PA 19038
Northwest Review, 369 PLC, Univ. of Oregon, Eugene, OR 97403
Notre Dame Review, English Dept., Univ. of Notre Dame, Notre Dame, IN 46556

O

Oasis, P.O. Box 626, Largo, FL 34649
Ogalala Review, P.O. Box 628, Guymon, OK 73942
Old Crow Review, P.O. Box 662, Amherst, MA 01004
Ontario Review, 9 Honey Brook Dr., Princeton, NJ 08540
Orchises Press, P.O. Box 20602, Alexandria, VA 22320
Orion, 136 East 64th St., New York, NY 10021
Osiris, Box 297, Deerfield, MA 01842
Other Voices, English Dept., Univ. of Illinois, 601 S. Morgan St., Chicago, IL 60607
Oxford Magazine, 356 Bachelor Hall, Miami Univ., Oxford, OH 45056

P

Palo Alto Review, Palo Alto College, 1400 W. Villaret, San Antonio, TX 78224
Pangolin Papers, Box 241, Nordland, WA 98358
Papier-Mache, 135 Aviation Way, #14, Watsonville, CA 95076
Paris Press, P.O. Box 267, Northhampton, MA 101061
The Paris Review, 541 East 72nd St., New York, NY 10021

Parnassus Literary Journal, P.O. Box 1384, Forest Park, GA 30051
Parting Gifts, 3413 Wilshire, Greensboro, NC 27408
Pearl, 3030 E. Second St., Long Beach, CA 90803
Peregrine, P.O. Box 1076, Amherst, MA 01002
Persephone Press, 53 Pine Lake Dr., Carthage, NC 28327
Pivot, 250 Riverside Dr., #23, New York, NY 10025
Plain Magazine, P.O. Box 100, Chesterhill, OH 43728
Ploughshares, 100 Beacon St., Boston, MA 02116
Plum Review, P.O. Box 1347, Philadelphia, PA 19105
Plympton Press International, 1225 Fair Oaks Pkwy, Ann Arbor, MI 48104
Pocahontas Press, P.O. Drawer F, Blacksburg, VA 24063
Poems & Plays, English Dept., P.O. box 70, Middle Tennessee Univ., Murfreesboro, TN 37132
Poet Lore, 4508 Walsh St., Bethesda, MD 20815
Poet Magazine, P.O. Box 54947, Oklahoma City, OK 73154
Poetry, 60 W. Walton St., Chicago, IL 60610
Poetry Miscellany, 3413 Alta Vista Dr., Chattanooga, TN 37411
Poetry Project, 131 E. 10th St., New York, NY 10003
Poets On, 29 Loring Ave., Mill Valley, CA 94941
Potpourri, P.O. Box 8278, Prairie Village, KS 66208
Prairie Schooner, P.O. Box 880334, Univ. of Nebraska, Lincoln, NE 68588
Prescott Street Press, P.O. Box 40312, Portland, OR 97240
Prologue Press, 375 Riverside Dr., #14C, New York, NY 10025
Provincetown Arts, 650 Commercial St., Provincetown, MA 02657
Puck Magazine, 47 Noe St., #4, San Francisco, CA 94114
Puerto Del Sol, College of Arts & Sc., Box 3E, New Mexico State Univ., Las Cruces, NM 88001

Q

The Quarterly, 650 Madison Ave., New York, NY 10022
Quarterly West, 317 Olpin Union, Univ. of Utah, Salt Lake City, UT 84112
QED Press, 155 Cypress St., Fort Bragg, CA 94537
La Questa Press, 355 Hamilton Ave., Palo Alto, CA 94301

R

Radiolarian Press, P.O. Box 1012, Inverness, CA 94937
Rain City Review, 7215 SW LaView Dr., Portland, OR 97219
Raritan, Rutgers State Univ. of N.J., New Brunswick, NJ 08903
RDR Books, 4456 Piedmont Ave., Oakland, CA 94611
Re/mapping the Occident, Box 11741, Berkeley, CA 94712
Red Cedar Review, English Dept., Michigan State Univ., East Lansing, MI 48823
Red Dancefloor Press, P.O. Box 4974, Lancaster, CA 93539
Redwood Coast Press, P.O. Box 9552, Oakland, CA 94613
The Review, Dept. of Languages, McNeese State Univ., Lake Charles, LA 70609
Review of Contemporary Fiction, Box 4241, Normal, IL 61790
Ridgeway Press, P.O. Box 120, Roseville, MI 48066
River Oak Review, P.O. Box 3127, Oak Park, IL 60303
Road Map Series, 13 Lapanday Rd., Panorama Homes, Davao City, Philippines 77466
Rocket Press, P.O. Box 672, Water Mill, NY 11976
Ronsdale Press, 3350 W. 21st Ave., Vancouver, B.C. V6S 1G7, CANADA
Rosebud, 4218 Barnett St., Madison, WI 53704

Rowbarge Press, P.O. Box 407, Monterey, CA 93942
Ruby, P.O. Box 5915, Takoma Park, MD 20913

S

Salmagundi, Skidmore College, Saratoga Springs, NY 12866
Sandstone Publishing, P.O. Box 36701, Charlotte, NC 28236
Santa Barbara Review, 104 La Vereda Lane, Santa Barabar, CA 93108
Satire, P.O. Box 340, Hancock, MD 21750
The Seal Press, 3131 Western Ave., #410, Seattle, WA 98121
Semi-Dwarf, Box 591, Albion, CA 95410
Seneca Review, Hobart & William Smith Colleges, Geneva, NY 14456
Sensations Magazine, 2 Radio Ave., A-5, Secaucus, NJ 07094
Seven Days, P.O. Box 1164, Burlington, VT 05402
Shenandoah, Box 722, Lexington, VA 24450
Shooting Star, 7123 Race St., Pittsburgh, PA 15208
Singing Horse Press, P.O. Box 30034, Philadelphia, PA 19106
Sistersong, P.O. Box 7405, Pittsburgh, PA 15216
Skylark, Purdue Univ., 2200 169th St., Hammond, IN 46323
The Slate, P.O. Box 581189, Minneapolis, MN 55458
Slipstream, Box 2071, New Market Sta., Niagara Falls, NY 14301
Edward R. Smallwood Inc., 4760 N. Oracle Road Suite 306, Tucson, AZ 85705-1674
Snowy Egret, College of Fine Arts, Ball State Univ., Muncie, IN 47306
So To Speak, George Mason Univ., 4400 Univ. Dr., Sub 1, Rm. 254A, Fairfax, VA 22030
Somersault Press, 404 Vista Heights Rd., Richmond, CA 94805
Sonora Review, English Dept., Univ. of Arizona, Tucson, AZ 85721
South Carolina Review, English Dept., Box 341503, Clemson Univ., Clemson, SC 29634
The Southern Anthology, 2851 Johnson St., Box 321, Lafayette, LA 70503
The Southern Review, 43 Allen Hall, Louisiana State Univ., Baton Rouge, LA 70803
Southwest Review, P.O. Box 750374, Southern Methodist Univ., Dallas, TX 75275
Sou'wester, English Dept., Southern Illinois Univ., Edwardsville, IL 62026
Spec, P.O. Box 40248, San Francisco, CA 94140
Spinster's Ink, 32 E. First St., #330, Duluth, MN 55802
Spout Magazine, 28 W. Robie, St. Paul, MN 55802
Steelhead Special, P.O. Box 219, Bayside, CA 94941
Steppingstone, P.O. Box 327, Chatham, MA 02633
Stone Bridge Press, P.O. Box 8208, Berkeley, CA 94707
Story, 1507 Dana Ave., Cincinnati, OH 45207
Story Quarterly, P.O. Box 1416, Northbrook, IL 60065
Sulphur River, P.O. Box 402087, Austin, TX 78704
The Sun, 107 No. Roberson St., Chapel Hill, NC 27516
Sycamore Review, English Dept., Purdue Univ., West Layette, IN 47907

T

Talking River Review, Div. of Lit. & Lang., Lewis-Clark State College, Lewiston, ID 83501
Tamaqua, Humanities Dept., Parkland College, 2400 W. Bradley Ave., Champaign, IL 61821
Tampa Review, 401 W. Kennedy Blvd., Tampa, FA 33606
Tar River Poetry, English Dept., East Carolina Univ., Greenville, NC 27858
Texas Christian Univ. Press, Box 30783, Texas Christian Univ., Ft. Worth, TX 76129
Texture Press, 3760 Cedar Ridge Dr., Norman, OK 73072

That New Magazine, Inc., P.O. Box 1475, Church St., Sta., New York, NY 10008
Thema, Box 74109, Metairie, LA 70033
Third Coast, English Dept., West Michigan Univ., Kalamazoo, MI 49008
13th Moon, English Dept., Univ. of New York, 1400 Washington Ave., Albany, NY 12222
Threepenny Review, P.O. Box 9131, Berkeley, CA 94709
Tomorrow Magazine, P.O. Box 148486, Chicago, IL 60614
Transfer Magazine, Creative Writing Dept., San Francisco State Univ., San Francisco, CA 94132
Trask House Books, 3222 N.E. Schuyler, Portland, OR 97212
Treasure House, 1106 Oak Hill Ave., #3A, Hagerstown, MD 21742
Tribes, P.O. Box 20693, Tompkins Sq. Sta., New York, NY 10009
TriQuarterly, Northwestern Univ., 2020 Ridge Ave., Evanston, IL 60208
Trout Creek Press, 5976 Billings Rd., Parkdale, OR 97041
Turning Wheel, 1631 Grant, Berkeley, CA 94703
Turnstile, 175 Fifth Ave., Ste. 2348, New York, NY 10010

U

University of Georgia Press, 330 Research Dr., Athens, GA 30602
University of Massachusetts Press, Box 429, Amherst, MA 01004
University of Pittsburgh Press, 127 N. Bellefield Ave., Pittsburgh, PA 15260
University of Wisconsin Press, 114 N. Murray St., Madison, WI 53715
The Urbanite, P.O. Box 4737, Davenport, IA 52808

V

Verve, P.O. Box 3205, Simi Valley, CA 93093
Viet Nam Generation, 18 Center Rd., Woodbridge, CT 06525
Vignette, 4150-G Riverside Dr., Toluca Lake, CA 91505
Vincent Brothers Review, 4566 Northern Circle, Riverside, OH 45424
Voices Israel, P.O. Box 5780, 46157 Herzlia, ISRAEL

W

Washington Review, P.O. Box 50132, Washington, DC 20091
Weighted Anchor Press, P.O. Box 1187, Hampshire College, Amherst, MA 01002
West Branch, Bucknell Univ., Lewisburg, PA 17837
The West Side Story, P.O. Box 776, New York, NY 10108
Western Humanities Review, Univ. of Utah, Salt Lake City, UT 84112
Whetsone, P.O. Box 1266, Barrington, IL 60011
White Eagle Coffee Store Press, P.O. Box 383, Fox River Grove, IL 60021
Whitefields Press, P.O. Box 3685, Louisville, KY 40201
Wild Duck Review, 419 Spring St., Nevada City, CA 95959
Wild Seed Publications, 664A Freeman Lane, Ste. 102, Grass Valley, CA 95949
William & Mary Review, P.O. Box 8795, Williamsburg, VA 23187
Willow Springs, EWU, 526-5th St., MS1, Cheney, WA 99004
Without Halos, 19 Quail Run, Bayville, NJ 08721
Witness, Oakland Community College, 27055 Orchard Lake Rd., Farmington Hills, MI 48334
Wolfsong, 3123 S. Kennedy Dr., Sturtevant, WI 53177
Women in Translation, 3131 Western Ave., Ste. 410, Seattle, WA 98121

The Worcester Review, 6 Chatham St., Worcester, MA 01608
Wordcraft of Oregon, P.O. Box 3235, La Grande, OR 97850
Wormwood Review, P.O. Box 4698, Stockton, CA 95204
Writ Magazine, Two Sussex Ave., Toronto, M5S 1J5, CANADA
Writers' Forum, English Dept., Univ. of Colorado, P.O. Box 7150, Colorado Springs, CO 80933
The Writing Self, P.O. Box 245, Lenox Hill Sta., New York, NY 10021

X

Y

Yale Review, P.O. Box 1902A, Yale Station, New Haven, CT 06520
York Press, P.O. Box 1172, Fredericton, N.B. E3B 5C8, CANADA

Z

ZYZZYVA, 41 Sutter, Ste. 1400, San Francisco, CA 94104

INDEX

The following is a listing in alphabetical order by author's last name of works reprinted in the first twenty-one *Pushcart Prize* editions.

603

604

605

606

607

610

613

614

615

617

619

620

621

622